HALF-A-HUNDRED

Tales by Great American Writers

Half·A·Hundred

Tales by Great American Writers

EDITED, WITH AN INTRODUCTION

BY CHARLES GRAYSON

THE BLAKISTON COMPANY—PHILADELPHIA

Contents

Overture

A HALF DOZEN OF US, an assortment of captains then out of the line for reasons as various as our branches, were billeted in a cold stone room in Ferdinand's gloomy pile at Caserta. Security closed down our little light, but after dark we would lie for a while with cold faces poked out of sleeping bags, to smoke and argue. If the talk got dull you just corked off. But usually it was the fatigue, for these were men full of bias and belief. Subjects spread far, and agreement was not usual—save on the topic of my failings as an anthologist.

The Overseas Editions people had issued in pocket form for the Forces, two books which years before I had compiled out of a taste for short stories of the more readable type and addressed to an audience with a similar liking. Once I had seen these volumes with some degree of pride (that of a midwife); now I was to learn that I was merely a neglectful, offensive scoundrel. I not only had left out the favorite author of two of my embattled companions, but in the other cases had not used favorite yarns by their particular enthusiasms. The dark streaked with abuse, acid, gentle, profane. It seemed that I was, at best, a revolving joker.

Yet while acknowledging that the absence of Louis Bromfield and John P. Marquand was deplorable ("I couldn't get everybody in, could I?") I still maintained a defense for the second charge. What, I held, is the sense of reshuffling packages of currently popular material, like those acts which kept coming back until they killed vaudeville? Later, when suggesting his own favorite story for this book, James Thurber mentioned that "Barney Haller" had never appeared in a compilation, and added: "What happens with anthologies seems to be that the editor does not have time to read all of a man's work and hence is forced to depend on other anthologies. For this reason only about seven of all my two hundred stories ever get into these collections."

vii

Another enemy of a fundamentally interesting scheme is the sort of doorstop which Orville Prescott may have had in mind when he commented so wryly on anthologies: "They have an irresistible attraction, seemingly so easy that anyone with a pair of scissors thinks he can assemble one. Any subject will do, old jokes, mediocre plays, poems newly translated from the Igorot, or selections from writers who lived near Lake Memphremagog between 1911 and 1913."

But this dreadful type of clambake (usually called something like *Holy Smoke: A Church-burning Miscellany*) isn't the final offender. As provoking, is the persistent gathering of "The Necklace," "An Occurrence at Owl Creek Bridge," "The Horla," "A Piece of String," "A Lodging for the Night," "The Canterville Ghost," "The Gold Bug," "A Municipal Report," "The Jumping Frog," "The Monkey's Paw," and similar threadbare "classics" under some such title as *The Greatest Short Stories of All Time*. What impudent nonsense! Those tired titles have been reappearing in compilations ever since the first assistant professor dreamed up the idea of publishing an estimable book without having to wrench it out of his own skull. Nor do they get any better. Just being famous doesn't make a story secure against time. For the most part the reputations of those venerable yarns are because they were first in the field, not because they have remained pre-eminent in it. Too many good ones have come along since, and too fast, and still are coming. Professional writers seldom hang up their gloves after having scored one knockout; stories are their trade, and they keep working at it until they die, one way or another.

Eventually my bedside wranglers agreed I had a point. In return I promised that if ever I should get together another collection—another rebellious gesture against the "boy meets, quarrels with, gets back girl" of the women's magazines, and the sad vignettes of the periodicals with a higher purpose—I would defer to their suggestions, if possible.

Despite the dubious probability it looked at the time, it so happened to be possible. Returned home, the notion of fixing up a book that would please those shadowy jockeys stayed with me. I began to see what I could do about it, and found, as it had to be at this time, that it would not be much of a task. Ever since the other books came out authors and their passionate friends have been sending me stories which they felt should be in a future set, if any. I looked over that mass of material, thought of my own discoveries in the decade since the first and subsequently much-followed volume, and began scratching together bits of paper marked with names, titles, or just vague descriptions of some tale which had pleased somebody, sometime. These last were nominations from readers who, like those in Italy, believe that in the short story modern American fiction is not only most characteristic, but at its general best.

Finally, this book is the result. The Bostonian's Marquand is in it, and the medico's Bromfield. So is "The Life of Riley," which had moved the young infantry officer for a personal reason the darkness finally let him admit. And a piece by S. J. Perelman, belligerently maintained by the Long Tom expert to be the funniest adjectival writer in the whole adjectival racket. And one, of course, by our good bald Boswell of the 5th Army, Ernie Pyle.

Well, the desperately in love appreciator of Captain Sherman's story won't read it again, nor will Sid's fan laugh at "The Pipe." But anyway, I have tried to line up an entertainment detail for the rest of that passing bunch of cosponsors. And, because they were sort of a cross section of those who favor stories with some meat on their good bones, perhaps for some others as well. For me, I find it pleasantly complete. Little of the manifest is readily available elsewhere, and that got in by the sheer pull of belonging.

One primary restriction, however, has been scrupulously observed—that the contributors be living Americans. The gentlemen herein represented are all contemporary storytellers of our country. They write in different manners of many types, scenes, and subjects. Some lean to mood, some to motion; but they have this in common: they write like a bat out of hell. As a group, I think, they form such a team as to end all anthologies like this for a long time to come. . . . Good evenings, friends—

C. G.

HALF-A-HUNDRED

Tales by Great American Writers

CONRAD AIKEN

Mr. Arcularis

MR. ARCULARIS stood at the window of his room in the hospital and looked down at the street. There had been a light shower, which had patterned the sidewalks with large drops, but now again the sun was out, blue sky was showing here and there between the swift white clouds, a cold wind was blowing the poplar trees. An itinerant band had stopped before the building and was playing, with violin, harp, and flute, the finale of *Cavalleria Rusticana*. Leaning against the window sill—for he felt extraordinarily weak after his operation—Mr. Arcularis suddenly, listening to the wretched music, felt like crying. He rested the palm of one hand against a cold windowpane and stared down at the old man who was blowing the flute, and blinked his eyes. It seemed absurd that he should be so weak, so emotional, so like a child—and especially now that everything was over at last. In spite of all their predictions, in spite, too, of his own dreadful certainty that he was going to die, here he was, as fit as a fiddle—but what a fiddle it was, so out of tune!—with a long life before him. And to begin with, a voyage to England ordered by the doctor. What could be more delightful? Why should he feel sad about it and want to cry like a baby? In a few minutes Harry would arrive with his car to take him to the wharf; in an hour he would be on the sea, in two hours he would see the sunset behind him, where Boston had been, and his new life would be opening before him. It was many years since he had been abroad. June, the best of the year to come—England, France, the Rhine—how ridiculous that he should already be homesick!

There was a light footstep outside the door, a knock, the door opened, and Harry came in.

"Well, old man, I've come to get you. The old bus actually got here. Are you ready? Here, let me take your arm. You're tottering like an octogenarian!"

Mr. Arcularis submitted gratefully, laughing, and they made the journey slowly along the bleak corridor and down the stairs to the entrance hall. Miss Hoyle, his nurse, was there, and the matron, and the charming little assistant with freckles who had helped to prepare him for the operation. Miss Hoyle put out her hand.

"Good-by, Mr. Arcularis," she said, "and bon voyage."

"Good-by, Miss Hoyle, and thank you for everything. You were very kind to me. And I fear I was a nuisance."

The girl with the freckles, too, gave him her hand, smiling. She was very pretty, and it would have been easy to fall in love with her. She reminded him of someone. Who was it? He tried in vain to remember while he said good-by to her and turned to the matron.

"And not too many latitudes with the young ladies, Mr. Arcularis!" she was saying.

Mr. Arcularis was pleased, flattered, by all this attention to a middle-aged invalid, and felt a joke taking shape in his mind, and no sooner in his mind than on his tongue.

"Oh, no latitudes," he said, laughing. "I'll leave the latitudes to the ship!"

"Oh, come now," said the matron, "we don't seem to have hurt him much, do we?"

"I think we'll have to operate on him again and *really* cure him," said Miss Hoyle.

He was going down the front steps, between the potted palmettos, and they all laughed and waved. The wind was cold, very cold for June, and he was glad he had put on his coat. He shivered.

"Damned cold for June!" he said. "Why should it be so cold?"

"East wind," Harry said, arranging the rug over his knees. "Sorry it's an open car, but I believe in fresh air and all that sort of thing. I'll drive slowly. We've got plenty of time."

They coasted gently down the long hill toward Beacon Street, but the road was badly surfaced, and despite Harry's care Mr. Arcularis felt his pain again. He found that he could alleviate it a little by leaning to the right, against the arm rest, and not breathing too deeply. But how glorious to be out again! How strange and vivid the world looked! The trees had innumerable green fresh leaves—they were all blowing and shifting and turning and flashing in the wind; drops of rain water fell downward, sparkling; the robins were singing their absurd, delicious little four-noted songs;

even the streetcars looked unusually bright and beautiful, just as they used to look when he was a child and had wanted above all things to be a motorman. He found himself smiling foolishly at everything, foolishly and weakly, and wanted to say something about it to Harry. It was no use, though—he had no strength, and the mere finding of words would be almost more than he could manage. And even if he should succeed in saying it, he would then most likely burst into tears. He shook his head slowly from side to side.

"Ain't it grand?" he said.

"I'll bet it looks good," said Harry.

"Words fail me."

"You wait till you get out to sea. You'll have a swell time."

"Oh, swell! . . . I hope not. I hope it'll be calm."

"Tut, tut."

When they passed the Harvard Club Mr. Arcularis made a slow and somewhat painful effort to turn in his seat and look at it. It might be the last chance to see it for a long time. Why this sentimental longing to stare at it, though? There it was, with the great flag blowing in the wind, the Harvard seal now concealed by the swift folds and now revealed, and there were the windows in the library, where he had spent so many delightful hours reading—Plato, and Kipling, and the Lord knows what—and the balconies from which for so many years he had watched the finish of the marathon. Old Talbot might be in there now, sleeping with a book on his knee, hoping forlornly to be interrupted by anyone, for anything.

"Good-by to the old club," he said.

"The bar will miss you," said Harry, smiling with friendly irony and looking straight ahead.

"But let there be no moaning," said Mr. Arcularis.

"What's *that* a quotation from?"

"The *Odyssey.*"

In spite of the cold, he was glad of the wind on his face, for it helped to dissipate the feeling of vagueness and dizziness that came over him in a sickening wave from time to time. All of a sudden everything would begin to swim and dissolve, the houses would lean their heads together, he had to close his eyes, and there would be a curious and dreadful humming noise, which at regular intervals rose to a crescendo and then drawlingly subsided again. It was disconcerting. Perhaps he still had a trace of fever. When he got on the ship he would have a glass of whisky. . . . From one of these spells he opened his eyes and found that they were on the ferry, crossing to East Boston. It must have been the ferry's engines that he had heard. From another spell he woke to find himself on the wharf, the car at a standstill beside a pile of yellow packing cases.

"We're here because we're here because we're here," said Harry.

"Because we're here," added Mr. Arcularis.

He dozed in the car while Harry—and what a good friend Harry was! —attended to all the details. He went and came with tickets and passports and baggage checks and porters. And at last he unwrapped Mr. Arcularis from the rugs and led him up the steep gangplank to the deck, and thence by devious windings to a small cold stateroom with a solitary porthole like the eye of a cyclops.

"Here you are," he said, "and now I've got to go. Did you hear the whistle?"

"No."

"Well, you're half asleep. It's sounded the all ashore. Good-by, old fellow, and take care of yourself. Bring me back a spray of edelweiss. And send me a picture post card from the Absolute."

"Will you have it finite or infinite?"

"Oh, infinite. But with your signature on it. Now you'd better turn in for a while and have a nap. Cheerio!"

Mr. Arcularis took his hand and pressed it hard, and once more felt like crying. Absurd! Had he become a child again?

"Good-by," he said.

He sat down in the little wicker chair, with his overcoat still on, closed his eyes, and listened to the humming of the air in the ventilator. Hurried footsteps ran up and down the corridor. The chair was not too comfortable, and his pain began to bother him again, so he moved, with his coat still on, to the narrow berth and fell asleep. When he woke up, it was dark, and the porthole had been partly opened. He groped for the switch and turned on the light. Then he rang for the steward.

"It's cold in here," he said. "Would you mind closing the port?"

The girl who sat opposite him at dinner was charming. Who was it she reminded him of? Why, of course, the girl at the hospital, the girl with the freckles. Her hair was beautiful, not quite red, not quite gold, nor had it been bobbed; arranged with a sort of graceful untidiness, it made him think of a Melozzo da Forli angel. Her face was freckled, she had a mouth which was both humorous and voluptuous. And she seemed to be alone.

He frowned at the bill of fare and ordered the thick soup.

"No hors d'oeuvres?" asked the steward.

"I think not," said Mr. Arcularis. "They might kill me."

The steward permitted himself to be amused and deposited the menu card on the table against the water bottle. His eyebrows were lifted. As he moved away, the girl followed him with her eyes and smiled.

"I'm afraid you shocked him," she said.

"Impossible," said Mr. Arcularis.

"These stewards, they're dead souls. How could they be stewards otherwise? And they think they've seen and known everything. They suffer terribly from the *déjà vu*. Personally, I don't blame them."

"It must be a dreadful sort of life."

"It's because they're dead that they accept it."

"Do you think so?"

"I'm sure of it. I'm enough of a dead soul myself to know the signs!"

"Well, I don't know what you mean by that!"

"But nothing mysterious! I'm just out of hospital, after an operation. I was given up for dead. For six months I had given *myself* up for dead. If you've ever been seriously ill you know the feeling. You have a posthumous feeling—a mild, cynical tolerance for everything and everyone. What is there you haven't seen or done or understood? Nothing."

Mr. Arcularis waved his hands and smiled.

"I wish I could understand you," said the girl, "but I've never been ill in my life."

"Never?"

"Never."

"Good God!"

The torrent of the unexpressed and inexpressible paralyzed him and rendered him speechless. He stared at the girl, wondering who she was and then, realizing that he had perhaps stared too fixedly, averted his gaze, gave a little laugh, rolled a pill of bread between his fingers. After a second or two he allowed himself to look at her again and found her smiling.

"Never pay any attention to invalids," he said, "or they'll drag you to the hospital."

She examined him critically, with her head tilted a little to one side, but with friendliness.

"You don't *look* like an invalid," she said.

Mr. Arcularis thought her charming. His pain ceased to bother him, the disagreeable humming disappeared, or rather, it was dissociated from himself and became merely, as it should be, the sound of the ship's engines, and he began to think the voyage was going to be really delightful. The parson on his right passed him the salt.

"I fear you will need this in your soup," he said.

"Thank you. Is it as bad as that?"

The steward, overhearing, was immediately apologetic and solicitous. He explained that on the first day everything was at sixes and sevens. The girl looked up at him and asked him a question.

"Do you think we'll have a good voyage?" she said.

He was passing the hot rolls to the parson, removing the napkins from them with a deprecatory finger.

"Well, madam, I don't like to be a Jeremiah, but——"

"Oh, come," said the parson, "I hope we have no Jeremiahs."

"What do you mean?" said the girl.

Mr. Arcularis ate his soup with gusto—it was nice and hot.

"Well, maybe I shouldn't say it, but there's a corpse on board, going to Ireland; and I never yet knew a voyage with a corpse on board that we didn't have bad weather."

"Why, Steward, you're just superstitious! What nonsense."

"That's a very ancient superstition," said Mr. Arcularis. "I've heard it many times. Maybe it's true. Maybe we'll be wrecked. And what does it matter, after all?" He was very bland.

"Then let's be wrecked," said the parson coldly.

Nevertheless, Mr. Arcularis felt a shudder go through him on hearing the steward's remark. A corpse in the hold—a coffin? Perhaps it was true. Perhaps some disaster would befall them. There might be fogs. There might be icebergs. He thought of all the wrecks of which he had read. There was the *Titanic*, which he had read about in the warm newspaper room at the Harvard Club—it had seemed dreadfully real, even there. That band, playing "Nearer, My God, to Thee" on the afterdeck while the ship sank! It was one of the darkest of his memories. And the *Empress of Ireland*—all those poor people trapped in the smoking room, with only one door between them and life, and that door locked for the night by the deck steward, and the deck steward nowhere to be found! He shivered, feeling a draft, and turned to the parson.

"How do these strange delusions arise?" he said.

The parson looked at him searchingly, appraisingly—from chin to forehead, from forehead to chin—and Mr. Arcularis, feeling uncomfortable, straightened his tie.

"From nothing but fear," said the parson. "Nothing on earth but fear."

"How strange!" said the girl.

Mr. Arcularis again looked at her—she had lowered her face—and again tried to think of whom she reminded him. It wasn't only the little freckle-faced girl at the hospital—both of them had reminded him of someone else. Someone far back in his life: remote, beautiful, lovely. But he couldn't think. The meal came to an end, they all rose, the ship's orchestra played a feeble fox trot, and Mr. Arcularis, once more alone, went to the bar to have his whisky. The room was stuffy, and the ship's engines were both audible and palpable. The humming and throbbing oppressed him, the rhythm seemed to be the rhythm of his own pain, and after a short time he found his way, with slow steps, holding on to the walls in his moments of weakness and dizziness, to his forlorn and white little room. The port had been—thank God!—closed for the night: it was cold enough anyway. The white and blue ribbons fluttered from the ventilator, the bottle and glasses clicked and clucked as the ship swayed gently to the long, slow motion of the sea. It was all very peculiar—it was all like something he had experienced somewhere before. What was it? Where was it? . . . He untied his tie, looking at his face in the glass, and wondered, and from time to time put his hand to his side to hold in the pain. It wasn't at Portsmouth, in his childhood, nor at Salem, nor in the rose garden at his aunt Julia's, nor in the schoolroom at Cambridge. It was something very queer, very intimate, very precious. The jackstones, the Sunday-school cards which he had loved when he was a child . . . He fell asleep.

The sense of time was already hopelessly confused. One hour was like another, the sea looked always the same, morning was indistinguishable from afternoon—and was it Tuesday or Wednesday? Mr. Arcularis was sitting in the smoking room, in his favorite corner, watching the parson teach Miss Dean to play chess. On the deck outside he could see the people passing and repassing in their restless round of the ship. The red jacket went by, then the black hat with the white feather, then the purple scarf, the brown tweed coat, the Bulgarian mustache, the monocle, the Scotch cap with fluttering ribbons, and in no time at all the red jacket again, dipping past the windows with its own peculiar rhythm, followed once more by the black hat and the purple scarf. How odd to reflect on the fixed little orbits of these things—as definite and profound, perhaps, as the orbits of the stars, and as important to God or the Absolute. There was a kind of tyranny in this fixedness, too—to think of it too much made one uncomfortable. He closed his eyes for a moment, to avoid seeing for the fortieth time the Bulgarian mustache and the pursuing monocle. The parson was explaining the movements of knights. Two forward and one to the side. Eight possible moves, always to the opposite color from that on which the piece stands. Two forward and one to the side: Miss Dean repeated the words several times with reflective emphasis. Here, too, was the terrifying fixed curve of the infinite, the creeping curve of logic which at last must become the final signpost at the edge of nothing. After that—the deluge. The great white light of annihilation. The bright flash of death. . . . Was it merely the sea which made these abstractions so insistent, so intrusive? The mere notion of *orbit* had somehow become extraordinarily naked; and to rid himself of the discomfort and also to forget a little the pain which bothered his side whenever he sat down, he walked slowly and carefully into the writing room, and examined a pile of superannuated magazines and catalogues of travel. The bright colors amused him, the photographs of remote islands and mountains, savages in sampans or sarongs or both—it was all very far off and delightful, like something in a dream or a fever. But he found that he was too tired to read and was incapable of concentration. Dreams! Yes, that reminded him. That rather alarming business—sleepwalking!

Later in the evening—at what hour he didn't know—he was telling Miss Dean about it, as he had intended to do. They were sitting in deck chairs on the sheltered side. The sea was black, and there was a cold wind. He wished they had chosen to sit in the lounge.

Miss Dean was extremely pretty—no, beautiful. She looked at him, too, in a very strange and lovely way, with something of inquiry, something of sympathy, something of affection. It seemed as if, between the question and the answer, they had sat thus for a very long time, exchanging an unspoken secret, simply looking at each other quietly and kindly. Had an hour or two passed? And was it at all necessary to speak?

"No," she said, "I never have."

She breathed into the low words a note of interrogation and gave him a slow smile.

"That's the funny part of it. I never had either until last night. Never in my life. I hardly ever even dream. And it really rather frightens me."

"Tell me about it, Mr. Arcularis."

"I dreamed at first that I was walking, alone, in a wide plain covered with snow. It was growing dark, I was very cold, my feet were frozen and numb, and I was lost. I came then to a signpost—at first it seemed to me there was nothing on it. Nothing but ice. Just before it grew finally dark, however, I made out on it the one word 'Polaris.' "

"The Pole Star."

"Yes—and you see, I didn't myself know that. I looked it up only this morning. I suppose I must have seen it somewhere? And of course it rhymes with my name."

"Why, so it does!"

"Anyway, it gave me—in the dream—an awful feeling of despair, and the dream changed. This time, I dreamed I was standing *outside* my stateroom in the little dark corridor, or cul-de-sac, and trying to find the door handle to let myself in. I was in my pajamas, and again I was very cold. And at this point I woke up. . . . The extraordinary thing is that's exactly where I was!"

"Good heavens. How strange!"

"Yes. And now the question is, *where had I been?* I was frightened when I came to—not unnaturally. For among other things I *did* have, quite definitely, the feeling that I *had been* somewhere. Somewhere where it was very cold. It doesn't sound very proper. Suppose I had been seen!"

"That might have been awkward," said Miss Dean.

"Awkward! It might indeed. It's very singular. I've never done such a thing before. It's this sort of thing that reminds one—rather wholesomely, perhaps, don't you think?"—and Mr. Arcularis gave a nervous little laugh—"how extraordinarily little we know about the workings of our own minds or souls. After all, what *do* we know?"

"Nothing—nothing—nothing—nothing," said Miss Dean slowly.

"*Absolutely* nothing."

Their voices had dropped, and again they were silent; and again they looked at each other gently and sympathetically, as if for the exchange of something unspoken and perhaps unspeakable. Time ceased. The orbit—so it seemed to Mr. Arcularis—once more became pure, became absolute. And once more he found himself wondering who it was that Miss Dean—Clarice Dean—reminded him of. Long ago and far away. Like those pictures of the islands and mountains. The little freckle-faced girl at the hospital was merely, as it were, the steppingstone, the signpost, or, as in algebra, the "equals" sign. But what was it they both "equaled"? The jack-stones came again into his mind and his aunt Julia's rose garden—at sunset; but this was ridiculous. It couldn't be simply that they reminded him of his childhood! And yet why not?

They went into the lounge. The ship's orchestra, in the oval-shaped balcony among faded palms, was playing the finale of *Cavalleria Rusticana,* playing it badly.

"Good God!" said Mr. Arcularis. "Can't I ever escape from that damned sentimental tune? It's the last thing I heard in America, and the last thing I *want* to hear."

"But don't you like it?"

"As music? No! It moves me too much, but in the wrong way."

"What, exactly, do you mean?"

"Exactly? Nothing. When I heard it at the hospital—when was it?—it made me feel like crying. Three old Italians tootling it in the rain. I suppose, like most people, I'm afraid of my feelings."

"Are they so dangerous?"

"Now then, young woman! Are you pulling my leg?"

The stewards had rolled away the carpets, and the passengers were beginning to dance. Miss Dean accepted the invitation of a young officer, and Mr. Arcularis watched them with envy. Odd, that last exchange of remarks—very odd; in fact, everything was odd. Was it possible that they were falling in love? Was that what it was all about—all these concealed references and recollections? He had read of such things. But at his age! And with a girl of twenty-two!

After an amused look at his old friend Polaris from the open door on the sheltered side, he went to bed.

The rhythm of the ship's engines was positively a persecution. It gave one no rest, it followed one like the Hound of Heaven, it drove one out into space and across the Milky Way and then back home by way of Betelgeuse. It was cold there, too. Mr. Arcularis, making the round trip by way of Betelgeuse and Polaris, sparkled with frost. He felt like a Christmas tree. Icicles on his fingers and icicles on his toes. He tinkled and spangled in the void, hallooed to the waste echoes, rounded the buoy on the verge of the Unknown, and tacked glittering homeward. The wind whistled. He was barefooted. Snowflakes and tinsel blew past him. Next time, by George, he would go farther still—for altogether it was rather a lark. Forward into the untrodden! as somebody said. Some intrepid explorer of his own back yard, probably, some middle-aged professor with an umbrella: those were the fellows for courage! But give us time, thought Mr. Arcularis, give us time, and we will bring back with us the night rime of the Obsolute. Or was it Absolete? If only there weren't this perpetual throbbing, this iteration of sound, like a pain, these circles and repetitions of light—the feeling as of everything coiling inward to a center of misery. . . .

Suddenly it was dark, and he was lost. He was groping, he touched the cold, white, slippery woodwork with his fingernails, looking for an electric switch. The throbbing, of course, was the throbbing of the ship. But he was almost home—almost home. Another corner to round, a door to be opened, and there he would be. Safe and sound. Safe in his father's home.

It was at this point that he woke up: in the corridor that led to the dining saloon. Such pure terror, such horror, seized him as he had never known. His heart felt as if it would stop beating. His back was toward the dining saloon; apparently he had just come from it. He was in his pajamas. The corridor was dim, all but two lights having been turned out for the night, and—thank God!—deserted. Not a soul, not a sound. He was perhaps fifty yards from his room. With luck he could get to it unseen. Holding tremulously to the rail that ran along the wall, a brown, greasy rail, he began to creep his way forward. He felt very weak, very dizzy, and his thoughts refused to concentrate. Vaguely he remembered Miss Dean—Clarice—and the freckled girl, as if they were one and the same person. But he wasn't in the hospital, he was on the ship. Of course. How absurd. The Great Circle. Here we are, old fellow . . . steady round the corner . . . hold hard to your umbrella . . .

In his room, with the door safely shut behind him, Mr. Arcularis broke into a cold sweat. He had no sooner got into his bunk, shivering, than he heard the night watchmen pass.

"But where," he thought, closing his eyes in agony, "have I been . . . ?"

A dreadful idea had occurred to him.

"It's nothing serious—how could it be anything serious? Of course it's nothing serious," said Mr. Arcularis.

"No, it's nothing serious," said the ship's doctor urbanely.

"I knew you'd think so. But just the same——"

"Such a condition is the result of worry," said the doctor. "Are you worried—do you mind telling me—about something? Just try to think."

"Worried?"

Mr. Arcularis knitted his brows. *Was* there something? Some little mosquito of a cloud disappearing into the southwest, the northeast? Some little gnat song of despair? But no, that was all over. All over.

"Nothing," he said, "nothing whatever."

"It's very strange," said the doctor.

"Strange! I should say so. I've come to sea for a rest, not for a nightmare! What about a bromide?"

"Well, I can give you a bromide, Mr. Arcularis——"

"Then, please, if you don't mind, give me a bromide."

He carried the little phial hopefully to his stateroom and took a dose at once. He could see the sun through his porthole. It looked northern and pale and small, like a little peppermint, which was only natural enough, for the latitude was changing with every hour. But why was it that doctors were all alike? And all, for that matter, like his father, or that other fellow at the hospital? Smythe, his name was. Dr. Smythe. A nice, dry little fellow, and they said he was a writer. Wrote poetry, or something like that. Poor fellow—disappointed. Like everybody else. Crouched in there, in his cabin, night after night, writing blank verse or something—all about the stars and flowers and love and death; ice and the sea and the infinite; time and tide—well, every man to his own taste.

"But it's nothing serious," said Mr. Arcularis, later, to the parson. "How could it be?"

"Why of course not, my dear fellow," said the parson, patting his back. "How could it be?"

"I know it isn't and yet I worry about it."

"It would be ridiculous to think it serious," said the parson.

Mr. Arcularis shivered: it was colder than ever. It was said that they were near icebergs. For a few hours in the morning there had been a fog, and the siren had blown—devastatingly—at three-minute intervals. Icebergs caused fog—he knew that.

"These things always come," said the parson, "from a sense of guilt. You feel guilty about something. I won't be so rude as to inquire what it is. But if you could rid yourself of the sense of guilt——"

And later still, when the sky was pink:

"But is it anything to worry about?" said Miss Dean. "Really?"

"No, I suppose not."

"Then don't worry. We aren't children any longer!"

"Aren't we? I wonder!"

They leaned, shoulders touching, on the deck rail, and looked at the sea, which was multitudinously incarnadined. Mr. Arcularis scanned the horizon in vain for an iceberg.

"Anyway," he said, "the colder we are the less we feel!"

"I hope that's no reflection on *you*," said Miss Dean.

"Here . . . feel my hand," said Mr. Arcularis.

"Heaven knows it's cold!"

"It's been to Polaris and back! No wonder."

"Poor thing, poor thing!"

"Warm it."

"May I?"

"You can."

"I'll try."

Laughing, she took his hand between both of hers, one palm under and one palm over, and began rubbing it briskly. The decks were deserted, no one was near them, everyone was dressing for dinner. The sea grew darker, the wind blew colder.

"I wish I could remember who you are," he said.

"And you—who are you?"

"Myself."

"Then perhaps *I* am yourself."

"Don't be metaphysical!"

"But I *am* metaphysical!"

She laughed, withdrew, pulled the light coat about her shoulders.

The bugle blew the summons for dinner—"The Roast Beef of Old England"—and they walked together along the darkening deck toward the door, from which a shaft of soft light fell across the deck rail. As they stepped over the brass doorsill Mr. Arcularis felt the throb of the engines again; he put his hand quickly to his side.

"*Auf Wiedersehen*," he said. " 'Tomorrow and tomorrow and tomorrow.' "

Mr. Arcularis was finding it impossible, absolutely impossible, to keep warm. A cold fog surrounded the ship, had done so, it seemed, for days. The sun had all but disappeared, the transition from day to night was almost unnoticeable. The ship, too, seemed scarcely to be moving—it was as if anchored among walls of ice and rime. Monstrous, that merely because it was June, and supposed, therefore, to be warm, the ship's authorities should consider it unnecessary to turn on the heat! By day, he wore his heavy coat and sat shivering in the corner of the smoking room. His teeth chattered, his hands were blue. By night, he heaped blankets on his bed, closed the porthole's black eye against the sea, and drew the yellow curtains across it, but in vain. Somehow, despite everything, the fog crept in, and the icy fingers touched his throat. The steward, questioned about it, merely said, "Icebergs." Of course—any fool knew that. But how long, in God's name, was it going to last? They surely ought to be past the Grand Banks by this time! And surely it wasn't necessary to sail to England by way of Greenland and Iceland!

Miss Dean—Clarice—was sympathetic.

"It's simply because," she said, "your vitality has been lowered by your illness. You can't expect to be your normal self so soon after an operation! When *was* your operation, by the way?"

Mr. Arcularis considered. Strange—he couldn't be quite sure. It was all a little vague—his sense of time had disappeared.

"Heaven knows!" he said. "Centuries ago. When I was a tadpole and you were a fish. I should think it must have been at about the time of the Battle of Teutoburg Forest. Or perhaps when I was a Neanderthal man with a club!"

"Are you sure it wasn't farther back still?"

What did she mean by that?

"Not at all. Obviously, we've been on this damned ship for ages—for eras—for aeons. And even on this ship, you must remember, I've had plenty of time, in my nocturnal wanderings, to go several times to Orion and back. I'm thinking, by the way, of going farther still. There's a nice little star off to the left, as you round Betelgeuse, which looks as if it might be right at the edge. The last outpost of the finite. I think I'll have a look at it and bring you back a frozen rime feather."

"It would melt when you got it back."

"Oh no, it wouldn't—not on *this* ship!"

Clarice laughed.

"I wish I could go with you," she said.

"If only you would! If only——"

He broke off his sentence and looked hard at her—how lovely she was, and how desirable! No such woman had ever before come into his life; there had been no one with whom he had at once felt so profound a sympathy and understanding. It was a miracle, simply—a miracle. No need to put his arm around her or to kiss her—delightful as such small vulgarities would be. He had only to look at her, and to feel, gazing into those extraordinary eyes, that she knew him, had always known him. It was as if, indeed, she might be his own soul.

But as he looked thus at her, reflecting, he noticed that she was frowning.

"What is it?" he said.

She shook her head, slowly.

"I don't know."

"Tell me."

"Nothing. It just occurred to me that perhaps you weren't looking quite so well."

Mr. Arcularis was startled. He straightened himself up.

"What nonsense! Of course this pain bothers me—and I feel astonishingly weak——"

"It's more than that—much more than that. Something is worrying you horribly." She paused, and then with an air of challenging him, added, "Tell me, did you?"

Her eyes were suddenly asking him blazingly the question he had been afraid of. He flinched, caught his breath, looked away. But it was no use, as he knew: he would have to tell her. He had known all along that he would have to tell her.

"Clarice," he said—and his voice broke in spite of his effort to control it—"it's killing me, it's ghastly! Yes, I did."

His eyes filled with tears, he saw that her own had done so also. She put her hand on his arm.

"I knew," she said. "I knew. But tell me."

"It's happened twice again—twice—and each time I was farther away. The same dream of going round a star, the same terrible coldness and helplessness. That awful whistling curve . . ." He shuddered.

"And when you woke up"—she spoke quietly—"where were you when you woke up? Don't be afraid!"

"The first time I was at the farther end of the dining saloon. I had my hand on the door that leads into the pantry."

"I see. Yes. And the next time?"

Mr. Arcularis wanted to close his eyes in terror—he felt as if he were going mad. His lips moved before he could speak, and when at last he did speak it was in a voice so low as to be almost a whisper.

"I was at the bottom of the stairway that leads down from the pantry to the hold, past the refrigerating plant. It was dark, and I was crawling on my hands and knees. . . . *Crawling on my hands and knees!* . . ."

"Oh!" she said, and again, "Oh!"

He began to tremble violently; he felt the hand on his arm trembling also. And then he watched a look of unmistakable horror come slowly into Clarice's eyes, and a look of understanding, as if she saw . . . She tightened her hold on his arm.

"Do you think . . . ?" she whispered.

They stared at each other.

"I know," he said. "And so do you . . . Twice more—three times— and I'll be looking down into an empty . . ."

It was then that they first embraced—then, at the edge of the infinite, at the last signpost of the finite. They clung together desperately, forlornly, weeping as they kissed each other, staring hard one moment and closing their eyes the next. Passionately, passionately, she kissed him, as if she were indeed trying to give him her warmth, her life.

"But what nonsense!" she cried, leaning back, and holding his face between her hands, her hands which were wet with his tears. "What nonsense! It can't be!"

"It is," said Mr. Arcularis slowly.

"But how do you know? . . . How do you know where the——"

For the first time Mr. Arcularis smiled.

"Don't be afraid, darling—you mean the coffin?"

"How could you know where it is?"

"I don't need to," said Mr. Arcularis. . . . "I'm already almost there."

Before they separated for the night, in the smoking room, they had several whisky cocktails.

"We must make it gay!" Mr. Arcularis said. "Above all, we must make it gay. Perhaps even now it will turn out to be nothing but a nightmare from which both of us will wake! And even at the worst, at my present rate of travel, I ought to need two more nights! It's a long way, still, to that little star."

The parson passed them at the door.

"What! Turning in so soon?" he said. "I was hoping for a game of chess."

"Yes, both turning in. But tomorrow?"

"Tomorrow, then, Miss Dean! And good night!"

"Good night."

They walked once round the deck, then leaned on the railing and stared into the fog. It was thicker and whiter than ever. The ship was moving barely perceptibly, the rhythm of the engines was slower, more subdued and remote, and at regular intervals, mournfully, came the long reverberating cry of the foghorn. The sea was calm, and lapped only very tenderly against the side of the ship, the sound coming up to them clearly, however, because of the profound stillness.

" 'On such a night as this——' " quoted Mr. Arcularis grimly.

" 'On such a night as this——' "

Their voices hung suspended in the night, time ceased for them, for an eternal instant they were happy. When at last they parted it was by tacit agreement on a note of the ridiculous.

"Be a good boy and take your bromide!" she said.

"Yes, Mother, I'll take my medicine!"

In his stateroom he mixed himself a strong potion of bromide, a very strong one, and got into bed. He would have no trouble in falling asleep: he felt more tired, more supremely exhausted, than he had ever been in his life; nor had bed ever seemed so delicious. And that long, magnificent, delirious swoop of dizziness . . . the Great Circle . . . the swift pathway to Arcturus . . .

It was all as before, but infinitely more rapid. Never had Mr. Arcularis achieved such phenomenal, such supernatural, speed. In no time at all he was beyond the moon, shot past the North Star as if it were standing still (which perhaps it was?), swooped in a long, bright curve round the Pleiades, shouted his frosty greetings to Betelgeuse, and was off to the little blue star which pointed the way to the unknown. Forward into the untrodden! Courage, old man, and hold on to your umbrella! Have you got your garters on? Mind your hat! In no time at all we'll be back to Clarice with the frozen time feather, the rime feather, the snowflake of the Absolute, the Obsolete. If only we don't wake . . . if only we needn't wake . . . if only we don't wake in that—in that—time and space . . . somewhere or nowhere . . . cold and dark . . . *Cavalleria Rusticana* sobbing among the palms; if a lonely . . . if only . . . the coffers of the poor —not coffers, not coffers, not coffers, oh, God, not coffers, but light, delight, supreme white and brightness, and above all whirling lightness, whirling lightness above all—and freezing—freezing—freezing . . .

At this point in the void the surgeon's last effort to save Mr. Arcularis' life had failed. He stood back from the operating table and made a tired gesture with a rubber-gloved hand.

"It's all over," he said. "As I expected."

He looked at Miss Hoyle, whose gaze was downward, at the basin she held. There was a moment's stillness, a pause, a brief flight of unexchanged comment, and then the ordered life of the hospital was resumed.

LOUIS BROMFIELD

Justice

THE SPECKS of dust danced in the long sunbeams that fell across the dim courtroom. The judge cleared his throat. He was a lean man, bald and with a not unkindly face, but impersonal, too intellectual, too calloused.

"The case of the people against Michael Rooney!"

The shuffling among the spectators died away. The clerk, a tired old man with long, drooping mustaches, fumbled among his papers, rattling a little, as if he, too, were desiccated and dusty. The district attorney, handsome, Jewish, urbane, intelligent, sat down by a table to run his pencil through the copy of the indictment. His manner spoke for him: "One among so many. I've forgotten the circumstances of this one." He was a little bored, a little weary. He was not in the least interested in sending Michael Rooney off to prison.

Below us—the twelve good men and true—sat the defendant Michael Rooney and his attorney.

"Gentlemen," continued the judge in his polite, incisive, colorless voice. "The defendant Michael Rooney is charged with grand larceny in the first degree. The case should not require much time. It is a simple one. The evidence is simple. There are no complications. The defendant Michael Rooney is charged with having acted as lookout during the robbery of one Patrick Love on the night of June 24." The judge rustled the papers before him. "He was indicted jointly with one Willie Fallon, who has already pleaded guilty to the charge of grand larceny in the first degree."

Feet shuffled nervously. The district attorney rose languidly. You liked him. He inspired confidence, a sense of impartiality. He addressed the jury.

Did any of us know him or the attorney for the defendant? Did any of us feel in any way prejudiced against himself, or the defendant, or the defendant's attorney? Did we understand that an indictment implied no guilt whatever? That it was simply a means of bringing a charge? We had a moment to answer if we had any answer to make. Silence. The machine rolled over us.

I examined myself. I *was* prejudiced against the attorney for the defendant. I knew this. I could not say so in court. I had never seen him before. There must have been others among the twelve men who felt dimly the same prejudice. The man was repulsive. He sat, like a toad, like a crawling thing you might find under a stone—oily, obsequious, with an air of maddening pomposity. He scratched a miserable existence by being appointed to defend unfortunate men who had no money to pay counsel. He hung about the court waiting for the judge to throw him a bone. A despicable character, whom it was impossible to respect. A shyster lawyer! Lawyers were bad enough, with all their tricks, but a shyster lawyer!

Did we understand that an indictment implied no guilt whatever? That it was simply a means of bringing a charge?

I understood that. No doubt the other eleven did. Yet . . . ? In the back of my mind, in some region beyond my control, a little voice kept saying, "There must be something in it. A jury believed enough of the story to bring a charge. It can't be false altogether." I instructed that portion of my mind to be still. It would not be still.

I am, I suppose, a man of average intelligence, but I could not still the voice. About me in the jury box were men less intelligent, men whose minds were little better than those of children, men whose minds were full of prejudices, of racial hatred, of a thousand bitter, twisted convictions. How many of them were like that? Who could say? Some of them certainly were. To some of them that little voice must be shouting.

The attorney for the defendant began the same set of questions. Again a slight pause in which to answer. The machine rolled on.

"I am satisfied," the toad told the judge. (I must not feel prejudiced against that man.)

The machine paused for a moment. More rustling of papers. A consultation. I fell to regarding the defendant Michael Rooney.

He sat with his cap in his hands, his eyes fixed upon a scrap of paper on the table before him. He was an ordinary youth, like a million others. He wore a shabby blue suit, bought on Eighth Avenue, high-waisted and fastened with a single button. His hair was dark, reddish. His hands large, clearly the hands of one who did manual labor. There was nothing unusual about him, save perhaps the breadth of shoulders and the faint swagger they carried.

He raised his head, looking straight at us, and I knew suddenly that there was something different about Michael Rooney. He was not at all like a million others. What was the difference, the distinction? The smoldering light in the blue eyes? The slightly pointed tip of the ears? That indiscernible air of swagger? Impossible to say. Yet the impression was vivid, unmistakable. There was a spark . . . something . . . which only a few men have in this civilized day. Who can say what it was? What marked him? What placed him? A gift of life which only a few men have? I think it was a sense of wildness and freedom.

On the table before him was a little spot of sunlight.

Amid a rustling of papers the machine was moving again.

"The circumstances of the case are simple," began the prosecuting attorney. "On the night of June 24 a police officer saw the defendant Michael Rooney and the codefendant Willie Fallon enter a doorway with one Patrick Love, who, it appeared, had been drinking heavily. A moment later he says he saw the defendant Michael Rooney step out from the hallway into the street and look up and down. Then the officer crossed the street and entered the hallway. He discovered the codefendant Willie Fallon with one hand in the trousers pocket of the complainant Patrick Love. At his approach Fallon withdrew his hand and two quarters fell to the floor. The defendant Michael Rooney, so the police officer says, was standing by. As the case progresses you will hear the stories of the various witnesses."

The case progressed.

The complainant, Patrick Love, stepped into the box. He was a man of perhaps forty, seared, bloated, savage in appearance, resembling a baboon. He was a creature, scarcely a man, unmistakably at the lowest rung of the human ladder. He spoke with an appalling brogue. He did not understand the simplest questions. The questions had to be repeated again and again. The machine terrified him. He had lost his wits.

He was a laborer, he said. He had been in the city about five weeks. Before that he worked in St. Louis. He went where he could find work. Sometimes a strikebreaker. On the day of the robbery he had been to Celtic Park to see the football matches. He had many drinks, so many he couldn't remember the number. At seven in the evening he had gone to the neighborhood of Ninth Avenue and Forty-ninth Street, where he heard there was a dance. No, he never got to the dance. He stopped at a saloon and had more drinks. How many? He did not know. He could remember nothing save that he left the saloon and started up Ninth Avenue. He had in his pocket, he believed, seventeen dollars. No, he wasn't sure, but he remembered changing a twenty-dollar bill sometime during the day. Did he know the defendant Michael Rooney? No. Had he ever seen him before? No. Had he seen him on the night of the robbery? He might have. He couldn't say. He remembered nothing.

The prosecuting attorney questioned and the attorney for the defense protested questions, he asked that they be struck out. The stupidity of the man! Even a layman could see his protests were idiotic. He was a toad trying to halt a steam roller. The judge, curt, dignified, denied his protests. Each time the shyster spoke people noticed him and that fed his sense of importance. Each time he rose to protest, he was for a second at least the center of attention. (I must not feel prejudiced against the man.)

He, too, questioned the complainant Patrick Love. The story remained the same. He had been robbed, the money taken from his pocket. He did not know how, he did not know when or he did not know where. He was too drunk. The dustman might have swept him up and dumped him into the river with no loss to anyone.

I looked again at the defendant Michael Rooney. Did he know the complainant? Had he robbed him? Who could say? Nothing in his face revealed the truth, or the lack of truth. He sat watching that speck of precious sunlight, crossing the table before him, moving slowly away, slipping down toward one leg of the table. The shoulders remained squared, a little defiant in the face of the machine.

Police Officer Redmond stepped into the box. Red-faced, hair *en brosse* like the comb of a fighting cock. Turned-up nose. Pale blue eyes. Awkward manner in the face of the machine. He told his story.

It followed closely the outline of the district attorney. He had found in the pockets of the defendant Rooney and the codefendant Fallon the total sum of one dollar and sixty-five cents. Together it was all they had. No, they could not have taken more than that amount from the complainant Patrick Love. It was all they had, both of them, together. He was certain of the identity of the defendant Rooney and the codefendant Fallon. He saw them enter the hallway with the complainant Love between them. Yes, there were other men standing near the doorway. Three or four, he couldn't be certain. No, he was sure that the defendant Rooney had been implicated. He wasn't simply standing beside the doorway. The time? The hour was ten minutes to two. "I had just happened to look at my watch. I seen it happen from the opposite side of the avenue."

I watched the face of Michael Rooney. He had forgotten the fleeting sunbeam. He faced Police Officer Redmond boldly. The light in his Irish eyes flamed a little higher. The shoulders squared more defiantly. Not the proper attitude for a prisoner. No cowering. Too much defiance. More like a leopard shut up behind bars.

The machine moved on.

The defendant Michael Rooney took the stand. With hand on the Bible, he swore the oath that every witness swears and some of them must break, since all cannot tell the truth. He sat down, still twisting the cap in his hand. The light was still in his eye. For a moment it dimmed, but instantly flared up again. He did not cringe. His body did not sag.

Yes. He was arrested at Ninth Avenue and Forty-ninth Street. He was on his way home. He had taken a girl home from a dance and was passing the corner when the officer arrested him. He lived with his sister and brother-in-law. He did not rob Patrick Love. He had never before seen the codefendant Willie Fallon. Yes. He lived on the same block with Fallon. He had lived there for five years. And still did not know Fallon, who had already pleaded guilty to the charge? No. Had never seen him until they were arrested together. The name of the girl he was seeing home? Nellie Rand. Where was she now? Why was she not in court? She had moved away. He did not know her new address. He had known her three years. They met on a street corner. Before she moved away she had lived near the scene of the crime, a block away.

I began to wonder. Nellie Rand! Was she a real person? Was she a woman at all? Was she simply a symbol of all women? Of street-corner encounters? The defendant Michael Rooney had the air of a man who

was death to the ladies. A cock among hens . . . that free swagger, that
sense of wildness, that light in the eye. A man born to live wildly. A man
born free. I began to believe that he was guilty. I also began to believe
that it made no difference.

The defendant Michael Rooney stuck to his story. He had not stepped
into the street. He had not aided in the robbery of Patrick Love. He did
not know the codefendant Willie Fallon.

Presently the machine had done with him. He got down and went
back to sit beside the toad.

Another pause; more rustling of papers.

I knew the town. I knew the block where Michael Rooney lived. Rows
of filthy brick houses, fifteen people living in three rooms. Streets littered
with garbage, flying dust, and old newspapers. Filth. Sweat. Hardship.
Poverty. Five years in that block where men and women, even children,
fought simply to live. Oh yes. I knew it!

The machine was rolling again.

The codefendant Willie Fallon stepped into the box. He, too, swore to
tell the truth, like the complainant Patrick Love, the police officer Redmond, the defendant Michael Rooney. He wore pants of khaki, a blue
shirt open at the throat. Tousled brown hair. Blue eyes close together. A
long nose. Manner bewildered.

He had been on the corner on the night of the arrest. He had picked
the complainant Patrick Love out of the gutter where he was lying in
the filth. He couldn't walk, so he dragged him into the hallway and
propped him up on the lower step. He could not remember quite clearly.
He had been drinking himself. He did remember loosening Love's collar.
He could not remember having robbed Love. He supposed he done it, if
the policeman said so.

There was a sudden halt. The polite voice of the judge interrupted the
questioning. He said that if Willie Fallon pleaded guilty only because the
police officer said he committed the crime the plea must be changed. A
man could not plead guilty unless he knew that he had committed a
crime.

"Mr. Clerk, change the plea of the codefendant Willie Fallon to not
guilty."

In the box the codefendant Willie Fallon sat wooden. Clearly it was
all the same to him. He didn't understand any of it. He, too, had a lawyer
who made a living by hanging about court.

The questioning began again. No, he did not know the defendant Michael Rooney. Had never seen him up to the night of the arrest. He had lived in the same block, but only a month. He had been out of work for two weeks. He had been out of work off and on ever since he got out of the Army. Why didn't he rejoin? Hell, nothing could get him back into the Army. He'd had enough of that. Being knocked around.

"That will do, Mr. Fallon."

The codefendant Willie Fallon shuffled off, led through a barred runway by a guard.

In his chair the defendant Michael Rooney sat upright, the cap clutched desperately in his hands. He was looking at the bit of paper. The spot of sunlight was slipping away, gently, easily.

One more witness. Giovanni Sardi. Blacksmith. Character witness. Short, powerful, swarthy, dressed for court in a Palm Beach suit and Panama hat. Very broken in English.

"A blacksmith, you say?" queried the judge with a twinkle.

"Yes . . . blacksmith . . . my card." He handed the judge a card.

"'Wagon repairing,'" read the judge to the court. "'Iron work, et cetera.'" He leaned toward Giovanni Sardi. "You don't shoe horses?"

Sardi grinned. "No shoe horses."

"I'm glad of that. Then you're not a real blacksmith. I'd hate to think of a real blacksmith in a Palm Beach suit. Spoils the illusion. Spreading chestnut tree . . . all that."

A compensating titter swept the courtroom.

Giovanni Sardi testified that the defendant Michael Rooney worked for him as a helper. Four years ago. Yes. Good fella . . . Good fella . . . Everybody like him. Especially the girls.

The Palm Beach blacksmith, grinning, confused, vanished.

Again a pause. A rustling of papers. The wall was closing in.

The prosecuting attorney and the attorney for the defense dispensed with summing up. Such a simple case. No need for it. The judge turned toward the twelve good men and true. The object of the trial, he said, was to prove the innocence or the guilt of the defendant Michael Rooney. The presumption, in our courts, was that a man was innocent until proven guilty. We must remember that. An indictment meant nothing, no indication of guilt. Our problem was to determine who was telling the truth. Was it probable that the defendant Michael Rooney happened to be on that one corner of all corners at the moment of the crime, to which the co-defendant Willie Fallon had already pleaded guilty—or, at least, said he must be guilty if the police officer said he was? We must be satisfied beyond a reasonable doubt. The law recognized no degree of guilt. If the defendant Michael Rooney stepped from the doorway to shield and protect the codefendant Willie Fallon, he was as guilty as if he himself had taken the money from the pocket of the intoxicated complainant Patrick Love. We must remember that. The amount of money charged in the indictment—the judge rustled his papers—one dollar and sixty-five cents, had nothing to do with the case. The charge was that a man had been held up and robbed in the nighttime. That was what made the affair serious. We must not allow the so-called crime wave to influence our judgment. If the defendant Michael Rooney was innocent, he was innocent whether or not there was any crime wave.

He told us a great deal more . . . a list of things we must do or must not do in reaching a judgment. The instructions seemed to carry an inverse meaning, as if each one meant exactly the opposite of what the judge intended them to mean. The indictment did carry an implication of guilt. We must be influenced by the crime wave. It is not clear. I cannot explain it. The speech was gently cynical, ironic—unconsciously so, I have no doubt. He must have said the same things so many times.

And at last, with a great shuffling of feet, we rose and filed out. I saw the eyes of the defendant Michael Rooney following us, wistfully. Again I was thankful I was not in his shoes. He still clutched the cap. The swagger had diminished a little. The spot of glowing sunlight had slipped away, quite to the edge of the table.

The twelve good men and true were shut up in a little room with a barred window at one end. We sat in twelve chairs about a long table. The room was bare. Nothing to distract our minds. Pure justice was our goal.

Silence. A thin, stooped, middle-sized man—a clerk, no doubt—cleared his throat officiously.

"Let's get the business over. I've work to do. It's the first time I've missed an hour from the office in ten years."

"To begin with," said I, "we might take a vote."

The foreman stood up, plump, goggle-eyed, kindly. "Gentlemen, how do we stand?"

We stood evenly divided, six for conviction, six for acquittal. I, with five others, remained seated.

One of those standing, a big man with a bullneck, in a checked suit, glared at me—hard as if I were a criminal.

"The fellow's guilty as hell!" he shouted. "Did you see him cringing there in the box? He couldn't look you in the eye. That's the way you can tell—every time!"

Michael Rooney had not cringed at all.

Another attacked the six seated jurors. A little man, full of importance, with jowls and a furtive eye. He spoke with a rich accent. I knew the sort. Man of property. Cloak-and-suit business. Worked his way up, by any sort of means.

"It's our duty to act, gentlemen . . . to protect society. No one is more softhearted than me. But if we let this fella go there'll only be more hold-ups, more robberies. Think of what the fur trade has lost in loft robberies alone. Something's got to be done. A fella ain't safe to walk a block at nighttime. You remember the judge pointed out it was nighttime. It's our duty to send this fella away."

I protested. I recalled to them what the judge had said, how he had counseled us to be fair, thoughtful.

One of those seated—a fat, good-natured old fellow—supported me. "It's a serious charge . . . grand larceny in the first degree . . . next to murder. They can give him a stiff sentence . . . five or ten years."

In the back of my mind a voice kept saying, "He's guilty. You know he's guilty."

A little insignificant man, one of those who had asserted himself for conviction, found an opening. He related a long and complicated story of the perils of the streets at nighttime. He worked in the nighttime. Every night the policeman on the corner escorted him home because he said it wasn't safe. A lot of fellas like this Rooney running around loose. You could tell by the way the fella swaggered that he was a bad one. In the box he was defiant. Not at all the proper attitude. What chance had a little fella in the nighttime against a guy like Rooney? It was an age-old cry of vengeance, the little fellow against the full-grown man.

The clerk who had not missed an hour from his office in ten years looked at his watch. He was eager to be back in his chains. To be free made him terrified and nervous.

"We might take another vote," suggested the mild foreman.

This time only two of us remained seated, the irresponsible fat man and myself.

"They haven't proved anything," I persisted, "not a thing. It's pretty hard to send a fellow away on such evidence."

The bull-necked gentleman turned on me savagely. "Ain't you got any intelligence? It's plain as day!"

In his wake the cloak-and-suit business followed in the attack. He was polite, oily. "Just look at that fella's face. Ain't it enough? Maybe someday you'll be robbed, eh? It ain't safe, I tell you. It ain't safe."

In the back of my mind a voice kept saying, "What's the use? If you disagreed there would be another trial. They'd only convict him. Anyway, you know he's guilty." I kept seeing things too. Michael Rooney's block and the kids in it that never escaped until they died.

The anxious clerk interrupted. "That other fellow—Fallon. You heard what he said about the Army. A fine way to talk. No patriotism. No cooperation. That's the kind they are."

"You could see Fallon was trying to shield him," added the gentleman in the checked suit. "Anybody could see that. Saying he didn't know Rooney. A lot of bunk!"

The foreman's monotonous voice again. "Gentlemen, we might take another vote."

This time I was deserted by my fat friend. He stood up. They waited. I was the ordinary citizen. Slowly I, too, got to my feet.

The cloak-and-suit business heaved a sigh of relief. "Well, that's done. Gentlemen, I congratulate you. We haff done our duty."

The little man regarded his watch. "It only took us ten minutes," he said. "Maybe the judge wouldn't like such a quick verdict."

"Maybe we'd better wait a little while," said the cloak-and-suit man.

"Sure," said the complacent fat gentleman. "We might enjoy another smoke before going in."

So we sat and smoked and talked of the crime wave for ten more minutes. We had to create with the judge an impression of our profundity, our deep deliberation.

When we entered, the courtroom was still. We took our places. The roll was called.

"Michael Rooney, face the jury and hear the verdict!"

The defendant Michael Rooney was brought before us. He looked at us squarely. His knees, I think, trembled a little. His face grew a shade

more pale. But the light did not go out of his eyes, nor the defiance from
his broad shoulders. He turned his cap round and round, awkwardly.
Somewhere in the background the attorney for the defense regarded us
with an oily smile. He was rubbing his hands all the while. His manner
said with oily confidence, "Gentlemen, don't think I'm in sympathy
with the prisoner. I'm appointed to defend him. I'm a good honest citizen
. . . one of the best!"

"Foreman of the jury, have you reached a verdict?"

"Yes, your honor."

I looked away from Michael Rooney. He seemed to accuse me . . . of
what? Of doing my duty. Simply that. Nothing more. Of betraying him
to those other men, the nervous clerk, the bully, the insignificant fellow,
the cloak-and-suit business—to all the ones who were not what he was
and hated him for it.

"Do you find the defendant Michael Rooney guilty or not guilty of
grand larceny in the first degree?"

"Your honor"—the voice of the foreman trembled a little—"we find him
guilty of grand larceny in the first degree."

My eyes, beyond control, sought Michael Rooney. He stared at us with
the air of a stoic, as if he did not see us at all. Then, slowly, his shoulders
drooped. The cap fell to the floor. The light, which had persisted through
everything, went suddenly out of his eyes.

We had killed Michael Rooney. The thing which was Michael Rooney,
the essence of him, the fire, the freedom, the swagger, the light in his
Irish eyes. This we had slain. For stealing . . . if he did steal it . . . one
dollar and sixty-five cents from a besotted animal, we had killed a rare
thing in an abominable civilized world.

The whole affair was over and finished in an hour and ten minutes.
One must hurry. So many cases.

Five years . . . Ten years! Michael Rooney after that? No, it was
better not to think of it, for it was the end of Michael Rooney.

The judge in his polite, incisive voice dismissed us, without comment.
I heard Michael Rooney answering his questions. "First conviction. . . .
Twenty-five years old. . . . Parents dead. . . . Single. . . ."

Twenty-five plus ten . . . Twenty-five plus five. One dollar and sixty-
five cents.

The machine began to roll on. "Bertha Fradkin to the bar!"

Curious, I waited for a moment. Bertha Fradkin was a bedraggled woman of perhaps thirty-five, in an ill-fitting tan suit. She had the face and the eyes of a moron. They were sentencing her. I heard that cold, polite voice of the judge, a voice like the voice of a machine.

"Bertha Fradkin, I sentence you to life imprisonment."

There was a curious empty silence and the muffled, sickening sound of a groan and a body crumpling upon the floor. It was her fourth offense.

I went out of the room. I had served the state and done my duty. I must forget the experience as quickly as possible. Life is too short to brood over things.

JAMES M. CAIN

The Baby in the Icebox

OF COURSE there was plenty pieces in the paper about what happened out at the place last summer, but they got it all mixed up, so I will now put down how it really was, and specially the beginning of it, so you will see it is not no lies in it.

Because when a guy and his wife begin to play leapfrog with a tiger, like you might say, and the papers put in about that part and not none of the stuff that started it off, and then one day say X marks the spot and next day say it wasn't really no murder but don't tell you what it was, why, I don't blame people if they figure there was something funny about it or maybe that somebody ought to be locked up in the booby hatch. But there wasn't no booby hatch to this, nothing but plain onriness and a dirty rat getting it in the neck where he had it coming to him, as you will see when I get the first part explained right.

Things first begun to go sour between Duke and Lura when they put the cats in. They didn't need no cats. They had a combination auto camp, filling station, and lunchroom out in the country a ways, and they got along all right. Duke run the filling station, and got me in to help him, and Lura took care of the lunchroom and shacks. But Duke wasn't satisfied. Before he got this place he had raised rabbits, and one time he had bees, and another time canary birds, and nothing would suit him now but to put in some cats to draw trade. Maybe you think that's funny, but out here in California they got every kind of a farm there is, from kangaroos to alligators, and it was just about the idea that a guy like Duke would think up. So he begun building a cage, and one day he showed up with a truckload of wildcats.

I wasn't there when they unloaded them. It was two or three cars waiting and I had to gas them up. But soon as I got a chance I went back there to look things over. And believe me, they wasn't pretty. The guy that sold Duke the cats had went away about five minutes before, and Duke was standing outside the cage and he had a stick of wood in his hand with blood on it. Inside was a dead cat. The rest of them was on a shelf, that had been built for them to jump on, and every one of them was snarling at Duke.

I don't know if you ever saw a wildcat, but they are about twice as big as a house cat, brindle gray, with tufted ears and a bobbed tail. When they set and look at you they look like a owl, but they wasn't setting and looking now. They was marching around, coughing and spitting, their eyes shooting red and green fire, and it was a ugly sight, specially with that bloody dead one down on the ground. Duke was pale, and the breath was whistling through his nose, and it didn't take no doctor to see he was scared to death.

"You better bury that cat," he says to me. "I'll take care of the cars."

I looked through the wire and he grabbed me. "Look out!" he says. "They'd kill you in a minute."

"In that case," I says, "how do I get the cat out?"

"You'll have to get a stick," he says, and shoves off.

I was pretty sore, but I begun looking around for a stick. I found one, but when I got back to the cage Lura was there. "How did that happen?" she says.

"I don't know," I says, "but I can tell you this much: if there's any more of them to be buried around here, you can get somebody else to do it. My job is to fix flats, and I'm not going to be no cat undertaker."

She didn't have nothing to say to that. She just stood there while I was trying the stick, and I could hear her toe snapping up and down in the sand, and from that I knowed she was choking it back, what she really thought, and didn't think no more of this here cat idea than I did.

The stick was too short. "My," she says, pretty disagreeable, "that looks terrible. You can't bring people out here with a thing like that in there."

"All right," I snapped back. "Find me a stick."

She didn't make no move to find no stick. She put her hand on the gate. "Hold on," I says. "Them things are nothing to monkey with."

"Huh," she says. "All they look like to me is a bunch of cats."

There was a kennel back of the cage, with a drop door on it, where they was supposed to go at night. How you got them back there was bait them with food, but I didn't know that then. I yelled at them, to drive them back in there, but nothing happened. All they done was yell back. Lura listened to me awhile, and then she give a kind of gasp like she couldn't stand it no longer, opened the gate, and went in.

Now believe me, that next was a bad five minutes, because she wasn't hard to look at, and I hated to think of her getting mauled up by them babies. But a guy would of had to of been blind if it didn't show him that she had a way with cats. First thing she done, when she got in, she stood still, didn't make no sudden motions or nothing, and begun to talk to them. Not no special talk. Just "Pretty pussy, what's the matter, what they been doing to you?"—like that. Then she went over to them.

They slid off, on their bellies, to another part of the shelf. But she kept after them, and got her hand on one, and stroked him on the back. Then she got ahold of another one, and pretty soon she had give them all a pat. Then she turned around, picked up the dead cat by one leg, and come out with him. I put him on the wheelbarrow and buried him.

Now, why was it that Lura kept it from Duke how easy she had got the cat out and even about being in the cage at all? I think it was just because she didn't have the heart to show him up to hisself how silly he looked. Anyway, at supper that night, she never said a word. Duke, he was nervous and excited and told all about how the cats had jumped at him and how he had to bean one to save his life, and then he give a long spiel about cats and how fear is the only thing they understand, so you would of thought he was Martin Johnson just back from the jungle or something.

But it seemed to me the dishes was making quite a noise that night, clattering around on the table, and that was funny, because one thing you could say for Lura was: she was quiet and easy to be around. So when Duke, just like it was nothing at all, asks me by the way how did I get the cat out, I heared my mouth saying, "With a stick," and not nothing more. A little bird flies around and tells you, at a time like that. Lura let it pass.

Never said a word. And if you ask me, Duke never did find out how easy she could handle the cats, and that ain't only guesswork, but on account of something that happened a little while afterward, when we got the mountain lion.

A mountain lion is a cougar, only out here they call them a mountain lion. Well, one afternoon about five o'clock this one of ours squat down on her hunkers and set up the worst squalling you ever listen to. She kept it up all night, so you wanted to go out and shoot her, and next morning at breakfast Duke come running in and says come on out and look what happened. So we went out there, and there in the cage with her was the prettiest he mountain lion you ever seen in your life. He was big, probably weighed a hundred and fifty pounds, and his coat was a pearl gray so glossy it looked like a pair of new gloves, and he had a spot of white on his throat. Sometimes they have white.

"He come down from the hills when he heard her call last night," says Duke, "and he got in there somehow. Ain't it funny? When they hear that note nothing can stop them."

"Yeah," I says. "It's love."

"That's it," says Duke. "Well, we'll be having some little ones soon. Cheaper'n buying them."

After he had went off to town to buy the stuff for the day, Lura sat down to the table with me. "Nice of you," I says, "to let Romeo in last night."

"Romeo?" she says.

"Yes, Romeo. That's going to be papa of twins soon, out in the lion cage."

"Oh," she says, "didn't he get in there himself?"

"He did not. If she couldn't get out, how could he get in?"

All she give me at that time was a dead pan. Didn't know nothing about it at all. Fact of the matter, she made me a little sore. But after she brung me my second cup of coffee she kind of smiled. "Well?" she says. "You wouldn't keep two loving hearts apart, would you?"

So things was, like you might say, a little gritty, but they got a whole lot worse when Duke come home with Rajah, the tiger. Because by that time he had told so many lies that he begun to believe them hisself, and put on all the airs of a big animal trainer. When people come out on Sundays, he would take a black snake whip and go in with the mountain lions and wildcats, and snap it at them, and they would snarl and yowl, and Duke acted like he was doing something. Before he went in, he would let the people see him strapping on a big six-shooter, and Lura got sorer by the week.

For one thing, he looked so silly. She couldn't see nothing to going in with the cats, and specially she couldn't see no sense in going in with a whip, a six-shooter, and a ten-gallon hat like them cow people wears. And for another thing, it was bad for business. In the beginning, when Lura would take the customers' kids out and make out the cat had their finger, they loved it, and they loved it still more when the little mountain lions come and they had spots and would push up their ears to be scratched. But when Duke started that stuff with the whip it scared them to death, and even the fathers and mothers was nervous, because there was the gun and they didn't know what would happen next. So business begun to fall off.

And then one afternoon he put down a couple of drinks and figured it was time for him to go in there with Rajah. Now it had took Lura one minute to tame Rajah. She was in there sweeping out his cage one morning when Duke was away, and when he started sliding around on his belly he got a bucket of water in the face, and that was that. From then on he was her cat. But what happened when Duke tried to tame him was awful. The first I knew what he was up to was when he made a speech to the people from the mountain-lion cage telling them not to go away yet, there was more to come. And when he come out he headed over to the tiger.

"What's the big idea?" I says. "What you up to now?"

"I'm going in with that tiger," he says. "It's got to be done, and I might as well do it now."

"Why has it got to be done?" I says.

He looked at me like as though he pitied me.

"I guess there's a few things about cats you don't know yet," he says. "You got a tiger on your hands, you got to let him know who's boss, that's all."

"Yeah?" I says. "And who *is* boss?"

"You see that?" he says, and cocks his finger at his face.

"See what?" I says.

"The human eye," he says. "The human eye, that's all. A cat's afraid of it. And if you know your business, you'll keep him afraid of it. That's all I'll use, the human eye. But of course, just for protection, I've got these too."

"Listen, sweetheart," I says to him. "If you give me a choice between the human eye and a Bengal tiger, which one *I* got the most fear of, you're going to see a guy getting a shiner every time. If I was you, I'd lay off that cat."

He didn't say nothing: hitched up his holster, and went in. He didn't even get a chance to unlimber his whip. That tiger, soon as he saw him, begun to move around in a way that made your blood run cold. He didn't make for Duke first, you understand. He slid over, and in a second he was between Duke and the gate. That's one thing about a tiger you better not forget if you ever meet one. He can't work examples in arithmetic, but when it comes to the kind of brains that mean meat, he's the brightest boy in the class and then some. He's born knowing more about cutting off a retreat than you'll ever know, and his legs do it for him, just automatic, so his jaws will be free for the main business of the meeting.

Duke backed away, and his face was awful to see. He was straining every muscle to keep his mouth from sliding down in his collar. His left hand fingered the whip a little, and his right pawed around, like he had some idea of drawing the gun. But the tiger didn't give him time to make up his mind what his idea was, if any.

He would slide a few feet on his belly, then get up and trot a step or two, then slide on his belly again. He didn't make no noise, you understand. He wasn't telling Duke, "Please go away"; he meant to kill him, and a killer don't generally make no more fuss than he has to. So for a few seconds you could even hear Duke's feet sliding over the floor. But all of a sudden a kid begun to whimper, and I come to my senses. I run around to the back of the cage, because that was where the tiger was crowding him, and I yelled at him.

"Duke!" I says. "In his kennel! Quick!"

He didn't seem to hear me. He was still backing, and the tiger was still coming. A woman screamed. The tiger's head went down, he crouched on the ground, and tightened every muscle. I knew what that meant. Everybody knew what it meant, and specially Duke knew what it meant. He made a funny sound in his throat, turned, and ran.

That was when the tiger sprung. Duke had no idea where he was going, but when he turned he fell through the trap door and I snapped it down. The tiger hit it so hard I thought it would split. One of Duke's legs was out, and the tiger was on it in a flash, but all he got on that grab was the sole of Duke's shoe. Duke got his leg in somehow and I jammed the door down tight.

It was a sweet time at supper that night. Lura didn't see this here, because she was busy in the lunchroom when it happened, but them people had talked on their way out, and she knowed all about it. What she said was plenty. And Duke, what do you think he done? He passed it off like it wasn't nothing at all. "Just one of them things you got to expect," he says. And then he let on he knowed what he was doing all the time, and the only lucky part of it was that he didn't have to shoot a valuable animal like Rajah was. "Keep cool, that's the main thing," he says. "A thing like that can happen now and then, but never let a animal see you excited."

I heard him, and I couldn't believe my ears, but when I looked at Lura I jumped. I think I told you she wasn't hard to look at. She was a kind of medium size, with a shape that would make a guy leave his happy home, sunburned all over, and high cheekbones that give her eyes a funny slant. But her eyes was narrowed down to slits, looking at Duke, and they shot green where the light hit them, and it come over me all of a sudden that she looked so much like Rajah, when he was closing in on Duke in the afternoon, that she could of been his twin sister.

Next off, Duke got it in his head he was such a big cat man now that he had to go up in the hills and do some trapping. Bring in his own stuff, he called it.

I didn't pay much attention to it at the time. Of course, he never brought in no stuff, except a couple of raccoons that he probably bought down the road for two dollars, but Duke was the kind of a guy that every once in a while has to sit on a rock and fish, so when he loaded up the flivver and blew, it wasn't nothing you would get excited about. Maybe I didn't really care what he was up to, because it was pretty nice, running the place with Lura with him out of the way, and I didn't ask no questions. But it was more to it than cats or 'coons or fish, and Lura knowed it, even if I didn't.

Anyhow, it was while he was away on one of them trips of his that Wild Bill Smith, the Texas Tornado, showed up. Bill was a snake doctor. He had a truck, with his picture painted on it, and two or three boxes of old rattlesnakes with their teeth pulled out, and he sold snake oil that would cure what ailed you, and a Indian herb medicine that would do the same. He was a fake, but he was big and brown and had white teeth, and I guess he really wasn't no bad guy. The first I seen of him was when he drove up in his truck, and told me to gas him up and look at his tires. He had a bum differential that made a funny rattle, but he said never mind and went over to the lunchroom.

He was there a long time, and I thought I better let him know his car was ready. When I went over there, he was setting on a stool with a sheepish look on his face, rubbing his hand. He had a snake ring on one finger, with two red eyes, and on the back of his hand was red streaks. I knew what that meant. He had started something and Lura had fixed him. She had a pretty arm, but a grip like iron, that she said come from milking cows when she was a kid. What she done when a guy got fresh was take hold of his hand and squeeze it so the bones cracked, and he generally changed his mind.

She handed him his check without a word, and I told him what he owed on the car, and he paid up and left.

"So you settled his hash, hey?" I says to her.

"If there's one thing gets on my nerves," she says, "it's a man that starts something the minute he gets in the door."

"Why didn't you yell for me?"

"Oh, I didn't need no help."

But the next day he was back, and after I filled up his car I went over to see how he was behaving. He was setting at one of the tables this time, and Lura was standing beside him. I saw her jerk her hand away quick, and he give me the bright grin a man has when he's got something he wants to cover up. He was all teeth. "Nice day," he says. "Great weather you have in this country."

"So I hear," I says. "Your car's ready."

"What I owe you?" he says.

"Dollar twenty."

He counted it out and left.

"Listen," says Lura, "we weren't doing anything when you come in. He was just reading my hand. He's a snake doctor, and knows about the zodiac."

"Oh, wasn't we?" I says. "Well, wasn't we nice!"

"What's it to you?" she says.

"Nothing," I snapped at her. I was pretty sore.

"He says I was born under the sign of Yin," she says. You would of thought it was a piece of news fit to put in the paper.

"And who is Yin?" I says.

"It's Chinese for tiger," she says.

"Then bite yourself off a piece of raw meat," I says, and slammed out of there. We didn't have no nice time running the joint *that* day.

Next morning he was back. I kept away from the lunchroom, but I took a stroll and seen them back there with the tiger. We had hauled a tree in there by that time, for Rajah to sharpen his claws on, and she was setting on that. The tiger had his head in her lap, and Wild Bill was looking through the wire. He couldn't even draw his breath. I didn't go near enough to hear what they was saying. I went back to the car and begin blowing the horn.

He was back quite a few times after that, in between while Duke was away. Then one night I heard a truck drive up. I knowed that truck by its rattle. And it was daylight before I heard it go away.

Couple weeks after that Duke come running over to me at the filling station. "Shake hands with me," he says. "I'm going to be a father."

"Gee," I says, "that's great!"

But I took good care he wasn't around when I mentioned it to Lura.

"Congratulations," I says. "Letting Romeos into the place seems to be about the best thing you do."

"What do you mean?" she says.

"Nothing," I says. "Only I heard him drive up that night. Look like to me the moon was under the sign of Cupid. Well, it's nice if you can get away with it."

"Oh," she says.

"Yeah," I says. "A fine double cross you thought up. I didn't know they tried that any more."

She set and looked at me, and then her mouth begin to twitch and her eyes filled with tears. She tried to snuffle them up but it didn't work. "It's not any double cross," she says. "That night, I never went out there. And I never let anybody in. I was supposed to go away with him that night, but——"

She broke off and begin to cry. I took her in my arms. "But then you found this out?" I says. "Is that it?" She nodded her head. It's awful to have a pretty woman in your arms that's crying over somebody else.

From then on, it was terrible. Lura would go along two or three days pretty nice, trying to like Duke again on account of the baby coming, but then would come a day when she looked like some kind of a hex, with her eyes all sunk in so you could hardly see them at all, and not a word out of her.

Them bad days, anyhow when Duke wasn't around, she would spend with the tiger. She would set and watch him sleep, or maybe play with him, and he seemed to like it as much as she did. He was young when we got him, and mangy and thin, so you could see his slats. But now he was about six years old, and had been fed good, so he had got his growth and his coat was nice, and I think he was the biggest tiger I ever seen. A tiger, when he is really big, is a lot bigger than a lion, and sometimes when Rajah would be rubbing around Lura, he looked more like a mule than a cat.

His shoulders come up above her waist, and his head was so big it would cover both her legs when he put it in her lap. When his tail would go sliding past her it looked like some kind of a constrictor snake. His teeth were something to make you lie awake nights. A tiger has the biggest teeth of any cat, and Rajah's must have been four inches long, curved like a cavalry sword, and ivory white. They were the most murderous-looking fangs I ever set eyes on.

When Lura went to the hospital it was a hurry call, and she didn't even have time to get her clothes together. Next day Duke had to pack her bag, and he was strutting around, because it was a boy, and Lura had named him Ron. But when he come out with the bag he didn't have much of a strut. "Look what I found," he says to me, and fishes something out of his pocket. It was the snake ring.

"Well?" I says. "They sell them in any ten-cent store."

"H'm," he says, and kind of weighed the ring in his hand. That afternoon, when he come back, he says: "Ten-cent store, hey? I took it to a jeweler today, and he offered me two hundred dollars for it."

"You ought to sold it," I says. "Maybe save you bad luck."

Duke went away again right after Lura come back, and for a little while things was all right. She was crazy about the little boy, and I thought he was pretty cute myself, and we got along fine. But then Duke come back and at lunch one day he made a crack about the ring. Lura didn't say nothing, but he kept at it, and pretty soon she wheeled on him.

"All right," she says. "There was another man around here, and I loved him. He give me that ring, and it meant that he and I belonged to each other. But I didn't go with him, and you know why I didn't. For Ron's sake, I've tried to love you again, and maybe I can yet, God knows. A woman can do some funny things if she tries. But that's where we're at now. That's right where we're at. And if you don't like it, you better say what you're going to do."

"When was this?" says Duke.

"It was quite a while ago. I told you I give him up, and I give him up for keeps."

"It was just before you knowed about Ron, wasn't it?" he says.

"Hey," I cut in. "That's no way to talk."

"Just what I thought," he says, not paying no attention to me. "Ron. That's a funny name for a kid. I thought it was funny, right off when I heard it. Ron. Ron. That's a laugh, ain't it?"

"That's a lie," she says. "That's a lie, every bit of it. And it's not the only lie you've been getting away with around here. Or think you have. Trapping up in the hills, hey? And what do you trap?"

But she looked at me and choked it back. I begun to see that the cats wasn't the only things that had been gumming it up.

"All right," she wound up. "Say what you're going to do. Go on. Say it!"

But he didn't.

"Ron," he cackles, "that's a hot one," and walks out.

Next day was Saturday, and he acted funny all day. He wouldn't speak to me or Lura, and once or twice I heard him mumbling to himself. Right after supper he says to me, "How are we on oil?"

"All right," I says. "The truck was around yesterday."

"You better drive in and get some," he says. "I don't think we got enough."

"Enough?" I says. "We got enough for two weeks."

"Tomorrow is Sunday," he says, "and there'll be a big call for it. Bring out a hundred gallon and tell them to put it on the account."

By that time I would give in to one of his nutty ideas rather than have an argument with him, and besides, I never tumbled that he was up to anything. So I wasn't there for what happened next, but I got it out of Lura later, so here is how it was:

Lura didn't pay much attention to the argument about the oil, but washed up the supper dishes, and then went in the bedroom to make sure everything was all right with the baby. When she come out she left the door open, so she could hear if he cried. The bedroom was off the sitting room, because these here California houses don't have but one floor, and all the rooms connect. Then she lit the fire, because it was cool, and sat there watching it burn. Duke come in, walked around, and then went out back. "Close the door," she says to him. "I'll be right back," he says.

So she sat looking at the fire, she didn't know how long, maybe five minutes, maybe ten minutes. But pretty soon she felt the house shake. She thought maybe it was a earthquake, and looked at the pictures, but they was all hanging straight. Then she felt the house shake again. She listened, but it wasn't no truck outside that would cause it, and it wouldn't be no state-road blasting or nothing like that at that time of night. Then she felt it shake again, and this time it shook in a regular movement, one, two, three, four, like that. And then all of a sudden she knew what it was, why Duke had acted so funny all day, why he had sent me off for the oil, why he had left the door open, and all the rest of it. There was five hundred pound of cat walking through the house, and Duke had turned him loose to kill her.

She turned around, and Rajah was looking at her, not five foot away. She didn't do nothing for a minute, just set there thinking what a boob Duke was to figure on the tiger doing his dirty work for him, when all the time she could handle him easy as a kitten, only Duke didn't know it. Then she spoke. She expected Rajah to come and put his head in her lap, but he didn't. He stood there and growled, and his ears flattened back. That scared her, and she thought of the baby. I told you a tiger has that kind of brains. It no sooner went through her head about the baby than Rajah knowed she wanted to get to that door, and he was over there before she could get out of the chair.

He was snarling in a regular roar now, but he hadn't got a whiff of the baby yet, and he was still facing Lura. She could see he meant business. She reached in the fireplace, grabbed a stick that was burning bright, and walked him down with it. A tiger is afraid of fire, and she shoved it right in his eyes. He backed past the door, and she slid in the bedroom. But he was right after her, and she had to hold the stick at him with one hand and grab the baby with the other.

But she couldn't get out. He had her cornered, and he was kicking up such a awful fuss she knowed the stick wouldn't stop him long. So she dropped it, grabbed up the baby's covers, and threw them at his head. They went wild, but they saved her just the same. A tiger, if you throw something at him with a human smell, will generally jump on it and bite at it before he does anything else, and that's what he done now. He jumped so hard the rug went out from under him, and while he was scrambling to his feet she shot past him with the baby and pulled the door shut after her.

She run in my room, got a blanket, wrapped the baby in it, and run out to the electric icebox. It was the only thing around the place that was steel. Soon as she opened the door she knowed why she couldn't do nothing with Rajah. His meat was in there; Duke hadn't fed him. She pulled the meat out, shoved the baby in, cut off the current, and closed the door. Then she picked up the meat and went around the outside of the house to the window of the bedroom. She could see Rajah in there, biting at the top of the door, where a crack of light showed through. He reached to the ceiling. She took a grip on the meat and drove at the screen with it. It give way, and the meat went through. He was on it before it hit the floor.

Next thing was to give him time to eat. She figured she could handle him once he got something in his belly. She went back to the sitting room. And in there, kind of peering around, was Duke. He had his gun strapped on, and one look at his face was all she needed to know she hadn't made no mistake about why the tiger was loose.

"Oh," he says, kind of foolish, and then walked back and closed the door. "I meant to come back sooner, but I couldn't help looking at the night. You got no idea how beautiful it is. Stars is bright as anything."

"Yeah," she says. "I noticed."

"Beautiful," he says. "Beautiful."

"Was you expecting burglars or something?" she says, looking at the gun.

"Oh, that," he says. "No. Cat's been kicking up a fuss. I put it on, case I have to go back there. Always like to have it handy."

"The tiger," she says. "I thought I heard him, myself."

"Loud," says Duke. "Awful loud."

He waited. She waited. She wasn't going to give him the satisfaction of opening up first. But just then there come a growl from the bedroom, and the sound of bones cracking. A tiger acts awful sore when he eats. "What's that?" says Duke.

"I wonder," says Lura. She was hell-bent on making him spill it first.

They both looked at each other, and then there was more growls, and more sound of cracking bones. "You better go in there," says Duke, soft and easy, with the sweat standing out on his forehead and his eyes shining bright as marbles. "Something might be happening to Ron."

"Do you know what I think it is?" says Lura.

"What's that?" says Duke. His breath was whistling through his nose like it always done when he got excited.

"I think it's that tiger you sent in here to kill me," says Lura. "So you could bring in that woman you been running around with for over a year. That redhead that raises rabbit fryers on the Ventura road. That cat you been trapping!"

"And 'stead of getting you he got Ron," says Duke. "Little Ron! Oh my, ain't that tough? Go in there, why don't you? Ain't you got no mother love? Why don't you call up his pappy, get him in there? What's the matter? Is he afraid of a cat?"

Lura laughed at him. "All right," she says. "Now you go." With that she took hold of him. He tried to draw the gun, but she crumpled up his hand like a piece of wet paper and the gun fell on the floor. She bent him back on the table and beat his face in for him. Then she picked him up, dragged him to the front door, and threw him out. He run off a little ways. She come back and saw the gun. She picked it up, went to the door again, and threw it after him. "And take that peashooter with you," she says.

That was where she made her big mistake. When she turned to go back in the house he shot, and that was the last she knew for a while.

Now, for what happened next, it wasn't nobody there, only Duke and the tiger, but after them state cops got done fitting it all together, combing the ruins and all, it wasn't no trouble to tell how it was, anyway most of it, and here's how they figured it out:

Soon as Duke seen Lura fall, right there in front of the house, he knowed he was up against it. So the first thing he done was run to where she was and put the gun in her hand, to make it look like she had shot herself. That was where he made *his* big mistake, because if he had kept the gun he might of had a chance. Then he went inside to telephone, and what he said was, soon as he got hold of the state police: "For God's sake come out here quick. My wife has went crazy and throwed the baby to the tiger and shot herself and I'm all alone in the house with him and—*oh, my God, here he comes!*"

Now that last was something he didn't figure on saying. So far as he knowed, the tiger was in the room, having a nice meal off his son, so everything was hotsy-totsy. But what he didn't know was that that piece of burning firewood that Lura had dropped had set the room on fire and on account of that the tiger had got out. How did he get out? We never did quite figure that out. But this is how I figure it, and one man's guess is good as another's:

The fire started near the window, we knew that much. That was where Lura dropped the stick, right next to the cradle, and that was where a guy coming down the road in a car first seen the flames. And what I think is that soon as the tiger got his eye off the meat and seen the fire, he begun to scramble away from it, just wild. And when a wild tiger hits a beaver-board wall, he goes through, that's all. While Duke was telephoning, Rajah come through the wall like a clown through a hoop, and the first thing he seen was Duke, at the telephone, and Duke wasn't no friend, not to Rajah he wasn't.

Anyway, that's how things was when I got there with the oil. The state cops was a little ahead of me, and I met the ambulance with Lura in it, coming down the road seventy mile an hour, but just figured there had been a crash up the road, and didn't know nothing about it having Lura in it. And when I drove up there was plenty to look at all right. The house was in flames, and the police was trying to get in, but couldn't get nowheres near it on account of the heat, and about a hundred cars parked all around, with people looking, and a gasoline pumper cruising up and down the road, trying to find a water connection somewheres they could screw their hose to.

But inside the house was the terrible part. You could hear Duke screaming, and in between Duke was the tiger. And both of them was screams of fear, but I think the tiger was worse. It is a awful thing to hear a animal letting out a sound like that. It kept up about five minutes after I got there, and then all of a sudden you couldn't hear nothing but the tiger. And then in a minute that stopped.

There wasn't nothing to do about the fire. In a half hour the whole place was gone, and they was combing the ruins for Duke. Well, they found him. And in his head was four holes, two on each side, deep. We measured them fangs of the tiger. They just fit.

Soon as I could I run in to the hospital. They had got the bullet out by that time, and Lura was laying in bed all bandaged around the head, but there was a guard over her, on account of what Duke said over the telephone. He was a state cop. I sat down with him, and he didn't like it none. Neither did I. I knowed there was something funny about it, but what broke your heart was Lura, coming out of the ether. She would groan and mutter and try to say something so hard it would make your head ache.

After a while I got up and went in the hall. But then I see the state cop shoot out of the room and line down the hall as fast as he could go. At last she had said it. The baby was in the electric icebox. They found him there, still asleep and just about ready for his milk. The fire had blacked up the outside, but inside it was as cool and nice as a new bathtub.

Well, that was about all. They cleared Lura, soon as she told her story, and the baby in the icebox proved it. Soon as she got out of the hospital she got a offer from the movies, but 'stead of taking it she come out to the place and her and I run it for a while, anyway the filling-station end, sleeping in the shacks and getting along nice. But one night I heard a rattle from a bum differential, and I never even bothered to show up for breakfast the next morning.

I often wish I had. Maybe she left me a note.

JOHN CHEEVER

The Single Purpose of Leon Burrows

LEON BURROWS was deferred from military service until the summer of 1944 because he was the sole support of a maiden aunt. He clerked in a grocery store in Philadelphia, lived with his aunt, and went to the movies three times a week, eating a bar of candy as soon as he was seated and saving a second candy bar for the feature. Once or twice a year he would drink himself into a frenzy and wake up in some hallway with a black eye and a cut hand. In the spring of 1944 his aunt died, and at a time when his life was at its most unsettled the draft board ordered him to report for induction. He sold his aunt's furniture, was accepted by the Army, and was assigned to an Infantry Replacement Training Center in the South. He was thirty-one years old at the time.

Leon became a neat and obedient soldier. He was a thin man with reddish, curly hair and a mouthful of false teeth. The lines on his face were so deeply cut that they appeared to be scars. On the little finger of his left hand he wore a brass ring. The brass left a bright stain on his skin. His part in the life of his company was unobtrusive and secure. He played poker in his underwear, drank beer on Saturday nights, and joined in every crap game. He was sometimes mistaken for a soldier of the old Army.

Burrows put on a uniform lightheartedly because he had been drafted so late in the war that he never expected to see action. He thought he would be assigned to troops of occupation and he imagined himself billeted in a small French village near a trout stream, drinking wine by candlelight, and talking French like a native with a pretty, white-skinned girl. But the optimism that Leon had brought from civilian life had not penetrated to the backwaters of Georgia Army camps. "It's either kill or be killed," Burrows' lieutenants told him. "There's still a lot of this war to be fought. Any of you guys think you're going to be used for occupation troops will find yourselves sewed up in a sack, occupying some lousy graveyard." Leon came to believe his lieutenants.

One day Leon's platoon was marched some distance from the camp for an exercise in river crossing. It was a broad river and the water was the color of yellow clay. The men were to ford the river with full field packs and rifles. As they advanced into the water they yelled and hollered like kids in a swimming hole. Leon was very quiet. He couldn't swim and water frightened him. He noticed that the water was up to the shoulders of the men who had gone ahead of him. He moved cautiously, trying to find a secure footing in the slippery clay. The water was so cloudy that the bottom could not be seen at all and he imagined it as an evil morass of rubbish and treacherous roots. When the water was nearly up to his chest, he stumbled on a root and the river closed over his head.

He dropped his rifle and thrashed around insanely with his arms, but his foot was caught in the root and he could not free himself or regain his balance. As he went down he could see the color of the yellow water, lighted by the sky, deepen until it was mud-brown and then black. The water burned as it forced its way into his throat and nostrils, and the harder he struggled to free himself the more securely he seemed trapped by his wet pack and the root. Then he saw a searing corona of light in front of his eyes and tasted what seemed like blood mixed with the water in his nose and mouth.

The men on either side of him got a grip on his arms at last and pulled him to the surface. Water spilled out of his mouth. He thrashed his arms like a windmill, broke from the grasp of the men who were holding him, and headed for shallow water. The lieutenant ordered him back, but Leon paid no attention to him. His panic was like insanity, and on his way to the shore he stumbled and fell a number of times. He reached the bank, sat down, and held his head in his hands. The air, when he began to breathe regularly again, seemed very sweet. "I nearly drowned," he told the lieutenant when the officer came up to him, carrying Leon's rifle and helmet. "I went down three times. I saw my whole past life in front of me."

The lieutenant listened sympathetically. He was hardly twenty. He looked behind him. No one was watching. No one would ever know, and so he broke all the iron laws of war and told Leon to rest. "Take it easy for a while, Pop," he said. "We're coming back the same way. Take a rest and you can pick us up on our way back."

The lieutenant waded back across the river and Leon sat on the bank, watching him go. He was still profoundly shaken. Those few seconds under muddy water had given him an insight, he thought, into the confusion and disorder of death in battle, and he didn't want any of it. That was the way you died. You tripped on a root or walked into a sniper's sight. It was not that he was afraid of dying, but he had discovered under the water an intense desire to live, a desire so passionate and strong that it still left him trembling. He lit a cigarette and filled his lungs with tobacco smoke. The smoke tasted very good. He noticed then how much like mountains the clouds above the parched fields around him seemed. He noticed the uneasy sound the September wind made in the stands of holly along the river and he remembered a vacation he had once taken at a mountain lake in September. He remembered sitting on the pier in a rented bathing suit, fishing for rock bass. He remembered the sound of oarlocks from a passing rowboat and the noise of a hunter's gun on the hill behind the hotel. Then Leon's platoon returned and he joined it and marched back to barracks. He was very quiet for the rest of the evening.

Anti-tank training was announced a few days after the river crossing. The few old soldiers in the company knew what the announcement meant. They said the men would dig five-foot slit trenches and remain in them while heavy tanks drove over their heads. On the morning for which anti-tank training was slated Leon went to the orderly room. He knew that what he was about to do was wrong, but he could not have stopped himself any more than he could have kept himself from whisky when he had a thirst. He told the first sergeant he was sick. "You're not sick, Burrows, you're gold-bricking," the first sergeant said, "and if you're not out there for the training this morning, I'll see that you get court-martialed for the deliberate evasion of arduous military duty."

The men fell out with packs and entrenching tools. Leon joined them. They marched into a valley where the ground was sand and hard clay. A light tank was parked on the crest of a hill. The sight of the tank excited Leon. A lieutenant—the young lieutenant who had forgiven Leon at the river—formed them for a lecture. "Infantrymen can protect themselves from tank attack," he began, "by digging narrow slit trenches to a depth of five feet, the length of the slit trench to be at right angles to the front or to the direction of the approaching tank. An enemy tank can destroy a slit trench and crush a soldier by spinning its tracks, but more often than not a tank driver will not notice a well-concealed slit trench." He talked by rote, stumbling over the involved language of the manual.

When the lecture ended the men were given a ten-minute break. "They won't dare drive tanks over us," Leon said. "Too many guys would get killed. They won't dare drive tanks over us."

After the break the men were assigned an area in which to dig their trenches. Leon took off his pack and his helmet and unstrapped his short-handled trench shovel. He had come to know the soil of Georgia very well. There would be a foot of loose sand, then hard clay in strata, some of it as white and as hard as caked salt. Leon dug slowly and wondered about the tanks.

It was hard work and he began to sweat. He made some effort to make the trench neat, strong-walled, and deep. He had always been a conscientious soldier who prided himself on his work, but digging a hole strong enough to bear the weight of a tank seemed hopeless to him. The edges would crumble as they crumbled under the light touch of his shovel, and the sand and the clay would pour down and bury him alive. The lieutenant came by to inspect the trenches. "Good work, Burrows," he said. Leon's shoulders were level with the edge of the trench.

When the officer completed his inspection he shouted, "The tanks are coming through in three minutes! Get into those trenches! Sit on the floor of the trench and keep your head down between your legs!"

Leon was standing beside his trench. Suddenly the sweat came out of his body in such quantities that he could feel his mouth go dry. "Get into that trench, Burrows!" he heard the officer yelling. "Get into that trench, you God-damned fool!" He saw that he was the only man who had not taken cover. He didn't move. "Get into that trench, Burrows!" the officer shouted again. Leon dropped into his trench. A lip of the trench broke and a lot of sand and clay followed him down, spilling onto his head and shoulders. He felt then that he was surely going to be killed. He would be sitting there with his head between his legs and the tank would crush him as easily as he would crush a roach with his shoe. "If any of you men want to pretend that you're throwing grenades," the officer shouted with a forced cheerfulness, "pick up a rock or something and throw it at the tank before it comes over!" Leon's clothes were black with sweat. He thought his heart would burst. All the strength had gone out of his legs. He thought of the reasons he should not be killed. For one thing, it should not be an ordinary morning in Georgia after a breakfast of heavy wheat cakes. For another, there were a lot of things he had to do. He had to go to night school and study mechanical drawing. He had always wanted to go to night school and study mechanical drawing. He wanted to get married. He had to get married. He wanted to see the Painted Desert. He had always wanted to see the Painted Desert. He wanted to buy a tuxedo and wear it to a night club. He wanted to have children. He wanted to come home from work and have his children go through his pockets looking for presents.

The tank had to turn in order to face the line of trenches. The motor backfired like a cannon and the tracks clanked as the vehicle pushed through some underbrush to make the turn. The tank siren moaned a little. Now Leon was thinking about the color of the sky at seven o'clock in the morning when he had walked to work in Philadelphia. He could remember the hearty singing at beer parties, picnics at beaches, a trip in a rented canoe, the strange color of the grass at a night ball game, and a waitress in a lunch cart who had once told him she loved him. The tank completed the turn and began to pick up speed, mangling the saplings and young pines in its path at the edge of the clearing. Leon looked over the rim of the trench and saw the tank coming down in a cloud of dust. As the tank went faster the siren began to shrill. He saw the tracks bear down on the trenches ahead of him. Then it seemed as though his heart exploded and as though the concussion wrung his bowels pitilessly, forcing the bitter remains of his breakfast up his dry throat. Just before the shadow of the tank touched his trench he scrambled out, ran a few yards, and fell. The tank passed at his back. The young lieutenant ran over to where Leon lay. He was sobbing convulsively and chewing the knuckles of his right hand.

"Don't cry, Pop," the lieutenant told Leon, and he put his hand on the man's thin back. "Everybody gets a yellow streak once in a while. Don't worry about it. You'll be all right next time. Once when I was playing football I felt like that. I should have tackled this man, but I was afraid of the spikes on his shoes and I fell a couple of feet short, on purpose. Everybody could see what I was doing and he made a touchdown." Leon had never played football and he didn't understand what the lieutenant was talking about. It was decided that he had been taken sick. A friend walked him back to barracks, where he took a shower and lay on his bed.

Leon felt well enough to get up for retreat and evening chow. His friends treated him considerately, as though his cowardice had been some misfortune beyond his own power, like a death in the family. He remained very quiet. After chow he went to his foot locker and took ten aspirins from a jar there. Then he went to the latrine, swallowed the aspirins two at a time, and washed them down with water. He lit a cigarette and waited there in the latrine until he thought he could feel the effect of the pills on his heart. The beating of his heart seemed to have become slower and louder. He walked over to the dispensary, where a medic and another soldier were playing checkers. "Sit down," the medic said. "I'll be with you in a minute."

"It's my heart," Leon said, and he put his hand over his heart. "It hurts. I feel dizzy."

"Then why in hell didn't you come here for sick call?" the medic said. He was losing the checker game and the interruption irritated him. "There's no doctor here now. They have sick call every afternoon, but there's always some dumb son of a bitch who comes here about half past nine."

"My heart didn't hurt until after chow," Leon said.

"All right, all right," the medic said. He left the checkerboard, took a small white pillbox from a cabinet, and tossed it to Leon. "There's some pills for your heart," he said. "They're officers' pills. Take them three times a day before meals. I'm doing you a big favor. If the captain knew I was giving you officers' pills, he'd ream me a couple new eye sockets."

"It's my heart," Leon said. "It sounds like a hammer."

"Take those officers' pills," the medic said. "You take one of these pills and you'll feel like a chicken colonel. They'll put curl in your hair." Leon left the dispensary, dropped the pills into an ash can, and went to bed.

The next day at noon, when the rest of the company lined up for chow, Leon went to the latrine and took ten more aspirins. At one o'clock he signed the sick book and went up to the dispensary. He waited in line for nearly an hour before he was examined by the doctor. "It's my heart, sir," he told the young captain. "It hurts me. I can't sleep at night." The doctor listened briefly to his heart, took his pulse, looked into his mouth, and gave him a bottle of yellow medicine. Leon threw this into an ash can as he left the building.

On the following day he took aspirin before lunch again and returned to the dispensary.

The doctor recognized him and listened more carefully to his heart this time. "Have you ever had trouble with your heart before?" he asked.

"I've always had trouble with my heart," Leon said. "I faint a lot."

"Has anyone else in your family ever had heart trouble?" the doctor asked.

"I don't remember. My people are dead," Leon said.

"What's your serial number, Burrows?"

"Three, two, three——" Leon began. "I can't remember," he said.

"Has there ever been any insanity in your family?" the doctor asked.

"I can't remember," Leon said.

"What did you do before you came into the Army?"

"I can't remember," Leon said, and he looked squarely at the doctor.

"Repeat these numbers after me," the doctor said. "Seven, four, three, two, one, zero, eight, four."

"Seven, three, two——" Leon began. "I can't remember," he said.

The doctor wrote something on a slip of paper and told him to go into another room. They drove Leon to the hospital in an ambulance that afternoon. He sat up in front with the driver. Before they committed him to a ward they took away his shoelaces, his belt, and his necktie.

No one in the company knew what had happened to Leon. He returned from the hospital in ten days, looking thinner and older, but when his friends asked him why he had been sent there he did not reply. Then, on the afternoon of his second day back in the company, Sergeant O'Neil, his section sergeant, was called down to the orderly room. "Get into your O.D.s," the first sergeant told him. "Burrows is bucking for a section eight and the board is meeting in the dayroom. They want to ask you some questions."

O'Neil reported to the dayroom and was told to wait outside. It was the end of a pleasant, cool afternoon. Smells of cooking came from the mess hall. The sky was green. The company areas seemed deceptively less like emergency billets than like a country village—contrite, provincial, and contented. " 'You are my sunshine, my only sunshine,' " the mess sergeant sang loudly as he threw open the screen door and dumped some coffee grounds. In the distance the regimental band played "I'm Dreaming of a White Christmas" while the officer of the day inspected weapons.

O'Neil could hear nothing through the closed door of the dayroom. He didn't know what was expected of him, he didn't know the officers of the board, he didn't know Burrows well, and he was nervous. He was kept waiting for so long that he went over to the mess hall and got something to eat. It was beginning to get dark when a lieutenant opened the door and told him to report to the board.

O'Neil stepped into the room and saluted the officers. They sat at a covered pool table.

"You're Private Burrows' section sergeant, is that right, O'Neil?"

"Yes sir."

"Do you know this sergeant, Private Burrows?"

O'Neil noticed Burrows then. He was sitting to the right of the table. His hair had been cut very close. He had left his false teeth out and this made his face look drawn and foolish. Burrows usually dressed himself carefully, but the fatigues he had on that day were rancid and black and there was dirt on his hands and his face. He grunted his reply and let a little saliva leak over his chin.

"Would you say that Private Burrows is clean?" one of the officers asked O'Neil.

"Yes sir."

"Has he many friends?"

"He keeps to himself."

"You'd say he was a solitary, then?"

"He keeps to himself," O'Neil repeated. He didn't know the meaning of "solitary."

"Can he learn what you have to teach him?"

"He hasn't qualified on none of the weapons," O'Neil said.

"Can he memorize things?"

"Yes sir," O'Neil said, "I mean no sir."

"Which do you mean?"

"No sir," O'Neil said.

"You say that he's a solitary and that he can't memorize. Have you anything else to say? Do you remember any incidents that might prove his mental unfitness for military duty?"

"No sir."

"That's all, Sergeant."

Leon sat with his head hung between his shoulders. He could tell that the interview was going his way. He had been interrogated for nearly three hours and he was very tired. He wanted a cigarette. The dirty fatigues he had dressed himself in stank of gun oil and sweat, and he was a man who liked to be neat. The members of the board were whispering. Then the ranking officer turned to Leon.

"What is the range rule for the M1 rifle?" he asked.

"I can't remember," Leon said.

"What is your sixth general order?" another officer asked.

"I can't remember," Leon said.

"What is your first name?"

"Burrows," Leon said.

"Your first name, your first name. Burrows is your last name."

"I can't remember," Leon said.

"Why can't you remember your first name?"

"They took it away," Leon said.

"They took what away?"

"They took my name away," Leon said.

Two of the officers smiled. The ranking officer lighted a cigarette. "That's all, Burrows," he said. "You're dismissed."

Leon shuffled past the officers and went out the door. Once he was out of the dayroom he straightened his shoulders and wiped the dirt off his hands and face. He knew that he had succeeded. In another two days he would be in civilian clothes. He was free. But now that he was free of his fear he did not understand why that freedom should have seemed so desirable. He did not understand why he had dressed himself in filthy clothes and rubbed dirt on his face. He did not understand why he should be so depressed. He had followed his passions before, but no vice had ever left him so weak or so filled with self-loathing. When he had awakened on a bench in some Philadelphia subway station after a night of drinking he had been a prouder man.

MARC CONNELLY

Coroner's Inquest

"WHAT IS your name?"

"Frank Wineguard."

"Where do you live?"

"A hundred and eighty-five West Fifty-fifth Street."

"What is your business?"

"I'm stage manager for *Hello, America*."

"You were the employer of James Dawle?"

"In a way. We both worked for Mr. Bender, the producer, but I have charge backstage."

"Did you know Theodore Robel?"

"Yes sir."

"Was he in your company too?"

"No sir. I met him when we started rehearsals. That was about three months ago, in June. We sent out a call for midgets and he and Jimmy showed up together, with a lot of others. Robel was too big for us. I didn't see him again until we broke into their room Tuesday."

"You discovered their bodies?"

"Yes sir. Mrs. Pike, there, was with me."

"You found them both dead?"

"Yes sir."

"How did you happen to be over in Jersey City?"

"Well, I'd called up his house at curtain time Monday night when I found Jimmy hadn't shown up for the performance. Mrs. Pike told me they were both out, and I asked her to have either Jimmy or Robel call me when they came in. Then Mrs. Pike called me Tuesday morning and said she tried to get into the room but she'd found the door was bolted. She said all her other roomers were out and she was alone and scared.

"I'd kind of suspected something might be wrong. So I said to wait and

I'd come over. Then I took the tube over and got there about noon. Then we went up and I broke down the door."

"Did you see this knife there?"

"Yes sir. It was on the floor, about a foot from Jimmy."

"You say you suspected something was wrong. What do you mean by that?"

"I mean I felt something might have happened to Jimmy. Nothing like this, of course. But I knew he'd been feeling very depressed lately, and I knew Robel wasn't helping to cheer him up any."

"You mean that they had had quarrels?"

"No sir. They just both had the blues. Robel had had them for a long time. Robel was Jimmy's brother-in-law. He'd married Jimmy's sister—she was a midget too—about five years ago, but she died a year or so later. Jimmy had been living with them and after the sister died he and Robel took a room in Mrs. Pike's house together."

"How did you learn this?"

"Jimmy and I were pretty friendly at the theater. He was a nice little fellow and seemed grateful that I'd given him his job. We'd only needed one midget for an oriental scene in the second act and the agencies had sent about fifteen. Mr. Gehring, the director, told me to pick one of them as he was busy and I picked Jimmy because he was the littlest.

"After I got to know him he told me how glad he was I'd given him the job. He hadn't worked for nearly a year. He wasn't little enough to be a featured midget with circuses or in museums so he had to take whatever came along. Anyway, we got to be friendly and he used to tell me about his brother-in-law and all."

"He never suggested that there might be ill feeling between him and his brother-in-law?"

"No sir. I don't imagine he'd ever had any words at all with Robel. As a matter of fact from what I could gather I guess Jimmy had quite a lot of affection for him and he certainly did everything he could to help him. Robel was a lot worse off than Jimmy. Robel hadn't worked for a couple of years and Jimmy practically supported him. He used to tell me how Robel had been sunk ever since he got his late growth."

"His what?"

"His late growth. I heard it happens among midgets often, but Jimmy told me about it first. Usually a midget will stay as long as he lives at whatever height he reaches when he's fourteen or fifteen, but every now and then one of them starts growing again just before he's thirty, and he can grow a foot or even more in a couple of years. Then he stops growing for good. But of course he don't look so much like a midget any more.

"That's what had happened to Robel about three years ago. Of course he had trouble getting jobs and it hit him pretty hard.

"From what Jimmy told me and from what Mrs. Pike says, I guess he used to talk about it all the time. Robel used to come over and see his agent in New York twice a week, but there was never anything for him. Then he'd go back to Jersey City. Most of the week he lived alone because after the show started Jimmy often stayed in New York with a cousin or somebody that lived uptown.

"Lately Robel hadn't been coming over to New York at all. But every Saturday night Jimmy would go over to Jersey City and stay till Monday with him, trying to cheer him up. Every Sunday they'd take a walk and go to a movie. I guess as they walked along the street Robel realized most the difference in their heights. And I guess that's really why they're both dead now."

"How do you mean?"

"Well, as I told you, Jimmy would try to sympathize with Robel and cheer him up. He and Robel both realized that Jimmy was working and supporting them and that Jimmy would probably keep right on working, according to the ordinary breaks of the game, while Robel would always be too big. It simply preyed on Robel's mind.

"And then three weeks ago Monday Jimmy thought he saw the ax fall.

"I was standing outside the stage door—it was about seven-thirty—and Jimmy came down the alley. He looked down in the mouth, which I thought was strange, seeing that he usually used to come in swinging his little cane and looking pretty cheerful. I said, 'How are you feeling, Jimmy?' and he said, 'I don't feel so good, Mr. Wineguard.' So I said, 'Why, what's the matter, Jimmy?' I could see there really was something the matter with him by this time.

" 'I'm getting scared,' he said, and I says, 'Why?'

" 'I'm starting to grow again,' he says. He said it the way you'd say you just found out you had some disease that was going to kill you in a week. He looked like he was shivering.

" 'Why, you're crazy, Jimmy,' I says, 'You ain't growing.'

" 'Yes, I am,' he says. 'I'm thirty-one and it's that late growth like my brother-in-law has. My father had it, but his people had money, so it didn't make much difference to him. It's different with me. I've got to keep working.'

"He went on like that for a while and then I tried to kid him out of it.

" 'You look all right to me,' I said. 'How tall have you been all along?'

" 'Thirty-seven inches,' he says. So I says, 'Come on into the prop room and I'll measure you.'

"He backed away from me. 'No,' he says, 'I don't want to know how much it is.' Then he went up to the dressing room before I could argue with him.

"All week he looked awful sunk. When he showed up the next Monday evening he looked almost white.

"I grabbed him as he was starting upstairs to make up.

" 'Come on out of it,' I says. I thought he'd make a break and try to get away from me, but he didn't. He just sort of smiled as if I didn't understand. Finally he says, 'It ain't any use, Mr. Wineguard.'

" 'Listen,' I says, 'you've been over with that brother-in-law of yours, haven't you?' He said yes, he had. 'Well,' I says, 'that's what's bothering you. From what you tell me about him he's talked about his own tough luck so much that he's given you the willies too. Stay away from him the end of this week.'

"He stood there for a second without saying anything. Then he says, 'That wouldn't do any good. He's all alone over there and he needs company. Anyway, it's all up with me, I guess. I've grown nearly two inches already.'

"I looked at him. He was pretty pathetic, but outside of that there wasn't any change in him as far as I could see.

"I says, 'Have you been measured?' He said he hadn't. Then I said, 'Then how do you know? Your clothes fit you all right, except your pants, and as a matter of fact they seem a little longer.'

" 'I fixed my suspenders and let them down a lot farther,' he says. 'Besides, they were always a little big for me.'

" 'Let's make sure,' I says, 'I'll get a yardstick and we'll make absolutely sure.'

"But I guess he was too scared to face things. He wouldn't do it.

"He managed to dodge me all week. Then last Saturday night I ran into him as I was leaving the theater. I asked him if he felt any better.

" 'I feel all right,' he says. He really looked scared to death.

"That's the last time I saw him before I went over to Jersey City after Mrs. Pike phoned me Tuesday."

"Patrolman Gorlitz has testified that the bodies were in opposite ends of the room when he arrived. They were in that position when you forced open the door?"

"Yes sir."

"The medical examiner has testified that they were both dead of knife wounds, apparently from the same knife. Would you assume the knife had fallen from Dawle's hand as he fell?"

"Yes sir."

"Has it been your purpose to suggest that both men were driven to despondency by a fear of lack of employment for Dawle, and that they might have committed suicide?"

"No sir. I don't think anything of the kind."

"What do you mean?"

"Well, when Mrs. Pike and I went in the room and I got a look at the knife, I said to Mrs. Pike that that was a funny kind of a knife for them to have in the room. You can see it's a kind of a butcher knife. Then Mrs. Pike told me it was one that she'd missed from her kitchen a few weeks before. She'd never thought either Robel or Jimmy had taken it. It struck me as funny Robel or Jimmy had stolen it too. Then I put two and two together and found out what really happened. Have you got the little broken cane that was lying on the bed?"

"Is this it?"

"Yes sir. Well, I'd never been convinced by Jimmy that he was really growing. So when Mrs. Pike told me about the knife I started figuring. I figured that about five minutes before that knife came into play Jimmy must have found it, probably by accident."

"Why by accident?"

"Because Robel had gone a little crazy, I guess. He'd stolen it and kept it hidden from Jimmy. And when Jimmy found it he wondered what Robel had been doing with it. Then Robel wouldn't tell him and Jimmy found out for himself. Or maybe Robel did tell him. Anyway, Jimmy looked at the cane. It was the one he always carried. He saw where, when Jimmy wasn't looking, Robel had been cutting little pieces off the end of it!"

JAMES GOULD COZZENS

Farewell to Cuba

FROM THE Calle Lamparilla the voices of the newsdealers crying late afternoon papers mounted at last to Martin Gibbs. In lengthening shadows, in sunlight diluted by a preparatory stir of evening air, these regularly chanted calls joined with the continuous hoot of taxi horns and the hard squeal of applied brakes where the traffic came together three reckless ways under the soft weather-marked masses of the Christo Church. To Martin Gibbs it seemed a sound peculiarly Havana's. Surely nowhere else did they drive so impetuously, or raise a wail so drowsy and so sad over final editorials. Similarly, you could not smell anywhere else the Havana smell, the blend of air-slacked lime, roasting coffee, and spilled anisette; reinforced now with a perfume of flowers, now with breath of butcher shops where the meat has been too warm all day. Although so many things had altered, things like that hadn't. Long, long ago Havana smelled and —though cars must have been few—managed to sound the same. Afternoon ended then as now, in sunlight limpid without being dim, clear and sad in its own way on ancient stone, on faded tints of colored plaster, and ribs of hoary tiles, red dulled to gray. The sky displayed a fine satin blue which it might be pleasant to touch. Martin Gibbs pushed back the tall shutters on the constricted hotel balcony, and the familiar noises came a little louder.

On one of the beds Celia stirred and said without opening her eyes: "Martin."

"It's half past five, honey," he told her. "How do you feel?"

She murmured: "All right." Her tawny hair was soaked with perspiration. Moisture shone unmistakable on her face, catching in ugly, artificial pallor the light twice reflected; up from the street, down from the pale blue walls. Her body lay awkwardly, inert; wrapped in a damp and wrinkled dressing gown of white silk. A vital energy which made her look always less than her age had ebbed very far; she looked more, now; over forty, certainly. Under the cool simplicity of her regular features and clear moderate coloring appeared a sharpness, a wasting of tissue which was drained of blood, and gray. Her arms were less slender than gaunt. Perhaps she felt some dismayed concern, for she protested suddenly, her eyes still closed: "Don't look at me. It must be awful."

Martin Gibbs said: "Never mind, honey. We'll be out of this tomorrow morning." His eyes had moved obediently away and he saw his own reflection in the shadowed pool of the mirror above the dressing table. The heaviness of his big plain face was always a surprise to him. Except the bold, slightly bent nose, no feature of it looked like Martin Gibbs. The nose had always been that way, but not the lines slanting past the ends of his mouth. The Southern sun, relentless, had formed the wrinkles at the corners of his calm eyes. His hair had receded so far that the central point, where he parted it, formed a lonely, isolated projection on his sun-browned skull. He was reminded at once of the fact that he was getting old—forty-four, in fact.

He said aloud: "We should have done this ten years ago." It was an appeal to what might have been, and it was a mistake, he realized. It prodded up in him an impotent and puerile rage; he would like without any warning to break things, but he steadied himself, consciously restrained and temperate. Leaving Cuba at his time of life, he was in a way staking everything on his capacity for exact judgment, his competence and coolness when situations new and unavoidably difficult would face him. As for leaving before, he knew that was nonsense, not to be argued about. He was leaving now, getting Celia away. He had done it just as soon as he was able to see how things really stood. Being young prevented any such view up to a certain point. You could stand anything easily while you believed that a lot lay ahead. When you saw that nothing remained, that was different. No rubbish about the country or the climate getting you. Age was the same everywhere, getting everyone, everywhere. A decade more, and age would have had him, fairly. Had him empty-handed. He had a positive, reassuring sense of his rightness in throwing it all up. There were thousands of careers and positions but only one life, and not much time left to be happy in it. He did look back at Celia now, and—for he himself had felt slowly safer and happier—he was jolted to see that her eyes were wet. While he watched, tears pushed slowly up through the closed lashes.

"Honey," he said, "what's the trouble?"

It was, of course, a silly thing to ask, and it took her a minute by the distinct ticking of his watch to find any answer. Her lips, looking almost blue in the thin queer light, worked a little, finally tightened, stiff over her teeth, and she said huskily: "Martin, what are we going to do? We don't know anyone in the North. We——"

She stopped it. Her courage was amazing; and Martin thought about such special qualities in her character with a wondering affection, a sort of harassed reverence. He wiped his forehead. "We've got some money," he said. "We're not poor. That's what matters."

Celia had none of most women's acute concern and sober practicality in such things. She was acquiescent, incurious; and for this he was grateful. There were difficulties which could only be made worse by explanations. "We have some money," he repeated. "There isn't a thing to worry about. Except getting away from here as soon as we can." He didn't, he told himself, actually believe that. He saw no limit to the things he must worry about; but they didn't dismay him. The platitudinous truth was so strong that he stated it: "As long as I have you they can't lick me. I won't have to, but I could start from the bottom, and in ten years . . ."

She moved her head in a minute gesture, as though of thanks or acknowledgment, rather than assent. She was nervous, and she was tired, but it wasn't in her to be difficult. A flood of tenderness and a moving gratitude heartened him. "Celia," he said, "why don't you have something to eat now? What would you like?" Practical questions helped him. Just in time they stopped a renewal, now helplessly on her behalf, of that congested feeling which rose with the sting of ridiculous tears to his eyes. The familiar useless anger, at what Cuba allied with the ruinous years had done to them, went down. He breathed again and repeated the question.

"Nothing," she said. "You go on. You mustn't be late." She did open her eyes now, a clear sad blue in her unhappy face. "I'll be all right. The heat and traveling. It's better for me not to eat anything."

He started to object, but the protest got not so far as words. Even in a matter like that he wanted her suddenly to have her way, to find things easy, to see him always on her side. "Can you sleep?" he said.

She nodded. "There's that medicine I could take if I didn't," she told him. "I hate to wake up and find it's not morning. . . ."

"You've got some?" he said. She nodded. "Enough. I won't need it in the North." That was true, Martin told himself. Her health would unquestionably be better in another climate.

"I'll stay until you get to sleep," he offered, but she shook her head, settling back. "No. If you stay it will take longer." She moistened her lips and smiled. "Lock the door, darling, and don't let them bother me."

He came and kissed her damp forehead. Her arms seemed so thin, her face so taut, that he said: "I love you, Celia. More than anything."

She put a hand on his arm, with a sort of nod. "I love you, Martin, too. I wanted to leave Cuba, darling. It's all right. I'll be asleep in a minute. Have a good time."

He was startled by the phrase, the idea of leaving her there and "having a good time." Rejecting that, he was startled again to wonder what, if not a good time, he was going to have. Carriker, George Biehl, Homer Loren— he never had anything but a good time with them. If he did not expect a last pleasant evening, why should he see them at all? Locking the door from the outside, he stood a moment in the corridor with its windows on the small dingy patio.

It might be a mistake; when he was leaving it all it was silly to bother to see people without future significance, whatever the past had been. Probably, he thought (scoffing at his overmastering desire, since he did not seem to be able to struggle with it), it would be a bore for them too. Only he knew better. Down here one kept friends. Even a man like Homer Loren, who had thousands of acquaintances, felt the fundamental loneliness. They drew together in defense. They fought off the underlying isolation of an atmosphere which no familiarity with the people, the language, the life, the climate could change from the permanently alien.

This sentimental, almost silly aspect of it troubled him, Martin knew. He might have been making a furtive escape to personal safety from a sorely besieged and dangerous fort where every man's presence counted. Counted a great deal, for never had he himself seemed to want so much the comfort of shared memories, the security of long acquaintance. Though a deserter, though he didn't deserve to, going finally away, he must see their faces, hear their voices. He could not help looking a last time on what he had to show for the vanished years and the outworn youth, the Cuba of their common past.

Martin Gibbs walked down two flights of stairs paved with stained, cracked marble, tossed his key onto the narrow desk. His wife, he said, was sleeping; on no account to be disturbed. Outside, the street was bright still with the level slant of the setting sun. He glanced at his watch and walked slowly.

"This is something like it!" Joe Carriker roared. "Martin, you old son of a gun!"

Carriker was enormously heavy, with a face broad and brick-colored. His hair, of which he retained plenty, stood up over his shining forehead in a short gray ruff. Martin Gibbs shook hands with him, and then with Homer Loren, across the table. Homer was lean-faced, deeply brown from mornings on the Marianao sands. He owned and edited an English-language daily. The *Evening Mail* was famous for its warm defense of the Cuban Administration, and everyone suspected that the Government subsidized it, at least indirectly. The President's nephew was widely believed to be the author of the lead editorials on local affairs. Some of its competitors were bitter, but Homer remained unmoved. He was rich now, for whatever reason; he was the only really prominent and influential man that Martin knew well in Cuba. "I see the *Wail* is worse than ever," Martin told him, happy.

"Ah," said Homer, "but did you see it tonight? You'd better buy a copy and frame it. I had them run a quarter inch on the front page lower right with a small head: 'Leading Santa Clara Banker Visits Havana.' No wonder the sheet is rotten."

Martin Gibbs nodded to him. "Much obliged for the buggy ride," he acknowledged. It would be just as well, he saw, to get this matter over at once. "Only you're wrong as always. I'm not visiting. I'm on the way out. I'm leaving Cuba for good."

"It would certainly be for good, if true," agreed Homer. His oblong brown face cracked in a smile. "What did you do? Ask for a raise and get turned down? Or are you running off with someone else's wife? Tell Uncle Homer so he can have a beat for Life in American Circles."

"I'm through," said Martin. "That's all. Homer, are you too poor to buy a drink? If the worst came to the worst, I'd treat you."

"Made your fortune?" asked Homer agreeably. "Listen, Martin, do you mean it about going?"

"You heard me," Martin said. He took a cocktail glass from the waiter's approaching tray. "Never mind such elegant service, *chico*," he told the man; "just run back and throw the stuff together again. Mud in your eye," he said to Homer and Carriker, "and I hope you rot to a ripe old age down here."

"Well, can you tie that!" grunted Carriker. "I'll bet he really is going!"

"Why don't you stick on in Havana, Martin?" asked Homer Loren. Homer made a practice of avoiding surprise. His long brown face with the patches of wiry gray hair lying close on his oblong skull above his ears, far behind his temples, showed a certain alertness. "One would pre-sume you understood figures," he said; "I'd risk it to the extent of a posi-tion in the Cuban-American Publishing Company. I expect to need a treasurer about next week. I can't say it has a future, but the present would be made about twice as good as anything your bank ever had."

"Thanks," agreed Martin, indifferent. Homer had the reputation for being singularly gifted in the choice of his executives. He would like to have Martin, and the generosity of his offer was flavored a little with his intelligent self-interest. "Thanks," repeated Martin, displeased by this realization, "that's nice of you, Homer. But I'm through with Cuba." He felt the gradual warmth of the cocktails in his stomach, and it helped him over a natural moment of doubt, a fear that he might be a fool to face the unfriendly North after all these years. "Stay and rot," he said. "Lots of good men are doing it."

"You must have made money," decided Carriker, who sold automobiles and knew ways of spending what he made faster than he made it. "If I could get a dollar ahead I'll bet I'd leave myself. Everything's going to the devil here. The tariff's going to bust every sugar mill in the island."

"What do you know about it?" asked Homer. He was suddenly aggres-sive, as though a button marked "Future of Cuba" had been pushed, switching on power.

"Homer believes all that drivel he prints in the *Mail*," Carriker said, recognizing it. "If people don't make money they can't spend it. How you made yours I'd like to know."

"You're crazy to go North if you haven't money, Martin," Homer said seriously. "When you've been away as long as you have it's no joke to break in."

"If the liquor doesn't kill you up there the climate will," Carriker promised. "When you've been in the tropics over fifteen years your blood gets thin. Fact. Scientific fact. You'll get pneumonia the first winter and that's the end of you."

"Bunk," said Homer. "Never mind what you will get. What have you got now, in cash? If you're bound you're going, I'd lend you five or ten thousand. So don't high-hat me. How much cash have you got?"

"I've got some," said Martin. "I have enough for another drink, anyway."

"What you need is about a hundred thousand," said Homer, almost malicious. He was a little hurt, Martin saw. He was used to arranging other people's business for them. Here, however, was one business Martin couldn't possibly hand to him. It was a matter strictly between Celia and himself. If she didn't mind the prospects of the future . . .

"You're a fool not to stay with the bank, at least," said Homer. "Wouldn't Spofford let you transfer? I'll bet you if I went and had a talk with him, he'd——"

"No, he wouldn't," snapped Martin. It would be like Homer to have, as he said, a talk with the general manager for Cuba. "Spofford's a good friend of mine. I can get anything out of him he has to give. I tell you, I'm sick of it. I've just been a sucker! They'd keep me down the island the rest of my life if they could. They know what I'm good for. I don't mind saying, and you know it's true, that I was the best man they ever had. Every branch they gave me I made a business of. I'll bet you I've been worth a million dollars to them in my day——" He stopped, surprised at the note of anger in this unbecoming boasting of his. "What do you suppose these glasses are for?"

"Let 'er go!" sighed Homer. "The least I can do is get pie-eyed over your departure. George isn't even here yet. We'll have to swim to dinner."

"Where is George?" asked Martin, conscious abruptly of this important absence.

"Believe his outfit dropped a peseta in the Calle Compostela. All hands helping to find it. No wonder bankers go loony. He's coming. He'll be here."

"There he is," said Carriker. "I'm glad I'm not a big money man, much as I like money. You never get to have a drink. All right, George, we're ready to start."

George Biehl was short, solid rather than heavy. His face was somewhat full, but firm and well shaped. "Good to see you, Martin," he said. His brown eyes were frankly affectionate. He shook hands hard. "Start?" he echoed Carriker. "Joe looks pretty near finished to me."

"Find your money?" inquired Homer.

"I expect I shouldn't answer that," said George, "but I will. Your rag will have it Tuesday anyway. We've had a horrible jolt, to be candid. A cashier who left us about a month ago had been taking us along—slickest system I've seen yet. They're in a panic, let me tell you. The auditors have out a hurry call to all branches to see how many other people thought up the same game. Sit still, Homer; I told you Tuesday would be time enough."

"That's tough," said Martin. He knew George's position so perfectly that he found himself already at mental work, his own long experience in the exigencies of local banking automatically operating. "It won't do you much good, will it? With tomorrow Sunday and the next day a holiday, you'll have a job rounding your branches up."

"Don't I know it?" groaned George Biehl. "When I left your outfit, Martin, I said that you people had the only system. Did these saps listen to me? They thought I'd better mind my own business. They——"

George, Martin told himself, never should have gone over. You could pass a tractor through those accounts. He—it was, thank heaven, George's business. He was through.

"You look surprised," marveled Homer dryly, "and I'll bet you between your two organizations I could name twenty men I've known personally who've walked out with the cash. Must be the climate, or do you suppose bankers are just naturally a little slow?"

"We aren't so slow," said George Biehl, plainly stung into exaggeration. "Every one of those twenty got caught, too. They only do it because they're sort of crazy, and when you're crazy you don't see things. They always do something so dumb you can't believe it."

"How much did he take along?" Homer asked.

"You may think you're pumping me," said George, "but you're not. How much he took is none of your business. It's the crazy system we use——"

"Ours wouldn't be any better if a really shrewd hand had a whack at it," said Martin soothingly. The system, he recalled, was, whatever its points, no longer his. "Yes," said George, "but you can watch really shrewd hands. They're big enough to watch usually. This boy got more than he's bonded for, I'll admit, but I'm surprised he didn't take the office furniture too. We never would have known it. Pretty nice for him, if we don't catch him. Wouldn't mind being young with a big pile like that for a start up North myself."

"So you think you have to be young and have a big pile," said Martin. He found himself facing with increased reluctance any mention of his own plans. "Well," he said, "better late than never seems plausible to me. I'm leaving Cuba, George."

"You're what?" said George.

It was a fact, Homer told him. "Martin's got the willies."

"Say, are you joking?" said George. He was blank with amazement and a dismay which made Martin wince a little. "Listen, did you have a scrap with Spofford? I can tell you right here and now that you can have—well, you can have Santiago right this minute, if you'll come over to us—"

"Wouldn't that be wonderful?" said Martin.

"I don't know what's come over him," said Homer. "He hasn't any money and he hasn't any sense and he's forty-five if he's a day."

"What I have got's quite a thirst," said Martin, impatient.

"Well," sighed Homer, "at least you haven't any family to worry about. If you invested your life savings nicely, in about five thousand years—"

"That's right," said Carriker; "that makes a lot of difference."

Carriker did have a family. A wife and quite a number of children in a Vedado bungalow. He never mentioned them, and, tacitly, neither did anyone else.

"All right," said George. He hadn't finished his objections, that was plain; he merely postponed them. "Martin can stand another drink. He can stand anything. Often wished I had his stomach." Martin wondered fleetingly if George thought anything would be gained by getting Martin drunk. He decided that George wasn't so simple. That would be the sort of thing Carriker might think of.

Homer Loren was showing what he had drunk already. He often did before dinner. "You shouldn't drink so much," Homer observed generally. "You can't stand it in this climate. Half Martin's willies are just those cocktails they make in the cane. No ice and who knows where the rum comes from?"

"It comes from Santiago," said Martin, "and every bohio has an electric refrigerator these days. It's called raising the standard of living, and it's what you yap about in the *Wail* every Thursday afternoon. Don't run it down now; people will think you aren't sincere."

"Matter of fact," said Homer, "I'm not. I wouldn't be found dead that way."

George Biehl groaned slightly. "This is going to be philosophy. We'll have to get some food into him." Carriker leaned back in his chair and shouted through the open arches into the street, "Taxi!"

"Do you good to walk," said George. "Something tells me this is going to be a hard evening."

"I've got to get in early," Martin told him. "Got a boat to catch early tomorrow."

"No, no," said Homer, "that's nonsense! Tomorrow's Easter. Don't you know that? Monday's a holiday. Tuesday you might leave, or a week from Tuesday."

"Can't be done," said Martin.

"What do you mean, it can't be done?"

"There are reasons," said Martin.

"He's got the willies," Homer repeated. "The tropics have ruined him. He was like to throw away his shoes and go native. He thinks this is the South Seas. This, let me tell you, is the Paris of America, and has the lowest death rate in——"

Sitting in the restaurant's electric-lighted cavern, they could see the dusk deepening on the green trees and gardens of the Parque Central. The lights of the Plaza roof were clear against the sky, and advertising signs about beer and chocolate had been turned on.

Carriker said that the trouble with Havana was that you couldn't do anything until twelve o'clock.

"We could get a carriage and drive down along the Malecon a ways," said Martin. "The water's nice. Or it used to be." He felt very comfortable, torpid perhaps; but a certain sadness constantly crept up in his mind. He even thought of Sancti Spiritus without impatience now. Its serenity of night coming down; the peace of the paved roof on his former house— he could sit and watch the moon, when there was a moon, in an amazing stillness over the stream and the three ancient humps of the Spanish bridge. There would be nothing like that in the North, nothing but trouble, doubts, and difficulties.

Homer said: "Who wants to drive in a carriage? Let's go down to the Sevilla bar."

Martin regretted the suggestion only a moment. It would be better, he saw, to get a little drunk. As soon as that happened he could trust an old instinct of his to nag at him until he broke away and went home. That was the bank still, he saw; as though it were in his blood. He had always had responsibilities, and he had learned to a hairsbreadth where responsibility wavered. Carriker said, pleasantly resigned: "You must want to make it a bat."

Moving down the Prado, it was George who put an arm through his, walking a little behind Homer and Carriker. "What's on your mind, Martin?" he said suddenly.

"I may tell you," Martin answered. It was unexpected even to himself.

He was surprised to realize that he wanted to talk to anyone, that he felt any need to get anything off his chest. They turned off, into the Sevilla, and in the bar they sat under a potted orange tree in the corner.

"Well," said Martin at once, "I might as well explain why I'm leaving tomorrow morning. This isn't any of your business, but I dare say I do owe you an explanation. As it happens, I'm not alone. That's all."

Out now, in unmistakable words, Martin at once wished that it wasn't. It was immediately tainted, as though their three minds got hands on it, leaving smears of the sordid and scandalous. Homer said with a vast, somber satisfaction: "Martin, I knew something was up. A woman, eh?"

Martin said: "I'll tell you what you need to know. Don't ask me." They all thought, he saw, that he meant a Cuban woman; some girl who might have been his mistress. George said finally: "Martin, you know how I feel about you, so you'll listen to me. You're crazy. I'm not going to let you do anything like that. I'll take care of it. I'll put you up at my place tonight and see that she gets sent back. Now——"

"You haven't got it right," Martin stated. "I wasn't asking for help. Everything is all arranged. I just wanted to tell you why I can't stay in Cuba."

George looked at him with intent concern. "Then it's that McLaughlin chap's wife," he decided abruptly. "I had an idea when I was up there a couple of years ago——"

"Never mind your ideas," requested Martin. "You'll have to think what you like, George, but don't say any of it."

Carriker ruminated: "McLaughlin." He concluded: "Federated Sugar. Jacinto. It's going to make a stink, isn't it?"

George Biehl was drinking Fundador. The brandy looked almost black in the small glass, twisting steadily in his fingers. Martin found himself imagining the hot and heartening taste of it. He said: "I'll have some of that, and then let's get out of here. I don't want to meet a lot of people."

"Right," nodded George. George could see well enough why he didn't want to meet a lot of people. "Where would you like to go, Martin?" George's voice was always gentler when he was troubled or dismayed. Turning a critical eye on these three friends, Martin realized that George was the only one who mattered to him—he started to say, the only decent one, but he checked himself. Joe Carriker and Homer were fine fellows. They didn't come finer. He had, in fact, owed them an explanation, and he ought to be glad that he had made it.

Carriker had changed the subject elaborately. He was suggesting, with a delicate indirection, to Homer that he himself might consider the job Homer had offered Martin. Carriker managed it with his usual loud and cheerful humor. Only now that he was older, his hair gray, the geniality seemed hollow. Close to panhandling, in fact. Carriker was probably in a tight place. His big hands were nervous on the table. Heaven only knew how much money he owed or how bad he was finding business in an era which had discarded the boisterous familiarities, the slipshod personal approaches of his youth.

Homer Loren was again a little drunk, but he was not unwary. He knew that Carriker was trying to get something out of him and he had—plainly to everyone but Carriker—no intention of allowing it to happen. His dark face was lopsided, with a chill small smile; his eyes were tightened in a cynical slant. Looking at him, it seemed to Martin that Homer had always been a trifle too astute. The faint evil miasma one sensed while reading the *Evening Mail* clung to him. He was tainted with the callous corruption, the unabashed bribes and shameless subsidies of the Government. Martin felt a chill, a cold malaise; for he seemed to have now Cuba, his past, his cherished friends spread before him. He saw their decay, the ruin of the years. Next, he knew, he would begin to think about himself, about Celia, about life and the future.

George said: "Let's take a motor out to Wirth's."

The others had drunk enough to go anywhere, anywhere rather than home. It was, indeed, the decisive moment. You had to choose now between departure—accepting the sad silence and depression of the night, satisfied to know that tomorrow things might look better—or staying, recklessly forcing things to look better right now, heedless of the certain miseries of the morning. George, he saw, had made up his mind. George was not going to desert him, George would be there when dawn came; Martin could count on this companionship to get him through until it was tomorrow and he left Cuba forever.

At midnight Homer was very drunk. Carriker, oddly enough, was considerably less so. He seemed to entertain some only half-tipsy notion that Homer might get drunk enough to promise him what he wanted. The party had been augmented by two slight, dark-eyed, tan-colored girls who sipped grenadine and water, submitting to Homer's attentions. Carriker's problem made him sweat. He didn't want to annoy Homer by interruptions, but neither did he want Homer to pass out altogether without giving him a chance to get a word in. When the latter occurred, about half past two, Carriker, in despair, defeated the girls' intention of taking this rich man in charge. Martin was cold with disgust and weariness, but George remained complaisant. He said: "Go on, Joe, take him home."

Carriker agreed. He'd see that no harm came to Homer. Homer was his dear old pal. They were the next thing to brothers. "So long, Martin, old scout," he said. "Better not leave. Stay around and have a wonderful time. Wonderful time every night." There was nothing to be done about this.

"Good-by," said Martin. "Good luck, Joe."

George said that they might as well go back to town, but he didn't purpose going to bed. "Neither do I," Martin agreed. "I'd like to see how Celia is. We can get some coffee."

In the taxi George remarked: "I don't get on so well with those two any more. I'm sort of sorry for Joe, but he's getting to be an awful nuisance. Homer's all right as long as you don't want him to do anything for you."

"He offered to lend me ten thousand dollars," Martin told him. "I think he really meant it."

"He did," admitted George. "He really respects you. You're one of the few people he knows who isn't a shyster of some sort. That's why I sort of hate to see you quitting, myself, Martin." He became suddenly voluble, faintly impatient. "I don't like this business about the lady. You know what you're doing, only I sort of wish it hadn't happened. I have an idea that you both got worked up. Just got bored and kicked the works over the mill. Either that—now don't get mad—or it was her idea. She sold it to you."

"That's not true," said Martin.

George looked at him in the dim moving light. "I guess maybe it is," he said. "If she hadn't been there you wouldn't have done it. You'd have hung on. I don't say she asked you, but I'll bet she just worked on you and——"

Martin sat with his legs thrust out, swaying to the jolt of the taxi. In his nervous, half-nauseated wakefulness he could understand George's point. There was, in a way, a perverted truth in it, he supposed. "Listen," he said, "it's true I couldn't do anything else, if that's what you mean. I simply couldn't stand it. Celia doesn't get on with McLaughlin and——"

George grunted with a sort of resignation. What he saw was perfectly plain. "Another good man gone wrong" would describe it well enough. One more irregular exit after many decent and devoted years. There was a miserable, even frightening monotony about men leaving Cuba that way. He said now: "How did Spofford take it?"

"I doubt if he knows yet," said Martin. "I wrote in. I didn't want him to get it until Tuesday, when I'd be gone. I've got a good assistant out there. He can carry on perfectly well."

George was plainly shocked. "You shouldn't have done that, Martin," he protested. "That's a rotten trick on Spofford."

Martin said wearily: "Maybe I shouldn't have technically. You don't seem to get the idea yet. I tell you I couldn't go it. And if I was going to leave, I had to leave like that; not after three weeks of chatter with Spofford and waiting around until he found someone else, with everyone knowing that I was going——"

"I'm not dumb," agreed George gloomily. "That's the lady, just as I said. You had to get off when you got the chance. Well, I guess you care a lot about her and that's your business. Only I don't mind saying that I hate to think of you getting out sort of secretly that way, leaving the bank in the lurch and taking along someone else's wife."

He said it without scorn or active accusation. He was simply depressed. Martin felt sorry, not resentful. George had still his own troubles to face; a scandal of his own, you might say, breaking on the front pages Tuesday. He glanced out and saw that they were passing the Christo Church. The doors were open and lights on; early Easter masses had begun, and he watched a moment, curious, while dark muffled figures went in. "Well," he said to George, "happy Easter. Here we are. We can probably get some coffee. I'll just run upstairs and see if Celia's all right."

George nodded. A sleepy clerk slouched in a chair behind the desk and George asked him about coffee. The clerk thought that there was a pot on the stove. He would see. Did the señor wish to use the elevator?

"I'll walk," Martin said.

His legs were tired and he couldn't think why he said it; he might have been trying to put off the moment when he would have to consider Celia as a concrete fact, not merely a theory of which George disapproved. He paused a moment in the shadows of the first floor. His stomach felt unpleasant, and his head swam slightly.

It was about four o'clock, he guessed, and he ought to have felt all right. Well, he was getting old! You mustn't expect to carry on the way you could once. He mounted the second flight and moved slowly down the hall, still breathing thickly. He waited a moment until this had quieted, and then he inserted the key.

Street light from the corner reached part of the wall, printing a slim column of radiance near the shutters. Celia lay much as he had left her, and he was obscurely reassured. He would not like to think that she had awakened and been worried. He sat down a moment on the edge of the other bed, looking at her in the shadows, trying halfheartedly to take some sort of stock of the situation. He could make out the lax, inert line of her hip; her hair, dark in this gloom, stood out against the pillow into which her face was half sunk.

He could not think of anything in particular. He was very tired, and only a disjointed series of recollections came to him: little informal dances at his house; small dinner parties at Jacinto, the American engineers from the sugar mill; Celia and the color of the dresses she had worn. George's remark remained with him—"taking along someone else's wife" —and it annoyed him. It carried a kind of contempt, which George had managed to expunge in the saying, but which was back now. He couldn't, somehow, think of Celia in such a position—open in any way to contempt. He might almost have left Celia behind. Here in this hot room he sat with somebody else. Despite everything, Celia might remain grave-eyed, without reproach, in the gardens at Jacinto.

This sense of change or error was so acute that he got up sharply. George might, then, be right. Kicked the works over the mill! Something like that would have to happen before he could persuade her. Now, at this truer point, he didn't think he would have tried; he wouldn't surely have been able to make her do anything so alien to her even if he had tried. Aloud he said: "What's done is done." It sounded rather silly, strained, in the darkness, and he looked back quickly, for fear that he might have awakened her. She made no move, however, and he turned to the door. His attention was taken a moment by something on the bureau.

His fingers found it to be an envelope and he was immediately angered, thinking that after all they had disobeyed his instructions downstairs. He was about to take it out with him when, standing still, he had another idea.

Without moving, barely breathing, he ripped the flap. He pressed a hand into his pocket and brought out a cigarette lighter. The wheel rasped his thumb twice and a flame jumped up, yellow on the enclosed sheet.

He looked at it quietly. He had never, it seemed to him, heard a silence so tremendous as Havana's at this hour before dawn. Not a sound, not a sound. No breathing but his own, and he looked slowly where the radiance extended onto the bureau, and saw that the veronal bottle was empty.

His solitary breath came hoarser now, quite loud, but he moved silently. He pushed the paper into his pocket, stepped out. The door caused a slight click, closing; and he locked it. He stood there a moment with the little flame of the lighter still burning in his hand, the small light shaking on his face. Then, starting, he snapped the cap down and went deliberately to the stairs.

George Biehl was sitting in the corner with coffee in front of him. He looked bad, Martin saw. His face was thickened, discolored under the damp skin. Shadows from the bare bulbs of the lamps clung to his chin like cobwebs. His eyes, dark, sunken a little, were bloodshot. "Hello," he said, "this will do you good." His cheerfulness was brittle. "Do you feel as rotten as I do?" he asked. "It's pretty nearly five o'clock."

Martin drew up a chair and set himself on it. "Well," he said, and his voice sounded remote to him, "this is a funny way for it to end. When did we first come down here, George? Twenty-two years ago. And here we are."

"Take some coffee," urged George, "and have a heart. I'm not going to say anything more. If I could get out of here I would. Go to it."

"Look," said Martin. He took a wallet from his pocket and removed a thick packet of American bills.

"All right," groaned George, "all right. I hope you have more."

"I have," said Martin. "It's no good to me. I'd give it to you if I could."

George Biehl stared at him. "What are you, crazy? Have a fight with a lady? Have——"

"Ninety thousand dollars in the brown suitcase," said Martin. "Here's the key. She knew. She couldn't go it."

George Biehl's thickened face, the wide eyes that looked bruised, remained on him, stupid.

"You could have figured it out," said Martin. "You said it yourself. We all do something so dumb you can't believe it. I had four days clear and everything clicked—it was good, George; not like a cashier. Only I should have stayed in last night. Turn it over to Spofford. Oh, Celia's dead, of course. I'll want about five minutes before you call the police."

George Biehl sat perfectly still. His throat made a sort of croak, but he didn't say anything. His hands with the swollen veins starting out of their backs lay in a paralysis on the round table top, palms to the marble. He could hear Martin's steps on the stairs for some time, receding. There followed at last a deep silence while he remained stiff, motionless. His heart seemed likely to stop if this lasted much longer.

His heart didn't stop, though; it beat on thickly, shaking him. He needn't have listened so hard, for the sound, breaking clean without a warning and with no echo, was muffled very little. His heart had jumped then; it seemed to hit his gullet and fall back; but it beat right on. The clerk had come to his feet, chair clattering, his head poking out blank and wide-eyed across the desk.

George Biehl made his hands lie quiet. "All right. That's all right," he said mildly. "Go on, boy. Go on. Telephone the police."

J. FRANK DOBIE

Old Bill

THEY TELL ME that Jeb Rider's log cabin is still standing, about a quarter of a mile up the slope from the spring on Elm Creek. Nobody has struck oil in this part of East Texas yet, and so things out of the past live on there. People still talk about the Civil War, though years and years ago they put what was left of Uncle Jeb Rider in the ground, in the little graveyard where wild trumpet vines cover the lane fence with red flowers all through the summer months and into the fall. Old Bill disappeared long before that, but Uncle Jeb's story of Old Bill seems to have a chance to keep on blooming with the trumpet vines. This is the way he told it:

When me and my wife married, it was her idear having the house so fur up the slope from where we got water outa the spring on Ellum Creek. She was skeered of floods. I was nacherly agin having to tote water so fur, but 'fore long I sometimes wished it were further. I could walk down that trail and set on the cypress log there at the spring and kinder get peaceful. She was always badgering me to clear more land and plant more sweet pertaters and hoe the corn cleaner and do things like that, and I jest nacherly kinder like to squirrel roun' with the dogs like I'd always done.

The best dog I ever had was Old Bill. He was out of a bitch Pa brung from Tinnissee; that is, figgering in several ginerations between. I never can remember whether it was July 13 or July 14 he died, the year before the war started. Anyhow, one cloudy day about a month after he died I was going down the trail to the spring uncommon low in the mouth and was about halfway when kinder unconscious-like I heard sumpin behind me. Maybe it was a rustle in the leaves. I didn't pay no 'tention till I heared a low rattle. Then I looked, and I'll be dogged if it wasn't the biggest diamon'back rattlesnake I ever see, right in the trail, not more'n six steps back.

When I stopped and looked, he stopped, too, and raised his head up in a curious way and looked at me without shaking his tail a-tall. It's that tail-shaking that makes a rattlesnake so fearsome, puts the jints in a human's backbone to shaking too. Well, I didn't have a thing with me to hit with, not even a water bucket, and when I glanced round fer a stick there weren't none in reach. I started on down the trail agin to a dead dogwood I could break off. Then I looked back and that diamon'back was coming on, too, keeping a respec'ful distance and looking like he didn't mean no harm.

When I got to the dead dogwood and broke off a stick and drew it back to lamm the snake, he looked more harmless than ever. I can't explain it. There he was keeping a respec'ful distance, and all at once he sorter seemed to me like a dog that wants to foller you and be friends but's afraid to come too clost. Well, I stood there a-holding the stick, and he had his head up a little watching me, and his eyes jest seemed to say he understood.

Then I done clear contrary to nature. I throwed the stick away and started agin on down to the spring. Ever' once in a while I'd turn my head and look back. The rattlesnake was still follering, humble and respec'ful. When I set down on the cypress log, he coiled up in a sliver of weak sunshine and kept looking right straight at me. D'reckly I begun to kinder talk to him. I was still a young man, remember, and a blamed fool about feeling sorry fer myself. And that old snake would nod his head aroun' and look like he felt sorry too.

When I started up to the cabin, he did the same, jest follering like a dog. About halfway up he dropped out, and I didn't see nothing more of him till the next day. I was going down to the spring agin to bring up some water fer Abbie to wash with. Right about the halfway place, he fell in behind me like he'd done the first time, and now his follering seemed jest as nacherl as a dog scratching fleas.

"See here," I says to him after we got settled at the spring, "I'm going to call you Bill. Bill, he was the best coon and possum dog I ever had, and he always understood me. When I wanted to squirrel aroun', he never had no idears about clearing off land or putting poles in the fence to keep the hawgs outer the field or anything like that. Yes sir, you're Bill to me from now on."

And Bill jest nodded his head and looked grateful out of his eyes and shore would've talked if he could of. It was real soothing to be with him, and when Abbie went to squalling fer me to hurry up and bring on the water he acturly winked.

Well, after that we was together lots at the spring. Whenever I went to the store I'd hear talk about the Aberlitionists up North working to take the darkies away from us Southern folks and make 'em our equals, and more talk about the Black Republicans. When I got back I'd tell Bill about 'em—sometimes afore I told Abbie—and, by hoeky, he'd coil up and look fierce enough to bite a crowbar. Then the war did come. I volunteered fer Captain Abercrombie's company and traded off some corn and a mule fer a good, gentle horse and bought Abbie a new ax and got all ready to go. The evening afore I was to set out, I went down to the spring to kinder ca'm myself and tell Bill good-by.

It looked like he understood all about the Yankees. I told him to look after things around the spring as best he could and I'd be back someday. The next morning after Abbie got my things all packed and I'd told her good-by, I turned by the spring to water my horse.

Well, jest as I was coming out under that leaning ellum over the trail between the house and the spring, I felt sumpin drop acrost my shoulders. It would-a scared me if it hadn't been so nacherl. "So you want to go to war too, do you, Bill?" I says.

"I don't know how the fellers in camps would take to you," I says. "They're all Texians, you know," I says, "and got about as much use fer a rattlesnake as a wildcat has for a lost puppy." You see, I hadn't told a soul about Old Bill—not even Abbie. I jest didn't think anybody would understand. But if Bill was so set on going with me, I decided right then I'd try to convert the heathen.

"If you'll promise," I says to him, "not to bother nobody and stay put where I puts you, I'll take you. I'll explain to the fellers and maybe they'll get the idear." He nods and we rode on.

Some of the fellers seemed to think at first that I was jest an idiot, but they left Bill alone and he left them alone. I shore didn't have no trouble with anybody trying to steal my blankets, and the way Jim Bowie—that's what I named my horse—and Old Bill got to be fren'ly with each other was a caution. Sometimes Jim Bowie would kinder noze Bill along the back, and many a when Jim Bowie was a-grazing I've seen Bill crawling out in front of him and scaring off devil horses so Jim Bowie wouldn't accerdently chew 'em up and swaller 'em. You know how a devil horse once it's inside the stumick of an animal can kill it. I fixed up a bag for Old Bill to ride comfortable in and, when we moved, hung it on the horn of my saddle.

Fer months we jest practiced marching and squads-righting and squads-lefting and so on. I'd leave Old Bill on the edge of the parade grounds, and I got to noticing how interested he seemed in our movements. When we'd have a parade, he'd get exciteder than the colonel's horse. The band music was what set him up. "Dixie" was his favorite tune, and he got so he could sorter rattle it. It shore was comical to see him histing his tail to get the high notes.

Finally our training was over. We crossed the Mississippi River and joined Gin'ral Albert Sidney Johnston's forces. Then when Shiloh opened up on that Sunday morning in April we was in it. We fought and we fit all day long, sometimes going forwards and sometimes backwards, sometimes in the brush and sometimes acrost clearings. We didn't know till next day that our gin'ral had been killed. If he had-a lived and if we'd-a had a few more like Old Bill, things would have turned out mighty different.

My rigiment was camped on Owl Creek, jest north of Shiloh Chapel, and jest before we went into battle that morning I took Old Bill over to a commissary waggin and told him to stay there and told the driver to kinder keep him. Late evening found us coming back into a long neck of woods that our colonel told us we'd have to clear of Yankees. They'd worked in between us and Owl Creek. We found 'em all right, but they was the deadest Yankees I ever see. At first we was bellying along on the ground, keeping behind trees and expecting fire. Then when we kept finding more and more dead uns, we figgered some other outfit had beat us to 'em. We got to breathing easy, and then somebody noticed that none of the dead Yanks bore bullet marks. It was all-fired strange, and the trees wasn't none of 'em creased neither.

I decided to make a little closer examination, and I pulled up the britches leg of one Yank. Jest above his shoe top on the outside, where the ankle vein runs, I noticed a pair of little holes about the size of pin points. I found the same marks on the leg of the next Yank, on another, on another, and then, all of a suddent, I knowed Old Bill'd been there. I told the boys. They went to looking at the dead Yankee legs and couldn't he'p being convinced.

We kept going through the neck of woods and counting dead Yankees till we got to Owl Creek, a little below camps. My ricollection is that the count run to 417, but it may have been a few less. Course, too, some few might've been counted twicet. I guess the official report would show, if it didn't get burned up at Richmond.

It wasn't more'n a rifle shot from the near side of the woods to camps. We got in a little before sundown, and there Old Bill was stretched out under the commissary waggin. He looked plumb tuckered out and as gant as a gutted snowbird. Well, the night before one of the boys happened to set a trap fer possum right in camps almost. He went to it as soon as we got in and found a big wood rat caught. He brung it in alive and put it in front of Old Bill. As a rule, Old Bill never et nuthin' hardly, but the way he nailed that rat and then swallered him whole was an eddicati'n in appertite. We all shore was proud of him. After that the boys quit figgering on frying him up fer beefsteak. They took to calling him Diamon' Bill and looked on him as a mascot and about the best soldier in the Confederate Army, too. Why, the colonel used to get me to send him out on scout duty. No telling how many Yankees he cleaned out of thickets it was dangerous fer a man to enter. He knowed the difference between Confederate gray and Union blue jest as well as Ab Blocker's old cow dog knowed the difference between a branded critter and a mav'rick.

Well, 'taint no use fer me to tell about all the battles we fought in. At Appermatox I was still alive and so was Diamon' Bill. Jim Bowie wasn't, though, and we rode home on a borrered mule. One day way long in the summer I put Bill down at the spring on Ellum Creek, and afore my saddle blanket was dry I was breaking land, putting up the old fences, hoeing weeds out of the patch Abbie had managed to plant, and doing all sorts of things. The dogs was all dead and there jest wasn't no time fer nothing but work. Lots of days I didn't even think about Old Bill.

Then one day in the spring of '66 while I was going in a hurry down to the spring, I heared something that made my mind whirl back. I wheeled around and saw a big diamon'back running towards me. Afore I could grab fer a stick, I seen it was Old Bill. I called out to him, "Bill," and he sorter nodded his head the way I'd seen him do a thousand times. But he made a new kind of motion that says he wants me to foller him. He turns off the trail and I follers.

About a hundred yards off he sidled up to another rattler, and looked back at me. "Mrs. Bill?" I says. He nodded, and the two went on. D'reckly we come to a nacherl clearing 'bout the size of our courthouse maybe. Old Bill stopped, raised up like a nacherl-borned commander, and give the derndest rattle a man ever heared. Then he moved on ahead about ten paces and rared up agin. By that time squads and troops and companies and battalions of young rattlesnakes was coming out of the brush on all sides. I'm afeared to say how many they was—hundreds, maybe thousands. They come out in regular formations, squads-righting and squads-lefting and fronting-into-line like old soldiers. Bill lined 'em up fer dress parade about the middle of the field. Then he sounded one rattle fer a signal and, keeping a perfect front, they begun advancing towards me, all rattles a-going and every dod-gumed one of um a-playing Dixie.

Old Bill knowed what he'd done in the war. The trouble was he was the only rattlesnake in it. He didn't seem to realize the war was over. Here he'd come home and raised this army, and now he was offering it to me. I ricollect how the Confederate boys useter always be quoting Gin'ral Bedford Forrest. He said, you know, that the gin'ral wins who gits there fustest with the mostest men. Well, it was jest too late to be fustest. I tried to explain to Diamon' Bill. And that was the last in a military way I ever seen of him.

WILLIAM FAULKNER

Two Soldiers

ME AND PETE would go down to Old Man Killegrew's and listen to his radio. We would wait until after supper, after dark, and we would stand outside Old Man Killegrew's parlor window, and we could hear it because Old Man Killegrew's wife was deaf, and so he run the radio as loud as it would run, and so me and Pete could hear it plain as Old Man Killegrew's wife could, I reckon, even standing outside with the window closed.

And that night I said, "What? Japanese? What's a pearl harbor?" and Pete said, "Hush."

And so we stood there, it was cold, listening to the fellow in the radio talking, only I couldn't make no heads nor tails neither out of it. Then the fellow said that would be all for a while, and me and Pete walked back up the road to home, and Pete told me what it was. Because he was nigh twenty and he had done finished the Consolidated last June and he knowed a heap: about them Japanese dropping bombs on Pearl Harbor and that Pearl Harbor was across the water.

"Across what water?" I said. "Across that Government reservoy up at Oxford?"

"Naw," Pete said. "Across the big water. The Pacific Ocean."

We went home. Maw and Pap was already asleep, and me and Pete laid in the bed, and I still couldn't understand where it was, and Pete told me again—the Pacific Ocean.

"What's the matter with you?" Pete said. "You're going on nine years old. You been in school now ever since September. Ain't you learned nothing yet?"

"I reckon we ain't got as fer as the Pacific Ocean yet," I said.

We was still sowing the vetch then that ought to been all finished by the fifteenth of November, because Pap was still behind, just like he had been ever since me and Pete had knowed him. And we had firewood to git in, too, but every night me and Pete would go down to Old Man Killegrew's and stand outside his parlor window in the cold and listen to his radio; then we would come back home and lay in the bed and Pete would tell me what it was. That is, he would tell me for a while. Then he wouldn't tell me. It was like he didn't want to talk about it no more. He would tell me to shut up because he wanted to go to sleep, but he never wanted to go to sleep.

He would lay there, a heap stiller than if he was asleep, and it would be something, I could feel it coming out of him, like he was mad at me even, only I knowed he wasn't thinking about me, or like he was worried about something, and it wasn't that neither, because he never had nothing to worry about. He never got behind like Pap, let alone stayed behind. Pap give him ten acres when he graduated from the Consolidated, and me and Pete both reckoned Pap was durn glad to get shut of at least ten acres, less to have to worry with himself; and Pete had them ten acres all sowed to vetch and busted out and bedded for the winter, and so it wasn't that. But it was something. And still we would go down to Old Man Killegrew's every night and listen to his radio, and they was at it in the Philippines now, but General MacArthur was holding 'um. Then we would come back home and lay in the bed, and Pete wouldn't tell me nothing or talk at all. He would just lay there still as a ambush and when I would touch him, his side or his leg would feel hard and still as iron, until after a while I would go to sleep.

Then one night—it was the first time he had said nothing to me except to jump on me about not chopping enough wood at the wood tree where we was cutting—he said, "I got to go."

"Go where?" I said.

"To that war," Pete said.

"Before we even finish gittin' in the firewood?"

"Firewood, hell," Pete said.

"All right," I said. "When we going to start?"

But he wasn't even listening. He laid there, hard and still as iron in the dark. "I got to go," he said. "I jest ain't going to put up with no folks treating the Unity States that way."

"Yes," I said. "Firewood or no firewood, I reckon we got to go."

This time he heard me. He laid still again, but it was a different kind of still.

"You?" he said. "To a war?"

"You'll whup the big uns and I'll whup the little uns," I said.

Then he told me I couldn't go. At first I thought he just never wanted me tagging after him, like he wouldn't leave me go with him when he went sparking them girls of Tull's. Then he told me the Army wouldn't leave me go because I was too little, and then I knowed he really meant it and that I couldn't go nohow noways. And somehow I hadn't believed until then that he was going himself, but now I knowed he was and that he wasn't going to leave me go with him a-tall.

"I'll chop the wood and tote the water for you-all then!" I said. "You got to have wood and water!"

Anyway, he was listening to me now. He wasn't like iron now.

He turned onto his side and put his hand on my chest because it was me that was laying straight and hard on my back now.

"No," he said. "You got to stay here and help Pap."

"Help him what?" I said. "He ain't never caught up nohow. He can't get no further behind. He can sho'ly take care of this little shirttail of a farm while me and you are whupping them Japanese. I got to go too. If you got to go, then so have I."

"No," Pete said. "Hush now. Hush." And he meant it, and I knowed he did. Only I made sho' from his own mouth. I quit.

"So I just can't go then," I said.

"No," Pete said. "You just can't go. You're too little, in the first place, and in the second place——"

"All right," I said. "Then shut up and leave me go to sleep."

So he hushed then and laid back. And I laid there like I was already asleep, and pretty soon he was asleep and I knowed it was the wanting to go to the war that had worried him and kept him awake, and now that he had decided to go he wasn't worried any more.

The next morning he told Maw and Pap. Maw was all right. She cried.

"No," she said, crying, "I don't want him to go. I would rather go myself in his place, if I could. I don't want to save the country. Them Japanese could take it and keep it, so long as they left me and my family and my children alone. But I remember my brother Marsh in that other war. He had to go to that one when he wasn't but nineteen, and our mother couldn't understand it then any more than I can now. But she told Marsh if he had to go, he had to go. And so, if Pete's got to go to this one, he's got to go to it. Jest don't ask me to understand why."

But Pap was the one. He was the feller. "To the war?" he said. "Why,

I just don't see a bit of use in that. You ain't old enough for the draft, and the country ain't being invaded. Our President in Washington, D.C., is watching the conditions and he will notify us. Besides, in that other war your ma just mentioned, I was drafted and sent clean to Texas and was held there nigh eight months until they finally quit fighting. It seems to me that that, along with your uncle Marsh, who received a actual wound on the battlefields of France, is enough for me and mine to have to do to protect the country, at least in my lifetime. Besides, what'll I do for help on the farm with you gone? It seems to me I'll get mighty far behind."

"You been behind as long as I can remember," Pete said. "Anyway, I'm going. I got to."

"Of course he's got to go," I said. "Them Japanese——"

"You hush your mouth!" Maw said, crying. "Nobody's talking to you! Go and get me a armful of wood! That's what you can do!"

So I got the wood. And all the next day, while me and Pete and Pap was getting in as much wood as we could in that time because Pete said how Pap's idea of plenty of wood was one more stick laying against the wall that Maw ain't put on the fire yet, Maw was getting Pete ready to go. She washed and mended his clothes and cooked him a shoe box of vittles. And that night me and Pete laid in the bed and listened to her packing his grip and crying, until after a while Pete got up in his night-shirt and went back there, and I could hear them talking, until at last Maw said, "You got to go, and so I want you to go. But I don't understand it, and I won't never, and so don't expect me to." And Pete come back and got into the bed again and laid again still and hard as iron on his back, and then he said, and he wasn't talking to me, he wasn't talking to nobody: "I got to go. I just got to."

"Sho' you got to," I said "Them Japanese——" He turned over hard, he kind of surged over onto his side, looking at me in the dark.

"Anyway, you're all right," he said. "I expected to have more trouble with you than with all the rest of them put together."

"I reckon I can't help it neither," I said. "But maybe it will run a few years longer and I can get there. Maybe someday I will jest walk in on you."

"I hope not," Pete said. "Folks don't go to wars for fun. A man don't leave his maw crying just for fun."

"Then why are you going?" I said.

"I got to," he said. "I just got to. Now you go on to sleep. I got to ketch that early bus in the morning."

"All right," I said. "I hear tell Memphis is a big place. How will you find where the Army's at?"

"I'll ask somebody where to go to join it," Pete said. "Go on to sleep now."

"Is that what you'll ask for? Where to join the Army?" I said.

"Yes," Pete said. He turned onto his back again. "Shut up and go to sleep."

We went to sleep. The next morning we et breakfast by lamplight because the bus would pass at six o'clock. Maw wasn't crying now. She jest looked grim and busy, putting breakfast on the table while we et it. Then she finished packing Pete's grip, except he never wanted to take no grip to the war, but Maw said decent folks never went nowhere, not even to a war, without a change of clothes and something to tote them in. She put in the shoe box of fried chicken and biscuits and she put the Bible in, too, and then it was time to go. We didn't know until then that Maw wasn't going to the bus. She jest brought Pete's cap and overcoat, and still she didn't cry no more, she jest stood with her hands on Pete's shoulders and she didn't move, but somehow, and just holding Pete's shoulders, she looked as hard and fierce as when Pete had turned toward me in the bed last night and tole me that anyway I was all right.

"They could take the country and keep the country, so long as they never bothered me and mine," she said. Then she said, "Don't never forget who you are. You ain't rich and the rest of the world outside of Frenchman's Bend never heard of you. But your blood is good as any blood anywhere, and don't you never forget it."

Then she kissed him, and then we was out of the house, with Pap toting Pete's grip whether Pete wanted him to or not. There wasn't no dawn even yet, not even after we had stood on the highway by the mailbox awhile. Then we seen the lights of the bus coming and I was watching the bus until it come up and Pete flagged it, and then, sho' enough, there was daylight—it had started while I wasn't watching. And now me and Pete expected Pap to say something else foolish, like he done before, about how Uncle Marsh getting wounded in France and that trip to Texas Pap had taken in 1918 ought to be enough to save the Unity States in 1942, but he never. He done all right too. He jest said, "Good-by, son. Always remember what your ma told you and write her whenever you find the time." Then he shaken Pete's hand, and Pete looked at me a minute and put his hand on my head and rubbed my head durn nigh hard enough to wring my neck off and jumped into the bus, and the feller wound the door shut and the bus begun to hum; then it was moving, humming and grinding and whining louder and louder; it was going fast, with two little red lights behind it that never seemed to get no littler, but jest seemed to be running together until pretty soon they would touch and jest be one light. But they never did, and then the bus was gone, and even like it was, I could have pretty nigh busted out crying, nigh to nine years old and all.

Me and Pap went back to the house. All that day we worked at the wood tree, and so I never had no good chance until about middle of the afternoon. Then I taken my slingshot and I would have like to took all my bird eggs, too, because Pete had give me his collection and he holp me with mine, and he would like to git the box out and look at them as good as I would, even if he was nigh twenty years old. But the box was too big to tote a long ways and have to worry with, so I just taken the shikepoke egg, because it was the best un, and wropped it up good into a matchbox and hid it and the slingshot under the corner of the barn. Then we et supper and went to bed, and I thought then how if I would-a had to stayed in that room and that bed like that even for one more night I jest couldn't-a stood it. Then I could hear Pap snoring, but I never heard no sound from Maw, whether she was asleep or not, and I don't reckon she was. So I taken my shoes and drapped them out the window, and then I clumb out like I used to watch Pete do when he was still jest seventeen and Pap held that he was too young yet to be tomcatting around at night, and wouldn't leave him out, and I put on my shoes and went to the barn and got the slingshot and the shikepoke egg and went to the highway.

It wasn't cold, it was jest durn confounded dark, and that highway stretched on in front of me like, without nobody using it, it had stretched out half again as fer jest like a man does when he lays down, so that for a time it looked like full sun was going to ketch me before I had finished them twenty-two miles to Jefferson. But it didn't. Daybreak was jest starting when I walked up the hill into town. I could smell breakfast cooking in the cabins and I wished I had thought to brought me a cold biscuit, but that was too late now. And Pete had told me Memphis was a piece beyond Jefferson, but I never knowed it was no eighty miles. So I stood there on that empty square, with daylight coming and coming and the street lights still burning and that law looking down at me, and me still eighty miles from Memphis, and it had took me all night to walk jest twenty-two miles, and so, by the time I got to Memphis at that rate, Pete would-a done already started for Pearl Harbor.

"Where do you come from?" the law said.

And I told him again. "I got to git to Memphis. My brother's there."

"You mean you ain't got any folks around here?" the law said. "Nobody but that brother? What are you doing way off down here and your brother in Memphis?"

And I told him again, "I got to git to Memphis. I ain't got no time to waste talking about it and I ain't got time to walk it. I got to git there today."

"Come on here," the law said.

We went down another street. And there was the bus, jest like when Pete got into it yestiddy morning, except there wasn't no lights on it now and it was empty. There was a regular bus deepo like a railroad deepo, with a ticket counter and a feller behind it, and the law said, "Set down over there," and I set down on the bench, and the law said, "I want to use your telephone," and he talked in the telephone a minute and put it down and said to the feller behind the ticket counter, "Keep your eye on him. I'll be back as soon as Mrs. Habersham can arrange to get herself up and dressed." He went out. I got up and went to the ticket counter.

"I want to go to Memphis," I said.

"You bet," the feller said. "You set down on the bench now. Mr. Foote will be back in a minute."

"I don't know no Mr. Foote," I said. "I want to ride that bus to Memphis."

"You got some money?" he said. "It'll cost you seventy-two cents."

I taken out the matchbox and unwropped the shikepoke egg. "I'll swap you this for a ticket to Memphis," I said.

"What's that?" he said.

"It's a shikepoke egg," I said. "You never seen one before. It's worth a dollar. I'll take seventy-two cents fer it."

"No," he said, "the fellers that own that bus insist on a cash basis. If I started swapping tickets for bird eggs and livestock and such, they would fire me. You go and set down on the bench now, like Mr. Foote——"

I started for the door, but he caught me; he put one hand on the ticket counter and jumped over it and caught up with me and reached his hand out to ketch my shirt. I whupped out my pocketknife and snapped it open.

"You put a hand on me and I'll cut it off," I said.

I tried to dodge him and run at the door, but he could move quicker than any grown man I ever see, quick as Pete almost. He cut me off and stood with his back against the door and one foot raised a little, and there wasn't no other way to get out. "Get back on that bench and stay there," he said.

And there wasn't no other way out. And he stood there with his back against the door. So I went back to the bench. And then it seemed like to me that deepo was full of folks. There was that law again, and there was two ladies in fur coats and their faces already painted. But they still looked like they had got up in a hurry and they still never liked it, a old one and a young one, looking down at me.

"He hasn't got a overcoat!" the old one said. "How in the world did he ever get down here by himself?"

"I ask you," the law said. "I couldn't get nothing out of him except his brother is in Memphis and he wants to get back up there."

"That's right," I said. "I got to git to Memphis today."

"Of course you must," the old one said. "Are you sure you can find your brother when you get to Memphis?"

"I reckon I can," I said. "I ain't got but one and I have knowed him all my life. I reckon I will know him again when I see him."

The old one looked at me. "Somehow he doesn't look like he lives in Memphis," she said.

"He probably don't," the law said. "You can't tell though. He might live anywhere, overhalls or not. This day and time they get scattered overnight from he—hope to breakfast; boys and girls, too, almost before they can walk good. He might have been in Missouri or Texas either yestiddy, for all we know. But he don't seem to have any doubt his brother is in Memphis. All I know to do is send him up there and leave him look."

"Yes," the old one said.

The young one set down on the bench by me and opened a hand satchel and taken out a artermatic writing pen and some papers.

"Now, honey," the old one said, "we're going to see that you find your brother, but we must have a case history for our files first. We want to

know your name and your brother's name and where you were born and
when your parents died."

"I don't need no case history neither," I said. "All I want is to get to
Memphis. I got to git there today."

"You see?" the law said. He said it almost like he enjoyed it. "That's
what I told you."

"You're lucky, at that, Mrs. Habersham," the bus feller said. "I don't
think he's got a gun on him, but he can open that knife da—I mean, fast
enough to suit any man."

But the old one just stood there looking at me.

"Well," she said. "Well. I really don't know what to do."

"I do," the bus feller said. "I'm going to give him a ticket out of my own
pocket, as a measure of protecting the company against riot and bloodshed.
And when Mr. Foote tells the city board about it, it will be a civic matter
and they will not only reimburse me, they will give me a medal too. Hey,
Mr. Foote?"

But never nobody paid him no mind. The old one still stood looking
down at me. She said, "Well," again. Then she taken a dollar from her
purse and give it to the bus feller. "I suppose he will travel on a child's
ticket, won't he?"

"Wellum," the bus feller said, "I just don't know what the regulations
would be. Likely I will be fired for not crating him and marking the crate
Poison. But I'll risk it."

Then they were gone. Then the law came back with a sandwich and
give it to me.

"You're sure you can find that brother?" he said.

"I ain't yet convinced why not," I said. "If I don't see Pete first, he'll see
me. He knows me too."

Then the law went out for good, too, and I et the sandwich. Then more
folks come in and bought tickets, and then the bus feller said it was time to
go, and I got into the bus just like Pete done, and we was gone.

I seen all the towns. I seen all of them. When the bus got to going good
I found out I was jest about wore out for sleep. But there was too much
I hadn't never saw before. We run out of Jefferson and run past fields and
woods, then we would run into another town and out of that un and past
fields and woods again, and then into another town with stores and gins
and water tanks, and we run along by the railroad for a spell and I seen

the signal arm move, and then I seen the train and then some more towns, and I was jest about plumb wore out for sleep, but I couldn't resk it. Then Memphis begun. It seemed like, to me, it went on for miles. We would pass a patch of stores and I would think that was sho'ly it and the bus would even stop. But it wouldn't be Memphis yet and we would go on again past water tanks and smokestacks on top of the mills, and if they was gins and sawmills, I never knowed there was that many and I never seen any that big, and where they got enough cotton and logs to run 'um I don't know.

Then I seen Memphis. I knowed I was right this time. It was standing up into the air. It looked like about a dozen whole towns bigger than Jefferson was set up on one edge in a field, standing up into the air higher than ara hill in all Yoknapatawpha County. Then we was in it, with the bus stopping ever' few feet, it seemed like to me, and cars rushing past on both sides of it and the streets crowded with folks from ever'where in town that day, until I didn't see how there could-a been nobody left in Mis'sippi a-tall to even sell me a bus ticket, let alone write out no case histories. Then the bus stopped. It was another bus deepo, a heap bigger than the one in Jefferson. And I said, "All right. Where do folks join the Army?"

"What?" the bus feller said.

And I said it again, "Where do folks join the Army?"

"Oh," he said. Then he told me how to get there. I was afraid at first I wouldn't ketch on how to do in a town big as Memphis. But I caught on all right. I never had to ask but twice more. Then I was there, and I was durn glad to git out of all them rushing cars and shoving folks and all that racket for a spell, and I thought, It won't be long now, and I thought how if there was any kind of a crowd there that had done already joined the Army, too, Pete would likely see me before I seen him. And so I walked into the room. And Pete wasn't there.

He wasn't even there. There was a soldier with a big arrerhead on his sleeve, writing, and two fellers standing in front of him, and there was some more folks there, I reckon. It seems to me I remember some more folks there.

I went to the table where the soldier was writing, and I said, "Where's Pete?" and he looked up and I said, "My brother. Pete Grier. Where is he?"

"What?" the soldier said. "Who?"

And I told him again. "He joined the Army yestiddy. He's going to Pearl Harbor. So am I. I want to ketch him. Where you-all got him?" Now they were all looking at me, but I never paid them no mind. "Come on," I said. "Where is he?"

The soldier had quit writing. He had both hands spraddled out on the table. "Oh," he said. "You're going, too, hah?"

"Yes," I said. "They got to have wood and water. I can chop it and tote it. Come on. Where's Pete?"

The soldier stood up. "Who let you in here?" he said. "Go on. Beat it."

"Durn that," I said. "You tell me where Pete——"

I be dog if he couldn't move faster than the bus feller even. He never come over the table, he come around it, he was on me almost before I knowed it, so that I jest had time to jump back and whup out my pocket-knife and snap it open and hit one lick, and he hollered and jumped back and grabbed one hand with the other and stood there cussing and hollering.

One of the other fellers grabbed me from behind, and I hit at him with the knife, but I couldn't reach him.

Then both of the fellers had me from behind, and then another soldier come out of a door at the back. He had on a belt with a britching strop over one shoulder.

"What the hell is this?" he said.

"That little son cut me with a knife!" the first soldier hollered. When he said that I tried to git at him again, but both them fellers was holding me, two against one, and the soldier with the backing strop said, "Here, here. Put your knife up, feller. None of us are armed. A man don't knife-fight folks that are barehanded." I could begin to hear him then. He sounded jest like Pete talked to me. "Let him go," he said. They let me go. "Now what's all the trouble about?" And I told him. "I see," he said. "And you come up to see if he was all right before he left."

"No," I said. "I came to——"

But he had already turned to where the first soldier was wropping a handkerchief around his hand.

"Have you got him?" he said. The first soldier went back to the table and looked at some papers.

"Here he is," he said. "He enlisted yestiddy. He's in a detachment leaving this morning for Little Rock." He had a watch stropped on his arm. He looked at it. "The train leaves in about fifty minutes. If I know country boys, they're probably all down there at the station right now."

"Get him up here," the one with the backing strop said. "Phone the station. Tell the porter to get him a cab. And you come with me," he said.

It was another office behind that un, with jest a table and some chairs. We set there while the soldier smoked, and it wasn't long; I knowed Pete's feet soon as I heard them. Then the first soldier opened the door and Pete come in. He never had no soldier clothes on. He looked jest like he did when he got on the bus yestiddy morning, except it seemed to me like it was at least a week, so much had happened, and I had done had to do so much traveling. He come in and there he was, looking at me like he hadn't never left home, except that here we was in Memphis, on the way to Pearl Harbor.

"What in durnation are you doing here?" he said.

And I told him, "You got to have wood and water to cook with. I can chop it and tote it for you-all."

"No," Pete said. "You're going back home."

"No, Pete," I said. "I got to go too. I got to. It hurts my heart, Pete."

"No," Pete said. He looked at the soldier. "I jest don't know what could have happened to him, Lootenant," he said. "He never drawed a knife on anybody before in his life." He looked at me. "What did you do it for?"

"I don't know," I said. "I jest had to. I jest had to git here. I jest had to find you."

"Well, don't you never do it again, you hear?" Pete said. "You put that knife in your pocket and you keep it there. If I ever again hear of you drawing it on anybody, I'm coming back from wherever I am at and whup the fire out of you. You hear me?"

"I would sure cut a throat if it would bring you back to stay," I said. "Pete," I said. "Pete."

"No," Pete said. Now his voice wasn't hard and quick no more, it was almost quiet, and I knowed now I wouldn't never change him. "You must go home. You must look after Maw, and I am depending on you to look after my ten acres. I want you to go back home. Today. Do you hear?"

"I hear," I said.

"Can he get back home by himself?" the soldier said.

"He come up here by himself," Pete said.

"I can get back, I reckon," I said. "I don't live in but one place. I don't reckon it's moved."

Pete taken a dollar out of his pocket and give it to me. "That'll buy your bus ticket right to our mailbox," he said. "I want you to mind the lootenant. He'll send you to the bus. And you go back home and you take care of Maw and look after my ten acres and keep that durn knife in your pocket. You hear me?"

"Yes, Pete," I said.

"All right," Pete said. "Now I got to go." He put his hand on my head again. But this time he never wrung my neck. He just laid his hand on my head a minute. And then I be dog if he didn't lean down and kiss me, and I heard his feet and then the door, and I never looked up and that was all, me setting there, rubbing the place where Pete kissed me and the soldier throwed back in his chair, looking out the window and coughing. He reached into his pocket and handed something to me without looking around. It was a piece of chewing gum.

"Much obliged," I said. "Well, I reckon I might as well start back. I got a right fer piece to go."

"Wait," the soldier said. Then he telephoned again and I said again I better start back, and he said again, "Wait. Remember what Pete told you."

So we waited, and then another lady come in, old, too, in a fur coat, too, but she smelled all right, she never had no artermatic writing pen nor no case history either. She come in and the soldier got up, and she looked around quick until she saw me, and come and put her hand on my shoulder light and quick and easy as Maw herself might-a done it.

"Come on," she said. "Let's go home to dinner."

"Nome," I said. "I got to ketch the bus to Jefferson."

"I know. There's plenty of time. We'll go home and eat dinner first."

She had a car. And now we was right down in the middle of all them other cars. We was almost under the busses, and all them crowds of people on the street close enough to where I could have talked to them if I had knowed who they was. After a while she stopped the car. "Here we are," she said, and I looked at it, and if all that was her house, she sho' had a big family. But all of it wasn't. We crossed a hall with trees growing in it and went into a little room without nothing in it but a nigger dressed up in a uniform a heap shinier than them soldiers had, and the nigger shut the door, and then I hollered, "Look out!" and grabbed, but it was all right; that whole little room jest went right on up and stopped and the door opened and we was in another hall, and the lady unlocked a door and we went in, and there was another soldier, a old feller, with a britching strop, too, and a silver-colored bird on each shoulder.

"Here we are," the lady said. "This is Colonel McKellogg. Now what would you like for dinner?"

"I reckon I'll jest have some ham and eggs and coffee," I said.

She had done started to pick up the telephone. She stopped. "Coffee?"

she said. "When did you start drinking coffee?"

"I don't know," I said. "I reckon it was before I could remember."

"You're about eight, aren't you?" she said.

"Nome," I said. "I'm eight and ten months. Going on eleven months."

She telephoned then. Then we set there and I told them how Pete had jest left that morning for Pearl Harbor and I had aimed to go with him, but I would have to go back home to take care of Maw and look after Pete's ten acres, and she said how they had a little boy about my size, too, in a school in the East. Then a nigger, another one, in a short kind of shirt-tail coat, rolled a kind of wheelbarrer in. It had my ham and eggs and a glass of milk and a piece of pie, too, and I thought I was hungry. But when I taken the first bite I found out I couldn't swallow it, and I got up quick.

"I got to go," I said.

"Wait," she said.

"I got to go," I said.

"Just a minute," she said. "I've already telephoned for the car. It won't be but a minute now. Can't you drink the milk even? Or maybe some of your coffee?"

"Nome," I said. "I ain't hungry. I'll eat when I git home." Then the telephone rung. She never even answered it.

"There," she said. "There's the car." And we went back down in that 'ere little moving room with the dressed-up nigger. This time it was a big car with a soldier driving it. I got into the front with him. She give the soldier a dollar. "He might get hungry," she said. "Try to find a decent place for him."

"Okay, Mrs. McKellogg," the soldier said.

Then we was gone again. And now I could see Memphis good, bright in the sunshine, while we was swinging around it. And first thing I knowed, we was back on the same highway the bus run on this morning —the patches of stores and them big gins and sawmills, and Memphis running on for miles, it seemed like to me, before it begun to give out. Then we was running again between the fields and woods, running fast now, and except for that soldier, it was like I hadn't never been to Memphis a-tall. We was going fast now. At this rate, before I knowed it we would be home again, and I thought about me riding up to Frenchman's Bend in this here big car with a soldier running it, and all of a sudden I begun to cry. I never knowed I was fixing to, and I couldn't stop it. I set there by that soldier, crying. We was going fast.

WALDO FRANK

A Place to Lay One's Head

THE NIGHT was like warm wine; his bag was light. As he stepped from the tiny station he spurned the boy and the motorbus which plied to the one hotel, four miles away on the sea—I'll walk. He wanted the night; he wanted to put off, as long as might be, the dull impersonal hotel room from which this murmurous summer would be barred, in which there would be nothing but sleep.

Sleep on such an evening in June! He walked under trees awake with leafy song. Fireflies were spangling star bits. And in the heaven the stars were fireflies.

When at last he saw the face of the hotel within the pines he rebelled that the hour's walk was over. The trees were a rebuke to his leaving them: warm, they enfolded him and tried to keep him. "Why not lie down with us?" He was tempted. He could make a pillow of the velvet lichen running on the roots of a hemlock. He could turn his face to the stars and the sea. With the pulse of the universe upon his eyes he could close his eyes and let dream's little universe, rhythmic within the great one, woo him and take him.

But while he wondered why he did not stay and sleep with the night he had stepped up the hotel porch and opened the door. The place seemed deserted. In the narrow lobby there was no guest. Two hooded lamps shadowed the panels of raw pine, cast brooding bits of darkness on a table littered with magazines and papers and on the cushioned nooks. Silence. Night was compressed in this room; its whisperings and songs crushed out. Night, here, was distilled into a heady liquor. He turned to escape. A thirst was in him for the cool cadence of outdoors. He did not like this hotel. He would go to the trees. . . .

"Are you looking for someone, sir?"

His eyes turned, almost guiltily, toward the voice. Behind a desk, close to a lamp, in a corner of the room stood a girl. He hesitated—from the open door came the breath of pines and the Pacific. Then he no longer heard. He shut the door and stepped nearer to the girl.

"Pardon me," he said. "Of course! I'm looking for a room."

"Oh, you missed the bus? What a pity! You walked?"

"It is not a pity. I liked the walk."

His gaze began to condense from the vague reverie of his hour with the wind and the trees; still, he scarce saw the girl—he saw merely that she looked at him.

"I hope it is not too late," he went on quickly, "to disturb you—for a room?"

She was silent. Then quite simply she repeated:

"It is a pity that you missed the bus."

He put her down for the usual country clod with no taste for anything but cars and city styles.

"You *have* a room?" He wanted to get away—why don't I go?

"I'm sorry," she said. "It is a pity. There is no room."

Then he first saw her: a chestnut cloud of hair over her eyes. She wore a waist flimsy and cool about the warm firm breast. Her arms were bare.

"No room?"

"There were four guests with the bus. And we had just four rooms. It's a pity, sir. If you had taken the bus . . . if you had stepped in quicker than one of the others."

He was close now to the desk; he placed his right hand on it. "This is a problem!" He had forgotten the inviting trees. Beside his hand was hers upon the wood. Her hand was an active presence; it disturbed the quiet of his own, making him conscious of it. He strummed on the wood.

"Nothing?"

"Nothing, sir. It is a pity."

"No other hotel, hereabouts?"

"At the station—across from it—the postmistress might take you in." She looked up and added, "If she is not asleep."

"I might phone at once."

"She is very deaf. If she's asleep you'll never wake her."

"Ah-ah." He thrummed with his fingers; grew aware of it. She took her hand away; he withdrew his.

"I might leave my bag and walk back. How many miles is it?"

"If you came"—her voice was oddly clear as if she talked to convince some stupid child—"if you came by the wood road, you walked four miles. There's a path by the sea that is six. A lovelier way."

Both had forgotten his suggestion of the phone; and he, the rebuking, inviting, sensuous trees.

There was silence, easy as if it were natural that he should pause ere he came to a decision on a weighty matter. His mind flew to chess—my move. Then he saw again . . . and alone . . . the girl who with a smile, polite but visibly indulgent, doubtless waited his going. He had forgotten utterly the woods; there was no outside. The room was alive and close about them.

"Not a nook for me *anywhere?*" he said.

"Not anywhere," she answered slowly.

"And all your guests have gone to bed?"

"We are early sleepers, here, sir. The night train is the last event of the day. Mail is not distributed till morning."

He held his hat in his left hand; he placed it on the desk. And his left hand, falling beside it, began again to strum the wood. The beat of the fingers was periodic, subtle . . . somewhat like telegraphic jottings. He felt beside his hand a presence that displaced it. He looked; her hand lay demurely at her edge of the desk. He watched her hand, and there came from it, through his hand to him, a tension bittersweet; soon, an intolerable tension.

"If you were kind," he heard his words come dry, he was outside his words, and they amazed him, "if you were kind you would not, at this hour, send me walking six miles back—to a deaf woman's door."

There was no saliva in his mouth; yet what he said seemed to concern him only mildly, as if it were a formula with a foregone conclusion.

"You would take me in. You would find—you would give me a place to lay my head." The room was breathing with them. His voice, clear as dry twigs, amazed him:

"*You* have a room?"

There, an instant, were his words between his eyes and hers; then his words were gone, as if her eyes had absorbed them.

Her face turned to a little stair behind her.

"Go up there, and wait."

Her face had been but a post to show the way. There was no feeling in it, no recognition. He took his hat, leaving his bag at the desk.

It was not the guest stair. It was a dark back stair that turned, halfway, so that the upper hall was black. In the balustrade below, a mere crack of light. He stood motionless in the black, and he waited.

There was no thought in him. He did not wait, unmoving because he feared if he moved he might rouse some sleeper. He waited, motionless and thoughtless, feelingless, because he was in equilibrium; cradled perfectly in some imminent presence.

He waited a long time.

There was a step below. The little crack of gleam within the balustrade winked out: so silent its demise that it was like a signal from a distance. He felt her coming toward him. Her shoulder faintly touched his. Then he followed her in the dark with a knowledge that was thoughtless, sightless. His following her was the mere wake of her walking—like some immutable effect of a cause in nature. A door shut behind them both; he heard it lock. . . .

Sleep softly pushed him to a dawn whose light was the stirring of his mingled senses. He turned his head, and only then opened his eyes which fell, already focused, on her face. The girl slept. Her hair was a chaos all about her ordered slumber. The shut eyes tremored slightly; a hand lay open on the coverlet. Still without thought he rose, dressed, and went.

When he reached the sea he again flung off his clothes and swam. The water on his flesh was, strangely, a salute: the sea seemed to accept him, infinitesimal and yet its equal.

At nine o'clock the sun stood high on the pines which margined the earth from the Pacific. He thought it safe, now, to return to the hotel. He had designed his little strategy. Thought, he had forced at last to come. And with thought, as he came out of the perfection of his trance in which act and impulse had been so miraculously attuned, came a waver of self-satisfaction—a self-salute at his prowess.

He strode, still glowing from the sea, into the hotel lobby. It was a dingy transformation from the night before: men and women were grouped in it like clumsy grotesques of a perverse creator gibing his own beauty.

Behind the old-fashioned desk squatted a round and ruddy woman, the proprietress.

"Good morning." He smiled at her.

She stared at this creature, as if his presence were impossible; indeed for her it was, coming in connection with no train or bus. Her bosom, high as a shelf beneath her dress, did not budge as she ducked her head.

He pointed to his bag which still stood where the girl had placed it.

"I arrived late last evening. There was no room for me. So I left my bag and went. It was a beautiful night. Can you accommodate me today? I want to stay some time."

The landlady's face took on a puzzled frown.

"You were here last night?"

He nodded.

"No room, you say?"

"I missed the bus. . . . The young lady was most kind. But there was no room."

"She said there was no room! Why, that is strange. And you had to tramp all the way back to the village! What a pity! How careless of the girl! *Of course* there was a room!"

ERLE STANLEY GARDNER

The House of Three Candles

THE Love of Loyalty Road in Canton is a wide thoroughfare cut ruthlessly through the congested district in order to modernize the city. Occasional side streets feed the traffic of automobiles and rickshas into it, but back of these streets one enters the truly congested areas, where people live like sardines in a tin.

The Street of the Wild Chicken is so wide that one may travel down it in a ricksha. But within a hundred feet of the intersection of the Street of the Wild Chicken and Love of Loyalty Road, one comes to Tien Mah Hong, which, being translated, means the Alley of the Sky Horse. And in Tien Mah Hong there is no room for even ricksha traffic. Two pedestrians wearing wide-brimmed hats must needs tilt their heads as they meet, so that the brims will not scrape as the wearers pass each other shoulder to shoulder.

Houses on each side of Tien Mah Hong, with balconies and windows abutting directly upon the Alley of the Sky Horse, give but little opportunity for privacy. The lives of neighbors are laid bare with an intimacy of detail which would be inconceivable in a less congested community or a more occidental atmosphere. At night the peddlers of bean cakes, walking through the Sky Horse Alley, beat little drums to attract attention, and shout their wares with a cry which is like the howl of a wolf.

Leung Fah walked down the Sky Horse Alley with downcast eyes, as befitted a modest woman of the coolie class. Her face was utterly without expression. Not even the shrewdest student of human nature could have told from her outward appearance the thoughts which were seething within her breast.

It had been less than a month before that Leung Fah had clasped to her breast a morsel of humanity which represented all of life's happiness, a warm, ragged bundle, a child without a father, a secret outlet for her mother love.

Then one night there had been a scream of sirens, a panic-stricken helter-skelter rush of shouting inhabitants, and over all the ominous, steady roar of airplane engines, a hideous undertone of sound which mounted until it became as the hum of a million metallic bees.

It is easy enough to advocate fleeing to a place of safety, but the narrow roads of Canton admit of no swift handling of crowds. And there are no places of safety. Moreover, the temperament of the Chinese makes it difficult to carry out any semblance of an air-defense program. Death in one form or another is always jeering at their elbows. Why dignify one particular form of death by going to such great lengths, so far as precautions are concerned?

The devil's eggs began to fall from the sky in a screaming hail. Anti-aircraft guns roared a reply. Machine guns sputtered away hysterically. Through all the turmoil the Japanese fliers went calmly about their business of murder, ignoring the frenzied, nervous attempts of an unprepared city to make some semblance of defense.

With fierce mother instinct Leung Fah had held her baby to her breast, shielding it with her frail body, as though interposing a layer of flesh and bone would be of any avail against this "civilized" warfare which rained down from the skies.

The earth had rocked with a series of detonations, and then suddenly Leung Fah had been surrounded by a terrific noise, by splintered timbers, dust, and debris.

When she had wiped her eyes and looked at the little morsel of humanity in her arms she had screamed in terrified anguish.

No one had known of Leung Fah's girl. Because she had no husband she had kept her offspring as a secret; and because she slept in one of the poorest sections of the city, where people are as numerous and as transient as bats in a cave, she had been able to maintain her secret. Since no one had known of her child, no one had known of her loss. Night after night she had gone about her work, moving stolidly through the heat and stench of the city, her face an expressionless mask.

Sahm Seuh, the man who had only three fingers on his right hand, and whose eyes were cunning, moving as smoothly moist in their sockets as the tongue of a snake, had noticed her going about her work, and of late he had become exceedingly solicitous. She was not looking well. Was she perhaps sick? She no longer laughed, or paused to gossip in loud tones with the slave girls in the early morning hours before daylight. Was it perhaps that the money she was making was not sufficient? . . . Sahm Seuh's oily eyes slithered expressively. Perhaps that, too, could be remedied.

Because she had said nothing, because she had stared at him with eyes that saw not and ears that heard not, her soul numbed by an anguish which made her as one who walks in sleep at the hour of the rat, Sahm Seuh had grown bold.

Did she need money? Lots of money—gold money? Not the paper money of China, but gold which would enable her to be independent? *Aiiii-ah-h.* It was simple. So simple as only the striking of a match. And Sahm Seuh flipped his wrist in a quick motion and scratched a match into flame in order to illustrate his meaning. He had gone then, leaving her to think the matter over.

That night as she moved through the narrow thoroughfares of the city her mind brooded upon the words of Sahm Seuh.

Canton is a sleepless city of noise. At times, during the summer months, there comes a slight ebb of activity during the first few hours after midnight, but it is an ebb which is barely perceptible to occidental ears. In the large Chinese cities people sleep in shifts because there is not enough room to accommodate them all at one time in houses. Those who are off shift roam the streets, and because Chinese ears are impervious to noise, just as Chinese nostrils are immune to smells, the hubbub of conversation continues unabated.

Daylight was dawning, a murky, humid dawn which brought renewed heat to a city already steeped in its own emanations; a city of silent-winged mosquitoes, oppressive, sweltering heat, unevaporated perspiration, and those odors which cling to China as an aura.

Sahm Seuh stood before her.

"That gold?" he asked. "Do you wish it?"

"I would strike a match," she said tonelessly, her face devoid of expression.

"Meet me," Sahm Seuh said, "at the house on Sky Horse Alley where three candles burn. Open the door and climb the stairs. The time is tonight at the last minute of the hour of the dog." And so, as one in a daze, Leung Fah turned down Sky Horse Alley and shuffled along with leaden feet, her eyes utterly without expression, set in a face of wood. . . .

Night found her turning into the Alley of the Sky Horse.

In a house on the left a girl was playing a metallic-sounding Chinese harp. Ten steps back of her a bean peddler raised his voice in a long, howling "o-w-w-w-w e-o-o-o-o." Fifty feet ahead, a family sought to scatter evil spirits by flinging lighted firecrackers from the balcony. They were scattered broadcast, in an impartial distribution. If a few firecrackers perchance flew across to the balconies of the adjoining houses and rolled in to explode under beds or chairs, who was there to object? Certainly no one would be so foolish as to wish to keep such evil spirits as might be in the room from being frightened away.

Leung Fah plodded on, circling a bonfire where paper imitation money, a model sedan chair, and slaves in effigy were being sent by means of fire to join the spirits of ancestors. Three candles flickered on the sidewalk in the heavy air of the hot night.

Leung Fah opened the door and climbed stairs. There was darkness ahead, only darkness. She entered a room and sensed that others were present. She could hear their breathing, the restless motions of their bodies, the rustle of clothes, occasionally a nervous cough The hour struck—the passing of the hour of the dog, and the beginning of the hour of the boar.

The voice of Sahm Seuh came from the darkness. "Let everyone here close his eyes and become blind. He who opens his eyes will be adjudged traitor. It is given to only one man to see those who are gathered in this room. Any prying eyes will receive the kiss of a hot iron, that what they have seen may be sealed into the brain."

Leung Fah, seated on the floor, her feet doubled back under her, her eyes closed tightly, sensed that men were moving around the room, examining the faces of those who were present by the aid of an electric flashlight which stabbed its beam into each of the faces. And she could feel heat upon her cheeks, which made her realize that a man with a white-hot iron stood near by, ready to plunge the iron into any eyes which might show signs of curiosity.

"She is strange to me," a voice said, a voice which spoke with the hissing sound of the *yut boen gwiee*—the Japanese ghosts of the sunrise.

"She is mine," the voice of Sahm Seuh said, and the light ceased to illuminate her closed eyelids. The hot iron passed by.

She heard a sudden scream, the sizzling of a hot iron, a yell of mortal anguish and the sound of a body as it thudded to the floor. She did not open her eyes. Life, in China, is cheap.

At length the silent roll call had been completed. The voice of Sahm Seuh said, "Eyes may now open."

Leung Fah opened her eyes. The room was black with darkness.

"Shortly before the dawn," Sahm Seuh said, "there will be the roar of many motors in the sky. Each of you will be given a red flare and matches. To each of you will be whispered the name of the place where the red flare is to be placed. When you hear the roar of motors you will crouch over the flare, as though huddling to the ground in terror. When the motors reach the eastern end of the city you will hold a match in your fingers. There will be none to watch, because people will be intent upon their own safety. When the planes are overhead, you will set fire to the red flares, and then you will run very rapidly. You will return most quickly to this place; you will receive plenty gold.

"It is, however, imperative that you come to this place quickly. The bombing will last until just before daylight. You must be here before the bombing is finished. You will receive your gold. In the confusion you will flee to the river. A boat will be waiting. It will be necessary that you hide for some time, because an investigation will be made. There are spies who spy upon us, and one cannot explain the possession of gold. You will be hidden until there is more work."

Once more there was a period of silence, broken only by the shuffling of men and of whispered orders. Leung Fah felt a round, wooden object thrust into her hands. A moment later a box of matches was pushed into her fingers. A man bent over her, so close that his voice breathed a thought directly into her ears, almost without the aid of sound.

"The house of the commissioner of public safety," he said.

The shuffling ceased. The voice of Sahm Seuh said, "That is all. Go, and wait at the appointed places. Hurry back and there will be much gold. In order to avoid suspicion you will leave here one at a time, at intervals of five minutes. A man at the door will control your passing. There will be no lights—no conversation."

Leung Fah stood in the darkness, packed with people whom she did not know, reeking in the stench of stale perspiration. At intervals she heard a whispered command. After each whisper the door would open and one of the persons in that narrow, crowded staircase would slip from the suffocating atmosphere into the relative coolness of the street.

At length the door was in front of her. Hands pushed against her. The door swung open, and she found herself once more in Sky Horse Alley, shuffling along with demure eyes downcast, and a face which was the face of a sleepwalker.

Leung Fah went only so far as the house where the sacrifices were being offered to the spirit of the departed. The ashes of the sacrificial fire were still smoldering in the narrow street, drifted about by vagrant gusts of wind. Leung Fah knew that in this house there would be mourners; that any who were of the faith and desired to join in sending thought waves to the ancestor in the beyond would be welcome.

She climbed the stairs and heard chanting. Around the table were grouped seven nuns with heads as bald as a sharp razor could make them. At another table flickering peanut oil lamps illuminated a painting of the ancestor who had in turn joined his ancestors. The table was loaded with sacrifices. There were some twenty people in the room, who, from time to time, joined in chanting prayers.

Leung Fah unostentatiously joined this group. Shortly thereafter she moved quietly to the stairs which gave to the roof, and within thirty minutes had worked her way back to the roof of the house of the three candles. She sought a deep shadow, merged herself within it, and became motionless.

Shortly after midnight a tropical rain came up without warning. It beat down in a deluge, from which there was no escape.

Leung Fah bent over, shielding the precious red fire and the box of matches from the downpour with her body, as a month ago she had tried in vain to shield the body of her baby from the rain of Japanese bombs.

After the rain it was cold; but Leung Fah remained hunched in one position, afraid to move lest some watchers on an adjoining rooftop should see her. Crouched in the shadows, she waited, wet, cold, and cramped.

Slowly the hours of the night wore away. Leung Fah began to listen. Shortly thereafter her ears, strained toward the east, heard a peculiar sound. It was like distant thunder over the mountains, a thunder which rumbles ominously, yet, because of distance, is all but inaudible.

With ominous rapidity the murmur of sound in the east grew into a roar. She could hear the screams of people in the streets below, could hear babies, aroused from their sleep as they were snatched up by frantic parents, crying fretfully.

Still Leung Fah remained motionless. The planes swept by overhead. Here and there in the city bright red flares suddenly blossomed into blood-red pools of crimson. And wherever there was a flare, a Japanese plane swooped down, and a moment later a mushroom of flame rose up against the night sky, followed by a reverberating report which shook the very foundations of the city.

No light bombs were these which were released on the flares, but aerial torpedoes that blasted to the very roots of the earth.

Leung Fah waited.

The planes circled and dipped overhead. Bombs screeched downward. The city shook on its foundations.

Leung Fah crept to the edge of the roof where she might peer over and watch Sky Horse Alley. She saw surreptitious figures darting from shadow to shadow, slipping through the portals of the house of three candles. Still Leung Fah waited.

At length a shadow, more bulky than the rest, the shadow of a fat man running on noiseless feet, crossed the street, and was swallowed up within the entrance of the house of three candles. The Japanese planes roared overhead.

Leung Fah placed her box of red fire on the roof and tore off the paper. With calm, untrembling hand she struck a match to flame, the flame to the flare.

In the crimson pool of light which illuminated all of the housetops Leung Fah fled from one rooftop to another. And yet it seemed she had only been running a few seconds when a giant plane materialized overhead and came roaring down out of the sky. She heard the scream of a torpedo. The entire street rocked under the impact of the terrific explosion. Glass windows tinkled into fragments. Houses became as cardboard.

Leung Fah was flung to her knees. Her eardrums seemed shattered, her eyes about to burst from their sockets under the terrific rush of pressure which swept along with the blast of the explosion.

Day was dawning when she recovered enough to limp down to Sky Horse Alley. The roar of the Japanese planes was receding into the distance, leaving the crippled city to silence and its wounds.

Leung Fah hobbled slowly and painfully to the place where had been the house of the three candles. There was now a deep hole in the Sky Horse Alley, a hole surrounded by bits of wreckage and torn bodies.

A blackened torso lay almost at her feet. She examined it intently. It was all that was left of Sahm Seuh.

She turned and limped back up Sky Horse Alley, her eyes downcast and expressionless, her face as though it had been carved of wood. Calmly she traced her painful way through the wreckage left by the air bombs.

The sun rose in the east, and the inhabitants of Canton, long since accustomed to having the grim presence of death at their side, prepared to clear away the bodies and debris, resume once more their daily course of ceaseless activity.

Leung Fah lifted the bamboo yoke to her sore shoulders. *Aiiii ah-h-h*, it was painful, but one must work if one would eat.

JAMES NORMAN HALL
Fame for Mr. Beatty

WILLIAM C. DOW AND COMPANY, wholesale dry-goods merchants, occupied a fourteen-story building covering half the block between Commercial and East River streets. The business offices of the firm were on the fourth floor. Here were to be found the sales manager with his staff, the manager of imports with his, the advertising manager with his. The remainder of the fourth floor, considerably more than half of it, was taken up by the accounting department, a miniature city laid out in orderly, rectangular fashion, with narrow passageways for streets and wire cages for houses, each of them six feet by six, each of them with its occupant. In one of the cages farthest from the main corridor was a man who had been in the employ of the Dow Company for more than twenty years. His name was Herbert Beatty.

It would be difficult to describe Mr. Beatty in any vivid manner. To say that he was quietly dressed, that his linen was immaculate and his boots carefully polished, is not to distinguish him from thousands of other self-respecting bookkeepers. Observing him in a crowd—but this is unthinkable: the most curious observer of human nature, touching elbows with him in a crowd, would not have noticed him, unless—which is equally unthinkable—Mr. Beatty had been guilty of some act of gross and unusual conduct, and even then the eccentricity would have been remembered rather than the man himself.

He was a lonely man, without close friends or any living relatives, so far as he knew, and his life flowed on from year to year in unbroken monotony. Although he spent forty-five hours weekly in his little wire enclosure, he neither spoke nor thought of it as a cage. He entered it, six mornings out of seven, as willingly as a bee enters its hive, and much more punctually. Having dusted off his boots with a flannel cloth which he kept in a drawer, he slipped into his black alpaca office coat. Then he marked out with a neat cross, in red ink, the date of the previous day on the calendar—two crosses on a Monday. Then he opened the ledgers in which he took such pride, and was immediately engrossed in his work. This was purely of a routine nature, as familiar to him as breathing, quite as necessary, and almost as instinctively performed. He was rarely disturbed, had no decisions to make, and was never asked for his opinion about anything.

At twelve-thirty he went out to lunch. He patronized always the same white-tiled restaurant on East River Street, a large, clean, impersonal sort of place catering to the employees of the wholesale houses in the vicinity. An immense sign on the wall of this restaurant read: "We serve more than three thousand lunches daily, between the hours of twelve and two." During the past ten years Mr. Beatty himself had alone been served with that number of lunches: three thousand lettuce sandwiches, three thousand pieces of custard pie, three thousand glasses of milk. But although his order was the same, summer and winter, none of the waitresses ever remembered what it was or appeared to recognize him as an old patron.

In winter he spent the whole of his luncheon hour in this place reading the *Morning Post*. On fine days in summer he would go, after his meal, to a small park near the City Hall, two blocks distant. There he would buy a bag of salted peanuts, and after eating a few of them would give the rest to the pigeons that frequented the square. They would eat out of his hand, perch on his outstretched arm, even on his head. He liked to think that they were his pigeons, and he enjoyed the moment of attention they brought him from other midday loungers in the park. When he had doled out the last of the peanuts he dusted the salt from his fingers and sat down to enjoy his newspaper.

Mr. Beatty was one of the numberless army of men and women who have made possible the success of the modern American newspaper, whose reading is confined almost entirely to its columns. It amused him, instructed him, thought for him. He found there satisfaction for all his modest needs, spiritual and cultural. He turned first to the comic section, smiling over the adventures of Mutt and Jeff and the vicissitudes of the Gump family. These people were real to him, and he followed their fortunes closely from day to day. Next he read the editorial of Dr. Francis Crake, whom he admired and respected as a philosopher of genius. Another feature of the *Morning Post* was the Enquirer's column. The Enquirer sauntered daily through the streets, asking of four people, chosen more or less at random, some question of current interest. Their replies, together with a small photograph of each individual, were then printed in the column. Mr. Beatty's interest never waned in this feature of his favorite newspaper. Indeed, there was so much on every page to engage his attention that his luncheon hour passed in a flash of time. At twenty minutes past one he would leave the park, and before the half hour struck was again at his desk and at work.

One sultry midsummer day, while he was enjoying his usual noontime recreation in the park, a young man wearing horn-rimmed spectacles and with a camera slung over his shoulder sat down on the bench beside him. Mr. Beatty was not aware of this at the moment, for he was in the midst of Dr. Crake's editorial for the day: "Clothes As an Index of Personality." In three short paragraphs Dr. Crake had evolved his philosophy on this subject. "Show me a man who is slovenly in his dress and I will show you one that is slovenly in his morals. A clean collar is the index of a clean mind. It matters not how modest your income or how humble your station in life, you cannot afford to be indifferent to the appearance you present to your fellow men. Neatness pays. It is investment at compound interest in the Bank of Success, and it will bring in dividends when you least expect them." So Dr. Crake in his first paragraph. Mr. Beatty heartily approved of these opinions and he thought, not without a touch of pride, that Dr. Crake would have approved of him.

Upon turning the page of his paper he noticed his companion on the bench. The young man nodded cordially.

"A scorcher, isn't it?" he said.

Mr. Beatty was slightly startled. It was not often that a stranger spoke to him.

"Yes, it *is* warm," he replied, a little apologetically, as though he were somehow to blame for the heat.

"Hottest day this summer," said the young man. "What do you suppose the thermometer at the *Morning. Post* building registered at noon?"

"Oh, I couldn't say. I fancy it was pretty high?"

"One hundred and two in the shade; and it's hotter than that inside. Pressroom like a furnace, city room worse. Glad I didn't have to stay there."

"Are you—do you mean that you are employed on the *Morning Post?*"

"Yes. I run what we call the Enquirer's column. You may have read it sometimes?"

"Oh yes! Well! Isn't that remarkable! Why, I always——"

"Well, that's my job on the *Post,* or one of them. I'm supposed to be working at it now. You know, that is really why I sat down on this bench. The question for tomorrow is, 'Do You Favor Restricted Immigration?' When I saw you sitting here I thought, There's a man, if I'm not mistaken, who has views on this subject. Would you mind letting me have them, Mr.—— But you haven't told me your name, I think."

"Beatty. Herbert Beatty."

"Are you in business in the city?"

"Yes. I'm a bookkeeper with William C. Dow and Company."

"That's fine! We'll be glad to have a man of your profession represented in the Enquirer's column. You don't object, do you, Mr. Beatty? You know, you can tell me precisely what you think our immigration policy should be. The *Post* wishes to offer its readers the opinions of intelligent men on both sides of the question."

Never, not even in his most sanguine moments, had it occurred to Mr. Beatty that he might one day be called upon to express, publicly, his opinion of any question. Now that the opportunity had come, he was dazed, stupefied. The sound of the young man's voice came to him with a strange, far-off effect. He understood in a dreamlike way that this reporter was preparing to direct the attention of a city of two million inhabitants to his, Herbert Beatty's, views upon a matter of great public concern. He watched, fascinated, while the young man drew a notebook from his pocket, slipped off the rubber band, opened it on his knee. What could he say? What *were* his views? Dr. Crake had dealt with this subject in one of his editorials only a few weeks before. If only he could remember what he had said, perhaps it would help him to——

Of a sudden he was conscious that the young man was speaking.

"I suppose you think there is something to be said on both sides, Mr. Beatty?"

"Oh yes! I—you see—you have taken me a little by surprise. One doesn't like to be too sure—I hardly know—perhaps——"

"But wouldn't it, in your opinion, be a good thing if the Government were to adopt a fairly cautious restriction policy, say for the next twenty-five years?"

"Well, yes, I believe it would."

"We would know by that time where we stand, don't you think, with respect to the great foreign-born population already in America? With this information to guide us, we could then decide what our future policy should be."

Mr. Beatty heartily agreed with this. It seemed to him a sound way of looking at the matter. The reporter made some rapid entries in his note-book, snapped on the rubber band, and clipped his pencil to his waistcoat pocket.

"Thanks very much, Mr. Beatty. You're the fourth man I've interviewed today. The views of the other three were rather extreme, both for and against restricted immigration. I'm glad to have found one man who favors moderation—a wise middle course. Now, then, you'll let me take your photograph? We like to print these with the replies in the column. I'll not be ten seconds. If you'll stand there—a little more this way—— Good! That will do. Snap! That's done it! Thanks once more, Mr. Beatty. To-morrow the whole city will know your views on the immigration problems, and I'll venture to say that nine out of ten men will agree with them. Well, good-by, I must be getting along."

Mr. Beatty was conscious of a feeling of profound relief as he entered his enclosure at the bookkeeping department. He rearranged the articles on his desk, flicked an imaginary fleck of dust from his adding machine, and resharpened a pencil whose point had been a little blunted with use during the morning. So great was the virtue in these familiar practices, and so strong the habit of a lifetime, that he was then able to resume his work with a certain measure of calm.

But his pleasantly disquieting thoughts returned at five o'clock. They seemed to be awaiting him in the street below, and occupied his mind to the exclusion of everything else. He entered the stream of homeward-bound pedestrian traffic, letting it carry him where it would, and presently found himself in front of the *Morning Post* building. One of the plate-glass windows bore an inscription in gold lettering: "The *Morning Post*. Your Paper—Everybody's Paper. Guaranteed Circulation Over 450,000." He gazed at this for some time as he thought over the events of the day. He could recall vividly the appearance of the young reporter and the kind of notebook he had used—opening at the end, with wide spaces between the ruled lines—and the round blue pencil with the nickel pocket clip. But he could not remember at all clearly the details of the interview. How long had it lasted? Five minutes? Ten minutes? Probably not more than five. The reporter had worked rapidly. . . . He had seemed pleased with his replies. . . . But just what was it he had said? . . . A circulation of four hundred and fifty thousand! And likely twice that many people actually read the *Post*.

After his customary solitary supper Mr. Beatty went to a moving-picture theater for the seven o'clock show. He returned to his lodgings at nine and went to bed. The following morning he awoke at a quarter to five, an hour before his usual time. It was impossible to sleep again, so he shaved, dressed, and went downstairs. The sky was cloudless; it would be another sweltering day. A horse-drawn milk wagon was just then making its rounds; otherwise the street was deserted.

The stationery shop where he usually bought his morning paper was not yet opened. He went on to another several blocks distant, but that, too, was closed. The papers had already been delivered there; they were lying on the doorstep, loosely wrapped in a brown paper cover. Mr. Beatty looked up and down the street; there was no one in view. Quickly opening his penknife, he cut the cord of the parcel and drew forth a copy of the *Post*. Then he discovered that he had only a penny, a quarter, and a half dollar in his pocket, and the price of the *Post* was three cents. He left the quarter on top of the parcel and hurried back to his lodgings, where Mrs. Halleck, his landlady, was standing in the entryway.

"Good morning, Mr. Beatty! Well! You *are* an early bird this morning! Wherever have you been at this time of day? My! Ain't this heat awful? I don't know what's goin' to happen if we don't have some rain soon to cool things off. You got the morning paper already?"

He murmured a hasty reply, went up to his room on the third floor, and shut and locked the door. Then he opened his paper at the editorial page.

ENQUIRER'S COLUMN

Question for the day: "Do You Favor Restricted Immigration?" Herbert Beatty, bookkeeper, with William C. Dow & Company, 400 Commercial Street.

"One hesitates in pronouncing an opinion upon a question of such far-reaching importance, but it would seem advisable that we should now adopt a cautious, well-balanced policy of restriction until such time as we shall have been able to assimilate the immense, foreign-born population already on our shores. Twenty-five years hence we shall have gathered sufficient data with regard to our immigration policy to enable us to decide with some measure of confidence what our future policy should be."

Mr. Beatty's photograph gazing at him from the page and the print of his own name looked so strange that he could hardly believe them his. He read the interview again, and a third and a fourth time. He had not been able to recall, before, just how he had worded his reply; he had been a little confused, of course, at the moment of the interview, and surprised at the suddenness of the question put to him by the reporter. What a faculty that young man had shown for getting immediately at the gist of his thoughts! That was a reporter's business, to be sure, but this one must be a particularly gifted interviewer. His own interview had been given the place of honor at the top of the column. He now turned to the views of the others:

Morris Goldberg, haberdasher, 783 Fourth Avenue.

"I don't think we've got room for any more foreigners in the United States. We ought to put the lid on tight, now. Business has been poor since the war, and there's too much competition already."

H. Dwight Crabtree, pastor, the Division Street Baptist Church.

"I often think of America as a great melting pot where all the various splendid elements which go to make up our Democracy are being fused, and the composite type, American, made perfect in the sight of the Father of us all. No, let us not forbid them, these brothers of ours from over the seas. Let us rather say: 'Welcome, ye poor and oppressed! We have room for you and more than room! Bask here in God's sunlight! Enjoy our opportunities! Partake of our fellowship! And may you bequeath to your children a rich heritage of health and love and beauty in this glorious land, America!' "

John J. Canning, architect, 45 First National Bank Building.

"This question would have been timely fifty years ago. My answer then would have been: 'I favor exclusion, not restriction.' That is my answer today."

Over his breakfast at the dairy lunchroom at the corner, Mr. Beatty again read the interviews, gaining the conviction, as he compared them, that his was by far the most sensible of the four. It was pleasant to think of the thousands of men who would that day read his opinions, learn of his name—college professors, lawyers, doctors, government officials, perhaps Dr. Crake himself. He remembered now that Dr. Crake, too, had counseled moderation in dealing with the question of restricted immigration. He would be pleased to see his views upheld in the Enquirer's column. He could fancy him saying, "Now *there's* a man that knows what he is talking about."

The walk to the office on this memorable August morning was like a dream to him. Every newsboy at every corner seemed particularly anxious to sell him papers, and every passer-by seemed to look at him with interest, with respect. He fancied several times that he had been recognized. He was almost afraid to enter the Dow building, and gave a sigh of relief when he was safe within his enclosure at the end of the corridor. He found it difficult to keep his mind on his work. The roar of traffic from the street was like a universal voice of acclaim loud with his name, Beatty—so loud, in fact, that he did not at first hear the voice of a small boy standing at the little window in front of his desk.

"Mr. Beatty! Mr. Dow wants to see you, Mr. Beatty."

He looked up quickly.

"Who did you say?"

"Mr. William Dow wants to see you. He says you are to come up at once if you are not too busy."

Arriving at the fourth floor, the boy who had escorted him pointed to a glazed door at the end of a passageway.

"Mr. Dow is in there," he said, and left him.

Mr. Beatty hesitated for a moment, then timidly approached the door and knocked, very gently. Receiving no reply, he knocked again, a trifle more firmly.

"Come in!"

Mr. Dow was busy with his morning correspondence. He finished the dictation of a letter before looking up.

"Good morning," he said. "Yes?"

"I beg your pardon, sir. I was told that you wished to see me."

"Oh yes. Are you Mr. Beatty? I've just been reading your little interview in the *Post*. It was yours, I believe?"

"Yes sir. That is——"

"I rather liked your reply to that question, Mr. Beatty. I merely wanted to tell you this. But just what do you mean by 'a cautious, well-balanced policy of restriction'? How would you put it into effect, supposing you had the power?"

"Oh, I should hardly like to say, sir. I haven't thought so very much—perhaps——"

"How would you begin? What nationalities do you think should first be restricted? Poles? Italians? Russian Jews?"

"Well, yes, perhaps the Russians—but I can't say that I am quite sure——"

Mr. Dow gave him a thoughtful, appraising glance.

"How long have you been with us, Mr. Beatty?"

"Twenty years, sir, the fourteenth of last April."

His employer pursed his lips in a soundless whistle.

"Have you! As long as that? What do you think of our accounting department? Is it efficiently managed?"

"Why, yes, I believe so, sir. At least—that is, I am sure that you know much better than I do."

"Have you any suggestions to make as to how it might be bettered?"

"Oh no, sir!"

Mr. Dow gazed silently out of the window for a moment.

"Well, I'm glad to have had this opportunity for a little chat with you, Mr. Beatty. That's all for the present. Thanks for coming up."

On a November afternoon several years later Mr. Beatty, having fed his pigeons in City Hall Park, dusted the salt from his fingers with his handkerchief and sat down to his customary after-luncheon perusal of the *Morning Post*. It was a raw, blustery day, too chilly for comfort out-of-doors. He decided that hereafter he would spend his luncheon hour at the restaurant. But this was not to be. The following day he came down with an attack of bronchial pneumonia. Within a week he was dead.

Mrs. Halleck, his landlady, was genuinely sorry to lose so old and dependable a lodger, but she could not afford to let sentimental regrets interfere with reletting at once her third-floor front, one of the best rooms in the house. Her new lodger, a law-school student, moved in immediately. She had the room all ready for him but had forgotten to remove from the wall a bit of cardboard which hung by a string by the side of the bed. A newspaper clipping, yellow with age, was pasted on it. The young man glanced idly at it as he took it down. "One hesitates," he read, "in pronouncing an opinion upon a question of such far-reaching importance, but it would seem advisable that we should now adopt——"

Whistling softly to himself, the new lodger arranged his belongings. He crumpled the piece of cardboard and threw it in the wastepaper basket. He hung a Maxfield Parrish picture in its place. The light was just right for it there.

DASHIELL HAMMETT

Nightshade

A SEDAN with no lights burning was standing beside the road just above Piney Falls bridge and as I drove past it a girl put her head out and said, "Please." Her voice was urgent but there was not enough excitement in it to make it either harsh or shrill.

I put on my brakes, then backed up. By that time a man had got out of the sedan. There was enough light to let me see he was young and fairly big. He moved a hand in the direction I had been going and said, "On your way, buddy."

The girl said again, "Will you drive me into town, please?" She seemed to be trying to open the sedan door. Her hat had been pushed forward over one eye.

I said, "Sure."

The man in the road took a step toward me, moved his hand as before, and growled, "Scram, you."

I got out of my car. The man in the road had started toward me when another man's voice came from the sedan, a harsh warning voice. "Go easy, Tony. It's Jack Bye." The sedan door swung open and the girl jumped out.

Tony said, "Oh!" and his feet shuffled uncertainly on the road; but when he saw the girl making for my car he cried indignantly at her, "Listen, you can't ride to town with——"

She was in my roadster by then. "Good night," she said.

He faced me, shook his head stubbornly, began, "I'll be damned if I'll let——"

I hit him. The knockdown was fair enough, because I hit him hard, but I think he could have got up again if he had wanted to. I gave him a little time, then asked the fellow in the sedan, "All right with you?" I still could not see him.

"He'll be all right," he replied quickly. "I'll take care of him all right."

"Thanks." I climbed into my car beside the girl. The rain I had been trying to get to town ahead of was beginning to fall. A coupé with a man and a woman in it passed us going toward town. We followed the coupé across the bridge.

The girl said, "This is awfully kind of you. I wasn't in any danger back there, but it was—nasty."

"They wouldn't be dangerous," I said, "but they would be—nasty."

"You know them?"

"No."

"But they knew you. Tony Forrest and Fred Barnes." When I did not say anything she added, "They were afraid of you."

"I'm a desperate character."

She laughed. "And pretty nice of you, too, tonight. I wouldn't've gone with either of them alone, but I thought with two of them . . ." She turned up the collar of her coat. "It's raining in on me."

I stopped the roadster again and hunted for the curtain that belonged on her side of the car. "So your name's Jack Bye," she said while I was snapping it on.

"And yours is Helen Warner."

"How'd you know?" She had straightened her hat.

"I've seen you around." I finished attaching the curtain and got back in.

"Did you know who I was when I called to you?" she asked when we were moving again.

"Yes."

"It was silly of me to go out with them like that."

"You're shivering."

"It's chilly."

I said I was sorry my flask was empty.

We had turned into the western end of Hellman Avenue. It was four minutes past ten by the clock in front of the jewelry store on the corner of Laurel Street. A policeman in a black rubber coat was leaning against the clock. I did not know enough about perfumes to know the name of hers.

She said, "I'm chilly. Can't we stop somewhere and get a drink?"

"Do you really want to?" My voice must have puzzled her; she turned her head quickly to peer at me in the dim light.

"I'd like to," she said, "unless you're in a hurry."

"No. We could go to Mack's. It's only three or four blocks from here, but —it's a nigger joint."

She laughed. "All I ask is that I don't get poisoned."

"You won't, but you're sure you want to go?"

"Certainly." She exaggerated her shivering. "I'm cold. It's early."

Toots Mack opened his door for us. I could tell by the politeness with which he bowed his round bald black head and said, "Good evening, sir; good evening, madam," that he wished we had gone someplace else, but I was not especially interested in how he felt about it. I said, "Hello, Toots; how are you this evening?" too cheerfully.

There were only a few customers in the place. We went to the table in the corner farthest from the piano. Suddenly she was staring at me, her eyes, already very blue, becoming very round.

"I thought you could see in the car," I began.

"How'd you get that scar?" she asked, interrupting me. She sat down.

"That." I put a hand to my cheek. "Fight—couple of years ago. You ought to see the one on my chest."

"We'll have to go swimming sometime," she said gaily. "Please sit down and don't keep me waiting for my drink."

"Are you sure you——"

She began to chant, keeping time with her fingers on the table, "I want a drink, I want a drink, I want a drink." Her mouth was small with full lips and it curved up without growing wider when she smiled.

We ordered drinks. We talked too fast. We made jokes and laughed too readily at them. We asked questions—about the name of the perfume she used was one—and paid too much or no attention to the answers. And Toots looked glumly at us from behind the bar when he thought we were not looking at him. It was all pretty bad.

We had another drink and I said, "Well, let's slide along."

She was nice about seeming neither too anxious to go nor to stay. The ends of her pale blond hair curled up over the edge of her hat in back.

At the door I said, "Listen, there's a taxi stand around the corner. You won't mind if I don't take you home?"

She put a hand on my arm. "I do mind. Please——" The street was badly lighted. Her face was like a child's. She took her hand off my arm. "But if you'd rather . . ."

"I think I'd rather."

She said slowly, "I like you, Jack Bye, and I'm awfully grateful for——"

I said, "Aw, that's all right," and we shook hands and I went back into the speakeasy.

Toots was still behind the bar. He came up to where I stood. "You oughtn't to do that to me," he said, shaking his head mournfully.

"I know. I'm sorry."

"You oughtn't to do it to yourself," he went on just as sadly. "This ain't Harlem, boy, and if old Judge Warner finds out his daughter's running around with you and coming in here he can make it plenty tough for both of us. I like you, boy, but you got to remember it don't make no difference how light your skin is or how many colleges you went to, you're still nigger."

I said, "Well, what do you suppose I want to be? A Chinaman?"

ERNEST HAYCOX
Weight of Command

DAYLIGHT was a violet pulse in the low east when the trumpets blew boots and saddles; and now the cavalry regiment moved in a sluggish serpentine line along the left bank of Lost Warrior Creek. Men rode stiff in the saddles, sulky and slow-witted from sleep; they rode in dismal silence. The white tops of the supply wagons emitted a vague glow; bare buttes and ridges slowly lifted from the night, from the desert's black sweep.

Cheadrick—Colonel William Starr Cheadrick—tarried briefly behind to have a last word with General Gibson, who commanded this expedition. For as the cavalry regiment moved out along Lost Warrior Creek three regiments of infantry were at the same time disappearing over a low ridge to the right, the two arms of the service embarking upon a nutcracker movement intended to close the hostile Sioux within its jaws.

Gibson was a dark and acrid little man, a sardonic beau sabreur on whose shoulders the single brigadier's star showed the tarnish of hard service. "You are," he said, "to continue up Lost Warrior Creek to its major fork and swing left, to cut the Sioux trail and make contact. I will be forty miles away from you at the far point of my swing, thereafter closing in. I'll meet you on the third morning. If you come upon Sioux in any considerable strength don't let them get away or we'll have all this dismal business to do over again. If it looks like a fight . . ." and he paused and shrugged his shoulders. "You're too old a campaigner to be given restrictive orders. I leave it to your judgment whether to attack or to wait for me. Good luck."

The two men shook hands. Gibson forded the creek and pursued the infantry with his aide and his orderlies behind him. Cheadrick set his horse into a slow gallop and overtook his command. The smell of extinguished campfires hung to the creek bottom, and all along the cavalry column a fine alkali dust boiled up. Cheadrick was sixty-two years old, better than six feet tall, and rode with his legs full down. He had spent most of his career in the saddle, so that the smell of horses and dust and leather was the principal smell of his life; he was a stringy, severe shape, with raw-boned shoulders and a silver-white goatee and mustache. He wore an old campaign hat with the brim tipped up, and his eyes, always half closed against sun and light, were agate-gray. There was but one definite mark of age on this cavalry commander—the two parallel streaks between chin and throat bottom. This, the skin on the colonel's throat, was loose and grizzled.

He passed the wagon train, viewing the mules for condition. He passed the troops one by one and saw a trooper's saddle blanket to be poorly folded. He checked in at once: "Drop out and refold that blanket. You'll gall your horse before ten o'clock." At the head of the column he pulled to a steady walk beside his civilian guide, Major Conn, and the correspondent from the Chicago paper. And now for Cheadrick the campaign had begun.

At eight o'clock the last bit of moisture had evaporated from the air. Sunlight glared on the monotonous flats of sage. The correspondent from Chicago said: "You know this country, Colonel?"

"Yes," said Cheadrick, "I know it."

He was tallying his regiment as a poker player would consider the laws of chance in a deck of cards. He had five hundred men, half of them good soldiers, half of them recruits from Jefferson Barracks. He had a set of tough noncoms, the backbone of his command. He had some good officers; he had a few who were green; he had some who were the sweepings of the Civil War. He had only one major, this Major Conn who rode heavily and choleric beside him, with a mind blurred by drink. Callahan, his senior captain, was half wild from slowness of promotion and might, in a pinch, throw away fifty men for the sake of making a reputation. Somewhere out in front of him the Sioux moved restlessly back and forth, stirred by their war chiefs and armed with repeating rifles that were better than the carbines of his own command.

This was how Cheadrick weighed his orders, the ability of his regiment, the enemy in front. This was what command meant, this insistent consideration of a hundred changing elements. At sixty-two it was a burden that added fifty pounds to his body and kept him awake at night and formed his mouth into a long, thin line. It was a thing you couldn't tell anybody; it was something only an old man knew, after years of experience.

At ten o'clock the full heat of the sun burned against exposed skin and flashed on metal gear, and dust rolled around them in cloudy billows. The advance guard rode a mile ahead, a line of flankers moved far out to either side of the column, and thus the regiment marched, a complete and self-contained unit on the face of emptiness.

Behind him the column slowly came alive from its morning's taciturnity; men were talking, men were laughing. Down in F troop Jack Studenburg said: "How does a woman get along when a man's away? Now I wonder."

Corporal Kanipe said: "There's other men."

"Now," grumbled Studenburg, "I could cut your heart out for puttin' the thought in my mind." He looked at Kistmiller in the file closers. "How you bettin' on that baby, Sarge?"

"A boy," answered Kistmiller, and said no more.

The column began to sing, and Cheadrick, listening to it, felt pleased.

He liked his men to sweat and eat dust and grow lank-muscled and quarrelsome, because that meant they had the vital salt of soldiering in them. He liked them to sing, for in singing he felt them pull together, he caught the unity and the single will of the command.

Cheadrick sent his scout detail into the southeast and listened to their reports on returning. At noon the command halted beside Lost Warrior Creek on the treeless plain, and was in motion again by one; fifty minutes of march and ten for rest, on through the piled-up haze, through a thin air and a furnace-blast heat, through a dust that collected on eyebrows in white drifts and stung the nostrils and settled as grit between shirt collar and flesh. Cheadrick sent the details out, one by one; they curled into the southeast and came back with their little sums of information, and at seven o'clock the regiment reached the major fork of Lost Warrior Creek and camped with the shadow of low hills fifteen miles ahead.

Cook fires burned pure yellow triangles into the enveloping dusk. The wagon train etched a broken line against the horizon, and men, bone-tired, murmured and lay still. The crunch of feeding horses, the tramp of the sentries, the shine of lanterns—all these details came to Cheadrick as he sat before his tent and debated with the civilian guide.

"They're coming out of the north and east," he said, "and meeting somewhere in the southeast."

The civilian guide said: "Beyond the second bunch of hills. There's a couple of high ridges, with a valley and Ash Creek flowin' between. It's been a meetin' spot of the Sioux for as long as I can remember."

"In considerable numbers. They've got their women along."

"They'll fight if you surprise 'em—because they got their women."

"How many would you guess?"

"Big party. Maybe a thousand—maybe two."

Coolness stirred on the desert. Cheadrick went into the tent and sat before the camp table, writing a letter to his wife. It was his lifelong habit to write something each evening when on campaign so that when his wife got the letters, back at Fort Lincoln, she would have the daily story. He wrote in a heavy, flowing hand and folded the letter and returned to the camp chair under the fly to catch some of the evening's coolness. Silence came to the camp, and five hundred men were sleeping, or lying awake with their memories and their dreams—and all these men's lives rested on a single command or one forward motion of his arm.

The ten o'clock call ran the sentry line and the last lights began to wink out, and sage and dust smell rolled steadily through camp, and coyotes were lifting their half howl and half yip along the desert, and mystery swept in from the dark horizons—the mystery of space and wildness. Cheadrick pulled off his pants and rolled into his blankets and lay awake. He remembered that Sergeant Kistmiller had a wife in Fort Lincoln expecting a baby. He remembered the trumpeter of L troop whose mother wanted his release. He thought about the company clerk of D, a man of education hiding his past in a uniform. Of this material was his regiment made. Each man had a life, but all those lives were at his disposal. This was the meaning, the stark responsibility of command.

In his tent Major Conn took a drink and rolled into bed with a grunt of fatigue and thought vaguely of the past and still more vaguely of the future. In the tent at the head of M troop, Captain Lewis Callahan said to Captain Van Horn: "This regiment could lick all the Indians on the plains. One charge would end this Sioux problem forever. All I want is just one chance at independent action. I'll take my troop through."

By the sallow glow of his candle the Chicago newspaper correspondent was writing:

"Five hundred men fall asleep tonight with the assurance they are one day nearer a meeting with the Sioux. That is a certainty rising from the caliber of the man in command of this regiment, Colonel William Starr Cheadrick. No man better knows Indians, no man is better equipped to find them and defeat them.

"Colonel Cheadrick is a six-foot, rawboned, ageless cavalryman, weaned on gunpowder and dust and toughened by violent action. He is cold, autocratic. He wastes no words and seemingly lacks the grace of human compassion. The troopers call him Vinegar Bill, sotto voce, and they fear his eye and grumble at his discipline. Yet fear him as they will, they sleep the sounder for knowing he is in command; for they know that, although he might lead them straight to perdition if he thought it in line of duty, he would never make a charge out of folly or pride. He is like nothing so much in the world as an old, tough hickory cask impregnated with the salts and bitter flavors of a thousand cargoes safely held."

By three o'clock the following day the regiment moved around the base of the low hill and faced three on-running ridges, roughly parallel; beyond them a smoky haze covered everything. All scouting parties had brought back one uniform story. Every sign indicated a concentration of bands somewhere in the southeast. Pony tracks showed everywhere through those hills; the main column itself had been crossing these tracks since noon. The civilian guide said: "We're gettin' warm."

Major Conn rode beside Cheadrick, the vein-netted surface of his face irritable for want of a drink. This, thought Cheadrick, was his second in command, an officer whose mind was filled with alcoholic vapors—inefficient and undependable. He called up Captain Callahan from the column and observed the rash gleam in Callahan's eyes; there was no caution in the man. Cheadrick said:

"I'm going down that central valley between the two ridges. Conn, you take two companies and swing into the ravine on the right of me. You will also take two companies, Callahan, and bear to the left. You will both be marching parallel to the main command. Watch sharp. Throw out advance parties. At seven o'clock cross over and join me. Do you understand?"

Cheadrick let the silence ride on, reviewing his orders to see that they were clear. Then he added: "If you meet Sioux and are offered a fight—refuse it. Come back at once."

Riding forward, Cheadrick watched Conn and Callahan take out their respective details to right and left. In a little while the high jaws of the narrow valley received the main column and Conn and Callahan disappeared.

The right ridge threw long shadows into the narrow valley; along the slope of both ridges were mounds of shale and rock and fine coverts of sage and juniper. Cheadrick's advance guard was too far ahead; he sent the trumpeter forward to pull it back. On right and left ridge the flankers were having trouble with the stiff grade. He beckoned up an orderly. "Tell them to climb to the backbone of those ridges." Heat lay solidly between the walls of this rock-sided valley; it was a kind of tissue through which Cheadrick pushed himself and his horse.

The correspondent from the Chicago paper lagged slightly behind to observe Cheadrick's face, for the correspondent fancied himself a keen judge of character. The regiment, he realized, was nearing decisive action. Behind him troopers sat upright on their saddles, and their faces veered from one ridge top to another, carefully searching. But Cheadrick rode flinty and serene, with his lids brought almost together and his head motionless. The correspondent tried to build up proper descriptive phrases:

"He feels nothing, fears nothing, cares for nothing except his job. He has looked at death and duty for so long that the minor sensibilities, like love or compassion, or the capacity for excitement, have been utterly destroyed. An ageless, tireless mechanism of bone and impervious hide and granite resolution." The correspondent thought it an excellent description that would look well in print.

The colonel, at this moment, was thinking of his long-past boyhood in Vermont—the smell of cut hay and the steady swing of his father's scythe, and the cook jug of sugar water in the shade of the rock fence. He was thinking of evening in the farmhouse when, with day's work done, he had sprawled on his belly and listened to his people talking—and he remembered how free and secure he had been, without care. That remembrance of golden irresponsibility was very strong.

At five the command halted for ten minutes. At six it turned a bend of the valley and faced a closure of the ridges and a low pass. Beyond the pass was a flare of sulphurous sunlight and thick heat smoke and the outline of other distant ridges. By seven they had crossed the pass and found a minor creek. Ahead of them was another sagebrush flat; across that flat, twelve miles distant, a low, short ridge—more like a butte—made a parapet against the horizon. Cheadrick said to the adjutant, "We camp here," and dismounted. An orderly took his horse away. Cheadrick sat on the ground, his back to a high boulder. He pulled his hat over his eyes, but he watched the country behind him with heavy attention, and part of the strain of this long day dropped from his shoulders when he saw Conn come down the rocky draws.

Callahan didn't appear for another hour. When he reported in, Cheadrick's voice struck him like an ax: "Hereafter, remember your orders or I'll relieve you of your command." There was no other way to grind the sense of exact duty into the soul of a careless officer.

Tents went up in regular pattern along the sagebrush, and the cook fires were burning livid holes through the blue swirl of dusk. A guard detail tramped by, and watering details went to the creek and returned, and the troops' horses stood picketed on each troop street. The civilian guide came back from his own private survey.

"They'll be yonder, Colonel," he said. "Beyond that ridge. It's the old meetin' ground. You got twelve, fourteen miles to go."

Cheadrick stripped to his undershirt and went to the creek to wash, and ate the hardtack and salt bacon and coffee brought by his orderly. He asked for a can of hot water and shaved by the pale spire of his tent candle, the sound of the razor like sandpaper against sandpaper. He wrote his nightly letter to his wife and returned to the front of the tent and sat in his camp chair, his long legs crossed and a stogie upward tilted between his teeth.

Lights went out one by one in the tents around him. Stillness swept off the ancient earth, and at last these five hundred men slept, each with his ambitions and his dreams and his sorrows; and all these men, with full freight of their lives, would move into the slash of gunfire at the sweep of his hand. Their lives were at his disposition, to be expended or saved as he saw fit. All that he had learned in the long years of his trade, all his watching and thinking, his self-denial of pride, would be squeezed into one single decision when morning broke.

He went into his tent and took off his boots and pulled a blanket over him. He put his watch beside him and said aloud, "Midnight," and pinched out the candlelight; and he lay there, listening to the camp settle, listening to the minor suspirations of the earth about him. His legs were hard with weariness, and the weight of the day was still on his chest; at last he slept.

At midnight he was awake, summoned by the mental alarm he had set; and he drew on his boots and stepped to the tent door and dispatched the guard for the adjutant. The adjutant came up in his undershirt, still half asleep. Cheadrick said: "We break camp at once."

At one the column moved forward without breakfast, and men rode lumped and taciturn in their saddles, and the white tops of the supply train glowed in the ink-stained shadows, and dust rose again. At two the column halted briefly and went on. At three the forward ridge began to grow and lift out of the plain. Eastward a long streak indicated soon-coming day. Cheadrick said to the adjutant: "Curtis' troop and McPherson's troop will guard the supply train. We will go ahead. Tell them to keep coming." The column stepped out at a longer pace; the ground began to lift and break into the first slopes of the ridge. Cheadrick said: "I remember this hill. There's an easy climb close by."

Cheadrick cantered forward with the civilian guide until the stiffer incline of the ridge brought him to a walk. They quartered the ridge, climbing to a crest littered by broken rock. The summit was nothing more than a thin wedge, and from this vantage point he saw the pale glitter of a creek in the valley below and a long row of conical shadows. This was a half mile onward, westward. Out of the valley's stillness came the irritable barking of an Indian dog.

The guide said: "There's your Sioux."

The head of the column came laboriously up the slope. Cheadrick spoke to the adjutant: "We occupy this position. Extend the line to the left. Send back a courier to the supply train. They will come up as far as the first bench. McPherson and Curtis will take up a position at the wagons."

One sudden ragged wedge of light broke through the eastern rim and widened. Cheadrick buttoned his blouse against the thin chill of the morning and watched the ten troops file along the brow of the hill. They were dismounting; horse holders moved back from the parapet. A raw voice said: "Better eat yere hardtack now, Johnny. We'll be swarmin' into that valley in a half hour." Cheadrick watched the supply train buckle and twist its way up the incline toward the first bench. Troopers attached tow-ropes to the wagons for the extra pull. Light shot across the sky suddenly. Turning around, Cheadrick watched day drop into the Indian village. Tepees lay in round-arranged units all along the creek, and smoke spiraled from the village, and women moved toward the creek. He had made his contact.

Conn and Callahan came up. The civilian guide said in a conversational voice: "They see us."

A woman ran back from the creek, and then all the women were running, and men appeared and raced for their horses. Horses and warriors broke through the village toward the creek. At this distance the Sioux warriors were dark, bare bodies, lank and flimsy on the ponies' backs. The guide said: "Big village. Thousand braves."

The warriors were gathering; they slashed across the creek and made irregular clusters. They stopped and seemed to be waiting.

Conn said in his husky voice: "The question's being put. To attack or run. I wish I had a cup of coffee."

Callahan's face was red and his eyes hung to Cheadrick and he was nervous, with the nervousness of wild hope. He said: "It takes two jaws to make a nutcracker. We're one, but where's the other? If they run we've lost them."

Cheadrick watched the Sioux arrange themselves. Warriors still streamed out of the village, galloping across the creek. A division took place before

Cheadrick's attentive eyes; part of the warriors broke away and started around the ridge at a dead gallop. The guide said: "They want to see whut we got on the other side."

Cheadrick said to Callahan: "Return to your battalion, sir."

As Callahan walked along the narrow ridge toward the extreme left of the strung-out regimental line he spoke bitterly under his breath: "I never expected to see the day when a regiment of United States Cavalry ran up a hill and permitted itself to be surrounded by a scurvy bunch of savages!"

Cheadrick watched the wagons arrive on the lower bench. Teamsters sprang down to unhitch, and the two covering troops of McPherson and Curtis were taking a line in the rocks; and when that defense was completed a part of the heavy care dropped from Cheadrick's shoulders. Nobody but an old man with a long memory of the disaster of split commands really knew what it meant to have the regiment in a compact fighting unit.

Presently Sioux swept around the base of the ridge and stopped to look at the wagon train's position. Cheadrick took a stogie from his pocket and lighted it and watched the Indians for a full five minutes, then put his attention on the main group of warriors in the valley. Those warriors were still waiting; they formed a wall between soldiers and squaws, and now the squaws, having the camp hitched to pony-drawn travois, were retreating toward the south end of the valley. The valley was no more than a mile broad, with low hills semicircularly closing it in on the far side. Cheadrick, sweeping those hills with an anxious eye, saw no infantry column breaking over them. Where was Gibson?

Gibson had said: "Keep them in hand until I come up, for if they scatter on us they'll play merry hell before we catch up with them again." There was a long-running burst of rifle echoes behind Cheadrick, and he looked around to see the Indians opposite the wagon train sweeping along the base of the ridge, parallel to the wagons. They fired as they raced by, and when they had passed the wagons they doubled back in another running line and fired again. All these shots would fall short; they had to get closer to do damage. Cheadrick thought: "The longer they have their fun the better it is." For the longer they delayed departure the nearer Gibson would be.

It was eight o'clock, and the sun was a low bright ball in the east and the rocks began to take on heat. The firing ceased, and the Indians in that quarter swept around the edge of the ridge to rejoin the main body of Sioux. The squaws were halfway up the valley, their departure marked by streaky runners of dust; presently the Sioux warriors slowly retreated across the creek and followed the squaws.

A thousand good fighting Sioux in that bunch, Cheadrick thought; they were slowly slipping away from him, and there was no sign of Gibson. Cheadrick put a fresh match to his stogie. He had five hundred men. If he took them down it would be a hell of a scrap. He had fought Indians a long time, and he knew the quality of those Sioux when they turned to defend their women with brand-new repeating rifles. But the summer was about done, and if the Sioux got away now there would be a long winter campaign and additional troops in the field and heavy casualties from a dozen running engagements. Casualties now, in a decisive engagement, would be better than casualties and a long-dragged-out campaign later. Gibson had said: "I leave it to your judgment."

Cheadrick spoke to the trumpeter. "Horses," he said. The trumpeter tossed up his instrument and flung that brief, peremptory summons through the day's heating stillness, and all along the ridge horse holders moved forward and men heaved up to the saddles. Cheadrick said to his orderly: "Bring up Captain McPherson's troop. Curtis will stay with the wagons." The orderly ducked down the hill slope.

The Chicago correspondent sat on his horse, and one hand rubbed the smooth top of his .45, which he had never before used, and he looked at the colonel and he thought: "No nerves, no sentiment. The man's a block of ice."

McPherson's troop grunted its way up the slope and fell into line. Cheadrick abandoned his stogie. The squaws were near the head of the valley, about to climb through the yonder pass. The warriors followed at a distance, forming a rear guard. There was no sign of Gibson.

Cheadrick moved his horse toward the middle of the long line, followed by his adjutant and his bugler and his orderly. The color sergeants had uncased the colors; they were close behind him. Cheadrick looked to either side of him, at this regiment he had built up by his care and discipline and affection. He saw the troopers, their sun-blackened jaws, their faces now hard-drawn by excitement. All these saddles were full, but many of them in another quarter hour would be empty. Kistmiller had pulled his hat down over his eyes, and he sat forward on the leather, alert and tough and wise in the kind of soldiering that would be presently needed; he saw

G troop's boy trumpeter and remembered the lad had a girl back at the post.

The colonel pulled the strap of his hat beneath his chin. It would have been nice to have taken the regiment back to the post intact, to have returned all these men to their women and their families, to the small and easy ways of life that were so sweet. This was what an old man thought when he sat at the head of his regiment. He took a grip on his reins, made a slow forward motion with his arm, and started down the slope at a walk, the long line of the regiment bellying and bowing behind him as it struck the steep pitch.

The Sioux warriors had halted their retreat. They were swinging around and breaking out of their compact formations. They were wheeling into individual fighting groups and stretching across the valley, awaiting the cavalry. The colonel took a professional look at the creek, estimated the possibilities of a small grove of willows near by, and mentally made his plans. The Sioux would fight their own way, which would be to flank his command; they were starting that wide-racing sweep already.

Half down the slope Cheadrick saw dust boil thicker at the head of the valley. Squaws and pony-drawn travois were turning back. Something rolled them back from the little pass up there, but the dust made a screen he couldn't see through. He came down to the valley's edge, the regiment in column of companies. There was a commotion among the warriors; they were recoiling from their flanking movement; they were rushing back toward the squaws. In a moment Cheadrick saw the sinuous glitter of guns in the pass. That would be Gibson.

Cheadrick said, "Gallop," and splashed over the creek. He wasn't aiming at the warriors; he was well behind them as he crossed the valley and plugged the lower end of it to block escape in that direction. The regiment was like a stopper in a bottle. Cheadrick brought the companies into front line. He said: "McPherson—take your company out to make a flank at the base of those hills." McPherson's company rushed away.

Out on the plain, squaws and warriors came together in a confusion of dust, and halted. Gibson's column poured through the pass, marching steadily forward; from this distance Cheadrick saw the column break into three smaller columns, each one forking out on the flat earth.

Presently the columns stopped. A group of Indians rode slowly from the main body and lifted their hands in signal of defeat. Gibson was riding up with his staff.

Cheadrick said, "Conn, take command," and trotted out to meet Gibson.

Gibson had stopped before the warriors. He was still in the saddle when Cheadrick came up; he was waiting for Cheadrick. Dust silvered his coat, and the sharp, acrid face of the man was a gray mask of alkali streaked with ragged sweat. Cheadrick reined in and made his salute. He was a stiff, autocratic shape in the sunlight; the upturned brim of his hat and the silver goatee and mustache gave him a cavalryman's flair.

"Well, Gibson," said Cheadrick, "here's your Sioux."

Gibson said, "Well done," and extended his hand. When Cheadrick took that hand he met Gibson's eyes and he knew that Gibson understood the strain of the past hours—for Gibson, too, had been through it. Nobody else would know; but Gibson did, and that was reward enough, the silent applause of one old commander to another. Weight slid from Cheadrick's shoulders. He remembered Kistmiller, and it was a fine, clean feeling to know he would be returning Kistmiller to his wife and new baby. The day was hot but the heat was good for his old bones, and some of the snap and resilience of his younger years returned to him.

Gibson said: "Where's the interpreter? I want to start this band back to the reservation."

It was a tremendous climax to the Chicago correspondent who stood aside to chronicle the meeting of these two men; and a tremendous anti-climax. Watching Cheadrick, he thought: "Unsentimental and untouched. Moved neither by excitement nor the thought of defeat nor the consummation of a bloodless peace. The man's a machine—but what a machine!"

BEN HECHT

Crime Without Passion

MR. LOU HENDRIX looked at the lady he had been pretending to love for the past six months and, being a lawyer, said nothing. Mr. Hendrix was a gentleman who could listen longer to female hysterics

without unbending than was normal. This, he would have said, was due
to his aloof and analytical mind. Then, also, the events which were taking
place in this boudoir at the moment were of a familiar pattern. Some eight
or nine times Mr. Hendrix had been the hero of just such climaxes as this,
when new love had entered his life and necessitated similar farewells.

The young lady who, this time, was doing the screaming was a nymph
of the cabarets known as Brownie. Her full name was Carmen Browne.
She danced, and very effectively, at the El Bravo Club where, devoid of
plumage as an eel, she led the Birds of Paradise number. In this she was
ravishing as a Dream of Fair Women.

Why so young and delicious a siren as Brownie should be so disturbed
over the amorous defection of Mr. Hendrix would have confused anyone
who knew this gentleman or merely took a one-minute look at him. He was
not Romeo nor was he Adonis, nor was he even such a male as one associ-
ates with the general practice of seduction. He was a little man with that
objectionable immaculateness which reminds one, instanter, of sheep's
clothing. He was one of those popinjays of the fleshpots with the face of a
tired and sarcastic boy. His sideburns were a wee too long, his smile unduly
persistent (like a ballet dancer's), his voice far too gentle to have deceived
anyone, except perhaps a woman, as to his spiritual composition. But one
can always depend on the ladies to misunderstand the combination of
gentleness and sideburns.

Brownie, who among her own kind was considered not only quite a
reader of books but a sort of practical authority on masculine characteristics,
had misunderstood Lou Hendrix, amazingly. Carry on as she would now,
she was no match for this caballero of the law who, out of a clear sky, was
engaged in giving her what she called "the go-by." As her monologue of
screams, epithets, and sobs progressed the lovely and muscular girl understood it all. She perceived, much too late for any use, that she had to do
with as purring a hypocrite, rogue, and underhanded soul as one might
flush in a seven-day hunt on Broadway, which, according to the chroniclers
Brownie most admired, is the world's leading water hole for human beasts
of prey.

Looking around at the pretty apartment in which Mr. Hendrix had
installed her and in which she had lorded it over her friends for the six
months and from which she must now exit—love's dream being ended—
Brownie spread herself on the couch and filled her sybaritic diggings with
a truly romantic din. From the more coherent utterances of this tear-stained

beauty it seemed that she was innocent of all dallyings with a certain Eddie White, an ex-college hero, and that since leaving this same Mr. White, whose love interest she had been before the Birds of Paradise number was staged, she had never once permitted him to lay a finger on her. She was, wailed Brownie, being wrongly accused. Then, sitting up, her greenish eyes popping with rage until they looked like a pair of snake heads, Brownie laughed, as she would have said, scornfully, and declared that she could see through Mr. Hendrix and his so-called jealousy. He was getting rid of her because he didn't love her any more. He was tired of her and putting her on the escalator—that was all there was to it.

To this Mr. Hendrix, thoroughly seen through, made no reply, and Brownie, announcing that she was not going to be made a sucker of, fell back on the couch, beat some cushions with her fists, and shook with grief. The telephone rang. Brownie straightened on the couch.

"It's probably for you," she said.

"More likely it's Mr. White," said Mr. Hendrix.

The taunt brought Brownie to her feet.

"If it's for me, by any mischance," said Mr. Hendrix, "say I'm not here." Brownie spoke into the phone.

"Who?" she asked. "No, he's not here. No, I don't know when he'll be here. No, no, I don't expect him." Hanging up, she looked bitterly at Mr. Hendrix. "Your office," she said. "Always making me lie for you."

"You might have been a bit more polite," said Mr. Hendrix.

The heartlessness of this suggestion sent Brownie back to the couch and her grief. She resumed her sobs. Mr. Hendrix continued to regard her with creditable, if villainous, detachment. His heart was in the highlands with another lassie. But even discounting that factor, Mr. Hendrix felt he was pursuing a wise course in ridding himself of so obstreperous an admirer as lay howling here. He had no use for overemotional types. They were inclined to drive diversion, which was Mr. Hendrix' notion of Cupid, out of the window with their caterwauling.

Mr. Hendrix' soul, in fact, was a sort of china closet, and he was firm in his aversion to flying hoofs. He belonged to that tribe of Don Juans, rather numerous at the Broadway hole, who never hang themselves for love. Tears he regarded as bad sportsmanship, and heartbreak was to him plain blackmail. Beauty—and by beauty Mr. Hendrix meant chiefly those delicious and agile Venuses of the cabaret floor shows—beauty had been put into Broadway (if not into the world) for man's delight; certainly not for his confusion and despair. And this little barrister lived elegantly, if rather villainously, by this conception.

A number of things, all obvious to the analytical Mr. Hendrix, were now operating in Brownie's mind and making her wail—Eddie's vengeful delight at her getting the go-by from his successor; the tittering of the little group of columnists, hoofers, waiters, and good-time Charlies whom she called the World; the lessening of her status as a siren—she might even be demoted from leading the Birds of Paradise number—and, through all these considerations, the nerve of the man, throwing her down as if she were some nobody! As for the more passional side of the business, the pain in her heart at losing someone she had so stupidly loved and misunderstood and at losing the foolish Broadwayish dream of wedlock she had cherished for half a year, Brownie chose not to mention these in her ravings, being too proud.

Mr. Hendrix, still preserving his finest courtroom manner of Reason and Superiority, watched on in silence and fell to wondering what he had ever seen in this redheaded, almost illiterate creature with her muscular legs and childish face to have ever considered her charming or desirable. But he was given small time to meditate this problem of idealization. Brownie, with a yell that set the base of his spine to tingling, leaped from the couch, stared wildly around, and then, emitting a series of shrill sounds, had at the furnishings of the love nest. She pulled a portiere down, hurled two vases to the floor, swung a chair against the wall and smashed it, beat Mr. Hendrix' framed photograph to bits against the edge of the piano, seized a clock from the mantelpiece and bounced it on the floor, and was making for Mr. Hendrix' derby, which he had placed on a chair near the door, when he, with an unexpected shout, headed her off.

The barrister, defending his derby, received a blow on the side of his face that sent him spinning. A thrown object caught him behind the ear. Brownie's pointed shoes belabored his shins. He retreated. But the hysteria to which he had been coolly and analytically listening seemed suddenly to have been injected, like a virus, into his blood stream. It had started with the tingling in the base of his spine. Smarting from blows, and full of some sort of electric current which gave off oaths in his head, the little lawyer began to outbellow his now ex-paramour. He came at the lady, and in his hand he held, almost unaware of the fact, a large brass candlestick.

What it was that made this popinjay, so renowned for coolness, strategy, and cynicism in his twin professions of amour and the law, so completely

shed his character, God alone, who was not at Mr. Hendrix' elbow at the
moment, could have told, and perhaps a psychiatrist or two might also have
made a guess at. But here he was much too far gone for analysis, his own
or anyone else's, charging at the lovely Carmen Browne like a bantam cave
man, screaming and swinging the heavy piece of brass in the air.

There was no precedent in Mr. Hendrix' life for such a turn of events
and no hint in any of his former love doings that passion could so blind
his faculties and hate so fill his heart. Yet blind he was, and full of a
clamorous hate that demanded something of him. From the oaths which
escaped Mr. Hendrix during this preliminary skirmish with the brass
candlestick, it seemed that what he hated was women; loathed and hated
them with a fury out of the Pit. Announcing this, he swung the piece of
brass, and the second swing exhilarated him the more. It had struck squarely
against Brownie's head, dropping her to the carpet. Mr. Hendrix, out of
breath, stood cursing and grimacing over her like a murderer.

Slowly the little lawyer's rage melted. His heart swelled with terror and
the nape of his neck grew warm. Brownie lay as she had fallen. He leaned
over. Her skull was cracked. Blood was running. Her eyes were closed. Her
legs, exposed in an incongruously graceful sprawl, were inert. He put his
ear to her bosom. There was no heart beating. He stood for several minutes
holding his breath and listening automatically for sounds outside the door.
The choking sensation in his lungs subsided, and the cool, analytical mind
that was Mr. Hendrix returned like some errant accomplice tiptoeing back
to the scene of the crime.

Carmen Browne lay dead on her hearthstone. No more would she lead
the Birds of Paradise number at the El Bravo Club. But Mr. Hendrix
wasted no time considering this sentimental phase of the matter. He had
committed a murder, without intent, to be sure, even in self-defense, looked
at factually. But no, self-defense wouldn't hold, Mr. Hendrix was thinking
swiftly. There rushed through his mind all the angles, holes, difficulties,
improbabilities, and prejudices of his case, and in less than a minute the
little lawyer had put himself on trial on a plea of self-defense and found
himself guilty.

Since a young man, Mr. Hendrix had always been close to crime. He
had had that unmoral and intellectual understanding of it which helps
make one type of excellent lawyer. In action, defending a criminal, Mr.
Hendrix had always been like some imperturbable surgeon. Guilt was a
disease that could be cured, not by any operation on the soul of its victim,

but by a process of mental legerdemain which convinced a jury that no guilt existed. Mr. Hendrix might have said that he served a cause beyond good and evil, that of extricating the victims of fleeting misadventures from the unjustly permanent results of their deeds.

Thus, far beyond most men who might have found themselves confronted by the strange and ugly dilemma of having unexpectedly committed a murder, Mr. Hendrix was prepared for his new role of criminal. He knew all the ropes, he knew all the pitfalls of the defense of such a case as this. He knew the psychology of the prosecution. And with an expert, if slightly still fevered, mind, he knew the perfect details by which his guilt might be cured, the ideal evidence, persuasive and circumstantial, by which a jury could be cajoled to the verdict of not guilty.

In less than a minute Mr. Hendrix had a full grasp of his case, seeing far into its convolutions and difficulties. He set about straightening these out.

But like some dramatic critic who, after observing plays for years with subtle and intimate understanding of them, is summoned suddenly on the stage and with the strange footlights glaring in his eyes told to perform the part whose words he knows, whose ideal gesture and intonation he has always dreamed about, Mr. Hendrix felt the panic of debut. To know and to act were phenomena surprisingly separate. This was what delayed the cautious barrister for another minute, a minute during which Mr. Hendrix' client, with beating heart and white face, mumbled for speed, chattered even of flight.

But at the end of this second minute Mr. Hendrix had elbowed this ignominious client into a far corner of his mind, seated him as it were at the counsel's table with orders to keep his mouth shut—and taken charge of the case. He leaned over and looked at the clock on the floor. The dial glass was broken. The clock had stopped, its hands at two minutes of four. Mr. Hendrix' thoughts were rapid, almost as if he were not thinking at all but knowing. He could move the hands forward to five o'clock. He could leave the premises undetected, if possible, and attach himself for the next two hours to a group of prospective alibi witnesses, remain with them during the hours between four, ten, and seven, and this would be the proof he had not been in the apartment at the time of the murder. Mr. Hendrix examined the watch on Carmen Browne's wrist. It, too, had stopped. It registered one minute after four. The two timepieces, evidently synchronized by their owner, told a graphic and substantially correct tale. At 3:58

the struggle had begun. At 4:01 the woman had been killed. He would have to set the wrist watch forward a full hour to preserve this interesting discrepancy in the stopped clocks.

The telephone rang. Mr. Hendrix straightened, not having touched either of the hour hands. He had actually anticipated a telephone ringing, and in this anticipation known the ruse of the forwarded time hands was stupid. At 3:50 Carmen Browne had answered a phone call, a record of which was with the switchboard man in the lobby. Now, at 4:03—he consulted his own watch—she failed to answer. Other phone calls might likewise come before five o'clock, all of which Carmen Browne would fail to answer, thus establishing an important series of witnesses against the fact that the murdered woman had been alive between four and five o'clock; thus rendering his alibi of his own whereabouts during that time practically futile. There was also the possibility that the neighbors had heard their quarrel and noted the time of the screaming. And more than all these the chance that someone, a maid or the building agent (Carmen Browne had been consulting him about subletting her place), might enter the room before five o'clock.

It was the hour preceding 4:01 for which Mr. Hendrix needed an alibi. He already knew its vital groundwork. At 3:50 Carmen Browne, alive, had told someone on the phone—probably Tom Healey of his own law firm—that he was not in her apartment. Mr. Hendrix' eyes had remained on his own wrist watch as his thought slipped through these pros and cons. It was 4:04. He glanced at the sprawled figure on the floor, shivered, but stood his ground. Another phase of his case had overcome him. He smiled palely, shocked at what had almost been an oversight. He must not only provide an alibi for himself but fortify it with evidence tending to prove someone other than he had done the deed. He must invent a mythical murderer—leave a trail of evidence for the sharp eyes and wits of the prosecution leading to Another, a never-to-be-found Another, but yet one always present in the case.

Carmen Browne's fingerprints were on the broken clock, the smashed chair, the battered photo frame. This was wrong. It would reveal that it was Carmen who had been in the rage, smashing things, demanding something that had resulted in her murder—and this sort of a situation, brought out by the prosecution, might easily point to Lou Hendrix, known to have been her lover. No, said Lawyer Hendrix swiftly, it must have been her assailant, demanding something of Carmen Browne, who had been in the

rage and done the smashing and struck the fatal blow. Mr. Hendrix established this fact circumstantially by wiping Carmen Browne's fingerprints
from the objects in question with a silk handkerchief. He wiped also, and
more carefully, the brass candlestick. The absence of fingerprints pointed
to a certain self-consciousness on the part of the assailant after the deed,
but that was both legitimate and normal. Men of the deepest passion, and
there was precedence for this, remembered to obliterate evidence.

At the door Mr. Hendrix, in his hat, overcoat, and gloves, paused. He
repeated to himself carefully, Carmen Browne had been attacked by some
suitor, jealous of her real sweetheart, Mr. Hendrix, as witness the destroyed
photograph of the latter. But why hadn't she used the gun the police would
find in the desk drawer two feet from the spot where her body lay? There
were, of course, normal explanations to be put forward. But Mr. Hendrix
did not admire them legally. For fifteen precious seconds Lawyer Hendrix
balanced the issue. During this space Mr. Hendrix listened rather than
thought. He listened to the prosecution pointing out to the jury that the
reason Carmen Browne had not reached for this available weapon with
which to defend herself was because she had not expected an attack
from the assailant, because the assailant was one familiar to her, against
whom she had no thought of arming herself; and, even further, because
the assailant, all too familiar with the premises, knew where this gun was
as well as did Carmen Browne and prevented her from reaching it. All
these values pointed shadowly, Mr. Hendrix perceived, at his client. He
removed the gun from the drawer and dropped it into his coat pocket. He
must be careful in disposing of the weapon, and Mr. Hendrix' mind dwelt
stubbornly on a dozen cases in which an attempt at postcrime evidence disposal had been the connecting link with guilt. But Mr. Hendrix assured
his client firmly that he would be more cautious in this regard than any
of his previous defendants had been.

With the gun in his coat pocket Mr. Hendrix stepped out of the apartment. Now he was, he knew, purely in the hands of luck. A door opening,
a neighbor appearing would ruin his case instantly. But no untoward event
happened. He had three floors to descend. He listened at the ornamental
elevator doors. Both cages were going up. Mr. Hendrix walked quickly
down the three flights and coolly, now like a gambler rather than a lawyer,
rehearsed the possible permutations of luck.

He had entered the apartment at three o'clock that morning with
Carmen Browne. But because it was his habit to preserve a surface air of
respectability toward the attendants of the place, though he fancied they

knew well enough what was going on, he had walked up to the apartment with Brownie. The switchboard operator, concealed in an alcove in the lobby, had not seen them come in, nor had the elevator boy on duty, as both were out of sight at the moment. If now he could leave the building with the equal but vitally more important luck of not being seen, his case would be more than launched.

The lobby was empty, but Mr. Hendrix did not make the mistake of slipping out too quickly and coddling the presumption that no eyes had observed him. He knew too well the possibility of the unexpected witness, and he paused to study the premises. The switchboard attendant, half hidden in the alcove, had his back to the lobby and was reading a newspaper. Both elevator cages were out of sight. There was no one else. Mr. Hendrix stepped into the street.

Here again he stopped to look for that unexpected witness. How often, he remembered grimly, had the best of his cases been tumbled by the appearance on the stand of those aimless, incalculable human strays who had "Seen the Defendant." Mr. Hendrix saw two of just that type. Two women were walking, but with their backs to him and away from the apartment. A delivery truck was passing. Mr. Hendrix noticed that the driver was talking to a companion and that neither of these passers looked in his direction. There was no one else. Mr. Hendrix turned his attention to the windows across the street. Only the first three floors mattered. Identification was impossible, or at least could be sufficiently challenged, from any greater height. The windows were empty. As for the windows of the building directly over him, if he kept close to the wall, none could see him from these.

Satisfied with this rapid but concentrated scrutiny, Mr. Hendrix started walking toward the corner. If the triumph of intellect over nerves, of reason over the impulses of the senses, may be called heroism, then this smiling, casually moving little popinjay in the black derby and snug overcoat might well be called a hero. Innocence, even aimlessness, was in his every movement; and in his refusal, despite a driving curiosity, to look at the time on his wrist—a telltale gesture were it recorded by anyone—there was something approaching the loftiness of purpose which distinguished the ancient ascetics. As he turned the corner Mr. Hendrix, still unruffled, still amiably rhythmic in his movements, looked back to make sure no taxicabs had entered the street. None had.

He was now on 6th Avenue, and he moved more briskly. He had four blocks to walk, and habit sent his eyes looking for a taxicab. But, alert to every variety of witness, he shook his head and stayed afoot. He smiled, remembering that his own bed in his own apartment was unmade. He had just turned in the night before when Brownie had telephoned and asked to meet him. Thus his housekeeper, who never arrived before noon, would establish simply the fact that he had slept at home. This was unnecessary, to be sure, unless some passer-by had seen Brownie and a man enter the former's apartment at three this morning.

Mr. Hendrix arrived now at a 6th Avenue cinema palace. He looked carefully over the small crowd waiting for tickets and then joined the line. In a few minutes he was being ushered into the roped enclosure at the rear of the auditorium. He slipped away quickly, however, and walked in the dark to the other side of the theater. He approached one of the ushers and demanded to know where he could report the loss of a pair of gloves. After a brief colloquy he was led to the office of the lost-and-found department, and here Mr. Hendrix, very voluble and affable, explained his mishap. He was not, he smiled, usually so careless with his belongings, but the picture had been so engrossing that he had forgotten all about his haberdashery. Then Mr. Hendrix gave his name, address, a description of the missing gloves, and watched with a glow of deep creative satisfaction the time being written down on the blank form used for cataloguing such matters. "Four-eighteen," the man wrote, and Mr. Hendrix, consulting his watch, pretended to be startled. Was it that late? he demanded: Good lord, he had had no idea of the time! It was quite a long picture. And the lost-and-found official, drawn into chumminess by Mr. Hendrix' affability, agreed that the film was a little longer than most but well worth sitting through—to which Mr. Hendrix assented.

Emerging from the movie palace, Mr. Hendrix rehearsed his case to date. The main body of his alibi was achieved. He had spent the time between two-thirty and four watching a movie. His continued presence at four-eighteen in this theater was written down in black and white. He had also taken care that it should be a movie he had already seen, so as to be able to recite its plot were he questioned in the next few hours. And he had also provided a motive for seeing this particular movie. The film had to do with the character and career of a mythical state's attorney, and a newspaper friend of Mr. Hendrix who conducted a gossip column had asked him to contribute a few paragraphs from a legal point of view carping at the improbabilities of the scenario.

Mr. Hendrix' next port of call was an elegant speak-easy. Here he had a drink, engaged in an exchange of views with the bartender, who knew him, asked the correct time so he might adjust his watch. At 4:50 he stepped into a phone booth in the place and called his office. He inquired whether anybody had been trying to reach him that afternoon. The law clerk on duty for the firm, Tom Healey, answered as Mr. Hendrix had expected. Mr. Healey said he had been trying to find him in relation to a disposition but had been unable to locate him. At this Mr. Hendrix feigned a light anger. Where had the incompetent youth called? He had, said Mr. Healey, tried everywhere, even Miss Carmen Browne's apartment.

At this bit of information Mr. Hendrix, in his mind's eye addressing one of his future star witnesses, changed his voice. He grew angry, and very obviously so, for he knew the laziness of people's memories and their slipshod powers of observation. He inquired sourly if Mr. Healey had spoken to Miss Browne. On hearing that he had, Mr. Hendrix said:

"Do you mind telling me how she seemed when you asked if I was there?"

"Well, I don't know," Mr. Healey said.

"Try and think," said Mr. Hendrix. "I'd like to know."

"Well," said Mr. Healey, "come to think of it, she struck me as a little curt or upset about something."

"Ha!" said Mr. Hendrix and, to the surprise of his office underling, called the young lady a villainous name.

"I don't want you to call me up at her place any more." He raised his voice. The clerk, Mr. Healey, said he would never do it again, but Mr. Hendrix, as though too enraged to notice this promise, continued. "I'm all washed up at that telephone number. Understand what I mean? You can just forget about it. Any other calls?"

"No," said Mr. Healey.

"O. K.," said Mr. Hendrix, and hung up the phone with an angry bang.

He walked from the speak-easy with the light step which to Mr. Hendrix' office colleagues always characterized a Not Guilty verdict in sight. Now that the tingling at the base of his spine as well as the annoying warmth on the nape of his neck, as if a prosecuting staff were actually breathing on him, had gone entirely, Mr. Hendrix was beginning to feel not only relaxed but even amused. He could hear the prosecution falling into this little trap he had just laid.

Question: So Mr. Hendrix told you that you needn't try to reach him at Miss Browne's apartment any more?

Answer: Yes sir.

And Lawyer Hendrix looked winningly at the jury that sat in his mind's eye. Gentlemen of the Jury, consider this. As if, having committed a crime, the defendant would be so gauche as to give himself away by some such oafish remark to a law clerk—a type of person trained to remember what he hears. Not a casual stranger, mind you, but a man with sharp and practiced wits.

Mr. Hendrix, skittering happily along the street, cleared his throat, beamed, and felt a desire to laugh. He had never quite so enjoyed a case. What subtle and yet vital psychological proof of his innocence was the fact that he had just said to Tom Healey what he had; what perfect proof of the fact that he had been the victim of an obvious coincidence in saying he was washed up with Carmen Browne when she lay dead in her apartment. No guilty man would ever have said that.

From a drugstore he was passing Mr. Hendrix made another telephone call. He called Carmen Browne. Inquiring for her of the apartment switchboard operator, a sharp excitement stirred him. Before his eyes the image of her body, sprawled gracefully and awfully on the floor at his feet, swayed for a moment. He hoped the crime had been discovered, although there were still chances to improve his case. But the switchboard man calmly plugged in for Carmen Browne's apartment.

"She doesn't answer," he said after a pause.

"This is Mr. Hendrix calling," said Mr. Hendrix. "Has she been in at all? I've been trying to get her all day."

"Hasn't come in while I've been here," said the man.

"How long is that?" said Mr. Hendrix.

"Oh, about three hours," said the man.

"Thank you," said Mr. Hendrix, and hung up.

He had told Tom Healey he was washed up with Carmen Browne, and now he was trying to reach her, and Mr. Hendrix considered this paradox, in behalf of his client, with a smile. It revealed, Gentlemen of the Jury, a distracted man, a lover full of confusion as a result of—what? Of the fact, gentlemen, Mr. Hendrix purred to himself, that my client was jealous of the attentions he had found out someone was paying to Carmen Browne; that he did not believe the poor girl's protestations of innocence and, driven from her side by suspicions, was yet lured back to her by his deep love.

Jealous, Gentlemen of the Jury, of the attentions being paid to Carmen Browne by this creature who that very afternoon had entered her apartment and against whom Carmen Browne had defended herself until struck down and killed.

To augment this phase of the case, Mr. Hendrix returned now to the apartment building in which Carmen Browne lay murdered. He approached the switchboard operator, who greeted him by name. Here Mr. Hendrix controlled a curious impulse that whitened the skin around his mouth. He felt impelled to ask this man whether he had noticed Mr. Hendrix in the building before, whether he had seen him during the few moments he had walked from the lobby an hour ago. Astonished at this impulse, Mr. Hendrix held his tongue for a space, aware that the switchboard man was looking at him with curiosity.

Question: How did the defendant seem?

Answer: Confused.

Gentlemen of the Jury, and how would a man consumed with jealousy seem while inquiring, against all his pride, if the woman he thought was wronging him was home?

"Has Miss Browne come in since I called?" asked Mr. Hendrix.

"I haven't seen her," said the man. "I'll try her apartment again."

There was no answer.

"Give her this note when she comes back," said Mr. Hendrix.

He wrote on the lower part of a business letter from his pocket:

"Darling, if you are innocent, don't torture me any more. Give me a chance to believe you. I'm willing to forget what I heard or thought I heard over the phone. As ever, Lou."

He placed this in a used envelope, scribbled her name on it, and sealed it.

Gentlemen of the Jury, can you imagine any man who had killed a woman he loved or had loved so lost to all human reaction, so fiendishly wanton as to have written that little plea when he knew she was lying dead at his hands?

That was merely a rhetorical overtone, the human rather than evidential side of the note, but Mr. Hendrix filed it away in his memory as a bit of decoration. His alibi, Lawyer Hendrix murmured to himself, was now complete. But the secondary phase of the case needed further effort. The beauty of a case lay always in the elaborateness of diverse but corroborating detail—as if the world were crying the defendant's innocence from every nook and cranny. And happily at work, Mr. Hendrix had, lawyer-like, so far forgotten the human existence of his client as to whistle cheerily the while he turned over and re-turned over the major psychological problem in his mind.

Defense—Carmen Browne had been murdered by a man to whom she refused, after perhaps leading him on, to surrender herself. Also it might be that the killing had been one of those passional accidents which the sex instinct, run amok, precipitates. It might be that Carmen Browne had led a double life and was discovered in this double life by her slayer.

Ergo—Lou Hendrix, sharp-witted, observant, a veritable connoisseur of women, must suspect the existence of this other man. And Defendant Hendrix must also be jealous of him.

Witness to this—his talk to Tom Healey; his note to Carmen Browne, now in the hands of the switchboard operator.

And Lawyer Hendrix, with the thrill of a gambler rolling a third lucky seven, remembered at this point a third witness—a veritable star witness, beautifully, if unwittingly, prepared for her role a few days ago. This was Peggy Moore.

Miss Moore danced at the El Bravo Club as a member of the ensemble. She had been Brownie's confidante for a year. Mr. Hendrix smiled blissfully recalling his conversation with Miss Moore less than a week ago and recalling also her general character, one made to order for the part he was to assign her.

This young lady was a tall, dark-haired Irish lassie with slightly bulging eyes and an expression of adenoidal and not unpleasing vacuity about her face. She was, as Brownie had frequently confided to him, a veritable love slave, a dithering creature incapable of thinking or talking on any subject other than the emotions stirred in her bosom by love or jealousy.

Some days ago Mr. Hendrix had selected this almost congenital idiot as the opening pawn in his decision to rid himself of Brownie. He had confided to Miss Moore's ears, so perfectly attuned to all tales of amorous agony, that he suspected Brownie of being still in love with his predecessor Eddie White. Miss Moore's eyes had bulged, her mouth opened as if to disgorge a fishhook, and simultaneously a shrewd, if transparent, emotion had overcome her. Miss Moore, the victim of so much perfidy, had been convinced instanter of her chum's guilt and had launched at once into a series of lies, all defending Brownie's integrity and offering idiotic details of her devotion to her lawyer lover. Mr. Hendrix, intent on laying some foolish groundwork for his subsequent defection, had persisted, however, and, for no other reason than that he delighted in playing the human fraud whenever he could, had feigned sorrow and talked of woe.

Now Mr. Hendrix summoned Miss Moore on the telephone to meet him at the speak-easy he had recently quitted. He spoke guardedly, hinting at a lovers' quarrel and pretending he needed her to verify some evidences of Brownie's guilt just unearthed. Miss Moore, full of a laudable and loyal ambition to lie her head off in Brownie's behalf, as Mr. Hendrix had foreseen, arrived in a rush. And the two sat down at a table in a corner, Miss Moore to invent innocent explanations and alibis for her chum, at which, like all overtearful addicts of passion, she was amazingly expert, and Mr. Hendrix to weave her artfully into his case.

But first Mr. Hendrix, aware of the lady's sensitivity toward all matters pertaining to love, proceeded to get himself drunk. He must be the lover stricken with jealousy and seeking to drown his pains in liquor, a characterization which this simple child and student of amour would remember only too vividly on the witness stand. Three drinks were consumed, and then, honestly befuddled from such an unaccustomed dose, Mr. Hendrix launched into cross-examination. And despite his thickened tongue and touch of genuine physical paralysis, Lawyer Hendrix remained as cool and analytical as if he were in a courtroom. He was not one to betray a client by any human weaknesses.

He put himself at Miss Moore's mercy. He must know the truth, and she alone could tell him. Otherwise, with too much brooding and uncertainty, he would be sure to go out of his mind. His law practice was already suffering. He would lose all his money. Miss Moore nodded tenderly and understandingly at this saga of love woes. In reply she could assure Mr. Hendrix that he was being very foolish to be jealous of Eddie White because Mr. White wasn't even in town and besides Mr. White was engaged to marry a society girl in Newport. Mr. Hendrix sighed appreciatively at this walloping lie.

"It's not Eddie," said Mr. Hendrix, "it's somebody else. You know that as well as I. You're in her confidence. Don't try to lie to me, dearie. I caught her red-handed, talking over the phone. She hung up when I came into the room. She was making a date—and not with Eddie White."

Miss Moore paled at the thought of this dreadful contretemps, but kept her wits. Her chum's guilt frightened her, but at the same time she saw through Mr. Hendrix' effort to lead her astray. Of course it was Eddie

White of whom he was jealous. Miss Moore was certain of this, and Mr. Hendrix, listening to her somewhat hysterical defense of Brownie, sufficient to have convicted that young lady of a hundred infidelities had he been interested, realized exactly what was in his companion's mind. He considered for a moment the plan of involving Eddie White in his case. He had thought of it before—Brownie's previous lover, a known hotheaded young gentleman given to nocturnal fisticuffs in public places. But for the second time he dismissed this phase. Eddie would have an alibi, and the establishing of Eddie's physical innocence, however psychologically promising his guilt might have looked, would embarrass his client's case.

For the next hour Mr. Hendrix drank and discussed his jealousy, pleading with Miss Moore to be kind to him and reveal what she knew, and hinting at gifts in return for such service. But Miss Moore only increased the scope of her lies.

"Have you seen Brownie today?" Miss Moore finally broke off, winded.

Mr. Hendrix waved in his seat and looked at her with bleary, drunken eyes.

"No," he said. "I don't trust myself to see her. God knows what I would do—feeling this way."

"You're just worked up about absolutely nothing," said Miss Moore, and rose. She had to toddle off to the El Bravo, where she performed during the dinner hour. Mr. Hendrix accompanied her to the door.

"Tell Brownie," he whispered, "I'll be over to the club tonight. And . . . and give her a last chance to prove her innocence."

"I'll give her the message," said Miss Moore, and sighed.

Alone, Mr. Hendrix returned to the phone booth. He sat down heavily and put in a call for Carmen Browne. His case was ready. He desired to hear the news of the finding of the body. An annoying tingle touched the base of his spine as he waited for the apartment switchboard to answer. He wondered how drunk he was. Drunk, to be sure, but sober enough to know exactly every phase and weigh every nuance. The moment he heard of the crime he would rush over, be detained by the police, and, with the aid of his intoxicated condition, act thoroughly irrational and grief-stricken. He would hint at no alibis, reveal not a shred of his case until the coroner's inquest.

The switchboard operator finally answered. Mr. Hendrix inquired thickly for Miss Browne. He was told Miss Browne was not in. He hung up. Rising and swaying for a moment, Mr. Hendrix, thoroughly at peace with the world, except for this intermittent tingle, decided on the best course. He would go to the El Bravo Club, order his dinner, and wait there till Brownie's absence was noticed and a search started.

The El Bravo orchestra was rendering a dance number. The dance floor was crowded. Mr. Hendrix looked dizzily at the circling figures. He had selected a table far to the side, one of those at which the performers and their friends grouped themselves during the evening. The stuffiness of the air made Mr. Hendrix feel drowsy. Looking up, he beheld a familiar figure approaching. It was Eddie White, whom he had pleased to style the ignorant drop-kicker. Mr. Hendrix smiled. He noticed tiredly that Mr. White seemed a little drunk.

The ex-college hero, still a sturdy, tanned, and muscular product of the Higher Education, greeted Mr. Hendrix calmly. He dropped into a chair at the table and inquired, with an eye roving over the place, how tricks were. Mr. Hendrix said they were fine.

There was a pause during which the music filled the café with glamorous and exciting sounds.

"Didn't know you were such a movie fan," said Mr. White apropos of nothing, and Mr. Hendrix felt himself sobering up as if in a cold shower.

"Just what do you mean?" Mr. Hendrix managed to inquire, and very casually.

His companion was busy looking them over on the dance floor and offering a roguish eye to a few of the tastier numbers. Mr. Hendrix stared at him in silence and felt the tingle return to his spine.

"Saw you going into the Roxy this afternoon," Mr. White resumed.

"You did," said Mr. Hendrix, and then added, as if he were looping the loop: "What time was that?"

"What time?" Mr. White repeated, looking at the little lawyer with a dull, athlete's stare. "Oh, a little after four, I should say."

"You're crazy," said Mr. Hendrix, "if you think you saw me going into the Roxy after four. Why, I came out about twenty after four, after seeing the whole show."

"I don't care what you saw," said Mr. White, "I saw you going in at about a quarter after. I was gonna say hello, but I thought the hell with it. How'd you like the picture? Ought to be in your line—all about one of those crooked legal sharks."

In the brief space during which Mr. Hendrix was now silent his thoughts

were very rapid. Mr. White, God help Mr. Hendrix, was that most objectionable of all humans known to a legal case—the aimless stray that the
prosecution was wont to drag, rabbit fashion, out of its hat with which to
confound the guilty. And Mr. Hendrix knew, without thinking, the full
significance of this witness, Eddie White. If the defendant had been seen
entering the movie theater after four, he had been seen entering after the
murder had been committed. But that was the least damaging phase. The
defendant had left the movie theater at 4:20, having lied to the attendants
and told them he had spent an hour and a half in the place. With the fact
of this lie established, the prosecution could take apart piece by piece the
obvious mechanism of his alibi. There was no alibi. There was no case. In
fact, to the contrary, Eddie White's simple statement of the time of day
—after four—revealed all of the defendant's subsequent actions as those of
a thoroughly guilty man, and Mr. Hendrix leaned across the table and put
a hand on the athlete's arm.

"It must have been somebody else you saw," he purred.

"Listen, don't tell me," said Mr. White. "I saw you looking around, buying your ticket, and ducking in."

Mr. Hendrix winced at the damning phraseology.

"I know it was about a quarter after four," pursued Mr. White, "because
I had a date outside. And don't get so excited. It wasn't with Brownie."

The tingle at the base of the Hendrix spine was almost lifting him out
of his seat.

"That's a lie," said Mr. Hendrix thickly.

"What's that?" Mr. White demanded.

"I said you're lying," Mr. Hendrix repeated slowly. "You didn't see me."

"Oh, that's what you said, is it?" Mr. White was unexpectedly grim.
"Listen, I never liked you, and I don't take talk off a guy I got no use for.
Get that."

And for the second time that day an unprecedented mood overcame the
little lawyer. He made an effort to stop the words which suddenly filled his
head, but he heard himself saying them and wondering confusedly who it
was who was drunk—he who was listening or he who was speaking. He was
telling Mr. White what a liar, numbskull, and oaf he was, and Mr. White
stood up. Words continued, Mr. Hendrix aware that he and Mr. White
were both talking at once. But the music made a blur in his ears and the
El Bravo Club swayed in front of his eyes. Then Mr. Hendrix realized, and
darkly, that the towering Mr. White's hand was on his collar and that he

was being lifted out of his seat. The El Bravo orchestra was rolling out a jazz finale, and nobody seemed to have noticed as yet the fracas taking place at this side table. As Mr. Hendrix felt himself being hoisted to his feet a sense of nausea and helplessness overcame him. He thrust his hand into his coat pocket.

"Calling me a liar, eh?" Mr. White was growling in the Hendrix ear. He added a number of epithets.

The little lawyer saw for an instant a fist pull back that never landed. Mr. Hendrix had removed a gun from his coat pocket, a gun of whose existence in his hand he was as unaware as he had been of the brass candlestick. The gun exploded, and Mr. White, with a look of suddenly sober astonishment, fell back into a chair. The music at this moment finished with a nanny-goat blare of trumpets. No heads turned. No waiters came rushing. Shaking as if his bones had turned into castanets, Mr. Hendrix stood looking at the crumpled athlete and watched his head sink over the table. The mouth was open. The athlete's fingers, hanging near the floor, were rigid.

Music started again, and Mr. Hendrix turned his eyes automatically toward the dance floor. Blue and pink floodlights were shining on it, and out from behind the orchestra shell came a line of almost naked girls. White legs kicked, smiles filled the air. Leading the chorus line Mr. Hendrix saw Carmen Browne. She was dancing.

The little lawyer grew sick. He shut his eyes. Then he opened them. They were full of pain and bewilderment. It was no hallucination. It was Brownie. Extending under her ear at the back of her head he saw strips of court plaster. She was alive and restored.

Mr. Hendrix knew exactly what had happened. The last time he had called her apartment the switchboard man, failing to recognize his liquor-thickened voice, had withheld the information he might have offered Mr. Hendrix—that Carmen Browne was alive, that she had summoned a doctor, that she had left the apartment.

And even as he was thinking of this tiny detail a hundred other details crowded into the Hendrix mind. He remembered his accusations to Brownie that she still loved Eddie White; his statement to Peggy Moore last week and this afternoon that he was too jealous to trust himself; his attack on Carmen Browne, his subsequent drunkenness, his idiotic antics in the movie theater—as if he were shadowing Eddie White—what else could his rushing in and rushing out mean? Everything Mr. Hendrix had accomplished since 4:02 this afternoon pointed only at one conclusion—that he hated Eddie White, that he had almost killed his sweetheart out of jealousy over White, that, still burning with this emotion, he had tracked White down and murdered him in cold blood.

Mr. Hendrix, during these brief moments staring at the crumpled athlete, wanted to scream, so macabre did all these events strike him, but his voice trailed off into a moan. What was this insane thing he had done for his client? Exonerated him! Mr. Hendrix, still shaking, slipped down into his chair. He, Lou Hendrix, the shining legal intelligence, had, like some Nemesis, convicted himself—and not of manslaughter, which might have been the verdict otherwise, but of premeditated murder in the first degree. There was no case. No defense was possible. There was nothing left to do but to flee like some thug.

Mr. Hendrix looked at his wrist. He had twenty minutes to make the ten o'clock train for Chicago. From Chicago he would travel to New Orleans and thence into Mexico. He had a wallet full of bills. The side exit of the El Bravo was ten feet away. But Mr. Hendrix, struggling to get to his feet, swayed and fell forward. The dozen drinks he had so shrewdly tossed down his gullet to help him act his part joined the hideous plot he had hatched against himself. He was too drunk, too dizzy to stand up and move quickly.

They found the little barrister hunched in his seat staring at the murdered athlete. The gun was still in his hand. Mr. Hendrix was mumbling passionlessly:

"Guilty. Guilty. Guilty."

ERNEST HEMINGWAY

The Capital of the World

MADRID is full of boys named Paco, which is the diminutive of the name Francisco, and there is a Madrid joke about a father who came to Madrid and inserted an advertisement in the personal columns

of *El Liberal* which said: PACO MEET ME AT HOTEL MONTANA NOON TUES-
DAY ALL IS FORGIVEN PAPA, and how a squadron of Guardia Civil had to
be called out to disperse the eight hundred young men who answered the
advertisement. But this Paco, who waited on table at the Pension Luarca,
had no father to forgive him, nor anything for the father to forgive. He
had two older sisters who were chambermaids at the Luarca, who had gotten their place through coming from the same small village as a former
Luarca chambermaid who had proven hard-working and honest and hence
given her village and its products a good name; and these sisters had paid
his way on the autobus to Madrid and gotten him his job as an apprentice
waiter. He came from a village in a part of Extremadura where conditions
were incredibly primitive, food scarce, and comforts unknown, and he had
worked hard ever since he could remember.

He was a well-built boy with very black, rather curly hair, good teeth,
and a skin that his sisters envied, and he had a ready and unpuzzled smile.
He was fast on his feet and did his work well and he loved his sisters, who
seemed beautiful and sophisticated; he loved Madrid, which was still an
unbelievable place, and he loved his work, which, done under bright
lights, with clean linen, the wearing of evening clothes, and abundant
food in the kitchen, seemed romantically beautiful.

There were from eight to a dozen other people who lived at the Luarca
and ate in the dining room, but for Paco, the youngest of the three waiters
who served at table, the only ones who really existed were the bullfighters.

Second-rate matadors lived at that pension because the address in the
Calle San Jeronimo was good, the food was excellent, and the room and
board was cheap. It is necessary for a bullfighter to give the appearance,
if not of prosperity, at least of respectability, since decorum and dignity
rank above courage as the virtues most highly prized in Spain, and bullfighters stayed at the Luarca until their last pesetas were gone. There is no
record of any bullfighter having left the Luarca for a better or more expensive hotel; second-rate bullfighters never became first-rate; but the descent from the Luarca was swift, since anyone could stay there who was
making anything at all and a bill was never presented to a guest unasked
until the woman who ran the place knew that the case was hopeless.

At this time there were three full matadors living at the Luarca as well
as two very good picadors and one excellent banderillero. The Luarca was
luxury for the picadors and the banderilleros who, with their families in
Seville, required lodging in Madrid during the spring season; but they

were well contracted during the coming season, and the three of these sub-
alterns would probably make much more apiece than any of the three
matadors. Of the three matadors one was ill and trying to conceal it, one
had passed his short vogue as a novelty, and the third was a coward.

The coward had at one time, until he had received a peculiarly atrocious
horn wound in the lower abdomen at the start of his first season as a full
matador, been exceptionally brave and remarkably skillful, and he still had
many of the hearty mannerisms of his days of success. He was jovial to
excess and laughed constantly with and without provocation. He had,
when successful, been very addicted to practical jokes, but he had given
them up now. They took an assurance that he did not feel. This matador
had an intelligent, very open face and he carried himself with much style.

The matador who was ill was careful never to show it and was meticu-
lous about eating a little of all the dishes that were presented at the table.
He had a great many handkerchiefs which he laundered himself in his
room, and lately he had been selling his fighting suits. He had sold one,
cheaply, before Christmas, and another in the first week of April. They
had been very expensive suits, had always been well kept, and he had one
more. Before he had become ill he had been a very promising, even a sen-
sational, fighter, and, while he himself could not read, he had clippings
which said that in his debut in Madrid he had been better than Belmonte.
He ate alone at a small table and looked up very little.

The matador who had once been a novelty was very short and brown
and very dignified. He also ate alone at a separate table, and he smiled
very rarely and never laughed. He came from Valladolid, where the people
are extremely serious, and he was a capable matador; but his style had
become old-fashioned before he had ever succeeded in endearing himself
to the public through his virtues, which were courage and a calm capability, and his name on a poster would draw no one to a bull ring. His novelty
had been that he was so short that he could barely see over the bull's
withers, but there were other short fighters, and he had never succeeded
in imposing himself on the public's fancy.

Of the picadors one was a thin, hawk-faced, gray-haired man, lightly
built but with legs and arms like iron, who always wore cattlemen's boots
under his trousers, drank too much every evening, and gazed amorously
at any woman in the pension. The other was huge, dark, brown-faced,
good-looking, with black hair like an Indian and enormous hands. Both
were great picadors, although the first was reputed to have lost much of

his ability through drink and dissipation, and the second was said to be too headstrong and quarrelsome to stay with any matador more than a single season.

The banderillero was middle-aged, gray, cat-quick in spite of his years, and, sitting at the table, he looked a moderately prosperous businessman. His legs were still good for this season, and when they should go he was intelligent and experienced enough to keep regularly employed for a long time. The difference would be that when his speed of foot would be gone he would always be frightened, where now he was assured and calm in the ring and out of it.

On this evening everyone had left the dining room except the hawk-faced picador who drank too much, the birthmarked-faced auctioneer of watches at the fairs and festivals of Spain, who also drank too much, and two priests from Galicia who were sitting at a corner table and drinking, if not too much, certainly enough. At this time wine was included in the price of the room and board at the Luarca, and the waiters had just brought fresh bottles of Valdepeñas to the tables of the auctioneer, then to the picador, and, finally, to the two priests.

The three waiters stood at the end of the room. It was the rule of the house that they should all remain on duty until the diners whose tables they were responsible for should all have left, but the one who served the table of the two priests had an appointment to go to an Anarcho-Syndicalist meeting, and Paco had agreed to take over his table for him.

Upstairs the matador who was ill was lying face down on his bed alone. The matador who was no longer a novelty was sitting looking out of his window preparatory to walking out to the café. The matador who was a coward had the older sister of Paco in his room with him and was trying to get her to do something which she was laughingly refusing to do. This matador was saying, "Come on, little savage."

"No," said the sister. "Why should I?"

"For a favor."

"You've eaten and now you want me for dessert."

"Just once. What harm can it do?"

"Leave me alone. Leave me alone, I tell you."

"It is a very little thing to do."

"Leave me alone, I tell you."

Down in the dining room the tallest of the waiters, who was overdue at the meeting, said, "Look at those black pigs drink."

"That's no way to speak," said the second waiter. "They are decent clients. They do not drink too much."

"For me it is a good way to speak," said the tall one. "There are the two curses of Spain, the bulls and the priests."

"Certainly not the individual bull and the individual priest," said the second waiter.

"Yes," said the tall waiter. "Only through the individual can you attack the class. It is necessary to kill the individual bull and the individual priest. All of them. Then there are no more."

"Save it for the meeting," said the other waiter.

"Look at the barbarity of Madrid," said the tall waiter. "It is now half past eleven o'clock and these are still guzzling."

"They only started to eat at ten," said the other waiter. "As you know, there are many dishes. That wine is cheap and these have paid for it. It is not a strong wine."

"How can there be solidarity of workers with fools like you?" asked the tall waiter.

"Look," said the second waiter, who was a man of fifty. "I have worked all my life. In all that remains of my life I must work. I have no complaints against work. To work is normal."

"Yes, but the lack of work kills."

"I have always worked," said the older waiter. "Go on to the meeting. There is no necessity to stay."

"You are a good comrade," said the tall waiter. "But you lack ideology."

"*Mejor si me falta eso que el otro,*" said the older waiter (meaning it is better to lack that than work). "Go on to the *mitin.*"

Paco had said nothing. He did not yet understand politics, but it always gave him a thrill to hear the tall waiter speak of the necessity for killing the priests and the Guardia Civil. The tall waiter represented to him revolution, and revolution also was romantic. He himself would like to be a good Catholic, a revolutionary, and have a steady job like this, while, at the same time, being a bullfighter.

"Go on to the meeting, Ignacio," he said. "I will respond for your work."

"The two of us," said the older waiter.

"There isn't enough for one," said Paco. "Go on to the meeting."

"*Pues, me voy,*" said the tall waiter. "And thanks."

In the meantime, upstairs, the sister of Paco had gotten out of the embrace of the matador as skillfully as a wrestler breaking a hold and said, now angry, "These are the hungry people. A failed bullfighter. With your ton-load of fear. If you have so much of that, use it in the ring."

"That is the way a whore talks."

"A whore is also a woman, but I am not a whore."

"You'll be one."

"Not through you."

"Leave me," said the matador, who now, repulsed and refused, felt the nakedness of his cowardice returning.

"Leave you? What hasn't left you?" said the sister. "Don't you want me to make up the bed? I'm paid to do that."

"Leave me," said the matador, his broad, good-looking face wrinkled into a contortion that was like crying. "You whore. You dirty little whore."

"Matador," she said, shutting the door. "My matador."

Inside the room the matador sat on the bed. His face still had the contortion which, in the ring, he made into a constant smile which frightened those people in the first rows of seats who knew what they were watching. "And this," he was saying aloud. "And this. And this."

He could remember when he had been good, and it had only been three years before. He could remember the weight of the heavy gold-brocaded fighting jacket on his shoulders on that hot afternoon in May when his voice had still been the same in the ring as in the café, and how he sighed along the point dipping blade at the place in the top of the shoulders where it was dusty in the short-haired black hump of muscle above the wide, wood-knocking, splintered-tipped horns that lowered as he went in to kill, and how the sword pushed in as easy as into a mound of stiff butter with the palm of his hand pushing the pommel, his left arm crossed low, his left shoulder forward, his weight on his left leg, and then his weight wasn't on his leg. His weight was on his lower belly, and as the bull raised his head the horn was out of sight in him and he swung over on it twice before they pulled him off it. So now when he went in to kill, and it was seldom, he could not look at the horns, and what did any whore know about what he went through before he fought? And what had they been through that laughed at him? They were all whores, and they knew what they could do with it.

Down in the dining room the picador sat looking at the priests. If there were women in the room he stared at them. If there were no women he would stare with enjoyment at a foreigner, *un inglés,* but, lacking women or strangers, he now stared with enjoyment and insolence at the two priests.

While he stared the birthmarked auctioneer rose and, folding his napkin, went out, leaving over half the wine in the last bottle he had ordered. If his accounts had been paid up at the Luarca he would have finished the bottle.

The two priests did not stare back at the picador. One of them was saying, "It is ten days since I have been here waiting to see him, and all day I sit in the antechamber and he will not receive me."

"What is there to do?"

"Nothing. What can one do? One cannot go against authority."

"I have been here for two weeks and nothing. I wait and they will not see me."

"We are from the abandoned country. When the money runs out we can return."

"To the abandoned country. What does Madrid care about Galicia? We are a poor province."

"One understands the action of our brother Basilio."

"Still I have no real confidence in the integrity of Basilio Alvarez."

"Madrid is where one learns to understand. Madrid kills Spain."

"If they would simply see one and refuse."

"No. You must be broken and worn out by waiting."

"Well, we shall see. I can wait as well as another."

At this moment the picador got to his feet, walked over to the priests' table and stood, gray-headed and hawk-faced, staring at them and smiling.

"A *torero*," said one priest to the other.

"And a good one," said the picador, and walked out of the dining room, gray-jacketed, trim-waisted, bowlegged, in tight breeches over his high-heeled cattleman's boots that clicked on the floor as he swaggered quite steadily, smiling to himself. He lived in a small, tight, professional world of personal efficiency, nightly alcoholic triumph, and insolence. Now he lit a cigar and, tilting his hat at an angle in the hallway, went out to the café.

The priests left immediately after the picador, hurriedly conscious of being the last people in the dining room, and there was no one in the room now but Paco and the middle-aged waiter. They cleared the tables and carried the bottles into the kitchen.

In the kitchen was the boy who washed the dishes. He was three years older than Paco and was very cynical and bitter.

"Take this," the middle-aged waiter said, and poured out a glass of the Valdepeñas and handed it to him.

"Why not?" The boy took the glass.

"*Tu*, Paco?" the older waiter asked.

"Thank you," said Paco. The three of them drank.

"I will be going," said the middle-aged waiter.

"Good night," they told him.

He went out and they were alone. Paco took a napkin one of the priests had used and, standing straight, his heels planted, lowered the napkin and, with head following the movement, swung his arms in the motion of a slow-sweeping veronica. He turned and, advancing his right foot slightly, made the second pass, gained a little terrain on the imaginary bull and made a third pass, slow, perfectly timed, and suave, then gathered the napkin to his waist and swung his hips away from the bull in a media-veronica.

The dishwasher, whose name was Enrique, watched him critically and sneeringly.

"How is the bull?" he said.

"Very brave," said Paco. "Look."

Standing slim and straight, he made four more perfect passes, smooth, elegant, and graceful.

"And the bull?" asked Enrique, standing against the sink, holding his wineglass and wearing his apron.

"Still has lots of gas," said Paco.

"You make me sick," said Enrique.

"Why?"

"Look."

Enrique removed his apron and, citing the imaginary bull, he sculptured four perfect, languid gypsy veronicas and ended up with a rebolera that made the apron swing in a stiff arc past the bull's nose as he walked away from him.

"Look at that," he said. "And I wash dishes."

"Why?"

"Fear," said Enrique. "*Miedo*. The same fear you would have in a ring with a bull."

"No," said Paco. "I wouldn't be afraid."

"*Leche!*" said Enrique. "Everyone is afraid. But a torero can control his fear so that he can work the bull. I went in an amateur fight, and I was so afraid I couldn't keep from running. Everyone thought it was very funny. So would you be afraid. If it wasn't for fear, every bootblack in Spain would be a bullfighter. You, a country boy, would be frightened worse than I was."

"No," said Paco.

He had done it too many times in his imagination. Too many times he had seen the horns, seen the bull's wet muzzle, the ear twitching, then the head go down and the charge, the hoofs thudding, and the hot bull pass him as he swung the cape, to recharge as he swung the cape again. Then again, and again, and again, to end winding the bull around him in his great media-veronica, and walk swingingly away, with bull hairs caught in the gold ornaments of his jacket from the close passes; the bull standing hypnotized and the crowd applauding. No, he would not be afraid. Others, yes. Not he. He knew he would not be afraid. Even if he ever was afraid he knew that he could do it anyway. He had confidence. "I wouldn't be afraid," he said.

Enrique said, *"Leche,"* again.

Then he said, "If we should try it."

"How?"

"Look," said Enrique. "You think of the bull but you do not think of the horns. The bull has such force that the horns rip like a knife, they stab like a bayonet, and they kill like a club. Look." He opened a table drawer and took out two meat knives. "I will bind these to the legs of a chair. Then I will play bull for you with the chair held before my head. The knives are the horns. If you make those passes, then they mean something."

"Lend me your apron," said Paco. "We'll do it in the dining room."

"No," said Enrique, suddenly not bitter. "Don't do it, Paco."

"Yes," said Paco. "I'm not afraid."

"You will be when you see the knives come."

"We'll see," said Paco. "Give me the apron."

At this time, while Enrique was binding the two heavy-bladed, razor-sharp meat knives fast to the legs of the chair with two soiled napkins holding the half of each knife, wrapping them tight and then knotting them, the two chambermaids, Paco's sisters, were on their way to the cinema to see Greta Garbo in *Anna Christie.* Of the two priests, one was sitting in his underwear reading his breviary and the other was wearing a nightshirt and saying the rosary. All the bullfighters except the one who was ill had made their evening appearance at the Café Fornos, where the big, dark-haired picador was playing billiards, the short, serious matador was sitting at a crowded table before a coffee and milk, along with a middle-aged banderillero and other serious workmen.

The drinking, gray-headed picador was sitting with a glass of cazalas brandy before him, staring with pleasure at a table where the matador whose courage was gone sat with another matador who had renounced the sword to become a banderillero again and two very houseworn-looking prostitutes.

The auctioneer stood on the street corner talking with friends. The tall waiter was at the Anarcho-Syndicalist meeting waiting for an opportunity to speak. The middle-aged waiter was seated on the terrace of the Café Alvarez drinking a small beer. The woman who owned the Luarca was already asleep in her bed, where she lay on her back with the bolster between her legs; big, fat, honest, clean, easygoing, very religious, and never having ceased to miss or pray daily for her husband, dead, now, twenty years. In his room, alone, the matador who was ill lay face down on his bed with his mouth against a handkerchief.

Now, in the deserted dining room, Enrique tied the last knot in the napkins that bound the knives to the chair legs and lifted the chair. He pointed the legs with the knives on them forward and held the chair over his head with the two knives pointing straight ahead, one on each side of his head.

"It's heavy," he said. "Look, Paco. It is very dangerous. Don't do it." He was sweating.

Paco stood facing him, holding the apron spread, holding a fold of it bunched in each hand, thumbs up, first finger down, spread to catch the eye of the bull.

"Charge straight," he said. "Turn like a bull. Charge as many times as you want."

"How will you know when to cut the pass?" asked Enrique. "It's better to do three and then a media."

"All right," said Paco. "But come straight. *Hugh, torito!* Come on, little bull!"

Running with head down, Enrique came toward him, and Paco swung the apron just ahead of the knife blade as it passed close in front of his belly, and as it went by it was, to him, the real horn, white-tipped, black,

smooth, and as Enrique passed him and turned to rush again it was the
hot, blood-flanked mass of the bull that thudded by, then turned like a
cat and came again as he swung the cape slowly. Then the bull turned
and came again, and, as he watched the onrushing point, he stepped his
left foot two inches too far forward and the knife did not pass, but had
slipped in as easily as into a wineskin, and there was a hot, scalding
rush above and around the sudden inner rigidity of steel and Enrique
shouting, "Ay! Ay! Let me get it out! Let me get it out!" and Paco slipped
forward on the chair, the apron cape still held, Enrique pulling on the
chair as the knife turned in him, in him, Paco.

The knife was out now, and he sat on the floor in the widening warm
pool.

"Put the napkin over it. Hold it!" said Enrique. "Hold it tight. I will run
for the doctor. You must hold in the hemorrhage."

"There should be a rubber cup," said Paco. He had seen that used in
the ring.

"I came straight," said Enrique, crying. "All I wanted was to show the
danger."

"Don't worry," said Paco, his voice sounding far away. "But bring the
doctor."

In the ring they lifted you and carried you, running with you, to the
operating room. If the femoral artery emptied itself before you reached
there, they called the priest.

"Advise one of the priests," said Paco, holding the napkin tight against
his lower abdomen. He could not believe that this had happened to him.

But Enrique was running down the Carrera San Jeronimo to the all-
night first-aid station, and Paco was alone, first sitting up, then huddled
over, then slumped on the floor, until it was over, feeling his life go out
of him as dirty water empties from a bathtub when the plug is drawn.
He was frightened and he felt faint, and he tried to say an act of contrition and he remembered how it started, but before he had said, as fast
as he could, "Oh, my God, I am heartily sorry for having offended Thee
who art worthy of all my love and I firmly resolve . . ." he felt too
faint, and he was lying face down on the floor and it was over very quietly.
A severed femoral artery empties itself faster than you can believe.

As the doctor from the first-aid station came up the stairs accompanied
by a policeman who held on to Enrique by the arm, the two sisters of
Paco were still in the moving-picture palace of the Gran Vía, where they

were intensely disappointed in the Garbo film, which showed the great star in miserable low surroundings when they had been accustomed to see her surrounded by great luxury and brilliance. The audience disliked the film thoroughly and were protesting by whistling and stamping their feet. All the other people from the hotel were doing almost what they had been doing when the accident happened, except that the two priests had finished their devotions and were preparing for sleep, and the gray-haired picador had moved his drink over to the table with the two houseworn prostitutes. A little later he went out of the café with one of them. It was the one for whom the matador who had lost his nerve had been buying drinks.

The boy Paco had never known about any of this nor about what all these people would be doing on the next day and on other days to come. He had no idea how they really lived nor how they ended. He did not even realize they ended. He died, as the Spanish phrase has it, full of illusions. He had not had time in his life to lose any of them, nor even, at the end, to complete an act of contrition.

He had not even had time to be disappointed in the Garbo picture which disappointed all Madrid for a week.

JOSEPH HERGESHEIMER

Triall by Armes

VIEWING HERSELF CAREFULLY in that stupendous mirror, she could yet discover nothing new or illuminating. Her features were not good—her nose, for example—they were not harmonious, and yet together they had not prevented the accomplishment of a very great deal. Really an enormous lot . . . and they seemed to have brought her more than a little trouble. It was the trouble that now concerned her. She turned slowly and faced her father-in-law. He was lighting a cigarette in his precise, despotic manner. "The question is," he said precisely, "if you want such a mirror in your dining room? Wouldn't it be better in the hall? I think so." The dining room, repeated in the glass which reached to the far ceiling, filling the wall between two far-removed windows, seemed absolutely endless, like a plain, a whole county, in the French taste.

"It does make it rather huge," she agreed.

But that wasn't important. It was spring, at last a really warm day, but she was oddly cold. She wanted to smoke—it could be a very useful act of defense—but she had left her cigarette case in another room, and she was incapable just then of searching for it. Even the effort of sending for it was beyond her. She couldn't, at that moment, explain her need to Mr. James Moderan. She was cold, the whole truth was, with fear. She had just recognized it. It was a quality she'd had very little knowledge of, and it left her decidedly sick. Like a weight, a cold weight of iron, in her stomach. But she would have to say something. "You're right, of course; but then you always are. About things like that. It would be better in the hall."

"About things like that?" He repeated her words in the form of an inquiry. "Aren't you limiting me just a little?" All she could think of in reply was—perhaps. She didn't say it. She was too tired, and then it would sound rude. It wasn't easy even for her to be rude to him. He dealt with that very finally and well. Yet God knew there was every reason why she—— After all, it would be perfectly reasonable if she left the room, his presence, forever. Forever. But, of course, she wasn't like that. She didn't want to be. It was so foolish. Still, something must be done. Purely for herself. And that surprised her. She had done so much for herself in the last year that to have to begin again so soon was disconcerting.

The man beside her was apparently lost in light and pleasant thought. He seemed to be the most remote, the most impersonal figure in the world. An idiotic impulse seized her to laugh; she wanted to laugh until even that immense room was completely filled with the sound of her scoffing mirth. For one thing, she was so very young. So ridiculously young. If she had been older, ten years older, thirty that was, the whole situation would be easier. Unimportant. Then she wouldn't have cared. But now it was harder than hell. Because she wanted something very positively. She wanted that something and not at all the other.

She knew what it was, too, and it was happiness. She had determined when she married—with her husband's feminine voice in her ears—to be happy. She even knew how to bring that about. By simplicity. She'd make her life up out of pleasant details never in conflict with its main accepted fact. In short she had determined to be rather old-fashioned—not because of the implied morality but because she decided that it was intelligent. The way to be happy. It all lay in the region of her mind, she had thought; a part of mere conduct and reason. But now her mental security was gone and its place taken by fear.

"I am getting some champagne," her father-in-law said. "I really need it. Will you have a glass? You know that I like you to be cheerful. I mean there is no good reason why you shouldn't." He took her hand casually, quite paternally, in fact. For the moment.

"No champagne, thanks," she answered clearly. "Somehow I've never liked it in daytime. I think it belongs to dinner, or afterward, but not before."

He said seriously that there was a question if champagne, or any other charged wine, was proper at all for dinner. "You never see it in France," he said. "At least you never did. Now you can see anything anywhere."

With that silently she agreed. Anything. It occurred to her that she might speak to him, at length, and carefully explain what was in her mind. Not about champagne. But she gave that idea, that hope, up at once. It would be no good. He'd pay no attention to her. He wouldn't believe her And then she couldn't tell him what was in her—her heart. It would all sound ridiculously ancient and unconvincing. It was, in view of the rest, even a little unconvincing and ridiculous to her. She wasn't quite the person, her situation wasn't quite the situation, for such feelings. They belonged to a different society. Definitely. She walked to a window. Turned her back on the room.

Below her the formal sunken gardens reached uninterrupted for more than half a mile to James Moderan's great house. At that distance it still showed itself to be immense, a gray immensity, formal and French. Between it and where she lived with Provost there were fountains sheeted in silver spray, broad graveled walks in geometrical patterns, close-cut turf, walls with urns and flights of steps and statues, and endless stiff bands and circles of flowers. Now mostly tulips. Orderly purple hedges of lilacs. Below her she mechanically counted fourteen gardeners busy setting in boxwood. Four carried each piece, its roots and earth carefully bagged, and put it in the prepared trench.

But it wasn't, she protested to herself, the Moderan money that threatened to overwhelm her. She hoped she wasn't as vulgar as that. And, after all, she had never been poor. Everyone in Canton who knew of him allowed her father his million. In reality they were looked on as rich. Only, of course, in the sense of the Moderans, they had no money at all. Simply none. The Moderans had so much that in effect it retired upon itself, it defeated its own bulk and vanished. In connection with it she could discover no sign of sheer possession. It was without limit and without form. It allowed no desires and no acquisitions. The money seemed to create things automatically outside of her wishes or needs. Dinners and dresses and motors and miles of gardens. There were around her boxwood mazes and pools and bowling greens and orchards, wall gardens and herb gardens and meadows just now gay with lambs, fields with brush-and-rail jumps and a track, groves of trees and too many buildings to remember. And against the Moderan money it was all rather less than nothing.

That was what confused her—the damned money was never apparent. It was a power, vague and limitless, rather than a reality. It couldn't be blamed or even talked about. To her, beyond such a formless realization, it had no substance. It meant nothing. It couldn't charm or seduce or reward her. It didn't even influence her. Except in its own strange way. She heard the servant come into the room and put down the tray with the champagne. "You won't change your mind?" her father-in-law suggested.

"Thank you, no. Do you mind very much if I look out the window?" she continued politely. "I have to see as far as possible."

He didn't, naturally. He stood beside her, so close that their shoulders nearly touched, a glass in his hand. "The box will look rather well there," he went on; "although it will have to be kept down to a foot high."

Suddenly she asked: "What was your father like? I'm so sorry he died before I could know him. When I look at all this I'm apt to think about him."

James Moderan said that his father had been a remarkable man. It wasn't, she thought, a remarkable description. "But I seem to find that you are always a little unfair to me. It's unfair to look at the gardens with my father in your head. He had nothing to do with them. He had no need for them.

"He deserves a great deal of credit but not all the credit. You could spare me some, a little, with justice. My dear child, his generation, his opportunities, were different from mine. And I believe it is even a greater responsibility to have money than to make it. Certainly it's more difficult. When he began there was only America, only the American market, to consider. I have the world. Then there is the world of beauty, and no one will deny that I've added to that."

"Of course not," she answered absent-mindedly. She was concerned by nothing he had said. The sense of dread was almost a tangible thing in her throat. More than half a mile of sunken gardens. The tulips were like ribbons laid on the grass, against the walls. The fountains wore silver veils like brides. Why, then, had she married Provost? But that wasn't important now. She mustn't get lost in a useless questioning. Perhaps she was wrong to bother. Perhaps her feelings were no better than conventional. The result of a large ignorance of actual life. Why did she bother?

Very well, then, she wouldn't; she'd stop acting like a child out of a Sunday-school book. She would be hard. That was the thing. It was the thing to be hard. Life was like a game, and she must play it as well, as coldly, as possible. She must match what she was against life and in that get as much as possible. Anyhow, she had begun splendidly. Married to Provost Moderan. Even if he had a feminine voice. Hands more flexible, softer, than hers. She could be stiff enough for both. But she must be more practical. For example, she must discover what it was that she was afraid of——

Why, it was herself! Could anything be more absurd? More ridiculous? It wasn't what the Moderans had or were, but just herself. That was, she had a few qualities she knew of, two or three determinations that gave her confidence; but outside of them she was ignorant. There were intimations of things in her that were distantly disturbing. She didn't know them by name, she couldn't single them out and regard them severely. She only realized them in the form of premonitions. Afterthoughts. It was extraordinarily dark inside of her. Against that she had put all she did know. She had backed it to win. And now it struck her sharply that she was in the rotten position of pulling a race.

She was amazed to find such a large and unexplored world within the narrow limits of her own body. She weighed a hundred and fourteen. Why, Columbus and Magellan might easily get lost in her. Never find the safety of the lands they looked for. She had scarcely put a foot into her own being. For that reason she rather hated to let go what she was almost certain of. Rather she wanted to make a good race. She had hardly started and already she was thinking of not riding. "That won't do," she said in a voice so unexpectedly clear and loud that it startled her. It had the sound of a cry for help.

"I don't know what it is that won't do," James Moderan said; "you've grown so secretive with me. But at least there is no doubt in your mind about it." Obviously she could add nothing but a nod to that. Since she couldn't go on with an explanation. The determination to be hard, reasonable, had left her; but whether it had been defeated by a contrary decision or the fear, she didn't know. But that, too, was unimportant. At present the fear, the dread of herself, was uppermost. Very well, then, she'd have to meet it. Discover more about it. All that was possible. It wasn't enough simply to realize there were parts of her she was uncertain of. Possibilities she couldn't predict. No, just that couldn't help her. Yet, even to herself, she couldn't put her exact position into words. It was so ugly. Anyhow, yet, it had no reality. It no more than threatened her.

To put it into words would give it too much importance. Too much reality. To put it into words, as a matter of fact, might give it reality. She felt that she didn't want to have it in her head. Pronounced. The thing to do, naturally, was laugh it off. Laugh it all off. If she could only be sure of doing that—of getting away with it—everything would be splendid again. But of course. However, she wasn't certain of succeeding. If she were, there could be no trouble. No fear. But she wasn't. And then if it had simply been a situation—like a situation in a book—she felt she could have met it. She would simply say so-and-so and so-and-so, and it would be over. But it wasn't clear like that. It was vague, like a storm just gathering above the horizon. Like the Moderan money. It might be nothing or it might leave the gardens and the houses in a broken tangle. The worst might pass directly over her, happen to her, and leave her untouched. She didn't know.

"Provost loves beauty too," she said, returning to James Moderan's explanation of himself.

He regarded her intently. "Yes," he admitted at last. "But Provost is even farther from the source than I am."

That, she recognized, was a devastating remark. Not the sort of thing a parent said. It had the detached air of having been spoken by one man about another. Just two men. It was even a little sharper than that. Instinctively she wanted to combat it, but she didn't know how. He had been so very searching. There was so much truth in what he had said. She could only acknowledge it. But she was a shade impatient.

"I know that," she told him. "But he might be farther from the source and nearer beauty, mightn't he? I mean in a sort of scale with you in the middle and your father and Provost at each end."

He laughed. "You didn't choose much of a position for my father. And after showing such a great interest in him." He touched her shoulder with his fingers. Very lightly. "Aren't you rather letting yourself get into what, I believe, is called a state? A little crosspatch. You mustn't be that, do you see?"

She turned and gazed intently into his face. Her body was tense with a repressed indignation. There was a pressure of words against her lips, but she kept them tightly closed. Silent. She felt that if she spoke now it would be fatal. Any advantage, any safety she still had might be lost. Forever. Always. She had an appalling momentary understanding of what always meant. It came and went like lightning and left her numbed. She was so harassed that she smiled at him. A smile like a whispered appeal. Faint. At the same time she moved back. And that left her arms out. In air. A gesture tired like her smile, and not longer in duration.

There were footsteps, and, to her enormous relief, she saw that it was Provost. He came directly up to them. "Anette," he said in a high-pitched excitement, "I stopped to see the baby, and I don't like the trained nurse we have at all. I really don't. She has hands like God knows what. She's too clumsy. I think we ought to get rid of her." If only he hadn't begun about, chosen, the nurse.

"She's very good, as a matter of fact," she replied. "Elinor had her for a year and thinks she couldn't be better. Anyhow, Provost, you mustn't bother about things like that. I can do them. I really can. You'd be surprised."

Provost Moderan dropped his hand inside her arm. "I don't doubt it," he assured her; "but I watched this woman, and she can't even tie a ribbon. She'll end by tearing everything. Don't you think we could get someone more sensitive?"

"We might, but I'm not going to try. I have perfect confidence in the one we have." She pressed his hand against her side. "Don't worry about ribbons." Suddenly she released herself and went out through a convenient door to the terrace. The sunlight was pale but distinctly warm, and yet she was cold. Stone steps led down to the sod, and she sat on them with her back definitely to the house. If only Provost hadn't complained about the nurse just then! However, being unfair to Provost would get her nowhere. She returned to herself:

To put it plainly, what was the matter with her? Did she, without realizing it, show some dreadful lack? Perhaps she was wrong. Perhaps she had always been wrong. Then it was hopeless. But she didn't quite think so. Not altogether. Very well, on the definite side—what was it, what was the happiness, she wanted? No, she had answered that. How could she get it? How could she be sure of it? At last she had asked herself an intelligent question. In the first place she had taken for granted that every possibility lay within her. She had depended, as usual, upon her own self. Exclusively. She'd had complete confidence in what she had called her character. She wasn't a weak person.

Now, she sharply realized, that wasn't enough. The truth was that she wanted something outside of herself. She was finding out that she couldn't stand alone. Tremendous discovery. She had always consciously thought of life in the terms of entire independence. And until now it had worked. Certainly it had worked in Canton, Ohio, and on the Maine coast: here and there she had picked out of life what she wanted, what attracted her, and added it to an amusing whole. She had composed her existence in the manner of a landscape painter, selected the colors and time of day, the background and the figures in the foreground. Specially the figures in the foreground. But it had all been exterior to her. A deliberate canvas. In return she had given a bright attention and uncertain presence. Noncommittal. Untouched, she had been enormously self-confident. Self-sufficient.

She had been until now entirely successful. But now, in the face of disaster, her confidence was leaving her. Her assurance had almost reached the vanishing point. She felt horribly lonely. If—for years—she had cried, she thought she could cry now. But at least there was no danger of that. I can't go on like this, she said to herself. Anyhow, that was something positive. A gain. But if she couldn't, what could she go on with? What was it that would make such a difference to her? A possible answer came into her mind, but it was so absurd, so stupid, that she disregarded it at once. She had thought of Provost.

In times of great difficulty a girl was supposed to turn to her parents. It was held to be the approved, the safe thing to do. And that, the idea of turning to her mother and father, now made her smile. A long while ago, ten years ago at least, she had stopped doing that. Even then it was useless. A nuisance. Her mother was so utterly different from her. A half of what was in her thoughts would have shocked her mother into a frenzy. Or at least she would have pretended the distress. Gone to bed. Oh, at once. Her mother's attitude toward life was very picturesque and innocent. Although the innocence had a peculiar quality. It wasn't always convincing. But it was maintained on the surface at any cost. With the greatest verbal extravagance. Looking back over their later contact, she realized that her mother's attitude toward her affairs, her daughter's affairs, had been dominated by a kind of questionable curiosity. Her mother got, she thought, a vicarious excitement out of her child's beginning experience. For that reason principally she had told her nothing.

Her mother showed the effects of an early and distinctly inferior social level. Life attracted and shocked her at the same time. She contradicted her feelings, her curiosity, by her words. She now talked incessantly about how few clothes women wore. Yes, she was like that. It was the same with regard to what she called society. She read everything the papers printed about, for example, the Moderans, and made sharp remarks about their divorces. The way they lived. But she never missed a notice. Her father was different:

The most evident thing about him was that he was frightfully bored at home. With his wife. But then he managed to be home very little. It was often necessary for him to go to Chicago or New York. He was quite possible-looking, quite young-looking, and she was certain that, away from Canton, he had a big time. The biggest imaginable. She could tell—if her mother couldn't—when he had been drinking. But at home he was conventional and dull and inattentive. He rather liked his younger daughter the best. At least he talked more to her, gave her more money. For example, he practically never had friends for dinner. At his house. The men almost never, and the women, naturally, not at all. When there was a formal dinner, a party, he was well enough; a little too pleasant, a shade too loud, and dull.

But all that, where she was concerned, had changed when she got engaged to Provost Moderan. Actually, her mother had grown afraid of her, and her father polite. He held long, meaningless conversations with her about God knew what. He recited to everyone, with enormous satisfaction, the homely history of the first Moderan to become imposing. "A plain man," he always said. He usually added that he hoped his daughter, in such luxurious circumstances, would keep on in the way she had been brought up. Of course he didn't. It was a lie. He wanted her to be continually in the papers. Draped with pearls. In England at a drawing room.

Drinking champagne at smart watering places. That was what he secretly wanted. Perhaps he even hoped she might introduce him to celebrated and very gay ladies.

Her mother, naturally, was worse. She continually referred to Provost and continually mispronounced his name. She had bought for her the most impossible sheer nightgowns. Nightgowns which, at the first opportunity, had gone to servants. Her mother had got for herself an extremely expensive town car and attempted a buffet breakfast, in the manner of the Moderans and England. She was certain that if Provost hadn't wanted to marry her, then her mother would not have seriously interfered with a more informal arrangement——

No, she couldn't go there for advice. For help. Perhaps she had been unfair. Too bitter. Her mother and father, actually, were very generally liked. It might be enough to say that they didn't understand her. They could have no idea of the life she had become a part of. They were useless. And with that she dismissed them. But the thought of Provost returned. It had been her intention to be very correct, very patient with him. She had thought this could be done by an effort of the will. Her will. She had seen their life together entirely as an arrangement of her own tact and determination. It was all to be a result of her own cleverness. This had been when her self-assurance was still unimpaired. When she had been certain of herself. She had really asked for nothing—certainly nothing like help—from Provost.

She had, she realized, accepted him as an obligation. She was intensely grateful to him, she felt she loved him; but all her responsibility had seemed to consist in watching and giving. She was the managing force.

When now she was considering going to him for assistance. Admitting that she was insufficient. She had thought of it, but of course it couldn't be done. It would be too dreadful. How could she put it in words? Yet she began to see that she had something very definite invested in Provost. He was like a bank where she had put a great deal of money. It wouldn't do for him to fail. This was a new attitude, a new conception of her marriage, and it amazed her. Why, she was married to Provost. He was hers. They'd had a child!

She wanted, she began to see, to admire him. To have a feeling not limited by his voice, the extreme flexibility of his wrists. She wanted, in short, someone other than herself she could depend on. Turn to. Her self-sufficiency, it seemed, had gone with a crash. She wanted to go to

Provost! And the great difficulty of her position was that she couldn't. It was impossible. Unthinkable. What engaged her was the further discovery that no one else would do. Not within the terms she had decided for herself. For her life. Someone later, perhaps. It might be a very definite, a very able someone. But that couldn't happen until what she was, what desperately she wanted to be, had died.

She looked out into the incredible extended beauty of the sunken garden. The fourteen gardeners had finished setting the boxwood hedge and they were walking soberly off. They were followed by trails of smoke from short, blackened pipes. Far away, on a terrace, there was a small activity—servants in short white coats with silver buttons arranging the tea table. Mrs. James Moderan always, in summer, had tea at that spot. At the hour of five. She lived that way, within an intricate timed schedule of events which she never ignored. Her appearances, her movements, were like the advertised, the perfectly planned appearances of a famous actress. They were as good as that, as effective, and as really meaningless. As James Moderan's wife she was magnificent. But you couldn't go to her. See her informally. She'd give you all the time you needed, listen attentively, with her fixed, comprehending smile. What good was that?

A shadow was widening down the length of the garden. Where it fell the sod was quite blue. The red-petaled tulips were like rubies. There was a shadow over the far activity of the tea table. She could see white dresses. The minute notes of hats. Servants in white and silver. On the left there was an impressive grove of oak trees. Bathed in an amber and still light. Not a leaf stirred. In imagination she felt the thick wetness of the sod. She knew where, in the meadow, there was a pale lavender sweep of quaker-ladies. Buttercups would be along. Water cress in the beds of the streams and mint under the banks. She liked the cool smell of mint and the secret smell of boxwood better than the scent of roses. Oh, infinitely better. She was really very nice, and it was too damned bad. To have it lost. Spoiled. She really wanted to do the nicest things. She liked little things—the quaker-ladies, for example.

None of the Moderans knew he had quaker-ladies. They simply never saw them. But then they were just as indifferent to the orchards. To their deer and their rare—and screamingly funny—water birds. She supposed they couldn't be aware of everything. There was so hideously much. She didn't love Provost, but she wanted to. That, at last, was the truth. She terribly needed to. Love, she discovered, was something you gave. Quite different from admirable conduct. Quite. You gave it, although it was an inseparable part of you, and naturally the giving hurt like hell. You gave yourself. That was it. A present. But you gave to something, someone, that could hold you. A feminine voice! Weak hands weren't so good for that. If she gave herself to Provost, really, could he hold her—against her fear? And could she do it? She meant was it possible against the present circumstances? Could she put it into words . . . to Provost?

It would be too awful. Very well, what else was there to hold her firm —safe—safely to the very little she recognized—the cherished determinations formed in ignorance and trust? Nothing. Simply nothing. It was Provost or nothing. A small quirk of bitterness ran through her. Why didn't Provost do something? Why didn't he demand her—all of her? How feminine, how sufficient without her, was he? An enormous danger was squarely before them, and he was sublimely ignorant of it. Or perhaps he wouldn't care. It might be that he had very little pride of that sort. Lord, she hoped he had! And while she might give him her love she couldn't give what she needed from him. That had to be Provost. Like a rope in a swift current. A current too swift for her without help.

How much of his grandfather—a plain man—was in him? James Moderan had intimated that he was far from the source. But was he too far? Wasn't anything left? The trouble was that if she did turn to him and it was a failure, it would be all over. Definitely. She could see, then, her following impatience. An impatience soon careless. She didn't like Mrs. James Moderan. She was too perfect. Good-by, Anette, she whispered. It was too bad when she had been so nice. But it wasn't over yet. Not altogether. There was Provost. Was it better to jump and perhaps land on the far, safe bank, or slide slowly into the water—the mud? Her instinct naturally was to jump. If only the details could have been different, there would have been no doubt in her mind. No difficulty. How could she express it? By the truth. But the truth included so much. So many people. Probably they would all regard it as no more than an impertinence. That aspect of the truth they had condemned forever as bad taste.

Someone came up behind her. It was Provost. "Where is your father?" she asked.

"He's sending some telegrams. The place here was closed and he had to telephone them to the city." He sat beside her. "Aren't the gardens sweet?" Provost went on. "And I can see that tea is on. As usual. I don't know how Mother does it. Everything is so exact, I mean. The truth is, she works like the devil. No rest. I don't see why she does it. Really. And she never makes a mistake—with names and all that—not one little mistake." At least he hadn't said tiny. That was in their favor. "Anette, you're so different. You do what suits you, and if they like it they can come along. If you see what I mean. You couldn't be funnier. I watch you all the time and I'm practically in spasms. The way you won't be influenced. You'll be yourself or absolutely nothing. The liberty bell is nothing."

"That sounds disagreeable," she observed. "As if I didn't realize there was any responsibility except myself. I'm trying to realize that more than anything else. Just now. I mean I've got to. I hope I will, Provost."

She would, of course, he replied. Provost patted her reassuringly on the arm. "Good girl. Everyone approves of you. I hear them talking about it, do you see? I think you are quite all right."

"Do you?" she said. "Really. That's a great help. I used to think I didn't need help. But I've changed my mind. I——" She stopped sharply, appalled by what she might say, where it might lead her. All of them. There were no words for what she wanted to tell him. Ask. Why, he might hate her. Oh, but very easily. Leave her. Outraged. When it should be she. But if he might kill the fear in her, it would be worth any risk. If he could. Were able. A question returned in a slightly new form. How much did Provost love her? Money, in great amounts, as a matter of fact, came between people. It made other people, more amusing or exciting people, so terribly easy to get. She had watched it with Provost at dinners. Parties. It held so much that it destroyed special, particular, things. Things like love, for example. It substituted simply everything outside for the few doubtful, the obscured, things within. The things within were such a bother. They required so much hard thought. Resolution. Then, too, no one was interested or helped you with them. They were a nuisance to other people.

With money you could take a fast car, or a faster private train, and get away. And you did. Oftener than not. And quite right, too, if you felt like that about it. Love rather stayed around the house. She could see that clearly. You had babies and saw that the windows were washed. The windows behind her were immaculate. But she had nothing to do with it. Nothing in the world. If she went away they would still be immaculate. She didn't even have to speak about it. A housekeeper did that. She could discharge the housekeeper, but she knew she wouldn't. What was the use? There were more amusing things to do than bother about windows. Ordering. All she did now was to say there would be ten for dinner. Or twenty.

Or two thousand. That was all. And she liked it that way. But love was different.

"You're pretty quiet," Provost said. "It's rather unnatural."

"I was thinking about money," she admitted.

"I hope you don't want any. I haven't had more than two dollars in my pocket for a week." He found a crumpled dollar bill, two quarters, a nickel, and some pennies. He dropped it into her lap. "Just like that. I'm a pretty generous husband, you'll find."

She returned it to him. "Don't be foolish. You'll need it for rent or the milk or something. I might waste it on silk stockings." Provost asked how much silk stockings did cost. She had no idea. "Those thick ones for golf were—— No, I can't remember."

"How about the ones with the panels of Venise rose point?"

"Don't, Provost," she begged him.

"There you make me quite a little sick," he replied. "That was a dreadful place you were brought up in. You have an idea it's a disgrace for a man to know about rose point. It's fearfully robust, of course, but silly. I wish I could get it out of your head."

"Well, I was thinking about money. Rather, what it did to you."

"You'll never have to bother about that."

"You're wrong," she said earnestly. Her fear turned into an acute fright. Fright at what she might say. She had a feeling that the situation was getting beyond her control. God, she hoped the rope would hold her. "It wasn't the silk stockings," she continued. "Different from that. A great deal more important. At least for me. I was thinking that after a certain amount money stopped being just money. It was something different. Power, perhaps. Like water changing to steam. Water changing into steam." She repeated that. It was so true. It expressed so exactly what she meant.

"And steam is dangerous," she added gravely. "It blows up things. Money is dangerous. I didn't suppose it was, but it is. I thought I could get away with it very nicely. A jump in a paddock. I've been patting myself on the back. The garden is sweet, Provost." He nodded, obviously surprised. "But, do you see, it's getting to be all in shadow? Even the youngest, the reddest, tulips. Yes, I thought I was quite able. That it was easy."

"Listen," Provost interrupted, "get somewhere. I don't care what it is, but reach it. In a little, if you keep on, I'll be crazy. I will. You've got a prayer-meeting sort of voice, and I haven't an idea what it is you are saying. Have you been buying some bad stock or just some subscription books from a bird at the door?"

"Don't interrupt," she warned him. "It's serious." He could see that, he added. "I'd like to be happy, Provost." Her voice had intimations of a wail. "I don't want to be upset. Changed. Not any. You see, I am now. Or at least I was. And I'd made up my mind how to do it. I thought it out before our wedding. Provost, I didn't marry you for money, but I wouldn't have married you without it. That's as clearly as I can say it. As honest. But I did have a decided feeling about you, too. Or it would have been impossible."

"I think you'd better stop," he told her. "I hate soul searching. Besides, it's so useless. Specially nonsense like this. Sheer nonsense." He grew shrilly indignant. "You married me, and that's enough. After all, I didn't find you outside a café. You didn't need money. You had plenty. And I don't want to listen to this. I know you're honest without it. And if you're getting around to something disagreeable, I wish you wouldn't. You don't want to leave me?" She smiled directly into his eyes. "Well, then, go to hell with it. Will you? And stop reading confession magazines."

He turned a little away from her. Almost sulky. Provost was really very good-looking. Delicate, of course, very fair, but good-looking. She couldn't imagine better clothes. Except for his socks, and they were too fragile a rose. He was young, too. She had forgotten to allow for that. Twenty-five. Perhaps he was too young for complete dependence. Perhaps, wanting to, he wouldn't be able to help her. It would take a great deal of understanding. Balance. The odds against them, against their ages, were frightfully long.

"Sometimes I have the strangest feeling about your father," she said. "He doesn't seem real to me. I mean the way you do. He's like a force instead of a person. He's so perfect where he is. With so much. No one else in the world could do it as well. Your mother is marvelous, of course. But he doesn't make the slightest effort. It's all so easy. So perfect. Do you know, I have never seen him with new clothes on. He must buy them. I can't think how he manages. His riding breeches. The polish on his boots. It's like preserved quinces. And then his manner, Provost. He takes everything for granted." She fell into a little silence. "Everything," she repeated. Although it was audible, the word was addressed to no one. To herself.

"I know what you mean," he agreed. "Lots of people feel that way about him. The way it affects me, you'll be surprised to know, is that it keeps me away from him. I never get near him. Not really. He won't let me. Or he can't. That's better. Anette, I wouldn't say this to anyone else, he's frozen by what he has. Or what he is——"

"Frozen," she interrupted him. "Oh, do you think so?"

"I know just what you mean," he reiterated. "He's like the thing that controls an enormous power. A switch. He puts it on and off. Anette, I don't believe he has a particle of feeling. Except perhaps for himself. And I've never seen that. He is always quite calm. Telling people what to do. He never does things himself. I don't mean that. He must. But you'd never guess it. I've seen him drink two quarts of champagne. But no one would have guessed it. It didn't do anybody any good. He was just a little quieter than usual." Provost fell silent. Then, "I wonder," he said. "I wonder?" She asked what he was wondering, but he only shook his head. "Little girls . . ." he told her, leaving his implication at once suspended and clear. "Damn it, he can't be a Puritan," Provost burst out. "He can't be. But no one, simply no one, gets a thing on him. I've watched him, but it's useless. He likes all the pretty ones. He's perfectly grand to them . . . all. He gives them beautiful presents, you know that, but just because they're a part of the picture."

"You'll remember I met your father before you," she proceeded. "When I was at French Lick. And he was divine to me. I almost always had his car, and he was almost never in it. Then when you came with the Fannings he had me to dinner the first night. He put us together. Provost, it was your father who married us! We really had nothing to do with it. I never realized that before, and you can't think how relieved I am. Do you see, I wasn't mercenary. I had nothing to do with it. You had nothing to do with it. Your mother didn't either. Since she wasn't there."

"Very well, then," Provost replied. "Why did he? Can you tell me? A small thing like that might explain him. I mean, Anette, to be perfectly frank, there were other girls you'd think he would back first. Girls near us here. People he's always known. You'd think he'd want an older wife with what was coming. Want me to wait." She said:

"He liked me, Provost."

Provost was impatient. "What's that got to do with it? We were talking about something really important to him."

"He liked me, Provost," she repeated.

There was a long silence. Except, where she was concerned, for the loud beating of her heart. Her fear grew into a sensation of impending calamity. It was no longer a cold weight inside her but the blackness of the storm about her head. I've ruined it all, she thought. I ruined it because I wasn't strong enough to stand alone. I couldn't meet life. I've failed. Suddenly she wasn't sorry for herself but for Provost. She had been only silly to think for a minute he could give up so much for her. Give so much to her. But then she had wanted him, wanted something special from him, so terribly.

In the end she would pay for it. She would lose all, little or big, that she'd had. And the littlest little might have been enough. More than enough. So much more than other women had. But she had wanted the most. He stirred sharply. Then he rose. She gazed up at him and saw that his face was white but composed. Except for his full lower lip. It trembled, but his hands were still. Provost put them in the pockets of his jacket and stood looking out over the sunken garden. It was now filled with shadow. The tea on the far terrace was at an end. Only servants, in white and silver, were left. Removing the tea things.

Provost didn't speak, and she couldn't. She had put him beyond the sound, the appeal or help, of her voice. She had made it impossible to help him. He must be lonelier now, more shockingly alone, than she had ever been. And he was younger than she had remembered. She had only thought of him as a man married to her. The man she had married. When the truth was he was hardly more than a boy. With a very special character. He was, to put it as brutally as possible, feminine. His voice was feminine, and his hands, his wrists, were weak. In so desperately wanting him to help her she had forgotten his great need to have her help him. She had promised herself to do exactly that. Always.

"You must excuse me." He was, at last, speaking to her. But in a strange voice. A strange manner. His manner was coldly formal, precisely courteous. Like his father. His voice was thin, as usual, but frozen.

She looked up questioningly. "But of course," she said.

He turned and left her. An enormous weariness settled over her. The shadow left the garden. In its place there was a pure transparent twilight. The amber radiance had faded from the oak trees. The quaker-ladies were exactly the color of evening, and they would be lost in it. The lambs quiet by their feeding mothers. There were footsteps behind her, but she didn't turn. She couldn't stir. It was Provost. He took the place beside her he had left.

"It was a good thing I went in," he said in his customary pitch. "Father was about to have the mirror taken out of the dining room. I told him at once that though the ground was his, any house we lived in was our house. I told him the mirror must stay where it was. I liked it there. I liked what it showed me." She laid a hand on his knee. "I told him," Provost Moderan said, "that if he moved it, if he touched it, I would kill him." The very quality of his voice took any bravado from his declaration. It was a literal and profoundly convincing statement. The twilight flowed up from the sunken garden, from under the oak trees, and made them one.

PAUL HORGAN

To the Mountains

JULIO lay as quietly as he could. Only his eyes kept moving, turning toward the open door that led into the other room, as if by looking there he could hear better what the women were saying. His brother Luis was asleep beside him. The same blanket of catskins covered them both. Luis could sleep no matter what happened. The firelight on the walls and the ceiling was enough to keep Julio awake, even if his mother were not weeping in the next room. It was a silent night outside, like all the other nights in this place of home.

"When the fire goes out I will go to sleep," thought Julio; his legs ached from holding them still. Four nights ago his mother had given birth to a baby girl. Josefina Martinez came nine miles from Bernalillo to assist. The father was in Mexico on a wagon train. The trade in the summer and autumn of 1800 was promising, and the weather very fortunate. Rosa's baby came with no one there but her two sons and Josefina the midwife. They made a huge fire in the front room and left the door open so that the heat would wave silently through. The boys stayed outdoors and shuddered like horses under the November moon. From within came the wafting firelight and the nimble sounds of repeated sufferings.

Each boy felt like the deputy of his father. Luis was sixteen and Julio was thirteen. Luis was a stout boy—legs and arms like cottonwood branch, round and wieldy. Julio was slender and something like a half-grown cat in his physical ways. He was wary and respectful of life's dangers. He had grown with caution, because fear slowly told him more as he grew up. Everything Luis did easily, because he was older, Julio had to learn to do because he was younger, and thus everything was harder for him. The boys had no one but each other for companions, mostly; for they lived in the Rio Grande Valley a way out from the village of Bernalillo. They sometimes went there on horseback, when their father could spare the animals from work in the fields. Once, riding to town, Julio's horse had stamped and run wild, because a hunter in the tall saplings by the field near the river had shot his musket at a rising goose. Julio often dreamed of it, and the triumph of regaining the horse's head.

The brothers slept and the firelight faded down.

In the back room Rosa presently slept too, and Josefina sat watching her and the new baby.

Josefina was greatly girthed, with two circles of fat at her middle. She was heavy-faced and her eyes were kind, even when her tongue was sharp and filthy. Thus her character: good heart, from instinct; wicked mind, from dealings in the hard world.

The baby lay by its mother's side.

"The face of a *piñón*," thought Josefina, staring at the tiny brown head and the little open mouth that breathed so roundly.

The house was thick as a fortress, with adobe walls. It stood on a little green flat of land above the fields, beyond which lay the Rio Grande. Over it went two mighty cottonwoods, planted by the grandfather of this house a long time ago, who himself had left the service of the governor of New Spain to scratch his own land and yield it to his own sons. To the east the fields faded into mesa country, rising face of gravelly sand that held dusty bushes. The mesa rolled away and lifted hills where little pine trees grew. In morning, distant under the early sun, the pine trees seemed to exhale a blue air; and from the blue air rose the mountains, whose mighty trees looked, far away, like scratches upon the face of blue rock.

The mountains were miles away from the house of the family, and sometimes they were altogether hidden by weather: cloud, or rain, or wind alive with dust. At other times the mountains were momentously close, as if moved in golden light by the hand of God, and every cañon, every wind course and water hollow in the rock, stood clear to the eyes of the wondering brothers. Hardly a day of their lives failed to be somehow influenced by the mountains off there to the east.

Josefina came into the front room to kick some more wood on the dying fire, for cold was quick to get through her petulant flesh.

She woke Julio, but he lay with his eyes shut, identifying the noises she made and the profane rumble of her musing. When she went back he heard his mother speak sleepily; then the baby squeaked and began to cry, what sounded to him like a mortal utterance and farewell of that alien little life in his mother's bed.

"Yes, if you all four of you get through the winter, that will be one of God's little jokes," said Josefina, slapping her hands on her cold belly. "This house never gets warm; and nothing to cover with, those boys out there, freezing on the dirt floor with a dirty old catskin . . ."

"My husband will bring back plenty of money and furs and clothes from Mexico," said Rosa. But she began to cry again and mumble little sad doubts against the baby's hot temple.

"So, I will stay as long as I can," said Josefina. "But you know that can't be forever. . . . Be quiet now. You will choke the baby. Here, I'll take her, though God knows she may freeze to death. Get back to sleep. I will warm her."

Josefina took the baby.

Julio leaned and crouched from his bed to see what they did. There was a coldly steady candle burning by the wooden saint in the corner of the bedroom. Josefina held the baby with one arm and with her other hand pulled her tight dress away in front, and her huge bosom lay open and cavernous with shadow. There, at her warmest and most copious being, she laid the baby and folded her breasts to it, and drew her dress together and held her arms like a cradle. Her cheeks quivered at the striving touch of the baby; some pleasure deepened in her being, and for no reason that she could recognize, out of her assortment of past events—midwife, servant, thief, and harlot—she began to blush.

Her eyes watered and she smiled and sighed.

Julio backed into his bed again. His brother Luis flinched and jerked like a dog that is tickled when it dozes. Julio held his breath for fear he would wake Luis. Yet he wanted to talk to him. He wanted to stir his brother into a fury of doing; to save this family; to prove that it was not a world for women—that it was their own little tiny sister who so blindly threatened their mother's life and will and who opened the disgusting bosom of a fat witch to lie there for warmth!

So his thoughts were confused and furious.

The fire was alive again in little flames like autumn leaves. He could not sleep. He could not forget. He hated his fears. They were with him, vaguely enlivened by Josefina's talk.

It was not long before winter.

In the broken darkness of firelight Julio lay awake and prayed until he was answered by the same thing that always answered prayers, the earliest voice he had been taught to recognize, which no one else had to hear —the voice of God Himself in his own heart. Father Antonio made him know when he was a very little boy that the stronger a man was, the more he needed the guidance of God. So when he felt afraid and feeble alongside his mild strong brother, he had only to pray, and shut his eyes, and remember Jesus, who would presently come to him and say, "I see you, Julio Garcia; it is all right. What is it?"

"The mountains, to the mountains," thought Julio in answer to his own prayer.

"*Blessed is the fruit of thy womb: Jesus . . .*"

"What is in the mountains?"

"*. . . now and at the hour of our death.*"

"There is much that my brother and I can do in the mountains, and as soon as he awakens I will tell him; we will take my father's musket and go hunting; we will bring home skins to keep our little sister warm, and show our mother that this is a house of men, who do what is right, no matter how hard it is to do."

"*Amen.*"

II

Against the mica panes of the small deep window the early daylight showed like fog, silvery and chill. Luis jumped alive from sleep and went like a pale shadow to the dead fireplace, where he blew ashes off a few remote coals and, shivering in his bare skin, coaxed a fire alive. Then he found his clothes and got into them. He began to laugh at Julio, curled like a cat under the mountain-cat skins, waiting for warmth in the room. Then he thought with pleasure of the work to be done outside, in the marching dawn; cold mist over the river; the horses stirring; animals to feed and release. He went out, already owner of the day.

Julio was awake all that time, and he squinted at the fire, judging nicely just when it would need more wood, lest it go out, and just when the room would be comfortable. He was soon up, listening for sounds in the other room. Presently Josefina came to make breakfast. She felt tragic in the cold morning, and her face drooped with pity for her heart which was abused.

"I am going home," said she.

"No, you can't do that," said the boy.

She looked at him with sad delight in his concern.

"Why can't I? What do I get around here for my pains? I was freezing all night."

"When my father comes home he will pay you plenty. Luis and I can —we will bring you a glorious piece of fur."

"Oh, indeed; and where from?"

"We are going to the mountains."

"A pair of fool children like you? Another thing for your poor mama to worry about! If she lives through the winter it will be very surprising."

"What do you mean?"

She had nothing to mean, and so she made it more impressive by quivering her great throat, a ridiculous gesture of melancholy.

Julio ran outside and found his brother. They did not greet each other, but fell into tasks together.

The sky was coming pale blue over the river, and pale gold edges of light began to show around the far mountain rims. The house looked like a lovely toy in the defining light, its edges gilded, its shadows dancing.

"Luis."

"What?"

"I have an idea."

"Well?"

"Did you feel cold all night?"

"No, but you would not lie still."

"I am sorry. I heard Josefina talking to Mama."

"The poor old cow."

"Do you realize that we are so poor that we haven't got enough things to keep us warm, especially with the new baby here? And an extra woman in the house? . . . She ought to stay with us until Mama is well again."

"What are you going to do about it?"

"You and I should take the musket and go to hunt cats in the mountains, and bring home enough furs to satisfy everybody."

"Yes," said Luis, without any surprise, "I have thought of that too."

"Then I can go?"

"I suppose so—if you behave yourself. It's no child's errand, you know."

"Of course not. Then will you tell Mama?"

"All right."

Now the smoke was thick and sweet above the house.

The light spread grandly over the whole valley.

Luis went to his mother's bedside and leaned down. The baby was awake and obscurely busy against her mother's side.

"Mama."

"My little Luis."

"Julio and I are going to the mountains for a few days, to get some furs."

"No, no, you are both too young! That little Julio is just a baby. Now, Luis, don't break my heart with any more troubles!"

"What troubles? We have no troubles!"

"Your father is gone, we have no money, my children shiver all night long, that Josefina is a fat crow, Father Antonio hasn't been near us since the baby was born."

She wept easily and weakly. Luis was full of guilt and ideas of flight. He leaned and kissed her cool forehead and laughed like a big man.

"You'll see. My brother and I will come back like merchant princes."

"Then you are going?"

"Yes, Mummie, we'll go."

She stared at him in a religious indignation. This was her son! So even sons grew up and went away and did what they wanted to do, in spite of all the things women could think of to keep them back!

Later Julio came to say good-by, and she shamelessly wooed him to stay, with the name of God, and her love, and his pure dearness, and various coquetries. He felt a lump in his throat, so he shrugged, like his father, and went to the other room, where he paused and said, "Thank you, Josefina, for staying until my brother and I get back."

"The devil takes many odd forms," said Josefina with a pout.

They had two horses and the musket which their father had left at home upon his last departure for Mexico. They had a rawhide pouch containing things to eat, loaves and chilies and dried meat. As soon as they were free of the little fields of home, Julio began to gallop; and Luis overtook him and, saying nothing, reached out for the halter and brought him down to a walk. Julio felt very much rebuked; he sat erect on his horse and squinted his eyes at the mountain rising so far ahead of them, and thought of himself as a relentless hunter.

The boys toiled over the land all morning.

They paused and looked back several times, touched by the change in the look of their farm, which lay now like a box or two on the floor of the valley; and they thought respectively, "When I have my farm, I shall want to be on higher ground," and "What if something dreadful has happened since we left home! If the baby choked to death, or a robber came, I should never forgive myself."

The mountains looked strangely smaller as they advanced. The foothills raised the riders up, and from various slopes the mountain crowns seemed to lean back and diminish. The blue air in cañons and on the far faces of rock slides and broken mighty shoulders was like a breath of mystery over the familiar facts of memory.

"Let me carry the musket now for a while."

"No, we might as well decide that now. I am to have it all the time."

"Why, that isn't right!"

"No, I have had more experience with it. It is our only arm. Now be sensible."

"Just because I am the younger, you always do this way. I tell you, I am an excellent shot."

"You may be. But I am nearly four years older, and—I just think it better this way."

"I wish I'd known before we started."

'Why don't you go back, then?"

"I will."

But they rode on together. Easily triumphant, Luis could afford to be indulgent; later on he rode close to Julio and knocked him on the back and winked.

"You think I am not as much of a man as you are," said Julio bitterly.

"Well, you're not."

"You'll see! I can show you!"

The brothers' love for each other was equally warm, but derived from different wells of feeling. Sometimes they felt only the love; at other times, only the difference.

Now in afternoon, riding on the windy November plain, and knowing that before nightfall they would be in the very shadow of the nearest mountain reach, they felt their littleness on that world. The air was lighter so high up above the river valley. They looked back: an empire of sand-colored earth, and there, in the far light, the river herself, furred with trees. They looked ahead, but in doing that had to look up.

It was a crazy giant land; a rock that looked like a pebble from here was higher than a tree when they got to it.

"We must find a place to leave the horses."

"What?"

"You idiot, we can't expect horses to climb straight up cliffs like that over there!"

"Sure, we'll find a place to leave them."

"It must be nearly too late to go into the mountains tonight."

"We'll make a fire here."

"If it is clear enough tonight, they could see our fire from home."

"They could?"

The thought made Julio shiver. But then it was already getting chill. The sun was going down.

III

They awoke the next morning under the cold mountains, and in their rested souls there was a mood of gods. They caught their horses and rode along the last little flat before the great rise, and before the sun was up over the rocky shoulder they had found a little box cañon where there was a growth of straw-colored grass and through which there washed a small creek. Leading the horses, they walked far into the narrow, shadowy cañon, and at last Luis said, "There!"

"What?"

"Here is the place to leave the animals. We can make a little fence down here, and then be safe when we go off to hunt."

"What will you build your fence with?"

"Some big rocks and then a lot of branches that will seem high to the horses."

"Where does that river come from, do you suppose?"

"If you'll stop talking long enough to get to work, we'll go and find out."

The light of builders came into their eyes, measuring, devising; after a few trials they had a system for their work; they moved harmoniously. Given need, materials, and imagination, nothing wanted. They grew warm and threw down their coats. The sun quivered in watery brilliance high beyond the rocky crown.

When they were done they untethered the horses and took up the food, the musket, the powder, balls, their knives, their tinder, and went up the cañon, following the creek. It led them into shadow; they had to wade;

the rocks widened—sunlight ahead; then a miniature marsh with moss and creatures' tracks; then a little waterfall, which they heard, a whisper in diamond sunlight, before they saw it; and under it a black pool plumbed by the sun to its still, sandy floor.

The fall came down from a rocky ledge halfway up the face of a gray stone cliff.

The forest shadows beyond it, which they saw looking up, were hazy with sunlight and noon blue.

"We'll swim!"

The boys took off their clothes and fell into the water; for a moment they hated the cold shock, and then they were happily claimed by the animal world. They were away from everything. They were let to their senses. They dived and splashed and bellowed, awakening the silences to echo, which only tempest and beast had awakened before them. This was a bath of a superman; not the idle, slow, muddy, warm current of the Rio Grande, which suggested cows and babies paddling and hot mud drugging boys who swam in summer.

They came out into the warmer air and slapped until they were dry; then they dressed.

"Up there—we've got to get up there some way."

Luis pointed up to the higher world beyond the fall. There were gigantic pines standing in light-failing ranks, and behind them a great plane of rock shaggy with its own breakage.

So they retreated from the waterfall and went around it, climbing and clawing until they had gained the upper level. They stood to listen. Enormous and pressing, the quiet of the mountains surrounded them. Their eyes, so long limited to a tame river world, hunted ahead. They were explorers, so far as they knew. What no man has ever seen before! There was a mysterious sense of awe in the first eye that owned it.

As they passed in and out of shadow they felt alternately cold and warm.

As they went they were often forced by the huge silence to stop and let their own sounds die away.

They would laugh at each other at such moments and then go on.

In midafternoon they thought they must plan to go back, since it took them so long to come. The horses would need company and perhaps protection against beasts.

The sun was yellower and cooler.

The way they had come no longer looked the same; coming, they had watched another face of it; now, retreating, they had to look back often to recognize their course. They lost it, or thought they had, when they came to a bench of gray stone in a spill of light through branches. They then looked aside and saw the ledge curve and vanish in a stout hillside and emerge a little farther on and there become the rocky shelf over which rustled their waterfall of the sunny noon.

"It is made by Heaven for our purposes!" said Luis.

"Yes, it certainly is. . . . How do you mean?"

"Well, the cats probably come and drink and lie here, and other animals. We could be here on this shelf, you see."

"And fire down on them?"

"Sure. Come on."

They started along the ledge and then shagged back and nearly fell down to the cañon floor below when a boom of air and shock arose and smote them from a few feet ahead. It was the thunder of a great bald eagle who beat his way off the rocks and straight up over them, his claws hanging down, his hot red eyes sparkling for one tiny second in the light of the sky. Then he wheeled and raised his claws and extended his head and drifted off in a long slanting line like the descent of the mountain edge over which he vanished.

The boys were breathless.

It scared them.

It also hushed them—the grandeur of that heavy bird leaving earth for air.

"How I should love to get a bird like that!"

"To kill him?"

"Or at least get some of his feathers."

"Maybe he dropped some."

Julio moved forward and then crouched and called for his brother.

"Luis, look! Hurry! Here is what he had!"

They were looking at a partially picked mountain-lion cub, off which the eagle had been feeding.

"Julio, you see, now? Here is where the big cats will come. They will roam until they find it, and they will watch. The eagle carried off the baby cat. He'll come back, too!"

Julio acted like a very small boy. He kicked the carcass of the cub off the ledge into the shaly slide below.

"What did you do that for?"

"I don't know."

"It was wonderful bait! Now it's gone!"

"Well . . ."

"Oh, come on!"

The godlike temper and power of the day were gone for them both—Luis exasperated, Julio tired and guilty.

As they went down to the cañon where the waterfall seemed to stand, not fall, in a mist of blue shadow now that the sun was sinking, they looked up and saw the eagle so high that he seemed like a spiraling leaf, and Luis shrugged and said, "Oh, cheer up! I suppose he would have come back anyway and carried his supper off!"

But Luis, though he was again friendly, could not offset the chilling of the whole day; and the rocky clear cold cupping of night in those walled places closed over Julio and confirmed his hunger, his bitterness, his youthful rue at the turn of happiness into misery, like the turn of day into dusk.

All right, if everybody was older than he was, let them parade and give orders. If Luis felt so superior, Julio would show him someday.

They scampered down the cañon as fast as they could, for where they had left the horses was like a station of home to them.

When it was dark enough they looked for stars, and saw some, but clouds had come, and a damp, warmish wind, and the cañon talked in wind, trees keening, and now and then an almost silent thunder of a wind blow when it met a distant high rock mountain face.

By the last light of their fire Luis examined his musket, to see that the day's toil over hard ground hadn't damaged it any.

"Let me see it," said Julio.

"What for?"

"Oh, can't I just see it?"

Luis handed it over.

Julio sighted along the barrel.

"She's a lovely one," he murmured. Then he gave it back, ready to go to sleep, chuckling with affection for Luis, who would be so surprised.

IV

Dawn came with a ghostly diffusion of misty light—the slow march of shapes.

Julio was ready.

He rolled with almost infinite slowness to the ground, free of the blankets, and left Luis slumbering like a mummy who knew the cold of centuries.

He crouched and slowly went around the other side of the bed and took up the musket and ammunition from the side of his brother.

He sniffed the air, and it was bittersweet with cold and some drifting new flavor.

He didn't know, in his excitement and caution, that it was the presage of snow.

He went up the cañon chewing on a hank of jerked meat from his pocket. He was abroad in his own wilderness, with his own gun; in effect, with his own destiny. He remembered yesterday's trail very well, and he toiled while the light grew; yet, there being no sun, everything had a new look, though he had seen it before. He came after a long time to the pool and the waterfall. There he stopped and looked back. Now he realized how far it was, how many hours divided him from Luis, who must have been awake and wondering hours ago.

What would Luis do?

Would he kick the hard ground in fury and halloo for him? Or would he set out in pursuit?

But which way would Luis decide to go?

Or perhaps he was weeping at the conviction that his beautiful young brother Julio had been carried off in the night by beasts of prey.

Then the image of a devouring lion shouldering a musket was too odd, and Julio laughed; then he smartly turned to see where another's laugh came from; then he laughed again, at his echo in the rocky room with the sky roof.

The waterfall was like a wraith made of heavier air than the gray essence that filled the intimate little cañon.

"The cats will come to the ledge," thought Julio, faithful to his brother's wisdom, even though he outraged it.

He went around the long way, slowly going across the fat roll of the rocky hillside, and found himself then in the tall forest up there. He knew that a hunter must wait, so he settled himself to do so on a tiled shelf of moss, between two big boulders, lacy with fern and dark with shadow.

His stomach was clutched by doubts and partly whetted hunger. Hardest of all was to keep the silence of the mountains, lest he startle his game.

Many times he was ready to get up, relieve the ache of his set legs, go back to Luis, and pretend that he had only wandered a few feet away from camp.

But he was afraid now. He was afraid of the way the sky looked, dark and soft, and wind very high up which pulled the clouds past the peaks as if tearing gray cloth on the sharp edges.

He was lost, really.

The musket was a heavy sin across his lap. It was loaded. Perhaps he should unload it and scamper back.

But then, if a mountain cat came to the ledge, he would be helpless.

Then he remembered for the first time that he might be in danger from the animals. It sent blood back through him, and he grew angry at such menace.

"If they think they can hurt me, they are crazy, those wildcats!"

So he spent the early day and noon in thoughts of himself and his furies, while the peace of the forest was held, and the sky now came down in darkness and again blew upward in windy jets of silvery light.

And he stayed, watching.

He was so alone and silent that the first touch on his cheek out of the air startled him, and he turned his head quickly to look; but what had touched his cheek was the snow, shortly after noon.

It came down, dandled by the odd currents of airy wind in the irregular mountains, like white dust sifting through the ancient stand of trees up the mountainside.

Julio blinked at the spotty snow falling before his eyes, and he licked the delicious flakes that starred his lips.

The rocks were beginning to look white. The air was white, and the distance was white.

The distance was reduced. When he tried to peer as far as he would, his sight seemed to go so far and then turn black.

All suddenly a most childish wave of lonesomeness broke over him, and he knew how far away he was, and how solitary; how subject to the mountains.

He got up.

Something else moved, too, in the whitening world.

He saw it, obscurely dark against the white stone shelf below him in line of sight. It was a mountain lion coming down the ledge with beautiful stillness and almost the touch of snow in its own paws.

Its heart-shaped nose was along the ground, smelling the fresh snow and whatever it covered.

Julio lifted the gun, which was as light as he wanted it in this moment, and watched, and licked the snow off his upper lip. Then, with his eyes wide open and his cheeks blown up, he fired.

He couldn't hear the lion cry, or the echo of the amazing blast through the cañons and the aisles. He was deaf from it. But he sat down behind his rock and watched while he reloaded, and saw the cat spilling its blood on the snow; and then gradually he could hear it moaning as his head cleared. Then it suddenly died. The snow continued on it passively, cooling the blood, and making it pale, and finally thickening over it entirely.

After a long time Julio came down from his rock and touched his game. He glanced around to see if any more cats happened to be there. There were none. He was exalted and indifferent. He rolled the heavy lion off the ledge down to the sloping hillside below it. There the snow was thinner. There he set to work to skin the cat, as he had watched his father skin animals at home, for leather, for fur, for rawhide.

v

His knife was so wet and cold that it tried to stick to his hands.

He was late in finishing. He felt proud.

Maybe Luis would be annoyed, but not for long. To bring home the first fur? He had a loving, warm, tender heart for all animals, now that he had conquered one of the greatest. He felt that animals must love men in return, and serve them humbly.

Done, then, he returned to thoughts of others, and then he could have groaned aloud when he really imagined what Luis might feel.

"Do you suppose my brother is in danger because I took away his gun? What if he has been attacked? What if I had not had the gun when the lion came? It would be the same with him, without any protection! Oh, my Jesus and my God, help me to get back in a hurry, and have him safe when I get there!"

Now, with heavying snow and night beginning to fall, the hunter could not scramble fast enough to undo what his day had done.

He shouldered his new skin, which was freezing and heavy, and his gun and his supplies, and went down off the shaly hill. In the bottom of the chasm, where the waterfall entered the stream, it was dark. The black water of the creek alone was clearly visible. He stopped and called out, then turned to listen, but the spiraling flaky darkness was vastly quiet.

He hurried on and sobbed a few times, but he said to himself that it was simply that he was cold, not that he was sorely afraid and sorry.

"Certainly I can see!"

But he paid for this lie when he struck a rock that cut his cheek and threw him down to the ground, where the soft copious snowfall went on secretly to change the mountains, to enrich stony hollows with soft concavities, to stand the bare ridges barer above snowy articulations.

He struggled to make a small fire, scratching twigs and needles and branches from the lee side of rocks, having to feel for his wants. At last he produced a flame, and his heart leaped up, the firelight on the snow was so lovely. In the light he saw where he was, and collected more branches, building craftily to bring up his flames, until the cañon was roaring with light and heat at that spot.

He sat, then lay on his new fur, with the raw side down.

The snowflakes made a tiny, fascinating little hiss of death when they fell into the fire.

"Luis will be all right. I will get to him early in the morning; as soon as it is light I shall start out."

He dozed and awoke, at last to see his fire gone. Then he knew he must stay awake.

What he knew next was so strange that he felt humble. In spite of trying not to, he had fallen asleep, and was then awakened afterward by wave after wave of sound, through the falling, falling snow which hushed everything but this clamor that had awakened him, the ringing of a bell. The bell clanged and stammered and changed with the wind; like the bell of the church at home, miles up the valley on a still, hot summer Sunday morning.

"But this is not—there can be no church in these mountains!" he said in the blackest density of the snowfall that night. And he listened again, but now heard nothing—nothing beyond the faint sense of hushing in the air made by the falling snow.

The bell was gone; it had served to awaken him; somewhere beyond this cold, separating fall it had rung out for him—true, even if it came to him as a dream of security. He did not lie down again, but sat, marveling, and sick for home.

VI

The snow continued with daybreak.

He set out again as soon as he could see a few feet in front of him. As the light grew, so did his sense of folly. It was as if he had dreamed of the things that might happen to his brother Luis.

All his greatness of accomplishment disappeared. What good was this smelling and frozen catskin now? He threw it down by an icy rock and found that he could now run, trotting, without the awkward burden of the cat hide, which was stiff and slippery—with its frozen leggings of fur which stuck out, ragged and indignant, the congealed ghost of the cat.

The snow died away as Julio hurried. The wind became capricious and bitter. It scratched in long sweeps down the cañon and bore out over the open plains, which Julio could begin to see as the day grew and he toiled farther down the shadowy chasm.

He kept staring ahead for sight of the spare pines which stood by their camp. He remembered seeing the pines against open sky the first night there—which meant that they were nearly out of the mountain's fold.

He thought he saw the sentinel trees once; broke into a hard run, and then stopped, panting, when he saw that the gray light on a wall of rock had looked for a moment like a misty sky out there over the plain.

The musket was heavy and cold in his grasp. He had it still loaded. Perhaps he ought to shoot it off, a signal for his brother?

But he would call first.

He cried out, and stood to listen, his whole body turned sideways to hear an answer.

There was none.

Now he knew that the bell he had heard last night, waking him up during the snowstorm, was a miracle, sent to keep him from freezing to death in his sleep.

So he began to run again, and his heart nearly burst. He thought perhaps there would be another miracle, to keep Luis safe and bring Julio back to him right away.

The boy crawled over the rocks that seemed cold enough to crack in the weather; he waded where he had to in the glazed creek. Suddenly it was lighter; the sky lay before him as well as above him; and at last he looked down on the miniature meadow of the cañon mouth where the horses were fenced. There! Yes, there were the guardian pine trees.

"Luis, Luis, I am back!" he cried, but he choked and made only a sobbing sound. There was no fire burning at the camp, and Julio was thumped in the breast by fear again, as if Luis had gone back home with the two horses and left him as he deserved to be left, alone in the mountains.

He hurried and then saw the horses, far down the way.

Then he heard a voice, talking to him from a distance; no words; level, careful sounds; it sounded like Luis.

"Luis, where are you?"

Julio came down farther.

He squinted around and then upward.

"I am glad to see you back. Stop where you are!"

"Luis!"

"Be careful."

At the same moment Julio heard how Luis spoke from the tree where he was hanging and he saw the wolf at the base of the tree, which sat staring upward, perfectly quiet and ready.

The wolf was huge and looked like a dog, except that he was gray, the color of rock—which was why Julio didn't see him for the first little while.

The wolf must have heard him, for his ears were standing up and the fur on his spine was silvery and alive. Julio stood shocking-still and was perfectly sure that the wolf's eyes were straining toward him as far as they could without the turn of the head, and the animal was ready to turn and attack him if necessary.

So there was a grotesque interval of calm and silence in the cañon.

Luis was hanging to the pine tree, which had a few tough fragments of branch about sixteen feet above the ground.

The sun tried to shine through the bitter and cloudy day.

Luis looked white and sick, half frozen; his eyes were burning black in new hollow shadows.

"Julio," said Luis as lightly as possible, never taking his eyes off the wolf; indeed, as if he were addressing the wolf.

"Yes, Luis," whispered Julio.

"You have the gun there with you, haven't you?" asked the older brother in an ingratiating and mollifying tone, to keep the wolf below him still intent upon his first design.

"Yes, Luis."

"Well, Julio," said his brother with desperate charm, velvet-voiced and easy, "see if you can load it without making much disturbance, will you?"

"It is loaded, Luis."

"Oh, that is fine. Then, Julio, pray Jesus you can manage to shoot the wolf. Julio, be easy and steady now . . . don't—move—fast—or—make—any—noise—Julio—for—the—love—of—God."

To Julio it was like coming back to the reward of his folly. He held his breath, to be quiet.

He thought Luis was going to fall from the tree—his face was so white and starving, his hands so bony and desperate where they clutched.

"Why, of course I can shoot the terrible wolf," said Julio to himself, slowly, slowly bringing the musket around to the aim.

Luis, from his tree against the gray pale sky, went on talking in tones of enchantment and courtesy to the wolf, to keep alive the concentration, until Julio fancied the wolf might answer, as animals did in the tales of early childhood.

"We shall see, my dear friend wolf, just sit there—one—more—minute— if you please—until—my—brother gets the thing ready. . . . Are—you— ready—Julio?"

The answer was the shot.

The wolf lashed his hind quarters around so that he faced Julio, whence the sound had come.

He roared and spat, but he could not move. His back was broken. He sat and barked and snapped his teeth.

Julio ran a little way forward, then was cautious. He stopped and began to reload.

Luis fell to the ground. He had his knife ready. But he could not move as quickly as he would. He was cold and stiff and cramped. He hacked his knife into the animal's breast, but the stab was shy and glancing. The wolf made a crying effort and scrabbled its body forward and took Luis by the leg.

"Now, Julio! Your knife!"

Julio dropped the musket and came down to them.

"Where, Luis?"

"Under his left forearm!"

"Wolf!" said Julio, and drove his knife.

VII

For a moment they all stayed where they were—the brothers panting; the animal dead, and slowly relaxing thus. The brothers sweated and couldn't speak, but hung their heads and spat dry spit and coughed and panted.

"Did he bite you bad?" asked Julio.

"No, he couldn't bite very hard, not even like a dog—he was too hurt."

"Let me see."

They peeled the cloth away from the leg just above the knee. The teeth had torn the cloth and the flesh. It did not hurt. It was numb. It bled very little. The skin was blue.

There was nothing to do to the leg except cover it again. They took as long as possible at it, but they had presently to come to the story of the young brother's folly, and as soon as that was done they felt elated—the one penitent and grave, the other pardoning and aware that the terrors of the experience were more useful to his young brother than any rebuke.

"And I know right where I left the lion skin; we'll get it later! We can get many more!"

Julio was ballooning with relief, now that it was all over and done with. He felt as he always felt after confession in church—airy and tall.

The physical misery in snow and wind and rocky mountain temper—this was their outer penalty. But the boys knew an inner joy at the further range of their doing. Simply being where they were, at odds with what menaced them—this was achievement; it was man's doing done.

Late that day the sun did break through and a little while of golden light seemed to relieve the cold. It didn't snow again that night. They kept their fire high. Luis was, oddly, too lame to walk. But he was glad to lie and watch the flames and smile at Julio's serious bearing, full of thoughtful play in his face which meant plans and intentions.

VIII

The day after the snowstorm the valley itself came back in a kind of golden resurge of autumn. The house at the little farm was soaked with melting snow; running lines of dark, muddy thaw streaked from the round-worn edges of the roof to the walls and the ground.

The temper of the river was warmer than the mountain weather. The willows and cottonwoods lost their snow by noon. The mountains were visible again, after the day of the blind white blowing curtain over the plain.

Not many travelers were abroad, but Father Antonio came down the road shortly after noon, and Josefina saw him, his fat white mare, his robe tucked above his waist, his wool-colored homespun trousers, and his Mexican boots. She went to tell Rosa that the priest was coming at last, and to stop crying, if that was all she was crying for.

The priest dismounted in the yard and let his horse move.

Josefina tidied herself in honor of the visit, and he came in, catching her wetting her eyebrows. She immediately felt like a fool, from the way he looked at her; and she bowed for his blessing, furious at his kind of power over and against women.

"I didn't get your message about the baby until two days ago, and then I said nothing could keep me from coming as soon as I could. Isn't it fine! Where is he? Or is it a girl? I hope you have a girl. Already those bad boys of yours—where are they?"

Rosa felt as if authority had walked into her house and that she need have no further fear.

Father Antonio was a tall, very spare, bony man nearly fifty, with straw-colored hair, a pale, wind-pinked face, and little blue eyes that shone speculatively as he gazed. He was awkward; he couldn't talk without slowly waving his great-knuckled hands in illustration of his mood; and he loved to talk, putting into words the great interest of his days. Everything suggested something else to him; he debated with himself as if he were two Jesuits, they said in Santa Fé, where he was not popular with the clergy because he preferred working in the open land among the scattered families of the river basin.

"Where are the boys?" he asked.

Rosa was at peace. Her cheeks dried and her heart seemed to grow strong. She felt a spell of calm, strong breath in her breast. She was proud.

"They have gone hunting. They have been gone several days now. In the mountains."

Josefina lingered on the outside of a kind of sanctuary which the priest and the mother made, a spiritual confine which she could not enter, a profane and resentful woman. But she could toss her opinions into it.

"They are little fools, a pair of chicken-boned infants, crazy, going to the mountains! It snowed there for two days. They will never come back."

Rosa watched the priest's face, ready to be frightened or not, by his expression.

He glanced at Josefina—a mild blue fire.

"They are probably all right."

Josefina mumbled.

"How will a man ever know what goes on," asked Father Antonio, "unless he goes out and looks at it?"

"How long can you stay, Father?" asked Rosa.

"Till we christen the baby."

"But——"

"I'll wait till the brothers come back, so the baby will have a godfather."

"I—godmother," simpered Josefina on the outskirts, making a fat and radiant gesture of coquetry.

"Why not?" said the priest mildly, taking the sting out of her scandalous contempt.

It sobered her. She blushed.

"When your husband comes back in the spring with the wagon train," said Father Antonio, "you can send some money to my church."

"Gladly," said Rosa.

"Those must be big boys by now. I haven't seen them for months. Luis? Julio? That's right. When I was a boy I had all the desires to go and look at what was over the mountains. Then when I was away, there, in Mexico, at the seminary, the world on this side of the mountains was just as inviting and mysterious. Eh? When I came back to go to work, everybody bowed to me and behaved properly as to a priest. But I always felt a little guilty for that, and went fishing or hunting. The animals had no respect for me, which was a relief, for they knew not of God, whose weight is something to carry, I can tell you!"

This was strange talk to the women.

"Next to catching a sinner and taking away his sin, I like best to fetch a trout or play a long game of war with beaver in the river pools. So now I know why your two big brown babies went off to the mountains."

"Oh," thought the women. "That explains it."

IX

Father Antonio stayed over a week. The boys were missing. The priest would go and look at the mountains in all times of day, to see if he could see anything, even in his mind, which might be played with as news for the distracted mother.

But all he saw were the momentous faces of the mountains; light or the absence of light; at dawn, a chalky black atmosphere quivering with quiet air; at noon, silvered by the sun, the great rock wrinkles shining and constant; at evening, the glow of rose, as if there were furnaces within the tumbled stone which heated the surface, until it came to glow for a few moments, then cooling to ashy black from the base upward until it joined the darkening sky like a low, heavy cloud.

"I have promised to stay for them, and I will," said the priest.

He spent the days making Rosa agree to get strong, until she finally arose from her bed and ordered her house again. He did the tasks of the outdoors. There was no need for Josefina to stay now; but stay she did, touched in her vanity by the godmotherhood which had been mentioned once.

She came in one day, still holding her arm over her eyes, as if staring into the distance, the golden chill of the open winter.

"I think I see them coming!" she cried.

They all went outdoors.

"You are crazy," said the priest.

They looked and looked.

The plain and the slow rise into the mountain lift were swimming with sunlight. They searched with long looks until they had to blink for vision.

"See! Like a couple of sheep, just barely moving?" insisted Josefina, pointing vaguely at the mountains.

"Where?"

"Yes, I do see! She is right! She must have Indian blood."

The mother was the last to see and agree.

There was an infinitesimal movement far on the plain, hardly perceptible as movement; some energy of presence, a fall of light and cast of shadow, just alive enough to be convincing. It was the hunters, coming on their horses on the second day's journey out of the mountains.

Late in the afternoon they arrived.

The marks of their toil were all over them.

To go and come back! This being the common mystery of all journeying, the mother could hardly wait for them to speak, to tell her everything.

She brought the baby, and the boys kissed the tiny furred head.

The priest gave them his blessing and they bent their shaggy necks under it.

Josefina stared and then squinted at them, whispering something.

"Luis, you are hurt!"

"Not any more."

"But you were!"

"I will tell you sometime."

"Now, now!"

"How long have we been away?"

"Ten days!"

The boys talked, confirming each other with looks.

Luis and the wolf; the bite; the fever; the body as the residence of the devil, and the raving nights. Julio and his amazing skill as a marksman; his reckless courage; the two of them together after Luis' recovery; shagging up and down rocky barriers, mountain sprites, and their bag of skins.

"Look at that!"

They got and opened out their two packs of furs, and there were cats, the wolf, a little deer, and a middle-sized brown bear.

"Who got the bear?"

"Luis! It was wonderful! The bear was in a tree, watching us, and what made him nobody knows, but Luis looked up, and *whang!* and *boo!* Down fell the bear, and all it took was the one shot!"

"But you should have seen Julio the time he saved my life, when the wolf was waiting for me to fall down, I was so cold and weak! Up in my tree!"

The silence was full of worried love: what had they not done! But safe. Yes, but—what if——

The brothers looked at each other.

Nothing would ever be said about the other thing. Nobody ever managed to grow up without being foolish at some time or other.

The priest thought, "The boy Julio looks taller. I suppose it is only natural; last time I was here he was——"

Luis took the baby sister to hold.

There was plenty of fur to keep her warm.

Julio sighed. It was a curiously contented and old man's comment.

Father Antonio felt like laughing, but there was some nobility of bearing in Julio's little mighty shoulders that did not deserve genial patronizing.

The priest glanced at Josefina. He knew his materials like a craftsman. He thought, "Josefina sees—she even smells as a female—what has taken place in Julio. She stares at him and then squints and whispers to herself. How little is secret! How much makes a life!"

The mother's arms were free of her infant. She went and hugged Julio, because, though she hardly thought it so clearly, she knew that he had gone and conquered the wilderness which was his brother's by birth. She knew that—and what lay behind it—as only a child's mother could know it; with defensive and pitying and pardoning love, so long as it might be needed.

X

"I wish I could write, now," said Luis.

"Why?"

"Then I would write to my father about it."

"But he could not read it."

"No, but he could get somebody to read it to him."

"Should I write and tell him about it for you?" asked Father Antonio.

"Oh, if you would, Father!"

"I'll be glad to—the minute I get back to my house where I have pens and paper. You have told me the whole adventure."

But when the priest did return home and sit down to keep his promise to the delighted brothers, what they had told him seemed to him man's story, and all he finally wrote was:

"DEAR GARCIA,

"Your wife has had a dear baby girl, and both are well and happy, with God's grace. Your two sons are proud of their family, and when you return, before hearing from their lips anything of their adventures during your absence, you will see that they are already proper men, for which God be praised in the perfection of His design for our mortal life."

CYRIL HUME

An Opinion on West Eden

In the night some wretched neighbor had poisoned my beautiful affable cat, and I was so shattered and enraged that when the postman came I told him about it.

I run across an instance of losing an animal, he said, easing his pouch down to the garden parapet without slipping the shoulder strap. It was when I used to deliver the route over to West Eden. It ain't what you'd call a high-tone district, but there's always something going on.

There was especially this big, shabby-painted old house in among a lot of brick buildings. It was the only one left on the block that had a yard, and there was a porch all around two sides of it with vines growing up it. A big colored family lived there, and they had a good time. I don't mean like *My Old Kentucky Home* in the movies, but they didn't worry any, and they lived all over the place. If the girls happened to be out in the yard they always had something good-natured to say when you passed by. A lot of singing went on inside, and hollering back and forth from one room to another, and usually it smelled like there was something good on the stove. I took a big interest because it was like somewheres in a foreign or European city, even while the family was the most American thing on the block, the way colored people always are.

Matter of fact, I got to stop in a couple of times a week. They was always getting letters from the South or New York City about how their race was doing in other parts of the country, and whenever I brought one the old lady would ask me in for a couple of the best doughnuts or something you ever eat.

What I'm aiming at, they had a small black dog name of Gyppie. He was just a mongrel with one of those big bushy tails curled up over onto his back, but he had a nice coat, and he was the smartest animal I ever seen. Anything any dog could do, that Gyppie could do.

He couldn't only just sit up and speak, and be a dead dog like a lot of them. They'd give him tough ones like go upstairs to the back room and bring down Louise's blue slipper. All the while they were telling him he'd be looking at them and listening, with his mouth open and his tail and ears hanging down, all worried and shaking inside, wanting to do it right. And when he finally got it he'd shoot upstairs and fetch the right thing back—not just Mattie's or anybody's slipper, but Louise's, the blue one. Then everybody would be pleased and laugh, and he'd dance around proud of himself until he got a piece of something for a prize.

I remember once the girls had been to a party the night before, and the old lady took it into her head to send him for Mattie's fan. Everybody said oh pshaw he couldn't do it, and tried to talk the old lady out of it, but she stuck to it and said Gyppie'd be able to. So they all began telling him very careful what they wanted.

He seemed to know it was a big test, and I was sorry for him, the way he shook and worried and tried to understand. Finally his nerve broke, and he scooted upstairs and came back with the wrong thing, and they all started to be scared that he wouldn't be able to do it. They kept up telling him, more and more solemn, what they wanted.

Finally I began wishing I wasn't there. They were all ashamed and disappointed, and mad at the old lady for thinking up such a crazy show-off idea in the first place. We'd sit there and listen to his paws on the stairs, and hold our breaths till he came back.

But finally damn if he didn't come back with the fan. And when he found out he was right he practically had a fit, and that family couldn't have been happier if they'd come into a fortune. I never seen an animal that thought more of any people, white or not, than that Gyppie thought of those people. And that meant a lot to them.

They were all crazy over him, but it seemed like the one that fussed most about him was Mattie, the younger girl. She was a nice-looking kid, with a gold-colored face, and a sharp-cornered smile, and very dark brown eyes you couldn't tell what she was thinking from. She was always at the gate to see if I had a letter, and if I did the old lady would holler out to her to bring me in, and she'd pass it on.

One winter after I'd been friends with the family for about a year there was an epidemic of smallpox. I don't know why, but the Board of Health put out an ordinance that any dog caught running loose off of his own property would be taken up and put out of the way. I spoke to Mattie about it when I saw her, but she just laughed and said it would take a horse to drag Gyppie out of his own front yard. The only time he ever went out was when he had to see about a lamppost.

Late one afternoon during the epidemic I was coming home along the route. It was just dark, and the street lamps were lighted. I passed the old house when I saw Gyppie coming back, trotting very fast the way he did, with his hind end off on one side for speed. I was glad to see him, and getting ready to say something, when I saw Doan the big young policeman crossing over from the other side of the street. He had his pistol out, and before I could think fast enough, he called, and the dog stopped.

I turned around and went back so I wouldn't be watching when it happened, but the report made my ears bang. When I'd gone a ways further I couldn't help looking once. Gyppie was down on the pavement, pushing around crazy, and Doan was standing under the street light, looking at him, with his pistol in his hand. Nearer to me the front gate had just squawked open, and Mattie was tearing down the block on her long legs, not making a sound.

I knew how they'd feel in the house, and I was afraid to go back there. When I finally had to, I tried to say something to Mattie about maybe the dog was better off. She didn't even look at me when she answered. She just said, as if it didn't matter much, that things like that happened. I was worried because I knew she was different, and I knew that was really the opinion she'd come to, and I didn't think she'd ever change her mind.

No sir, they didn't do anything about it. Nothing to do then. Anyway, colored people in this country don't often figure you can do anything about a white man in a uniform. They just took it, and weren't so nice afterwards. I don't mean they were ever fresh or anything when I brought the mail. But they stopped being friends, and the old lady didn't ask me in for pie and so on. I'd go on past, feeling that I was just a dumb letter carrier.

Funny thing though. I never had much to do with Doan or any cop, but one day when I met him on the route I was feeling dirty, and I asked him if he'd shot any pets lately. Well right away that cop look come off his face, and he fell in beside me, hurrying to keep up.

I had my orders, he says, I couldn't do nothing about it.

He seemed awful worried.

You could have give the dog a boot home, I says. It was only a half a block.

I'm just a member of the force, he says. I couldn't do nothing about it.

I felt sorry for the big kid with his gun and his uniform, acting like he owed me money.

It wasn't so good, he says, looking off down the street. When I give it to him, he right away sits up with his paws toward me, like that was what I wanted. There wasn't much more than half of him still holding together, but the damn dog sits up and speaks.

I wanted to get out of there, but he took hold of me. Look, he says, I often thought if at the time I'd maybe had the pooch stuffed for them . . . But I don't guess that would have done no good.

No, I says, I don't guess it would.

NUNNALLY JOHNSON
Twenty Horses

IT WAS AT LUNCHEON at the Statisticians' Club that Mr. Ogburn, of Ogburn, Balch & Harrison, auditors, explained his stand in the matter to Mr. Kruger, of Kruger Bros. & McAllister, stocks and bonds, and Mr. Kruger, it turned out, felt precisely the same way.

"If it isn't educational," Mr. Ogburn said, "I won't have anything to do with it."

"That's me," Mr. Kruger said.

"One of these educational games—why, you're learning something. Like I said about crossword puzzles; you do a crossword puzzle every day for a year and you will have twice as big a vocabulary."

"The other night I learned a new jewel, named lapis," Mr. Kruger pointed out. "I never heard of it before."

"I heard of it," Mr. Ogburn said, "but not definitely."

"This game where you just stand off and throw cards into a hat—that's just a waste of time."

"Nothing else! Nothing else at all! You mean serious businessmen play a game like that?"

"I saw two brokers playing it."

"Well," Mr. Ogburn said, signaling for the check, "I have no patience with businessmen who will waste their time like that when they could just as well be improving their mind at the same time they are playing. I like to play as well as the next one, but I like to realize I'm also doing something educational."

"You're never too old to learn," Mr. Kruger said.

"Me?"

"Anybody. That's what the old copybooks used to say—you're never too old to learn."

"What about tomorrow afternoon?" Mr. Ogburn asked. "Meet you at the caddie house at three-thirty?"

"Good," Mr. Kruger said. "I'll be there."

Mr. Ogburn did not return directly to his office. On the way he called at his broker's and there learned something that curdled all the good nature that his highly satisfactory conversation with Mr. Kruger had brewed. Through carelessness or ignorance or rush of business, some idiot had mislaid a stop order he had put in, and the error had cost him a sum of money. It was not altogether the amount, which, fortunately, was not large, but the stupidity of the thing that infuriated him. When he reached his office he was in a very bad temper indeed, directed mainly against employees who hadn't their hearts in their duties.

As he passed through his filing department this mood was scarcely soothed by the sight of at least seven of his own clerical staff gathered idly near a window about a young woman typist whose name he remembered as Miss Farrell. With him out of sight, it seemed, they preferred to loaf and listen to this vapid-looking young blonde, whom Mr. Ogburn immediately identified as a shining example of the type of employee that had just cost him a matter of nearly three thousand dollars.

With a malignant eye on her, he drew near, unnoted, and listened for a full moment before making his presence known.

"What was the other one?" he heard a filing clerk ask.

"Well," said the blonde Miss Farrell, "a man had twenty horses and he had three stalls. He wanted to put these horses in the three stalls, but he didn't want to put an even number in any stall. How did he do it?"

"Twenty horses, three stalls, and he didn't want an even number of horses in any stall."

"That's it." Miss Farrell smiled. "How did he do it?"

This was enough for Mr. Ogburn. He cleared his throat, and the effect was as dramatic as he could have hoped.

"I beg your pardon," he said with ominous gentleness, "but am I paying you young ladies and gentlemen to learn how to put horses in stalls?"

Under the fishy coldness of his presence the young ladies and gentlemen exchanged uncomfortable smiles and then, in a pained silence, melted away—all but Miss Farrell, who, eyes wide with alarm, was the obvious object of Mr. Ogburn's particular interest.

"Your name," he said, "is Farrell, I believe."

"Y-yes, sir."

"I gather that you are responsible for this—er—pleasant little party on the company's time."

"Why, we—we were——"

"Whatever your other qualifications, Miss Farrell," he interrupted suavely, "you obviously do not grasp the essential quality of industry in a position."

"I—I'm sorry, sir. We were——"

"If you will go to Mr. Hudlin, the chief clerk," Mr. Ogburn continued, "he will present you with whatever pay is due you, and you will then be at liberty to spend your entire time elsewhere, with your calculations relating to stables."

He turned and strode, not walked, away. Miss Farrell remained stockstill for a second and then started after him. She called his name twice and then stopped. The door to his office slammed, and she went back to her desk slowly, to get whatever she had in its drawers.

Inside his office Mr. Ogburn sat at his desk, bolt upright, still angrier, he realized furiously, than the occasion demanded. He rang for Mr. Hudlin.

"That girl Farrell," he said when the chief clerk came in, "I've just fired her."

"What for?" Mr. Hudlin asked in surprise. "She's pretty good."

"She was telling riddles," Mr. Ogburn said, uncomfortably aware this seemed a bit inadequate for so drastic an action. "Telling riddles on the company's time."

"Riddles!"

"Riddles about horses."

"Horses!"

"Don't keep repeating words," Mr. Ogburn said irritably. "When I came in she had a whole bunch of the staff around her and she was telling them about a fellow who had twenty horses and three stalls and no even number in any stall."

Mr. Hudlin sat down. "Well?" he said.

"Well what?"

"How did he do it?" Mr. Hudlin asked, clearly interested in the problem.

"How should I know how he did it? I just told her she was fired. But a fool riddle like that—all you got to do is work it out mathematically."

"Well," said Mr. Hudlin thoughtfully, "you could put one horse in the first stall, three horses in the second stall, and——" He stopped.

"Don't be stupid," Mr. Ogburn said. "You put seven horses in the first stall, five in the second, and——" He stopped also. "You could put eleven horses in the first stall, one horse——" He stopped again. "No," he said thoughtfully, "that wouldn't do it."

"If he put nine horses in the first stall," Mr. Hudlin said slowly, beginning to figure on a slip of paper.

"Five in the second," Mr. Ogburn added, with the air of a man who is slipping up with the idea of pouncing on the solution before it got away, "and—"

They exchanged thoughtful stares.

"Come, come," Mr. Ogburn said disgustedly; "that's enough of this nonsense. I've got work to do. Send somebody in with the Fox Hills correspondence. They want some kind of answer this evening."

He picked up a heap of papers and dismissed Miss Farrell's problem from his mind to get down to business. Mr. Hudlin left, studying his slip of paper with a puzzled look. As he reached the door Mr. Ogburn spoke with elaborate casualness.

"Oh, by the way," he said, not looking at Mr. Hudlin, "when the Farrell girl comes for her pay, see if you can find out about those horses—just for the fun of the thing," he added, laughing merrily.

For fifteen minutes, when the Fox Hills correspondence was brought in, he went through the records, searching for just the right estimate, neither too high nor too low; and then he laid the papers down and, leaning back in his chair, stared at the ceiling.

Whatever his rumination, this brought no answer, so he dug a pencil out of a drawer, and a slip of paper, and jotted down two figures, scratching them out almost immediately. He tried two more and scratched them out also. Still another two, and as the door opened behind him he dropped his calculations hurriedly into a drawer and turned with a disarming smile to Mr. Hudlin.

"Conway's on the wire," the latter said after a suspicious pause. "Want to speak to him?"

"No. Tell him to use his own judgment."

Mr. Hudlin started to withdraw.

"Er—by the way!" Mr. Ogburn started, and stopped.

"Yes?"

"Oh, never mind! It doesn't matter."

Mr. Ogburn stared resentfully at the closing door. The idiot might at least have said whether he spoke to Miss Farrell, he reflected. He needn't be so mysterious about it.

After another half hour with the Fox Hills correspondence, he called in a stenographer and dictated three letters. He was in the midst of the third—to the Laney people about the Albany situation—when, so suddenly that the young woman taking down his words went pallid, he gave a little excited bleat, snatched her pencil from her, and scratched two figures on the pad on his desk—clearly a gentleman to whom a long-sought solution had come like a bolt of lightning and who intended to get the impression down in black and white before it flashed as quickly from his consciousness. Then, looking at the two figures, he snorted with disgust, and the stenographer—a Miss Gosling—looked around warily for the door, just in case of emergency.

"That's not it!" he snapped.

"I beg your perdun!" Miss Gosling said.

"Nothing," Mr. Ogburn said. "Where was I?"

Shortly before five, instead of sending for Mr. Hudlin, Mr. Ogburn went himself to his office and, opening the door, was just in time to see the chief clerk, with almost criminal haste, fumbling some slips of paper into his desk. Mr. Hudlin smiled at him innocently. Mr. Ogburn asked two or three routine questions, the answers to which he knew, and knew Mr. Hudlin knew he knew the answers; and it all nettled Mr. Ogburn considerably. But he answered his chief clerk's set smile with another just as set.

"Well," he said then with an extremely dubious-looking yawn, "guess I'll call it a day. M-m-m-m! By the way, did you happen to get hold of that Miss What's-Her-Name—about the horses?"

"Horses?" Mr. Hudlin appeared to rack his memory for any pending matter of horses. "Horses?"

"Oh, you know!" Mr. Ogburn laughed good-humoredly. "That Miss Farrell's riddle about the horses."

"Oh, that!" The chief clerk joined his employer in the laugh. "No, I didn't get to see her. Joe'd fixed her up before I got there." He resumed his air of innocence. "Why?"

"Nothing, nothing!" Mr. Ogburn replied hastily. "Nothing at all! Just sort of thought, idly, maybe you'd got the answer to it, that's all. Just sort of thought you might have got it, I mean."

"No," Mr. Hudlin said with a most bland and offensive indifference. "No, I never got it."

"Oh well"—Mr. Ogburn laughed again, indulgently—"purely a matter of mathematics."

"Purely."

"Mountain out of a molehill," he hazarded.

"Nothing more."

The first part of Mr. Ogburn's journey home in the subway he devoted to loathing Mr. Hudlin. The reasons he was able to summon were vague, but the results were fairly definite. Mr. Hudlin was not the man he had always believed him.

Around Forty-second Street Mr. Hudlin faded from his thoughts, and the remainder of the way he stared at a large foreign family standing near the center door, unnerving them with his protruding eyeballs, and tried to imagine that they were horses to be inserted into three stalls, represented by imaginary lines he drew across the car.

At dinner, smiling casually at his own interest, he posed the problem for Mrs. Ogburn.

"Why didn't he want to put an even number of horses in a stall?" she asked practically.

"I don't know that," he admitted.

"He must have been crazy," she decided.

"Perhaps so," he insisted, "but that doesn't answer it."

"Well, I can't be bothered working out why crazy people do things," she declared, and added, after a moment of thought, "and besides, I don't like horses."

At ten o'clock, in the library, where he alternately worked at a crossword puzzle and stared into the fire, he decided to fetch for himself the drink of water he wanted. In the pantry, as he opened the door, was Robert, the butler, and Robert was figuring with a stub of a pencil on a grocery bill, and as they stared at each other, both startled, it clicked in Mr. Ogburn's mind that perhaps this was all a gigantic plot to annoy him.

"What's that?" he demanded.

Robert continued to stare at him.

"Let's see it!" He put out a stern hand, and Robert, after a pause, gave him the bill. On the back of it were innumerable numbers in pairs, all scratched out.

"The horses!" Mr. Ogburn exploded.

"It's cook, sir." Robert smiled weakly, apologetically. "I couldn't help overhearing, sir, and cook, when I told her, was insistent, and I was merely——"

"Tell cook," Mr. Ogburn said angrily, "to stick to her pans of whatever they are and leave the horses to me."

"Very good, sir."

The incident so upset him that, forgetting the drink of water, he returned to the library, threw the crossword puzzle in the fire, and went to bed, where he lay awake for an hour, maneuvering a squadron of phantom horses about the black ceiling in a search for spectral stalls.

He reached his office the next morning in a poisonous temper. He was sore—sore at himself, sore at that blasted Miss Farrell, and sore at her double-blasted horses. The thing floated in his mind like the intolerably wearisome strains of some idiotic popular song. Try as he would, he couldn't get away from it.

Forthwith, the door of his private office closed, he called up all the half-witted people he knew, on the theory that only half-witted people would be likely to know the answer to such a question, and, one and all, they failed him.

This settled it. He rang for his chief clerk.

"Hudlin," he said darkly, "about those horses."

"Horses?"

"Horses is what I said. I saw you figuring those horses out. I caught you in the very act."

"Well, you weren't so indifferent——" Mr. Hudlin began indignantly.

"I got a full right," Mr. Ogburn began, and stopped, an inspiration arriving most providentially. He smiled amiably. "Personally," he said more gently, "they can take those twenty horses and dump them in the North River, as far as I'm concerned. What I'm worrying about," he added solemnly, "is my wife."

Mr. Hudlin looked at him suspiciously.

"Yes," Mr. Ogburn went on, laughing with relief at the happiness of this explanation, "I told Mrs. Ogburn about them last night, and I haven't had a minute's peace since. You know how women are."

"Yes?" Mr. Hudlin said warily.

"You never heard such goings on in your life, Hudlin! All evening, half the night, and the last thing this morning, 'Don't come home without the answer!' Last thing I heard, Hudlin."

"Yes?"

"So," Mr. Ogburn said briskly, "if you'll just get somebody to give Miss Farrell a ring—say one of the boys she was talking to yesterday—we'll just clear that little matter up and get down to business."

"She hasn't got a phone," Mr. Hudlin said.

"No phone!" His chief turned on him like a tiger. "What's she doing without a phone? Everybody has phones."

"She hasn't. I tried to get her last night."

Mr. Ogburn sat down, a look of anguish in his face. "But everybody's got phones," he insisted, as though explaining something to a child. "Everybody's got phones these days."

"Everybody but Miss Farrell," Hudlin said.

"What'll we do?"

"I think," the chief clerk said slowly, "we better hop in a taxi and go right over to her house."

"Good!" Mr. Ogburn sprang to his feet. This was action. This was getting somewhere. "Get your hat, Hudlin. We'll run right over, clear the little matter up, and then we can get down to business."

Mr. Hudlin gave the chauffeur an address which Mr. Ogburn recognized as somewhere in Brooklyn. The meter showed $2.25 before he realized how far in Brooklyn it was.

"Quite a long way," he observed—his first words in the cab.

"Miles," Mr. Hudlin said.

"Don't suppose she's moved, do you?"

"That was her address yesterday."

The meter was but a few dimes short of five dollars when at last the cab stopped in front of a frame house in south Brooklyn.

"No," Mr. Ogburn commented after surveying the wires that ran from its eaves, "no phone."

They ordered the driver to wait; then, in answer to a long press on the bell button, a gangling boy of seventeen appeared.

"Where's Miss Farrell?" Mr. Ogburn asked eagerly.

"She's gone to business," the boy replied doubtfully.

"Business!" Mr. Ogburn said indignantly. "Why, she has no business. She was discharged yesterday."

"She got another job. Who's this wants to know?"

"I'm Mr. Ogburn." He hesitated. "I've come to get her to go back to work for me."

"She wouldn't do it," the boy said definitely. "She says you're nuts."

"Wait a minute," Mr. Hudlin interrupted as Mr. Ogburn seemed on the point of striking the minor. "Let's get this straight. It just happens," he explained slowly, seeking words that would soften the reflection on their sanity as much as possible, "that your sister—she is your sister, isn't she?—

asked a riddle just before she left, but didn't tell the answer. Now, for business reasons we would like very much to get the answer to that riddle. It's very important. Do you know the riddle?"

"What riddle?"

"Listen," Mr. Hudlin said, wiping his forehead. "A man had twenty horses, and he wanted to put them in three stalls but didn't want to put an even number in any stall. How did he do it?"

"Why didn't he want to put an even number in?"

"He was crazy." Mr. Hudlin brushed hastily over that aspect of the situation. "How did he do it?"

The boy thought a minute. Then: "I give up," he said. "How did he do it?"

"Great heavens!" exploded Mr. Ogburn. "We haven't come all the way out here to ask you a riddle! We're after the answer. Don't you know it?"

A high, cheery voice drifted out from the rear of the house: "Who's there, Joe?"

"Man from New York," Joe called back, "asking riddles!"

"Don't want any today, sonny boy," the cheery voice replied.

"Come on," snapped Mr. Ogburn, "let's get out of here." He addressed Joe again: "Where's your sister asking riddles today?"

"I don't know the number."

"You know where it is?"

"Yes, but——"

"Get your hat," Mr. Ogburn said. "Stop talking and get your hat."

After some delay Joe joined them and gave the driver a series of involved and complicated directions. Then he sat back and revealed himself as a young man who appreciated an outing like this. He was willing, moreover, to contribute his share to the fun, and, assuming that riddles were the order of the day, he asked several dozen, answering them all himself very quickly, so that his companions were not put to the strain of mulling over them. The cab stopped finally in Williamsburg.

"That's it," Joe said. "Garner's."

"This is beginning to run into money," Mr. Ogburn said, peering at the meter.

"You want to stop?" Mr. Hudlin asked.

"No," Mr. Ogburn said thoughtfully, "my wife is very anxious for something definite."

Joe led them up a flight of stairs and into a large room where a number of typists were at work. Their first survey failing to find Miss Farrell, the impetuous Mr. Ogburn started down the aisles, staring into each face he passed. A short fat gentleman who watched this behavior for what he apparently believed to be a reasonable length of time inserted his presence in Mr. Ogburn's path.

"You looking for something?" he asked.

"We're looking for a young lady named Farrell," Mr. Hudlin said. "She came to work here this morning."

"Myrtle Farrell," Joe said.

"I know her," the fat gentleman said. "She ain't here."

"I knew it!" Mr. Ogburn said.

"Why ain't she here?" asked Joe. "She came here this morning. Why ain't she here now?"

"Never mind that," Mr. Ogburn said, pushing Joe aside, the better to address the fat gentleman. "Do you like riddles?"

"Riddles?" the gentleman repeated, obviously surprised.

"Riddles," Mr. Ogburn said. "Questions and answers."

"Sure," the gentleman said. "What is the difference between a cow with a crumpled horn and a corn with——"

"Listen," Mr. Ogburn interrupted impatiently. "A man's got twenty horses and three stalls, and he wants to put the horses in the stalls but no even number in any stall. How does he do it?"

The gentleman looked at the ceiling. "I give up," he said then.

"Let's go," Mr. Ogburn said without further ado.

"Hey!" called the gentleman. "What's the answer?"

"I'm trying to tell you," Mr. Ogburn said, "I don't know the answer."

"You mean you ask me a riddle," the gentleman exclaimed, obviously indignant, "and you don't know the answer!"

"We're looking for my sister," Joe explained. "She knows the answer."

"Well," said Mr. Garner thoughtfully, "it's purely a matter of mathematics——"

"We know that," Mr. Hudlin cut in shortly. "Let's go, chief."

"All you got to do," Mr. Garner continued confidently, "is put three horses in the first stall and seven in the second——"

A minute later, as Mr. Ogburn and his staff of two investigators descended the stairs, they heard running feet behind them, and Mr. Garner, his hat on, was at their heels.

"If you don't mind," he said apologetically, "I'll go along with you. I want to hear what this young lady says—because it can't be done."

"Which way?"

"She ain't been gone ten minutes," Mr. Garner said. "She just up and said she didn't like the place, not ten minutes ago."

He went off to get his own cab, as there were signs in the first group that he was not wanted there. Hurrying to where their cab was parked, Mr. Ogburn gave Mr. Hudlin a startled stare.

"Did you hear what he said?" he whispered.

"Yes."

"Do you suppose she'd ask a riddle that didn't have any answer at all?"

"Well," Mr. Hudlin replied evasively, "I didn't know her very well."

"Would your sister ask a riddle that didn't have any answer to it?" Mr. Ogburn asked Joe.

"She never has," Joe said.

They got in the cab, and Mr. Ogburn took another look at the meter. It registered $8.60. He looked at his watch. It was two-thirty.

"Well?" Mr. Hudlin asked. Mr. Ogburn thought. "No," he said then, "it would make us look bad if we came all this way and then didn't get it. Besides," he added after another pause, "Mrs. Ogburn is interested."

"It might work," Mr. Hudlin said suddenly, "if you put one in the first stall, seventeen in the second——"

"No, I tried that. I put three in the first——"

"There she is!" Joe shouted suddenly. "Pull up, driver—pull up! There she is coming out of that drugstore!"

The drivers pulled up simultaneously, and Miss Farrell's view of the situation was this: She was coming out of this drugstore where she'd been drinking a soda, as she had every right to, when two ominous-looking taxi chauffeurs rushed up to the curb in front of her and a large crowd of excited men burst from the doors of the cab and made directly for her, shouting incoherently. She did what any lady would do under like circumstances—she made a dive for the drugstore.

Inside the store it all happened so quickly that the pale young man behind the prescription counter, who took his hands off his hips and walked right out to speak sternly to those responsible for the disturbance, was scarcely able to relate later what took place.

As best he saw it, a mob of some twenty men burst into the door after a terrified young woman. Ducking around a counter, she got into a telephone booth. The gang located her almost immediately. There were shouts, objections, complaints, and wails, and then, as suddenly as they had entered, they dashed out, whisking the terrified young woman away in their midst. Hurling her into one of the several high-powered cars drawn up at the curb, with motors running, they were all off like the wind. It was one of those occurrences, the prescription clerk explained afterward, that give a fellow quite a turn.

Broadly speaking, this was an accurate enough account, and back in the taxi even Mr. Ogburn appreciated Miss Farrell's mounting hysteria, for in the scuffle Mr. Garner had also managed to work his way into the first cab, so that, counting Joe's sister, it now held five people, and it was not a large cab.

Behind them came Mr. Garner's empty cab, and behind him a third cab, also empty, whose driver Mr. Garner's driver had persuaded to come along, in case there should be trouble in collecting his fare from the elusive Mr. Garner.

Having identified a majority of her captors, Miss Farrell jumped to one conclusion and stuck to it. "I never took a thing!" she sobbed unhappily. "I'm honest and I never took a thing from either place!" She started to wail.

"Miss Farrell," Mr. Ogburn tried to assure her in his most melting tones, "it is furthest from my thoughts——"

"I won't say a thing until I see a lawyer!"

This alarmed Mr. Ogburn. "If you will only listen, Miss Farrell," he said earnestly, "you'll understand——"

"I demand a lawyer! I've got a right to see my lawyer before I say a thing—and you can't bully me!"

"Speak to her," Mr. Ogburn ordered Joe. "Tell her we don't mean anything wrong."

"Listen, Sis——"

"She can't do it," Mr. Garner said calmly. "You can't put twenty horses in three stalls——"

"Strangle that fool," Mr. Ogburn ordered his chief clerk. "What's he doing in here, anyway?"

"It's mathematically impossible——"

"Listen, Sis," Joe said. "All they want is you should answer a riddle, and that's all."

Miss Farrell took her handkerchief from her eyes and, after looking her surprise at her brother, studied the others thoughtfully.

"That's all," Mr. Ogburn added coaxingly; "just answer a riddle—that's all."

"No"—Miss Farrell buried her face in her handkerchief once more—"I ain't in a mood for riddles."

"She can't do it," Mr. Garner said.

"Listen here!" Mr. Ogburn shouted at her so furiously that she sat up, frightened. "A man's got twenty horses and three stalls, and he don't want to put an even number in any stall—understand?"

She gazed at him with wide eyes.

"Understand?"

She nodded.

"All right, how does he do it?"

She stood the concentration of tense attention for a full moment, and then, her nerves a little weakened by the excitement, her face screwed up into wrinkles, her mouth widened, and tears flowed from her eyes.

"I don't know!" she cried. "I can't remember—and I want a lawyer!"

"You don't need a lawyer to answer a riddle!" Mr. Ogburn said furiously. "All you got to do is answer it!"

"I want to get out of this cab," she mumbled in her handkerchief. "I can't remember any riddles—you shout at me so, I can't hardly remember my own name! Let me out, I say!"

"I told you," Mr. Garner said.

Mr. Ogburn turned to him, obviously holding himself in with an effort. "If you say that again," he said deliberately, "I'll knock you clean out of this cab."

Mr. Garner shut up, but wiggled his eyes defiantly.

"Now, my dear," Mr. Ogburn resumed soothingly, "all you've got to do is concentrate. Just concentrate on horses—twenty horses and three stalls. Nobody's going to harm you—not while Mr. Ogburn's here. So just see if you can't concentrate."

There was a long silence. Then Miss Farrell, who never removed her handkerchief from her eyes, began sniffling again.

"I'm frightened," she wept. "I want to go home."

"Mr. Ogburn will take you right home," Mr. Ogburn promised softly, "just as soon as you tell Mr. Ogburn about the horses."

Another long silence.

"It's all gone," she mumbled. "You frightened me and I can't remember. I want to go home."

Mr. Ogburn sat back with tight-pressed lips and then turned suddenly to Mr. Garner, but Mr. Garner, staring innocently, indicated with his hands that he had nothing to say.

"Look, Sis," Joe said. "Ain't that one of the riddles you got from Artie?"

"Uh-huh!" she nodded.

"Good!" Mr. Ogburn exclaimed, once more the executive. "Now we're getting somewhere. How can we get hold of this Artie? What we want to do," he explained briskly to Mr. Hudlin, "is just clear this little matter up, get it settled, and get back to business."

Joe opened the driver's window. "Fourteenth Street, Manhattan," he ordered. "Just follow the cross-town streetcar line."

"What's this?" Mr. Hudlin asked.

"Artie's a conductor on the Fourteenth Street cross-town line," Joe explained. "We'll just find his car and hop it."

"Capital!" Mr. Ogburn said, and sat back as the driver, still leading Mr. Garner's two empty cabs, turned his radiator cap in the direction of the Queensboro Bridge. "Funny thing for a man to be," he commented conversationally to Mr. Hudlin. "I mean a conductor on the Fourteenth Street cross-town line. I never thought of a man being that."

"No more did I," admitted Mr. Hudlin.

"You don't think this is beginning to make us look ridiculous, I hope," Mr. Ogburn went on with sudden anxiety. "I mean, after all, that meter, you see, and everything."

"It's for Mrs. Ogburn," Mr. Hudlin reminded him.

"Can't be helped," Mr. Ogburn shrugged.

They crossed the bridge and drove downtown through Park and Fourth avenues, and on Joe's advice turned east, moving slowly along the car tracks and watching the conductors on the crowded cars that passed. Three went by and no Artie.

"I say, Miss Farrell," Mr. Hudlin said, "did the answer by any chance have to do with switching the horses suddenly?"

"Switching the horses?" Mr. Ogburn said, puzzled. "Why should the horses be switched?"

"In some riddles," Mr. Hudlin explained apologetically, "things are switched around suddenly."

"I see. I thought you meant whipping the horses."

Miss Farrell shook her head. "I don't remember."

"Artie!" The alert Mr. Joe Farrell was halfway out of the window, waving frantically to a dingy-looking little conductor on the jammed back platform of a car. Mr. Ogburn's head went out of the same window and he waved also, while Mr. Hudlin and Mr. Garner signaled vigorously from the opposite side.

Recognizing no one at first, Artie waved merrily back and said something to his passengers, who laughed heartily and all waved good-humoredly. The taxi passengers waved again, and again the streetcar passengers responded. It was a game in which many joined; it even attracted amused attention from pedestrians. Mr. Ogburn began to perspire.

"The man must be an idiot," he muttered.

"Hey!" An enormous gentleman wearing a corduroy suit and carrying a lunch pail was hailing them through cupped hands from the streetcar. "Go soaka da head! You gotta too mocha da hooch, hey?" His friends aboard roared.

Mr. Ogburn looked at Mr. Hudlin, appalled. "He thinks we're drunk!" he gasped. "Here!" He seized Joe, hauled him out of the window, and, seizing Miss Farrell by the neck, thrust her blonde head into the opening. "Look, you idiot!" he shouted.

The maneuver was successful. One sight of Miss Farrell and the dingy conductor yanked his bell cord once, and the car came to a sudden stop. Jumping off, he met the occupants of the taxicab, Miss Farrell in their midst, in the middle of the street.

"What's the idea," he demanded, "trying to throw this girl through the window like that?"

"I'm not trying to throw anybody——"

"I seen you," Artie stated. "I seen you trying to throw her through the window of that cab. Well, if you keep that up——"

"Artie," Miss Farrell said breathlessly, "listen to what they got to ask and let them beat it! In all my life I never had so many lunatics——"

"All we want," Mr. Ogburn said, "is that you should answer a riddle."

"Riddle or no riddle, you can't throw girls through taxi windows like that, you know!"

"Listen, Artie!"

"Go ahead. What is it?"

"Listen," Mr. Ogburn said hurriedly as a crowd began to assemble, "you told Miss Farrell a riddle about a man had twenty horses and three stalls——"

"What's all this?" The crowd pressed back as a tall traffic cop pushed his way in. "What's all this about?"

"Just a minute, Officer! It's a riddle——"

"You can't tell riddles in the middle of the street!"

"Twenty horses, three stalls, and no even number in any stall!" Mr. Ogburn said frantically to Artie. "Quick! How's he do it?"

"How many stalls?" shouted someone in the rear of the crowd.

"Three!" Mr. Ogburn called back obligingly. "Quick! How's it done?"

"Well," said the traffic cop, "you could put three in the first stall, five in the second——"

"Just a minute, Officer! . . . How is it done, Artie?"

Artie grinned. "Easy," he said. "He puts one horse in the first stall."

"Yes."

"Nineteen in the second."

"And the third?"

"He don't bother with the third," Artie grinned. "The riddle don't say he's got to put horses in all the stalls. It just says he's got three of them. One in the first, nineteen in the second. That's all."

"But say——" began the cop.

"It's a trick," Mr. Garner stated. "I told you it couldn't be done on the level."

"Is that—is that the way the riddle goes?" Mr. Ogburn asked, looking at Artie pathetically.

"Fooled you, eh?" Artie was very happy. "That riddle always fools 'em. Nine times out of ten they can't answer it."

Mr. Ogburn looked at Mr. Hudlin. "I guess we'd better get along," he said weakly. "We've got a lot to do."

"Hey!" called Artie as he started to edge away, but Mr. Ogburn did not stop. He sent Mr. Hudlin back. "Anything," he said mildly; "give him anything." He pressed his way on out through the curiously staring crowd. "The very idea," he said bitterly to himself, "of his leaving one stall empty—the very idea!"

A half hour later, in his private office, Mr. Ogburn fluttered a sheaf of papers briskly.

"Now," he said, "we've got that little matter off our hands, we better get down to brass tacks. What about those Hanover papers? Get me those Hanover papers and we'll brush right through them."

"Aren't you going to call Mrs. Ogburn?" Mr. Hudlin asked.

The fluttering of papers halted. Mr. Ogburn looked around slowly at his chief clerk, but Mr. Hudlin's face was pure innocence. "No," he said. "I'll tell her tonight."

"Won't she be worrying?"

Once again Mr. Ogburn looked at him. "No," he said. "I'll tell her tonight."

"I really think," Mr. Hudlin said, "you ought to let her know, so she'll have some peace."

A pause. Then: "Oh well!" He lifted the receiver and got his home. "Mrs. Ogburn," he said. "Tell her Mr. Ogburn is calling." He looked around, but Mr. Hudlin was making no move to leave. "Hello, hello! Is this you, dear?" A pause. "Yes, dear, about those horses." Pause. "Those horses. Those twenty horses. Those twenty horses in that riddle." Pause. "Horses, I say. Twenty horses in a riddle." Pause. "Listen, dear, that riddle I was telling you last night." Pause. "Riddle, I say!" He was becoming a little warm, and particularly conscious of a grim and vicious smile on Mr. Hudlin's face, even though it was behind him.

"Listen, damn it, darling. I'm talking about that riddle about horses— horses—horses!"

"Crazy over horses," he heard Mr. Hudlin murmur.

"Well, whether you remember or not," Mr. Ogburn said between set teeth, "it's one in the first stall, nineteen in the second, and none in the third." He jammed the receiver on the hook and, without looking around, picked up the Hanover papers.

"That must have relieved her," Mr. Hudlin said guilelessly. "Things like that upset a woman."

"I'll see you later," Mr. Ogburn snapped.

Mr. Hudlin got up.

"This Farrell woman," Mr. Ogburn said, "is she coming back here?"

"No. That Artie called me back to see what we were going to do, but she said—well, she said she didn't think she'd want to come back." He paused. "She was a little exercised over it all."

"It's just as well," Mr. Ogburn said. "Telling riddles like that—it upsets the staff. Can't get a bit of work done. I wish you could have seen them loafing around here when I came in yesterday!"

MACKINLAY KANTOR

Whear Ha' Ye Ben, My Laddie?

Oh! I ha' ben wi' Gordon's men—
Dinna ye hear th' bagpipes play?
SCOTTISH SONG.

THE FIRST kilted Scotsman whom Sam ever met was Sir Harry, in the days before he was Sir Harry. It was at the old Classic-Imperial Theater in Detroit; Sam was covering a lucrative territory which his firm had recently given him as a reward for shrewd and diligent services.

Sam was enjoying a free evening and he had gone over to call on a boyhood friend named Hillman, who was manager of the Classic-Imperial. It would be good to see Hillman; Sam would possibly receive a complimentary seat in the orchestra; from both lines of his ancestry Sammy had inherited strong reluctance to pay for a seat if, with all dignity, he might have one free.

The minstrel's full-length pictures were leaning against the theater façade, and Sam paused to admire them. He had never heard Harry sing; of course he knew Harry's phonograph records. Once, in Hillman's office, Sam had expressed anticipated pleasure at the thought of hearing the great performer.

"Sure," said Hillman. "He's been playing all week, Sam. He's been packing 'em in. You want to go back and meet him?"

The delighted Sammy was escorted backstage, and Mr. Hillman introduced him to the great man. For a few moments Sam, usually glib and self-possessed, was stricken dumb by his proximity to greatness.

Harry wore a gay little jacket with ornate buttons on the sleeves, and a heavy pleated kilt. He had a leather sporran with silver on the front, and his famous Balmoral cap with dice and feathers. Sam's eyes devoured Harry greedily; amazingly he was thrilled by Harry's huge head, his coal miner's shoulders, his solid knees, and the little dagger with gleaming hilt which was thrust into his plaid stocking.

Harry Lauder beamed, and chatted with Hillman about the house and the hotels in Detroit and their prices; he was wholly affable. Presently Sam plucked up courage to tell Harry Lauder that his own mother was a Davidson.

"Of that, laddie," said Harry, "there can be no doubt!" and he led off a series of chuckles in which Hillman joined.

"No," said Sam, "I mean she was Scotch."

"Scottish is the worrd, laddie. She was a Scottish lady?"

"All right," said Sam. "You understand, I was raised an orphan by some folks in New York, you understand; but my mother was Scotch." And when Harry looked at him frosty-eyed, Sam corrected himself hurriedly and said, "Scottish."

He told Harry more, before the minstrel went on stage. Sam said that his Grandfather Davidson kept a grocery store and his mother clerked there; Sam's father had a tiny tailor shop across the street and he used to buy food at Davidson's grocery. He fell in love with Mary Davidson and married her, and was promptly run over by a coal wagon. A few months later Sam's mother died when Sammy was born; so that made him an orphan and he was raised by some good people named Frank. But he was always proud that his mother had been Scotch. Scottish.

"Aye," said Harry Lauder. "A fine family, a fine Highland family, the Davidsons." Then he spoke in "braid Scots," as was his bounden intent so often. "Ye ha' nae mony Hielan' Davidsons i' America."

His speech was incomprehensible to Sam.

"Not many Davidsons," Harry Lauder translated, and the bagpipes began to moan and he went on stage.

Sammy was led around to the front; he came down and sat in the orchestra—in a free seat, surely enough. He contemplated Harry Lauder with blissful awe; his senses swam confused amid the droning of the pipes.

He had heard bagpipes before—he did not know just when—in vaude-ville, no doubt. He had heard the pipes, but he had never been aware of them. Now it seemed that a warlike Highland spirit, for twenty-odd years buried within his slim, swarthy body, came burningly alive. He pounded his feet upon the floor, he breathed heavily, his eyes were wild; people in near-by seats turned to look at him with curiosity and annoyance.

When the entertainment was over he brazenly deserted Hillman, who had wanted to go for a late beer and sausages at a swell place called Louie's. Sam took his post in the alley and watched the stage door. At last he was gratified by the sight of Harry Lauder, still wearing his kilt and a gray raincoat, too, walking bandy-legged up the alley and out of Sammy's life for that season.

But never out of Sammy's memory nor out of his affections. Sam swung down the street toward his hotel; now he was a Highlander; he imagined that the pipes were crying ahead and behind and all around him. He squared his shoulders and tried to walk like a majestic piper. He imagined that his new button shoes were buckled brogans. He looked down at the swishing hem of his topcoat and wondered what it would be like to wear the kilt.

In his mind Sammy said, "wear kilts," but soon he learned the incorrectness of this term. He began to learn a great deal about Scotland in general and his ancestral Davidsons in particular.

In bookstores of Detroit, Cleveland, and Buffalo he bought books about Scotland. Some of them were prissy, trivial travel books, written by prissy, trivial old ladies in petticoats and in trousers alike, who went into peeping ecstasies over the Trossachs and Stirling. Some were wordy histories which required a scholarly background for their proper interpretation, and this background Sammy did not as yet possess. Rapidly, enthusiastically, he began to acquire it.

Before the year was out, men in his firm were calling him "Scotty" and hooting his mania. After all these years of bourbon, they said, it was amazing to see Sam buying scotch, because scotch was expensive. But Sam declared that the smoky barley taste was infinitely preferable; no gentleman of Highland blood could swallow a whisky made from corn.

The music of the pipes he drank voraciously. He haunted side-street variety houses where, not so frequently as Sam could have wished, bagpipers played their vaudeville turns.

It might have been suspected that his work as a salesman of tailors' trimmings and imported fabrics would suffer as a result of the Scottish obsession which now ruled Sam's life. But this did not happen to be the case. He became an authority on tweeds, and he could discuss the process of tweed manufacture with infectious delight. His employers took away his line of trimmings and put him on tweeds exclusively. The first month after this happened he made an extra one hundred and forty-four dollars in commissions, and some of that amount he contributed to the passion which had become his private and public religion.

In the Madison Avenue hotel which Sam called home, in New York, he plastered the walls with colored prints or stained-steel engravings found in secondhand shops. There ruled Walter Scott, Bobby Burns, The Meeting of Burns and Scott, The Highlanders' Assault on Gibraltar, Sir Colin Campbell's Entrance into Lucknow, The Young Pretender's Entrance into Edinburgh, The Parting of Burns and Highland Mary, The Parting of Prince Charlie and Flora MacDonald, The Twa Brigs of Ayr. And, of course, a photograph of Harry Lauder—which, after difficulty, Sammy managed to have signed by the minstrel when Harry returned for his next farewell tour.

No longer, rocking through the hinterland in smoking compartments, did he trade Jewish and Irish stories with the other boys. He told Scotch jokes only, but with a "braid Scots" accent which kept most of his hearers from understanding them. Since people did not appreciate his jokes, Sammy retired more and more from talkative crowds in the smokers and rode alone, reading.

He learned the complicated and sanguinary history of battles in Sutherland or Perth which he had never heard of before, and which most of his fellow Americans had never heard of either. He began to learn pipe tunes. This music, no longer an uncertain moan of the drones and a whining spasm from the chanters, separated itself logically into clan record and regimental movement. It became specifically: "Cock o' the North," "The Seventy-fourth Highlanders' Farewell to Edinburgh," "Blue Bonnets over the Border," "The Barren Rocks of Aden," and scores of other reels, pibrochs, strathspeys.

Well aware that he and his muscular enthusiasm would go down to the dust as millions of valiant clansmen had gone before them, Sammy did not neglect the coronachs. These were the dirges. These were the most moving, the most tender and compelling of all. They were the tunes that cried along misty roads when coffins lay beneath the Union Jack on gun carriages, when officers paced slowly with arms reversed, when drums were dulled and muted by death and the rain.

As a saint of old wrestled with an outlandish opponent, so Sammy wrestled with the distraction of his common life and ambitions, one August night in a Toronto hotel room.

He had heard the thud of leather feet slamming the pavement all through the previous afternoon and part of the previous evening. The braying of pipes haunted his dreams; occasionally Sam got up in his nightshirt and sat on the window ledge, face pressed against the dirty screen.

If Sam kept on, the way he had been going, he would certainly clear six or seven thousand dollars in this year. Six or seven thousand dollars are not to be sneezed at, when you know the value and importance of money—when, within your personal recollection, you have endured inconvenience or pain for the lack of it. Sammy envisaged the astonishment—even consternation—which would prevail in New York if the sales manager learned that Sam's madness had ruined a promising business career.

It was well enough to think about the firm. But, he kept feeling, it was more important to think about the Davidsons.

He fetched them out of Kinrara's history. "The Davidsons, styled of Invernahaven, in Badenoch, were . . . originally a branch of the Comyns." So they were; and then came Donald Du who married a daughter of the Mackintoshes, and then came internecine feuds within the Clan Chattan. Sammy could count the dead at Invernahaven and the dead at the North Inch; and he could pile them with the dead of other Scottish families of other wars, tribal and international alike. He could feel that he should be numbered among them.

It seemed silly that Toronto could be the steppingstone. He had always thought of Toronto as a place where he liked to eat chicken and dumplings at Fisher's Restaurant; a place where he sold certain American goods to Curtis & Mulvaney, a place where sometimes he met Mr. Pryor, of his firm's importing department, in a noisy and profitless game of poker with Mr. Pryor's friends. He had never thought of Toronto as the gateway to the Highland wars, as the gateway to any wars whatsoever. Haggard above the breakfast counter, Sammy decided that Toronto was the gateway, and a thousand dead Davidsons were compelling him to walk through it.

Late that forenoon he closed his order books and put rubber bands around them, in the office of Curtis & Mulvaney. He told the younger Mr. Curtis, "You understand, I've written my last order for a while," and left the younger Mr. Curtis gaping.

Shortly thereafter Sam was standing in front of a folding table in a barren armory—a long room, filled with the hollow voices and whistles of young men. He was looking alternately into an officer's small black eyes and onto the pink bald top of that officer's head.

"Name?"

Sammy told him.

The officer smiled. "Are you sure you're not joining up with the wrong outfit, my lad?"

"Aren't you recruiting for the Forty-eighth Highlanders?"

"That's right."

"Then this is the outfit for me," said Sam. "My mother was a David-son."

"Are you a Canadian?"

"Yes sir," lied Sam.

"Born where?"

Sammy told a prodigious lie about being born in Vancouver; afterward he was worried about that, because it seemed to him that Vancouver was a city in the United States. But the recruiting officer wrote it down without a murmur. Sam was sent to be poked at and punched by the doctors.

When they issued him his first uniform he fell into a state of quiet delirium akin to drunkenness. True, he felt that he should be wearing the soft green tartan of the Davidsons. But this red-and-black marvel which draped his thighs was woolen plaid; it was a kilt; he had only dreamed of kilts, he had never thought that he might actually wear one.

Sam turned himself out for every parade and inspection like a toy soldier, a candy soldier on a Christmas tree. The brass of his buttons hurt the sergeants' eyes; his bonnet tails were as thin and flat as black paper. The buckles of his equipment looked like jewelry; and he mourned the dull rain of August twenty-ninth, for the regiment had to go off to Long Branch without a color flying.

By no means were they all Scotsmen in the Forty-eighth Highlanders —though most of the officers were Scots, and Sam rejoiced especially that the colonel's name was Currie. There were some Irish, some Norwegians, a few Englishmen; more of the war-trained English had gone out with the Pats and were in France and in action before the Forty-eighth Highlanders ever waded off Salisbury Plain. There was one soldier who looked like a Greek. There were men with Scottish names whose features and patois were decidedly French-Canadian. But the regiment had more fun with Sam than with any of them.

They made rich whimsy out of Sam's every excitement. They asked him about the price of goods in Vancouver and whether the goods were good goods. But they found themselves admiring him more all the time, and Sammy found himself loving the whole battalion. Even when they burned the pay show at Valcartier, and one riotous comrade carried his celebration into quarters on his return, and said things about Sammy's ancestry which he thought were witty—even with a black eye and torn knuckles and a sore jaw and a confinement staring him in the face, Sam still adored the battalion.

He didn't care what they called the battalion at Dominion headquarters, or in the office of the Secretary for War. They might call it the Fifteenth Battalion, Third Brigade, First Division, C.E.F. But it was only one thing to Sammy: it was the Forty-eighth Highlanders, and of these words the last was the most important.

Though soon a dowdy khaki apron supplanted the scarlet and black of the tartan kilt, though the sporran became only a pocket, though the mud demanded rubber boots instead of the gaudy leg gear which the soldiers had worn before—though France cried out her eyes about the First Canadian Division, Sammy could only laugh in his heart. At last, he cried, a bold, bright Davidson had climbed from foreign slumber and was marching behind the pipes once more.

Neuve-Chapelle disappointed Sam considerably. He had wanted to stand knee-deep in heather, target on arm, claymore in hand, striking against the hated invader who had fired his cottage thatch. Instead, it seemed that the people of Flanders regarded him as much an invader as they did the Germans. There were no rocky eminences on which to burn the fiery crosses Sam's spirit longed to kindle. If there grew heather in France, it was conspicuous by its absence around Neuve-Chapelle.

All he could remember of Neuve-Chapelle, at long last, was a tall Michigander who bent in the litter with a wafer of a precious American tobacco sack dangling from his pocket. He was saying, over and over, "Some days you can't lay up a cent. No sir, some days you can't lay up a cent!" As a rallying cry that might have done very well for a man from Michigan; it was fair insult to one of the Davidsons, styled of Invernahaven, in Badenoch.

St. Julien appeared as more of a battle, more the way a battle should be, until the gas messed things up. The black-faced men in torn breeches who came stumbling and coughing across the beets would never have been permitted to put in an appearance at the battle of North Inch. Still, the Forty-eighth Highlanders were fighting hard; so was the entire Third Brigade; so were other Canadian brigades alongside.

Sammy had run until he was as dark in the face as the miserable Turcos. He had fired exactly seventeen rounds into the close ranks of helmeted people who pressed before him, when somebody swung a board and struck him smartly on the thigh.

The impact sent him tumbling over the edge of the manure pile where he had been warring, and he looked up in fury to see what traitor among his companions could possibly have swatted him with a board. But it was not a board; it was a metal-jacketed bullet which had made hay out of his upper right femur, and that was not the way bullets were supposed to feel. They were supposed to feel like red-hot pokers or stabs of steel; Sam had read about them often enough. He had not read that they felt like somebody hitting you with a board.

With which summary dispatch, Sam was retired from active warfare in the ranks of the Fifteenth Battalion, Third Brigade, First Division, C.E.F. For the next twenty-five years, despite all surgery, his femur corroded within his thigh.

When he crutched back to work in New York in 1917, he wore upon his lapel a disk as resplendent as a new quarter dollar. It bore a British shield and the words, FOR SERVICE AT THE FRONT C.E.F.

But in his pocket he carried the badge of the Forty-eighth Highlanders —complete with its numeral, its brass, its angry little falcon cock, its buckled belt with the delightful Gaelic inscription: "*Dileas gu brath.*" That was just as good a rallying cry as anything else, when you got down to it. People told Sam that most assuredly he had done his bit, but it didn't seem like a very large bit to him.

He kept his battalion badge in the pocket of whichever tweed suit he wore. He turned it over frequently, as an especial petition for good luck. He must have turned it over the day he limped into the office of Apgar Brothers, in Philadelphia, and saw Miss Jennie at the switchboard.

They were married late in November of 1918, after Jennie had cried upon Sam's shoulder. This happened during Sam's seventh trip to Philadelphia, in the time of his life which may be labeled A. J., or, in other words, After Jennie. It was on the evening of their ninth dinner together.

Early during their friendship Sam had talked affectionately about Scotland. Jennie said that she had often wanted to see the Highlands; she wondered whether they were higher than the Catskills, where once she had vacationed.

"Ben Nevis," said Sammy in his authority, "is the great monarch of Scottish mountains, rising to a height of forty-four hundred and six feet, and is said to take its name from Gaelic words meaning the 'cloud-kissing hill.'"

Jennie said, "I think it's simply wonderful, Sam, the way you know all about Scotland."

Sam shrugged. "That's what it said in a book," he admitted. "I haven't ever yet been to Ben Nevis."

"Maybe you'll go sometime."

"I ask you, how can I go to Scotland while the war is going on, and maybe get myself torpedoed? I went over once and I came back all right; I don't want to crowd my luck, Jennie."

"Couldn't you go to Scotland while you were in the war?"

He explained, "Some of them went when we were on Salisbury Plain, but I couldn't get leave then."

He could have told her more. He could have told her that his dreams were nightly redolent of heather, that, waking or sleeping, he heard the pipes. But he told her that he wanted to go to Scotland, and let it go at that.

He was tired and lame. He had worked like a slave since re-entering civil life; those were the piping times of war, with no pun suggesting itself when Sam looked at his little bankbook. His employers urged him, much against their own financial interest, to take an extended rest. But there was no place he wished to go except to Scotland, and too many difficulties attended such an adventure.

Therefore, no one celebrated the Armistice more fervently than Sam, and some ten days afterward he staged a second and quieter celebration with Jennie, when business took him to Philadelphia. Then it was that he told her that he was going to Scotland; then it was that she burst into tears. Two weeks later found them married, bedded snugly in a B-deck stateroom, feeling their way through fog along the Newfoundland Banks.

They landed at Plymouth; Sam wore his Forty-eighth Highlanders' badge on his overcoat, and was teased about it by tired, thin-faced boys who crowded their second-class carriage on the way up to London. Forthwith he bought himself some medal ribbons.

He wanted to be orthodox or nothing. He went around with red-white-and-blue of the 1915 Star, and the blue-white-black-and-orange of the General Service ribbon gay upon his breast pocket. Jennie thrilled with pride. When later Sam added the prismatic glories of the Victory ribbon, she told him that, like Joseph in olden days, he wore a coat of many colors.

They went from London to Edinburgh by night train, and at ten o'clock next morning Sam was stumbling through the cold keep and passages of the castle in a kind of drooling daze. He stood with Jennie on Princes Street that afternoon and watched a funeral procession pass. A body was being fetched home from France. Yes, the British flag swaddled the coffin; yes, the attendant officers wore crape and carried their arms reversed; ghosts walked with the sorrowing pipers and led them in the wailing threnody, "My Home." Sam was crying; Jennie had never seen him do that before. She slipped her hand into his; he put the print of his bones upon her flesh.

They did not return to the United States for nearly four years, and when they went it was only for a visit, and they stayed only two months. They took their small son with them, of course, and Sam insisted upon the boy's wearing Highland dress complete to the very shoe buckles.

Sam had wanted to buy a house far up in the Grampians and a little business of some kind there as well, but Jennie balked at that. Their son would need to have the advantages of a city close at hand, she contended; Sam never guessed how well Jennie herself loved the grumble of traffic.

So they settled in Fife, on a road northwest of Cowdenbeath, in a village called Dunbayne. There Sam bought a small hotel with the money he had saved in the United States; there eventually he acquired the license to operate a public house which he named Sam's Rest. There, in due season, American tourists marveled at his "braid Scots" accent and at the philabeg of Davidson tartan which brushed his knobby knees.

The little boy was named Isaac; that had been his paternal grandfather's name, but Sam's researches taught him that also many of the Davidsons had been named Isaac. It seemed the only name wholly appropriate, when you considered the circumstances.

His Scottish neighbors were incredulous and amused when Sam and Jennie first settled in Dunbayne. Still, the newcomers encountered little downright hostility; only the suspicion invariably accorded visiting Americans. As years went on and as their child, born in the village, grew older, Sam's family took a respectable and respected place in the community.

Sometimes the natives found Sam's Highland mania a little hard to take. There was a redheaded plumber named Forrester, who became annoyed one evening at Sam's persistent rendition of a historic Highland chant in pidgin Gaelic. Forrester arose, broke his ale glass against the stove, and bellowed, "I can bear no more of this man! He's but an imitation Scotsman!"

The room exploded with noise and struggling figures, as the combined efforts of the group became necessary to restrain Sam, who tried to fly at

Forrester with a loaded bottle, shrilling meanwhile the war cry of the Mackintoshes.

Sam declared, when capable of coherent speech, that Forrester's remark had been a slander against his mother; she was as pure a Davidson as David Du himself; and with this statement the neighbors concurred. They invited Mr. Forrester to apologize. He did so in due season handsomely, and he and Sam were fast friends from that time forth.

Indeed Forrester's uncle, a middle-aged and disheveled inebriate named John Cameron, became factotum and handy man at Sam's Rest. Old John built fires, carried wood, made beds, and scrubbed floors with moderate efficiency, but never forgot that for nine glorious years he had piped with the Gordon Highlanders. He told young Isaac, Sam's son, the most fantastic tales of his military wanderings.

John Cameron owned a pair of pipes still, and on pleasant summer evenings the screech of "Cock o' the North," "My Huntly Braw," or the livelier notes of "Roy's Wife of Aldìvalloch" would come wheedling through the Dunbayne street. Men might chuckle, down at the butcher's shop, about the fervent antics of him whom they called "the American Scotsman." But Sam's family and Old John himself took the pipe music very seriously. And when little Isaac was grown tall enough to send to a better school, they counted their shillings happily and sent him to Edinburgh, where each day he might see the castle walls frozen against the gray sky. On occasion, there, he might watch the changing of the guard; the spots of the drummer's leopard skin would be no foreign spots before his eyes.

When the family went on holiday—that was all too seldom, with Isaac's education costing them down to the last scraped threepenny bit—they headed north, always north, in their old Morris car. Sam would arouse Jennie at the crack of dawn with

> *Bonnie lassie, will ye go*
> *To the birks of Aberfeldy?*

and, wholly in keeping with the song, Jennie was never reluctant to "let fortune's gifts at random flee." She would join the excursion and exclaim about the rocks and foam when they crossed the river at Rumbling Bridge. Long hours later, with the heather-tufted slopes of the Middle Almond and Strath Bran behind them, the three would come jolting down the long hill into Aberfeldy. There they feasted at last amid beauty which somehow they felt that Bobby Burns had preserved for them alone.

Once they took old John Cameron with them—he had expressed a desire to visit Killiecrankie. They rattled on through Pitlochry; in the narrowest part of the pass, with the River Garry trickling clean and the black-faced sheep astonished, Old John mounted a rock and played "The Battle of Killiecrankie." His pipes were never more humming, never more kindly tuned.

Sam stood listening, resting his weight on the left leg, which was less sore and aching than the right, with his arm around his son's shoulders. He knew Isaac was growing taller and taller. He was a braw laddie; it was well enough for him to plan to study pharmacy in Edinburgh, as he wished, but it was time to be thinking about his regiment.

Commissions in line regiments, in famous regiments like the Black Watch or the Argyll and Sutherland Highlanders, are not readily obtainable for youths of Isaac's situation. But there should be a chance for him in the Blue Bonnets. In the United States they would have called the Blue Bonnets a National Guard outfit; the modern organization stemmed from the famous parent regiment of the same name. The deeds of His Majesty's Blue Bonnets had been sung in legend and in whisky advertisements for many years. Quebec, Ticonderoga, Malta, Balaclava, Khyber, Ladysmith, Mons, Ypres, Loos, the Somme—both Sommes, 1916 and 1918: all these battle honors might have been flaunted from the colors of the Blue Bonnets had they cared to stretch a few historical points and paint them there.

There was O.T.C. training available to young Isaac in Edinburgh. The then colonel of the Blue Bonnets, who was a genial fatty named Mulross who came often to Sam's public room because he liked the kind of ale Sam served and because Colonel Mulross, like Sam himself, had fought at the second battle of Ypres, though not with the Canadians.

As for Sam himself, when talk got around to the war, he never said, "I was with a Canadian battalion." Instead he said, "I was with the Forty-eighth Highlanders." Which puzzled certain military-minded Scotsmen no end.

Isaac secured his commission in the winter of 1938–39, and it happened to be Burns' Night when the news reached Dunbayne. Traditionally there was plenty of haggis eaten and whisky served; a generous open house was kept at Sam's Rest. But whisky flowed like the tides of the Forth, on this night of nights. Not since John Cameron, in an extremely elevated condition, won piping honors at the Inverkeithing games, five years earlier, had Sam allowed himself and his friends the luxury of such dissipation.

Sam was dragged to bed at last by the embarrassed Jennie. He mumbled Gaelic words, words of thanksgiving, while she was undressing him.

In the blackest silence before dawn Sam awoke with throbbing head and parched throat. His mind had sharpened once more; he had his wits, and he used them enough to go for a glass of water. When he padded back through the cold he snuggled warmly beside his wife, and his thin hand clutched her fat one ecstatically.

"I wanted to do it," Sam said. "Oh, Jennie, long, long I hoped to do it! The Boche didn't let me."

Jennie mumbled in a sleepy puzzle, "What was it you wanted to do, Sam?"

"I longed to die for Scotland," said Sam. "I didn't get to, but maybe he will. Maybe Isaac will."

"Oh, my God!" sobbed Jennie, and she shivered for a time. Sam was asleep.

Some seven months later the Blue Bonnets were indeed called up, and of course Isaac was called with them. There had been parades before this. Sam had stood in the streets of Perth and let his soul drip in happy anguish as young Isaac swung by, dark-faced, haughty, callow, hook-nosed, with a blue bonnet on his head, with the gaudy gold-and-scarlet of the MacMillans belted around him—for, as everyone knows, the first colonel of the Blue Bonnets was a MacMillan.

But it was a procession of a different sort when the regiment was actually called up for service. Their kilts had been taken from them, despite tearful and indignant protestations emanating from Dunbayne and other villages—most of all, perhaps, from Dunbayne.

The men were allowed to keep their bonnets, for the time being; soon enough would be substituted the drab helmets that humped behind their shoulders. They wore regulation khaki with long, full, baggy trousers; they looked like slim Teddy bears, like athletic children turned loose in sleeping garments. Still, no children ever marched with such heavy rifles growing up from slings behind their right shoulders, and no dictum of war ministers had yet taken the bagpipes away.

The regiment pounded to the station with drums roaring like thunder and the pipes squealing "The Blue Bonnets." Also some angel—a spectral Canadian angel, perhaps—whispered in the pipe major's ear. . . . "Ye'll Take the High Road" came dinning aloft somewhere along the route. It was the marching-out tune of the Forty-eighth Highlanders, on another late summer day exactly twenty-five years before; and Sam couldn't see much of the parade after that.

He had cleared his eyes in later seasons when big Junkers and Dorniers began to wheel and smoke in the sky above the Firth of Forth bridge. True, Sam had a very bad leg—had had, for a quarter of a century—but that didn't prevent him from lying upon a petrol-depot roof top with a pair of binoculars in his hand—German binoculars, sure enough, and very good ones, too. He could glare up into the Scottish sky, with every regulation promulgated by the A.R.P. stenciled on his brain.

In that situation old John Cameron found him—Old John's whisky-soaked eyes being unfit for any service, be it A.R.P. or what-have-you. Old John found Sam on a June day in 1940. John's scabby hands made non sense out of an orange-covered *Times Weekly Edition* fresh from London. He shook the paper as Sam himself might have shaken a cocktail shaker, in other years when American tourists sat at the inn.

Sam had to take the paper away and hold it himself, before he could read the B.E.F. awards.

It didn't seem real. It was too wonderful to be real; it was like wearing a kilt for the first time, or setting foot on Scottish soil. It was like hearing again the mettlesome drums of Harry Lauder's troupe. . . .

"The following appointments to the Distinguished Service Order," said the *Times Weekly Edition,* "are included in War Office lists . . . in respect of recent operations."

There followed Isaac's name, tiny but bold in black type, with his rank and regiment. "On May 28, 1940," read the appointment, "this officer was sent to Dixmude . . ."

There was something about blowing up bridges over the Yser Canal. "By his skillful dispositions and bold leadership, he inflicted so many casualties on the head of an enemy column that he was able, when reinforced by other troops, to contain the enemy east of the Yser Canal for over seven hours, by which time more than 250 vehicles had been counted entering Dixmude, and the road Dixmude–Roulers was a solid mass of transport. Had he failed, by less bold action, to deceive the enemy as to his true strength and thus to contain this overwhelmingly superior force, the enemy would, during the first few hours, have had a clear road to two beaches from which the B.E.F. finally embarked."

The pipes screamed in Sam's Rest that night; people sang themselves

hoarse. Their howl went along the black little road that twisted through
Dunbayne and into the hills beyond—"the lands beyond Forth"—until John
Cameron's stiff and ancient fingers could squeeze the chanter no more.

Again the patient Jennie helped her lord to bed. "There are brave
Duinhewassels three thousand times three," was the only sensible thing
which Sam could say, "will cry, 'Hey for the bonnets!' " And Jennie whispered in her worried spirit that if Isaac had indeed died for Scotland, his
father's passion could scarcely have been of more ferocious intensity.

That final accolade was laid upon them, very soon afterward, when the
Times Weekly Edition began to lump the embarkation casualties on its
grim orange page, when horrid little telegrams began to creep, slow and
bitter, from the War Office. Again Sam was upon the depot roof, watching
for enemy aircraft, and again it was John Cameron who brought him the
tidings.

That night Sam could not drink—nor has he been drinking since. Instead, he sat silent in his empty public room, with shriveled dry face gone
grim and hard. He was composing an announcement which he would send
to the paper. It would be published in the department picketed, On Active
Service, and Sam would pay for it at the regular rate of two shillings per
line (three lines minimum), or thirty shillings per inch (if displayed).

GINSBERG—Died of wounds, Lieut. Isaac Davidson Ginsberg, D.S.O.,
The Blue Bonnet Highlanders, dearly loved only son of Sam Ginsburg,
late 48th Highlanders, C.E.F., and Jennie (*née* Levinsky), of Sam's Rest,
Dunbayne, Fife.

RUFUS KING

Knock on a Door

THEY DIDN'T KNOW the door was unlocked, and that was funny,
really funny. Mr. Warburton complimented himself on being amused as
he backed towards the opened window. His face was wet with sweat. He
was young.

They would expect, he knew, to have to batter the door down; on the other hand they might have sense enough to try the knob first, but even if they did so they would open it cautiously, knowing that his back was against the wall, which also was awfully funny, as where his back would literally be would be against the opened window. He would have plenty of time to say: "Come in!" and then let them find the room empty. It was a sixteen-floor drop, uninterrupted by any projections, to the concrete pavement of the street.

They wouldn't knock again. He felt sure of that. They were probably deliberating now, out in the hallway. Breeze fanned the sweat on the back of his neck, chilling the skin, and he wondered petulantly why his whole life wasn't revealed to him in swift review between that knock and the turning of the handle of the door, as it was to people who were drowning, with the space-and-time-devouring rapidity of a dream.

Consciously he tried to force this phenomenon, as he felt doubtful of its occurrence during the drop. His hands, stretched behind him, contacted the sill, and the raucous medley of the city was thinned by depth against him. It would be a pity to hit anybody on the street, but he had studied statistics, and the chances of doing so were slim. Someone always saw, and shouted a warning, in time.

One thousand dollars a floor; that was very funny too, the coincidence of such an accurate payment of his debt. He wondered whether some reporter would be smart enough to notice it; they should, and the possibility that it might be overlooked annoyed Mr. Warburton a lot. Sixteen thousand dollars, sixteen floors, and yes, by God, the sixteenth of the month. Oh, something surely would have to be done about that. One second had passed since the knock on the door.

They did the most amazing things with crushed bodies; take Harry's, for instance, after that explosion on the yacht, all built over when you came right down to it, from a photograph, and what a hell of a lot of bother just for a final look. People were queer that way, in wanting a last nice thing to remember. His people would be too.

He deliberately loosened the strained tension of his fingers upon the metal sill, and a series of photographs flashed across a mental vision, cabinet ones that were pretty fancy and too hazed by art to be of much use, snapshots which were really better. They'd pick, he supposed, the one done by that Jap on the Avenue; there was an ethereal quality about it which he'd always pointed out as a big laugh, that light in back of his head turning his hair into a sort of nimbus. He should wear a nimbus. They were being pretty damned deliberate about their deliberations out there in the hallway. Two seconds had passed since the knock on the door.

He wanted to shout: "Come in!" and get it over with, and on the other hand he didn't. It was a good act, so why rush it? Timing was everything in life, and, it amused him to add, in death; the velocity of an inert mass weighing one hundred and seventy pounds falling from a height of three hundred and ten feet would be—well, it would be pretty quick and not worth quibbling about. Consciousness would be lost almost at once, although there were two schools of thought about that, and it would be fun, finally, to know which one was right. If there were only some way of his leaving a record, like writing "Now!" on a scrap of paper at the exact instant during the drop when he felt his senses slipping, but that was silly. It couldn't be done. He was unaware that his fingers had tightened convulsively, but he did know that the handle of the door had turned.

It was an experimental turn, rather apologetic, for the handle came to rest again and the door stayed closed. His smile cupped drops of sweat as he realized that they probably thought of him as being desperate. They'd be the ones who would laugh if they could only see through the panels and look at him shaking and lonely and all in a sweat, instead of crouching behind a steel filing case, say, with a gun in his hand.

They must have tried the door, imperceptibly, when the handle had turned, and realized that it was unlocked. Naturally that would puzzle them; and they'd go into more planning, the better to preserve their skins. My dear. And what big teeth you've got, Grandma. Mr. Warburton pulled himself up short. It was all right to be funny, but not insane. Three seconds had passed since the knock on the door.

Just the same it always had astonished him that they'd read such things to children. Annie, his first nurse, a big-boned Irish woman, had sent him into his first convulsion with Rock-a-bye Baby, when the bough broke and the poor brat fell out of the treetop, cradle and all, and what a hot lot of detail that was, even the cradle had to be damned well smashed up too. Oh great, just the sort of stuff to send a child to sleep on, and again, if they wanted to be Freudian about it, what a break that angle would be for a bright reporter, baby-treetop, man-sixteen-story-window, everyone should really write his own obit, so many choice points were always otherwise missed.

The handle was turning again *so few people had ever understood him, the athletic coach at prep school, chemistry had been hard at college not because he hadn't had the ability to cope with it but simply because it was so damn dull and skiing at Lake Placid down that fir-plashed hill with yes,* the door was opening now *hot toddies at the Waldorf in Bertha's apartment at sixteen thousand a year if he knew his rentals and add that to the other sixteens* there was quite a crack between the edge of the door and the jamb, widening, *and Bertha would still have married him if he'd let her, which was the funniest thing of all, anything in pants, and she'd have paid the sum up with the scratch of a pen* quicker, now, that widening *Mr. Harrison's eyes had been hard as stone when he'd called him into the president's office and given him until yesterday and all our yesterdays have lighted fools the way to dusty death, out, out brief candle, life's but a walking shadow (how the hell did the rest go?) a poor player who struts and frets his weary hour upon the stage (let the damn crack widen)* "Come in!" *and then is seen no more.*

Four seconds had passed since the knock on the door. The woman turned, as she opened it, and said with a bright smile to their family lawyer: "I was afraid he might have locked the door, and when he's brooding he sometimes refuses to open it, but everything's all right now, Mr. Winterbottom, I just heard him say, come in."

MANUEL KOMROFF

A Day of Pleasure

So EARLY IN THE MORNING and the day was already shot to hell. He got into his car at the side of the road and for a moment sat blankly at the wheel. He could not make up his mind. He drew a large railroad watch from his pocket and looked at the time. Only seven o'clock. He could drive home and be there in an hour, but there was no good going home. His foot touched the starter, and while the car was warming up he placed his hand to his inside breast pocket to make certain that the envelope was deep down and secure. He had not bothered to open it, but he knew it contained a hundred-dollar bill. "Well, that is something, anyway, even though the day was shot to hell." And he started off down the road.

There was a lunch wagon about a mile down the state road, and here he stopped. It was a clean place painted in gay colors and patronized mainly by truck drivers, but at this time in the morning there were only two men beside the chef in the wagon. They were eating pancakes and talking about something or other, but as soon as he opened the door he saw the chef place a finger to his lips and suddenly the place was silent.

"Give me a cup of coffee," he said. And as the chef was pouring it out he added, "You haven't a glass of whisky you could give me?"

"Sorry, boss. We're not allowed to sell the stuff."

"Didn't ask you to sell it. No law against giving it away. And no law to prevent me giving you a couple of good cigars."

"Not a drop around here, boss."

"What else is there?"

"Not a drop of anything."

"This is a hell of a place."

The two truck drivers looked at each other and poured more maple syrup over their pancakes.

"You want the coffee?" inquired the chef.

"Okay, and cut me a slice of that apple pie."

While he was eating, the stranger tried to make some conversation, but he got little response from the chef.

"Turned out a nice day after all. Looked like rain when I got up. This is my second breakfast. Been up since four o'clock. It don't get light until a quarter past five, then it comes on suddenly this time of the year."

The chef did not reply; he merely stood back near the stove and nodded his head. You could see him nod very definitely because he had a large clean linen cook's cap on his head. His white jacket, however, was hanging on a hook. What seemed most prominent, however, were a pair of extra-strong suspenders, almost brand new, that went over his flannel shirt. The leather ends were bright yellow, and the nickel-plated buckles, stamped with the popular brand mark "Police," glistened. All this you could see very plainly as he stood there nodding his head. Not once did he open his mouth.

The stranger finished his coffee and pie. Again he drew out his big railroad watch (it does not lose a minute in a month) and looked at it. He held it in both hands, which were strange and shapeless. His fingers were very fat and tapered sharply at the ends, and the nails were very small for so big a man. His thumbs turned back with a definite hook and there was a glisten in his palms due to excessive perspiration. The lines in his palms were a bright pink and divided the fat folds in strange irregular spaces.

He gazed a long time at his watch and then said, "Well, I guess this is just one day out." Then he paid for his coffee and pie and was about to leave. He paused behind the truck drivers and said, "How many miles do you reckon from here to Silver Lake?"

The drivers looked at each other, and finally one of them replied, "I make it about fifty-two."

The other nodded his head to indicate that this was correct.

"Fifty-two miles to Silver Lake. Well, the day is shot to hell anyway," he thought.

As he was getting into the car he saw that the three men in the lunch wagon had put their heads together and were again talking about something. He slammed the door of the car and started off for Silver Lake, which, as everyone knows, is the amusement park about ten miles this side of the city.

"Might just as well forget it and turn it all into a day of pleasure," he said to himself.

He touched his hand to his inside pocket, for here is where he had the envelope with the hundred-dollar bill. He looked at the gas gauge on the dashboard. There was plenty of gas. "Okay. We'll let her rip." And with these words in his mind he stepped hard on the accelerator because it was fifty-two miles to Silver Lake. Fifty-two miles before he could get a drink of whisky and put a nickel in the slot of the mechanical piano. The day of pleasure could not begin until he got there, and so he tore along the concrete state road at sixty miles an hour and only slowed down to take the curves.

When he stopped before the saloon in Silver Lake he took out his watch, the same large railroad timepiece that does not lose a minute in a month, and noticed that he did the run of fifty-two miles in an hour and ten minutes. Well, that was pretty good. But it was still quite early in the morning.

The porter was mopping the floor of the saloon, and the bartender, without his white coat, was polishing the brass beer faucets. He paused to look up at the stranger.

"A glass of whisky."

He drank it down quickly, and his big shoulders shuddered as the liquor passed his throat. Then he filled the glass a second time, and now he sipped his drink slowly.

The porter passed his wet mop around the stranger and went on with his cleaning. "Stay right where you are, mister. I'm just cleaning up."

The words "cleaning up," for some reason or other, struck him as being funny, and his thick lips smiled.

"Kind of dead around here this time of the morning."

"Well, it's a bit early yet," the bartender replied. "Things don't start going until the afternoon."

Yes, it was true; no place seemed as dead as an amusement park that was closed. Across the street from the saloon he could see the gay entrance to Dreamland, but there was a chain across the gate. The peanut wagon on the sidewalk was covered with a canvas, and he could see the gypsy fortuneteller's booth with its large "phrenology" poster on which was boldly printed—"Happiness—Fortune—Power. Are these coming to you? 25c." This place was also closed.

High above the fence he could see the timbered scaffolding of the roller coaster. At night there would be piercing screams as the little cars would plunge down the great dip. And these screams, mingled with shouts and laughter, would all be part of the fun. But now all was silent and hardly a soul was about.

Anyone could see that at this time in the morning the place was dead.

"Yes, it is dead," he said to himself. "And it gives you a creepy feeling. And the only thing to kill a creepy feeling is . . ." He pushed his glass forward and spoke out loud. "Fill her up again."

He put five cents into the mechanical piano, and it started off at breakneck speed with a noisy racket and badly out of tune. Then he drew the white envelope from his breast pocket. There was some printing in the corner, and written with a bold hand in blue pencil was his given name: "Jim." He looked inside and then addressed the bartender. "I don't suppose you could change a hundred-dollar bill?"

"At this time in the morning I'd have a hard time changing a five."

The porter paused from his labors when he heard the mention of a hundred-dollar bill and, leaning on his mop, drew a deep breath and scratched his head. "Some people are surely lucky," he thought.

The bartender volunteered the information. "No bank in Silver Lake.

Just a summer business here. About three months in the year, and then it is as dead as a doornail. Wouldn't pay to have a bank. We all send down to the city for what we need."

But nothing was going to stop his day of pleasure. He was determined to get that hundred-dollar bill changed and perhaps blow it all in, and nothing was going to stop him. He had some small change in his pocket, enough to pay for his drinks, and, having done so, he saluted the bartender, got back into his car, and started off for the city. It was only a short run, but the traffic was fairly heavy and he took it easy. Besides, the whisky seemed to buck him up and he was not quite so impatient as when he left the lunch wagon.

While he was driving along a hundred things seemed to course through his mind. He said to himself: "Never knew Silver Lake could be so dead. And when a thing is dead it sure is dead. All lights out. Nothing doing. It's as though the bottom has dropped out of everything. Guess I better have a shave when I get to town. Funny I don't feel sleepy. Anybody else getting up before daylight . . . I could eat again. A big plate of something cold and . . . Those fellows in the lunch car stopped kind of short when I opened the door. Guess they were talking about something or other. Well, what do they know? A man ought to keep his business to himself, then nothing will ever bother him and everyone will be happy. And there is no reason why a man should not be happy. In fact, it's the duty of every man to be happy. It's his privilege. A man owes it to himself, and even if it kills him he ought to burst out once in a while and have a good time. A whole day of pleasure from morning until night. He owes it to his fellow citizens. Oh boy! I just feel like raising hell. Wish I had someone with me. A nice-looking Jane would help things. And say, what a soft time she'd have. She'd think I was a yokel from the country with plenty of cash for a good time. Okay, then I will be a yokel. It's all the same to me. And I'll tell her the story of my life and . . . Sure, I can talk plenty and not say anything. No one ever found out anything from me. Guess I better slow down a bit. City limits. And the car tracks probably lead you straight in. Never saw anything so dead as Silver Lake this morning. Well, it might be a bad morning for some people, but that don't say a man don't owe it to himself . . . The sun is out. What the hell! Well, another mile and then . . . Say, a nice cold lobster wouldn't be a bad idea. I haven't eaten a lobster in . . . Can't even remember the last time. A man owes himself a little something once in a while. It's a duty."

With these thoughts flowing through his head he arrived in the center of the city, and for a moment he thought he might park his car in front of the city hall, but something made him change his mind and he drove into a parking lot where you can leave your car a whole day for twenty-five cents.

He walked around the block and into the entrance of the Merchant's Bank. Here he presented his hundred-dollar bill and changed it into tens and fives which he returned to the envelope and into his inside breast pocket. Now there was nothing to stop the day of pleasure, and out he went.

At a barbershop he got a haircut and a shave. The barber was filled with local politics and the news of the day. His tongue wagged in beat with his scissors.

"Turned out a nice day," he said. "I'll use the clipper on the back of the neck. Yes sir. Looks like they are going to have some trouble in Europe. They never know when to stop. I tell you, when you read all the things that are going on in Europe it makes you feel good that you are living in a free country."

"Bet your life," replied the stranger in the chair.

"And I guess Mrs. Klopp paid the penalty this morning. Haven't seen the afternoon paper yet, but on the radio last night they said that the governor refused to interfere any further in the case. Some of the women's clubs in the state sent a petition for clemency because no woman was ever hanged before in this state."

"She killed her husband, didn't she?"

"Oh yes. No question of it, only it was a matter of sentiment, and no woman was placed on the gallows in this state before. And so they thought the governor might change the sentence to imprisonment for life."

"That's only a slow form of dying. Besides, the law is the law, and men and women are the same before the law. She killed her husband, didn't she?"

"Sure, she killed him, all right," replied the barber. "But you know I don't think he was much good. But anyway she had no business to kill him."

"No, the law is the law. And you can't try to beat it. The law is designed to protect property and life and limb. Its courts and officers are doing a service to humanity. They do their duty."

"Sure, that's what I always said. The police know who the gangsters are, and so why don't they lock them up? . . . You think that's short enough on top?"

Then they spoke about other things, and in this way the haircut and shave were accomplished and the stranger walked out of the shop a little freshened up and, due to the clipper, the fat rings on the back of his neck showing more plainly than before.

On his way to find a sea-food restaurant he paused in front of a hatter's window and went in and bought himself a nice big felt hat with a broad brim, for which he paid ten dollars. It was a good hat, and at the moment he thought that nothing was too good for him. The old hat, with its sweat-stained band, was not even worth taking along. He left it there.

In the restaurant he changed his mind, and instead of having cold lobster he ordered a whole broiled lobster with hot butter sauce. This, he thought, would be juicier. And while he waited for the lobster to broil he had a plate of oysters and drank two cocktails.

It was noon when he left the restaurant, and he was feeling pretty good. He stuck his chest out, and with the brand-new hat on his head he walked down the street as though the whole city belonged to him. He bought himself some extra-fancy cigars and wandered into a movie called *The Price of Love*. The name attracted his attention, and he was curious to know what the story was about. But it proved to be quite different from what he expected, and he left the movie house a little disappointed.

The newsboys had the afternoon papers on the streets as he came out of the theater, but somehow or other the news did not interest him. He lit a fresh cigar and climbed into a taxi and told the driver to take him through the park. It was a pleasant afternoon, not too cold and not too hot. He leaned back in the cushions of the cab and puffed on the cigar. He saw the children in the park wading in the pool and sailing their toy boats, and he ordered the driver to stop. "That's a pretty sight," he said. "Why can't people be kids all their lives?" Then he saw two pretty nurse-maids in uniforms wheeling perambulators along the walk, and he said to the driver, "I haven't been here in some years. Is the Cat and Mouse still going?"

"It's a cabaret place, boss."

"What time does it open?"

"Nighttime."

"Where are the Janes in the afternoon?"

"Don't know, boss. Most anywhere. Park, movies, in the department stores; some stay home; most anywhere, boss. Some go to Billy's for a drink and to see what they can pick up. It's in back of the Commercial Hotel and a great place for traveling salesmen."

It was not many minutes later that he found himself in Billy's place buying a drink for a young woman with blonde hair.

"You know," she said, "I only came in here to see if my sister was here because she has a crush on a fellow who hangs out here. And I don't often get around to these places but I went to the movie this afternoon. Did you see that picture also? Well, I don't see why they are raving about that girl at all. Say, you don't know me, mister man, and I don't know you, but if she's an actress then honest to God I'm only a piece of cheese. I guess she must be the girl friend of some director in Hollywood or some big shot. Well, some people get the breaks and some people . . . My sister and I played big time across the country. We had a song-and-dance act, and then the whole vaudeville business blew up and so—— Yes, I'll have another. And so we came home and waited for a call from Hollywood!"

"Don't often come down this way myself," he said. "But once in a while a fellow owes himself a day off. It does him good. A man gets kind of lonesome."

"Where's your wife?"

"I have none."

"Work all the time?"

"No. Not all the time. I take it easy. I have a shop in Westville. Wagon wheels. But I don't go out for business. Some special orders come to me and sometimes some repairs. But it's all automobiles these days and not much wagon business."

She was feeling sorry for him already. "Say, it's not easy for a young girl these days, either. My name is Dolly; what's yours?"

"Jim," he said. "Just plain Jim."

"And my sister's name is Peggy. You'd like Peggy."

"Where is she?"

"Well, that's what I've been telling you. I came in here looking for her because her boy friend George, he hangs out here."

"Why don't you get hold of her and we will have a swell party? A fellow can't have a party alone."

"She might have a date with George."

"Well, ask George to come along; the more the merrier."

"Say, Jim, you're all right. Well, let's have another drink, and maybe they will be along."

He signaled the waiter. "Anything you say is okay with me, Dolly."

After a slight silence she asked, "You live all alone in Westville?"

"Yes."

"Don't it get on your nerves to be alone?"

"That's why a fellow must come away from the place and have a party and a little fun once in a while."

As he said this the waiter brought the drinks and Jim drew a five-dollar bill from the envelope.

In a little while her sister Peggy arrived with George, who turned out to be a furniture salesman for an installment house. They joined them at the table and things grew livelier. They all thought it would be a good idea to have a nice party.

A newsboy came through the place with evening papers, and George bought one. Dolly opened it up and exclaimed, "Gee, they hanged her this morning!" Then she read aloud: "After the governor had refused a plea for clemency last night, Mrs. Klopp walked her last mile this morning and mounted the scaffold to pay the penalty for the murder of her husband. She is the first woman to be executed in this state. She was accompanied across the prison yard by the prison matron and the chaplain. Her step was steady and her gait even until it came to mounting the six wooden steps of the scaffold. She seemed dazed and hesitated on the second step, but the hangman reached down and drew her up. She put her arms about him and clung to him as though he were the last living thing left on earth. Her eyes were dry and not a word passed her lips. He put the freshly greased rope over her head while she embraced him. It was with some difficulty that the hangman could free himself and plunge back to spring the trap."

She threw down the newspaper and whispered, "It's terrible. Terrible!"

Jim said, "Well, she killed her husband, didn't she? The law is the law. The governor is a square man, and if he didn't think it was right he could have— Say, how about going to the Cat and Mouse after supper? I haven't seen a cabaret show in years."

"All right, Jim," all agreed. And they thought he was a good fellow.

The sisters, Dolly and Peggy, went home to dress up in their very best and get ready for a big evening while Jim went upstairs to the hotel room occupied by George the furniture salesman. Here he had some photographs of furniture that he wanted Jim to see. A new combination couch that can be opened up to a full-sized bed was the main subject of conversation.

But the furniture man was also anxious to tell Jim that he made no mistake in his choice of companions.

"Those sisters," he said, "are a damn fine pair of girls. A man couldn't fall in with better company. They are a couple of straight shooters. Yes sir. Just a little down on their luck, could happen to anybody, but they are no gold diggers. Why, a million dollars couldn't buy one of them if she didn't like you. But if she liked you, well then, if you didn't have a nickel, it would be all right with her. That's the kind they are."

"Say, I can tell a person a mile away," Jim boasted.

And soon the girls, dressed in evening gowns, were announced and the men came down into the hotel lobby. They went to a swell place to have a good dinner and a nice bottle of wine.

It was evening now, and all day long he had been seeking pleasure and some of the things he had hoped would be joyous did not turn out so well. But now this was the real thing. The girls were quite pretty and they were pleasant and gay. And they knew all kinds of stories that they related in an entertaining manner. And as for George, the furniture sales-man, he too was a good fellow. He was no grafter, either, for twice he apologized for having horned his way into a nice party. And each time he did so Jim assured him that it was a pleasure to have him "because three is a bad number."

Yes, these were all fine people, and it was a great pleasure to have them on a party. And the sky was the limit. Turkish cigarettes for the girls, a good Havana cigar, the best in the house, for George, and a round of "What's the name of the French liquor made by the monks? Yes. That's it. Four of those with the coffee."

Now things were getting really gay. And about nine o'clock that eve-ning they decided to go to the Cat and Mouse and dance and see the cabaret show. They took a taxi to the place.

At one time when Peggy was dancing with George and Dolly and Jim were alone at the side table, she leaned over and, touching his large hairy hand, said, "You know, Jim, I could like you a whole lot."

He pressed her hand, but then the waiter passed and she drew it away. And when the waiter got to the bar the bartender said to him, "I think I know that fellow's face. But I can't place him."

At eleven o'clock the floor show went on, and people showered streamers at each other and made lots of noise with rattles provided by the management. Also paper caps were distributed to add to the gaiety.

The floor show ended at a quarter of twelve, and by this time three tables were drawn together and "friends" had joined Jim's party. Now Jim was feeling good, and one of the girls wanted to know if the orchestra would play "My Old Kentucky Home."

"I never was in Kentucky," she said, "but I just love that song. It makes me feel good to hear it."

The orchestra played the song, and there was a great silence in the place. Jim drew some bills from the envelope and asked the waiter to give these to the musicians. He glanced at the remaining bills in his hand. There was enough left to pay for the party and a little over. He folded them and, placing the roll in his trouser pocket, crumpled up the envelope and threw it on the floor.

A minute later the waiter picked up the envelope and brought it to the bartender, who, opening it, read the word "Jim" written in blue pencil. He also saw the printing in the upper-left-hand corner and, showing it to the waiter, whispered something in his ear.

This was the beginning. One whisper led to another. Some people left the place quite abruptly. One girl said she had a sick headache, and Dolly overheard something and, signaling to her sister, they excused themselves for a moment. But they did not return. In less than five minutes George and Jim were left alone at the table. Something was up.

Jim took out his big railroad watch and looked at the time. It was a minute to twelve o'clock. "This big onion," he said proudly, "does not lose a minute in a month."

But the bartender caught George's eye and beckoned to him. When he came over he said to him: "The ladies are waiting for you in the lobby of the Commercial. I thought I recognized that fellow; he was in here a long time ago." Then he held out the envelope on which was printed "State Penitentiary" and leaned over across the bar and whispered, "He's the hangman!"

"Funny they all walked out on me," Jim said as he paid the check.

He put on his new felt hat and, without glancing to the right or left, walked straight out of the place. He walked the streets for several blocks and presented the ticket for his car at the parking place. He was feeling good. He looked up overhead and saw the stars and remarked to the boy, "It's been a nice day."

Now the day of pleasure was over and he was driving back to Westville. Somehow or other on his hands there still lingered a rancid odor of grease.

HAROLD LAMB

The Empress' Yankee

I WAS ASLEEP when the order came to me to go to the war. But before the cocks started crowing I was in the saddle of my Kabarda horse. A Cossack of the Terek does not stop when he hears of fighting.

Instead of joining the squadron I went around to my girl's cottage. Leaving the horse, I scratched on the shutter farthest from where the old people slept. When Babitka looked out, rubbing her hair back, I whispered to her what had happened.

"What war?" she asked.

"How do I know? When an order comes, a Cossack rides, he does not ask questions. It is for the empress!"

Babitka would not let me kiss her. "It is always for that woman, the empress," she whispered. Then she hugged me. "Wait."

So I tied up my horse and went to wait at the haystack. I thought Babitka was a fine girl, and so quick. Strong, too—only stubborn at times. And, of course, I would be away at the war a long time.

She kept me waiting until the trees showed against the sky, and she came pulling a pony behind her. Instead of sitting down on the hay she cracked the whip in her hand, and I saw she had put on men's broad trousers and boots.

"Ivak," she said, "listen. This time I am going with you."

I laughed, thinking of Babitka, who milked the cows and brought in the cherries and baked barley cake, riding off with Ivak, who had smelled the smoke of powder often, who was a *sotnik* of the squadron.

"Why do you fight this time?" She came close to see my eyes.

How could I say? "For honor, little pigeon, for glory." And when this did not satisfy her: "Nay, I will bring you a shawl and pearls for your necklace from Tsargrad—for that is how we call Constantinople. The brothers say we will take Tsargrad this time for our empress."

She pushed me away, so I almost fell down. "*Tfu*—I could spit when you speak of her. I am coming with you to the war."

Now if the devil himself, who knows how to talk to girls, said no to Babitka, she would say yes to him. She is strong as two devils when she feels stubborn. And in her long coat, with her hair tucked up into her woolly cap, she looked almost like a boy. The thought came to me, Why not? My blood felt warm because she was so near me.

"You need someone, Ivak, to be wise for you."

I heard the horses snort together. "A good omen," I told her.

That is how I suffered Babitka to ride with me to the Charnomar, that you call the Black Sea. And when we saw the dark sea, the omens were not so good. For pale white lights gleamed along the edge of the stagnant water. I have heard officers say that this light is the phosphorescent salt in the water, but we Cossacks know it is the souls of the dead running along the edge of the sea seeking a resting place. Babitka looked long at the sea that was not a sea but a huge estuary into which the great rivers ran, making sand bars and currents.

"Those lights," she said, "are not good. Perhaps they are a sign to us."

"Look farther, girl," I told her.

Other lights shone in the channel where Father Dnieper pours himself into the salt estuary. They were on the masts of ships, large and small, all waiting together like a herd of cattle.

When I tried to find my squadron at the encampment, I learned the meaning of the ships. My brothers had been sent on them, and before long these ships were to make a march out into the sea. The war, it seemed, would be on the water, not on the land. What matter? A Cossack is at home anywhere under the sky. But Babitka could not go on a ship of war, stuffed with men. Impossible.

When I told her, she still wanted to go. "Take me on the ship, please, Ivak," she begged. "And as God lives I will ask for nothing more."

Because she was weeping and men began to stare and edge over to us, I took her behind the woodpile and whacked her shoulders with my whip. At once she stopped crying and took the reins of the two horses and marched off, holding her chin down on her chest. And I felt empty inside. Better if she had thrown her knife at me.

I went down quickly to the water, before she could be stubborn again. I went to a man under a lanthorn who shouted in bad Russian. Under his cocked hat his scalp lock was tied with a ribbon, and it was stiff with white flour paste. When I poked my finger into it, he swung up his cane as if to strike me. But he thought better of that. And it was well for him he did so. He looked like a weasel, and the weasel is no fool.

"Get your carcass into that boat, brainless!" he yelped.

Then I knew he was not a Russian. The German Prussians call us dumb because we do not speak German. I wondered why he gave commands on the fleet of the empress.

"Tie up your riband, darling," I told him, and walked away feeling his eyes on my shoulders.

And on the boat I found much more to wonder at. It was the biggest of the ships, with the masts stretching up like trees. And it smelled of sheep and hot tar and dirt, what with the rivermen on her deck—and snuff-stinking Tatars, and pale jailbirds trying to sleep around the guns. Already this *Vladimir,* as they called the big ship, felt the pull of the current and the floors moved under our feet. *Ekh-ma,* I went up on the roof to breathe freely, and there I found some of my brothers from the squadron, and other Cossacks, all knowing little of why we had been set on this castle of the sea. They said the officers walking about wore the caftans of hussars.

Now it was bad to be quartered among the scourings of the river. It was more than bad to be commanded by hussars. Every Cossack who has served his time knows that a hussar is good only to parade and kill flies.

I felt truly empty, and I thought of Babitka, the sweet one, sleeping in the hay with the horses on good dry earth. I sat on the poles, where the motion of the sea was not so great, and borrowed a light for my pipe from a man of Irivan who wore sheepskins.

"Eh, kunak," I said, "what passes?"

"Much."

Now, being an Armenian, Kushel by name, he knew everything that went on. He had been selling rugs before they put him on the *Vladimir.*

"Will we march forward into the sea tonight?"

Kushel spat. "No."

"Tomorrow, then?"

"Not tomorrow, or next month. Impossible."

"How impossible?"

Kushel pointed down the bay, to where a point of light showed, far, far.

Down there were the enemy ships, where the water of the bay ran out into the true sea. They were waiting in the mouth of the bay.

"Those dogs will bite," he said. "Those Turks and Corsairs and such."

Now it seemed to me if the sultan's ships waited there, our ships would go and drive them away. But Kushel thought otherwise. "Then there would be calamity."

"How calamity?"

The man from Irivan touched the pole we sat on. "Green wood." He pointed his pipe at the men snoring among their bundles. "Green sap."

He explained how the ships had been made in haste, out of wood that was still green, so it rotted in the water, and when all these guns went off together—*bourra-oum*—they might break through the rotting wood and let in the water. Besides, he said, the ships were too big to run down among the sand bars. They would sit in the sand. And the crews were not accustomed.

"So will be calamity."

Shaking his fists, Kushel swore. All these frigates, as he called them, and gunboats had been made for a whim. They had been made in such haste to please the empress when she visited the Black Sea, a year or so before, so she could see a fleet sailing and go on it herself. "Think of that!" He tore at his beard. "For a parade!"

Truly Kushel was a wise man, to know all that.

"And now," he groaned, "comes Pavel."

"What is he?" I asked, wondering at this fleet made for a parade.

"A pirate. Worse, an American."

No American, Kushel explained, had ventured into our Russian land before. They grew tobacco, far over the sea, to chew. And they built ships to fight on the sea. Pavel's name was really Paul. John Paul Jones.

He came during a feast that our commanders made for ladies. These ladies smelled of honey, for they were visitors from the court of the Empress Catherine at Petersburg. One of them had her hair piled up, as if bees had hived in it. Eh, she was a beauty, the Lady Anna. She drank wine out of little glasses and she brought her maid to carry her fan.

That maid was Babitka. The little devilkin tripped about the ship where I had told her not to set foot. Ay, she had tied a Persian shawl around her head and put red on her cheeks, and she rolled her eyes at the younger officers when they winked at her. But not a glance for me.

"Babitka!" I called from behind the fence across the deck.

She smoothed down her new shawl. "Eh, animal," she said, "do not bother a maid in waiting. Be off to your stables."

She waited, smiling at me. But some of the officers laughed, trying to get their arms around her, and I said nothing. It is not good to be laughed at.

So I hardly saw Pavel, the American, when he came over the side of the ship with an escort and walked up the rump. A small, straight figure of a man, without flour in his hair or ornaments on his sword. He was gay in his blue coat as if glad to be among us.

Champing over the notions of that fool girl, Babitka, I paid no heed to him then. Only Kushel saw what happened in the after cabin—although how Kushel came to be in the admiral's cabin then, I do not know.

All our high commanders bowed to Pavel—to Jones—and praised him, because he brought a letter from the empress herself. There was the Brigadier Alexiano, who commanded the *Vladimir*, and also the prince of Nassau Siegen, from Prussia, who wore splendid gray and gold and commanded all the fleet. And between them was the Lady Anna, who was Nassau Siegen's *dushenka,* his girl. She sparkled upon Jones, giving him wine in a little glass.

Now to have this Jones come to share the command with Nassau Siegen was not a good thing. One man can drive two horses, but two men cannot drive one horse without calamity. No, never.

Besides, this Jones could speak only one word of Russian, as I came to know. Being dumb like that, he had to have a man to speak for him. Then, too, he had little money, having spent all his life on ships instead of at court, like Nassau Siegen. Ay, Jones had come with all these other foreign officers, as bees swarm around the queen bee, to serve our little mother the empress for gold, titles, honor and glory, and the like.

"We must give you a voice, my chevalier," Nassau Siegen told him. "Rely upon me to explain your directions to these ignorant Russians."

Jones laughed and said he wished he had Lady Anna's voice always at his side, to make music for him. And she gave him her hand to kiss. Nassau Siegen did not seem angry. He already wore decorations, and he spoke as a man sure of himself—a handsome man who made many friends, and used them. Lady Anna looked inside of Jones, and it was clear she thought much of him.

When the women left us, Jones turned to the brigadier. "Captain," he said, "will you call the men to stations?"

Rousing ourselves, we went to stand by the cannon and the ropes as we had been told. Jones walked among us, looking at everything—at our faces and boots, and the wheels of the big cannon, and up at the masts where the sails were tied as they had been all summer. With his hands he turned over ropes and gear. By his manner we knew that he was accustomed. He even went down into the cellar where we kept our wine and goats for fresh meat. He was gone so long that we could smell the kasha pots cooking. When he came up he no longer looked like a man of honey—eh, he had become a man of stone.

Then he stared into the blaze of sunset, at the Turkish ships, tiny in their place at the mouth of the sea. I saw then that he had gray in his hair, and when he did not smile he looked tired.

"Where are the charts?" he asked Nassau Siegen, still making a picture with the eyes of his mind.

Neither Nassau Siegen nor Alexiano knew anything about charts. Then Jones asked for something unwonted—for the bags to put powder in, to carry to the guns.

"The devil, my dear chevalier," said Nassau Siegen. "Perhaps they will be in the warehouse of the encampment. I will have inquiry made tomorrow."

"Tomorrow! Tonight—now!"

Jones seemed to be gnawed by a fear, while Nassau Siegen felt no fear. A spark was struck between them, because of this.

And the spark grew hotter with every question Jones asked, in his strange fashion. If the bags for the powder were not brought before dark, he said, he would order us of the crew ashore.

"But what if the Turks come?" the prince asked. "We would lose the ships."

Jones was still looking at something with the eye of his mind. "They are top-heavy enough, with their build. We have no right to risk the men——" He stopped, thinking.

"Impossible to run away." Nassau Siegen held his head high. "I, for one, have the courage to take a risk."

We who heard this only understood that the spark between them was growing to a fire.

"Only a fool," said Jones, "would run such a risk as this."

Nassau Siegen put his hand on his silvered sword hilt; then he shrugged his shoulders and turned away. "I think," he said loudly to Alexiano, "that our new admiral is afraid. He shows his breeding."

But he said this in Russian, and Jones did not understand.

After that the American wandered about as if seeking something he could not find. We Cossacks were then gathered at the rail, singing because the brandy had been poured out. When Jones wandered up with the interpreter, we felt sorry for him because, like us, he was far from his home, and afraid—which we were not. For a while he listened to the singing, looking over the rail at a skiff tied there.

A thought came to him, and the interpreter explained the thought. "The admiral," he said, "has a whim. He wants rags tied around the middle of the oars, and a rudder rigged up with a stick in that skiff."

Perhaps because I was the biggest of the brothers, or the best singer, the interpreter picked on me to do the work, although he took care himself to disappear after that.

I was working in the skiff—it being then nearly dark—when someone came down the ladder. By his frog's voice I recognized the Prussian sergeant who had sent me on the ship.

"Eh, Cossack," he said, "you like rix-dollar for tobacco?"

In his hand silver coins chinked softly. I waited, fastening a pikestaff to a board, to serve for the rudder.

"Good soldier," he said, as if to a horse. "Like me, the drill sergeant, you serve the empress?"

"At command," I muttered.

"Then, here!" He put five coins into my fist, and they felt like good silver.

Coughing, he told me that I should watch out what Jones did. Because some of the senior officers did not trust Jones. If the admiral tried to send a message to the enemy, I should report him. That was all.

"Fine soldier," he said again. "You."

The silver being good silver, I kept it. I began to smell smoke in this, but I could not see any fire. Why should a Prussian sergeant want to turn in the new admiral?

Then I heard Jones coming down the ladder. Eh, he might have heard our words, if he understood. Even in the dark the Prussian saluted as if made of iron, stepping aside for Jones.

"*Stuppai!*" said Jones. "Forward!"

That word of ours at least he knew. But what did he mean? I could only think of the oars, and I took them up, while he sat in the stern, putting his hand on the new tiller.

The Prussian on the ladder watched us row out into the mist, the two of us alone in the skiff. By the lights of our fleet I saw that we were heading out toward the Turkish ships. Then the mist hung around us like a veil.

Seaweed pulled at my oars, like the fingers of dead men reaching up, and my heart began to feel cold.

For Jones sat in his shirt sleeves, without his hat but with a pistol and sword in his belt. And he kept throwing into the water a strong cord, knotted along its length and weighted with a stone. That cord was strong enough to tie a man's arms. The stone did not go down far on account of the shoals. When he pulled it out, Jones counted the knots.

Because of the rags, the oars did not grate against the thole sticks, and we made no noise. After a time we slipped past an anchored ship, and I heard voices. The skin felt cold inside my belt then—the voices were Turkish. Jones was steering me through the Turkish fleet, tossing out his line as if fishing!

A guard boat rowed past us in the mist. That night, by ill luck, seemed to be full of boats. We were passing a great ship with three rows of cannon when a barge almost bumped into us. Jones put his hand on my knee.

"*Ya muslimin*," a Turk in the barge called. "O men, do you carry arak to drink? Our throats are dry."

Jones never moved or spoke. Glory to the Lord, I could understand and answer: "We have salt. We come from the island."

Without more words they cursed us and went on. Why should they think that two Christians were rowing a skiff among their ships of war? The sweat was cold on me, but Jones laughed. "*Stuppai*, Ivak," he said.

Forward again! We passed the feluccas lined up under the guns of their fort at the bay's mouth. I rowed until my hands bled, while Jones kept measuring the water of the sea. Truly, his whim was a queer whim. For sometimes he felt of the stone at the end of the line. And sometimes he licked the finger that felt of the stone.

The next morning the Prussian sergeant drew me aside. "Well, Ivak, what?" he asked. "Did this pirate Pavel speak with the Turks?"

"How could he?" I said. "He cannot speak to me. How could he talk to a Turk?"

He looked at me and slapped his coat pocket. Silver coins clinked loud in it. He slapped my shoulder. "Ten rix-dollar for you, Ivak," he said, "if Pavel sends *any* message to the Turks." Winking, he put his finger against his nose. "Understand—*hein?*"

With so much smoke, I began to understand where the fire might be: Nassau Siegen. That prince did not want Jones here to command the fleet.

Every night Jones would call for me and go out in the skiff to measure the water, first turning to this side, then to that. And at times he made marks on a sheet of paper.

In the day he drove all the souls on the *Vladimir*, as if taking a whip to them. He ordered half of the guns on the upper decks to be hauled ashore in barges. The remaining guns he had us run in and out on their wheels, and load with the heavy balls until we were wet down with our sweat.

Nassau Siegen protested when the cannon were lowered away—saying we would be weak without all the guns. But Jones said the empress had made him admiral of the fleet, and he would pistol any man who refused to carry out an order. After that Nassau Siegen went away, to the gunboats along the shore, where the men drilled little if at all.

Probably he was glad to go, because just then His High Wellbornness arrived at the encampment on the land—the Prince Marshal Potemkin, the favorite of the empress. Eh, he arrived with coaches and pavilions, and green and red officers of the guard, and two nieces—all to see the new fleet being made ready. And Nassau Siegen was the first to greet him.

I thought of Babitka, with that Persian shawl tied on her, in all this splendor, and my tobacco tasted like dried oak leaves in the pipe. Kushel also felt afraid—more afraid than before.

"Look, Ivak," he whispered to me, "you can take out the skiff at night. The guards will let us over the side, and tonight you and I can be safe on the shore."

But I could not take the skiff and leave Jones, who might want to measure the water some more. Kushel went away without arguing. And that night he found some way to escape from the *Vladimir*. He was wiser than we.

He was not on the ship when the calamity came. Mist hid the lower bay in the morning, and we were sitting at the kasha pot when the lookouts began to shout and feet pounded on deck. When I poked my snout up into the air I saw Alexiano running, pulling his caftan over his nightshirt and yelling, "They come—they come!"

Through a break in the mist I could see sails of ships moving toward us. Sails upon sails, coming slowly in the light breeze.

On the rump of our ship Alexiano's officers argued, while we waited for orders. Some of us went to stations, not knowing what else to do. Then I heard a voice of command calling: *"Stuppai!"*

It was Jones's voice, and he called to us as he cut the lashings from the wheel. He knew only that one word, forward. Alexiano ran up to him to argue, but Jones motioned us to our stations. Then they dragged out his interpreter, and he could tell us what was in his mind. *Tfu*—orders for everyone. Up with the anchor, down with the sails. Powder bags from the magazine! He acted like a man who was no longer afraid.

"Quick, lads, or you will be late for the dancing."

Eh, he made a jest, while we were stumbling around, pulling at ropes. *Bourra-oum* sounded over the water, and something splashed close to us. I climbed up the ladder of ropes to the platform on the mast.

And I saw twenty-one Turkish and Levantine ships sailing toward us, their guns flashing and smoking.

We were all afraid—who was not afraid?—when we marched thus out toward the sea.

I watched Jones when the powder smoke cleared away. He stood without moving by the wheel, sometimes putting his hand on the wheel. He turned the ship first this way and then that, passing through the shoals. And I thought of the nights when we had measured the water, so Jones could see the shoals in the eye of his mind.

Behind us the other five frigates followed, struggling with their sails. I saw a bomb fall—*kerrumph*—into the nearest one, and it turned on its side. It staggered and lay down on the water, like a wounded horse. But the *Vladimir* did not lie down. She felt her way forward toward the biggest of the Turkish ships, the one with three rows of cannon.

I heard Alexiano shout that we would go aground. He ordered the brothers up in the bow to drop the anchor—Jones understanding nothing of the command. When the anchor pulled at the ship, the mast shook and the sails cracked. But Jones would not turn the wheel, and the *Vladimir* forged on, until the anchor chain ripped away. Jones said something to Alexiano, and after that the brigadier gave no more commands.

So we marched into the mass of the enemy ships, our guns making explosions on each side. *Tfu*—how things smoked up!

A Cossack came up the ladder of ropes, wiping the blood from his mouth. "Liven up, lads," he told us. "Little Father Jones says the dancing is just beginning."

So we on the platform laughed and began firing off our muskets, as if shooting tigers. Little Father Jones, that's what he was!

And the guns barked. We, who were not accustomed, did not even aim. For with the Turks all around us, every ball hit something. Yet they, when they fired at us and missed, hit one another.

I watched the flashes, through the smoke. And I saw a strange thing happen. The *Vladimir* marched on, toward the sea; but the Turks began to move this way and that. They began to circle away from our guns. When they circled, some of them stumbled on the shoals and sat. The biggest of their ships sat thus, leaning over, so its guns pointed up uselessly at the sky.

Then the others tried to go one way and another, heading toward the sea. Something splintered above me, and the smoke grew black. . . .

When I could see again, I felt dried blood on my head. A splinter had slapped me on the scalp lock, and I sat there on the platform looking into the sun. And that sun was setting over the water. The smoke had gone, and we were far from the river, out beyond the bay.

Rubbing some gunpowder and brandy into the split on my scalp, I felt alive again. "Fire away, lads!" I yelled.

The others on the platform looked at me queerly. For hours, they said, I had been blind and snoring, and now the battle was over. Ay, they showed me the sails of the remnant of the Turkish fleet escaping to sea.

"May the dogs bite them," I said. "But what guns are shooting?"

Because I could hear guns, far off. Nay, it was not well for us that we followed the battle so far to sea. When we turned home, we saw what guns were shooting. Nassau Siegen's. That officer had not followed Little Father Jones at all into the battle. But he had come up afterward with the flotilla of gunboats and bomb boats, and now he was shooting fire bombs into the Turkish ships sitting on the shoals.

Ay, he was firing into the ships that had surrendered to us and could not shoot back at him because they sat on the shoals, all six of them. They were burning like haystacks, with men dying inside. Jones, angered by this, hailed Nassau Siegen to stop the destruction, but he would not. What could we do?

When we came back to our anchorage, we found the encampment lighted up as if for a feast, with Prince Potemkin and his ladies and officers watching the fireworks down the bay.

Alexiano, who had all his uniform on now, put his arm around Jones. As for us Cossack brothers, we were glad to be alive—those of us who lived —and to have won the victory. For the *Vladimir* looked like a floating wreck.

I thought that even Babitka, the devilkin, would admire me now, after the battle. And that night she came again to the *Vladimir*.

It was after Jones had inspected the wounded. In his shirt sleeves he was sitting in the big after cabin, writing out his report of the action. One wall of the cabin had been shattered into beams. He smiled at me as I smoked my pipe. "Eh, Ivak," he said, "we did well."

He was writing thus, carefully, his report to the empress, when we heard shouting, and in came Alexiano, bowing before the Prince Marshal Potemkin, who wore a cloth of gold cloak, and kissed Jones on both cheeks. The Lady Anna and Nassau Siegen followed after, both sweet as honey to the American. Then my blood felt warm, because of Babitka, the darling, running up to me and catching me in her arms, so I could feel the beating of her heart.

"Ivak—you are on your feet!" She stared up at me. "For the love of good St. Nikolka, wash your face!"

Such a notion she had to wash my face! She went away from me, as if I was useless, just because I wasn't dead. But then I heard the interpreter talking. Potemkin was chewing his beard, thinking. They were telling him, because he asked, what Jones wrote to the empress. Eh, he wrote of the battle, as I had seen it—of the *Vladimir* and his officers and much of us of the brotherhood.

Still I could see well enough that Nassau Siegen was not pleased. "Chevalier Jones," he said, "I also saw the action."

He had been in the camp, miles away. But no one mentioned this—not before the prince marshal. Potemkin seemed to be thinking. He no longer smiled. "It is true, Chevalier Jones," he said then, "that you handled your ship well."

At this Jones, who had been puzzled by the talk, flashed out angrily. Eh, he was tired, not having slept much in that week, as I knew.

"If the Prince Marshal please," he said, "I did not come here to be an apprentice."

The interpreter wriggled when he said this, and Potemkin looked long into the snuffbox he was holding. Truly he was used to softer answers.

"Your report, Chevalier Jones, might prove misleading." He tapped the snuffbox. "The heroism of the prince of Nassau Siegen was responsible for our great victory, with your assistance."

As I live, he said that. Who had done the fighting, if not we of the *Vladimir?*

I chewed on my pipe and waited, while Jones stared at the papers he had been writing.

"My prince," he said at last to Potemkin, "I am thinking of the officers and men who served under me today."

"Of course, my dear admiral!" Potemkin was pleasant as a tavern keeper. "Of course you must think of such things. Do not write tonight, but come and breakfast with me in the morning."

And he went out with all the rest following like a bevy of birds. Only the beautiful Lady Anna left her fan on the table by Jones and smiled at him over her shoulder. And his brown eyes brightened at that.

Yet when the Lady Anna swished out, Babitka ran over to me and took the pipe from my mouth, putting her hand on my lips. "Listen, Ivak," she whispered swiftly, "don't try to think or to speak—only listen. This admiral of yours does not understand the Russians. Nay, he is blind. He must do as the prince marshal says, because Potemkin is like a god to your little mother, the Empress Catherine the Great. And *my* lady can twist Potemkin around her finger. Don't you understand how she loves Nassau Siegen?"

What words! Babitka swore they were true. She had heard the reports of the spies who told Potemkin and Lady Anna what passed on the fleet. Ay, Kushel was such a spy. Already they had tried to make Jones appear to be a pirate, by paying gold.

"Only give Nassau Siegen the praise for the victory, and Jones can have honor and glory—my lady spoke of lands in Russia and serfs and a thing like a decoration. You must tell your Jones, so his eyes will be opened. He must talk in another tone to Potemkin tomorrow."

She ran away quickly. What notions she had since she had risen to be maid in waiting, as she called it. We of the *Vladimir* had done the fighting, and whoever said otherwise was a brother of a dog. Being angered, I told the interpreter to say to Jones what that Babitka had told me.

Jones sat long in silence, his brown eyes troubled. Truly he was like a man alone, except for Ivak the Cossack. Taking up the fan of the Lady Anna, he opened it, to stare at the flowers and gold painted on it. "The empress," he said then, "is a great lady."

Then he began to write again, slowly, as if tired. When he finished the last page he signed his name and sprinkled sand on the paper. Folding it all, he sealed it and made the mark of his ring on the seal.

Nor did he go to take breakfast with Potemkin the next morning. Nay, he gave his sealed report to two of his officers to take to the empress. He said nothing of what was written.

But I had a thought as to that. I thought that Jones had told the truth about us of the *Vladimir*. And after many days had passed, another thought came to me. Potemkin also might have written a report.

At last the couriers came from the empress. Eh, she was happy because of the victory. And she sent rewards—a diamond-set sword of honor for Potemkin, and a sword with sapphires for Nassau Siegen, with promotion to rank of admiral, and a deed to lands in Russia, and the splendid Cross of St. George. To Alexiano, also promotion and reward. And twenty-four gold swords of honor—to Nassau Siegen's officers.

To Jones she sent only a letter. And I heard the words of the letter because it was an order. The order demanded that the Chevalier Paul Jones depart at once and without ceremony from the fleet to the court—his sphere of activity was no longer with us on the fleet.

That is how Jones went away from us, in his blue coat, with his plain sword at his side. I wondered if he could find a ship to take him back to his own land, now that his career with us was ended.

For the Russians gave him no honors when he went over the side of the *Vladimir*. Only we Cossacks rowed him ashore. He waved back to me. "Eh, Ivak," he called the only word he knew, "*stuppai!*"

Now that he had gone, I could see everything clearly. Jones had been afraid for us, all the time, and the prince of Nassau Siegen had been afraid for his own reputation. That's how it was.

When I understood that, I felt empty inside. The earth felt good under my feet. I did not want to go back to the *Vladimir*, where Nassau Siegen was now our admiral. To the devil with Babitka and careers at court! I wanted to ride back into the steppe, to my hut on the banks of the Terek.

But I had to see Babitka for one thing. Finding my way through the pavilions of the Russians, I arrived in the entrance of the pavilion of that Lady Anna. Some of the lackeys were holding to my arms and bleeding through their noses where I had cuffed them when they tried not to let me arrive. When they yelled, as if I were a wild boar, Babitka came running out.

"Ivak!" she cried, as if seeing a ghost.

As sweet as honey, gripping those lackeys, I bowed to the girdle. "May it please Your High Wellbornness," I said politely, "to know that I have found out it smells bad to me around here. Will your painted maidship tell me where you left my Kabarda horse?"

She caught her breath, her eyes big.

"What do you want of the horse?"

"To ride back to the Terek."

"It's in the stables of the Hussars' tavern, Ivak."

To the devil with all those brothers of dogs! I found the stables, and I found my black horse standing there fat and with a smooth coat. There beside him Babitka's nag was tethered, and I wondered what a maid in waiting wanted of a pony. I was swinging the saddle up on the Kabarda when I heard feet running.

Babitka rushed in. And I felt empty in my body. For the red was washed from her cheeks, the Persian shawl was gone—her dark hair tangled over her shoulders, and she wore men's trousers, just as if she were out singing in the high grass of our steppes.

"I knew you wouldn't go without the horse!" she cried.

Think what that darling wanted! Not to be lady's maid in waiting, but to ride back with me, Ivak, to my hut! We were far from the edge of the salt sea, riding together, before I felt sure that Babitka was again herself as she used to be, without thought of a career of glory. Then I began to see everything clearly, because it is easier for a Cossack to think in the saddle.

"*Tfu*—what brought Potemkin to our ship, after the battle?"

"I did," Babitka told me. "I begged Lady Anna, and she persuaded Potemkin to go."

"But why?"

She hung her head, so I could not see her face behind the dark hair. "I had to see if you were hurt, buffalo!" She looked at me, and her eyes were wet and shining. "When you beat me back of the lumber pile, my dear, I knew that you loved me. I was so happy I cried."

That's how it is with a girl. Drive them one way and they go another.

JACLAND MARMUR

Cape Horn Pilot

NORTH of the Cape of Virgins, after eastward passage of Magellan Strait, the tramp steamer *Trinipal* was taking the cold blasts of weather with a great to-do. Her ash chutes hissing, brown smoke flat at her funnel lip, she splintered each comber into acres of white, slipped headlong into the deep hollow beyond, and regained her pace with cataracts spilling from her topgallant fo'c'sle like long gray beards flowing in the wind. Captain Blessing, in the habit of skippers in those dangerous latitudes, restlessly paced the master's bridge. Up aloft, Mr. Barnaby, the chief officer, had an air of not trusting the mists that walked the ocean in the first dogwatch; his eyes kept darting around as much of the shifting horizon as he could see. But Harry Stacey, the second mate with the dusty-colored hair, stood easily behind the stuttering weather cloth, his young face composed, his lean body giving instinctive adjustment to the quick angles the *Trinipal* made with her thrusting pitch and roll. Mr. Stacey was alert enough; he simply saw no reason for premature alarms. And down on the foredeck the two apprentice boys were listening goggle-eyed to a hoary sailor yarn.

"He's a tough ol' shellback with a big white beard who wants to get home to Fiddler's Green. Can't blame the poor bucko, Jaimey. That's the happy place all honest sailors find, after they make their last landfall an' pass away beyond. Everybody knows that. They get all the rum they want down there, of a special kind to make nobody drunk; just feelin' fine. An' they spend their time yarnin' an' drinkin' from one big payday to the next. But mostly just makin' love to the girl they should never have left behind in the first port of home when they were young." The bos'n shifted his cud, spat to leeward, and readjusted himself on the No. 2 Hatch with a vastly prodigious sigh. "But they won't let this feller in down there 'cause his sailor record ain't clean. So he has to get his penance done. That's why he beats around these latitudes."

The bos'n's rough-throated bass funneled easily to the bridge where the two mates stood. Mr. Barnaby looked down for long enough to grin indulgently. His gray head even gave a short paternal nod, doing instinctive honor to the simple faiths of his calling. But it made Mr. Stacey smile. He'd heard that dogwatch yarn before. What blue-water sailor hadn't? It's a wind-ship legend of the Cape Horn trades, and this was the place for it. But Mr. Stacey knew for certain the windbag's day was done. Coal and steam were the things today; the war with Spain proved it conclusively. He had had enough of sail, wanting no more.

Harry Stacey was a skillful, efficient officer who meant to sit for master when the *Trinipal* reached the port of New York. He had a schedule for a well-planned life. He wanted a captain's handle to his name, so he could step ashore and take over his father's ship-fitting yard at Hunters Point on Frisco Bay. Then he would marry Alice Colby regardless of what her father thought. He saw no reason why Erasmus Colby's inexplicable hate of him should stand in the way of well-made plans. So Harry Stacey smiled at what he heard the bos'n say. He was just a little too old, and certainly much too young, to believe in singular nonsense such as that. Still, that sailor voice had strange compulsion in its tone. It made the second mate look down, amusement in his clear gray eyes.

"Bless us, Jaimey, that's a fact!" The lamp trimmer, on his way aft with the night lights in his arms and a rag wrapped around his throat, stopped long enough to give corroboration to a shipmate's tale. "Right here is where the Cape Horn pilot comes aboard all westbound ships. Don't laugh! That's truth."

The bos'n nodded his head, not ceasing the movement of his jaws. But Jaimey, the junior apprentice boy with the rosy cheeks, grinned merrily, the cynical disbelief of extreme youth in his eyes.

"What's his name, then, bose?" his thin voice demanded urgently. "Hey? Tell us what's his name."

"That's what everyone wants to know," the bos'n rumbled with unruffled calm. "I've heard some fellers call him Francis Drake, and others name him Roger Hawkes. But I don't take no stock in that. I never heard tell of them fancy navigators at all. He——"

"There you are!" the apprentice cut in gleefully. "Did you ever see him, bose?"

"See him?" The bos'n shifted his balance casually as the *Trinipal* slipped far over, dipping down her rail. "Why, bless you, Jaimey," he boomed then, solemnly, "a feller like him don't have no truck with the likes o' us. He belongs to the afterguard. He won't even talk to anything less'n the chief mate of a skys'l-yarder. He beats around these latitudes in a shallop with a patched gray sail. And anywhere south of fifty, down where the Cape Horn graybeards run, he's liable to board a westbound ship to help a master in trouble weather the stormy corner. If he loses a vessel he gets a bad mark, but each one he helps around Cape Stiff they put to his credit in the Old Man's big logbook down below. And that's all about it I know. Except I mind a barkentine I was down here in got taken all aback an'——"

The *Trinipal* lunged angularly over just then, her main deck freeing ports clanging with two distinct reports. The ash hoist clattered in the ventilator abaft the bridge, and they heard no more aloft of the bos'n's dog-watch tale.

The second mate, still faintly smiling over such pleasant nonsense, summed it up with precision for Mr. Barnaby. "The yarns," he said flatly, "the yarns you hear at sea!"

The chief officer made no response. He was frowning at something he saw across the heaving ocean waste before he pointed it out. For some moments the two officers were silent, swinging in the sky. Then Harry Stacey gave his quick, decisive judgment first: "Cape Horner, all right. Ship. Three t'ga'n's'ls set. Bound south. Starboard tack. Damme, Mr. Barnaby! I'm glad I'm not in her. I've had my bellyful of them."

Mr. Stacey's eyes were keen. To a landsman's gaze there was nothing there at all except a grayly tossing flood with mist banks streaming before the wind in failing light. Till distantly three slim black spars, like pencils, swung for an instant in unison through an arc of the cloud-swept sky. They disappeared at once, as if pulled with violent ease below the curving rim of the earth. Then all at once the veil parted again. And there she was, ascending with an upward lunge that for a moment showed a lean dark hull all drowned in white. Then it went down once more, deep in a valley between two great, green, running hills. But her bare upper spars remained this time and her topgallant cloths, swinging like three gray banners making lonely celebration in an empty place. Behind their backs the officers of the *Trinipal* heard Captain Blessing's heavy tramp on the ladderway.

"Mister, get the signal book. Ring up slow ahead," he said. "That's old Captain Slocum's ship, *Madrigal*, flying our own house flag. She will want to speak us to be reported in the Plate."

When Harry Stacey could look again, that wanderer over there had her mainsail laid against the mast. Signal buntings broke along the halyard to her mizzen peak. Captain Blessing deciphered, a thick forefinger on the pages of his signal book. He pulled at his muttonchop side whiskers and looked up, startled.

"Something wrong, sir?" Mr. Stacey asked, knowing it not unlikely. "Scurvy, sure as fate!"

"Captain Slocum. Heart. They buried him off the River Plate. I knew him well." The master shook his head, frowning severely. "Her mate wants urgently to know can we spare him an officer. He's the Horn to weather yet, you know. It—it's very irregular."

Irregular! Well, by the gods, young Mr. Stacey thought, so it was. He turned to look. The full-rigged *Madrigal* arced her trucks in the drift of the steamer's funnel smoke, plunging her martingale stays deep one moment, pointing her dripping jib boom aloft the next. In between there was loud, familiar noise: the hissing crash of ocean, the lonely whimper of a rising wind toward dark. And Captain John Blessing's solemn voice, reflecting what he thought out loud: "That mate wouldn't ask a thing like that unless he knew he must. If she didn't fly the house flag of Brawnlee-Holt, I would say no at once. Still, I can't order a man under my articles to go, and I certainly couldn't spare Mr. Barnaby."

It was enough to bring Harry Stacey's strong young head around. "That, sir," he said, "seems to leave it up to me."

"Entirely up to you," the master agreed. "It would be entered in both vessels' logs, for your protection. I can tell you only it would do you no harm at all when Mr. Brawnlee hears of it on Water Street. Give you a great shove for master, too. But the decision, Mr. Stacey, must be entirely your own."

Young Harry Stacey let a youthful grin slip swiftly along his lips. "I've made some pierhead jumps, sir, in my time," he said, "but never in a place like this."

"Aye. Well?"

Perhaps the second mate had an inkling this was the time of his changing tide. But it isn't likely. That quick instant slaps itself all in a moment before a man, and largely passes by unrecognized. It found Harry Stacey thinking, a little scornfully, that if he were mate of the *Madrigal,* and the captain died, he'd take her through himself. Then his shoulders lifted imperceptibly. This wasn't really important. He would sit for master in Frisco instead of the port of New York; he would see Alice Colby the sooner, and take her out to inspect that ship-fitting yard that was his when he stepped ashore for good. So the fine-drawn moment of decision passed, leaving Harry smiling at it calmly self-possessed.

"Very well, sir," he said in a voice that might have been tossing off the most casual of remarks. "I'll go."

And that's how Harry Stacey, who was certain that all he needed to fill his fortune and his manhood out was a captain's handle to his name, joined his new ship *Madrigal* almost off the pitch of the Horn. He went, toward dark of a cold gray South Atlantic day, in an open boat under Mr. Barnaby's charge.

He took his sextant with him in its hardwood case, and he took his sea chest too. These outward symbols of the sailor craft Mr. Stacey thoroughly understood, and the planing force of heavy gales. What more important thing than this could there possibly be that a captain had to know. Maybe that silly yarn the bos'n told. Because he was reminded of it before he went away.

"Well, bose!" He heard the voice of Jaimey, high-pitched and boyish on the wind, just as the falls ran out. "If it was only a shallop with a patched gray sail, you could say there was the Cape Horn pilot himself going to join that ship. Imagine!" The little fellow laughed in glee. "We had him aboard here all the time! Why didn't you tell us, booo?"

Harry Stacey heard that with singular clarity, and it stuck in his mind, somehow. Then Mr. Barnaby was crying good luck from the stern sheets of an open boat that dropped abruptly out from under as he seized a dancing pilot ladder. Grizzled faces were staring down. He heard the hard slap of water against a wooden hull. Then he came over the bulwark, the familiar restlessness of the decks of sail beneath his feet once more as he gave his first order in the ship he joined in so unorthodox a way.

"Bos'n, have my dunnage taken aft." And, turning, he strode toward the place of command, climbing the windward ladder to the poop.

He went up briskly. And then—abruptly!—Harry Stacey stopped in his tracks at what startling thing he saw. The traditional captain's rattan chair was lashed to the deck against the cabin skylight. It held an emaciated man, stretched full length, one extended leg stiff with splint and bandage. His chest, too, was tightly strapped beneath an open reefer coat, and there was a yellow muffler wrapped around his throat where muscles bulged like whipcord. He remained motionless. Except his eyes! Under a shapeless felt hat they glittered and burned with fierce intensity out of deep hol-

lows in a gray-stubbled face. They flew wide instantly at sight of the man
with the dusty-colored hair erect on the threshold of the deck of command. They faced each other for a moment of taut and silent opposition.
Then the mizzen topsail fluttered loudly, and that man's eyes narrowed to
flaming points. "You!" The thin lips barely parted to let that hoarse explosive through. "Why did it have to be you!"

"Sorry, Mr. Colby." Harry quickly recovered his efficient poise. "Alice.
told me you were mate in the *Parsifal,* or I——"

"Transferred in New York on sailing day," Erasmus Colby snapped. "I
was to take over the *Madrigal* when Captain Slocum retired ashore in
Frisco." His lips curled acidly. "My command came a little ahead of
schedule. It almost always does." Then his voice went thin and harsh. "If
I'd known it was you they'd send—I'd sooner take her round alone! Busted
leg, cracked ribs, and all!" Then swiftly his hate and scorn came pouring
out: "Didn't get your master's ticket yet, did you, Harry Stacey? I expect
not, or you wouldn't be at sea at all. You don't know what I've got against
you? Well, that's it. You're just putting in your time out here; you're worse
than a passenger. All you want of us is a captain's ticket. When you get it,
you'll hustle ashore and keep it safely tucked away like a bit of loot you've
plucked to hang in a fancy picture frame! Like a deer-head hunter's stuff.
To hell with that! That does no honor to the cloth you wear. I want no
son-in-law like that for mine! You don't pass for master in New York or
in the Frisco customhouse. Down here is where the examiners come aboard!
It's time you learned. It's time——"

He stopped, gasping. It dawned on Harry that Erasmus Colby had the
burning eyes, the flaming cheeks of fever, or he wouldn't talk that way.
So Mr. Stacey smiled with self-possessed indulgence.

"Let's leave that, sir, for another time," he murmured quietly. "Where's
the second mate? Let's get the ship along."

"The second!" The man stretched out in the rattan chair let go a quick,
hoarse laugh, startlingly strong from such a shaken frame. "Great Caesar's
ghost!" he roared. "Do you think if I had a second mate I'd ask for help
from a smoking tin pot? The second mate's in a thousand fathom, or else
he's safe in Fiddler's Green. Swept off the main t'gallant yard in that pam-
pero off the Plate. Now, if you want to go back to your *Trinipal,* you
better make your mind up quick! There she goes, tootling us good-by."

Harry's head came up at those three sharp whistle blasts. He was in time
to see the last puff of steam torn from that distant funnel lip. Then he

slowly turned. On the *Madrigal's* main deck a solid row of upturned faces eyed him, grizzled, silent, appraising. He put his head on his shoulder toward the wheel.

"Helm up!" He faced forward again with deliberation. "Hands to the main braces! Get the yards swung round!" The time of Harry Stacey's trial had begun.

It came on him suddenly, without warning. It just reached out and lightly touched him to let him know he'd got the nod at last. When he had time to take his first pacing measure of the poop, there was no sign left of the *Trinipal.* The sea was dark and empty, loud with a hard rush of weather, the hiss of boarding sprays. Then the steward came up, a worried man with his cap in his hand, looking fearfully toward Captain Colby in his chair, where a faint gleam, upflung through the cabin skylight, caught him in dim outline.

"He's been up here, sir, ten solid days like this," the steward whispered. "He ought to be below, so he can mend." He lifted a wrinkled face to his new officer, patient with appeal. "He'd skin me alive if he knew I was saying this. But I'm scared of pneumonia, sir, if he stays up here in the weather when we get off the Horn."

Mr. Stacey looked down on the granite face of Alice Colby's father. Nothing but an iron will had kept that man in charge. Now the hollow eyes were closed beneath the shaggy brows, the cheeks sunken and burning.

"Fetch him below, steward." Harry Stacey's voice was strangely quiet. "Then tell the bos'n to come aft. He'll have to spell me when the weather will allow."

Harry remembered making that decision. He remembered poring over the chart in the little cuddy to burn the ship's track and her last day's work in his mind. Then he blew out the hurricane lamp. When he did, and the sudden solid darkness fell over him, it was like turning off the light on everything that had ever happened before. Because the wind went to the west before the middle watch, starting to head the *Madrigal.* It backed steadily into the southern quarter to let him know he was down near Stormy Corner, where the great gales blow. And after that he moved through instinct, and his memory was blurred.

Out of the south and west the weather came, roaring with sleet and hail, herding the mile-long seas before it. Harry was ready: preventer gear rove, an extra hand at the wheel, relieving tackles on the helm. Under shortened canvas the ship's upper spars were bare, like trees naked in winter, violently arcing through a soil of lower scud. She began her endless struggle, knot by knot, for westing, only to be hurled away again. Till Time became eternal and unbroken. Except for short flashes of vivid memory. Haphazard things loomed out of the turmoil of chaotic storm. He remembered once passing the weather earing himself out on the foreyard-arm; he remembered the pitiful look of the men flailing on the drunken footropes, blue-lipped, blood at their finger tips from fisting ice-stiff canvas, body-and-soul lashings on their ragged waterproofs. He remembered an age with the *Madrigal* hove to, her yards pointed almost in the screaming wind, pressure on the after sides, weather oil bags dripping while all the South Atlantic banshees howled. But mostly he remembered the ocean —its smoking, wild, and terrible look, as if ultimate good and evil were in contention, deadly and final.

Lashed by the mizzen fife rail, he faced forward with hollow eyes. Sleep was a blessed thing he had heard about but would never know again. The *Madrigal's* track on the brine-soiled chart took on the look of a pattern a madman might have traced. And Harry Stacey never knew how long he faced that torture. A day, a week, perhaps whole months went roaring overhead. Exhaustion had him by the throat. This was a thing he had not ever known before. Oh, he had stood here other times, efficient and self-contained, taking the freezing blasts of weather in his eyes. Yes! But another man had always stood beside him then, a man with the hard, unyielding face that plainly spoke command. Or else that man was stretched in a chair lashed by the cabin skylight, making believe he slept. You could shake him out when it got too much for you. You could shove the dreadful burden off on his shoulders for a little while at least, certain it would be accepted without question to give you a moment's ease. Well, there was a chair there now, too. But it was empty. There was no one to fill it but himself. And Harry Stacey's soul rebelled.

He cursed Erasmus Colby from the bottom of his heart. Raging with fever, that man was in his cabin underneath the poop, where the sea washed odds and ends of litter back and forth. But Harry, in streaming oilskins and sou'wester, raised his dripping face to a sky exploding sleet and hail. And his spirit cried out in agony. He never came aboard for this. This wasn't what his schedule said! He didn't have his captain's ticket yet; the best he had was mate. He was skillful, capable; he knew his job. But a man had to have some help before exhaustion drowned him out. There was limit to a man's endurance when he was by himself. "Damn you, Erasmus Colby!" Harry's spirit cried. "A man can't last this out. Why the blazes should he? Not alone! Not without some help!"

Whether he actually cried aloud his desperate rebellion or whether he just imagined it, he didn't know. But that's when it happened. Right then. It was a most astonishing thing. Through the blinding sheets of spindrift he saw that lugger lift along the mountainous ridge of a Cape Horn sea not half a cable length away. He tried to cry out, but he couldn't. So he watched it, fascinated. How easily she ran! Dry as a bone, fore and mainsail set in a full hurricane, skillfully swinging alongside. And then a spry little man leaped briskly from those stern sheets to the deck of the *Madrigal*, to come quickly up the ladder to the poop with mincing steps. He was a most amazing fellow! He wore a fine corselet of mesh steel under a doublet of brilliant red, and a sea cape of blue. There was a dirk at his hip, a small round hat on his head, and he had a clipped, brown, curly beard. An odd-looking, ancient seafarer's instrument Harry recognized for a big wooden astrolabe hung around his throat by a golden chain. He had merry eyes that sparkled and bubbled, and he minded the cruel weather not at all.

"Well, hello there, Harry Stacey," he said in the clearest, thinnest voice. "I've been wondering how long before you'd ask my help. I can't come aboard until you do, you know. High time! . . . You lads won't ever learn to put the pilot ladder over. I'm not as young as I used to be. Well, no matter. Here I am."

Harry moved his head a little. How odd! There was some vague thing about this fellow he thought he recognized. He struggled with memory, but it wasn't any good—he was too stupefied with fatigue. And then it came to him like a sudden burst of light. Why, this was that yarn the bos'n always told! Right here in front of him! Harry stared out of hollow-socketed, red-rimmed eyes.

"Why," he managed to gasp at last, "you must be the Cape Horn pilot I've so often heard about!"

"But of course," the little fellow said, casting a smart look aloft to what canvas Harry had on the *Madrigal*. "Who else did you expect?"

"No one at all," Harry said quickly. "It's just that you don't look the way the bos'n said you would. He said you'd have a big white beard."

"Bos'ns!" He gave a laugh of careless scorn. "Bos'ns always get things wrong. . . . Let's sweat up that lower maintops'l brace. Hey, Harry Stacey? Let's try."

So they did. And Harry noticed that even in the waist-high boil of sea along the deck with the watch, the Cape Horn pilot never left his side. His jovial face retained its look of happy serenity. It was a great comfort. He felt easier. He suddenly understood the vague look of gratitude he'd often seen on a skipper's face when the pilot comes aboard in the offing to some harbor dangerous and little known. And he thought that here he was, face to face at last with a famous seaman he'd heard so many bos'ns yarn about. He ought to learn the truth this time! So he went about it slyly, not wanting to appear rude, or ignorant, or too nosy about another man's affairs.

"I almost missed you altogether, sir," he murmured, back in his lashings by the weather mizzen shrouds. "I always understood you used a shallop with a patched gray sail."

"There you go! Just like all the rest. Looking for the wrong thing all the time. That's the bos'n's doing, I expect." The Cape Horn pilot peered through the sights of his astrolabe at a sun no other man could see, giving a sharp look to the reading of his arc. "I gave that shallop up a hundred years ago. Fine seaworthy boat, too. But a man's got to keep up with the times. I really don't know why, except it seems to be expected."

"A hundred years!" Harry grinned astutely to himself. Here was just the opening he wanted. "Have you been down here as long as that?"

The bluest, brightest eyes turned on Harry. "You think that's long?"

"Well, isn't it?"

The Cape Horn pilot shook his head. His eyes went solemn and he drew himself erect. It was amazing how his stature seemed to grow. His voice wasn't thin any longer, either. It was deep and low; it boomed like the booming of a heavy gale. "I have seen the carracks of Portugal and Spain go driving past on this patrol. I've boarded big Dutch caravels and English men-o'-war. I showed them Falkland Islands and I showed them the pitch of the Horn. I've done my share!" he wildly cried. "You think a hundred years is long? By your reckoning, it will be almost four times as long that I have sailed these seas to help you lads around."

"Four hundred——" Harry was aghast. "But you speak English as if——"

"Of course!" His mood changed instantly, bright and merry as a lark again. "You've got to speak all kinds of tongues, the trade I'm in. Now, why don't you come out with it? You want to know my name. They all do. I've told hundreds of them, but they just can't pass the proper word along." He chuckled. "And you want to know how long before the Big

Four-Striper who walks the quarter-deck in Fiddler's Green will let me get back home. Now, ain't that right?"

"Well, yes." Harry felt a little uncomfortable. "I was just afraid it would be impolite."

"Not a bit. That's what I'm really here for." He leaned closer, in a very confidential way. "I am Juan de Cartagena, a nobleman of Spain. In what you call the good old days, I missed my one big chance and gave little honor to the cloth I wore. Just the way a lot of fellows do. That was when that Portuguese we hated, Fernão de Magalhães, sailed this ocean in a time when no man knew what terror and what fury lived down here. You came through the passage he discovered, Harry, before you left the *Trinipal*. Anyhow, we did a fearful thing. Four hundred years ago, that dreadful April in Port San Julian, we mutinied." He paused an instant, sadly to contemplate that unforgivable sailor crime. "Magellan marooned us as our punishment," he went on with hollow sorrow. "Myself and a lay priest name of Pedro Sanchez de la Reina. He's got that shallop with the patched gray sail you spoke about. He uses it in his work along the Tierra del Fuego coast. It's a fearful penance he has, trying to make men understand the truth about their gods. Because you know how mutiny's considered by the Old Man down in Fiddler's Green. I have my penance too. I've got to help a thousand ships in trouble round Cape Stiff before he'll let me swing my hammock in that happy sailor place."

"Yes, I know," Harry murmured, wanting to give comfort for a dreadful fate like that. "That's what the bos'n said."

"Did he?" The Cape Horn pilot looked sharply at him with a sly, ecstatic grin. "Of course a steamer hardly counts at all; and if I lose a ship, my record drops two points in the Old Man's big logbook down below. They have a devil of an inquiry; you know how those things go."

"Well, you don't seem a bit downhearted over it."

"Downhearted? I should say not! I got those ships all entered and accounted for at last. All except two! Why shouldn't I be gay? Because, you see, a ship like the *Madrigal* here, with only one officer able to keep the deck—— Well, I generally get the Old Man to give me an extra mark. If he's in real good humor, I can sometimes get him to count a ship like that for two. So if we can only shove her round, Harry, you and me, and pick up an easterly slant, my long penance will be done! Oh, I'm happy as a lark about it, let me tell you that."

"Yes, I can imagine. I'll do the best I can for you."

And then, thinking of the loveliness of Alice Colby, Harry ruefully murmured, "Four hundred years! How lonely it——"

"Ho! Now it's the girls you're worrying about. Sailors are all alike!" The Cape Horn pilot chuckled. "Of course I'm a little too old to try my luck. I gave that sort of thing up a couple of hundred years ago. But we've all kinds of girls. You'd be surprised. All the girls who wouldn't marry men they loved because they went to sea—they're all down here. They do their penance just the same as anyone. Poor things! They know now what they missed; they wail about it constantly. They're very much worse off than me."

His bright face took on a look of the profoundest commiseration, thinking of all those lovely women who had never known a sailor's hearty love. It made Harry Stacey feel a little sad himself. But they had to get a lower tops'l set just then, feeling a breath more southing in the icy wind. And that's how Harry's conversations with this wonderful fellow went: in odd, broken bits. Some of it by the mizzen fife rail, lashed by a turn of the topsail sheet against smothers of sleet and spume; some of it while he staggered along the main deck driving the men, with that fellow spryly whispering in his ear. But the next thing Harry could recall with any clarity, the men were gathering in ominous clusters down by the break of the poop.

They were half frozen, in patched oilskins and sodden rags. Some of them peered upward to the deck of command with hollow eyes; others just swayed where they stood, growling. The ship plunged and soared, tight on half a moderating gale, the long gray seas sweeping past the bulwarks like wild white horses running. Harry stared down, stupid with exhaustion. Till one man stepped out before the rest with a fid clutched tightly in one paw.

So Harry had to stagger to the head of the ladderway, swaying. "Well?"

The man's head shot up, fire in his eyes. "We're fed up! We'll never get the blasted hooker round!"

A loud muttering sounded behind his back. Harry took one step down, hanging to the handrail. He was glad the Cape Horn pilot was beside him. He knew he couldn't manage this alone.

"That's nonsense, Joe! Don't be a fool." He barely recognized his voice, it was so taut and brittle with fatigue. "The weather's spent. Fog's pouring from the south. We've got a slant due soon. . . . Get for'ard, men."

"Be damned to that! We're freezing!"

Harry Stacey took another downward rung. "So am I."

"We're starved!"

"So am I."

They watched the officer with a peculiar fascination. That, Harry thought, was because of that bizarre little fellow at his side. He descended the ladderway slowly and stood on deck, weaving from side to side, a gaunt man with stubbornness in his eyes.

Till the giant in front of him humped his shoulders, his voice exploding, "The ship's bewitched! Master and second mate gone, Mr. Colby laid up, and you don't belong in her at all! You'll never get the damned tub round. Never! Turn her, we say! Turn her and run to the east around Good Hope while we still got strength enough to swing the yards!"

"No."

That's all that Harry said, and he wasn't really sure, but he thought he heard the Cape Horn pilot's chuckle at his side. "That's the ticket, Harry! Tell 'em no. When you say no to other men, to yourself you're really saying yes."

Then the man with the fid took half a pace, blazing, "I tell you we mean it!"

"No!" Harry thrust out his arm. "Give me that pin, Joe!"

"Now you're talking, Harry! For a minute you had me scared. We got to get this vessel round. It means an awful lot to me."

That's what Harry Stacey heard the Cape Horn pilot whisper in his ear, that moment he stood face to face with his victory or his defeat. But all the rest was a funny blur. It was all mixed up with a sudden icy breath of wind and with that seaman, hopeless with fatigue, leaping at him all at once with his eyes ablaze and the fid upraised. Harry ducked, out of the sheerest instinct. He heard a whistling through the air, felt a glancing blow on his shoulder blade. Then his fists slammed out to impact yielding things. Something staggered away, fell in a heap to the deck. Other weaving shapes closed in, and he fought blindly on.

Till a voice, shrill and fierce, knifed to his consciousness. "Stow that, you blasted fool! Ice! Ice on the weather bow! Helm up! Helm up, you idiot!"

It shocked Harry to his senses instantly. He had one sharp sight of Erasmus Colby, his pinched face covered with stubble, standing ghostlike under the break of the poop with an open mouth. He had a piece of dunnage for a crutch, his other arm clutching the frightened steward's shoulder for support. That's all Harry saw before he leaped to the poop, desperately crying up the helm, struggling with the spokes himself, roaring orders down the deck. Then he stood there, taut and breathless.

The ship's head swung with throat-catching slowness, her jib boom penciling across the face of a floating blue-white mountain. It reared up with unhurried deliberation, a dreadful shape with an icy breath, shouldering the fog aside. It made a vast sucking noise before it plunged with a deafening crash to hurl a sea wash for a mile around. The men stood rooted to the plunging deck, wide-eyed with terror. It seemed to Harry Stacey that he stood unblinking there and held his breath for half an age before that monstrous thing, soundless and still for all its noisy passage, slipped astern to be swallowed up in haze.

When Harry, in one great exhaling gush, released the bands of steel that bound his lungs, he found he was trembling. He found he had to cling to the binnacle stand. He was lightheaded, feeling a breath of weather on his cheek he couldn't believe. So he tested it. It came again. He looked across the ocean waste, then aloft to the lower rack of cloud.

He found his voice once more. Or maybe it wasn't his voice at all, but the voice of the Cape Horn pilot who could bellow with such strength as this. "Out tops'l reefs!" he roared. "Move to it, blast you all! Get the t'gallants on her too!"

He screamed out innocent blasphemy with a wild, unreasonable joy. He went lurching for the ladder to lend a hand. "There you are!" he cried to the little fellow with the bubbling eyes who was prancing along beside him. "You're going to be all right now! Here's our slant for sure!"

"Of course!" The Cape Horn pilot's face looked very sly, and his curly beard kept bobbing up and down. "We done it, Harry Stacey! Yes, we did!"

The *Madrigal* flung full topsails and her three topgallants to a southing wind that freshened steadily. Harry remembered drinking in the look of it—gray seas marching, sprays flying, leaning towers of canvas taut aloft. And he remembered lifting old Erasmus Colby in his arms to carry him bodily to his bunk below.

"You stay here! Till you're fit to keep the deck! You're Alice Colby's father, and I mean to bring you home to her alive!" Harry spoke wildly, fierce exultation in him. "I brought the ship as far as here without you. I can take her the rest of the way."

Erasmus Colby's thin lips stirred. "I saw that fellow fling the fid. Log him. I saw it plain as——"

"No! They've stood enough, those men; they'll do. You saw nothing, Mr. Colby."

"No?" His feverish eyes fluttered open. His voice was sharp with scorn. "You near smashed my ship! I suppose you'll say it was the Cape Horn pilot cried out warning when——"

"That's right. That's——"

"Go tell that silly yarn to Alice! See what——"

"I will! I'll tell her about it when we're married and she sails with me in all the fine big ships I will command."

Captain Colby raised himself on one elbow, hearing that. He saw a tall youthful man, haggard and swaying, his wet face deeply tooled by utter weariness. Sea water sloshed around his sea-booted feet; trickles of it drained steadily from his oilskins. But the look of him was different from that of the lad who wanted nothing better than a cushy job ashore, once he got a captain's handle to his name.

It was enough to let the bitter hate drain out of Mr. Colby's granite face, and what he said was startling. "You won't have any trouble, Harry. You can sit for master any time." He fell back weakly in the bunk. "The examiners must have been aboard."

Then Harry had to do serious battle with his leaden legs to make them climb aloft. He found himself clutching the rail at the break of the poop, and things were spinning round. But he knew the wind was fair. It came pouring over the *Madrigal's* quarter with a hard and solid rush. It made a great booming sound alow and aloft, like a noise from very far away. Fair wind! The ship sang with it. The hands at the braces forward, backs bent on the ropes, had already forgotten the conflict and the terror. Fair wind at last! They, too, were singing in celebration. Their rough voices roared while Harry Stacey, swaying with exhaustion, drank in the sight and the sound of his vague and obscure victory. Till he sensed there was someone beside him. *It must be the Cape Horn pilot, coming to say "Thank you" and "Good-by,"* he thought. But it wasn't. It was just the bos'n, plucking him persistently by the sleeve.

"You got to take a spell, sir," he was insisting over and over again, to make his officer understand. "You been up here for days and nights on end." He was urging Harry along, helping him stagger toward a rattan chair lashed close against the cabin skylight. "She'll do now. I'll watch her good. You got to take a spell."

So Harry sank back into heavenly ease. He was in the captain's chair.

He never believed he'd fit, it seemed so huge to him. But it just drank up his weary frame. It seemed to him the bos'n, bending down and urging him to rest, had eyes like the Cape Horn pilot had. But that was silly, he knew. Because here was that little fellow himself, with his absurd hat and his ancient astrolabe around his throat, standing at his elbow now, smiling very cunningly.

"Well, Señor Juan de Cartagena," Harry told him, struggling to keep awake long enough for that, "we got the ship around, and you can call your penance done at last. You got to forgive me, sir, for sitting down while a famous sailor like yourself is standing up. But I'm pretty well done in. It costs a lot, a thing like this."

The little fellow grinned, nodding. "Yes, Harry Stacey, I know. It's quite all right. I got to be going anyhow. Here comes my lugger. You're all right now, and that's as long as I can ever stay." He waved his hand, half turning away. "I'll be seeing you next trip."

"Next trip!" Harry was startled. "I thought you said you could go home to Fiddler's Green if——"

"So I did. So I did." What a cunning look he had, stopping with his head cocked over his shoulder to look back toward Harry in the master's chair. "But then——"

"You mean that stuff you told me isn't true?" Harry was furious. "You mean you're a fraud, the way I always——"

"There you are! You see? I have to tell you fellows yarns like that, or young skippers wouldn't ever believe in me. I've seen it too many times. I know."

"But look here! I've got to know the truth! I can't go giving my wife a pack of lies. If you aren't Cartagena who led the mutiny in Port San Julian, then who——"

"Oh, I am him all right." Harry Stacey saw the Cape Horn pilot draw himself erect and saw his eyes take on a look imperious. "Whatever a man calls me, that I am." His voice boomed loudly, like the booming of the ocean when the great gales blow. "Some men say I'm Francis Drake and others name me Roger Hawkes. The truth is I am all of them. I am all the skippers who ever sailed these frozen seas, needing help from me. I'm Captain Colby, too, and John Blessing, who is master of the *Trinipal*." He came closer. His shadow fell hugely across the captain's chair. "As a matter of fact, Harry Stacey, I am really *you!* I'm what makes you hold on when it seems there isn't any use; I'm what makes you honor the cloth you wear.

If you believe it, you're all right. But if you don't, then I can't be standing ever at your side. And if I'm not there, you'll never get a ship around Cape Horn. Or ever weather any other dreadful cape. . . . So long, Harry Stacey. I'll be seeing you next trip."

He seemed to leap to the bulwark, springing to the stern sheets of his lugger. Then he put the tiller over and she fell away; the mist came down; he disappeared from sight at once.

Harry struggled up. "Here!" he wanted to cry out. "You can't go off like this! We've got to talk this through, so it will make some sense!" But he felt the bos'n's big hand on his shoulder, strong and unyielding.

"There's no need to be shouting this way, sir," he was growling. "The ship's all right, I tell you. Easy now. Easy, sir."

Harry sank back. But it seemed a little clearer now. No wonder they all said they knew that fellow's name but couldn't pass the proper word along. You could imagine funny things when you were all burned out. Best put it to the bos'n, who was still looking down, anxious worry in his eyes. That's what Harry thought.

So he mumbled, "Bose! You know that yarn they tell about the Cape Horn pilot who——"

"Lord love us, yes!" The bos'n's growl sounded very far away indeed. "He's a tough ol' shellback with a big white beard who wants to get home to Fiddler's Green. Can't blame the poor bucko, sir. That's the happy place all honest sailors find, after they make their last landfall and pass away beyond. Everybody knows that. We sure could-a used his help this voyage, sir. Now, isn't that a fact?"

There was good comfort in that gruff voice, speaking the familiar idiom of bos'ns everywhere. Harry could faintly smile. There you were! No one even knew that fellow'd been aboard. No one but himself. Well, wasn't that enough? He could tell the truth to Alice Colby now; he wouldn't have to lie. That was the last thing Harry remembered before rest stole over him like a sweet warm bath. It crawled along his limbs. It crept like an exquisite delight into the marrow of his tired bones. It gave his spirit peace. That smile could remain on his haggard, youthful face, lined with the torture of exhaustion and fatigue. He knew the ship ran easy now. Free of Stormy Corner. Boiling to the west and north. And he knew that he could safely sleep. He could sleep the blessed, blessed sleep. Because he was snug in the captain's rattan chair—and he knew the Cape Horn pilot's name at last.

JOHN P. MARQUAND

You Can't Do That

SINCE THE YEAR 1806 a cloak of red-and-yellow feathers has hung in the hallway of the March house on the Ridge, with a helmet made from the same plumage suspended above it. These two articles have always held the same position on the wall, except for such times as they have been put away in camphor to protect them from the moths. The cloak was brought there by John March and indicates very accurately the first venture of the March ships in the fur-and-sandalwood trade with China. It was hung there by John March when he returned as supercargo on the brig *Polly*, Moses March, owner, and Elihu Griggs, master. A single glance at that cloak in the shady, spacious hallway of that square Federalist house is startling to anyone who is even remotely familiar with the curiosities of the South Seas.

It hangs there, an alien object, and yet, through association, somehow strangely suitable to a house like the old March house in a New England seaport town. Granted that its presence there is known to many scholars, familiarity cannot avert a shock of surprise at a sight of that vivid garment, for it is one of the most beautiful objects ever conceived by the mind or executed by the hand of man. It is strange, too, to realize that if that cloak and the helmet above it were sold today, their price would probably equal the March profits in their precarious trade of another century. It is a long, fine cloak—and the Marches have always been careful of everything they have laid their hands on—one of the best of the hundred-and-some-odd feather garments which are known to be extant today, and there will never be another made. The o-o which supplied those yellow feathers, only one beneath each wing, a shy bird which once fluttered through the crimson-blossomed ohia and the tree-fern forests of the Hawaiian mountains, is virtually extinct, and the bird that wore the red plumage is in hardly a better case. He is vanishing from the face of this earth like the genial race whose ancestors collected and attached those feathers to their delicate base of fiber netting in a manner so admired by Captain Cook. Granted that the labor which went into the making of that garment is beyond all accurate calculation, the result was worth it. The reds and yellows are nearly as vivid as when the coat was new. They glisten there in the hallway, jewel-like, with a depth of luster and lacy velvet texture that is more vital than inanimate. On an evening when the lights are lit, John March's cloak glows like flame and there is an element of awe in its splendor.

This is not odd, for it was intended to indicate greatness. The red lozenge pattern upon the yellow marks it as belonging not alone to one of the *alii* but to a Hawaiian chief of a royal lineage that was very near to kingship. Its size and the amount of yellow is a sufficient indication of its former owner's greatness. If the shadow of a commoner were to touch the shadow of the man who wore it, that commoner would suffer death, for the man who wore it was sublimated in the complicated feudal ritual of his islands into a being more than human. The feather kahili was carried behind him; an attendant bore his calabash of koa wood to preserve his spittle, his nail parings, and his fallen hair, so that they might not fall into the hands of enemies whose kahunas, or witch doctors, might use them in fatal incantations. When the man who wore that cloak walked abroad, the populace assumed a prone position on pain of death. Some trace of the majesty of its first owner's presence still seems to linger about that feather cloak, incongruously, in a New England town.

The cloak was owned by the chieftain Kualai, as his name is spelled, probably incorrectly, in the March letter books and the log of the brig *Polly,* since there were no missionaries then to bring order to the Hawaiian phonetics—no missionaries, no mosquitoes, no red ants to kill the kou trees, no colds, and no disease. Kualai ruled his share of the Kona coast on what is now known as the Big Island, under the protection of the great king Kamehameha in the days when John March was young. In Kualai's youth he had been one of the king's best warriors; in the war exercises he could evade six spears thrown at him simultaneously from varying directions; and he could trace his descent from one of the gods who had sailed with his attendants from the south.

Kualai gave his cloak and helmet to young John March when the *Polly* anchored in a bay on the Kona coast to exchange Yankee notions for sandal-wood before proceeding to Canton. There is no doubt that John March valued the gift, for it is mentioned in his will. The clause reads:

"Item, the Feather Cloak that was given me by my friend Kualai on my first voyage to the Sandwich Islands, and the feather hat that goes with it, I leave to my daughter, Polly March, and I ask her to guard it carefully."

John March sailed other seas before he died and brought back other curious things, but there is every reason why the cloak should have had a value to him which was more than intrinsic; and his descendants have never sold that cloak because of the reason why it was given him, a reason that is closely connected with honor and integrity. John March was a shrewd trader, but he was an honest man.

In the New England harbor town which was the home port for the March ships, a voyage around the world was not an unusual matter when John March was young. As long as John March could remember, his town had been a port of travelers, although a part of it was cast in the narrow mold of puritanical tradition. When John March was young, no music was allowed in the white church with the rooster on its spire where merchants and clerks and shipwrights and returned mariners listened for three hours each Sunday to discourses on original sin. Not even the note of a pipe was allowed, to indicate the pitch for the singing of the psalms, because such a concession was considered an encouragement to the idolatrous errors of papacy. Yet in such surroundings of a Sunday one could see from the square box of the March pew a distinctly cosmopolitan congregation, for the world across the seas was closer to the town in those days than it has ever been since. Nearly every man and boy and most of the women in the pews and the Reverend Thomas himself, who thundered forth his nasal sermon while the sands ran from his hourglass on the pulpit, knew their geography as well as they knew the intricacies of their catechism. They could talk familiarly of the Baltic ports and of St. Eustatius and St. Kitts. There were plenty who knew the ivory factories and the slave pens on the Grain Coast and the anchorages along Fernando Po. There were plenty who had seen the sand upon the lead from soundings off Madagascar. The weather off Cape Horn was common talk. A restless, burning energy that made the town a lively place, except on Saturday nights and Sunday, had driven others to the factories at Canton. The townspeople were familiar with nearly every world port where money could be gained, for the town lived from shipping. One had to go, of necessity, a long way to make money then, what with European wars and privateers and orders in council and blockades. It was a time for gambling with lives and ships, a time of huge losses and huge gains, and no one could judge which until the ships came in.

It seemed hardly more than a piece of everyday business to John March when his father called him into the square parlor of the March house on the Ridge. It was an evening in April; a bright, fresh fire was burning in the parlor, and the candles were lighted on the mahogany table in the center of the room. Moses March and a man whom John March had never seen before were seated somewhat stiffly by the table with a punch bowl between them. When John March saw the punch, he knew that they were discussing important business, for his father, particularly in his later years, was abstemious with liquor. Moses March had not changed much since John March could remember him. His brown hair, done in a queue, was heavily streaked with gray, and the shrewd lines around his eyes and mouth were deeper and more pronounced. There was an added stoop to his lanky shoulders, but his eyes were as bright as ever and his voice was vibrant, without any quaver of age.

"John," said Moses March, nodding at his guest, "this here is Captain Griggs from Boston. Captain Griggs, he's been sailing for the Perkinses in the fur trade."

In many ways it seemed to John March that Captain Griggs was a younger replica of his father. The captain had the same bony facial contours and the same slouch to his shoulders. When he spoke he had the same flat voice, but his eyes were different—more mobile and less steady. The captain raised a hand before his tight-lipped mouth and coughed, then he rose from his chair with a creaking of his joints, a tall, somber man who might have been a deacon in a church. His eyes met John's and looked away toward some invisible object on the floor, then darted back and looked away again.

"Pleased to meet you," he said. . . . "I compliment you, Mr. March; he's handy looking, that's a fact."

"He's kind of peaked," said Moses March, "but John here's almighty quick at figures."

There was a silence. Captain Griggs ladled himself a fresh tumbler of punch, drank it at a gulp, and said, "He needs to be. It pays to be sharp, don't it, Mr. March?"

Moses March smiled in faint embarrassment. He had never been able to acquire a manner with his captains, nor to stop undue familiarity.

"Yes," he said, "I guess so. . . . John, Captain Griggs is taking out the *Polly*. You're sailing with him, supercargo."

John March looked at Captain Griggs again. The captain was staring intently at a lemon peel in the bottom of his glass. The news was entirely unexpected.

"Where to, Father?" he asked.

"Where you haven't been, Son," said Moses March, "but you've heard the talk, I guess. Up along the Northwest Coast for sea otter, trading with the savages, then to these new islands you've heard Enoch Mayo talk about, to put aboard sandalwood, then the whole cargo sold at Canton for tea. The *Polly*, she's sailing the end of the month. You'll start in working over the cargo tomorrow. Your mother, she'll get your things packed."

John March nodded without speaking, and he showed no emotion. It was not the first time that his father had surprised him, because it was one of his father's maxims never to talk about what he proposed to do until he was ready. His father was always reaching for something new; his mind was always working. Probably he had been pondering over the matter all winter, and now, as though he were speaking about arrange-ments for hauling firewood, he was making plans to send one of his vessels where a March ship had never gone before.

It was strange to think that while he sat there, a homely, uncouth man, his mind could reach around the world and back. His life had never seemed so plain or matter-of-fact. The order of the March house, each piece of furniture exactly in its place, had never seemed so perfect as when he spoke of that voyage. That literal order of the letter books and the columns in the ledger were all a part of the business. There was no ex-pression of doubt, because they all knew by then that a ship could go wherever there was water.

Captain Griggs ladled himself another tumbler of punch and blew his nose on a long blue handkerchief which seemed to have imparted some of its own color to his nose. Not having been asked to sit down, John March stood examining his new captain, comparing him with other sea-faring men whom he had met. The captain was evidently a heavy and competent drinker and no doubt a capable master, but behind his lantern jaws and his high, narrow forehead there were hidden convolutions of character beyond John March's grasp. He only knew that by the time the voyage ended he would know the captain like a book. At the present time all John March could do was to stand staring at the pictures of his own imagination, striving to conjure up the sights which he and Captain Griggs would see. Captain Griggs was staring at him moodily across the brim of his glass.

"He'll do. He'll fill out," he said. "He'll be aft with the mate and me, of course. Does he know navigation, sir?"

"Yes," said Moses March; "he ain't a fool, but I hadn't aimed to make him a sailor. He'll handle this business ashore when I get through."

Captain Griggs nodded in a melancholy way. "I hope he ain't squeamish," he said. "He'll see some rough sights, like as not. We have a saying on the coast: 'You hang your conscience on the Horn.'"

"Yes," said Moses March, "I've heard it, but you, Captain, I'd like for you to keep your conscience on your ship."

"God bless you, sir," Captain Griggs said quickly, "no owner's ever complained of me. I'm always in my owner's interest. It's just dealing with these here savages, I mean. They've killed crews on the coast and they're murdering thieves on the islands." He rose stiffly. "You'll be satisfied, Mr. March. You'll be pleased as punch with me. There ain't no tricks in the trade that I don't know thereabouts. Four fourpounders and a bow chaser will be enough, and the grapeshot and plenty of small arms, and thanking you, I'll pick my own mate, and now I'll be under way, and I'll wish you a very good evening, and you, mister." He nodded to John March.

When the captain was gone, Moses March called to John March again.

"John," he said, "set down. You've been to the Baltic; you've been to the Indies; and I'd proposed keeping you ashore, but I want for you to learn this trade when it's still new." Moses March paused and rubbed his jaw. "I hear tell there's money in it, and we're going where there's money."

"Yes sir," said John March.

"It seems," his father continued, staring at the fire, "as how these savages put aboard furs, and these other savages put aboard sandalwood, for nothing more than notions and novelties in trading goods. Well, I got 'em for you; you and Griggs can get the rest. He'll try hard. He has his money and more than the usual prerequisites."

"Yes sir," said John March.

"And sandalwood and furs are worth a mint of money in Canton."

"Yes sir," said John March.

"You know about it, do you?"

"Yes sir," said John March; "I've heard 'em talking."

His father smiled. "That's right," he said; "listen to 'em talk, but keep your own mouth shut. Have you anything to say?"

John March thought a moment. He had a number of things to say, but he kept them to himself. "No," he said. "I can obey orders, I guess. You know what you're doing, I guess, Father."

Moses March stroked his chin slowly, and then he asked a sudden question: "How did you like Griggs?"

"He looks too sharp to me," John March said, "but I guess we'll get along."

"Yes," said Moses March, "he's sharp, but maybe that's all right. But mind you watch him, John. I'm sharp, but I guess I'm honest. Mind you watch him."

Even when he was three thousand miles away from town and farther than that by water, something of the town was always with him. The *Polly* was a part of the town because she had been built in the yards by the river, a good tight brig of two hundred and fifty tons. The crew was a part of the town, because most of the men before the mast had been born within its limits. The sense of the nearness of things he knew gave John March a certain peace when everything else was strange. The emptiness of the Pacific coast, the incredible size of its fir trees, the frowning menace of its mountains, would have oppressed him if it had not been for that sense of home. As it was, everyone stood together and behaved, in order to keep reputations intact when they got home.

John March was used to work. He was satisfactory to Captain Griggs, and he was treated well because he was the owner's son. Once they began bartering for furs off the Northwest Coast, there was no doubt that the captain knew his business, and John March admired in silence the way the captain worked. Martin Sprague, the mate, knew his business, too, in caring for the ship. The men were armed; there was a sharp lookout day and night. The fourpounders were loaded with grapeshot, and the matches were kept burning. Only a definite number of the painted dugout canoes of the Indians were allowed alongside, and only a certain number of savages were permitted on deck to trade. There were very few ships off the coast that year, so that the selection of pelts was particularly fine. Sea-otter pelts came aboard in great quantity in exchange for powder, shot, nails, muskets, beads, and blankets. It was a pretty sight to see the captain read faces and weigh the desire to sell. He seemed to have an intuitive sense of when to bargain and when to buy immediately.

"If there's any trade goods left after the islands," he said, "we'll stand back here again and use 'em up. It's a pity to see this fine fur wasting here. I wish we had six ships."

John March could feel the excitement as small goods turned suddenly into a valuable cargo. It was better than any figuring in the countinghouse to see the fur pelts come aboard and to estimate their probable value in a Chinese port.

"Yes sir," said Captain Griggs, "it seems a pity to haul off and leave this. We ought to buy the villages out and to the devil with the islands and the wood."

They were in the cabin at the time, the captain and Sprague, the mate, a heavy muscular man, and John March, a thin blond boy.

"Mr. Sprague," said the captain, "pass the rum. What do you think, mister? Shall we do all the trading here and simply water at the islands?"

Martin Sprague rubbed the palm of his left hand over the knuckles of his right. "I never seen trading so easy," he said. "Yes sir, I think I should."

Then John March spoke up; it was the first time on the voyage that he'd made a positive statement. "We can't," he said.

Captain Griggs set down his glass and scowled. "Young man," he said, "I'm surprised at you. You ought to know better. You do know better. You've behaved yourself fine up till now, my boy. You've done your duty, and more, and I shall be pleased to report favorably to your father if you continue, but there's two things for you to get inside your head. The first is, you were sent here to learn to trade. You don't know this business, and don't you forget it. The second is, I'm captain, and this brig goes where I tell it to. I'm sorry to be obliged to tell you straight."

John March did not shift his position at the table. He knew that he was young and that he was green. He had interrupted solely from a conscientious sense inherited from his race. It had come over him that he was a representative of the March family and of the March cargo. Now that the eyes of the older men were upon him, he found himself stammering, because he was shy in those days, but his hesitation only made him the more determined to speak out.

"Captain," he said, "I understand what you say. This is your ship, of course, but you are under owner's orders, just as I am. A portion of these trade goods was allotted for furs and the rest for sandalwood. The owner's orders are to stop and trade at the Sandwich Islands. There may be more profit here, but we are to establish relations there. We may send out another ship."

Captain Griggs leaned half across the table. "Young man," he inquired, "are you insinuating I'm not looking after owner's interests? Because if you are, I will not tolerate it. I'm thinking of my owner all the time, and a sight better than you are, maybe. We'll make for the islands tomorrow, and there's an end to that, but if there's any trade goods left when we're through there, why, then, with your kind permission, we'll come back here. I hope that satisfies you."

"Yes," said John March, "it does, and I ask your pardon, Captain."

Mr. Sprague rose. "I must be up with the watch," he said, "if you'll excuse me, sir. . . . Will you come with me, Mr. March?"

It was a fine night on deck, clear, with bright stars and a faint, quivering circle of the northern lights. The night was cool, without a breath of wind. The ship, with her own small lights, was like an insignificant fragment of a distant world anchored there in space. The mate took out his pipe and tinderbox. There was a flash of spark as he expertly hit the flint against the steel, and then the tinder glowed.

"Johnny March," he said, "I've kind of got to like you. Now you listen to what I say. This kind of spark's all right, but not the kind that you were striking in the cabin. You leave the old man be. He's as good a master as there is, and he's honest with the owners, and that's all we have to care for. I've sailed with Griggs before. I don't need to tell you that a master's king aboard his ship, and you know it makes 'em queer. I've never seen a skipper yet who liked to be crossed. You better leave him be."

"Yes sir," said John March.

"And listen, Johnny," the mate said, "the islands are a fine place. You'll like the islands. The islands are like heaven, pretty near. The captain will take you ashore, of course, to make the bargain. You'll see plenty of funny sights, but keep your mouth shut, Johnny, except to say 'Yes sir,' to the captain. We've got a long way yet to go."

"Yes sir," said John March.

"That's right," said Sprague, "that's right. I like a tight-lipped boy."

It was said in the forecastle of the *Polly,* just as it was said aft, that Johnny March was taciturn. As a supercargo he had no fixed duties in working the ship, and few knew much about him except that he was March's son. They only saw him as a thin, brown-faced, gray-eyed boy with yellow hair who made no trouble or complaint. They did not know the impression which strange sights made upon him, because he was studiously silent on that voyage to the islands, hardly ever venturing a remark, only answering courteously when addressed. No one on the *Polly* knew—and perhaps it was just as well—that his thoughts were poetic, because there was no room for poetry on a Yankee trading brig.

The evening before they sighted land, he had a sense of the land's nearness. The banks of clouds off the port bow as the sun went down were pink and gold, and were more like land clouds than sea clouds. The *Polly* was moving in the steady breath of the trades, and the setting sun struck the bellying sails forward, making their colors soft and golden. The only sounds were the creaking of wood, the straining of ropes, and the splash of waves on the bow. He had seen many evenings like that one, but subtly this was different. There was a mystery in the warmth of the air, an intangible unreality in the cloud banks. Captain Griggs came and stood beside him, smelling strongly of rum.

"Mr. Sprague," he said, "you've got everything locked up, I hope. To-morrow we'll be overrun by black thieves and their women. Clew up the courses and continue under topsails. Set a watch up in the crosstree and keep an eye out for breakers. We must not get in too close tonight. . . . And, Mr. March——"

"Yes sir," said John.

"You and I will go ashore."

"Yes sir," said Johnny March, and then he cleared his throat: "How will we speak to them, sir?"

"You'll soon learn, boy," said Captain Griggs. "You've got a lot to learn. These islands have kings, or chiefs, and the chiefs will have some-one who can speak trading English. The sandalwood is up in the moun-tains. It will be the property of the king, or chief. We will agree to purchase so many piculs, and he'll send his people to cut it. The chief will come aboard to see our goods, and we will make a bargain for the cargo, payable when the wood is safe aboard, you understand. There's no need to make our crew work when the chief will make his people load it. The islanders are handy men on ships. We'll go to see the chief, and we'll make the chief a present. Break out that clock that strikes the hour, and two cutlasses. That will be enough, and maybe"—Captain Griggs paused and hesitated—"three yards of bright print calico; he ought to like it—paper's all they dress in."

"Yes sir," said Johnny March. "Did you say that they dressed in paper?"

The hard lines of the captain's face wrinkled into an indulgent smile.

"Young man," he said, "it's a fact they dress in paper, when they dress at all, which isn't often. The women, they pound it out of the bark of a tree. They have nothing else on the islands, or almost nothing. Time was when they'd sell a pig for three tenpenny nails, and their women sell their virtue for less than that, which isn't strange, because they have no morals. Why, their menfolk bring 'em right aboard for the time we stay. Will you come below for a glass of rum?"

"No, thank you, sir," said Johnny March. "I'll stay on deck—that is, if you don't mind."

The sun had dipped out of sight behind a bank of clouds, and then suddenly the light was gone. Without a prelude of dusk, the dark came over them like a warm black garment. It seemed only a second before that the sky had been red and gold. Then, in another second, the sky was a void of darkness, filled with the trade wind and with stars. He stood for a while listening to the wind singing through the ropes, and then he went below. It was still dark when John March was awakened by a long-drawn-out call and by Mr. Sprague's voice shouting, "Where away?" and he knew that they had come in sight of land. Once he was up on deck, the topsails were slatting sleepily, and off the starboard bow there was a glow in the sky like fire.

"We've hit it to a second, sir," the mate was saying to Captain Griggs. "Yonder's the volcano; we're in the lee of the mountains."

Captain Griggs was a shadow in the starlight. It was too dark to see his face, but his voice was satisfied. "A pretty piece of navigating," he said, "if I do say so, mister. There'll be an inshore breeze by dawn, and then we'll make the bay." He sniffed the air. "We can't be far from land," he said, "but there's no use heaving lead. It shelves off here as deep as hell. There'll be an inshore breeze with dawn."

"Is that a light yonder, sir?" asked Johnny March.

Near the horizon there was a twinkling, glimmering point.

"Your eyesight's good," the captain said. "Yes, that will be a fire. We're close to land."

The dawn came as suddenly as the dark, in a swift rush of light, as though a hand had snatched away a veil, and John March saw the land. It was a solemn sight to see land which seemed to have risen out of nowhere. Off the bows of the *Polly* was a mountain, black and green, that rose in a gradual slope up into snow and clouds. The coast was dark from volcanic rock which made ugly black gashes between green forests. Close to the water's edge there was a fringe of palms and beeches between black lava headlands. The sea was smooth and calm and streaked with violet; the air was as soft as the air of spring at home and was subtly laden with the smells of land. All the colors were soft in a faint, early-morning haze. The black rocks merged into reds and purples. The greens of the upland forest blended subtly from shades of silver to emerald, and Captain Griggs was right—a soft breeze was filling the sails, moving the *Polly* gently along the coast.

"That's where the sandalwood comes from," Mr. Sprague was saying, "up yonder in the mountains. The coast hereabouts is the favorite place of the kings. Do you see the stone walls and the yellow thatch of the houses of the villages? The chiefs own straight from the tops of the mountains to the sea. How do you like it, son?"

The question made John March tongue-tied. "I think it's very handsome, sir," he said, "a very pleasant island."

The *Polly* was moving under topsails into a small bay. It opened out before them, a smooth amphitheater of water, surrounded by high cliffs. "Yonder's where the kings are buried," the mate said. "They scrape the flesh off their bones and tie them up in paper cloth and put them there in caves with their canoes."

At the head of the bay John March could see a beach fringed with tall palm trees, the leaves of which moved idly in the breeze, and he could see the thatch of houses beneath them. There was a dark crowd of people on the beach, pushing canoes into the water, log dugouts, balanced by an outrigger and manned by naked paddlers. Captain Griggs was wearing clean linen and a black broadcloth coat, although the day was hot.

"Mister," he said, "we'll anchor. Let go falls and clew up lower topsails and order the stern boat cleared. You can allow the women aboard, Mr. Sprague."

By the time the anchor struck the water, the *Polly* was surrounded by canoes and the water was full of swimmers who were pulling themselves up the anchor chain, smiling and laughing; men and women as beautiful as statues, their straight dark hair glistening with the water. Captain Griggs stared at his visitors sourly from the quarter-deck.

"They've got the minds of children," he said. "The chief's man should be here. Look at those shameless hussies, will you? There's no decency on these islands. They don't care for decency; no, they don't care."

As Captain Griggs finished speaking, a native pushed his way through the crowd at the waist and walked aft; evidently a man of importance, because the crowd gave way respectfully. He wore a pair of sailor's castoff trousers, and his skin was lighter than the others'. His voice rose above the babel of strange words in English.

"Mr. Captain," he called out, "I am Kualai's man."

"Who's he?" asked Captain Griggs. "The chief?"

The other nodded, bobbing his head up and down, still smiling. "Yes," he said, "yes, yes. And he sends me because I speak English good. I've been a sailor on a Boston boat. I speak English very good. Kualai sends me to say *aloha*. He is glad to see you. He asks you will you trade for wood?"

"Yes," said Captain Griggs, "we're here for wood. What's your name?"

"Moku," said the native. "Billy Adams Moku. Kualai ask what name."

The captain nodded condescendingly. "Captain Griggs," he said, "brig *Polly*. Moses March, owner. We're carrying very fine calicoes, ironware, tinware, lead and copper, and even a few muskets. Has your chief got wood?"

Moku nodded. "The wood is coming down. Kualai, he will see you." He pointed to a laden canoe. "Kualai sends you food."

Captain Griggs looked at the canoe carefully as it drew alongside. "Very good," he said. "When will he see me?"

"Now," said Moku. "He waits on the shore."

"Mister," the captain called, "have the stern boat lowered. Mr. March and I will go ashore, and, Mr. March, give that man a pocketknife and bring along the presents."

The dark sand of the beach at the head of the bay seemed insecure under John March's feet, since he had been so long on the water. In the sunshine like a warm June day at home, every sight and sound was new. The crowd of natives standing on the beach drew back from them shyly and smiled, but their tongues kept chattering busily; commenting, probably, on the way these strangers looked. The chief's man walked first, then Captain Griggs, nonchalant and cool, and then John March behind him. They walked along a path beneath a grove of coconut palms and beneath large broad-leafed trees such as he had never seen. They were threading their way through a settlement of houses made of dried grass, past small gardens inclosed between walls of black volcanic rock. His memory of that day always brought back living green against dark rock, and dark smiling faces and red hibiscus flowers. In his memory of the place a soft breeze was always blowing and there was always a strange dry rattle from the leaves of the coconut palms. There was a group of larger houses not far back from the beach which evidently belonged to a man of importance. Natives were busying themselves about a fire in a pit; women and children were staring from open doorways. There was an open pavilion near the center of this group of buildings, and the chief's man led them toward it. Seated in a Cantonese armchair under the pavilion was one of the largest men that John March had ever seen. He was middle-aged, and so corpulent that the chair seemed to creak beneath his weight. A single look at his face was enough to indicate that he was the ruler, Kualai, of whom the man had spoken. The face was set in benign lines that could only have come upon it through suave and complete authority. It was all that was necessary to indicate his rank, but he also had the exterior show of office. He was wearing a yellow-and-red cloak of feathers, dazzlingly bright, which fell below his waist, and an attendant stood behind him holding a large stick which bore a tuft of colored feathers on the end. Moku stopped dead still at the entrance of the pavilion, and the great man rose from his chair and stepped slowly forward, gracefully, in spite of his heavy paunch. It was plain that he had seen other white men and knew something of their manners, because he smiled graciously and held out his right hand. At the same time he spoke melodiously in a language that was all vowels, so that his words sounded like rippling water.

"What's he saying?" asked Captain Griggs.

"Kualai," Moku translated, "he say he's, oh, very glad to see you."

"Well, I guess we're glad to see him too," said Captain Griggs as he shook hands. Then John March saw that Kualai was looking at him.

"He wants to know," said Moku, "who is the other man?"

"Tell him he's the son of the man who owns the vessel," said Captain Griggs.

"He wants to know," said Moku, "is he a chief's son?"

"Tell him yes," said Captain Griggs.

"He would like," said Moku, "to feel his hair. He would like to know if it is real."

"Take off your hat," said Captain Griggs, "and let him feel your hair. Don't be afraid of him. He won't hurt you."

"All right," said Johnny March. He felt very much like a child as he walked toward Kualai, for the man, now that he was standing, must have been close to seven feet in height. His skin was glistening with coconut oil. He was stretching out his arm. He touched Johnny March's hair gently and then he pulled it softly. Johnny March looked up at him and smiled, and Kualai smiled back.

"Break out the presents," said Captain Griggs, "bow to him and put 'em on the ground."

Kaulai's face lighted up at the sight of the clock when John March held it toward him. It was evident that he had never seen such a mechanism —a battered ship's chronometer whose useful days were over. He touched it gingerly and imitated its sound.

"Tick-tick," he said, and John March nodded and repeated after him, "Tick-tick." That interchange of words always seemed to him ridiculous, but somehow there was an exchange of thought with the words which made them friends.

"He asks you to stay and eat," said Moku. "He will come on the ship tomorrow and see the goods, and he asks the young man to stay with him until the trade is over, to sleep inside his house."

Captain Griggs muttered something beneath his breath, and then he said, "March, you'd better stay."

"Yes sir," said John March, "I'd be very glad to stay." He turned to Moku. "Tell him I'll be glad."

Then Moku spoke again: "Kualai says he will trade with the young man."

"All right," said Captain Griggs, "as long as I'm there too. And tell him"—Captain Griggs's eyes shifted toward the bay and back—"you tell him I want the wood measured on the beach and put aboard by his people. Tell him my men are tired." And then he drew a bottle of rum from his pocket and added plaintively: "Ain't we had enough of this? Let's everybody have a drink, and bring on the dancing girls."

Some half-perceptible change in Captain Griggs's voice made John March turn to watch him. The captain's face was bleak and impassive, but his eyes were shifting from point to point, from the chief to John March, then away to the matting on the ground, then to the houses of the settlement. John March knew him well enough by then to know that the captain was turning over in his mind some thought which he wished entirely to conceal.

"Ah," he said suddenly, "here comes some wood," and he nodded toward a path which led upward to the mountains.

A dozen men and women were staggering down the path in single file, each bearing a burden of long sticks, and John March knew from

hearsay that these were the chief's people, who had been sent to the
upland forests where the sandalwood grew. The chief called out an order,
which Moku ran to obey, and a few moments later a pile of the sandalwood lay on the matting before his chair, a heap of sticks which varied in
size from a few inches to a foot in diameter. The bark had been stripped
off, leaving a heavy wood of deep yellow which verged on orange. Captain Griggs ripped out his clasp knife, whittled at the sticks, and sniffed
the shavings.

"It ain't bad," he said; "in fact, it's prime."

He was right that the wood was fine, since sandalwood was plentiful
in the islands then, when the trade was new, and John March did not
suspect that he would live to see the time when hardly a stick would be
left standing on the entire island group. Captain Griggs stood there,
staring at the pile of wood, apparently lost in thought.

"Tell him we'll pay him well for it," he said, and his voice was soft and
almost kindly, "once he lands it on the deck."

But all the while John March was sure that Captain Griggs was concealing some other thought.

It took nearly two weeks to collect the wood and measure it, a space
of time which moved in a peculiar series of days and nights, but it was
strange to John March how soon the life there grew familiar. Though
he could hardly understand a word which was spoken, though nearly every
sight and sound in those two weeks was new, he became aware immediately
of certain human values. Kualai, in his way, was a cultivated man of gentle
breeding, who had developed his own taste for the arts, and qualities of
understanding which were the same on that isolated island as they were
elsewhere. He would sit for hours of an evening watching interpretive
dances and listening to his minstrels sing of the exploits of his ancestors.
He had a good eye for patterns in the tapa cloth, and a nice skill in
various games of chance, which he played daily with his choice companions, but, above all, he had a sense of hospitality. He lost no occasion
to make John March feel politely that he was a welcome guest. He took
him fishing in his war canoe; he took him to the caves and the lava rocks;
he took him to watch the young men perform feats of strength; he was
even careful that John March's privacy should not be disturbed unduly.
When he came aboard the *Polly*, he kept John March beside him. He
was greatly pleased with the calico and nails and lead and copper in the

trading cargo, but he went through the intricacies of the bargain in a detached way, like a gentleman. In those days trading was easy on the islands, before the chiefs were glutted with material possessions.

"He say he want you to be happy," Moku said the last time Kualai came aboard; "he want you to come again."

"Tell him we're happy," said Captain Griggs. "He understands when all the wood's aboard that we'll give out the goods."

Moku nodded. "He understands," he said; "he knows you're good men."

Captain Griggs coughed slightly. "I shall want Mr. March back with me," he said, "tomorrow morning. . . . Mr. March, you come here; I want to speak with you in the cabin."

It occurred to John March, when they were in the cabin, that it was the first time since they had been on the islands that he and Captain Griggs had been alone. Captain Griggs rubbed his long hands together and poured himself a glass of rum.

"Young man," he said, "you've done fine. You've kept that old heathen happy, and that's all we needed—to keep him happy—and now we're all finished shipshape. We'll get the wood stowed tonight"—Captain Griggs smiled happily—"and tomorrow they can come and take off their goods, but I want you aboard first, understand?"

"Yes sir," said John March, "but there's one thing I don't see. I don't see why you haven't put the goods ashore before this, sir."

Captain Griggs poured himself a second tumbler of rum.

"Young man," he said, "when you take a few more voyages you'll understand you can't trust natives. How do you know we'd get the wood if we put the goods ashore?"

"Because Kualai's honest," John March said.

Captain Griggs looked thoughtfully at the ceiling. "Maybe," he said, "and maybe not. Anyways, we've got the wood. You come aboard tomorrow." And Captain Griggs smiled genially, but even when he smiled, John March had a suspicion that something had been left unsaid, that there was some thought in the captain's mind of which he had not spoken.

Mr. Sprague came up to get him the next morning, carrying a bundle of small presents and perspiring in the heat of the early sun.

"Say good-by to the chief," he said. "The captain's orders are to leave right now. You're to stay aboard until we sail. The quarter boat's waiting at the beach."

John March was sorry, now that it was time to go. He walked to Kualai and held out his hand. "Thank you very much," he said, and the interpreter, Moku, gave him back the chief's answer:

"He say for you to come back soon."

The canoes were gathering about the *Polly* already, by the time he reached the beach. He and Mr. Sprague sat in the stern sheets of the quarter boat while two men rowed, helped by a light breeze offshore.

It was only when they were halfway out that John March was aware of something disturbing.

"Look," he said; "they're setting the lower topsails!"

"Yes," said Mr. Sprague shortly, "so they are. We've got a fair breeze, haven't we?"

"But it'll take a good six hours to put off those goods," said Johnny March.

Mr. Sprague put a heavy hand on his knee and smiled. "Don't you worry, boy," he said. "Captain Griggs will see about those goods."

They were beside the companion ladder by that time, and even John March was puzzled, but nothing more. He was not aware of Captain Griggs's idea until he was on the poop, then he saw that the tarpaulins were off the guns and that men were beside them with matches, and then he saw that the decks were clear and that the sandalwood and the trade goods were all back in the hold. Captain Griggs grinned at him.

"Safe and sound," he said. "You've done very well, Mr. March; your father will be very pleased, I think. . . . Mister, you can man the capstan now."

John March found himself stammering: "But what about the goods, Captain? We haven't put the goods ashore."

"No, boy," said Captain Griggs, "we ain't, and we ain't going to. What's the use when we've got the wood aboard? Those goods are going to go for skins."

Even then John March did not entirely understand him. "But you can't do that," he said. "We owe the chief the goods."

"Listen, boy," said Captain Griggs, "this ain't like home. There're plenty of other chiefs, and plenty of other islands. Let 'em come and get the goods, and I'll blow 'em out of water. There ain't no law out here. Now you be quiet, boy."

For a moment John March found it impossible to speak. Now that the whole matter was completely clear, he knew that he should have suspected long ago what must have been in the back of the captain's mind.

Captain Griggs proposed sheer robbery, but he would not have called it that. He would have called it a clever piece of business in a place where there was no law.

"You see," Captain Griggs was saying, "it isn't as though they were white people, Mr. March. More fools they, that's all."

Then John March found his voice. "Captain," he said, "this is a March ship. You don't leave until you've set those goods on shore. We don't do things that way, Captain. You can't——"

Captain Griggs turned toward him quickly.

"That'll be enough from you," he said. "Who says I can't? I'm trying to make a profit on this voyage. I can, and I will, and I'm taking full responsibility. If you don't like it, get below."

John March's tongue felt dry and parched as he tried to speak. Even in that short while a hundred things were happening. The fore-and-aft staysails and the lower topsails were set by then, and the call came from forward, "Hawser short!" A glance toward the beach was enough to show him that the islanders were aware of the captain's trick. Men were running toward the water. He could hear the beating of a drum. Men in canoes were gesticulating and shouting. Men with spears and clubs and slings were hurrying to the beach.

"Break out anchor, mister," shouted Captain Griggs, "and stand by them guns! Forward there, pass out the small arms! By God, we'll show 'em!"

"Captain," said John March suddenly. He knew there was only one thing to do as he spoke. "If you go, you'll leave me here. I'm going back ashore."

Captain Griggs looked at him and laughed. "They'll kill you back ashore," he said. "Look at 'em on the beach."

John March spoke with difficulty. "You and I are different sorts of men," he said. "You can either set those goods ashore or I'm going."

"May I inquire," said Captain Griggs, "how you're going to go? Keep your mouth shut, boy!"

In the haste of getting under way, the quarter boat was still drifting alongside, and the captain must have perceived John March's intention from his glance.

He made a lunge at John March, but John March broke away, and then he went on the bulwarks.

"Get ahold of that damned fool!" shouted Captain Griggs. "Lay ahold of him!"

Two of the crew ran toward him, and he jumped crashing into the quarter boat. "Get in there after him!" Captain Griggs was shouting. "Don't let him go!"

And then John March cut the painter, and the quarter boat was drifting from the side.

"You damned fool!" shouted Captain Griggs. "You hear my orders! Come back here or they'll kill you, March!"

Once the boat was drifting from the side, John March was amazed at himself. His anger and his lack of fear amazed him. He was standing amidships in the quarter boat, shouting back at Captain Griggs.

"I'd rather be killed ashore," he shouted, "than stay aboard with you!" Then he picked up the oars and began to row ashore, slowly, because the boat was heavy for a single man to handle.

"You hear me?" Captain Griggs was shouting. "Stay there and be damned to you!"

John March saw that the anchor was aweigh and the *Polly* was standing slowly out to the open sea. His back was to the beach as he pulled toward it, but he heard the shouting and the beating of the drums. It must have been his anger at Captain Griggs that did not make him afraid, or an assurance within himself that he was right and Captain Griggs was wrong. A glance astern of the quarter boat as he strained at the oars showed him the *Polly* standing out to sea, but he did not look over his shoulder toward the beach. He did not look until the bottom of the quarter boat grated on the sand, then he shipped his oars carefully and stepped ashore. He found himself surrounded by shouting men who waved their spears and their fists in his face, but somehow they were not so real to him as the reality which lay inside himself. He only realized later that a single gesture of fear might have meant his death, but then he was so involved in his own preoccupation and with the single desire which was in him that he walked calmly enough across the beach toward the palm trees and the thatched houses; the crowd in front of him gave way as he walked, and then followed on his heels. He was taking the path to Kualai's house, and the shouting around him died away as he drew near it.

Then he saw Kualai walking toward him in the feather cloak which he had worn the first day they had met, carrying a light throwing spear in his right hand. Kualai was shouting something to him—obviously a question which he could not understand—and Moku was standing near him.

"Tell Kualai," John March said, "that I come from honest people. Tell him that I have come here to stay until he is paid for his wood." He saw Kualai listening intently to his answer, and then Kualai raised his right arm and drove his spear into the earth.

"He says you are his son," Moku said. "He asks you: Will you please to shake his hand?"

The reaction from what he had done came over him when Kualai grasped his hand. He knew the harsh and accurate consequences of his action then, as the smells and sounds of that Polynesian village came over him like a wave. Captain Griggs had left him, and every vestige of home was gone. He was a stranger among savages, and he might be there forever, for anything he knew, yet even then he knew that he had done the only proper thing. Suddenly he found that he was homesick, because the chief was kind.

"Ask him if I can be alone," he said. "Tell him I want to be alone."

He was given a house of his own that night, next to where the chief slept. He was given a pile of woven mats for his bed and a piece of tapa cloth to cover him. He was given baked pig and sweet potatoes and the gray paste made from the taro root, called poi, for his evening meal, and mullet from Kualai's fishpond. He was as comfortable as he could have hoped to be that night. For a moment, when he was awakened early the next morning, he thought he was at home, until he saw the rafters and the thatch above him. Moku was standing near him in his ragged sailor breeches, and Kualai himself was bending his head, just entering the door.

"Wake up!" Moku was saying. "The ship is back!"

John March sat up on his bed of mats and rubbed his arm across his face. Although he spoke to Moku, his eyes were on Kualai.

"The ship?" he asked. "What ship?"

"Your ship," said Moku. "She come back, and now the captain, he unloads the goods."

John March stood up. He had no great capacity for showing emotion.

"Ask Kualai if he is satisfied," he said.

Moku nodded. "He says, 'Yes, very much,'" he said, and Kualai nodded back. "He asks for you to stay a long time—always."

"Thank him, please," said John March, "but tell him it's my ship. Tell him I must go to see that the goods are right."

"Kualai," Moku answered, "says he will go with you to the beach."

Mr. Sprague had landed in the longboat by the time they had reached the shore, and the beach was already covered with bolts of calico and small goods and ironware and lead and copper. Mr. Sprague nodded to John March formally, as though nothing had happened. "The captain sends his compliments," he said, "and asks you to come aboard, so that he can resume the voyage." And then Sprague grinned and added, "It's damned lucky for you, John March, that you're the owner's son."

John March looked at the goods upon the shore. "You can thank the captain for me for coming back," he answered. "You can tell him that I hope we both can forget what has happened, but the complete consignment is not landed yet. I'll stay here until the list is checked."

"You're an accurate man," said Sprague.

John March nodded. "I've been taught to be," he said, and he stayed there on the beach until every item was verified. Then he turned to Kualai and his interpreter.

"Tell the chief," he said, "that I believe that everything is right. Ask his pardon for the delay, but tell him our house will make any mistakes correct. Thank him, and tell him that I am going."

Moku spoke quickly in the musical language of the islands while Kualai stood, looking first at John March and then at the ship that brought him. After Kualai had listened, he stood silently for a moment. Then he smiled and spoke swiftly. He raised a hand and took off his feather helmet, and one of his men very carefully removed his feather cloak from his shoulders.

"He says there will always be wood for you," said Moku. "He asks you to take his coat."

HORACE McCOY

The Girl in the Grave

I was eating a hamburger at Ma's Place, next to the Giant Slide, when Charlie came running in, saying that Gloria wanted to see me.

"In a minute," I said.

"Now," he said. "She wants to see you right now."

"What's the rush? She ain't going anywhere," I said.

How could she? She was buried alive, twenty feet under the ground. It cost a dime, ten cents, the tenth part of a dollar, to go in and talk to her through the periscope. She had been buried two hundred hours, which was only fifty hours short of the record; and she was the hottest thing on the Midway. We were beating the customers off with sticks.

"That's what you think, she ain't going anyplace," Charlie said, laughing. "She's going someplace tonight. You better come on."

I didn't know what he meant (and I was afraid to ask him), so I went. The tent was full of customers.

"Look at 'em," said the Deacon, the spieler and ticket seller. "I learned that trick with Forepaugh and Sells."

"Nuts," I said. "I could get that crowd with a phonograph record. No more tickets till I talk to her."

"What's the matter?" he asked. "Something wrong?"

"That's what I'm gonna find out," I said.

I hung around till this batch went out. Gloria ran them through in about fifteen minutes. The last customer out was a skinny woman who had worked herself into a lather. (A lot of them did.) "This is outrageous!" she said. "It's unsanitary. How does that girl——"

I almost laughed in her face. "Madame," I said, "everybody wants to know the same thing. I'll call my assistant. Hey, Charlie," I called. "Give this lady the answer to Problem One."

I left her outside the tent talking to Charlie, and went in. Everybody was gone. I picked up the speaking tube and looked down the periscope. (We had a piece of thick glass down near the bottom of the periscope. It used to all be open, but a lot of wise guys would drop things down it or spit down it and Gloria raised so much hell we had to put the glass in there to act as a screen.)

"Gloria," I said.

"You finally got here," she said.

"I been here. I had to wait till we got some privacy. What's on your mind?"

"I want to get out of here," she said.

I felt like I'd been hit in the navel with a blizzard.

"Are you crazy?" I said. "Why? What's happened?"

"You heard me. I want out," she said.

"But why? We got the world's record in the bag——"

"I also got a date tonight," she said.

"A date?" I said.

"Yeah. I gotta see him tonight."

"What's the rush? It'll keep."

"He's leaving town," she said. "I gotta see him tonight."

I was beginning to get a little sore.

"Look," I said. "Be reasonable. You're the hottest thing on the Midway."

"You don't know the half of it," she said. "Dig me up."

"You make it sound damned simple," I said. "I got an investment here. I got a contract with you."

"And I got a date at midnight," she said. "You got just three hours."

"You're nuts," I said. "I should dig you up to keep a date with some hayshaker you never even laid eyes on——"

"I didn't have to lay eyes on him," she said, and all the harshness suddenly went out of her voice. "I heard him. He's got the most wonderful voice in the world. I still get goose bumps——"

My God, I thought, getting madder and madder, the things that happen to me. "Just because you got hot pants for some guy with sex appeal in his voice is no reason I should ruin a good living," I said. "I'm just getting off the nut. You'll get over this. You've had yens for guys before and got over 'em."

"I'll never get over this," she said. "There never was a voice like this in the whole history of the world!"

My God, I thought . . .

"You stay there and like it," I said. "Look," I said. "I'll make everything right with you. On the level, I will. Look, Gloria, me standing here talking is costing us both a lot of money. I'll let another batch in——"

"The hell you will," she said. "By God, I'll get the law after you. I haven't forgotten what those clubwomen told me. I mean it. I'll send for 'em so fast it'll make your head swim. You dig me the hell up from here and fast."

"Look, Gloria," I said.

"Okay," she said. "Run another batch through here. Run 'em through and listen to what I tell 'em."

I was so mad I could have cut her throat, but what could I do? She had me where the hair was short. "All right," I said.

Ten minutes later they started digging her up. I yanked down the signs out front, tearing them to shreds.

"Too bad," the Deacon said. "I was just getting the feel of the crowds. You know a barker is no good until he gets the feel——"

"Tough luck," Charlie said. "But we'll think of something. Maybe that cannon gag. Shoot a guy out of the cannon into the ocean——"

"Yeah," I said. "Look. You see the guy Gloria likes?"

"Sure. He's been hanging around here an hour or more."

"Where?"

"There," he said, pointing.

I looked around. I didn't see anybody.

"Where?"

"There. That one. The one you're looking at."

"Him?"

"Sure. Him. He's the one."

I still didn't believe it. This guy was a dwarf, as broad as he was tall, with a face that looked like it might be a mask for a nightmare. He was the most deformed man I've ever seen in my life, and I've made a business out of it.

I strolled over to the guy.

"I'm the concessionaire here," I said. "More properly speaking, I *was* the concessionaire here. You the guy Gloria's got a date with?"

"Yes," he said. "And I'm truly sorry to occasion all this trouble and confusion."

In spite of everything, I couldn't help smiling. Gloria was right. This guy had a milk-and-honey voice that would charm the birds right out of the trees.

"I'm sorry too," I said.

He smiled, shrugging.

"Well," he said, "there're some days when not even the banks can return a profit. Can you let me have a guess on how long before she'll be out?"

"Three hours," I said.

"Three hours!" he said. "Three hours!"

There was a look of relief on his face, behind all the wrinkles. He actually seemed happy that it would be that long. That's funny, I thought. "You seem glad it's that long," I remarked.

"Oh, I am, indeed," he said.

I didn't get it.

"But Gloria can hardly wait," I said.

"I wish it were thirty hours instead of three," he said. "Tell your men not to hurry, will you?"

"Pardon me, brother," I said. "This is no longer any of my business, but why aren't you in a hurry too?"

He smiled at me.

"Because," he said, "when she sees me she'll be terrified. Then she'll be disgusted. Most women," he said, "find me singularly repulsive. She's under the impression that she's going to be with me. But of course she won't. When she sees me she probably won't even speak to me."

Maybe, I thought, I'm the one who's crazy.

"But," I said, "if you know that, if you know she's gonna brush you off when she sees you, why make us go to the trouble of digging her up and ruining our concession and everything?"

"Because," he said quietly, "no woman before has ever wanted me to the exclusion of all other men. For the next three hours I am Casanova and Don Juan and all the great lovers of history rolled into one——"

"I don't understand," I said.

"A woman wants me passionately, fiercely—for the next three hours. I need that. I need a woman wanting me."

"I still don't understand," I said.

"I didn't think you would," he said softly.

WILLIAM McFEE

Deckers on the Coast

DOWN ON THE AFTERDECK, shielded from sun and rain and the idle stare of the promenade, they were spread in a sprawling heap on number three hatch. Sixty, counting the children, as the ship left Colón. Nine hours later, what with the motion of the vessel and money troubles, the great Negress in the purple kimono set up a roaring, and she was got out of the crowd somehow; and then there were sixty-one.

In that congested microcosm, however, this was no more than an ephem-

eral inconvenience. It was more or less perplexing to a spectator how so
many of them, with their diversities of sleeping paraphernalia, had con-
trived to embed themselves in a species of human mosaic, upon a thirty by
twenty-five hatch. Nevertheless, it was not adequate. They overflowed on
all four sides, spilling from camp bedsteads set solidly athwart the gang-
ways, snoring on bags of dunnage draped upon the winches (which were
still hot, and caused occasional squeals as some small darky clutched the
pipes and cylinders), and dispersing upon the bulwarks, where several
were holding secret communication with the heaving waters.

As it grew dark a huge wired bowl was suddenly turned on, and the
assembled voyagers were flooded with yellow rays. It was easy to see that
some of these people were accustomed to this method of traveling and had
grown expert in dealing with the minor problems of existence in such
circumstances. There was a girl, for instance, on the port side, who had
brought her own narrow iron bed, with sheets, and who revealed the skill
of a quick-change artist in divesting herself of her shore finery and appearing, as if by magic, in a scarlet peignoir, her hair cascading over brown
shoulders, and between her lips a cigarette offered by an appreciative saloon
waiter, who, with one eye cocked to watch the long port alley for the
second steward's approach, was laying the foundations of, let us hope, an
enduring friendship.

There was the aged Negro, so grizzled that he seemed incredible and
out of place save in an advertisement, who sat on a basket suitcase on the
deck and read slowly, and with devastating enunciation, from the Old
Testament.

There was the perennial and solitary vagabond, in dire need of a shave,
his feet thrust into soiled rope-soled canvas shoes, his head bound in a
calico underskirt borrowed from a neighbor, already sound asleep.

Others were less easy. Again and again they rose from their chairs and
beds, and settled themselves in supposedly more comfortable attitudes. A
mother, with her three, all on one strip of canvas and laid out as if for
interment, was periodically aroused by her offspring in monotonous rota-
tion. Fed, their dark little faces still moist from the suckling, they fell back
and slept instantly, lying in utter and innocent nakedness like statues of
polished chalcedony. A couple, man and woman, perplexing enough to
the European unversed in the life of the coast, fondled one another and
chuckled at intervals at their own whispered remarks. Perplexing, since he
was a heavy blond young man with a silky beard concealing a weak chin,

while she was a vigorous and beautiful quadroon, the wedding ring conspicuous on her finger as she lolled in her chair, alert, intelligent, bright as a new penny when she leveled her gaze upon an appraising saloon waiter or scullion who meditated an advance. Less easy, these, since they were just married, and the future in Calomar, whither he was bound as a clerk, was uncertain.

Beyond them, and engaged in rapid converse with some of the crew, stood a man of uncertain age. His cap was of some furry fabric spotted to resemble the skin of a leopard, and his soiled linen suit hung loosely upon him. His face was drawn into vertical lines, into harsh furrows, and the expression of his irascible and bloodshot eyes was that of a man engaged in secret warfare with fate. At times he turned, and the light from the cargo cluster illumined that ravaged countenance with dreadful fidelity. There was an air of excitement about him, too, since he talked with the rapidity and gestures of one who lacked time to complete his story; and he looked around into the glare of the light as if he saw someone in the distance, overtaking him.

And he had competitors: from the recumbent forms arose a murmurous cacophony of diverse organs. Children whimpered and squalled; four Negroes snarled and gabbled as they shot craps; a piratical creature strummed on a banjo and hummed; while on the starboard side a furious uproar raged around a gray-haired virago, fit model for the Eumenides herself, who was accusing a smiling youth of stealing a bottle of eau de cologne from her bag. This was the most popular show of the evening. The dame sat there on her bed, her chemise sliding from her incredible shoulders, her bony arms and jaws moving in a convulsive synchronism. Men stood over her, with folded arms, and watched every movement, as if she were some monotonous automaton they had wound up and set going. This impression, that she was not human, but a clockwork affair, gained force when, of a sudden, without warning, as she foamed and choked, and lunged toward her adversary to strike him down to death, some word spoken amid the din made her stop and, collapsing upon her pallet, she shrieked with laughter. She seemed to have run down, her spring broken, her interior mechanism gone derelict.

But the man on the other side of the hatch took no notice of these distractions. He was driven by something more than a mere momentary gust of animal passion. His incessant watchfulness, as he turned his head again and again toward the light, reminded one of a wild animal devouring his prey in an alien jungle. Like a wild animal, too, he took no notice of the snapping jackals near him, or of the natural noises—the booming of the wind now rising, the rattle and flap of the awning, the sough and spit of the sea along the side. He held the three men in white jackets in subjection to his vibrating finger and swift impetuous speech. They made no sign, save to spit and flick ash from cigarettes, but they remained. Here was necromancy, since they knew the steward was already searching angrily for them. They remained. The dinner gong thrummed musically along the corridors as the bellhop moved to and fro. They remained. The figure of the second steward, spick and span, shaven to pink perfection, emerged smartly from the port alley. They saw him and moved, yet dominated by the cadaverous being in his dirty linen suit, who was offering them, so to speak, the kingdoms of the world. And then the steward saw them, and they rushed into the starboard alley toward the kitchen, leaving the necromancer to sink down on a yellow leatherette suitcase and fumble in his pocket for a cigarette.

All his life he had been an imaginative man. There had come to him, with the romantic tales of childhood, a shameful yet alluring conviction that he would be able to know those desperate doings in reality, be able to rip away the baffling veils hung between himself and the things he desired. There was a dark significance in the way he sat there, his chin on his clenched hands, recalling the vivid moments of his life. He surveyed with stoical courage his boyhood dreams, which were always of material import—dreams of gold and silver, or slaves, and houses of barbaric solidity. What he wanted had always to die, and when it was dead he no longer wanted it. So, as he grew older, he thought more and more of wealth, hard minted bullion, never finding that mysterious idealism which is the key to the riches of the world. Now, on the eve of success, he was poor.

He looked back. The soilure of the deck at which he stared through his unwashed fingers became transmuted into a dark mirror, in which he saw his life in a series of episodes. Yet were they episodes? Were they not rather a series of sudden irretrievable crashes to lower levels of industrious resignation? For he had been industrious. He had been a clever boy at school, and the scholarship which had sent him to the university was easy to him. Yet it was the first stage in his unlucky career. He saw that now. It had started him up the rickety ladder of learning. While his real self, his imagination, was concerned with the things you could get hold of, money and its transmutations. That was the first drop, when he found himself a book-

maker's clerk at Newmarket, instead of student in cap and gown at
Cambridge, a dozen miles away. He had not regretted the change at the
time; he had defiantly enjoyed it, and it might have been his career. But
the favorites won day after day, and he had been forced to beg a ride to
London.

He recalled all the succeeding years, and saw no flaw in himself. Bad
luck. He had asked no more than some of the wealth in the world, yet
people got the habit of regarding him with contempt and disdain, as if he
suffered from some moral lesion. And he was sometimes a little bitter with
the gentry who preached that a man, to succeed, should concentrate upon
his ambition. Had he not done just that? Yet he had failed very badly
indeed.

And it came to him, as he sat on his poor and inadequate valise, staring
at the deck, that his struggle had been very much with simple circumstances, and not with people. Neither he nor they had been evil. And also
there was this fatal gift of his, of talking with terrible facility. Why was
that? Always he had suffered from it. Give him a listener, and he was
"away to the races," as they used to say at home. Even when he had got a
business position, this gift of tongues, as one might say, was no asset. Once,
when he had been admitted to an interview, and he was tearing along,
thinking that he was doing finely, his client had shot half out of his chair
thundering, "Shut up!" There had been a silence, a moment of paralysis,
and then a mutter from the man: "What d'you think you're doing? . . .
Drive a man crazy," and suchlike comments.

Why was that? Never got anywhere in spite of his education and
fecundity of speech. Even this evening, when he confronted the ship's
doctor in the surgery, and was identified on the list of deck passengers, he
had somehow launched into an uncalled-for loquacity, and had found the
man, his eyeglass screwed into his experienced blue eye, examining him
critically. And had there not been a faint sound like "cacoëthes loquendi"
as he went out? The doctor thought himself safe, no doubt, in talking
Latin to a decker. But had he really gabbler's itch?

He stared at the deck and wondered. Even as he did so he found his
lips forming the words that he had "no animus, no animus whatever."
There it was—cacoëthes loquendi—gabbler's itch. He frowned. It was a
grave disadvantage, this lack of animus. Because a simple fellow had no
consideration in the world, if he talked. They shouted, "Shut up!" or just
stared and moved out of earshot. His wife, for example, had simply cleared

out, left him for good. Of course he had failed to support her. Ah! But there was another side to that. He had never been successful with women. Nobody could hold it against him that he had done them any harm. It was true that he ought to have supported his wife. But he had a humorous conviction that she would have gone—anyway. Saw it in her eye, one day, while he was talking very fast.

There was something about him, he was well aware. He made a momentary comparison of himself with that doctor, for instance, with his finely wrinkled yet healthy-looking parchment skin, his alert poise, his superior, monocled scrutiny. About the same age. Thirty years ago they might have been contemporaries at the same college. And he, the doctor, had never said a word beyond "What's your name?" and that valedictory mutter in Latin. Was that the difference? No. Something else, he felt quite sure.

He was apparently unaware of the turmoil surrounding him, the buzz and chatter that arise always from a huddled mass of humans, who are being carried, like cattle, to their desired havens, and who become garrulous and musical and quarrelsome, merely for lack of responsibility and employment. He did not notice how, in the course of ceaseless rearrangements of baggage and persons, he had become isolated. He sat now on his valise, on the deck, a solitary being, apart. The deck was now like a large chamber walled in by the wind. Above the great bowl of light which poured its rays diagonally upon them and threw immense black shadows into the after-gloom, the canvas awning seemed to be struggling to escape. It bellied out from the halyards in a concave vault of quivering fabric, and then suddenly descended and began to flap viciously in the gusts that came over the bulwarks at intervals. Beyond those bulwarks was darkness and heaving waters, and a wind that gave out great booming sighs as it fled over the sea.

He looked up at last, and found himself as if shunned. And his undisciplined imagination took it as an omen when a wave suddenly reared up over the bulwarks and fled aft, splashing him contemptuously with spray. Nobody touched but him! He shook the water from his eyes and stood up, glancing round to discover the witnesses of his misfortune. But the occupants of the hatch were preoccupied with the problem of existence. The eddying wind and the beating canvas were giving trouble. Children were crying, and the mothers, reared up from their beds, were looking about for more secluded quarters. Several had already moved stealthily aft, and were lost among the crew.

The ship took a long careening roll, and the sea leapt out of the darkness, sparkled and gleamed in the light, and detonated upon the deck. Murmurs and cries mingled with the sough of the water through the scuppers. The forms of men, safe in the shelter of the alleys, were silhouetted against the far brightness of the kitchens, whence had come great crashes of falling metal. Above the straining canvas the guy ropes hummed and tackle squeaked as it was flung about by the wind and the scend of the ship. As she drew out from the horns of the Dark Gulf she began to wallow on the outer edge of a hurricane.

Yet the fact that no one had seen his discomfiture with that first wave was for him a source of satisfaction. His mind ran swiftly over the situation as he edged in between two massive bollards under the lee of the bulkhead. He saw one of those to whom he had been confiding his plans peering out upon the deck as if looking for him, and wearing an expression of hard curiosity.

He drew back. He must think. His trouble was, of course, money. Money for an adequate boat and tackle. But for that he would not have mentioned a word to these supercilious beings who would be in Sovranilla for a few hours, and then gone, to Curaçao, to Port-au-Prince, to Havana and New York. No! Much rather would he have depended upon the people he knew in Sovranilla. Perhaps it would have been better if he had never left it. And he would never have heard that conversation, carried on in growls behind the latticework where he sat smoking a cigarette after he had washed the dishes for Jovita's Chinese cook.

Jovita was the proprietress of the Love Nest Café for Officers, in a discreet back street in Colón. The café was upstairs over the street, and was screened all round with romantic greenery trellised over painted lattice. Jovita's two daughters, as big as herself, were the sirens. They danced and looked ponderously languorous at young ensigns from Indiana and Ohio. But the growls came from maturer throats. Captains of ships, he reflected, smoking cautiously, and lowering his ear until it was on a level with the voices. The latticework had creaked as the owner of the growl leaned against it. Outside the Love Nest in the arcaded street the tropical rain was descending in wavering sheets. It poured like a momentary cataract over the corrugated iron roof of the kitchen. So the captains of ships replenished their glasses and growled on.

The word "Sovranilla" came out. One of the speakers grumbled that "they could do what they liked with it, once they got it to Sovranilla." And then "six hundred thousand dollars. Gold, in little barrels a strong boy could run off with!" The speaker became indignant. "And nowhere to put it but a cupboard on the boat deck, with a rotten old ship's lock on it. Of course"—here the growl became very thick, and almost inaudible—"nobody knowing it, just as safe, eh?" And, "What the eye don't see the heart don't grieve for"; and a reference to the "worries of life," followed by guttural laughter and contralto badinage from a daughter of Jovita.

The watcher looked critically at her through a crevice in the heavy foliage. That was not his weakness. It exasperated him at times, that men should abandon realities for such ephemeral solace as women afforded. Yet they had their uses, he reflected. They were kind enough. At Sovranilla, when he was so utterly on the beach that he had but one pair of pants, a brown-skinned creature with soft black eyes and gentle voice had sewn industriously on his behalf. He had bought her a bottle of perfume when he won eleven dollars on the commandant's bird at the village cockpit. But for the idolater of tangible riches there was no lure in feminine softness. Indeed, he had this much feminine about him—and it may be some explanation—that he loved the things they loved: the glitter of gems, the seductive feel of amber and ivory, the smooth caresses of silk, and the satisfying solidity of coins. He experienced a sensation almost of vertigo as he imagined those "little barrels a strong boy could run off with." The cigarette burned his fingers sharply as he crouched with closed eyes by the latticework, listening to the syncopations of the phonograph.

And they were up there now, a hundred feet away from him, those little barrels. He snuggled down between the bollards and tried to visualize them —clean, solid little affairs with fat scarlet seals, exquisitely portable even for "a strong boy." But with a mysterious lack of logic his mind would not be preoccupied with them. He discovered that his vividly imagined fortitude was undermined by a desire to return to Sovranilla. Do what he would, he could not evade a secret conviction that he regretted his departure. Why had he left?

He drew hard on a cigarette as he recalled that unkempt coast town that sprawled along the crumbling edge of a shabby bluff. He liked it. There was no appearance to keep up. The streets were lanes of mud or dust, with steep gullies cut here and there athwart them; and pigs and fowls wandered in and out of the houses. He liked it. They were kind to him. Always, when he had been in low water, there was a meal somewhere for him. He could always get a canoe and paddle around to a sheltered cove for an afternoon's swimming. And the brown-skinned girl liked him, for she would always iron a shirt when he asked her.

And he had left it all suddenly, without a word of good-by, because of his fatal facility of speech. There was no doubt that, once started, he could not stop. He told that passenger an astounding tale as he walked up the long jetty carrying the gentleman's valise. And what he realized now, as he sat with his back to the vibrating bulkhead and watched the white water spring upon the bulwarks, was that "when he got going" he was not himself but the person he imagined he was—that alert and efficient image in the rear of his brain! He would have to carry that other magniloquent self upon his back all his days, suffering for the follies of one who seemed to be a fantastic and irresponsible kinsman.

Carrying the gentleman's valise, and carried away himself upon a swift gust of speech, he was aware suddenly that he had been presented with a decker's ticket to Colón. He had shown conclusively and exhaustively that, if he could only get away from Sovranilla, he could regain his position in life. He had invited a college man to consider the agony of spirit another college man suffered in that shaggy dump beside the emerald-green combers of the Caribbean. He saw himself, as he talked, flung down in uttermost misery behind some convenient wattled hut. He saw life unfolding for him amid the glare and rattle of the night life in Colón, wealth coming to him in heaps of paper and metal, followed by the respect of his contemporaries. So it had befallen, and he had walked out of the great docks, his own small satchel in his hand, his head high, until he was out of sight. Then he knew he was better off, far better off, in that little town of Sovranilla.

And as he thought it out now from his refuge behind the bollards he saw himself as the owner of a secret which would make them all rich. He imagined himself walking about among them, able at a word to turn the whole place upside down. But he would never speak it. He saw himself again when he came to die, handing on the secret of the money he had cast into the sea at such and such a place, giving the bearings of the lighthouse and the buoy on the sunken wreck. He even saw in imagination the stir that would arise in Juan Pierella's botiga when the news went round. Gamecocks and roulette wheels would be forgotten while they discussed it in whispers. Little barrels!

And then, seeing those white-coated men by the door, their glances falling at times in hard curiosity upon him, hiding there between the bollards, he made a determined gesture and turned his mind resolutely from these fancies. And this resolution of his, like a grapnel, caught upon the first thing convenient in his mind. He would have nothing to do with these people on the ship. They had scarcely concealed their amusement while he had sounded them as to their willingness to go into a venture that might be a good thing. He ought to know by now that these people had no ideas above smuggling drugs or egret feathers in their underwear, or perhaps pilfering trinkets from a passenger's trunks. He hated them, when they came ashore in Sovranilla. On one occasion he had risen in a paroxysm of disgust because a crowd of them had walked into the room where he was talking to that brown girl while she ironed. Even they, tough as they were, had seen something ominous in the gestures of the thin, unshaven man in shirt and pants, the cigarette trembling in his fingers as he lashed them with his incomparable tongue. A mistake, they muttered, and withdrew, ashamed. Neither he nor the girl had said a word for a long time, and then he had slipped away into the darkness.

As the evening wore on it was evident that the people lodged beneath the straining awning, and attacked by the seas that leaped the bulwarks at uncertain intervals, would be in distress. The chief officer, in dirty white uniform and long rubber boots, came down the ladder from the bridge deck and consulted with the bosun, a harassed expression on his face as he looked around. The man crouching between bollard and bulkhead watched him with dislike. It was part of his character to hate uniforms; but behind that human trait there lurked the subtler reason that these men could not be induced to talk. They barked, or snarled, or grunted, or were sullenly silent. You couldn't get near them. He recalled the doctor, with his monocle, his spotless white and gold regalia, his cool, silent appraisal. They symbolized for him, these men, a world in which he had failed to get a footing. Thinking of them, Sovranilla, with its pigs and fowls walking in and out among the humans in the adobe huts, was, by comparison, home. There everybody talked, interminable rigmaroles in Spanish, about nothing at all—about the pimple on the nose of the conductor just in on the train from Calomar, or the new white enameled basin Emilia Gurmesindo had ordered from New York through Wong Choy's general store, or the bottle of perfume which the assistant commandant had smuggled for his wife, but which he had given to Vina Muñez, who was not esteemed.

And there was another and subtler reason hiding like a shadow behind all this. He was unable to appreciate their fidelity to an abstraction. He could be inspired by those he knew. As he flinched from a great wave that roared along the rail and vanished without coming inboard, he had a sudden vivid consciousness of his affection for the folk in Sovranilla. But to work all one's life for people one never saw was folly. An idea! A chimera! And no doubt flung aside when they were too old, eh?

He would have plunged into a fresh depth of imaginative reflections had not the whole ship sprung to life before his eyes. The officer stiffened to an alert rigidity as the whistle whined and blared suddenly above them, three long blasts, and then he ran to the side. The sailors followed suit, lining the bulwarks. The sound of men running came to the ears of the man crouching out of sight. He could remain in this position no longer. He rose and, looking earnestly at his little valise, walked to the side.

At first nothing could be seen save the great foam-flecked planes of the sea, a series of enormous and advancing ridges with toppling white crests as they passed; and the glare of the portholes so illuminated them that beyond was a place of vague darkness. But as he gazed he saw, away on the starboard bow, a slow rising globe of intense light, a globe that exploded into a cascade of distant spangles. As the radiance died out and the ship sloped sharply forward down the weather side of a wave he saw something else, which evoked from his troubled and weary spirit a sigh of relief. Only for a moment he caught the deep red glow of the wreck buoy outside Sovranilla, and then it disappeared.

At once, as that rocket ascended into the distant darkness, the officer and his crew abandoned their plans of moving the deckers to some other part of the ship and ran up the ladders to the boat deck away above them. And it was easy in the confusion for the man who had stood beside them at the bulwarks to follow unobserved. The mere act of ascending was an inspiration to him. For a moment he shrank back as he found himself confronting the long smooth camber of the promenade deck, with its colored lights and recumbent forms; and then he sprang on up the next ladder, and came out upon a place of baffling obscurity and a masterful rushing wind.

For here was no water, only a ceaseless pressure of air. It roared about him as he stumbled over deadeyes and guy ropes. It tore at the collar of his shirt and flapped the trousers about his knees and ankles. But he gained what he wanted, a high clear view of that ruby light; and he clung to the corner of a deckhouse and watched it. All about him were men shouting as they toiled above one of the boats. The wavering beam of a flashlight suddenly threw them into brilliant relief, and their eager faces as they turned gave them the appearance of a party of conspirators. He shrank back into the shadow of the house as the light advanced. No one, as far as he could imagine, had noticed his hurried ascent with the crew. And now, while they were putting the boat out over the water, his mind became clogged with sensations.

He became aware that he was concealed from view by the very thing he had set out to seek. He could no longer see either the men at work or the ascending rockets from the bark on her beam-ends below the bluff, or the ruby light winking from the wreck buoy. He was in deep shadow, and sheltered from the roaring wind. And an ecstasy assaulted him, a desire, not so much to do what he had vividly imagined, as to see if for once his imagination had not played him false. And he began to explore, concentrating in a few moments some of those discoveries often spread over years.

For while he was feeling for the door, behind which lay the money that had obsessed him, he was also exploring his own nature. He was conscious of standing beside himself and watching with painful curiosity what he would do. The door, of course, would be locked, but there was a window, a round scuttle opening inward and too small even for the strong boy the captain had sardonically specified. And he saw himself reach an arm into that window, and felt beneath his hand the rough edges of a barrelhead. For an instant he was almost in a swoon as he saw the enterprise crowned with success. A determined struggle with the door, a dozen swift journeys to the deserted lee rail, a quick fixing of position in his mind, and then away down to the raucous uproar of the deckers, stage by stage, emerging from some dark corner where he had been sleeping in innocence through the storm. How could they suspect him? He fondled the smooth perfection of the plan.

For once his imagination had not fooled him. Here it was, at last, the authentic foot of the rainbow. He saw himself in Sovranilla, telling the children, as the passing rain squall fled over the emerald and silver waves, that there was a cask of gold at the foot of yonder colored arch. He would make an allegory of it, until the time came when they could go out and see how truly he had spoken.

And that thought made him shrink back as if he had been struck suddenly in the darkness. He felt the hot plates of the funnel against his hands and shoulders. There it was again, that devil with the forked tongue as it were, the devil of loquacity. He sprang away and stumbled aft until he came to the rail overlooking the awning. It was going, the wind was ripping it, halyard by halyard, and he could discern the hullabaloo of the helpless folk dodging the ruthless lashings of the canvas. Could he accomplish nothing without this ebullient verbiage? His hands closed desperately on the rail, as if the rushing wind was a fate trying to bear him away.

And as he stood there fate came to him, in the guise of a man in oilskins who bumped into him in the darkness, who asked him who he was, and without waiting for an answer bade him go forward and man the boat.

He thought, afterward, when he had reached it, had clambered into it as it swayed on the outswung davits, that he must have spoken at length to the man in the oilskins—a man with a voice both furry and hoarse, redfaced and solemn under the sou'wester tied below his chin. Must have done that. The words of that man sang in his ears like harp strings: "For the Lord's sake, shut up . . . not so much conversation . . . talk later . . . see the rockets . . . get in . . . Ready, bosun? . . . Then lower away!"

The ship had been stopped, and by the time the boat began to descend all way was gone from her. And it seemed to him, as he sat in the boat among a half dozen of silent men, that their rapid passing by lighted deck and bright portholes, row on row, into the darkness below, was a symbol of life. Consecrated to a high purpose, they descended into unknown perils as if from another world; and suddenly they were afloat and the falls unhooked, and they were pulling with a mystical union of energy toward a cascade of falling stars.

Here, for a stark materialist, the episode would have ended in failure. But for him it was a revelation of his own potential character. Sitting there in the obscurity of the storm, joined with unseen and unknown men in a common beneficent endeavor, he shed the pretentious trappings of an irksome life habit and comprehended resolutely his true bearings. He saw them as, when he was poised high upon a lofty wave crest, the ruby light of the wreck buoy shone across to him. He saw them when, after enormous labor, they had won to the lee side of the great bark, dismasted and careened upon the white-toothed rocks below the bluffs. He saw them as those frightened and weary men tumbled aboard with a shout and a whimper of delight. But he saw them best of all when, after the long, long pull, they gained the little harbor and stood at last upon the jetty below the silent huts of Sovranilla. It was the moment of dawn, and the steamer was standing in toward the anchorage. None of the strangers noted his gesture as he faced the eastern ranges where the sun had touched the snowy summits of the Andes with rose. It was a gesture of surrender and illumination, a symbol of what he now comprehended and believed.

And often, in after days, the children would see him pause in his talk when a rain squall fled away over the Caribbean, and make that gesture toward the rainbow, watching in silence where the shaft of it sank into the emerald sea.

GEORGE MILBURN
The Cowboy Sang Soprano

THIS KID come riding up to the chuck wagon while we was eating. He's a peakèd-faced boy with dreamy eyes. He's got on orange-colored chaps and a ten-gallon hat and the varnish is still on his mail-order boots. He climbs off his spavined pinto, comes over to Ab, the trail boss, and allows he's heard back at Fort Griffin we was needing a hand.

We was a month out of Bandera on the old Western Trail with two thousand head, and hadn't even crossed the Brazos yet. Our herd never had got road-broke proper, and thunderstorms had caused one stampede after another.

Ab was the meanest-dispositioned trail boss any man ever rode with. If he'd ever had a heart in him the size of a pecan, it had petrified. He was quick on the draw. He could knock the pips out of the six of spades at twenty yards. His trail hands had a way of drifting off without even calling for their time.

Ab hands the Kid a lariat and tells him to go over to the remuda and rope him out a horse. The Kid makes a brave start, but he gets all tangled up. Ab calls the Kid back and asks if they was to be a night stampede, would he drift along in front, or circle them to a mill? The Kid says he would drift along in front, which of course was just one hundred per cent the wrong answer. Ab was purely disgusted. He says, "Tell me what you figger your qualifications as a trail hand are."

The Kid thinks a minute, and then he says, "Well, I've got a good singing voice."

A good singing voice does help to keep a herd quieted down. There wasn't 'ary one of us could carry a tune if we had it in a poke. Even a greenhorn who could sing soothing on night guard, especially to a herd as restive as ours was, wasn't a hand to be passed lightly by.

So Ab says, "I tell you what—if you want to ride along to Dodge with us for your beans, okay."

The Kid was purely overjoyed. Ab put him on the drag with me, bringing up strays. He didn't know riding herd from sour apples, and I kept him so busy he didn't have a chance to sing.

We crossed the Brazos that day. It was in flood, and the Kid lost six steers. Ab cussed him out and the Kid just shivered.

That night Ab put me and the Kid on the second shift of night herd. We had been circling the bed grounds for about ten minutes when I says: "Come on, Kid. Now's your chance to sing." He let out the awfulest caterwauling that ever struck a man's ears. The steers all begin lowing and struggling to their feet. I knowed it wouldn't take much more to set them off across the prairie. But before I could stop the Kid, here come Ab Dunn, just a-faunching.

"You call that singing?" he says. "You've purt' near got the cattle scared into a stampede. We'd never get these steers to Dodge with you along."

The Kid whimpered, "Please, Mr. Dunn. I got my feet wet crossing the river today, and I must've lost my singing voice."

"You'll lose more'n your voice if you ain't away from this camp before morning. Vamoose!"

When the shift changed and me and Ab got back to the chuck wagon, the Kid was waiting. He pleaded for Ab to just let him get his throat cleared up and then he'd prove he could sing. Ab finally agreed to let him stay till we got to Doan's Crossing, which took a week. The Kid spent most of his time gargling salt water, but he still hadn't got his voice back when we reached Red River.

Red River was full from bank to bank. Only a trail boss as mean as Ab would expect his men to put two thousand rambunctious steers across that flooded stream. There was no question of firing the Kid then, because we needed every hand. We swum thirty head across at a time, and made it with less trouble than I figured.

As I reached the north bank behind the last bunch I looked around in time to see the Kid's horse go under with him in the current. I jumped off my horse. Ab Dunn came up and grabbed me.

"Leave go me," I says. "I've got to save that kid."

"No, you ain't. That kid's of no account to us. You'll get pulled under. I can't afford to lose another trail hand if I'm ever going to get these steers to Dodge."

By this time the Kid, swept clear of his saddle and grabbing out blind, had caught hold of his horse's tail, and the horse was swimming for shore with him in tow.

Well, we dreened might near a coffeepot full of water out of that kid before we brung him to. We put him in the chuck wagon, more dead than alive. Ab Dunn rared and faunched about it.

Laying up in the cook wagon, away from the dust of the herd and keeping his feet dry, it wasn't long till the Kid got his voice back.

That kid had the most wonderful singing voice I have ever heard on a human. He sang soprano. No, I don't mean tenor. Soprano. Yodeled some, too. He had learned all them songs like "Poor Lonesome Cowboy" and "Cielito Lindo" and "The Letter Edged in Black." We used to lay awake listening while he was on night guard. The steers seemed to appreciate his singing voice as much as we did. They rested easy while he was out there singing.

The rest of us worked three shifts at night guard, but Ab made the Kid stay out all night. The Kid was so anxious to be a cowboy he never beefed. Every night he would yodel to them steers in the starlight until it would might near break your heart.

We had fine weather all the way across the Territory, so we made good progress. But when we struck Dodge City, Ab learned that the K.C. market had dropped. In spite of it setting in to rain again, he concluded to drive on to Ogallala and ship over the U.P. to Chicago. Meanwhile the boys had dispersed themselves around the various centers of entertainment in Dodge. Ab located me, and we set out to round them up so we could hit the trail next morning.

We was coming up Main Street when we heard pistol shots. We looked and over in front of the Lady Gay Dance Hall Bat Wilson was shooting at a tenderfoot's toes. It was the Kid, picking them up and putting them down in a puddle of rain water, with the bullets splashing around his feet. Ab Dunn's hand flicked to his hip and his .45 cracked twice. Across the way Bat's two guns clattered on the boardwalk.

"Ab," I says, "that's as fine a thing as ever I've seen a man do. You've got a good heart, after all."

"You didn't think I'd stand by and watch him shoot holes in the Kid's boots, did you?" Ab says.

"If I ever suspicioned that of you, Ab," I says, fervent-like, "I apologize to you now. I'm proud to know a man that would come to a kid's rescue the way you done."

"Yeah," Ab says, blowing the smoke out of his gun, "I ain't taking no chances on the Kid getting holes in his boots. Why, if he was to get his feet wet and lose his singing voice just now, we never would get them steers to Ogallala."

CHRISTOPHER MORLEY

Continuity

THERE WAS ALWAYS a stir and movement among the leaves, in that strip of woodland beyond the empty house. The dim blank windows, with dusty scarves of cobweb in the sash corners, looked into alcoves of green perspective where, at the bottom of the vista, clear twinkles of sky sifted through. No matter how still the day, how heavy the air, there seemed a gentle trouble in the boughs. Among the tangle of blackberry briers and dying chestnut trunks matted with robes of poison ivy were some dogwood trees. In a light spring air their blossoms of four white twisted petals tossed and spun like tiny propellers. The tall oaks lifted rough gray rafters under the lattice of tremulous green. There was always an eddy and chiming under the eaves of that airy roof. What word is soft enough to say it? A whisper, a murmur, an audible hush, a sigh.

Paths that men have made persist surprisingly. Behind the old faded blistered barn a still visible way among the thickets led to a deserted dump heap among the trees. Here, quietly rotting in a flicker of sun and shadow, lay the cast-off rubbish of former tenants—broken china, rusted cans, a skeleton umbrella, an old slipper, warped and stiff. Poison ivy had grown up again along that path. The blackberries softened, and then withered, unpicked.

The two men who walked up the hill did not see all this. Their first glimpse of the house, seen by chance from the road, pleased them. The faint sadness of any dwelling, lonely and stripped, was at that moment only an agreeable air of strangeness. In the transparent blaze of light and warmth under a golden pour of late afternoon sunshine the place was ideal for their bivouac. They had tramped far, were tired and hungry. The rich green of mint and cress on the hill slope led them to the spring: when the paste of dead leaves and twigs and seed clots had been scummed off, the water was cold and sweet. There was dry hay in the loft of the barn. Here they spread their blankets. By an old log, scarred with ax cuts, they lit a small cautious fire, made tea, and fried bacon. In the valley they could see opal shadows gathering, rising, a lake of dusk, a blue tide making up a green estuary. Daylight retreated on the great tawny hillsides, slipping quietly among scattered gray boulders.

"Now let time stand still awhile," said Dunham, lighting his pipe and stretching out at ease. "I didn't know how tired I was until I got out here away from all the meaningless pressure of the office. I'm too tired even to think. I couldn't think if I wanted to."

"There's a good many in the same case," said Grimes with a faint grin. "But not for the same reason."

They gazed about them with a sort of vacant satisfaction.

"My mind feels like that old house there," said Dunham. "A dusty shell, vacant, lifeless, and yet somehow aware that it was once alive. Just a foggy memory that I was, forty-eight hours ago, a hustling businessman tied down by telephone wires."

"Yes, you're tired," said Grimes. "Everyone's tired. The world itself is tired. I'm glad it is. If it gets tired enough, desperate enough, it'll come to its senses. Think of a place like this, close to the main road, in this heavenly country, and lying empty. I suppose the people who lived here moved to the city. I can imagine them, huddled in some mean crowded street, going to the movies every evening."

There was a throbbing down the road, and round the curve that embraced the hillside flashed a big touring car, lifting a swirl of powdery dust. They watched it disappear, with the small pitiful smile of two ghosts, just stepped off earth and reviewing the quaint futilities from which they were now released.

"These arcadian spots aren't always what one imagines," Dunham said. "It doesn't do to live too close to nature. I've always noticed it's the loveliest places that lie vacant. That's just it—they're too lovely. People get frightened. There are days, like today, when the very harmony of air and sunlight terrifies me. Days so excellent they trouble the heart. They make you suspect that life is only a queer dream, one of those nightmares in which your limbs are paralyzed in the face of sure disaster. Perhaps we will wake up in the fourth dimension, who knows?"

"Yes, it's all a disordered mix-up. But life is rather like a detective story. No matter how badly written, or how clumsy the plot, somehow you generally want to read it to the end."

"You admit, then, it's a kind of fiction. Exactly. But if life is fiction, then what represents biography?"

Grimes laughed. "My dear boy, we're getting uncomfortably subtle for two tired loafers. Let's wash the frying pan and take a stroll."

The rusty old pump, under the grape arbor near the back stoop, was found to yield water after some priming. And then Dunham, poking about, noticed that the outside cellar door was unfastened.

"Hullo," he cried. "Here's a way in! Let's explore. I never can resist an empty house."

Through a dark earth-smelling basement they felt their way gingerly. Grimes lit a match and they found the stairs. The door at the head of the flight was hooked on the inside, but not tightly: there was enough gap to insert a penknife blade and lift the fixture. They were in the pantry.

Nothing is more fascinating to a thoughtful mood than rambling through a deserted house, imagining it peopled with one's own domestic gods, and also conjecturing the life of the former occupants. A home keeps so many subtle vestiges. The creak of the stair, the stain on the wallpaper, the hooks in the cupboard, the soot of the fireplace, all these are mysterious and alluring whispers out of that unknown household. You can feel the vanished reality, obscurely existent and yet dumb, intangible. There must be some way, you would think, of wiping the dust from that old mirror and seeing the lingering reflection.

"They were good housekeepers," said Grimes. "I never saw a place more scrupulously clean. No scraps of paper or curtain rings or flabby toothbrushes lying about. The woman had an upstate conscience, evidently."

"*Too* clean," said Dunham. "I don't like it. It's too—too naked. I don't think they loved the place. If they had, they'd have left something for it to remember them by."

"I'm going upstairs before it gets too dark to see. It's interesting. I wonder why they closed all the shutters just on this side of the house and not on the others?"

Dunham was examining a large cupboard under the stairway. He heard his friend's footsteps go upward over his head. The heavy walking shoes moved slowly from room to room; he could hear them strike sharply on the echoing floor. At the back of a cupboard like this, he was thinking, would be the likeliest place for things to be forgotten. He groped carefully into the dark corner, with a curious feeling that he would find something. Above him was a sudden soft pattering. Mice, he thought. Then he heard Grimes calling.

"Here's some evidence!" he was saying.

Dunham turned—perhaps with an irrational feeling of relief—from the stuffy blackness of the closet. He went upstairs and found Grimes standing in a fair-sized room on the sunset side of the house.

"There were children. See the Mother Goose wallpaper, all scrawled over with pencil marks."

"Pretty tall children," Dunham said. He pointed to some of the scribbles, which were just at the height of his shoulder.

"They do it standing in their cribs." Grimes smiled. "I know that from home experience."

Dunham opened a closet door in one corner.

"Funny," he said. "They left all their toys."

On the floor of the cupboard, neatly arranged, lay an assortment of childish treasures: a clockwork locomotive and battered tracks, building blocks, a tin shovel and pail, some small tools.

"Children had grown up when they moved away," Grimes suggested.

In the darkening room they seemed to see the little tin rails set out in a circle on the splintery floor, the toy engine clattering round until, like all such contrivances, it reeled over and lay with a loud buzzing, like a kicking beetle turned on its back. From some faraway imagined childhood the picture presented itself. The room seemed very lonely.

"Let's go outdoors," Dunham said.

They walked quietly up and down the rough driveway that lay between the house and the woods. Among the trees was an occasional blink of fireflies. The evening air was cool, and Grimes rebuilt a small blaze, but Dunham still paced around the house. The place moved him with a grave appeal. As the last green light drew westward darkness crept in from under the trees, where it had lain crouching. The wood itself drew closer and whispered more certainly. It loomed immensely high, like a wall of blackness, darker than the dark. The house seemed smaller and had lost that look of established confidence that houses have. Happy houses welcome the night; built to conquer it, their gallant windows hold swords of brave yellow lamplight to pierce our first enemy. But here, Dunham thought, this lonely steading quailed beneath the shadow. Darkness invaded it and triumphed over it; it lay passive, but still afraid.

At last he joined his companion, who was lying comfortably propped against a log.

"This is just the sort of place I'd like to live in," said Grimes.

Above them the ruddy shine of their bonfire was caught upon the boughs; it hung like a bright mist among the softly shaking leaves. Each way they looked was warm glow, but the dark was always just behind them.

"Curious how much closer the woods come at night," said Dunham. "Sunlight keeps them at a distance, but now they press nearer. They seem to lean right over the house. If I lived here I'd clear out some of the trees. I like a bit of open space around me, to give the stars room to move about in."

"I don't like trees at night," he continued presently. "I'm not surprised those people shuttered their windows on this side. There's something strange about that towering blackness. You might think it goes all the way up."

"All the way up?" said Grimes, lazily tapping out his pipe. "It probably does."

"I guess not. It's only earth's little shaft of shadow, waving through the empty brilliance of space. There must be sunlight away up, or we shouldn't see the stars. They haven't any light of their own—have they?"

"My astronomy's rather vague. Come on, let's turn in: I'm tired. I'll pour a pan of water on those embers."

The barn loft was airy, with a faint dry sweetness a little ticklish to the nose. They swung open a big upper door that looked upon a yard, and arranged their blankets on the hay. Dunham was thinking of the people who had lived here once. A broken pitchfork stood against the wall: its wooden handle was dark and slippery from the moisture of many palms. As he settled himself comfortably he had a sense—with the sudden clear vision of the mind—of the *past*, of all humanity's past: the endless broken

striving of men, their fugitive evasions of disaster, their hazardous momentary happinesses. And when you realize (he was thinking) how everything
vanished, surroundings once dearly familiar pass out of one's life, with what
an emotion you remember things you once loved and will never see again!
This plain house, deserted under the dark profile of the trees, had once
been filled with life. To someone, every sill and corner had had meaning.
Now, in the tremulous summer evening, it had an air of defeat, of flight,
the air of tragedy worn by abandoned things. This is a sadness felt by all,
a personal and selfish sadness, the universal pang of the race troubled by
time's way with men. To his mind came words half remembered:

> All things uncomely and broken, all things worn out and old,
> The cry of a child by the roadway, the creak of a lumbering cart,
> The heavy steps of the ploughman . . . the ploughman . . .

How did it go?

"By the way," said Grimes, "what was that you said about——" The hay
rustled as he turned over.

"Said about what?"

Grimes paused.

"Never mind," he said. "I was going to ask you something. I've forgotten
what it was."

They fell asleep.

Dunham woke as one does in middle night—not drowsily, but sharply,
definitely, with a mere opening of the eyes. As he lay he could see out
through the open door: everything was lovely with a pallor of moonlight.
In that wan, delicate shining the trees were a milky gray: every leaf distinct and separate, limned upon seeping chinks of shadow. The crickets
and other night sounds had fallen still. A comfortable calm possessed him.
The feeling of sadness and oppression had passed. In this clear tranquillity
he was necessarily placid. The old hypnotism of the moon, as she passes
her silver mirror gravely before humanity's face, makes all passions and
perplexities seem vain. He rose, quietly, for Grimes lay solidly asleep, and
descended the ladder to the barn floor.

He walked out softly, for there was sure enchantment in the night.
Moonlight never fails of her spell upon the imaginative; but this was a
brightness so hushed, so secret, so crystalline, he seemed drowned at the
bottom of an ocean of light. He trod, as he had dreamed in childhood of
doing, on a clean sandy sea bed where light struck radiantly down through

leagues of clear water, gilding corals and shipwrecks and green caverns with a tremble of pale colors. Again the tall proscenium of woodland seemed to have receded under the flow and purity of that thin gleam. A straight white barrier lay between the house and the trees.

He walked almost on tiptoe. This was a different world from that shadow of loneliness and trouble that had lain across the hillside a few hours before. Sometimes from sleep men rise like Lazarus from the dead; their eyes see newly. Fears and fevers were dissolved in this pearly luster. Not with horror but with tenderness he saw the splintered lives of men, whose weakness alone makes them lovable; and even this poor shell of a house, once dear to men, shared in that generous emotion.

A faint reiterated rhythmical sound reached him as he strolled quietly beside the house. He wondered, at first, whether it was bird or insect. It seemed partly a whistle, partly a squeak; and as he halted to listen it queerly conveyed a sense of something revolving. It was always on the other side of the house. A bat, perhaps, he thought idly. But then he detected in the sound a small rattling or jolting.

He stood under the grape arbor, with just a subtle prickling of nerves. The soft creaking seemed to pass now along the stony roadway under the trees. There was a suggestion of metal in the sound. It ceased and then was renewed, irregular, but with a rhythm of its own.

Men are easily frightened at night, but Dunham was not frightened. In some curious way he felt that this was part of the destiny of the evening. He felt only an unexplained sense of pity. He had known this was going to happen. Ever since he had first divined the quiet misery of this house under the horror of the trees he had known . . .

But it was quite different from his expectation. Round the corner of the house, into a pool of moonlight, rode a child on a velocipede. He was about four years old and wore a sailor suit. There was a faint squeaking from the unoiled cranks of his toy. A crumpled sailor cap was carelessly tilted on his head; his face was bright with gaiety. With a kind of reckless dash and glee he twirled the tricycle round and rode briskly, with a merry up-and-down of bare knees, down the bumpy drive. What on earth is that child doing here at this time of night? thought Dunham, his tension suddenly relaxed. Some neighbor's youngster, strayed away from home? He followed slowly, not to frighten him. But the child, absorbed in his escapade, had not noticed any watcher. He had halted the velocipede and was sitting thoughtfully, bent over the handlebars.

"Hullo!" Dunham called gently. "What are you up to, sonny? You ought to be in bed."

The figure turned on the saddle. Through the overhanging trees the blanched light fell hazily upon the small face; Dunham could see it change, first to shyness, then to alarm. He pedaled swiftly, bumping over the stones, down the hill to the highway, and disappeared in the mottled shadow at the turn in the road.

For no reason he could analyze, Dunham looked up at the house. At an upper window, white in the glitter on the pane, was a woman's face, colorless, staring, horrified; with a sudden dreadful movement her hands flew to the sill, as if to throw up the sash. Her mouth opened in a soundless cry.

Dunham ran to the bottom of the hill and looked along the road. There was no one there.

As he walked up the driveway again he looked, against his will, at the window where he had seen that anguished face. It was closely shuttered.

The next morning Grimes went among the trees to collect sticks for the breakfast fire.

"Look here!" he called. "Here's an old dump heap. More evidence!"

Dunham followed the old track among the bushes. There, quietly rotting in a flicker of sun and shadow, lay the cast-off rubbish of a vanished household—broken china, rusted cans, a skeleton umbrella. Among the litter, broken and badly twisted, lay an old velocipede.

After breakfast, while Grimes was packing up their kit, Dunham slipped into the house. In the morning light, that broke in golden webs across the dusty rooms, the place was only faintly sad. In the cupboard under the stairs, far at the back, he found a child's sailor cap.

As they were setting off down the road a farmer passed in a hay wagon.

"How long's it been empty?" he said. "Oh, five, six years, I guess. The folks moved away after their little boy got killed by a car. They was all wrapped up in that kid, too. He was riding his tricycle, right here in the road. That bit of woods, you see, it shuts off the view of the curve."

The wagon was creaking on when Dunham turned and ran after it.

"Say," he called, "when will it be full moon, d'you know?"

The man meditated.

"Why, the full o' the moon was about two weeks back. Another fortnight, I guess. Nights are pretty black just now, I reckon." He went on down the road.

As Dunham joined his companion Grimes said: "Oh, I remember what I was going to ask you. You said something yesterday about the fourth dimension. That interests me. Just what did you mean?"

"Lord knows," said Dunham. "Sometimes I've thought that the fourth dimension is what the moving-picture people would call continuity. When you paste all the little shots of film together it goes on and on and never stops. Everything that ever happened is happening still."

"In other words, the fourth dimension is memory?"

Dunham looked off down the valley, where great areas of shadow were moving, subtending the silver floes of wind-drifting cloud.

"Put it this way," he said. "It's the shadow that life casts on eternity."

"Or maybe the other way round. The shadow eternity casts upon life?"

They walked on round the hillside, skirting the patch of woodland that hid the house from the road. An eddy and trembling rustle of leaves was chiming under that airy roof. What word is soft enough to say it? A whisper, a murmur, an audible hush, a sigh.

JOHN O'HARA

The Lieutenant

AT THE FOOT of the rather steep stairs Bresnahan began to smile, partly because he wanted to be smiling and partly because there was Haley, sitting behind his cash register and at work on the crossword puzzle which he practically never finished. It was just like old times, or anyway that much was like old times. Bresnahan wanted everything to be like old times. It was the middle of the afternoon and men and boys were playing various kinds of pool games at four or five of the ten tables. That was about normal. Haley's place was always crowded at night; you always had to wait for a table if you came after seven o'clock, but it did all right in the afternoon too. Something Bresnahan had never particularly noticed before, though: even when a poolroom is half full in the afternoon it is always much quieter than you'd expect. Maybe because everybody just came in out of the daylight and you didn't feel like acting up or yelling your head off in the daylight. Whatever the reason for it, there it was: the place was quieter than you would expect from a half-filled poolroom.

Bresnahan made his way to the cigar counter, where Haley was working on his puzzle. Haley looked up casually and looked back again at his puzzle. Then he recognized Bresnahan. "Hello, Red," said Haley. He got off his stool and put out his hand.

Bresnahan grinned. "Hello, Jerry."

"I didn't hardly know you in the uniform. You look all right, kid."

"Well, feeling okay."

"How long you got?" said Haley.

"Here, or altogether?"

"Altogether," said Haley.

"Well, I'll only be in New York till Thursday. Then they're sending me out making speeches in defense plants."

"Yeah," said Haley. By this time several of the young men of Bresnahan's age came over to say hello, and he was busy shaking hands, but there wasn't anyone he knew very well or liked very much, and something in the way Haley said, "Yeah," worried him. It was what he was afraid of, what he had been afraid of secretly ever since he had left Guadal. It made him more polite than he would otherwise have been to jerks like Haas, for instance, who used to go to Bund meetings and shoot off his mouth about what a wonderful guy Hitler was. He was polite, too, to Murphy and Griffiths, who were for Coughlin, and once asked him did he have English blood, joining the Marines when the right thing for us to do was stay the hell out of it. But these jerks didn't matter. It was Haley he worried about. Haley had been in a war, too, the other one. He was different.

"What's this one, Red?" said some kid whose name he didn't remember.

"That's the Purple Heart," said another kid. "I know that one, but what's this one? I never saw one like this. The stripes are going the wrong way."

"That's a unit citation," said Red. "We all got it."

"What's this one?"

"The Distinguished Service Cross," said one kid. "Isn't it, Red?"

"Yeah, that's right. The D.S.C.," said Red.

"What's these two, or are they the same one?"

"One's for being in before Pearl," said Red.

"Yeah, my brother got one of them."

"The other's for being in the Pacific," said Red.

"And you're a lieutenant. First or second?"

"Second, you dope," said a kid. "First is silver, gold is for second. Why is that, Red?"

"Christ knows. I don't," said Red. He wished they would go away.

"How'd you get along at City Hall?"

"Yeah. You and La G'ardia, how about that? You tell him about the banquet? You tell him about the club giving you a banquet?" said Murphy.

"Yeah. Is La G'ardia coming to the banquet?" said Griffiths.

"I don't know. Did you invite him?" said Red.

"Are you kidding?" said Murphy. "La G'ardia?"

It was coming, and Red knew it. Murphy and Griffiths were putting the needle in. He would lose his temper, take a poke at them, and they would all say what he was afraid they would say, and what was not true: swelled head. Then Haley spoke.

"Why don't you guys go back and play pool and stop being a God-damn nuisance?" They didn't all go right away, but it was enough to break it up, and pretty soon Bresnahan was alone with Haley.

"Have a drink, Red?" Haley kept a bottle of whisky hidden illegally behind the cigarettes.

"I'll take a beer, thanks, Jer'."

Haley set up the beers on the cigar counter. He raised his glass. "All the best, Red," he said.

"Best to you, Jerry," said Red.

"You didn't marry that movin'-picture actress," said Jerry. "The one it said in the paper."

"I was never going to. I'm not gonna marry anybody—not for a while yet. Why should I?"

"Yeah, I guess you're getting plenty," said Haley.

"I didn't mean that."

"Maybe not, but there's plenty around." Haley pointed his glass at Bresnahan's chest.

"Well, I guess you ought to know," said Red.

"No, it was different in my day. We all came back together, those that were left of us. I guess every son of a bitch in the regiment got the Crah de Guerre. Well, so did the regiment, for that matter. They hung it on the regimental colors."

"Yeah, I know," said Bresnahan.

"Anyway, I was married and had two kids by that time. I come back and went to work drivin' a team of horses. Through truckin' was how I got into selling booze. No, there was no movin'-picture actresses after us. No newsreel movies. John F. Hylan was mayor then, I remember, but the only time I ever got close enough to shake hands with him was years later when he come to the club one night."

"Well, everything's publicity nowadays, I guess," said Red.

"You can say that again," said Haley.

"And anyway, you got this before I was born," said Red, pointing with his thumb to the D.S.C. ribbon that Haley had in his lapel.

"Yeah. We use to have a saying, that and a nickel will get you a ride on the subway," said Haley. "Have another beer?"

"I'll buy one."

"Cut it out," said Haley. "I won't be at your banquet." He drew two beers, talking the while. "Have to drink to you here."

"I'm sorry you won't be there."

"Oh, I bought a couple tickets, but I'm alone here half the time. Notice they rack 'em up themselves. I put a new rule into effect a couple months ago. No knocking the cues on the floor. Be go to hell if I'm gonna chase up and down, back and forth, racking up for these punks. If they don't like it they can go someplace else."

"Yeah, I don't blame you," said Red.

"You know anybody you'd like to give the tickets to for the banquet?"

"No. If it wasn't for my old man I wouldn't be there myself."

"Oh," said Haley.

"Wuddia mean oh, Jerry? You meant something by the way you said it."

"Well, if it was the Waldorf-Astoria——"

"If you got something to say come on out and say it. You mean I don't want to go to the banquet because it's our district club. You're trying to say I think it ain't good enough for me only you're afraid to come right out with it."

"Afraid? Afraid of what?" said Haley.

"Afraid if you come out with it I'll take you apart."

"Where, Lieutenant? You want to come back here or will I come over on your side of the counter, where there's more room?" Haley laid down his glass.

"Aa-a-h," said Red. "You're getting childish." His hand was not steady as he finished his beer.

"Don't have pity on me, Lieutenant. A man makes a threat to take me apart, I'd like to see if he can do it." He started to come around the counter.

"So long," said Bresnahan, and walked fast to the stairway. Haley started to follow him but halted when he saw Bresnahan was halfway up the steps. He called out something about moving-picture actresses which Bresnahan could not make out over the sound of his own footsteps. Whatever it was, he didn't want to hear it, and when he got outside he didn't like the sunlight and a feeling that he had lost.

S. J. PERELMAN

The Pipe

AT APPROXIMATELY four o'clock yesterday afternoon the present troubadour, a one-story taxpayer in a wrinkled twenty-two-ounce basket weave and a repossessed Panama, was gaping into the window of Alfred Buntwell Inc., the celebrated tobacconist in Radio City. Above his balding, gargoyle head floated a feathery cloud containing a Mazda bulb labeled "Idea!" Buntwell is a name revered by pipe smokers everywhere; his briars have probably penetrated farther into the earth's far places than the Union Jack. From the steaming jungles of the Gran Chaco to the snows of Kanchanjanga, from the Hook of Holland to the Great Barrier Reef, the white dot on the Buntwell pipestem is the sign of the sahib.

Deep in equatorial Africa, surrounded by head-hunters, Mungo Park clenched a Buntwell pipe between his teeth to maintain his fortitude; it was a battered Buntwell mouthpiece that yielded up the fate of the Franklin polar expedition.

Peering into the shop, jostled by crisp, well-fed executives hurrying toward million-dollar deals, it suddenly struck me that a Buntwell pipe was the key to my future. Here at last was a magic talisman that would transform me from a wormy, chopfallen cipher into a forceful, grim-lipped tycoon. A wave of exultation swept over me; I saw myself in the club car of the Twentieth Century Limited puffing a silver-mounted Buntwell and merging directorates with a careless nod. I, too, could become one of those enviable types who lounged against knotty-pine interiors in four-color advertisements, smoking their Buntwells and fiercely demanding Old Peg-leg Whisky.

"Give me Old Peg-leg's satin smoothness every time," I would growl. "I like a blended rye."

I squared my tiny shoulders and, baring my teeth in the half snarl befitting a major industrialist, entered the shrine. To my chagrin, no obsequious lackey sprang forward to measure my features for the correct model. A cathedral hush enveloped the shop, which had the restrained elegance of a Park Avenue jeweler's. At a chaste showcase displaying a box of panatelas marked down to a thousand dollars, a glacial salesman was attending a fierce old party with white cavalry mustaches redolent of Napoleon brandy. In the background another was languidly demonstrating a cigarette lighter to a dowager weighed down under several pounds of diamonds. I coughed apologetically and gave the salesman a winning smile to indicate that I knew my place. The old grenadier scowled at me from under beetling brows. "Confound it, sir," he roared, "you're not at a cockfight! Blasted place is gettin' noisier than the durbar!" I cleared my throat, in which a fishbone had mysteriously lodged, and made myself as inconspicuous as possible. The salesman hastily explained that the war had brought an influx of foreigners, but his client refused to be mollified.

"Should have caned the bounder," he sputtered. "Country's goin' to the demnition bowwows, dash it all! Now then, Harkrider, what's this infernal nonsense about my Burma cheroots?" He waved aside the salesman's excuse that a convoy had been sunk, commanded that Buntwell himself be summoned.

"But Mr. Buntwell has been dead sixty years, Major," Harkrider protested.

"None of your poppycock!" barked the major. "You tell Buntwell to bring 'em around personally by noon tomorrow or I close my account!" He stamped out, his wattles scarlet with rage, and I sidled forward timidly. In a few badly chosen words I indicated that I required a pipe.

"H'm-m-m," murmured Harkrider grudgingly, surveying my clothes. "Just a moment." He disappeared through a curtain and engaged in a whispered consultation with the manager. I dimly overheard a phrase that sounded like "buttersnipe"; the two were obviously discussing their lunch. At length the salesman re-entered and conducted me sullenly to a showcase. After some deliberation he extracted what appeared to be an old sycamore root fitted with a steel flange that covered the bowl.

"Know anything about pipes?" he inquired patronizingly.

"Well, not exactly," I hesitated. "I had a corncob when I was a little boy——"

"I'm not interested in reminiscences of your youth," he snapped. "Hold still." With a quick gesture he jammed the root into my mouth and backed off, studying my face critically.

"Wh-what is it for?" I stammered.

"Big-game hunting," he returned loftily. I was screwing up my courage to inquire out of which end the bullet came when he suddenly plucked it from my teeth. "No, I don't care for you in that. Let's see now—what's your club?"

"Why—er—uh—the Williams After-Shave Club," I replied politely. "You know, for men whose skins welcome that zestful, bracing tang——"

"No, no," he broke in irritably. "Where do you keep your yacht?" His face darkened and he took a threatening step forward. "You have a yacht, haven't you?"

"Oh—why—er—bub—certainly," I lied skillfully. "He's—I mean, she's laid up right now, the man's scraping her chimney. It got full of seaweeds."

Harkrider glared at me suspiciously, clearly unconvinced.

"Yo heave ho, blow the man down," I hummed nonchalantly, executing a few steps of the sailor's hornpipe. "Thar she blows and sparm at that! A double ration of plum duff for all hands, matey!" The stratagem was successful; with a baffled grunt, Harkrider produced a green velvet jewel case and exhibited a small, charred stub encrusted with salt.

"That's been used before, hasn't it?" I faltered.

"Of course it's been used," he grated. "You don't think you're going to get a new pipe for sixty-seven dollars, do you?"

"Oh no, naturally," I agreed. "Tell you the truth, I had in mind something a bit smaller."

"Smaller?" snorted Harkrider. "You ought to have a calabash to go with that jaw of yours!"

"That's what I was telling the wife only this morning," I chuckled. "Gee, did you ever see anything like it? It's worse than an English bulldog's."

"Well, do you want a calabash or not?" he interrupted. "They're twenty dollars—though I guess you don't see that much money in a year, do you?"

Blushing like a lovely long-stemmed American Beauty rose, I explained that I merely wanted something to knock around in, a homely old jimmy pipe I could suck on while dispensing salty aphorisms like Velvet Joe. After a heart-rending plea, he finally consented to part with a factory second for thirteen dollars, equipped with an ingenious aluminum coil which conveyed the nicotine juice directly into the throat before it lost its potency. To prove my gratitude, I immediately bought a tobacco jar in the shape of a human skull, two pounds of Buntwell's Special Blend of chopped rubies and attar of roses, and a cunning all-purpose reamer equally useful for removing carbon from a pipe or barnacles from a boat. Peeling eighty-three rugs from my skinny little roll, I caught up my purchases and coursed homeward, whistling gems from *The Bartered Bride.*

Right after dinner I disposed myself in my favorite easy chair, lit a cheery blaze in the pipe, and picked up the evening paper.

When I regained consciousness there was a smell in the apartment like a Hindu suttee, and a stranger in a Vandyke was taking my pulse and what remained of my roll. If I go on improving at this rate he's promised I can get up tomorrow. That means I can go out Wednesday and go to jail on Thursday, because in the meantime I've got a date to heave a brick through a plate-glass window in Radio City.

ERNIE PYLE

Captain Waskow

CAPTAIN WASKOW was a company commander in the 36th Division. He had led his company since long before it left the States. He was very young, only in his middle twenties, but he carried in him a sincerity and a gentleness that made people want to be guided by him.

"After my father, he came next," a sergeant told me.

"He always looked after us," a soldier said. "He'd go to bat for us every time."

"I've never known him to do anything unfair," another said.

I was at the foot of the mule train the night they brought Captain Waskow down. The moon was nearly full, and you could see far up the trail, and even part way across the valley below.

Dead men had been coming down the mountain all evening, lashed onto the backs of mules. They came lying belly down across the wooden packsaddles, their heads hanging down onto one side, their stiffened legs sticking out awkwardly from the other, bobbing up and down as the mules walked.

The Italian mule skinners were afraid to walk beside dead men, so Americans had to lead the mules down that night. Even the Americans were reluctant to unlash and lift off the bodies when they got to the bottom, so an officer had to do it himself and ask others to help.

I don't know who that first one was. You feel small in the presence of dead men, and you don't ask silly questions.

They slid him down from the mule and stood him on his feet for a moment. In the half-light he might have been merely a sick man standing there leaning on the others. Then they laid him on the ground in the shadow of the stone wall alongside the road. We left him there beside the road, that first one, and we all went back into the cowshed and sat on water cans or lay on the straw, waiting for the next batch of mules.

Somebody said the dead soldier had been dead for four days, and then nobody said anything more about it. We talked soldier talk for an hour or more; the dead man lay all alone, outside in the shadow of the wall.

Then a soldier came into the cowshed and said there were some more bodies outside. We went out into the road. Four mules stood there in the moonlight, in the road where the trail came down off the mountain. The soldiers who led them stood there waiting.

"This one is Captain Waskow," one of them said quietly.

Two men unlashed his body from the mule and lifted it off and laid it in the shadow beside the stone wall. Other men took the other bodies off. Finally there were five lying end to end in a long row. You don't cover up dead men in the combat zones. They just lie there in the shadows until somebody comes after them.

The unburdened mules moved off to their olive grove. The men in the road seemed reluctant to leave. They stood around, and gradually I could sense them moving, one by one, close to Captain Waskow's body. Not so much to look, I think, as to say something in finality to him and to themselves. I stood close by and I could hear.

One soldier came and looked down, and he said out loud, "God damn it!" That's all he said, and then he walked away.

Another one came, and he said, "God damn it to hell, anyway!" He looked down for a few last moments and then turned away and left.

Another man came. I think he was an officer. It was hard to tell officers from men in the dim light, for everybody was bearded and grimy. The man looked down into the dead captain's face and then spoke directly to him, as though he were alive: "I'm sorry, old man."

Then a soldier came and stood beside the officer and bent over, and he, too, spoke to his dead captain, not in a whisper but awfully tenderly, and he said, "I sure am sorry, sir."

Then the first man squatted down, and he reached down and took the captain's hand, and he sat there for a full five minutes holding the dead hand in his own and looking intently into the dead face. And he never uttered a sound all the time he sat there.

Finally he put the hand down. He reached over and gently straightened the points of the captain's shirt collar, and then he sort of rearranged the tattered edges of the uniform around the wound, and then he got up and walked away down the road in the moonlight, all alone.

The rest of us went back into the cowshed, leaving the five dead men lying in a line end to end in the shadow of the low stone wall. We lay down on the straw in the cowshed, and pretty soon we were all asleep.

ELLERY QUEEN

The Hanging Acrobat

LONG, LONG AGO in the Incubation Period of Man—long before booking agents, five-a-days, theatrical boardinghouses, subway circuits, and *Variety*—when Megatherium roamed the trees, when Broadway was going through its first glacial period, and when the first vaudeville show was planned by the first lop-eared, low-browed, hairy impresario, it was decreed: "The acrobat shall be first."

Why the acrobat should be first no one ever explained; but that this was a dubious honor everyone on the bill—including the acrobat—realized only too well. For it was recognized even then, in the infancy of show business, that the first shall be last in the applause of the audience. And all through the ages, in courts and courtyards and feeble theaters, it was the acrobat—whether he was called buffoon, *farceur*, merry-andrew, tumbler, mountebank, Harlequin, or *punchinello*—who was thrown, first among his fellow mimes, to the lions of entertainment to whet their appetites for the more luscious feasts to come. So that to this day their muscular miracles are performed hard on the overture's last wall-shaking blare, performed with a simple resignation that speaks well for the mildness and resilience of the whole acrobatic tribe.

Hugo Brinkerhof knew nothing of the whimsical background of his profession. All he knew was that his father and mother had been acrobats before him with a traveling show in Germany, that he possessed huge smooth muscles with sap and spring and strength in them, and that nothing gave him more satisfaction than the sight of a glittering trapeze. With his trapeze and his Myra, and the indulgent applause of audiences from Seattle to Okeechobee, he was well content.

Now Hugo was very proud of Myra, a small, wiry, handsome woman with the agility of a cat and something of the cat's sleepy green eyes. He had met her in the office of Bregman, the booker, and the sluggish heart under his magnificent chest had told him that this was his fate and his woman. It was Myra who had renamed the act "Atlas & Co." when they had married between the third and fourth shows in Indianapolis. It was Myra who had fought tooth and nail for better billing. It was Myra who had conceived and perfected the dazzling pinwheel of their finale. It was Myra's shapely little body and Myra's lithe gyrations on the high trapeze and Myra's sleepy smile that had made Atlas & Co. an "acrobatic divertissement acclaimed from coast to coast," had earned them a pungent paragraph in *Variety*, and had brought them with other topnotchers on the Bregman string to the big circuit.

That everyone loved his Myra mighty Brinkerhof, the Atlas, knew with a swelling of his chest. Who could resist her? There had been that baritone with the dancing act in Boston, the revue comedian in Newark, the tap dancer in Buffalo, the adagio in Washington. Now there were others—Tex Crosby, the Crooning Cowboy (Songs & Patter); the Great Gordi (Successor to Houdini); Sailor Sam, the low comic. They had all been on the same bill together now for weeks, and they all loved sleepy-eyed Myra, and big Atlas smiled his indulgent smile and thrilled in his stupid, stolid way to their admiration. For was not his Myra the finest female acrobat in the world and the most lovely creature in creation?

And now Myra was dead.

It was Brinkerhof himself, with a gaunt suffering look about him that mild spring night, who had given the alarm. It was five o'clock in the morning and his Myra had not come home to their theatrical boarding-house room on Forty-seventh Street. He had stayed behind with his wife after the last performance in the Metropole Theater at Columbus Circle to try out a new trick. They had rehearsed and then he had dressed in haste, leaving her in their joint dressing room. He had had an appointment with Bregman, the booker, to discuss terms of a new contract. He had promised to meet her back at their lodgings. But when he had returned—*ach!* no Myra. He had hurried back to the theater; it was locked up for the night. And all the long night he had waited. . . .

"Prob'ly out bummin', buddy," the desk lieutenant at the West Forty-seventh Street station had said with a yawn. "Go home and sleep it off."

But Brinkerhof had been vehement, with many gestures. "She never haf this done before. I haf telephoned it the theater, too, but there iss no answer. Captain, find her, please!"

"These heinies," sighed the lieutenant to a lounging detective. "All right, Baldy, see what you can do. If she's piffed in a joint somewhere, give this big hunk a clout on the jaw."

So Baldy and the pale giant had gone to see what they could do, and they had found the Metropole Theater locked, as Brinkerhof had said, and it was almost six in the morning and dawn was coming up across the park and Baldy had dragged Brinkerhof into an all-night restaurant for a mug of coffee. And they had waited around the theater until seven, when old Perk, the stage-door man and timer, had come in, and he had opened the theater for them, and they had gone backstage to the dressing room of Atlas & Co. and found Myra hanging from one of the sprinkler pipes with a dirty old rope, thick as a hawser, around her pretty neck.

And Atlas had sat down like the dumb hunk he was and put his shaggy head between his hands and stared at the hanging body of his wife with the silent grief of some Norse god crushed to earth.

When Mr. Ellery Queen pushed through the chattering crowd of re-porters and detectives backstage and convinced Sergeant Velie through the door of the dressing room that he was indeed who he was, he found his father, the inspector, holding court in the stuffy little room before a gang of nervous theatrical people. It was only nine o'clock and Ellery was grumbling through his teeth at the unconscionable inconsiderateness of murderers. But neither the burly sergeant nor little Inspector Queen was impressed with his grumblings to the point of lending ear; and indeed the grumblings ceased after he had taken one swift look at what still hung from the sprinkler pipe.

Brinkerhof sat red-eyed and huge and collapsed in the chair before his wife's dressing table. "I haf told you everything," he muttered. "We rehearsed the new trick. It was then an appointment with Mr. Bregman. I went." A fat hard-eyed man, Bregman the booker, nodded curtly. "Undt that's all. Who—why—I do not know."

In a bass sotto voce Sergeant Velie recited the sparse facts. Ellery took another look at the dead woman. Her stiff muscles of thigh and leg bulged in rigor mortis beneath the tough thin silk of her flesh tights. The green eyes were widely open. And she swayed a little in a faint dance of death. Ellery looked away and at the people.

Baldy, the precinct man, was there, flushed with his sudden popularity with the newspaper boys. A tall thin man who looked like Gary Cooper rolled a cigarette beside Bregman—Tex Crosby, the cowboy crooner; and he leaned against the grime-smeared wall and eyed the Great Gordi—in person—with flinty dislike. Gordi had a hawk's beak and sleek black mustachios and long olive fingers and black eyes; and he said nothing. Little Sam, the comedian, had purple pouches under his tired eyes and he looked badly in need of a drink. But Joe Kelly, the house manager, did not, for he smelled like a brewery and kept mumbling something drunken and obscene beneath his breath.

"How long you been married, Brinkerhof?" growled the inspector.

"Two years. *Ja.* In Indianapolis that was, Herr Inspektor."

"Was she ever married before?"

"*Nein.*"

"You?"

"*Nein.*"

"Did she or you have any enemies?"

"*Gott, nein!*"

"Happy, were you?"

"Like two doves we was," muttered Brinkerhof.

Ellery strolled over to the corpse and stared up. Her ropy-veined wrists were jammed behind her back, bound with a filthy rouge-stained towel, as were her ankles. Her feet dangled a yard from the floor. A battered stepladder leaned against one of the walls, folded up; a man standing upon it, he mused, could easily have reached the sprinkler pipe, flung the rope over it, and hauled up the light body.

"The stepladder was found against the wall there?" he murmured to the sergeant, who had come up behind him and was staring with interest at the dead woman.

"Yep. It's always kept out near the switchboard light panel."

"No suicide, then," said Ellery. "At least that's something."

"Nice figger, ain't she?" said the sergeant admiringly.

"Velie, you're a ghoul. . . . This *is* a pretty problem."

The dirty rope seemed to fascinate him. It had been wound tightly about the woman's throat twice, in parallel strands, and concealed her flesh like the iron necklace of a Ubangi woman. A huge knot had been fashioned beneath her right ear, and another knot held the rope to the pipe above.

"Where does this rope come from?" he said abruptly.

"From around an old trunk we found backstage, Mr. Queen. Trunk's been here for years. In the prop room. Nothin' in it; some trouper left it. Want to see it?"

"I'll take your word for it, Sergeant. Property room, eh?" He sauntered back to the door to look the people over again.

Brinkerhof was mumbling something about how happy he and Myra had been, and what he would do to the *verdammte Teufel* who had wrung his pretty Myra's neck. His huge hands opened and closed convulsively. "Joost like a flower she was," he said. "Joost like a flower."

"Nuts," snapped Joe Kelly, the house manager, weaving on his feet like a punch-drunk fighter. "She was a floozy, Inspector. You ask *me*," and he leered at Inspector Queen.

"Floo-zie?" said Brinkerhof with difficulty, getting to his feet. "What iss that?"

Sam, the comic, blinked his puffy little eyes rapidly and said in a hoarse voice: "You're crazy, Kelly, crazy. Wha'd'ye want to say that for? He's pickled, Chief."

"Pickled, am I?" screamed Kelly, livid. "Aw right, you as' *him,* then!" and he pointed a wavering finger at the tall thin man.

"What is this?" crooned the inspector, his eyes bright. "Get together, gentlemen. You mean, Kelly, that Mrs. Brinkerhof was playing around with Crosby here?"

Brinkerhof made a sound like a baffled gorilla and lunged forward. His long arms were curved flails and he made for the cowboy's throat with the unswervable fury of an animal. Sergeant Velie grabbed his wrist and twisted it up behind the vast back, and Baldy jumped in and clung to the giant's other arm. He swayed there, struggling and never taking his eyes from the tall thin man, who had not stirred but who had gone very pale.

"Take him away," snapped the inspector to Sergeant Velie. "Turn him over to a couple of the boys and keep him outside till he calms down." They hustled the hoarsely breathing acrobat out of the room. "Now, Crosby, spill it."

"Nothin' to spill," drawled the cowboy, but his drawl was a little breathless and his eyes were narrowed to wary slits. "I'm Texas an' I don't scare easy, Mr. Cop. He's just a squarehead. An' as for that pie-eyed sawback over there"—he stared malevolently at Kelly—"he better learn to keep his trap shut."

"He's been two-timin' the hunk!" screeched Kelly. "Don't b'lieve him, Chief! That sassy little tramp got what was comin' to her, I tell y'! She's been pullin' the wool over the hunk's eyes all the way from Chi to Beantown!"

"You've said enough," said the Great Gordi quietly. "Can't you see the man's drunk, Inspector, and not responsible? Myra was—companionable. She may have taken a drink or two with Crosby or myself on the sly once or twice—Brinkerhof didn't like her to, so she never drank in front of him—but that's all."

"Just friendly, hey?" murmured the inspector. "Well, who's lying? If you know anything solid, Kelly, come out with it."

"I know what I know," sneered the manager. "An' when it comes to that, Chief, the Great Gordi could tell you somethin' about the little bum. Ought to be able to! He swiped her from Crosby only a couple o' weeks ago."

"Quiet, both of you," snapped the old gentleman as the Texan and the dark-mustachioed man stirred. "And how could you know that, Kelly?"

The dead woman swayed faintly, dancing her noiseless dance.

"I heard Tex there bawl Gordi out only the other day," said Kelly thickly, "for makin' the snatch. An' I saw Gordi grapplin' with her in the wings on'y yest'day. How's 'at? Reg'lar wrestler, Gordi. Can he clinch!"

Nobody said anything. The tall Texan's fingers whitened as he glared at the drunken man, and Gordi the magician did nothing at all but breathe. Then the door opened and two men came in—Dr. Prouty, assistant medical examiner, and a big shambling man with a sea-red face.

Everybody relaxed. The inspector said: "High time, Doc. Don't touch her, though, till Bradford can take a look at that knot up there. Go on, Braddy; on the pipe. Use the ladder."

The shambling man took the stepladder and set it up and climbed beside the dangling body and looked at the knot behind the woman's ear and the knot at the top of the pipe. Dr. Prouty pinched the woman's legs.

Ellery sighed and began to prowl. Nobody paid any attention to him; they were all pallidly intent upon the two men near the body.

Something disturbed him; he did not know what, could not put his finger precisely upon the root of the disturbance. Perhaps it was a feeling in the air, an aura of tension about the silent dangling woman in tights. But it made him restless. He had the feeling . . .

He found the loaded revolver in the top drawer of the woman's dressing table—a shiny little pearl-handled .22 with the initials MB on the butt. And his eyes narrowed and he glanced at his father, and his father nodded. So he prowled some more. And then he stopped short, his gray eyes suspicious.

On the rickety wooden table in the center of the room lay a long sharp nickel-plated letter opener among a clutter of odds and ends. He picked it up carefully and squinted along its glittering length in the light. But there was no sign of blood.

He put it down and continued to prowl.

And the very next thing he noticed was the cheap battered gas burner on the floor at the other side of the room. Its pipe fitted snugly over a gas outlet in the wall, but the gas tap had been turned off. He felt the little burner; it was stone cold.

So he went to the closet with the oddest feeling of inevitability. And sure enough, just inside the open door of the closet lay a wooden box full of carpenter's tools, with a heavy steel hammer prominently on top. There was a mess of shavings on the floor near the box, and the edge of the closet door was unpainted and virgin fresh from a plane.

His eyes were very sharp now, and deeply concerned. He went quickly to the inspector's side and murmured: "The revolver. The woman's?"

"Yes."

"Recent acquisition?"

"No. Brinkerhof bought it for her soon after they were married. For protection, he said."

"Poor protection, I should say," shrugged Ellery, glancing at the headquarters men. The shambling red-faced man had just lumbered off the ladder with an expression of immense surprise. Sergeant Velie, who had returned, was mounting the ladder with a penknife clutched in his big fingers. Dr. Prouty waited expectantly below. The sergeant began sawing at the rope tied to the sprinkler pipe.

"What's that box of tools doing in the closet?" continued Ellery, without removing his gaze from the dead woman.

"Stage carpenter was in here yesterday fixing the door—it had warped or something. Union rules are strict, so he quit the job unfinished. What of it?"

"Everything," said Ellery, "of it." The Great Gordi was quietly watching his mouth; Ellery seemed not to notice. The little comedian, Sam, was shrunken in a corner, eyes popping at the sergeant. And the Texan was smoking without enjoyment, not looking at anyone or anything. "Simply everything. It's one of the most remarkable things I've ever run across."

The inspector looked bewildered. "But, El, for cripe's sake—remarkable? I don't see——"

"You should," said Ellery impatiently. "A child should. And yet it's astounding, when you come to think of it. Here's a room with four dandy weapons in it—a loaded revolver, a letter cutter, a gas burner, and a hammer. And yet the murderer deliberately trussed the woman with the towels, deliberately left this room, deliberately crossed the stage to the property room, unwound that rusty old rope from a worthless trunk discarded years ago by some nameless actor, carried the rope and the ladder from beside the switchboard back to this room, used the ladder to sling the rope over the pipe and fasten the knot, and strung the woman up."

"Well, but——"

"Well, but why?" cried Ellery. "Why? Why did the murderer ignore the four simple, easy, handy methods of murder here—shooting, stabbing, asphyxiation, bludgeoning—and go to all that extra trouble to *hang* her?"

Dr. Prouty was kneeling beside the dead woman, whom the sergeant had deposited with a thump on the dirty floor.

The red-faced man shambled over and said: "It's got me, Inspector."

"What's got you?" snapped Inspector Queen.

"This knot." His thick red fingers held a length of knotted rope. "The one behind her ear is just ordinary; even clumsy for the job of breakin' her neck." He shook his head. "But this one, the one that was tied around the pipe—well, sir, it's got me."

"An unfamiliar knot?" said Ellery slowly, puzzling over its complicated convolutions.

"New to me, Mr. Queen. All the years I been expertin' on knots for the Department I never seen one like that. Ain't a sailor's knot, I can tell you that; and it ain't Western."

"Might be the work of an amateur," muttered the inspector, pulling the rope through his fingers. "A knot that just happened."

The expert shook his head. "No sir, I wouldn't say that at all. It's some kind of a variation. Not an accident. Whoever tied that knew his knots."

Bradford shambled off and Dr. Prouty looked up from his work. "Hell, I can't do anything here," he snapped. "I'll have to take this body over to the morgue and work on it there. The boys are waiting outside."

"When'd she kick off, Doc?" demanded the inspector, frowning.

"About midnight last night. Can't tell closer than that. She died, of course, of suffocation."

"Well, give us a report. Probably nothing, but it never hurts. Thomas, get that doorman in here."

When Dr. Prouty and the morgue men had gone with the body and Sergeant Velie had hauled in old Perk, the stage-door man and watchman, the inspector growled: "What time'd you lock up last night, mister?"

Old Perk was hoarse with nervousness. "Honest t' Gawd, Inspector, I didn't mean nothin' by it. On'y Mr. Kelly here'd fire me if he knew. I was that sleepy——"

"What's this?" said the inspector softly.

"Myra told me after the last show last night she an' Atlas were gonna rehearse a new stunt. I didn't wanna wait aroun', y'see," the old man whined, "so, seein' as nob'dy else was in the house that late, the cleanin' women gone an' all, I locked up everything but the stage door an' I says to Myra an' Atlas, I says: 'When ye leave, folks,' I says, 'jest slam the stage door.' An' I went home."

"Rats," said the inspector irritably. "Now we'll never know who could have come in and who didn't. Anybody could have sneaked back without being seen or waited around in hiding until——" He bit his lip. "You men there, where'd you all go after the show last night?"

The three actors started simultaneously. It was the Great Gordi who spoke first, in his soft smooth voice that was now uneasy. "I went directly to my rooming house and to bed."

"Anybody see you come in? You live in the same hole as Brinkerhof?"

The magician shrugged. "No one saw me. Yes, I do."

"You, Texas?"

The cowboy drawled: "I moseyed round to a speak somewhere an' got drunk."

"What speak?"

"Dunno. I was primed. Woke up in my room this mornin' with a head."

"You boys sure are in a tough spot," said the inspector sarcastically. "Can't even fix good alibis for yourself. Well, how about you, Mr. Comedian?"

The comic said eagerly: "Oh, I can prove where I was, Inspector. I went around to a joint I know an' can get twenny people to swear to it."

"What time?"

"Round midnight."

The inspector snorted and said: "Beat it. But hang around. I'll be wanting you boys, maybe. Take 'em away, Thomas, before I lose my temper."

Long, long ago—when, it will be recalled, Megatherium roamed the trees—the same lop-eared impresario who said: "The acrobat shall be first," also laid down the dictum that: "The show must go on," and for as little reason. Accidents might happen, the juvenile might run off with the female lion tamer, the ingénue might be howling drunk, the lady in the fifth row, right, might have chosen the theater to be the scene of her monthly attack of epilepsy, fire might break out in Dressing Room A, but the show must go on. Not even a rare juicy homicide may annul the sacred dictum. The show must go on despite hell, high water, drunken managers named Kelly, and the Fantastic Affair of the Hanging Acrobat.

So it was not strange that when the Metropole began to fill with its dribble of early patrons there was no sign that a woman had been slain the night before within its gaudy walls and that police and detectives roved its backstage with suspicious, if baffled, eyes.

The murder was just an incident to show business. It would rate two columns in *Variety*.

Inspector Richard Queen chafed in the hard seat in the fifteenth row while Ellery sat beside him sunk in thought. Stranger than everything had been Ellery's insistence that they remain to witness the performance. There was a motion picture to sit through—a film which, bitterly, the inspector pointed out he had seen—a newsreel, an animated cartoon. . . .

It was while "Coming Attractions" were flitting over the screen that Ellery rose and said: "Let's go backstage. There's something——" He did not finish.

They passed behind the dusty boxes on the right and went backstage through the iron door guarded by a uniformed officer. The vast bare reaches of the stage and wings were oppressed with an unusual silence. Manager Kelly, rather the worse for wear, sat on a broken chair near the light panel and gnawed his unsteady fingers. None of the vaudeville actors was in evidence.

"Kelly," said Ellery abruptly, "is there anything like a pair of field glasses in the house?"

The Irishman gaped. "What the hell would you be wantin' *them* for?"

"Please."

Kelly fingered a passing stagehand, who vanished and reappeared shortly with the desired binoculars. The inspector grunted: "So what?"

Ellery adjusted them to his eyes. "I don't know," he said, shrugging. "It's just a hunch."

There was a burst of music from the pit: the overture.

"'Poet and Peasant,'" snarled the inspector. "Don't they ever get anything new?"

But Ellery said nothing. He merely waited, binoculars ready, eyes fixed on the now footlighted stage. And it was only when the last blare had died away, and grudging splatters of applause came from the orchestra, and the announcement cards read: "Atlas & Co.," that the inspector lost something of his irritability and even became interested. For when the curtains slithered up there was Atlas himself, bowing and smiling, his immense body impressive in flesh tights; and there beside him stood a tall smiling woman with golden hair and at least one golden tooth which flashed in the footlights. And she, too, wore flesh tights. For Brinkerhof, with the mildness and resilience of all acrobats, had insisted on taking his regular turn, and Bregman the booker had sent him another partner, and the two strangers had spent an hour rehearsing their intimate embraces and clutches and swingings and nuzzlings before the first performance. The show must go on.

Atlas and the golden woman went through an intricate series of tumbles and equilibristic maneuvers. The orchestra played brassy music. Trapezes dived stageward. Simple swings. Somersaults in the air. The drummer rolled and smashed his cymbal.

Ellery made no move to use the binoculars. He and the inspector and Kelly stood in the wings, and none of them said anything, although Kelly was breathing hard like a man who has just come out of deep water for air. A queer little figure materialized beside them; Ellery turned his head slowly. But it was only Sailor Sam, the low comic, rigged out in a naval uniform three sizes too large for his skinny little frame, his face daubed liberally with grease paint. He kept watching Atlas & Co. without expression.

"Good, ain't he?" he said at last in a small voice.

No one replied. But Ellery turned to the manager and whispered: "Kelly, keep your eyes open for——" and his voice sank so low neither the comedian nor Inspector Queen could hear what he said. Kelly looked puzzled; his bloodshot eyes opened a little wider; but he nodded and swallowed, riveting his gaze upon the whirling figures on the stage.

And when it was all over and the orchestra was executing the usual *crescendo sostenuto* and Atlas was bowing and smiling and the woman was curtsying and showing her gold tooth and the curtain dropped swiftly, Ellery glanced at Kelly. But Kelly shook his head.

The announcement cards changed. "Sailor Sam." There was a burst of fresh fast music, and the little man in the oversize naval uniform grinned three times, as if trying it out, drew a deep breath, and scuttled out upon the stage to sprawl full length with his gnomish face jutting over the footlights to the accompaniment of surprised laughter from the darkness below.

They watched from the wings, silent.

The comedian had a clever routine. Not only was he a travesty upon all sailormen, but he was a travesty upon all sailormen in their cups. He drooled and staggered and was silent and then chattered suddenly, and he described a mythical voyage and fell all over himself climbing an imaginary mast and fell silent again to go into a pantomime that rocked the house.

The inspector said grudgingly: "Why, he's as good as Jimmy Barton any day, with that drunk routine of his."

"Just a slob," said Kelly out of the corner of his mouth.

Sailor Sam made his exit by the complicated expedient of swimming off the stage. He stood in the wings, panting, his face streaming perspiration. He ran out for a bow. They thundered for more. He vanished. He reappeared. He vanished again. There was a stubborn look on his pixy face.

"Sam!" hissed Kelly. "F'r cripe's sake, Sam, give 'em 'at encore rope number. F'r cripe's sake, Sam——"

"Rope number?" said Ellery quietly.

The comedian licked his lips. Then his shoulders drooped and he slithered out onto the stage again. There was a shout of laughter and the house quieted at once. Sam scrambled to his feet, weaving and blinking blearily.

"'Hoy there!" he howled suddenly. "Gimme rope!"

A papier-mâché cigar three feet long dropped to the stage from the opposite wings. Laughter. "Naw! Rope! Rope!" the little man screamed, dancing up and down.

A blackish rope snaked down from the flies. Miraculously it coiled over his scrawny shoulders. He struggled with it. He scrambled after its tarred ends. He executed fantastic flying leaps. And always the tarred ends eluded him, and constantly he became more and more enmeshed in the black coils as he wrestled with the rope.

The gallery broke down. The man *was* funny; even Kelly's dour face lightened, and the inspector was frankly grinning. Then it was over and two stagehands darted out of the wings and pulled the comedian off the stage, now a helpless bundle trussed in rope. His face under the paint was chalk-white. He extricated himself easily enough from the coils.

"Good boy," chuckled the inspector. "That was fine!"

Sam muttered something and trudged away to his dressing room. The black rope lay where it had fallen. Ellery glanced at it once and then turned his attention back to the stage. The music had changed. A startlingly beautiful tenor voice rang through the theater. The orchestra was playing softly "Home on the Range." The curtain rose on Tex Crosby.

The tall thin man was dressed in gaudiest stage-cowboy costume. And yet he wore it with an air of authority. The pearl-butted six-shooters protruding from his holsters did not seem out of place. His big white sombrero shaded a gaunt Western face. His legs were a little bowed. The man was real.

He sang Western songs, told a few funny stories in his soft Texan drawl, and all the while his long-fingered hands were busy with a lariat. He made the lariat live. From the moment the curtain rose upon his lanky figure the lariat was in motion, and it did not subside through the jokes, the patter, even the final song, which was inevitably "The Last Roundup."

"Tinhorn Will Rogers," sneered Kelly, blinking his bloodshot eyes.

For the first time Ellery raised the binoculars. When the Texan had taken his last bow Ellery glanced inquiringly at the manager. Kelly shook his head.

The Great Gordi made his entrance in a clap of thunder, a flash of lightning, and a black satanic cloak, faced with red. There was something impressive about his very charlatanism. His black eyes glittered and his mustache points quivered above his lips and his beak jutted like an eagle's; and meanwhile neither his hands nor his mouth kept still.

The magician had a smooth, effortless patter which kept his audience amused and diverted their attention from the fluent mysteries of his hands. There was nothing startling in his routine, but it was a polished performance that fascinated. He performed seeming miracles with cards. His sleight of hand with coins and handkerchiefs was, to the layman, amazing. His evening clothes apparently concealed scores of wonders.

They watched with a mounting tension while he went through his bag of tricks. For the first time Ellery noticed, with a faint start, that Brinkerhof, still in tights, was crouched in the opposite wings. The big man's eyes were fixed upon the magician's face. They ignored the flashing fingers, the swift movements of the black-clad body. Only the face . . . In Brinkerhof's eyes was neither rage nor venom; just watchfulness. What was the matter with the man? Ellery reflected that it was just as well that Gordi was unconscious of the acrobat's scrutiny; those subtle hands might not operate so fluidly.

Despite the tension the magician's act seemed interminable. There were tricks with odd-looking pieces of apparatus manipulated from backstage by assistants. The house was with him, completely in his grasp.

"Good show," said the inspector in a surprised voice. "This is darned good vaudeville."

"It'll get by," muttered Kelly. There was something queer on his face. He, too, was watching intently.

And suddenly something went wrong on the stage. The orchestra seemed bewildered. Gordi had concluded a trick, bowed, and stepped into the wings near the watching men. Not even the curtain was prepared. The orchestra had swung into another piece. The conductor's head was jerking from side to side in a panicky, inquiring manner.

"What's the matter?" demanded the inspector.

Kelly snarled: "He's left out his last trick. Good hunch, Mr. Queen. . . . Hey, ham," he growled to the magician, "finish your act, damn you! While they're still clappin'!"

Gordi was very pale. He did not turn; they could see only his left cheek and the rigidity of his back. Nor did he reply. Instead, with all the reluctance of a tyro, he slowly stepped back onto the stage. From the other side Brinkerhof watched. And this time Gordi, with a convulsive start, saw him.

"What's coming off here?" said the inspector softly, as alert as a wren. Ellery swung the glasses to his eyes.

A trapeze hurtled stageward from the flies—a simple steel bar suspended from two slender strands. A smooth yellow rope, very new in appearance, accompanied it from above, falling to the stage.

The magician worked very, very, painfully slowly. The house was silent. Even the music had stopped.

Gordi grasped the rope and did something with it; his back concealed what he was doing; then he swung about and held up his left hand. Tied with an enormous and complicated knot to his left wrist was the end of the yellow rope. He picked up the other end and leaped a little, securing the trapeze. At the level of his chest he steadied it and turned again so that he concealed what he was doing, and when he swung about once more they saw that the rope's other end was now knotted in the same way about the steel bar of the trapeze. He raised his right hand in signal and the drummer began a long roll.

Instantly the trapeze began to rise, and they saw that the rope was only four feet long. As the bar rose, Gordi's lithe body rose with it, suspended from the bar by the full length of the rope attached to his wrist. The trapeze came to a stop when the magician's feet were two yards from the stage.

Ellery squinted carefully through the powerful lenses. Across the stage Brinkerhof crouched.

Gordi now began to squirm and kick and jump in the air, indicating in pantomime that he was securely tied to the trapeze and that not even the heavy weight of his suspended body could undo the knots; in fact, was tightening them.

"It's a good trick," muttered Kelly. "In a second a special drop'll come down, an' in eight seconds it'll go up again and there he'll be on the stage, with the rope on the floor."

Gordi cried in a muffled voice: "Ready!"

But at the same instant Ellery said to Kelly: "*Quick!* Drop the curtain! This instant. Signal those men in the flies, Kelly!"

Kelly leaped into action. He shouted something unintelligible and after a second of hesitation the main curtain dropped. The house was dumb with astonishment; they thought it was part of the trick. Gordi began to struggle frantically, reaching up the trapeze with his free hand.

"Lower that trapeze!" roared Ellery on the cut-off stage now, waving his arms at the staring men above. "Lower it! *Gordi, don't move!*"

The trapeze came down with a thud. Gordi sprawled on the stage, his mouth working. Ellery leaped upon him, an open blade in hand. He cut quickly, savagely, at the rope. It parted, its torn end dangling from the trapeze.

"You may get up now," said Ellery, panting a little. "It's the knot I wanted to see, Signor Gordi."

They crowded around Ellery and the fallen man, who seemed incapable of rising. He sat on the stage, his mouth still working, naked fear in his eyes. Brinkerhof was there, his muscular biceps rigid. Crosby, Sailor Sam, Sergeant Velie, Kelly, Bregman. . . .

The inspector stared at the knot on the trapeze. Then he slowly took from his pocket a short length of the dirty old rope which had hanged Myra Brinkerhof. The knot was there. He placed it beside the knot on the trapeze.

They were identical.

"Well, Gordi," said the inspector wearily, "I guess it's all up with you. Get up, man. I'm holding you for murder, and anything you say——"

Without a sound Brinkerhof, the mighty Atlas, sprang upon the man on the floor, big hands on Gordi's throat. It took the combined efforts of the Texan, Sergeant Velie, and Manager Kelly to tear the acrobat off.

Gordi gasped, holding his throat: "I didn't do it, I tell you! I'm innocent! Yes, we had—we lived together. I loved her. But why should I kill her? I didn't do it. For God's sake——"

"*Schwein,*" growled Atlas, his chest heaving.

Sergeant Velie tugged at Gordi's collar. "Come on, come on there. . . ."

Ellery drawled: "Very pretty. My apologies, Mr. Gordi. Of course you didn't do it."

A shocked silence fell. From behind the heavy curtain voices—loud voices—came. The feature picture had been flashed on the screen.

"Didn't—do—it?" muttered Brinkerhof.

'But the knots, El," began the inspector in a bewildered voice.

"Precisely. The knots." In defiance of fire regulations Ellery lit a cigarette and puffed thoughtfully. "The hanging of Myra Brinkerhof has bothered me from the beginning. Why was she *hanged?* In preference to one of four other methods of committing murder which were simpler, more expedient, easier of accomplishment, and offered no extra work, as hanging did? The point is that if the murderer chose the hard way, the complicated way, the roundabout way of killing her, then he chose that way *deliberately*."

Gordi was staring with his mouth open. Kelly was ashen pale.

"But why," murmured Ellery, "did he choose hanging deliberately? Obviously because hanging offered the murderer some peculiar advantage not offered by any of the other four methods. Well, what advantage could hanging conceivably offer that shooting, stabbing, gassing, or hammering to death could not? To put it another way, what is characteristic of hanging that is not characteristic of shooting and the rest? Only one thing. *The use of a rope*."

"Well, but I still don't see——" frowned the inspector.

"Oh, it's clear enough, Dad. There's something about the rope that made the murderer use it in preference to the other methods. But what's the outstanding significance of this particular rope—the rope used to hang Myra Brinkerhof? *Its knot*—its peculiar knot, so peculiar that not even the Department's expert could identify it. In other words, the use of that knot was like the leaving of a fingerprint. Whose knot is it? Gordi's, the magician's—and, I suspect, his exclusively."

"I can't understand it," cried Gordi. "Nobody knew my knot. It's one I developed myself. . . ." Then he bit his lip and fell silent.

"Exactly the point. I realize that stage magicians have developed knot making to a remarkable degree. Wasn't it Houdini who . . . ?"

"The Davenport brothers, too," muttered the magician. "My knot is a variation on one of their creations."

"Quite so," drawled Ellery. "So I say, had Mr. Gordi wanted to kill

Myra Brinkerhof, would he have deliberately chosen *the single method that incriminated him,* and him alone? Certainly not if he were reasonably intelligent. Did he tie his distinctive knot, then, from sheer habit, subconsciously? Conceivable, but then why had he chosen hanging in the first place, when those four easier methods were nearer to his hand?" Ellery slapped the magician's back. "So, I say—our apologies, Gordi. The answer is very patently that you're being framed by someone who deliberately chose the hanging-plus-knot method to implicate you in a crime you're innocent of."

"But he says nobody else knew his confounded knot," growled the inspector. "If what you say is true, El, somebody must have learned it on the sly."

"Very plausible," murmured Ellery. "Any suggestions, signor?"

The magician got slowly to his feet, brushing off his dress suit. Brinkerhof gaped stupidly at him, at Ellery.

"I don't know," said Gordi, very pale. "I thought no one knew. Not even my technical assistants. But then we've all been traveling on the same bill for weeks. I suppose if someone wanted to . . ."

"I see," said Ellery thoughtfully. "So there's a dead end, eh?"

"Dead beginning," snapped his father. "And thanks, my son, for the assistance. *You're* a help!"

"I tell you very frankly," said Ellery the next day in his father's office, "I don't know what it's all about. The only thing I'm sure of is Gordi's innocence. The murderer knew very well that somebody would notice the unusual knot Gordi uses in his rope-escape illusion. As for motive——"

"Listen," snarled the inspector, thoroughly out of temper, "I can see through glass the same way you can. They all had motive. Crosby kicked over by the dame, Gordi . . . Did you know that this little comedian was sniffin' around Myra's skirts the last couple of weeks? Trying his darnedest to make her. And Kelly's had monkey business with her, too, on a former appearance at the Metropole."

"Don't doubt it," said Ellery somberly. "The call of the flesh. She was an alluring little trick, at that. Real old Boccaccio melodrama, with the stupid husband playing cuckold——"

The door opened and Dr. Prouty, assistant medical examiner, stumped in, looking annoyed. He dropped into a chair and clumped his feet on the inspector's desk. "Guess what?" he said.

"I'm a rotten guesser," said the old gentleman sourly.

"Little surprise for you, gentlemen. For me too. The woman wasn't hanged."

"What!" cried the Queens together.

"Fact. She was dead when she was swung up." Dr. Prouty squinted at his ragged cigar.

"Well I'll be eternally damned," said Ellery softly. He sprang from his chair and shook the physician's shoulder. "Prouty, for heaven's sake, don't look so smug! What killed her? Gun, gas, knife, poison——"

"Fingers."

"Fingers?"

Dr. Prouty shrugged. "No question about it. When I took that dirty hemp off her lovely neck I found the distinct marks of fingers on the skin. It was a tight rope, and all that, but there were the marks, gentlemen. She was choked to death by a man's hands and then strung up—why, *I* don't know."

"Well," said Ellery. "Well," he said again, and straightened. *"Very* interesting. I begin to scent the proverbial rodent. Tell us more, good leech."

"Certainly is queer," muttered the inspector, sucking his mustache.

"Something even queerer," drawled Dr. Prouty. "You boys have seen choked stiffs plenty. What's the characteristic of the finger marks?"

Ellery was watching him intently. "Characteristic?" He frowned. "Don't know what you mean . . . Oh!" His gray eyes glittered. "Don't tell me. . . . The usual marks point upward, thumbs toward the chin."

"Smart lad. Well, these marks don't. They all point *downward.*"

Ellery stared for a long moment. Then he seized Dr. Prouty's limp hand and shook it violently. "Eureka! Prouty, old sock, you're the answer to a logician's prayer! Dad, come on!"

"What is this?" scowled the inspector. "You're too fast for me. Come where?"

"To the Metropole. Urgent affairs. If my watch is honest," Ellery said quickly, "we're just in time to witness another performance. And I'll show you why our friend the murderer not only didn't shoot, stab, asphyxiate, or hammer little Myra into kingdom come, but didn't hang her either!"

Ellery's watch, however, was dishonest. When they reached the Metropole it was noon, and the feature picture was still showing. They hurried backstage in search of Kelly.

"Kelly or this old man they call Perk, the caretaker," Ellery murmured, hurrying his father down the dark side aisle. "Just one question . . ."

A patrolman let them through. They found backstage deserted except for Brinkerhof and his new partner, who were stolidly rehearsing what was apparently a new trick. The trapeze was down and the big man was hanging from it by his powerful legs, a rubber bit in his mouth. Below him, twirling like a top, spun the tall blonde, the other end of the bit in her mouth.

Kelly appeared from somewhere and Ellery said: "Oh, Kelly. Are all the others in?"

Kelly was drunk again. He wobbled and said vaguely: "Oh sure. Sure."

"Gather the clans in Myra's dressing room. We've still a little time. Question's unnecessary, Dad. I should have known without——"

The inspector threw up his hands.

Kelly scratched his chin and staggered off. "Hey, Atlash," he called wearily. "Stop Atlash-ing an' come on." He swayed off toward the dressing rooms.

"But, El," groaned the inspector, "I don't understand——"

"It's perfectly childish in its simplicity," said Ellery, "now that I've seen what I suspected was the case. Come along, sire; don't crab the act."

When they were assembled in the dead woman's cubbyhole Ellery leaned against the dressing table, looked at the sprinkler pipe, and said: "One of you might as well own up . . . you see, I know who killed the little—er—lady."

"You know that?" said Brinkerhof hoarsely. "Who is——" He stopped and glared at the others, his stupid eyes roving.

But no one else said anything.

Ellery sighed. "Very well, then, you force me to wax eloquent, even reminiscent. Yesterday I posed the question: why should Myra Brinkerhof have been hanged in preference to one of four handier methods? And I said, in demonstrating Mr. Gordi's innocence, that the reason was that hanging permitted the use of a rope and consequently of Gordi's identifiable knot." He brandished his forefinger. "But I forgot an additional possibility. If you find a woman with a rope around her neck who has died of strangulation, you assume it was the rope that strangled her. I completely overlooked the fact that hanging, in permitting use of a rope, also accomplishes the important objective of *concealing the neck*. But why should Myra's neck have been concealed? By a rope? Because a rope is not the only way of strangling a victim, because a victim can be *choked* to death by fingers, because choking to death leaves marks on the neck, and because the choker didn't want the police to know there *were* finger marks on Myra's neck. He thought that the tight strands of the rope would not only conceal the finger marks but would obliterate them as well—sheer ignorance, of course, since in death such marks are ineradicable. But that is what he thought, and that *primarily* is why he chose hanging for Myra when she was already dead. The leaving of Gordi's knot to implicate him was only a secondary reason for the selection of rope."

"But, El," cried the inspector, "that's nutty. Suppose he did choke the woman to death. I can't see that he'd be incriminating himself by leaving finger marks on her neck. You can't match finger marks——"

"Quite true," drawled Ellery, "but you *can* observe that finger marks are on the neck *the wrong way*. For these point not upward but downward."

And still no one said anything, and there was silence for a space in the room with the heavily breathing men.

"For you see, gentlemen," continued Ellery sharply, "when Myra was choked she was choked *upside down*. But how is this possible? Only if one of two conditions existed. Either at the time she was choked she was hanging head down above her murderer, or——"

Brinkerhof said stupidly: "*Ja* I did it. *Ja.* I did it." He said it over and over, like a phonograph with its needle grooved.

A woman's voice from the amplifier said: "But I love you, darling, love you, love you, love you . . ."

Brinkerhof's eyes flamed and he took a short step toward the Great Gordi. "Yesterday I say to Myra: 'Myra, tonight we rehearse the new trick.' After the second show I see Myra undt that *Schweinehund* kissing undt kissing behind the scenery. I hear them talk. They haf been fooling me. I plan. I will kill her. When we rehearse. So I kill her." He buried his face in his hands and began to sob without sound. It was horrible; and Gordi seemed transfixed with its horror.

And Brinkerhof muttered: "Then I see the marks on her throat. They are upside down. I know that iss bad. So I take the rope undt I cover up the marks. Then I hang her, with the *Schwein's* knot, that she had once told me he had shown to her——"

He stopped. Gordi said hoarsely, "Good God. I didn't remember——"

"Take him away," said the inspector in a small dry voice to the policeman at the door.

"It was all so clear," explained Ellery a little later, over coffee. "Either the woman was hanging head down above her murderer, or her murderer was hanging head down above the woman. One squeeze of those powerful paws . . ." He shivered. "It had to be an acrobat, you see. And when I remembered that Brinkerhof himself had said they had been rehearsing a new trick——" He stopped and smoked thoughtfully.

"Poor guy," muttered the inspector. "He's not a bad sort, just dumb. Well, she got what was coming to her."

"Dear, dear," drawled Ellery. "Philosophy, Inspector? I'm really not interested in the moral aspects of crime. I'm more annoyed at this case than anything."

"Annoyed?" said the inspector with a sniff. "You look mighty smug to me."

"Do I? But I really am. I'm annoyed at the shocking unimaginativeness of our newspaper friends."

"Well, well," said the inspector with a sigh of resignation. "I'll bite. What's the gag?"

Ellery grinned. "Not one of the reporters who covered this case saw the perfectly obvious headline. You see, they forgot that one of the cast is named—of all things, dear God!—Gordi."

"Headline?" frowned the inspector.

"Oh, Lord. How could they have escaped casting me in the role of Alexander and calling this the Affair of the Gordian Knot?"

JOHN RUSSELL

The Price of the Head

THE POSSESSIONS of Christopher Alexander Pellett were these: his name, which he was always careful to retain intact; a suit of ducks, no longer intact, in which he lived and slept; a continuous thirst for liquor, and a set of red whiskers. Also he had a friend. Now no man can gain friendship, even among the gentle islands of Polynesia, except by virtue of some quality attaching to him. Strength, humor, villainy: he must show some trait by which the friend can catch and hold. How, then, explain the loving devotion lavished upon Christopher Alexander Pellett by Karaki, the company boy? This was the mystery at Fufuti.

There was no harm in Pellett. He never quarreled. He never raised his fist. Apparently he had never learned that a white man's foot, though it wobble ever so, is given him wherewith to kick natives out of the road. He never even cursed anyone except himself and the Chinese half-caste who sold him brandy: which was certainly allowable because the brandy was very bad.

On the other hand, there was no perceptible good in him. He had long lost the will to toil, and latterly even the skill to beg. He did not smile, nor dance, nor exhibit any of the amiable eccentricities that sometimes recommend the drunken to a certain toleration. In any other part of the world he must have passed without a struggle. But some chance had drifted him to the beaches where life is as easy as a song and his particular fate had given him a friend. And so he persisted. That was all. He persisted, a sodden lump of flesh preserved in alcohol. . . .

Karaki, his friend, was a heathen from Bougainville, where some people are smoked and others eaten. Being a black, a Melanesian, he was as much an alien in brown Fufuti as any white. He was a serious, efficient little man with deeply sunken eyes, a great mop of kinky hair, and a complete absence of expression. His tastes were simple. He wore a red cotton kerchief belted around his waist and a brass curtain ring suspended from his nose.

Some powerful chief in his home island had sold Karaki into the service of the trading company for three years, annexing his salary of tobacco and beads in advance. When the time should be accomplished, Karaki would be shipped back to Bougainville, a matter of some eight hundred miles, where he would land no richer than before except in experience. This was the custom. Karaki may have had plans of his own.

It is seldom that one of the black races of the Pacific shows any of the virtues for which subject populations are admired. Fidelity and humility can be exacted from other colors between tan and chocolate. But the black remains the inscrutable savage. His secret heart is his own. Hence the astonishment of Fufuti, which knew the ways of black recruits, when Karaki took the worthless beachcomber to his bosom.

"Hy, you, Johnny," called Moy Jack, the Chinese half-caste. "Better you come catch this fella mahster b'long you. He fella plenty too much drunk, galow."

Karaki left the shade of the copra shed where he had been waiting an hour or more and came forward to receive the sagging bulk that was thrust out-of-doors. He took it scientifically by wrist and armpit and swung toward the beach. Moy Jack stood on his threshold, watching with cynic interest.

"Hy, you," he said; "what name you make so much bobeley 'long that fella mahster? S'pose you bling me all them fella pearl; me pay you one dam' fella good trade—my word!"

It annoyed Moy Jack that he had to provide the white man with a daily drunk in exchange for the little seed pearls with which Pellett was always flush. He knew where those pearls came from. Karaki did forbidden diving in the lagoon to get them. Moy Jack made a good thing of the traffic, but he could have made a much better thing by trading directly with Karaki for a few sticks of tobacco.

"What name you give that fella mahster all them fella pearl?" demanded Moy Jack offensively. "He plenty too much no good, galow. Close up he die altogether."

Karaki did not reply. He looked at Moy Jack once, and the half-caste trailed off into mutterings. For an instant there showed a strange light in Karaki's dull eyes, like the flat, green flicker of a turning shark glimpsed ten fathoms down. . . .

Karaki bore his charge down the beach to the little thatched shelter of pandanus leaves that was all his home. Tenderly he eased Pellett to a mat, pillowed his head, bathed him with cool water, brushed the filth from his hair and whiskers. Pellett's whiskers were true whiskers, the kind that sprout like the barbels of a catfish, and they were a glorious coppery, sun-gilt red. Karaki combed them out with a sandalwood comb. Later he sat by with a fan and kept the flies from the bloated face of the drunkard.

It was a little past midday when something brought him scurrying into the open. For weeks he had been studying every weather sign. He knew that the change was due when the southeast trade begins to harden through this flawed belt of calms and cross winds. And now, as he watched, the sharp shadows began to blur along the sands and a film crept over the face of the sun.

All Fufuti was asleep. The houseboys snored in the back veranda. Under his netting the agent dreamed happily of big copra shipments and bonuses. Moy Jack dozed among his bottles. Nobody would have been mad enough to stir abroad in the noon hour of repose: nobody but Karaki, the untamed black, who cared nothing for customs nor yet for dreams. The light pad of his steps was lost in the surf drone on the barrier reefs. He flitted to and fro like a wraith. And while Fufuti slept he applied himself to a job for which he had never been hired. . . .

Karaki had long ago ascertained two vital facts: where the key to the trade room was kept and where the rifles and ammunition were hidden. He opened the trade room and selected three bolts of turkey-red cloth, a few knives, two cases of tobacco, and a fine small ax. There was much else he might have taken as well. But Karaki was a man of simple tastes, and efficient.

With the ax he next forced the rifle chest and removed therefrom one Winchester and a big box of cartridges. With the ax again he broke into the boat sheds. Finally with the ax he smashed the bottoms out of the whaleboat and the two cutters so they would be of no use to anyone for many days to come. It was really a very handy little ax, a true tomahawk, ground to a shaving edge. Karaki took a workman's pleasure in its keen, deep strokes. It was almost his chief prize.

On the beach lay a big proa, a stout outrigger canoe of the kind Karaki's own people used at Bougainville, so high of prow and stern as to be nearly crescent-shaped. The northwest monsoon of last season had washed it ashore at Fufuti and Karaki had repaired it, by the agent's own order. This proa he now launched in the lagoon, and aboard it he stored his loot.

Of supplies he had to make a hasty selection. He took a bag of rice and another of sweet potatoes. He took as many coconuts as he could carry in a net in three trips. He took a cask of water and a box of biscuit. And here happened an odd thing.

In his search for the biscuit he came upon the agent's private store of liquor, a dozen bottles of rare irish whisky. He glanced at them and passed them by. He knew what the stuff was, and he was a savage, a black man. But he passed it by. When Moy Jack heard of that later he remembered what he had seen in Karaki's eyes and ventured the surprising prediction that Karaki would never be taken alive.

When all was ready Karaki went back to his thatch and aroused Christopher Alexander Pellett.

"Hy, mahster, you come 'long me."

Mr. Pellett sat up and looked at him. That is to say, he looked. Whether he saw anything or not belongs among the obscurer questions of psychopathy.

"Too late," said Mr. Pellett profoundly. "This shop is closed. Copy boy! Give all those damned loafers good night. I'm—I'm goin'—bed!"

Whereupon he fell flat on his back.

"Wake up, mahster," insisted Karaki, shaking him. "You too much strong fella sleep. Hy-ah, mahster! Rum! You like'm rum? You catch'm rum any amount—my word! Plenty rum, mahster!"

But even this magic call, which never failed to rouse Pellett from his couch in the mornings, fell now on deaf ears. Pellett had had his skinful, and the fitness of things decreed that he should soak the clock around.

Karaki knelt beside him, pried him up until he could get a shoulder under his middle, and lifted him like a loose bag of meal. Pellett weighed one hundred and fifty pounds; Karaki not much more than a hundred. Yet in some deft coolie fashion of his own the little black man packed his burden, with the feet dragging behind, clear down to the beach. Moreover, he managed to get it aboard the proa. Pellett was half drowned and the proa half swamped. But Karaki managed.

No man saw their departure. Fufuti still dreamed on. Long before the agent awoke to wrath and ruin their queer crescent craft had slipped from the lagoon and faded away on the wings of the trade.

The first day Karaki had all he could do to keep the proa running straight before the wind. Big smoky seas came piling up out of the southeast and would have piled aboard if he had given them the least chance. He was only a heathen who did not know a compass from a degree of latitude. But his forefathers used to people these waters on cockleshell voyages that made the venture of Columbus look like a ride in a ferryboat. Karaki bailed with a tin pan and sailed with a mat and steered with a paddle: but he proceeded.

Along about sunrise Mr. Pellett stirred in the bilge and raised a peagreen face. He took one bewildered glance overside at the seething waste and collapsed with a groan. After a decent interval he tried again, but this was an illusion that would not pass, and he twisted around to Karaki, sitting crouched and all aglisten with spray in the stern.

"Rum!" he demanded.

Karaki shook his head, and a haunted look crept into Pellett's eyes.

"Take—take away all that stuff," he begged pathetically, pointing at the ocean. . . .

Thereafter for two days he was very, very sick, and he learned how a small boat in any kind of a sea can move forty-seven different ways within one and the same minute. This was no trifling bit of knowledge, as those who have acquired it can tell. It was nearly fatal to Pellett.

On the third day he awoke with a mouth and a stomach of fumed leather and a great weakness, but otherwise in command of his few faculties. The gale had fallen and Karaki was quietly preparing fresh coconuts. Pellett quaffed two before he thought to miss the brandy with which his breakfast draught was always laced. But when he remembered the milk choked in his throat.

"Me like'm rum."

"No got'm rum."

Pellett looked forward and aft, to windward and to lee. There was a great deal of horizon in sight, but nothing else. For the first time he was aware of a strangeness in events.

"What name you come so far?" he asked.

"We catch'm one big fella wind," explained Karaki.

Pellett was in no condition to question his statement nor to observe from the careful stocking of the proa that they had not been blown to sea on a casual fishing trip. Pellett had other things to think of. Some of the things were pink and others purple and others were striped like the rainbow in most surprising designs, and all were highly novel and interesting. They came thronging up out of the vasty deep to entertain Christopher Alexander Pellett. Which they did.

You cannot cut off alcohol from a man who has been continuously pickled for two years without results more or less picturesque. These were days when the proa went shouting across the empty southern seas to madrigal and choric song. Tied hand and foot and lashed under a thwart, Pellett raved in the numbers of his innocent youth. It would have been singular hearing had there been any to hear, but there was only Karaki, who did not care for the lesser Cavalier poets and on whom whole pages of *Atalanta in Calydon* were quite wasted. Now and then he threw a dipperful of sea water over the white man, or spread a mat to keep the sun from him, or fed him with coconut milk by force. Karaki was a poor audience but an excellent nurse. Also he combed Pellett's whiskers twice every day.

They ran into calms. But the trade picked them up again more gently, so that Karaki ventured to make westing, and they fled under skies as bright as polished brass.

> "My heart is within me
>   As an ash in the fire;
> Whosoever hath seen me
>   Without lute, without lyre,
> Shall sing of me grievous things,
>   even things that were ill
> to desire——"

Thus chanted Christopher Alexander Pellett, whose face began to show a little more like flesh and a little less like rotten kelp. . . .

Whenever a fair chance offered, Karaki landed on the lee of some one of the tiny islets with which the Santa Cruz region is peppered, and would make shift to cook rice and potatoes in the tin dipper. This was risky, for one day the islet proved to be inhabited. Two white men in a cutter came out to stop them. Karaki could not hide his resemblance to a runaway nigger, and he did not try to. But when the cutter approached within fifty yards he suddenly announced himself as a runaway nigger with a gun. He left the cutter sinking and one of the men dead.

"There's a bullet hole alongside me here," said Pellett from under the thwart. "You'd better plug it."

Karaki plugged it and released his passenger, who sat up and began stretching himself with a certain naïve curiosity of his own body.

"So you're real," observed Pellett, staring hard at Karaki. "By George, you *are*, and that's comfort."

He was right. Karaki was very real.

"What side you take'm this fella canoe?"

"Balbi," said Karaki, using the native word for Bougainville.

Pellett whistled. An eight-hundred-mile evasion in an open boat was a considerable undertaking. It enlisted his respect. Moreover, he had just had emphatic proof of the efficiency of this little black man.

"Balbi all same home b'long you?"

"Yes."

"All right, Commodore," said Pellett. "Lead on. I don't know why you shipped me for supercargo, but I'll see you through."

Strangely—or perhaps not so strangely—the whole Fufuti interval of his history had been fading from his brain while the poison was ebbing from his tissues. The Christopher Alexander Pellett that emerged was one from earlier years: pretty much of a wreck, it was true, and a feckless, indolent, paltry creature at best, but ordinarily human and rather more than ordinarily intelligent.

He was very feeble at first, but Karaki's diet of coconuts and sweet potatoes did wonders for him, and the time came when he could rejoice in the good salt taste of the spray on his lips and forget for hours together the crazy craving for stimulant. They made a strange crew, this pair—simple savage and convalescent drunkard—but there was never any question as to which was in command. That was well seen in the third week when their food began to fail and Pellett noticed that Karaki ate nothing for a whole day.

"See here, this won't do," he cried. "You've given me the last coconut and kept none for yourself."

"Me no like'm eat," said Karaki shortly.

Christopher Alexander Pellett pondered many matters in long, idle hours while the rush of foam under the proa and the creak and fling of her outriggers were the only sounds between sea and sky. Sometimes his brow was knotted with pain. It is not always pleasant to be wrenched back into level contact with one's memories. Thoughts are no sweeter company for having long been drowned. He had met the horrors of delirium. He had now to face the livelier devils of his past. He had fled them before.

But here was no escape of any kind. So he turned and grappled with them and laid them one by one.

When they had been at sea twenty-nine days they had nothing left of their provisions but a little water. Karaki doled it out by moistening a shred of coconut husk and giving Pellett the shred to suck. In spite of Pellett's petulant protest, he would take none himself. Again the heathen nursed the derelict, this time through the last stages of thirst, scraping the staves of the cask and feeding him the ultimate drop of moisture on the point of a knife.

On the thirty-sixth day from Fufuti they sighted Choiseul, a great green wall that built up slowly across the west.

Once fairly under its headlands, Karaki might have indulged a certain triumph. He had taken as his target the whole length of the Solomons, some six hundred miles. But to have fetched the broadside of them anywhere in such a craft as the proa through storm and current, without instrument or chart, was distinctly a feat of navigation. Karaki, however, did no celebrating. Instead, he stared long and anxiously over his shoulder into the east.

The wind had been fitful since morning. By noon it was dead calm on a restless, oily sea. A barometer would have told evil tales, but Karaki must have guessed them anyway, for he staggered forward and unstepped the little mast. Then he bound all his cargo securely under the thwarts and put all his remaining strength into the paddle, heading for a small outpost island where a line of white showed beach. They had been very lucky thus far, but they were still two miles offshore when the first rush of the hurricane caught them.

Karaki himself was reduced to a rattle of bones in a dried skin, and Pellett could scarce lift a hand. But Karaki fought for Pellett among the waves that leaped up like sheets of fire on the reef. Why or how they got through neither could have said. Perhaps because it was written that after drink, illness, madness, and starvation the white man should be saved by the black man again and a last time from ravening waters. When they came ashore on the islet they were both nearly flayed, but they were alive, and Karaki still gripped Pellett's shirt. . . .

For a week they stayed while Pellett fattened on unlimited coconut and Karaki tinkered the proa. It had landed in a waterlogged tangle, but Karaki's treasures were safe. He got his bearings from a passing native fisherman, and then he knew that *all* his treasures were safe. His home island lay across Bougainville Strait, the stretch of water just beyond.

"Balbi over there?" asked Pellett.

"Yes," said Karaki.

"And a mighty good thing too," cried Pellett heartily. "This is the limit of British authority, old boy. Big fella mahster b'long Beretani stop'm here, no can go that side."

Karaki was quite aware of it. If he feared one thing in the world, he feared the Fiji high court and its resident commissioner for the Southern

Solomons, who did sure justice upon all who transgressed in its jurisdiction. Once beyond the strait he might still be liable for the stolen goods and the broken contract. But never—this was the point—never could he be punished for anything he might choose to do over there in Bougainville.

So Karaki was content.

And so was Christopher Alexander Pellett. His body had been wrung and swept and scoured, and he had downed his devils. Sweet air and sunshine were on his lips and in his heart. His bones were sweet in him. As his vigor returned he swam the lagoon or helped Karaki at the proa. He would spend hours hugging the warm sand or rejoicing in the delicate tracery of some tiny sea shell, singing softly to himself, while the groundswell hushed along the beach, savoring life as he never had done.

"Oh, this is good—good!" he said.

Karaki puzzled him. Not that he vexed himself, for a smiling wonder at everything, almost childlike, filled him these days. But he thought of this taciturn savage, how he had capped thankless service with rarest sacrifice. And now that he could consider soberly, the why of it eluded him. Why? Affection? Friendship? It must be so, and he warmed toward the silent little man with the sunken eyes and the expressionless face from which he could never raise a wink.

"Hy, you, Karaki, what name you no laugh all same me? What? You too much fright 'long that fella stuff you steal? Forget it, you old black scamp. If they ever trouble you, I'll square them somehow. By George, I'll say I stole it myself!"

Karaki only grunted and sat down to clean his Winchester with a bit of rag and some drops of oil he had crushed from a dried coconut.

"No, that don't reach him either," murmured Pellett, baffled. "I'd like to know what's going on under that topknot of yours, old chap. You're like Kipling's cat, that walks by himself. God knows I'm not ungrateful. I wish I could show you——"

He sprang up.

"Karaki! He one big fella friend 'long you: savee? You one big fella friend 'long me: savee? We two dam' big fella friend, my word! . . . What?"

"Yes," said Karaki. No other response. He looked at Pellett and he looked away toward Bougainville. "Yes," he said, "my word," and went on cleaning his gun—the black islander, inscrutable, incomprehensible, an enigma always, and to the end.

The end came two days later at Bougainville.

Under a gorgeous dawn they came into a bay that opened before their prow as with jeweled arms of welcome. The land lay lapped in bright garments like a sleeper half awakened, all flushed and smiling, sensuous, intimate, thrilling with life, breathing warm scents . . .

These were some of the foolish phrases Pellett babbled to himself as he leaped ashore and ran up on a rocky point to see and to feel and to draw all the charm of the place to himself.

Meanwhile Karaki, that simple and efficient little man, was proceeding methodically about his own affairs. He landed his bolts of cloth, his tobacco, his knives, and the other loot. He landed his box of cartridges and his rifle and his fine tomahawk. The goods were somewhat damaged by sea water, but the weapons had been carefully cleaned and polished. . . .

Pellett was declaiming poetry aloud to the alluring solitude when he was aware of a gentle footfall and turned, surprised, to find Karaki standing just behind him with the rifle at his hip and the ax in his hand.

"Well," said Pellett cheerfully, "what d'you want, old chappie?"

"Me like," said Karaki, while there gleamed in his eyes the strange light that Moy Jack had glimpsed there, like the flicker of a turning shark; "me like'm too much one fella head b'long you!"

"What? Head! Whose—my head?"

"Yes," said Karaki simply.

That was the way of it. That was all the mystery. The savage had fallen enamored of the head of the beachcomber, and Christopher Alexander Pellett had been betrayed by his fatal red whiskers. In Karaki's country a white man's head, well smoked, is a thing to be desired above wealth, above lands and chiefship's fame, and the love of women. In all Karaki's country was no head like the head of Pellett. Therefore Karaki had served to win it with the patience and single faith of a Jacob. For this he had schemed and waited, committed theft and murder, expended sweat and cunning, starved and denied himself, nursed, watched, tended, fed, and saved his man that he might bring the head alive and on the hoof—so to speak—to the spot where he could remove it at leisure and enjoy the fruits of his labor in safety.

Pellett saw all this at a flash, understood it so far as any white could understand it: the whole elemental and stupendous simplicity of it. And standing there in his new strength and sanity under the fair promise of the morning, he gave a laugh that pealed across the waters and started the sea birds from their cliffs, the deep-throated laugh of a man who fathoms and accepts the last great jest.

For finally, by corrected list, the possessions of Christopher Alexander Pellett were these: his name still intact; the ruins of some rusty ducks; his precious red whiskers—and a soul which had been neatly recovered, renewed, refurbished, reanimated, and restored to him by his good friend Karaki.

> "Thou shouldst die as he dies,
>   For whom none sheddeth tears;
> Filling thine eyes
>   And fulfilling thine ears
> With the brilliance . . . the bloom
>   and the beauty . . ."

Thus chanted Christopher Alexander Pellett over the waters of the bay, and then whirled, throwing wide his arms:

"Shoot, damn you! It's cheap at the price!"

WILLIAM SAROYAN

Dear Baby

THE ROOM was a large one on the seventh floor of the Blackstone Hotel on O'Farrell Street in San Francisco. There was nothing in it to bring him there except the portable radio-phonograph, the one record, and darkness.

He came into the room smiling, and walked about, trying to decide what to do. He had six hours to go, and after that a time so long he didn't like to think about it.

He no longer saw the room. During the day the blind of the only window was drawn to keep the place dark. At night he turned the light of the bathroom on and kept the door almost shut so that only enough light came into the room to keep him from walking into something. It happened anyway. It wasn't that he couldn't see as well as ever. It was simply that he was alone again all the time and wasn't looking. There was no longer any reason to look.

He remembered everything.

At the core of everything was his remembrance of her.

He walked about quietly, turning, bumping into the edges of doorways and chairs and other objects in the room, moving unconsciously, his eyes unable to see because of the remembrance. He stopped suddenly, removed his hat and coat, stretched and shook his head as he did when he was confused in the ring.

It was nothing.

He could go on as if he had never known her. He could be boisterous in act and loud in laughter, and someday be all right again. He could go on like everybody else in the world, but he didn't know if he wanted to. Lazzeri said he was in better shape than ever, but Lazzeri didn't know what he knew.

The odor of her hair, the taste of her mouth, and the image of her face came to him. His guts sickened. He smiled and sat on the bed. After a moment he got up, went to the portable machine, turned the knob, and put needle to disk. Then he stretched out on the bed, face down, and listened to the music, remembering her, and saying: "Dear Baby, remembering you is the only truth I know. Having known you is the only beauty of my life. In my heart there is one smile, the smile of your heart in mine when we were together."

When the phone rang he knew it was Lazzeri. He got up and turned off the machine.

"Joe?" Lazzeri said.

"Yeah."

"Are you all right?"

"Sure."

"Remember what I told you?"

"What did you tell me?"

"I want you to take it easy."

"That's what I'm doing."

"Don't go haywire."

"Okay."

"What's the matter?"

"I've been sleeping."

"Oh," Lazzeri said. "Okay. I'll see you at nine."

"Okay."

"Something's the matter," Lazzeri said.

"Don't be silly."

"Something's the matter," Lazzeri said again. "I'm coming right up."

"I've been sleeping," Joe said. "I'll see you at nine."

"You don't sound right," Lazzeri said.

"I'm fine."

"You haven't got somebody in that room with you, have you?"

"No."

"Joe," Lazzeri said, "what's the matter?"

"I'll see you at nine," Joe said.

"You're not going haywire on me again, are you?"

"No."

"Okay," Lazzeri said. "If you're all right, that's all I want to know."

"I'm all right," Joe said.

"Okay," Lazzeri said. "If you want to be alone, okay. Just don't go haywire."

"I'll see you at nine," Joe said.

He went back to the machine, turned the knob, and then decided not to listen to the music any more. That's what he would do. He wouldn't listen to the music any more. He would break the record. He would give the machine away. He would lift the blind of the window. He would turn on all the lights and open his eyes. He would come to the room only to sleep. He would go down to the poolroom on Turk Street and find a couple of the boys. He would shoot pool and listen to the boys talking about cards and horses and the other varieties of trouble they knew. He would go up to a couple of the places he used to visit and find some girls he used to know and buy them drinks and ask how they'd been and hear them tell of the troubles *they* knew. He would stop being alone.

He began to laugh, at first quietly and then out loud. He laughed at himself—the wretched comedy of his grief. Then he laughed at everybody alive, and began to feel everything was going to be all right again. If you could laugh, you could live. If you could look at it that way, you could endure *anything*. While he was laughing he heard *her* laughing with him, as clearly as if she were in the room. He became sick again and stopped laughing, knowing it was no use.

He remembered her as if she were still alive, walking beside him along one of many streets in one of many cities, her face childlike and solemn, her movement beside him shy and full of innocence, her voice so young and lovely he would stop anywhere to hold her in his arms while she said seriously: "Joe, people are looking."

He remembered her alone with him in one of many rooms, her presence the first goodness and beauty in his life. He remembered the sweetness of her mouth and the soft hum of her heart growing to the sudden sobbing that brought out in him a tenderness so intense it was ferocious, a tenderness he had always hidden because there had never been anyone to give it to.

He walked about in the dark room, remembering how unkind he had been to her the night he had come home and found her listening to the record. He pointed at the machine and said, "Where did that come from?"

He remembered the way she ran to him and put her arms around him and the way he pushed her away. He remembered the way she moved away from him and said, "I only made a down payment on it. I'll tell them to come and take it back if you want me to. I thought you'd like it."

The record was playing, and although he knew it was something he liked very much, and needed, and should have known long ago, he went on being unkind. She was on the verge of crying and didn't know where to go or what to do. She went timidly to the machine and was going to shut it off when he shouted to her to let it play. She hurried, almost ran, into the other room, and he stood in front of the machine with his hat on and listened to the record until it finished. Then he shut off the machine and went back to town and didn't come home till after five in the morning. She was asleep. He couldn't understand what right he had to know her, to speak to her, to live in the same house with her, to touch her. He bent over her and touched her lips with his own and saw her eyes open. "Please forgive me," he said.

She sat up smiling and put her arms around him, and he kissed her lips and her nose and her eyes and her ears and her forehead and her neck and her shoulders and her arms and her hands, and while he was doing so he said, "Please remember one thing, baby. No matter what I say to you, I love you. I'm liable to go haywire any time, but don't forget that I love you. Please remember that."

He took off his clothes, got into his bed, and went to sleep. When she got in beside him he woke up and embraced her, laughing, while she whispered his name the sorrowful, serious way she always did when she knew he was all right again.

That was in Ventura, where they had taken an apartment because he had three fights coming up in that vicinity; one in Los Angeles, one in Hollywood, and one in Pismo Beach. He let her come to the fight in Hollywood the night he fought Kid Fuente, the Indian, because he knew how much she wanted to see him in the ring. He got her a ringside seat and after the fight she told him she had sat next to Robert Taylor and Barbara Stanwyck and they had been very nice to her.

"I hope you didn't ask them for an autograph," he said, and she became embarrassed and said, "Yes, I did, Joe."

"Well," he said, "they should have asked *you* for one."

"Oh, they were swell," she said. "They sure liked you."

"Oh sure," he said. "Sure. Sure. That dumb Indian almost ruined me. I don't know how I won. I guess he got tired trying. I'll be punch-drunk in another three or four months."

"You were wonderful in the ring," the girl said.

He remembered the fight because she had talked about it so much. It was six rounds. He was almost out in the fourth. She had known it and kept talking around it, but one day she said, "I almost cried."

"What are you talking about?" he said.

"I mean," she said, "at the fight. Everybody was yelling and I didn't know whether they were for you or against you and I almost cried."

"When was that?" he said.

"I don't know," she said. "I was so excited. He was fighting hard and you were in a corner and everybody stood up and was yelling. I thought he was hitting *me*."

He remembered being in the corner, taking a lot of bad ones, not being able to do anything about them, not knowing if he wasn't going to be out and saying to himself, "You'll be punch-drunk in no time at this rate." He kept trying to move away, but there was nowhere to go, and all of a sudden the Indian slowed down, he was tired, and he remembered saying to the Indian, "Okay, Kid, that's all." He knew he was going to be all right now because there weren't more than fifteen seconds to that round. He gave the rest of the round everything he had. The Indian was tired and couldn't do anything, and just before the bell the Indian stopped a bad one and fell backward, looking up at him with an amazed expression because the Indian couldn't understand how anybody could take so much punishment and come up so strong.

The bell saved the Indian, but for the rest of the fight the Indian was no good, and he knocked him down once in each of the last two rounds.

"That was a bad spot," he told her. "By rights I should have been out, but the Indian got tired. You can't start slugging that way in the middle of a round and expect to keep it up till the end of the round."

"You looked fine," she said, "and you didn't look sore. Don't you get sore?"

"Sore?" he said. "Who's there to get sore at? That poor Indian is only out to earn a little money, the same as me. He's got nothing against me and I've got nothing against him. If he can floor me he's going to do it, and if I can floor him I'm going to do it."

"Well," she said, "I almost cried. You looked so fine all the rest of the fight, but when you were in the corner the only thing I could see was somebody being hit over and over again."

"I didn't like that myself," he said.

He was glad she hadn't seen some of his bad fights—the earlier ones, the ones in which he had taken a lot of punishment. Lately he'd learned enough about the racket not to get into a lot of trouble. He seldom took advantage of a chance to clinch, but if the worst came to the worst and there was nothing else to do he would do it, rest a few seconds to try to figure out what to do in the remaining seconds of the round. He usually ended every round nicely, coming back if he had been hurt earlier. Of course he had the reach, his legs were good, and even when he was hurt they didn't wobble and he could stay solid.

After seeing the fight with Kid Fuente she didn't want to see any more. The day of a fight she would be sick, sick in bed, and she would pray. She would turn on the phonograph and listen to the record, which had become their music, the song of their life together. And when he'd come home he'd find her pale and sick and almost in tears, listening to the song. He would hold her in his arms a long time, and he would hear her heart pounding, and little by little it would slow down to almost normal, and then he would hold her at arm's length and look into her eyes and she would be smiling, and then he would say, "It only means fifty dollars extra, baby, but I won." And she'd know there was no vanity in him, she'd understand what he was talking about, and she would ask him what she could get him. Ham and eggs? Scotch and soda? What would he like? She would rush around in an apron and fool around with food and dishes and put the stuff on the table.

He used to eat even if he wasn't hungry. Just so he hadn't lost. If he'd lost he'd be mean, he'd be so sore at himself that he'd be mean to her, and she wouldn't know what to do, but in the midst of being mean to her he would suddenly say in a loud voice, "And don't be a fool, either; don't pay any attention to anything I'm saying now because I'm out of my head. I made a mess of the whole fight."

When he came home from the fight with Sammy Kaufman, of New York, he was pretty badly hurt. His head was heavy, his lips were swollen, his left eye was twitching, every muscle of his body was sore, and he was swearing all the time, even though it had been a good fight and a draw. He wasn't mean to her that night, though, and she said, "Joe, please give it up. You can make money some other way. We don't need a lot of money."

He walked around the apartment and talked to himself. Then suddenly he calmed down and shut off the lights and put the record on the machine and sat down with her to listen to their song. It was a piece by Jan Sibelius, from the *King Kristian Suite*, called "Elegie." He played the record three times, then fell asleep from exhaustion, and she kept playing the record until he woke up a half hour later. He was smiling, and he said, "I'd like to quit, baby, but I don't know any other way to make money."

The following week he tried gambling and lost.

After that he had stuck to fighting. They had traveled together up and down the coast—north to San Francisco, Sacramento, Reno, Portland, and Seattle, and then south to the towns along the coast and in the valley that were good fight towns, and Hollywood and Los Angeles and San Diego—when he found out about it. From the beginning he was scared to death, in spite of how good it made him feel. He tried his best not to be scared and tried to keep her in good spirits, but he was worried about it all the time. She was a child herself. She was too little. He didn't know what to do. He remembered her saying one night, "Please let me have it, Joe. I want it so badly."

"Do you think I don't want it?" he said. "Do you think I don't want you to have it? That's *all* I want. That's all I've ever wanted."

Then he began to mumble, talking to himself.

"What, Joe?" she said.

"Do you feel all right?" he said. "Do you feel you can do it? You're not scared, are you?"

"I'm a little scared," she said, "but I guess everybody's scared the first time."

The months of waiting were the happiest of his life. Everything that was good in him had come out—even though he was worried all the time.

Even in the ring he had been better than ever. His fights were all good, except one, and that was the fight with the champion, Corbett, which had been a draw, but very close, some sports writers saying he had won and others saying that Corbett had won, and everybody wanting a rematch, especially Lazzeri.

So tonight he was fighting Corbett again. He had six hours to go. If he won this fight he and Lazzeri would be in the big money at last. He believed he could take the fight, but what if he did? What did he care about money now? Suppose he did take the fight? Where could he go *after* the fight?

"I'm dead," he said. "What's the use bluffing?"

Remembering the girl, he fell asleep, and when he woke up he went to the telephone, without thinking, and asked the hotel operator to get him Corbett at Ryan's Gymnasium, and call him back. A moment later the telephone rang. He answered it, and Corbett said, "Hello, is that you, Joe?"

"Ralph," Joe said, "I want to tell you I'm out to win tonight. I think it's about time you retired."

At the other end of the line Corbett busted out laughing and swore at his friend in Italian.

"I'll take care of you, kid," he said. "You know I like an aggressive fighter."

"Don't say I didn't tell you," Joe said.

"See you in the ring," Corbett said.

In the ring, when they shook hands, Joe said, "This is going to be your last fight." Corbett didn't know he was talking to himself.

"Okay, Joe," he said.

The first round was fast and wild. Even the sports writers couldn't understand. Lazzeri was sore as hell.

"Joe," he said, "what do you think you're doing? You can't beat Corbett that way. Take it easy. Fight *his* fight."

The second round was faster and wilder than the first. They were probably even, but that was only because he wasn't tired yet. The music was humming in him all the time, getting into the roar of the crowd and sweeping along in him, while his heart kept talking to the girl, dreaming that she was still alive, at home listening to their song, waiting for him to come home and take her in his arms.

Lazzeri wanted to hit him after the second round. "Joe," he said, "listen to me. Fight Corbett's fight. He'll kill you."

("That's okay with me," his heart said. "Dear Baby, that's okay with me.")

The third round, if anything, was faster than the first and second, and coming out of a clinch, Corbett said, "What do you think you're doing, Joe?"

"I'm knocking you out," Joe said.

Corbett laughed at him and they began slugging again, one for one, with the sports writers looking at each other, trying to figure out what was going on.

Lazzeri was furious.

"Joe," he said, "I'm not talking to you. I've worked with you six years. I changed you from a punk to a great fighter. Now you're throwing away the championship—the chance we've been working for all these years. You can go to hell, Joe. I hope he floors you in the next round."

During the fourth round things began to go haywire. Corbett's left eye was cut and bleeding badly, and it seemed he was bewildered and less strong than he had been.

("What the hell," his heart said. "Is Corbett going to go haywire at a time like this?")

After the round Lazzeri said, "Joe, I think you've got him—but I'll talk to you later. Your next fight will be in Madison Square Garden. We'll go to Florida for a while. But I'll talk to you later."

In the fifth round Corbett was slow, his punches were weak, and he seemed confused. Toward the end of the round he fell and stayed on one knee to the count of nine.

"You're fighting the most beautiful fight you've ever fought," Lazzeri said. "The sports writers are crazy about you. You're a real champion, Joe."

The fight was stopped near the end of the sixth round because Corbett's eye was so bad.

Lazzeri was crazy with joy but unable to understand what had happened. It was obvious that Joe had fought a great fight—that his style had been perfect for *this* fight. And yet Lazzeri knew something was wrong somewhere.

"Joe," he said in the cab, "you're a champion now. What's eating you?"

"I'm not fighting for three or four months, am I?" he said.

"Two or three, anyway," Lazzeri said. "Why?"

"We've got more money than we've ever had before, haven't we?"

"We've got enough for both of us for two years at least," Lazzeri said. "But why? What are you driving at?"

"Nothing," he said. ("Dear Baby," his heart said.) "I think I'm entitled to a little celebrating."

"Sure, sure," Lazzeri said. "I don't want you to go stale. What do you want?"

"I want laughs," he said. "I'll go up to my room. Get a couple of girls. Bring some scotch. I want *laughs*."

"Sure," Lazzeri said. "Sure, Joe. We'll have a little party. I need laughs myself after the scare you gave me."

When he got to his room he turned on all the lights, took the record off the phonograph, and for a moment thought of breaking it. He couldn't, though. He put the record under the bed, as if to hide it. He walked around the room until the sickness caught up with him again, only now it was worse than ever, and he sat down on the bed and began to cry.

When Lazzeri and the two girls came into the room it was dark except for a little light coming from the bathroom. The phonograph was playing, and the fighter was sitting on the bed with his head in his hands and he was crying.

"Get the hell out of here," he said softly.

Without a word Lazzeri led the two girls out of the room. "He'll be all right," he said.

"Dear Baby," the fighter kept saying over and over again.

ROBERT L. SCOTT, Jr., and HORACE S. MAZET

Squadron Leader

Army communiqué: Last night several squadrons of enemy planes attempted to attack positions in the Panama Canal region, but were beaten off with severe losses. Some of our planes failed to return.

SQUADRON LEADER RUTHERFORD looked anxiously around the pilots' ready room, at the relaxed faces of younger men who were shortly to take off over the Panama Canal. There was no outward sign of fear here, or hesitancy to obey orders of the Air Corps HQ, despite the knowledge of everyone that perhaps even now an enemy was winging in through the night to bomb the Canal into ruins. Each man knew that perhaps before morning he would be lying dead in his wrecked plane, hidden by the treacherous jungle that covered the entire country in every direction.

Rutherford knew it too. And he was afraid. All his lengthy flying career he had been afraid. His first solo, for example, had found him practically paralyzed, but his inferiority complex had made him struggle through with it. His first pursuit flight had been a nightmare, and never since had he felt secure when guiding his throbbing pursuiter through the skies at better than four hundred miles an hour. He feared and disliked that job. And now, particularly, during the long night flights he had come to feel that fear rode in the cockpit with him. He could not shake it off. But never could he reveal it, even by the slightest sign, or squadron morale would be a mockery.

He recalled that horrible moment when, some weeks ago, Deputy Squadron Leader Griffin had said, "The trouble with you, Rutherford, is that you think too much about what might happen. You always figure everything out in your mind, then conclude that our chances are poor, and naturally it gets under your skin. I've seen you thinking it all out many times. If you don't stop worrying and join us in a good drunk you'll grow afraid to fly at all!"

Afraid to fly—afraid to fly—there it was, spoken out loud in the barroom. Rutherford had sensed a great emptiness where his stomach should have been. He knew the others at the bar had stopped talking and had turned to watch. He felt every eye on him. He had forced his hand to remain steady as he picked up his glass.

"Afraid to fly!" he had mocked scornfully. "That's for new cadets. You can't remain in this business for years and still be afraid to fly. Simply can't. You know that. And with what's coming, it would be suicide to fly in combat without forgetting everything except shooting down the other fellow." He had turned to the other members of the squadron. "Get this, lads. Once you're up there in a scrap you *have* to forget your own feelings, or you're a goner!"

Well, here it was right now, the combat he had talked about that day. At any minute these chaps here in the room, Griffin, himself, would be called to fly up into the frightening night and repel enemy aircraft, trading burning slugs with enemy cannon, facing instant destruction—or worse, a lingering death by starvation in the trackless jungles below, after a jump from a wrecked ship.

If only he could be indifferent to it all, like Griffin, now, or like any number of these kids here just recently out of the advance training school, who took to pursuit "pea-shooters" like generals to a desk. Most of all, Griffin believed that he was a good leader, and he could not betray his command in the slightest without permanent disgrace. He would have to meet the future as he had met every crisis in his past, with clenched hands and the knives of agony cutting into his brain. If only it were not night but daytime. . . .

Eighteen pursuiters from the 78th Squadron were up there in the darkness now. Another eighteen were standing by on the ground, alert pilots playing cards, with radio headsets close at hand. They were unnaturally quiet; ready.

Rutherford and Griffin were standing by, listening with one ear to the guard radio frequency for the alarm signal Gee-Aye, if and when it should come.

Like sudden gunfire it snapped from the speaker: "G A to all squadrons: enemy bombers reported by Air Warning from Pointo Obaldia to be converging on Canal. The following orders to squadrons: all ships in the air and cover your zones by Plan Five. . . . Acknowledge. . . ."

Interference quivered through the set into the room. Rutherford tuned as finely as possible, then looked at his deputy leader. His anxiety did not betray itself in his blank eyes. "Jammed!" he announced. He swung to secondary frequency. It was also unreadable because of blanketing signals.

"Let's go," he said with dry lips to listening pilots who were already standing, headsets in their hands and helmets donned. "If they're coming on in, the best we can do is get up there, forget about radio, and intercept them." He flicked the receiver back to guard frequency only to find it oscillating—intentionally jammed by the enemy.

Rutherford, as he went out the door, yelled to the mechanics, "Turn them over!" To fat Sergeant Morse he said, "Wind them all up, Morse. Every ship takes off as soon as possible. Full ammunition. No bombs." He strode out into the night toward his plane, betraying nothing of the inner conflict that was gnawing at his effort.

Like cold water creeping up the sides of a well, he felt the chill of anticipation rising over his body. Fear of the coming action, of the unknown, of the night all around him crept up and covered him. He was tortured by the knowledge that the 78th Pursuit, a group of the finest lads on earth, would be led by an incompetent. No matter that he was looked up to by all his command. They never knew of his horror from the gut-sinking turns, the blackout recovery from dives, the taut-scalp trepidation of imminent crashes at night when coming back to the black field for a landing at a hundred and twenty miles an hour, when you couldn't even see your own wing tips.

In the mounting roar of warming engines a hand touched his shoulder. He turned to find Griffin at his side. His deputy grasped his hand. "So long, old boy," he was saying. "See you when we get back!" And Rutherford was alone again. . . .

The second section of the 78th Pursuit Squadron climbed to its appointed sector. Search formation. It was already after midnight. They would be up there until at least 4 A.M., unless they had to high-tail it at full throttle or dog-fight. Their mighty Allisons ate up gas too fast for much of that high-speed action. But it would be a long, lonesome detail, for undoubtedly something big was up. This was it. This was what he had dreaded; all the years had warned him against this night.

One element stuck in his mind. The jammed radio bands. *They* were on their way now! That sense of impending terror began to flood again over his equilibrium, and he fought it, consciously, almost as if he could see it there in the dark.

Over the clouds the stars shone, but the storm of the late afternoon had long turned and gone south into the Pacific. Above thirty thousand, oxygen masks were adjusted again to lessen the uncomfortable facial pressure. It was miserably cold.

Rutherford's assigned sector was next to that of the 74th. Echelons flicked their blue recognition lights. Rendezvous was established at 01:15 o'clock. The leader of the 78th circled three-sixty degrees to the right, the signal for the entire squadron to split and search the sector in eighteen two-ship elements. He knew now that every square mile of the Zone, as well as hundreds of square miles to either side, was covered in staggered altitudes from forty-two thousand feet down to eight thousand.

Rutherford's pale face relaxed a bit in the dim reflected glow of the stars as he thought of big Griffin flying on his wing. It was comforting to have the lanky Texan with him, for Rutherford knew that in a tight spot he could rely on his deputy implicitly. His sweaty hands in thick gloves gripped the plane controls and, peering apprehensively now into the black ahead, he searched the sector constantly with darting glances. He was afraid of what he might see, but overcome with dread that he would not see them first before he himself was spotted. In this activity there was no "second chance."

Shivering, he cruised with Griffin from Gamboa to Portogandi and back toward the Canal by Bayamo. No activity, but intense anticipation, almost palpable in the cold darkness, and constant peering for telltale exhausts streaking back in the night brought strain to his eyes. He pressed them tight shut more and more often, and began to feel a headache whose roots lay deep in the turmoil of his brain. He wondered how long, how many hours, how many days, a man could live in constant fear of his life, and yet cover up so that his closest friend would never know. The doubts of all the past long months' preparation for the coming conflict aroused themselves anew, so that he groaned aloud. The old question: Why did I ever become a pilot? arose, and futile answers chased themselves around in his aching head until he forced himself to read and reread his pressure gauges, keeping his brain active on the immediate present. It would do until he could get down on the ground again.

"Christ, it's cold!" he muttered to himself as the two planes swung through the frosty night on their search. His wing thermometer registered —50 Centigrade, although they were only a few degrees above the Equator.

Formation trains of gliders, loaded with invading troops, sounded fantastic despite information direct from HQ. Yet Rutherford and every pilot knew from the recent events in this hemisphere war that almost anything was not only possible but probable. Every so often his glance swept the black sphere around him, seeking those gliding planes against the cold darkness, fearing that he would find them. Perhaps he would be able to spot them first against the lighter blackness overhead, silhouetted against the fixed stars.

They are coming tonight . . . tonight . . . tonight. . . .

Far to the south he could spot the inky dots of the fortified islands; directly below lay the San Blas islands, now completely hidden by clouds. Back toward the south where lights of Balboa and Panama City should have glowed warmly, nothing was visible save the faint phosphorescent rim of the vast Pacific bordering those two blacked-out cities. Yes undoubtedly they were coming tonight, and the conviction sent a shiver through him.

At first he thought clouds had unaccountably formed even up there at forty thousand feet. Then in a sudden realization his throat contracted with excitement. He tried to pierce that darkness as tension mounted in his brain. He inhaled deeply and his nostrils expanded.

Finally he could make it out. Less than a thousand feet above him he saw dimly the blue stream of an exhaust. He pulled slowly up to identify it, keeping well under the glow of the flame. Two exhaust plumes appeared, and Rutherford forgot to breathe. They were enemy exhausts. Suspecting two more would appear to his left, he skidded his ship automatically and immediately picked up the left-wing exhausts, four in all! An enemy bomber, a four-engined giant, one of many rolling in with full bomb bays. With these loads of demolition bombs they would blast the locks of the Canal in preparation to invasion by glider trains that would follow at once. There was no time to lose.

This was it!

Rutherford looked around. His heart missed a beat. Griffin was nowhere to be seen. Griffin had deserted him just before combat. Or was he off stalking another enemy ship in the darkness? The squadron leader looked once more at the giant bomber above and imagined turrets with heavy-caliber machine guns manned by alert gunners, waiting for him, trained on his ship. Should he attack this enemy plane, or should he . . . ? Years of training for just such an emergency as this resolved the doubts. Automatically his hand charged his guns. Fail to attack now and he could never face his squadron again.

Keeping well forward of the tail turret to escape detection, Rutherford spotted his fighter directly beneath the big attacking bomber. He tried to gauge his distance from the widening space between the two inboard engine exhaust flames ahead, and slowly closed. He was hardly breathing through his oxygen mask now. He could make out the four engine nacelles bulging from the wing in the faint starlight. No four-engine job was ever carrier-based, and he knew he had found his target. This was the real thing.

At point-blank range Rutherford put his prop into low pitch. With a hand that trembled he pulled the nose of his plane up and then aimed his luminous sights on the invader. He could not miss. He eased back-pressure on the stick, his index finger squeezing the trigger of his nose cannon. The solenoid switch closed and he felt the recoil of the heavy guns. Tracers, like balls of a huge roman candle, burned into the bowels of the bomber. They disappeared into the section where the curving left wing joined the bomb bay.

The soft underbelly was vulnerable. The tracers seemed to sail very slowly toward the enemy. His hand tried to squeeze the top of the stick off as he pressed the trigger, and there was a faint, cooling wind of relief as action relieved the tension in his muscles.

A flame licked out. Burning gasoline flared blindingly back from the bomber into the slip stream of one of its own inboard engines. Rutherford, frightened, skidded his fighter out from below and then over his shoulder saw the plume of fire grow wide and immeasurably long. At first he thought perhaps the heavy plane would continue on to its destination wrapped in fire. Then the left wing slowly sank and an explosion flashed brilliant before his eyes. Burst asunder like a huge fuel tank, the bomber disintegrated, parts of fuselage and wing flaming in all directions. Rutherford involuntarily ducked to his instrument board. Burning remnants of the attacker streaked downward for the jungle.

After the first shock of combat the pursuit pilot had time to catch his breath. He trembled with the reaction of what he had just seen, his own work sending men plunging down to death. In the chill darkness he seemed now utterly alone and abandoned, tearing at infinite speed toward some distant rendezvous yet more dreadful and unpredictable, like a chip whirling ever closer to the brink. The fear of failure had lessened, and now his old incubus returned as the night seemed to cut him off from all his fellow men.

Then his eye was caught by something. Off to one side the darkness was shattered anew by other blazing planes. Rutherford climbed desperately as he saw another combat off to his left. Tracers were cutting angry streaks across the sky in all directions. As he neared a second bomber, vaguely discernible in the light overhead, he felt a hail of machine-gun bullets strike his engine cowling.

Frightened suddenly, he skidded violently to one side and, before he realized it, sent a burst from his eight .50-calibers at the enemy. He dove steeply and nearly ran into one of the 78th pursuiters coming up from below. It looked in that split second like Griffin's plane, and then it disappeared. My God, he thought, if Griff is gone . . . !

From the bomber's tail the Axis gunner raked the uprushing P-59, and Rutherford saw it hesitate in its climb, stall lazily, then fall into an inverted

spin for the jungle, a thin streak of fire tracing and rapidly enveloping the
entire plane. Rutherford set his teeth to keep from crying out. What was it
Griff had said to him that day, aeons ago? "Afraid to fly!" Wasn't that it?
Yes, that was it—*afraid*. God, but it all seemed remote and silly now. . . .

A cold feeling took possession of him. The squadron leader hurriedly
groped for altitude in a way that was automatic. Turning in a chandelle,
he headed for a point ahead of the big ship, quartering its course almost
at right angles. Now its nose crossed his luminous sight ring. Now it was
in position. He led the bomber slightly and pressed the solenoid. Tracers
burned rivers of fire from cockpit to bomb bay.

A flood of keen satisfaction swept over Rutherford as he saw fire spurt
from the top of the cockpits. He watched the crew trickle through hatches
from the stricken ship. Then it fell off on one wing, and finally plunged
like a comet into the well of blackness below.

The actual attack on those two ships had taken only seconds, and during
that seemingly endless time Rutherford had not been able to think clearly,
logically, of his reactions. Now, solo once more, that overwhelming sense
of loneliness swept in over him. Griffin was gone. Well, they might get
him too. But if they did he would take a lot of them with him first.

Far off to the right another burning ship dived for the ground thousands
of feet below. Friend or foe, he could not tell, but the Air Corps was
making a night of it.

As scheduled, after the first encounter with enemy bombers, Rutherford
now turned to effect a rendezvous with his squadron above Pointo Obaldia.
At forty thousand feet, with a flood of relief, he found the blue formation
lights of his outfit, or what was left of it. Over toward the west and the
Canal, flares of burning ships could be seen. Other Air Corps fighters were
intercepting the enemy bombers. Now Rutherford led one of the four
defense pursuit squadrons combing the sky at staggered altitudes to intercept the expected soaring trains coming from the east. Their job would not
be easy, and the squadron leader sucked in great draughts of increased oxygen from his tube. Either this night the 78th would win its spurs, or
Rutherford would not come back. Griff was gone—maybe ten, a dozen
others would never return. They had not been afraid to fly. . . .

Suddenly he jumped to alertness. Not far away a magnesium flare
spurted to life. That was the signal! Gliders had been encountered. Rutherford tensed anew and sweat started under his helmet. He squinted into the
darkness, fearful of what was out there.

Over farther to the east another flare exploded and drifted down with its chute. Then to his left he saw a dark shadow passing between him and the stars. Turning, he edged in. The dim outline was hard to follow in the night, and as he closed he reasoned by the absence of exhaust flames that the craft was a glider. He reconnoitered ahead and saw another, dimly silhouetted against the heavens. Diving sharply, he went under the train and sought out the towing plane. If he could knock down the tow ship here some hundred and forty miles from the Canal, even from their great altitude the gliders would fall short by a hundred miles at least. And the jungle would take care of them.

There it was! A trimotor job of the Junkers type. Behind, in tandem on the towlines, were five large gliders, each carrying at least ten men with invasion equipment. Those poor fools, Rutherford breathed into his oxygen tube—those poor damn fools in there. He sucked in, sharply.

Quickly he came in from below and behind and raked the towing plane from center engine to the pilot's cockpit. The first burst fired the fuel tanks and flames streaked back almost to the first glider in the train. He zoomed and dropped a flare to light the motorless craft as they cut their useless towlines. He maneuvered to the left. The brilliancy of the magnesium flare was temporarily blinding, but as its shadow swung toward him he made out the first glider on its own, grimly holding its course for the Canal. He cut in swiftly and tried to hold it in his sights, but ran over it before firing a single burst. There was no fear of heavy-caliber fire from a glider, and Rutherford sensed relief.

The throttled fighter passed the glider as though it were stationary. His ship was making one-eighty; the speed of the sailplane was less than fifty now. He dove then far below, keeping his eyes on the glider vainly trying to maneuver out of the flare light. Again he approached at reduced speed. Hanging on his prop, he pressed the trigger of the gun switch. The short burst from his eight guns ate into the elongated pod of the glider, struck the outrigger root, and the glider broke into two pieces. Wing and pod swung crazily for the earth.

Strangely exhilarated, the squadron leader spotted several of his command picking off the unlucky soaring planes. The sky was brilliant now with parachute flares dropped by the fighters. Gliders were trapped in a night which had been lit as white as noontime. Rutherford picked out another craft frantically trying to dodge a flare light. He pulled his nose up and put his prop back into low pitch, then flew straight at the tail of the turning glider. He saw the heavy burst actually riddle the pod of the glider. Confident that he had raked the entire passenger compartment, he resumed his patrol. From another glider he shot the complete tail assembly away. A third tried to dive to low altitude and escape, and Rutherford saw the wings snap off from the unnatural strain. Not a parachute opened, he noted subconsciously. Evidently the invasion troops were not equipped.

The 78th worked back in close to the Canal where searchlights were crisscrossing the sky. Every hill around the waterway seemed to spurt with a battery of lights. Anti-aircraft guns belched explosive shells at the enemy bombers coming over in decimated waves. Every now and then the blinding flash of an exploded plane showed against the brilliance of the searchlights and the velvet backdrop of tropical night. But some few enemy bombers must be filtering through the screen because there were heavy flashes very near the Canal itself.

Rutherford, tired beyond experience, dreading any further action, went in now to the third assembly rendezvous with his squadron. Out there to the eastward other fighter ships were encountering more enemy gliders. Flares still blossomed out far away toward Obaldia. The reassembled squadron flew now at twenty-two thousand feet. About an hour's fuel remained. They would probably have to refuel and get right back into the air before this night was over, and the thought of renewing the patrol was almost more than Rutherford could bear.

And then, suddenly, the large bomber formation came in with its convoy of enemy fighters. Before he was completely aware, the air about Rutherford seemed filled with two-engined bombers and their waspish escorts. Carrier-based enemy planes! No fighters could possibly convoy bombers from Aruba without auxiliary bases, which simply did not exist!

Climbing in a steep turn to the left, Rutherford dodged, then tried to close in. He could see the flaring exhausts of many enemy fighters against the black sky, and he was fatigued, and the stabbing pain of the headache had become a dull throbbing so that this night's operations seemed already to be a year old.

It was almost continuous full throttle for thirty minutes. Rat races and squirrel cages were tame compared with that melee, even maintaining a semblance of formation against the invaders. At one time Rutherford took his ships into perfect position above and behind three bombers and blew them into eternity. The sight of enemy plane parts being actually shot into fragments displayed the destructive power of eight synchronized wing guns to him as no practice run ever had, and Rutherford grinned for the first time that night.

Then a fighter got on his tail. His first realization of danger was when the nose cannon of the E.A. blasted through his canopy, knocking a great hole in his instrument panel and armored cockpit. He was almost numbed by fright. He dove, skidding down from side to side. Below in the jungle, he knew, dozens of fires from burning wrecks still glowed, and he already saw himself in a raging furnace of bent metal, oil, and gasoline. The old fear returned. He must get out of this somehow. . . .

He was clear again—unbelievingly, shakingly. An enemy hurtled after him in flames from somewhere, evidently shot down by a prowling 78th pilot. Off to one side two fighters ran together, spinner to spinner, and there was nothing left after the explosion but fragments. The squadron leader inhaled deeply and groaned. His goggles fogged up and he wiped them with a gloved hand. He was sweating profusely despite the piercing cold of substratosphere air, and he shivered, thinking of the narrowness of his escape.

"If I get down safely," he muttered to himself, "they'll have a hell of a job putting me back in the air again tonight!"

Anti-aircraft fire dotted the heavens, but Rutherford knew that if those enemy bombers were to be knocked down before they reached the Canal either fighters or interceptors of both would have to do it. As he climbed back from his dive a squadron of swift two-engined interceptors streaked past. He could see their exhausts as they knifed up to engage the enemy with long bursts of fire from the .50-caliber guns and four nose cannon. Then back to bases for more fuel. Fuel for only fifty minutes, but their concentrated fire power was terrific, he remembered half fearfully.

Rutherford glanced at his instrument panel, wrecked by that burst. He tasted salty blood where flying glass of the broken canopy had cut his mouth. He had to lean far over to the left in his seat to avoid the cold blast of air coming through the holes in the windshield. He tried stuffing a crumpled map into the largest of the holes, but the slip stream sucked it out. He climbed on up to the bomber flight level, hoping there to meet up with members of his squadron.

For just a moment there was nothing visible, then suddenly a giant bomber tore by under him. Its swift appearance startled him and left him shaking again. Grimly he set his teeth and gripped his controls. Lining his sights mechanically for the tenth time that night, he pursued the enemy ship and pulled the trigger. Simultaneously his world seemed to explode as everything went white before him.

He felt the plane hit from the bomber's rear gunners. Then he opened his eyes into darkness, to realize that he was still alive, still flying smoothly behind his great Allison, and for the moment quite safe. Gradually he became aware that the beam from one of the defense searchlights had picked him out of the night, then passed on. The impact of relief flooded him so completely that he released his controls and sat, shaking.

Slowly he regained his equilibrium, and he knew that he must gratify the nervous tension within him with action. Positive action against the enemy. Now once again in darkness, he readjusted his eyes. Below him, somewhere, anti-aircraft fire burst with brilliant effect and a sound like continuous coughing. At intervals Rutherford was conscious of the tactical efficiency of other members of the 78th—his own squadron—whose small formations in shot-up elements still sent bomber after bomber down in flames. Without radio, without visual contact except close aboard, they were carrying on in the best tradition of the Air Corps, with superb air discipline as the vital moments ticked away. . . . All except their leader, who sat alone high above the fight, a solitary watcher ashamed of his own weaknesses and the fate which had thrust him into a position from where there was no turning back. Well, by God, he'd show them. . . .

Something like a cool desperation was growing inside him. He went down again after a lone bomber. As the target loomed in his sights he began to fire. Red bursts from machine-gun turrets in the sides of the big bomber and in its tail, and pounding in the forepart of his plane, told him that the enemy was scoring hits on him also. One struck his prop. Rutherford felt the impact, then a continuous vibration that nearly shook him out of the seat. His engine sputtered, but he dove in recklessly with guns full on. The recoil, combined with the loss of revs from his chattering engine, nearly stopped him in mid-flight. He sensed rather than saw hundreds of tracers eating into the bomber's vitals, noticed the tail gunner's turret nearly shot away, and then the enemy plane spouted fire.

Rutherford's Allison sputtered again and as flames from the stricken bomber swept back toward him he realized with a pounding heart that he himself was afire!

His engine roared out, vibrated wildly, and then the holed propeller gave way to the unequal strain. His engine ran, released from metal blades, to infinite speed and burst.

Hot oil struck him full in the face, coming through holes in the windshield and canopy. With left arm raised to guard his eyes, he pulled the emergency release of the hatch cover and started to climb over.

All the world had taken a moment to catch its breath and was strangely silent. Only the wind sound as it rushed through the jagged holes in his plane came to his ears against the backdrop of roaring flames. He would have to jump, but he couldn't. Not down there in that darkness. Suppose the chute failed to open. A man did not pass out in a free fall, he knew that. He would drop, screaming, for twenty thousand feet to smash into pulp in the jungle below.

If only he could stay with the ship up here. But he could not wait. He gripped the cockpit cowling and pulled himself upright. He would take advantage of the next yaw when the plane fell off behind him.

"There is really nothing to it," he remembered a veteran jumper had told him. "All you do is jump out and down, then wait until you are clear and pull the ring. You never feel the jerk of the chute as it opens. Suddenly you realize that you are floating down quietly and easily, and it's like a ride on a boardwalk wheelchair. But keep your feet crossed for the landing, if you jump at night. . . ."

Night? It was night, and he was jumping. Not afraid now? N-o-o, not afraid of the jump, or the long float to the ground. Or of the landing down there. Not afraid of the night, even, or of the enemy.

The hell he wasn't! He was shaking with fear.

The plane yawed back and flames reached for his face.

Rutherford jumped for the jungle far below. With closed eyes he felt for the elusive ring and jerked the pilot chute loose. The snap was audible above the roaring in his ears; he knew his chute had opened. He swung softly from his risers and wondered where he would land.

A gentle wind rushed up past his face. It was an unreal world all around him now, suspending him in mid-air, hanging, gently falling, falling. . . .

Far off he could see the direction of greatest activity; that must be the Canal. Well, his pocket compass would aid him in making the trip on foot. After all, it was not too far away. If the Chuchunaque head-hunters did not get him, or a panther jump him, or if he did not fall victim to the swamps or fever.

Below, Rutherford could make out a few dark splotches of trees through holes in the clouds, some lit by burning wreckage. Swinging like a pendulum, he watched his flaming plane swoop in a comet arc into a low cloud above the jungle. He heard the terrific explosion as it hit.

Rutherford kicked his legs, strained his eyes as he sought a clear space in the mat toward which to slip his chute, but he could see nothing clearly. He did not see accurately enough to gauge his height above the trees. His feet brushed a branch and then a gnarled limb struck him heavily in the small of the back. He felt his left arm crack against a heavy branch.

Gasping for breath, he braced himself for hitting the ground. Overhead the silken chute tore loudly; then it jerked to a halt and he hung suspended from the treetops far above the ground in the shattering silence of the tropical night.

Above him, toward the reflected light from searchlights and fires raging in isolated points, he could see the strained silk spread out across the top of a giant jungle tree. His left arm hung limply at his side, fractured in the fall, aching as if it were being jabbed with needles.

Hanging from the shroud lines, he swung gently high up, although every now and then, at first, the silk tore and he'd slip a few inches lower. He stared down into the blackness but could not see the ground, and shifted his weight. In trying to swing nearer the tree trunk to release his harness and slide down, the chute tore again and slipped dangerously. Alarmed that he might drop and thus become easy prey to jungle animals, he remained still.

Overhead now the hole that he had made in the tree roof slowly closed and hid the sky. No one could spot him now from the air, even in broad daylight.

Around him the silent rain of the tropics began. His body swung back and forth silently. The rain at least cooled his face, scorched from the flames of the burning ship. Now it was cool, but tomorrow it would stop raining, and the sun would beat down. Tomorrow . . . and tomorrow . . .

Far off, even the noise of the attack had stopped. The sky reflection died as storm clouds moved in, and the jungle was as dark as the inside of a huge cave.

Rutherford took a deep breath. The night pressed close around him, swinging by shroud lines from a jungle tree.

IRWIN SHAW

Faith at Sea

LIEUTENANT PETER GIFFORD LAWRENCE, U.S.N.R., stood on the foredeck of the SS *Rascoe*, holding lightly onto the canvas-sheathed three-inch gun as the bow dipped and trembled in the harsh chop of the North Atlantic. Five men of the gun crew stood at ease before him, shifting easily with the soaring lift and fall of the *Rascoe* as she chewed busily into the slate waves that had been hacking at her for six days, getting stronger and stronger as the six-thousand-ton freighter plowed at nine knots toward England.

"The duties of the gun captain," Constantini was reciting, like a child in school. "A, on manning gun, reports through sight setter to group control officer when gun is ready. B, operates plug as necessary. C, calls, 'Ready,' to pointer when breech is closed. . . ."

Lawrence only half listened as Constantini's voice droned on in the regular Thursday afternoon gunnery class that Lawrence conducted to keep the Navy gun crew alert and interested on the long, monotonous trips. He looked at the five men outlined in mufflers and coats against the low-hanging, cold sun. These, plus the five men on duty now at the after gun, had been given him by the Navy to guard the gray and shabby and valuable life of the *Rascoe,* and, as always, when he saw them assembled he felt with a mixture of amusement and pity how old he was.

He was only thirty-five, but except for Farrell, the chief petty officer, who was older than he, and Benson, the gunner's mate, who was twenty-five, all the men were under twenty-one. Their faces, bronzed and unlined and boyish, were always solemn and youthfully important when they were assembled like this for any official function, and were especially solemn today, because they had lost the convoy the night before in a storm and were now plodding over the gray wastes toward port vulnerable and alone.

"He is responsible for the conduct, efficiency, and spirit of the crew,"

Constantini was saying, "and must be made to realize that he is the representative of his battery officer. . . ."

"Very good," Lawrence said. "Harris."

"Yes sir." Harris stood stiffly at attention.

"The duties of the sight setter."

"To set the sights," Harris rattled off glibly, "and to transmit all communications between gun and group control officer. . . ."

Lawrence looked up over Harris' head to the bridge. Captain Linsey, his beard patchy and crooked in the wind, was peering angrily down at what he called the Navy kindergarten.

"To call, 'Set,'" Harris was saying, "to pointer when sights have been set. . . ."

Suddenly Harris stopped. Lawrence turned from looking at Captain Linsey on the bridge. The man next to Harris, William Doneger, was on his knees by Harris' side, gripping Harris' arm with a tortured, clutching hand. Harris stood there stupidly, frightened, looking blankly at the sweating, tense face.

"Doneger——" Lawrence started toward him. Doneger let loose his grip, dropped to the deck, and lay there, bent over and rocking.

Constantini sank swiftly to his knees and took Doneger's head in his hands, tenderly.

"What is it?" Lawrence kneeled beside the two of them, with the other men crowded silent and helpless around them.

Doneger looked up wildly, sweat breaking from his forehead.

"He's been sick all day, sir," Constantini said, his hands almost unconsciously going slowly and soothingly over his friend's forehead. "Terrible bellyache, sir."

Lawrence looked down at the suffering boy. His lips were bleeding from biting them and his face had grown terribly, greenly pale, morbid, and alarming in the cold Atlantic dusk.

"Let's get him below," Lawrence said. "To my quarters." There was no doctor on board and Lawrence's quarters had the medical chest and served as clinic for the Navy men.

Constantini got Doneger under the armpits and one of the other men, Crowley, got him around the knees and they started down with him.

Lawrence looked out across the ocean for a last survey. The water hissed by the *Rascoe* and the gray waves piled endlessly and monotonously on top of one another and the clouds came down, and that was all. He swallowed a little dryly, thinking of Doneger, racked and contorted, waiting for him, then braced his shoulders consciously and walked slowly toward his quarters.

When Lawrence opened the door of his cabin Doneger was lying on the extra berth and Constantini was whispering to him, a steady, soft stream of comforting words. "Nothing at all, William, nothing at all." Constantini was the only one on the ship who called Doneger William. All the other men called him Bill and Billie, but Constantini gave him his full and proper name, like a doting mother. "Something you ate. I've had bellyaches in my time." Constantini was seventeen years old. "I thought I was going to split down the middle and two hours later I'd be out eating two plates of spaghetti and a quart of dago red——" When he saw Lawrence come into the room he stopped his whispering and stood up at attention, trying to make his face impassive and martial. But he had a child's face, with deep, soft, brown Italian eyes, heavy, curled black eyelashes, and a full, almost girlish mouth, and the martial mask at the moment was not deceptive. Crowley, too, had jumped to attention.

Lawrence looked down at the suffering boy. Doneger looked up at him wanly. "Sorry, sir," he whispered.

"Sh-h-h," Lawrence said.

"He's been puking, sir," Constantini said. "All day, sir."

Lawrence sighed and sat down on the edge of the berth next to Doneger. That's what it's going to turn out to be, he thought as he put his hand on the boy's side. The worst possible thing.

The right side was swollen and tight, and Doneger jumped even at the slightest pressure.

"He has a very sensitive belly, sir." Constantini was speaking quickly and anxiously, as though somehow his words and explanations could make Donegar's condition less dangerous. "I took him to my cousin's wedding and he got drunk faster than anyone else, even faster than the sixteen-year-old girls. We had a stew yesterday that was a little greasy and maybe——"

"He has appendicitis," Lawrence said slowly.

Constantini looked at his friend's face in silence. Doneger closed his eyes. Lying down here, in the warm stateroom, on a dry bed, he seemed more comfortable, better able to meet the pain.

"Everything will be all right, William," Constantini murmured to Doneger. "The lieutenant's already diagnosed the disease."

The door opened and Captain Linsey came in. He stood above Doneger, staring down at him, his mouth curled, as always when he had anything to do with the Navy men on board his ship, into a sour and ancient snarl.

"Sick," Linsey said. "This sonofabitch is very sick."

"Yes," Lawrence said. Captain Linsey would make amusing conversation after the war at dinner parties in Boston. Crusty old merchant sea dog. Ignored the Navy. Ignored the war, even in the middle of a pack of submarines.

"This sonofabitch'll die." Captain Linsey leaned over and peered harshly into the pale, suffering face.

Very amusing after the war at dinner parties, Lawrence thought. Right now I'd like to kill him.

"We'll take care of him," Lawrence said.

Suddenly Captain Linsey poked Doneger in the side with a huge, wrinkled finger. Doneger cried and jumped. "Sorry, sonny," Captain Linsey said. He turned to Lawrence. "Ready to bust. Boy out with me on the way to Wilhelmshaven in 1931 died in three days. Same thing."

Out of the corner of his eye Lawrence saw Constantini look quickly down at Doneger, then look up and take a long, deep breath.

"Please," Lawrence said. "I'll come up to the bridge later and you can tell me whatever you——"

"This sonofabitch needs an operation."

"There's no doctor on board."

Captain Linsey sucked at the wet ends of his mustache and looked with crazy slyness at Lawrence. "We won't make port for seven days. At least. He ain't going to last no week."

I'd like to kill him, Lawrence thought, looking up at Captain Linsey's old, harsh seaman's face. I'd like to kill him, but he's right, he's right.

"I thought we could freeze it," Lawrence said. "After all, we have ice. Maybe it'll subside."

"Too late." Captain Linsey wagged his head. "Surgery. Surgery or nothing."

"There're no surgeons here," Lawrence said loudly. "If you insist on arguing, let's get out of this room."

"You ever see an operation?" Captain Linsey asked.

"Yes." Lawrence's brother-in-law was a surgeon and over a period of ten years Lawrence had seen seven or eight operations. "That isn't the same thing."

"There was a Dutchman we took to Capetown in 1927," Captain Linsey said. "A doctor. Studied in America. He left a book on board. All kinds of operations. Every once in a while I read in it. Very interesting reading. I bet it's got appendicitis in it."

"That's ridiculous." Lawrence stood up and went over to the door. "Thank you for your interest, Captain."

Captain Linsey touched Doneger's head. "Fever. I bet it's over a hundred and four. An operation really isn't so much. A little common sense and a little nerve. What the hell, what has this boy got to lose?" He leaned close to Doneger and spoke with surprising softness. "Sonny, you got any objections to being operated on?"

Doneger stared at Constantini. Constantini turned away, giving no answer one way or another with his eyes.

"I have no objections," Doneger said faintly.

Captain Linsey strode briskly toward the door. "I'll send the book down," he said cheerfully. "We'll save the sonofabitch yet." He clapped Lawrence on the back. "I'd do it myself, only I'm old and jumpy and I've drunk too much whisky in my day. I'll be on the bridge. I'll keep this tub as steady as possible." He went out quickly.

Lawrence closed his eyes so that he wouldn't have to look at Doneger or Crowley or Constantini.

A moment later a seaman came in with a worn and broken-backed book. He put it on the table and went out. Crowley and Doneger and Constantini and Lawrence all looked at the book, lying alone on the table.

Lawrence stood up and went over and opened to the index. Under A, Appendectomy—p. 941. The first time he read through it, the words were a weird and incomprehensible blur. He looked up once or twice, only to see the staring, serious eyes of the three other men scanning his face as though they somehow could tell from that distance whether or not the words he was reading were of any value to him.

Lawrence took off his coat and started slowly to read the passage from the beginning once more:

"Before operating try to locate the situation of the appendix. The incision should be over the seat of the disease. In the rare left-sided cases and in median cases the incision is median. . . ."

The words began to group themselves in his mind into coherent sentences capable of being understood by a man who could read and write.

"In an acute case in a man I separate the muscular fibers. Battle's inci-

sion at the outer edge of the rectus muscle is preferred by many surgeons. . . ."

In a biology course in college Lawrence had dissected the earthworm,
the frog, the white rat, but all dead, beyond the reach of pain, unmoved by
clumsiness or error.

"If there be infection, surround the region involved with packs of plain
gauze, each strip being two and a half inches wide, fifteen inches long,
and four layers in thickness. Pass a ligature through the meso appendix
as shown in Fig. 691A, tie the ligature, and . . ."

Fig. 691A was very simple, and if flesh and muscle and organ were anything like the diagram, it was conceivable that a deft though unpracticed
man might be able to manage.

"William," Lawrence said. "Are you sure?"

Doneger sighed. "I'm sure."

"Crowley," Lawrence said, "go to the galley and get a pot of boiling
water."

"Yes sir," Crowley said, and went out softly, already making a hospital
of the room.

Lawrence went back to the close print of the book. He read and reread, studied the diagrams until he felt that he could draw them with
his eyes closed.

He stood up and unlocked the medical chest. He threw open the doors
and stared at the rows of bottles, the serried bandages, the fateful, gleaming instruments. Behind him he heard the voice of Constantini, rough
with the accent of the streets of New York, soft with compassion and fear.

"It ain't hardly nothing, William. A cousin of mine had this and he was
operated on and three days later he slept with the nurse." Constantini had
a cousin for all eventualities of discussion, naval and civilian. "Everybody
ought to have his appendix out. They don't do you no good. None at all.
If I had the time I'd have 'em out myself."

Lawrence stared at the bottles, the bandages, the steel instruments. He
made his eyes go slowly and calmly from one thing to another in the
chest, taking a deliberate inventory. The thing is, he thought, not to hurry.
After all, men have done more difficult things than this. The instruments
are there, the one can of ether, the bandage, the scalpel, the needles, the
catgut, the clamps, the sponges, the alcohol, the sulfanilamide. And the
Navy had given him a course in first aid. How to stop bleeding. How
to avoid gangrene. How to set a broken leg.

"You hardly feel it," Constantini was saying in his deep, melodious boy's voice. "You take a little nap. You wake up. Appendix absent. You feel a little stiff for a day or two, you get a good rest, the other guys stand your watches, you read the magazines and drink hot soup. You get to England, you get three weeks' sick leave, you'll have the time of your life. The English girls're crazy about American sailors. I got a cousin in the Merchant Marine and he says that an American in London is like a king far as the girls're concerned. They can't do enough for them."

Why, Lawrence thought with a remote and bitter detachment, did this have to happen the first time we lost a convoy? In a convoy the boy could be transferred to one of the cruisers accompanying them and there a first-rate naval surgeon in a shining, brilliantly equipped operating room would do the job in ten minutes as a matter of simple routine.

Crowley came in with the pot of hot water and Lawrence put the scalpel, the needles, and the clamps into it.

"Anything I can do," Constantini said as Lawrence watched the steel gleaming dully as it sank among the bubbles of the boiling water. "Anything at all."

Lawrence nodded. "There'll be plenty for you to do. Clear that table and get a sheet out of the locker and spread it over it." Constantini listened eagerly and nodded. "Wash your hands first."

While Crowley and Constantini scrubbed their hands and the strong smell of the soap pricked his nostrils, Lawrence reread, slowly, the entire description of the operation. Even after he had finished and after the gentle, watery sound of scrubbing behind him had long ceased, he sat with his head in his hands, staring at the page before him. At last he stood up. Well, that was that.

He turned briskly, and without words he and Constantini and Crowley lifted Doneger onto the white-covered table. He washed and scrubbed his hands with alcohol. Gently he shaved the slight, downy fuzz from the boy's belly. Then he washed it with alcohol.

Crowley behaved wonderfully. He was a little, impassive Irishman to whom all things seemed to come as a matter of course—promotions, overwork, murders, drownings, wars. Lawrence was glad it was Crowley who had silently volunteered for this job.

Constantini, too, handled Doneger with soft hands, lifting him gently and securely, making no unnecessary move. Together they bound Doneger to the table with linen bandage, so that the roll of the ship would not throw him off the table.

Lawrence noticed that the ship had swung around and was heading directly into the wind and was much steadier now. He would remember to thank Captain Linsey later.

He took the ether cone and stood at Doneger's shoulder. Doneger and Constantini and five of the other boys had had their heads shaved when they were last in the States. They had done it as a joke after Lawrence had complained at inspection that they were letting their hair grow too long. All seven of them had marched solemnly back onto the *Rascoe* from their shore leaves and had with one gesture swept their hats off their heads as they reported in. Lawrence had stared at the seven shining pates, scarred with the incredibly numerous battles of childhood, and had lowered his eyes to keep from laughing, and had said, "Very good." They had saluted and swept out and he had heard them roaring with laughter on the deck.

Doneger's head, now with a slight baby fuzz standing up all over it, lay flatly in the shadows on the table in the small cabin as the old plates of the *Rascoe* creaked and wailed under the attack of the sea.

"All right, William," Lawrence said softly. "Are you ready now?"

"I'm ready, sir." Doneger spoke in a whisper and smiled up at him.

Lawrence put the cone gently over the boy's face and said, "Breathe deeply." He poured the ether in and the smell, sweet and morbid, leaked into the cabin, making it suddenly strange and deathly. "Count," Lawrence said. "Keep counting."

"One, two, three," Doneger said clearly, "four, five, six, seven, eight"— the young voice began to blur and thicken—"nine, ten, eleven, twelve, thir . . . thir . . ." The voice mumbled heavily and wearily through the cone. The long, chubby body on the table relaxed for the first time and Crowley gently straightened the legs out. The voice died away completely and the noise of the creaking plates of the old ship was the only sound to be heard.

Lawrence lifted the ether cone. Doneger's face was calm and showed no trace of pain. Lawrence gave the cone to Constantini. "If I tell you to," he said, "put this over his face. In case he moves."

"Yes sir," Constantini said, and moved quickly to Doneger's head.

Lawrence went to the pot of boiling water and with a forceps took out the instruments he had put there to sterilize. Crowley had arranged a clean towel on the bunk and Lawrence put the instruments there in a neat and shining row, remembering how dentists who had filled his teeth had done the same thing.

He picked up the scalpel and adjusted the lamp so that its full glare fell on the bare stomach of the sleeping boy.

The skin was very pink and there seemed to be a firm, small layer of fat under it. Doneger was very young and his belly still had a round little baby swell. He was breathing softly and the muscles trembled rhythmically and gently.

How smooth, how subtle, how complex, Lawrence thought. How close to death. How vulnerable to knife and powder. How irrevocably naked to damage. He closed his eyes for a moment, unable to look any more at the smooth, childish skin. With his eyes closed and the moaning and creaking of the tumbling ship in his ears, it all seemed dreamlike and impossible. He, Peter Gifford Lawrence, gently reared, nursed and fed and tended all his years by mother and aunt and teacher and doctor, every boyhood scratch mercurochromed and overbandaged; soft-blanketed sleeper in neat, well-ventilated room; student at Harvard, where he had taken notes on Plato and Geoffrey Chaucer, on the architecture of the Renaissance and the metrics of John Milton—Peter Gifford Lawrence, gentleman, formal guest at pleasant dinners, polite talker to old ladies at Lenox garden parties, dealer in books and fine prints, now standing, scalpel in hand, in the cramped, peeling stateroom of a wheezing freighter groaning and heaving in a middle Atlantic gale, with four miles of black sea water and countless drowned sailors under the keel, the prey of deadly vessels that struck unseen and mortal in the turn of a man's head. . . .

"Battle's incision at the outer edge of the rectus muscle is preferred by many surgeons. . . . After opening the peritoneum, examine very gently to detect the situation of the . . . This divides the mucous membrane, submucous tissue, and muscular coat . . ."

Lawrence opened his eyes and looked up. Constantini was staring at him. In the soft, girlish eyes, besides the worry for his friend's agony, there was deep trust, deep confidence, that this kindly, efficient, understanding, courageous man, this officer who had been designated by great authority to guide his wartime fate, would, this time and all times, do well what had to be done. There was no doubt in the soft, steady eyes of Salvatore Constantini.

Lawrence bent his head and firmly made the incision.

When the operation was over and Doneger had been gently lifted into the extra bunk and Constantini had silently taken the watch at his side, Lawrence opened the door and stepped out onto the deck. The black wind flung bitter spray into his face and he had to half shut his eyes against it. But he stood there, holding onto the rail, peering sightlessly into the roaring darkness, hardly thinking, hardly feeling, rolling crazily and aimlessly with the roll of the ship.

He stood there drunkenly for a long time, then suddenly turned and went into his room. Doneger was lying there, motionless, the ether still in control. Constantini sat quietly at his side, never taking his eyes off the pale, exhausted face.

Lawrence lay down in his clothes and slept immediately.

When Lawrence awoke he opened his eyes slowly and came up from the deep well of sleep, as though he had slept for weeks on end. Slowly he became aware of Constantini sitting across the room from him, still looking steadfastly at Doneger, as though he hadn't moved all night.

Lawrence opened his eyes wide.

"Good morning, Lieutenant." Constantini smiled shyly at him. His eyes were sunken and he rubbed them like a sleepy infant.

"Morning, Constantini." Lawrence sat up suddenly, remembering in a rush that across from him lay a man whom he had operated upon a few hours before. Doneger was awake, and drowsily smiled, his face creased by a kind of remote pain.

"Hello, Lieutenant," Doneger whispered.

Lawrence jumped out of his bunk. "How are you?"

"Fine," Doneger whispered. "First class. Thanks."

Lawrence peered at him closely. There were wrinkles of pain in the boy's face, but there was a little color in the cheeks and something in the eyes that seemed to announce that death had once and for all passed by.

Lawrence looked at Constantini. "You get any sleep last night?"

"Not much, sir. I'm pleased to watch William."

"Get below and get some sleep. Someone else'll watch William."

"Yes sir." Constantini looked shyly at him and then turned to Doneger. "My God," he whispered as Lawrence poured some water to wash, "will you have a picnic with those English girls!" He touched his friend's forehead lightly and chuckled as he went out. And deep, deep from the depths of his eighteen years and recovery from death, Doneger chuckled softly in return.

Later in the day Lawrence started forward toward the bow gun, where the men were assembled for the interrupted examination in gunnery. The sun was shining and the ocean was a sharp blue, the whitecaps in the distance looking like the bobbing sails of a regatta with a million entries. He had left Doneger smiling and sipping tea, and the bright wind felt festive and alive against his freshly shaven face. He saw the cluster of blue uniforms and the ruddy faces of the gun crew around the gun and heard Constantini's voice, melodious and terribly earnest, chanting in final review before his arrival. Lawrence smiled to himself and was proud of the Navy and the red-faced, earnest boys and the gun and the *Rascoe* and himself, abroad, dependable, and unafraid, on the wide ocean.

" 'Tention!" Benson called as the lieutenant approached, and the boys stiffened rigidly, their faces stern and set, their hands tight at their sides. Lawrence looked sternly at them, carrying out his share of the martial drama. He looked at them and felt once more, with the old amusement and pity, how old he was at the age of thirty-five, confronted by and responsible for these large, determined, valuable, fearless children. "At ease," he said. Out of the corner of his eye he saw Captain Linsey, his face as sour and scornful as ever.

The tight little knot relaxed and the men shuffled about, making themselves comfortable. They kept their eyes on Lawrence, seriously. Constantini's lips mumbled inaudibly as he ran over the list of questions he might be asked to answer.

"We'll go right into it," Lawrence said. "Harris"—he started with the boy nearest him—"what're the duties of the first loader?"

"To receive the shell from the second loader," Harris said, "and to load the gun."

"Levine." Lawrence spoke to the next man. "Duties of the second loader?"

"To pass shells to the first loader," Levine said carefully. "To arrange shells on deck in rear of gun in probable arc of train."

Lawrence went down the line. "Constantini." He saw Constantini's face tense almost painfully with anticipation. "What are the duties of the third loader?"

Constantini's lips started to move. Then he licked them uneasily. He took in a deep breath, looked suddenly blankly and despairingly at Lawrence. Lawrence glanced at him and saw that all knowledge had fled from his head.

A deep red flush surged up over Constantini's collar and stained his cheeks, his ears. He licked his lips in misery, looked straight ahead, hopelessly.

Lawrence looked away for a moment, then called the next man, Moran. Moran answered briskly.

One by one, Lawrence went down the line of men. Each man snapped out his answer, their voices ringing clear and triumphant in the bright wind. Once more it was Constantini's turn.

Lawrence looked surreptitiously at him. He was standing as stiff as though all the admirals of all the fleets of the world were passing him in review. His jaws were clenched and the muscles stood out like rope. His eyes stared ahead of him like a man watching the execution of his father— wild, hopeless, full of guilt.

Lawrence knew in his heart that no matter what question he put to Constantini, no answer would come from that mourning brain, no word pass those locked, despairing lips. For a moment Lawrence thought of passing him up and going on to the next man. But then to the shame of Constantini's ignorance and defection would be added the ignominy of official pity.

"Constantini," Lawrence said as crisply as he could, hoping to shock him out of his trancelike trauma. He carefully sought out the simplest, most transparent, most easily answered question in the whole book. "Constantini," he said, slowly and clearly and loudly, "what is the purpose of shrapnel?"

Constantini did not move. The tongue froze between the lips, the eyes stared without hope across the Atlantic Ocean, while no answer came to show this good man, this Boston lieutenant who had done a brave and noble thing to save his friend's life, that he, Salvatore Constantini, loved and admired him and would be grateful to him for the rest of his life. The blush settled like a permanent blight on his cheeks, but no answer came from the rock-bound brain. The deep, ordinary thanks that a man could give by the crisp performance of his duty could not be given. William lived and Salvatore had failed the man who had saved him. Suddenly the tears started from his eyes and rolled down his rigid cheeks.

Lawrence looked at the weeping boy, staring blindly out to sea, among the men who kindly stared out to sea with him. Lawrence saw the bitter tears and almost put out his hand to comfort the boy, but held back just in time, since comfort now, before his ten friends, would be agony later.

Lawrence glanced once more at him and tried to call the next man's name and ask him the purpose of shrapnel, but the name stuck in his throat and he turned his back on the men to keep them from seeing what was plain in their lieutenant's face.

RICHARD SHERMAN
The Life of Riley

ALL THAT DAY, that long summer's day, the sky was blue and cloudless. From the sun's rising somewhere out of Brooklyn and Queens to its disappearance somewhere beyond the Palisades, there were almost fifteen hours of varying shades of light to be seen and to see by: first the gray light of dawn, which softened mistily into a wash of pink, and then the strong, clear, flat light of midday, and after that the long, slanting light of late afternoon, and then the lingering glow of sunset, and finally the deepening shadows of twilight. The day was warm, yet not too warm, and although on the whole it was windless there was nevertheless a gentle breeze whenever and wherever a breeze was needed. All in all, it was as nearly ideal as a day could be, one that might well have been deposited in the time capsule and labeled "Summer Day. American. Twentieth Century. Perfect Specimen."

And yet, perfect though it was, there was no reason he should remember this particular day in preference to thousands of other days. It was not a birthday or an anniversary or even strictly a holiday, although in a sense it was a holiday, of course, because that whole summer was a holiday. "The last real holiday you'll probably be having until you're so old that holidays won't mean much," his father had warned him gravely. "So you'd better make the most of it." All of which was his father in one of his conscientiously parental moods, as distinct from his usual mood of laissez faire. The good thing about his father, or rather one of the many good things, was that he frequently found it difficult to remember to act like a father. But when he did remember, he remembered furiously, as if trying to make up for lost time, giving solemn counsel and earnest admonitions until at last he would become embarrassed and say, "Mm, well, I guess that's enough of that," and then relievedly lapse into a human being.

At any rate, in accordance with his father's wish, even command, this entire summer was to be his own, and not until September was he to set about that mysterious procedure known as "earning a living"—which in his case seemed to point to his running up and down Madison Avenue as an only slightly glorified messenger boy for his father's advertising agency, at a salary of twenty-five dollars a week.

His mother, who was very serious about being a mother, was inclined to doubt the wisdom of this nepotic proposal, and she had announced her views during that informal Commencement Day conference they had had as they had sat—all five of them, Sheila and Tim, too, the Rileys reunited —beneath the elms of the Harvard Yard. In her opinion, she said, it might be better if Rick "struck out for himself." And when his father had asked, "Meaning what, my love?" she had replied with uncharacteristic vagueness: "Well, I don't know exactly. Just—strike out. You know. The way you did. After all, your father didn't set you up in business."

Rick's father had answered: "I'll say he didn't. He didn't even have any business for himself. Anyway, I'm not setting Rick up in business. I'm just giving him a job. What's the use of working yourself up to the point where you're able to give people jobs if you can't give one to your own son?"

Mrs. Riley had remained reluctant and uneasy, as if she felt that the plan was either too simple to be logical or was somehow not quite honest. She had said, "But don't you think he ought to have a chance to be—well, self-reliant?"

"Don't worry. He'll have plenty of chances to be self-reliant during the next fifty years or so."

Mr. Riley had gazed at the green sweep of lawn and at the families strolling in the dappled shade of the leafy trees. Sunlight on time-worn red brick, the dark, waxy gloss of ivy, the creamy whiteness of entryways, women in summer dresses, and the sound of a fountain playing. Although there was no self-pity in his voice, there was perhaps a little envy and certainly a little regret. "I never went to college, but my son has," he had said. "And I never had two months to myself to do nothing in, but he's going to have them." He had looked at Rick sternly. "And mind you do nothing. You can develop your forehand and your crawl and maybe your rumba. You can even read now and then, if you like; but you'd better stick to detective stories and comic strips. The point is, I don't want to catch you at anything that might be useful. None of this improving your mind. Remember that."

Rick had smiled. "I'll remember," he had said.

And his mother had sighed. "Really, Michael," she said. "Honestly."

"That's one of the privileges of being a self-made man," Mr. Riley had said cheerfully. "One of the rewards. You can ruin your children."

"You will ruin them, too."

"Oh, I don't know," he had said. "I don't think so. Anyway, even if I do, we'll all have a good time at it. We could do worse." Then he had reached over and placed his hand on Tim's thick, strawberry-colored thatch. "I tell you what. We'll experiment my way with Rick, and then if that doesn't work out we'll try your way with Tim. When the time comes we can let Tim strike out in all directions. When he's twenty-one we'll blindfold him and set him down in the middle of Times Square in his underwear and with a clean shirt in a bandanna and tell him to take it from there. He can sink or swim."

"In his underwear in Times Square," Sheila had giggled. She was thirteen and at the prim stage. "Daddy, the things you say."

"How could I swim in Times Square?" had asked Tim, who was nine and practical. "And how could I sink?"

His mother had been silent and reflective. At last she had seemed to resign herself despite her principles. She even had made an attempt to rationalize and justify a situation they all suspected her of secretly anticipating with pleasure. "Well, of course it will be nice, having him at home," she had admitted. "I suppose he can be helpful, too. On errands and things like that."

"No errands," his father had said. "The main thing is for him to be idle and spend his time wastefully."

"It certainly looks like a full summer for Angie Fisher," Sheila had remarked. "My goodness, if he's going to have nothing to do but go over and hang around her place she'll be worn to a frazzle."

"Now, Sheila," his mother had said, and Rick had merely smiled and contented himself with an amiable "Shut up."

And a few minutes later they had got up and gone toward the canvas enclosure, where, in company with several hundred similarly black-gowned and mortar-boarded figures, Rick had ascended wooden steps, walked across a platform, and been welcomed into "the fellowship of educated men." And that had been a memorable day too.

But, curiously, it was not so memorable as this other day, two weeks later, this day that had no significant, identifying ceremony, being in many ways like days that had gone before it and days that would come after it, and yet which somehow stood alone and apart.

They were occupying the same South Shore house they had been renting for the past several seasons—a rambling, shingled, many-porched affair, situated within easy walking distance of the beach. It was not a very modern or even a very attractive house, just as the community on whose edge it stood was not a fashionable one. But his father said that the whole point in moving to the country for the summer was to take things easy and that therefore he refused to "try to keep up with the Hamptons, East, South, or even West." Also this place was comfortable and commodious and they all liked it, even Sheila, who was unsparingly critical.

This, then, was the house in which Rick woke up that day.

The blinds were still drawn, and the room was filled with a green, aqueous light; but he could tell by the finger of sun inching up over the rumpled sheets of Tim's empty bed that it must be almost nine o'clock. Through the open window, from the badminton court below, he could hear the shrill shrieks of Sheila and Tim at play. Rising, he padded barefooted to the windows, snapped up the blinds, and leaned out into air that had the good smell of fresh-cut grass in it.

"Hi," he said. "You certainly make a lot of racket for so early in the morning. Can't you let a person sleep?"

"Early!" said Tim. "It's practically noon. Didn't you hear me getting up?"

"Angie phoned," said Sheila. "Twice. She says for you to be sure not to be late." She smiled up with a winsomeness he had every reason to distrust. "You know, I was wondering if maybe you wouldn't like me to go with you. I've only been once, and there are a lot of things I'd like to——"

"No," he said, and turned away. Of the some hundred and thirty million people who might have accompanied him and Angie, Sheila was probably the last he would have chosen. She was a nice girl, Sheila, and he was fond of her, but the fact remained that she was his sister and thirteen years old.

He took a shower, donned shorts, a crew shirt, and sneakers, and descended to the dining room, where he found his mother lingering over her second cup of coffee.

"Hello," he said, kissing her cheek, and then he sat down and gulped his orange juice. "Dad get off on time?"

Mrs. Riley nodded. "He left early. He drove in. He said it was such a nice day, and he thought it would be a good chance to put on more mileage." She shrugged. "That car. He'll wear it out before he's even broken it in. He thinks that as long as he's going thirty-five he's only standing still."

"Well," Rick said, grinning, "isn't he?"

"Like father, like son," she said darkly. "And how fast did you drive last night?"

"Twenty-five all the way," he said solemnly. "We just crept."

"Mm. I can imagine," she said. And after a moment added: "Crept where? I heard you come in. The dance couldn't have lasted that late, could it?"

"No, but afterward we drove around for a while, and then we went back to Angie's and talked." But most of the time they hadn't talked. Just sat in the swing, the chains squeaking as they rocked gently to and fro, patches of moonlight slanting through the porch vines, everything quiet, everything still.

"Oh," she said. "I see." And Rick had an idea it was more than possible that she did see. And then she said, "Well, what are your plans today?"

"I'm picking up Angie at noon, and we're going to the Fair with Bingo and Dot. We're staying out there for dinner."

His mother shook her head in mystification. "I really don't understand how you can go so often. All those crowds, and all that walking. And when you've seen it once, you've seen it."

"It's the 'Greatest Spectacle of the Century,'" he said, quoting.

"Perhaps. But I'll be glad when it's over. It's like living with a carnival, and the traffic seems to get worse and worse. Every time I drive past and look at that spire thing and that hideous ball——"

"Trylon and Perisphere," he corrected.

"Well, whatever it is, it's a monstrosity and I wish they'd take it down." She rose, a list in her hand. "I'd better be getting started. There's lots to keep me busy." And then she added ironically, "But of course you wouldn't know about being busy, would you?"

He smiled. "I guess you think I'm pretty useless."

She hesitated, and then she smiled too. She placed her hand lightly on his shoulder. "Yes," she said, "I do. But I'd rather you were useless now than later." She paused. "And it's just that—well, that your father's so much the lighthearted Irishman and I suppose I'm so much the——" She stopped and walked toward the kitchen. "Tell Angie and Mrs. Fisher that we're expecting them for Sunday," she said, and disappeared.

Rick sat sipping his coffee. It might not be an appropriate or even a nice way to think of your mother, but the fact was that her bark was worse than her bite. And she did like Angie. In fact his whole family liked Angie. Of course there was no reason why they shouldn't—they had known her most of her life. But the tradition of literature, from *Romeo and Juliet* on, invariably indicated that your own family should be opposed to the girl you wanted to marry, and the somewhat disappointing truth was that his wasn't: disappointing because he would have liked so much to have defied someone—the world, even—for Angie's sake. But no, they were crazy about her, all of them. It sometimes seemed to him that they were crazier about her than they were about him. Especially his mother, who in her sterner moments said: "Wait till Angie gets hold of you. She'll take you in hand. You won't leave a bathroom in this state in her house, I assure you."

He finished his breakfast, reached for the newspaper, and after a few minutes devoted to the sports column, idly scanned the front page. There didn't seem to be much news. The King and Queen had arrived back in England, the Dixie Clipper had landed at Lisbon, Portugal, after making the first commercial passenger flight from the United States to Europe (Just imagine, he thought. Flying across the Atlantic Ocean. Boy!), and there had been a murder in the Bronx. Otherwise nothing much appeared to have happened during the past twenty-four hours. In China the Japanese had occupied a place called Swatow; but that wasn't news, because something like that was always going on in China and neither he nor anyone he knew had ever been able to make head or tail of it.

He strolled onto the side porch and stood watching Sheila and Tim on the badminton court. He commented critically on their proficiency and offered to take on both of them at once. The offer was accepted. They beat him badly, though with considerable exertion.

"I know what," said Sheila. "Let's take a swim."

Tim said: "Sure. Let's. Rick too."

"Okay," he said, and they all headed for the house to change.

The Rileys always regarded that particular strip of beach as "their" beach, although it wasn't really theirs at all. It was anybody's who happened to come along; but they usually had the place to themselves.

This morning, as usual, the wide white sands were trackless and deserted. The surf roared in, wave after wave, and they fought it, plunging their glistening brown bodies into the foamy mountains of green and white that swept fiercely toward them. But the fierceness was merely assumed, for it was not an angry ocean. It was an ocean at play, just as they were at play. They stayed in the water for almost an hour, and then they dropped on the warm sand and lay with the sun biting pleasantly into their backs.

"What a day," Rick thought, turning over and squinting up at the cloudless sky. "Boy, what a day. Just about perfect."

Tim drew himself up on his elbows and, chin cupped in hands, gazed at the sea. He launched into a typically Timlike speculation. "If a person were to swim out in a straight line from here," he said, "just where I'm looking now, as far as he could go, what would happen?"

"He'd probably drown," Rick said, "if he went far enough."

"No, you dope. I mean, if he could just go on and on. Where would he get?"

"Oh—Spain, I guess. Or maybe the northern part of Africa."

"Not that way he wouldn't," observed Sheila. "He'd get to South America." She glanced witheringly at Rick. "My goodness, and to think you're a college graduate."

"South America—Africa." Tim shifted his eyes, and after a period of global indecision said, "I think I'd rather go to Africa—wouldn't you, Rick?"

"Mm?" he said lazily. He had turned over on his stomach again and had pillowed his head on his arms and was on the verge of sleep. His eyes were closed, although the brilliance of the sun prevented complete darkness— behind his closed lids was an iridescent velvet curtain on which showers of stars danced—and in his ears was the rhythmic boom of surf. And then he did sleep, in the hot sun and the cool ocean breeze, and dreamed of Angie.

Suddenly someone was poking him and Sheila was saying: "Hey, wake up. Look. Out there."

He sat up and looked, and in the distance saw the white shimmer of a liner, outward bound. A curl of smoke smudged itself against the blue.

"I wonder which one it is," said Tim.

"It's the *Normandie*," he said. "You can tell by her stacks."

"On its first trip over," said Sheila, out of her inexhaustible store of miscellaneous information, "it crossed in four days, three hours, and twenty-five minutes."

"Gee," said Tim dreamily, "how'd you like to be out there on her?"

"Not me," said Rick, but what he really meant was: "Not now. Not yet." Because he had an idea, a plan, and had had it for some time. It was that he and Angie should go to Europe on their honeymoon, and on the *Normandie*. As yet he hadn't mentioned it to anyone, even to Angie, for he wasn't sure where the money would come from. It would be a little difficult to manage on twenty-five dollars a week, he supposed, although by that time he'd probably be making more. . . . He gazed out at the ship, and in his mind he saw himself and Angie strolling the deck, arm in arm, while the other passengers turned around to look at them and whispered: "They're just married. Name's Riley. Mr. and Mrs. Rick Riley. Isn't she lovely? Isn't he lucky?"

Back in his room, he dressed carefully—tan gabardine suit, white canvas shoes, white shirt, white handkerchief fluffed up just the proper length from his breast pocket, and blue tie. No hat, because he didn't like wearing hats. His final gesture was to pick up his wallet and finger the bills in it. Yes, he had enough. Maybe not enough for the French Pavilion, but if they did decide to go there, he could always borrow from Bingo.

He got the car and drove off, and turned finally onto the parkway. The traffic was thick with Fair-bound cars, but he weaved in and out expertly and illegally. He switched on the radio, and in a moment a soprano voice swelled out:

> "Sum-mertime, and the liv-in' is eas-y.
> Fish are jumpin', and the cot-ton is high. . . .
> Oh, your daddy's rich, and your maw is good-look-in'. . . ."

That was it, he thought. Summertime, when the living is easy. However, although his mother was good-looking—there wasn't a gray hair on her head, and golf kept her figure like a girl's—his father wasn't exactly rich. Or was he? As a matter of fact he had never been able to determine what the family's economic status was. They belonged to a beach club, but it was a considerably less elegant one than the Atlantic Beach Club. His father's advertising agency was larger than some; but on the other hand, it was a great deal smaller than most. In town their apartment on West

Twelfth Street was multiroomed and well furnished; but it bore little resemblance to the apartments of the really wealthy as he had seen them in the movies and the rotogravure sections.

Once, when talking with his father, he had happened to say something about "us in the middle-income bracket." His father had said, "Who's in the middle-income bracket?" And he had answered, "Well, I guess we are, aren't we?" His father had laughed. "Three cars, even if two of them are secondhand. Two servants. The country in the summer. Your mother's mink coat. Do you call that 'middle-income bracket'? Is that what they teach you at Harvard? Listen, in comparison with people who really are in the middle-income bracket, we're up in J. P. Morgan's class. We're those rich Rileys—comparatively speaking. We're among the blessed."

And without being either smug or self-satisfied, that was the way Rick had thought of them ever since—as being neither rich nor poor, as having not too much yet more than enough. As being "among the blessed." And he himself was twice blessed, because he had Angie.

He saw her now as he drove up to her house. She was sitting on the porch steps waiting for him, and as always when he first glimpsed her, something sang within him. It was like poetry—"My heart leaps up when I behold . . ." And then, after leaping up, settled back into a heart's normal pace and routine. It happened every time. He had started to tell her about it once, trying to describe it. But it hadn't been necessary, for she had said: "I know. Me too."

She got up from the steps and went toward him as he drew the car to the curb. Except for the sheen of the beige stockings on her wonderful legs, she was all in white—white shoes, white dress, white gloves, and a huge white cartwheel hat. Her lips and fingernails were scarlet, her arms and face a golden tan, her eyes green, and her hair black with blue lights in it.

"Hello," she said.

"Hello."

The way they looked at each other, they might have been meeting again after a separation of twelve months, instead of a few hours.

Rick swung open the door, and she got into the seat beside him and placed her hand in his. "Isn't it a marvelous day?" she said. "Isn't it?"

"Perfect," he said. "It's been perfect from the minute I woke up, and now it's even better."

"A thing can't be better than perfect," she said. "It isn't possible."

"Oh yes, it is."

Mrs. Fisher rounded the walk from the garden, her hands full of flowers. "Hello, Rick," she called.

"Hello, Mrs. Fisher," he called back. "Mother wanted me to remind you about Sunday."

"As if we'd forget," she said, smiling, and headed toward the steps. "Have a nice time at the Fair."

"Thanks," he said.

That was another thing that wasn't working out the way it did in books, he reflected—his liking Mrs. Fisher so much and her liking him. You weren't supposed to like your future mother-in-law. But he liked his. And his mother and father did too. They played bridge with the Fishers, and went to the club dances with them, and saw them throughout the winter in town. Mrs. Fisher was certainly a friendly and easy sort. Take the way she had spoken to him just now. She hadn't said, "Don't make Angie stay out too late," or "Be careful driving," or any of the things she might have said. Instead she had just said, "Have a nice time." Furthermore, which was an added satisfaction, whenever he looked at her he could see Angie as she would be twenty-five years from now—a woman still beautiful, still young with a youthfulness that had nothing to do with age. Only, of course, Angie would be even better. "Something's wrong," he thought. "There ought to be some complication, some problem. Another girl or another man, or maybe money. The path of true love shouldn't be this smooth." Actually, of course, there was some slight difficulty about money, or there would be when they were married, but perhaps even that would disappear. Surely he wouldn't be earning twenty-five dollars a week forever.

"Among the blessed." Yes, that was it. That certainly was what it amounted to.

Suddenly there were the shrill and startling notes of a musical horn, and they looked around and saw that Bingo had driven up silently behind them, with Dot in the seat beside him. If Rick had doubts about his own family's financial status, he had none at all about Bingo's—and if anyone ever had had, the sight of Bingo's car would have removed them. It had a hood that seemed to extend indefinitely, and its leather upholstery was rich and red, and it bristled with gleaming chromium accessories. Looking at that car, you could picture everything that went with it—the penthouse on Park Avenue, the winters in Palm Beach, the place at Southampton. Yes, whatever Rick himself was, Bingo was definitely "upper-income bracket."

"Hi," he called. "Well, which car?"

"I guess we'd better go separately," said Bingo. "That is, unless you want to come back before dinner. Dot and I have to go and have dinner with her folks."

"Why don't you come too?" Dot asked.

"No, thanks," Rick said. "We'll have dinner at the Fair. Let's meet by the Trylon, and then we can get lunch somewhere."

"Okay," said Bingo, and the huge car swerved past them noiselessly —a multitude of cylinders, a minimum of sound—and in a moment was out of sight.

They followed. "Well," Rick said, "what do you want to see today?"

"Oh, I don't know," Angie said. "Let's just poke around. Maybe we could see the Futurama, or the Perisphere. After all, I suppose we ought to see the Perisphere sometime. That's what the whole thing's about."

"Yes," he said with an equal lack of enthusiasm, "I suppose so."

Their tours of the Fair had been confined chiefly to the Amusement Area. The Aquacade, Jungleland, Old New York, the freak shows from the circus and the girl shows from Forty-second Street—these they had explored thoroughly. And they had given brief inspections to most of the international exhibits—from Albania, which two months before had ceased to be Albania, to Yugoslavia, which still was Yugoslavia.

But what the Fair meant mostly to them was Billy Rose and Michael Todd rather than Norman Bel Geddes and La Guardia. They had respectfully viewed Railroads on Parade, and had watched hygienic cows being milked hygienically, and had visited the House of Magic, and had watched glass being blown into incredible shapes. Yet what they remembered most vividly were the fat lady and the live trout flashing through a woodland stream in the Maine exhibit and the day Angie had won a kewpie doll by tossing a ring onto a cane. It wasn't because they were unappreciative or unintelligent. It was because he was twenty-one and she was nineteen.

Descending at the motorists' entrance and leaving the car to be parked, they went through the turnstiles and made their way to the Trylon, where Bingo and Dot were waiting. Past them ran sight-seeing trucks, whose warning signal was a few bars from "The Sidewalks of New York," and in the sunlight the white surfaces of the buildings cast blinding, flat light.

"Well, where shall we eat?" said Bingo, and after the usual argument they decided on the Polish restaurant.

They ordered strange dishes, which were served by a girl in an embroidered peasant costume, and as they ate they looked around at the rustic interior and the painted walls and wondered what it would be like to be in Poland. The real Poland, that is; not Poland-in-Flushing. And they agreed that it would probably be very nice—very quaint, very Old World, like a movie travelogue.

"All I know about Poland is that Paderewski came from there," said Angie.

"And Pola Negri," added Bingo. "Or maybe she's German."

"Who's Pola Negri?" said Dot, for whom the history of the motion picture began with Greta Garbo and to whom everything before that was a cinematic Ice Age.

After lunch they went onto the crowded, sunny pavements and began to walk aimlessly, Bingo and Dot ahead, Rick and Angie trailing. They walked slowly, leisurely, and Angie removed her cartwheel hat and carried it in her hand. One of the nicest sights in the world, Rick decided, was a girl on a summer day carrying her cartwheel hat in her hand. This girl, anyway.

"What do they call this place?" Angie asked as they strolled past flags and banners.

"The Court of Peace."

Bingo called back over his shoulder. "There are sixty different countries represented here," he said proudly, as if he were personally responsible for the presence of each of them. "It certainly makes you think, doesn't it?"

It didn't particularly make Rick think—except to reflect that he was glad he didn't have to name the sixty countries or identify their flags. Some of them he knew, of course—the British Union Jack and the French Tricolor —but most of the others were just pieces of colored silk. Czechoslovakia, for instance. Did Czechoslovakia have a flag, and if so, which was it? And Iceland—or maybe Iceland wasn't a country: he wasn't sure. In fact whenever he went to the Fair he came across names he either had forgotten or never had known. Like Thailand and New Guinea. On the whole, it was very educational.

They ambled past the cascade of water on the Italian building ("Very pretty," they said. "But what does it mean?"), past the huge British Empire building, past lavish Belgium and modest Greece. They peered into the patio of the Turkish building, where a fat woman sat sipping coffee, and wandered over the miniature bridge and past the lily pools of the Japanese gardens, shepherded by a small, smiling, spectacled man and two equally small and smiling women in kimonos. ("Aren't they darling?" said Dot. "Honestly, I think the Japanese are the most adorable little people in the world. And did you ever see anyone so polite?") Then, their internationalism dwindling, they found themselves at the Telephone Company's exhibit, standing with earphones around their heads and listening to the conversations radiating to all parts of the country.

To Angie and Rick this was a never-ending source of fascination and delight. They listened to a sailor talking to a girl named Irene in San Francisco. At first Irene couldn't seem to understand that her remarks were being heard by several thousand other people, and she was interestingly intimate and uninhibited, while the sailor blushed. After that they listened to a woman talking to her husband in Lowell, Massachusetts. And to a little girl speaking to her grandmother in Dallas, and to a man in Minneapolis who had domestic troubles, and to Miss Claudette Colbert in Hollywood, who informed a fan that she was delighted that he had chosen to call her, and to a girl in New Orleans who said that she had received Joe's letter and who did he think he was, having the nerve to write her things like that?

"Who would you call?" said Bingo. "I mean, if you won, who would you pick?"

"I'd call Bing Crosby," said Dot, "and ask him to sing to me. Just imagine. Wouldn't it be wonderful?"

Bingo said that he would call somebody named Fruity Wallace, who, it developed, was a classmate of his at Yale and who now lived in Seattle, and Angie said she wasn't sure, but she thought she'd probably call her aunt Florence in Chicago. And then the inquisition got round to Rick.

"I don't know," he said. "If I were here alone I'd call Angie." Yes, and he would, too, even though she lived only twenty miles away. And Dot laughed teasingly; but Angie gave him a quiet smile which made his gallantry worth while. "And if I were here with Angie—well, I guess maybe I'd call—oh, President Roosevelt."

"Um-hum," said Bingo. "And if you got him, which you wouldn't, what would you say?"

Well, that was a fair enough question. What *would* he say? He didn't know. "H'm—just 'Hello.'"

"If my dad could talk to him he'd say a lot more than that," said Bingo. "But they'd cut him off before he got very far." He looked around at the crowd. "Well, anyway, it's a very smart promotion stunt," he said wisely.

"Good showmanship. Gets a lot of people used to the idea of long-distance calls who otherwise would probably never think of them."

"Come on, Rick," said Angie, and took his arm. "Let's go over to the Perisphere." She was reluctant to leave the earphones and the private lives that filtered through them, yet it was obvious that she knew where their duty lay. "We really ought to go sometime, you know, and we might as well get it over with." She turned toward Dot and Bingo. "You coming?"

But Dot and Bingo already had paid their respects to the Perisphere. It was very interesting, they said, very instructive, but it wasn't really necessary to see it twice. So they would stay here for a while and meet them later in the Amusement Area.

So Angie and Rick walked toward the huge ball, and after the usual waiting they found themselves moving up the escalator, part of an endless belt of humanity. You looked behind you and saw a descending ladder of faces—male, female, young, old, black, white—and beyond them what originally had been a meadow and then a dump heap and was now the wonder of the world.

They smiled at each other, and Angie linked her arm more closely in his.

At this moment, in this place, Rick had all he ever wanted to have. This girl, this day. Mere weather didn't make a day (he had been happy on rainy days and miserable on sunny ones); but it helped, like frosting on a cake.

Then they were in the dim interior of the ball and were being shunted onto a moving balcony. The hum and buzz of conversation that had been going on during the escalator's ascent had quieted now, and the atmosphere was hushed, almost cathedrallike. An invisible and amplified orchestra played, and then from somewhere came the voice of Kaltenborn, substituting for the voice of the Future: "This is Democracy. The City of Man, The sun rises, and . . ."

Yes, and there it was, the morning light. The people stood side by side, circling the immense scene and looking down on it.

"Well, there you have it," Rick whispered. "The World of Tomorrow."

They saw the towers and the gardens and the streets, which were wider and cleaner than any streets they had ever walked. The sun moved across the heavens, and to the accompaniment of music they heard the story of "this brave new world built by united hands and hearts." Of men and women working, of children playing. Slowly those of today revolved around the spectacle of tomorrow.

It lasted—how long? Rick didn't know. He couldn't have said. Fifteen minutes—maybe twice that. Here, within this prophetic shell, there was no time.

Then the unseen sun had made its arc and dusk was falling and the music swelling and the voice saying, "As day fades into night, each man seeks home. . . ." And after that they were outside again, on the Helicline, making their descent. The sun they felt now had heat in it, and the people were real—they jostled, pushed, perspired, talked. The spell was broken, gone.

"Well," Rick said, "how do you think we'll like it?"

"What?" Angie asked.

"The World of Tomorrow. How do you think we'll like living in it? Because that's what we will be living in. Things are going to be different. Everybody says so. The airplane and all that."

She was silent, gravely considering. "It looks awfully *clean,*" she admitted. "And everything seems to be very well arranged. I mean, it's all very carefully thought out and planned. But——"

"But what?"

"Oh—nothing."

He didn't persist in questioning her, because somehow he felt he wouldn't care to be questioned about it, either. The fact was that, although he was impressed, he found it difficult to summarize his impressions. What he had seen, in combination with what he had read, was the shape of things to come. The airplane spanning seas and continents, television in full color and even three dimensions, the wizardry of the electric eye and the photoelectric cell, radio-telephones for automobiles, portable and pre-fabricated houses, electronic cooking, the helicopter—all that magic, just around the corner, waiting.

They were edging their way through the increasing crowds. "If that is the future," Rick reflected, "I guess maybe I'm not ready for it yet. Of course I will be eventually, and so will everyone else. Angie too. We'll be educated to it and prepared for it. But right now—well, the present is more understandable. Until something better comes along, I'll take what I've got."

"Let's do something, or get something to drink, or something," Angie said nervously, and he realized that neither of them had spoken for several moments. They had been walking apart, and now she again took his arm. "It isn't tomorrow yet. And I'm glad it isn't. It's today. It's 1939."

He smiled. He knew what she meant. If it had been tomorrow their life would have been behind them, or most of it at least. Now it lay ahead.

"How about the parachute jump?" he said.

"Wonderful!"

They met Bingo and Dot and with them made the parachute jump, with Dot and Angie screaming with laughter and fear and with Rick and Bingo being very nonchalant about it all. And then a visit to the Amazons, and then idle, aimless meandering through the streets of pleasure and forgetfulness. There was no flinching from the unknown here. This was the known. Those rouged cheeks and spangled thighs on the platform were real. This boy with his dirty face smeared with crackerjack was real, too, and familiar. These shuffling throngs, these beckoning barkers, the brass that brayed, the calliope that raced, the tired-eyed woman comforting a crying child, the red-faced man with the straw hat on the back of his head —they were all real, and the fact that they were real was somehow pleasant after an excursion into the antiseptic but intangible realm of tomorrow.

Then it was late afternoon, and from across the water came the chiming of the carillon on the Florida building. The day crowds were leaving, and the evening crowds were coming in.

"Well," said Bingo, "I guess it's time Dot and I got going."

"I wish we could stay," said Dot.

"Another time," said Angie solacingly.

"Sure," said Rick. "There'll be lots of other times."

They watched Dot and Bingo disappear through the crowds, and suddenly they realized that they were tired. They sat on a bench. "Oh dear," said Angie. "My feet." And then, "Where shall we have dinner?"

Rick made a rapid mental calculation. They had spent most of the afternoon at free exhibits, and therefore his wallet had suffered less than he had expected. "Well, there's the French Pavilion."

"No," she said firmly. "It's too expensive for dinner. Anyway, I feel like some American food. Why don't we stop somewhere and then maybe go to the French Pavilion afterward? We could sit there for a while and listen to the music."

Always thinking of him. Always being on the watch, so that he didn't spend too much money on her. Always looking ahead. She was the balance wheel, the one who planned and foresaw. "She's like Mother," he thought suddenly. "And I suppose I'm like Dad. It's history repeating itself. History or life or something."

"All right," he said. "Sure."

Their schedule arranged, she left him and a few minutes later returned, refurbished and revived. She had put her hat on, and lipstick, and the smudges on her white shoes had disappeared.

"There," she said, smiling. "Now I feel better. Come on, let's go."

So they wandered back toward the restaurant center. Critically they surveyed golden-brown chickens turning slowly on spits, and mounds of lobsters, and great red roasts of beef, and pink hams studded with cloves and crusted with brown sugar, and the plump, tender breasts of turkeys. Behind plate glass lay a roast pig with an apple in its mouth, and in another window rows of steaks were displayed in refrigerated isolation—thick, purplish, protectively netted with gauze.

"I really can't decide," she said. "I don't know what I want. You decide."

"Let's have a steak," he said. That was one thing about the American restaurants as contrasted with the international ones—whenever you were in doubt you could always settle for a steak. "These in here look good. Let's try 'em."

So they had their steaks at the steak place and then, progressively, ice cream at an ice-cream booth, which offered twenty-four different flavors, and coffee at one of the many coffee stands. It was, they agreed, a good and satisfying meal. Nothing fancy, but it filled you up.

Later, as twilight fell and the lights began to come on, they sat at a white-clothed table on the terrace of the French Pavilion and looked out at the fountain and the Lagoon of Nations. Rick studied the enormous menu card handed him and finally chose champagne, even though Angie said: "You oughtn't to, Rick. We aren't celebrating anything."

"I know," he said, "but your mother wouldn't mind your having just a glass."

"Of course not. That isn't it. But—you ought to be saving your money."

"For what?" he said, smiling. As if he didn't know. "Anyway, this isn't my money I'm spending. It's Dad's."

"If it were yours you'd still be spending it. And you shouldn't get into champagne habits, because we're going to have to be careful at first. It won't be as if each of us were still living at home, you know. It'll be different."

He looked at her. "It'll be wonderful."

The champagne came, cold and pale and bubbly, and they sipped it. She glanced up at the glass curtain that was closed in bad weather, around at the tables, where there was the hum of conversation and laughter, and down at the orchestra, which was playing its usual muted and adroitly aimed version of "April in Paris." "Ap-ril in Pa-ris, chest-nuts in blossom . . ."

"It is like Paris, isn't it?" she said. "That is, it's the way I imagine Paris to be. Sitting outdoors and drinking champagne."

"We'll see for ourselves sometime."

"I hope so," she said. "Sometime. It would be wonderful if we could go abroad, wouldn't it?"

"Maybe we'll go sooner than you think." The champagne seemed to be having its effect in loosening his tongue and expanding his self-confidence. "How would you like to go over on our honeymoon?"

She caught her breath. "Oh, Rick! Wouldn't it be beautiful?"

"It wouldn't be bad." And then he went on. Yes, he certainly was feeling it. "On the *Normandie,* for instance."

"Not on the *Normandie,* of course. That's completely out of the question."

"Why? We could——"

"Darling, don't be silly. But we *might* be able to go student third on one of the smaller boats. I've got something saved, and Daddy will want to give us a wedding present, and——"

The orchestra played on: "Holi-day tables under the trees . . ."

"We could make sort of a Grand Tour of it," he said, and he edged his glass aside, because he didn't need it any more. He was feeling another sort of intoxication now. "Paris, and London, and maybe even Italy. I've always wanted to see Italy. And in a way it'd be very sensible if we did that, because then afterward we could come back home and settle down and just sort of vegetate."

"Paris," she said dreamily. "You know, there's a department store there called Au Printemps. 'In the Spring.' Isn't that a nice name for a store? Isn't it sweet? It sounds so much prettier than—well, Gimbel's."

His imagination was mounting extravagantly. "We could go up north too—to Norway. Golly, we could even go to Russia."

"Oh no." Her face was mildly reproving. "Not Russia."

"Why not?"

"Well, darling, you know what Russia is. It's Bolshevistic and Communistic, and they don't want to have anything to do with America or Americans. No," she concluded placidly, "not Russia."

"There's the rest of it at least," he said, now that Russia had been out-lawed. "There's Holland and——"

But geography had ceased to interest her, and practicalities came first. "When do you think it'll be, Rick?"

"Well," he said soberly, "you'll have to graduate first. I wouldn't want you to leave college just in order to get married—it wouldn't be fair to you. Let's see. I start work in September. . . . I think in a year and a half or so. I ought to be able to swing it by then." He smiled at her. "Are you willing to wait that long?"

"Of course. Anyway, I don't suppose it will seem so long, really. You'll be busy working and I'll be busy finishing college. No, it'll be all right. Mother says we ought to wait a little while, anyway. She says, how can we be so sure, how do we know? She says we're young and one of us might meet somebody else."

They laughed hilariously at the very thought of such an impossibility.

The fireworks began then, and they watched them—the rainbow rockets arching upward, the whirling kaleidoscope of colors falling into the eve-ning sky, the fountain whose waters were now white, now crimson, now green. The hiss and boom of fireworks echoing across the Lagoon of Nations and into the Court of Peace. And then, faintly, the acrid smell of gun-powder.

They drove through the moonlight back to Angie's house, and once Rick glanced over his shoulder and saw the floodlighted spire and ball growing smaller in the distance. The parkway was one long procession of cars, so thick they ran bumper to bumper; but when Rick turned off onto the secondary road there was no traffic at all—only a frightened rabbit leaping past the glare of his headlights, blinded and no doubt regretting its noc-turnal adventurousness. He made another turn, into Angie's street, and, arriving at her house, they got out and headed toward the steps, walking quietly, for the house was dark.

"Well," Rick said as they stood on the porch. "Good night." He took her in his arms and kissed her.

"Good night, darling," she said.

"Look, you don't have to go in just yet, do you?" he asked and led her toward the swing. Only one kiss during the whole day—that was hardly enough.

She smiled. "Well, all right," she said. "Just for a little while."

They sat down, and he drew her toward him. "There," he said. "There."

Then, later, he was at home, driving the convertible into the garage between the station wagon and the gleaming bulk of the new sedan. He got out, locked the garage, and went toward the house, whistling softly. His house was dark also.

He let himself in and felt his way noiselessly up the stairs. He began to undress in the semidarkness. Tim lay curled into one of those contortionist's knots that were his customary sleeping posture. One hand hung limply over the side of the bed, pale and ghostlike in the moonlight. Funny kid, Rick thought. A good kid too. . . . Then, in his pajamas, Rick went to the windows to pull down the blinds, so that the sun wouldn't wake him in the morning. Looking out, he saw the moonlight on the badminton court, the lawn, the roses. There was no sound except the distant rolling of the surf.

"Wonderful day," Rick thought. "Wonderful night."

And after that he pulled down the blinds and got into bed. For a time he lay awake, thinking, tracing each hour. He thought of his father's getting up early in order to put more mileage on the car, of his mother's saying at breakfast, "I'd rather you were useless now than later," of Sheila and Tim on the beach, of the *Normandie,* of Bingo and Dot, of the Fair and Angie, and of Angie and himself watching the rockets shoot up into the night. And the last thing he thought of as he drifted into sleep was himself and Angie in the World of Tomorrow. Would that be wonderful too? he wondered drowsily. Wonderful the way today had been?

That was the day he remembered. Out of all the other and more important days he might have chosen—Christmases and Fourths of July, and the day he was graduated from high school, and the day he first wore long trousers, and the day he first began to shave, and the day he was inducted, and his wedding day—he remembered this day.

And he remembered it, all of it, in less time than it takes for a bullet to leave a gun and strike a heart. He remembered it as he fell and lay there on the shores of Sicily. And he knew then that this was his World of Tomorrow, but that he wasn't living in it. He was dying in it.

ROBERT E. SHERWOOD

"Extra! Extra!"

FROM THE STREET BELOW came that most terrifying of sounds, the full-chested roar of two men shouting, "Extra! Extra!" through the rainy night.

"Extra! Extra!"

Mr. Whidden, reading his evening paper (it was the home edition, published at noon, containing no news whatsoever), wondered what the trouble was. He could gather nothing from the ominous shouts that assailed his ears. The two men might have been lusty-lunged Russians for all of him. But there was an ominous note in their voices—the warning of dark calamity—the grim suggestion of wars, plagues, holocausts.

"Where do they get those men with voices like that, and what do they do between extras?" he thought.

Mrs. Whidden emerged from the kitchen, whither she had retired to bathe the supper dishes.

"There's an extra out, Roy," she announced.

"So I hear," said her husband, who was not above an occasional facetious sally.

She walked over to the window, opened it, and thrust her head out into the rain. In the street, five stories below, she could see the two news vendors.

"Extra! Extra!"

Mrs. Whidden turned from the window.

"Something must have happened."

There was an overtone of complaint in her remark that Mr. Whidden recognized only too well. It was a tone that always suggested unwelcome activity on Mr. Whidden's part. He wished that she would come right out and say, "Go downstairs and get the paper," but she never did. She always prefaced her commands with a series of whining insinuations.

"I wonder what it was?" she asked, as though expecting her husband to know.

"Oh, nothing, I guess. Those extras never amount to anything." Mrs. Whidden turned again to the window.

"Something awful must have happened," she observed, and the counterpoint of complaint was even more pronounced.

Mr. Whidden shifted uneasily in his chair—the one comfortable chair in the flat—the chair which he himself had bought for his own occupancy and about which there had been so much argument. He knew what was coming; he didn't want to move, and walk down and up four flights of stairs for the sake of some information that would not affect his life in the remotest degree.

"Don't you intend to find *out?*" asked Mrs. Whidden, and it was evident that she had reached the snappy stage. Her husband knew that, if he didn't go down and buy that damned paper, he would provide fuel for an irritation that would burn well into the night. Nevertheless that chair was so comfortable, and the weather was so disagreeable, and the stairs were such a climb . . . !

"I guess I won't go down, Emmy. Those extras are always fakes, anyway, and, besides, if it is anything important, we'll find out about it in the morning paper."

The roars of the men shouting "Extra! Extra!" reverberated through the street, beating with determined violence against the sheer walls of the walk-up apartment houses, shuddering through the open window of the Whiddens' living room, jarring the fringed shade of the reading lamp, the souvenirs on the bookshelves, the tasseled portieres that led into the little hall.

"You're just lazy, Roy Whidden," said Mrs. Whidden. "You sit there reading your paper—night after night—night after night." She turned as though to an invisible jury, to whom she was addressing a fervent plea for recognition of her prolonged martyrdom. Then, with all the dramatic suddenness of an experienced prosecutor, she snapped at the defendant: "What *do* you read, anyway? Answer me that! What *do* you read?"

Mr. Whidden knew that the question was purely rhetorical. No answer was expected.

"You don't read a *thing*. You just sit there and stare at that fool paper—probably the death notices. When anything important happens, you don't even care enough to step out into the street and see what it is."

"How do *you* know it's important?" Mr. Whidden inquired, being inclined, albeit unwisely, to display a little spirit.

"How do you know it *isn't?*" Mrs. Whidden backfired. "How will you ever know *any*thing unless you take the trouble to find out?"

Mr. Whidden uncrossed his legs and then crossed them again.

"I suppose you expect *me* to go down and get that paper," cried Mrs. Whidden, whose voice was now rivaling the news vendors'. "With all I've got to do—the dishes, and the baby's ten o'clock feeding, and . . . all right! I'll *go!* I'll walk down the four flights of stairs and *get* the paper, so that Your Majesty won't have to trouble yourself." There was a fine sarcasm in her tone now.

Mr. Whidden knew that it was the end. For seven years this exact scene had been repeating itself over and over again. If there had only been some slight variation in his wife's technique . . . but there never had. At first he had tried to be frightfully sporting about it, assuming the blame at the first hint of trouble and doing whatever was demanded of him with all possible grace; but that pose, and it had not been long before he admitted that it *was* a pose, was worn away by a process of erosion, a process that had kept up for seven years—seven years of writing things in ledgers in an airless office on Dey Street; seven years of listening to those endless scoldings and complaints at home. Whatever of gallantry had existed in Mr. Whidden's soul had crumbled before the persistent and ever-increasing waves of temper. He knew that now, if he gave in, he did so because of cowardice and not because of any worthily chivalrous motives.

He threw his paper down, stood up, and walked into the bedroom to get his coat. Little Conrad was asleep in there, lying on his stomach, his face pressed against the bars of the crib.

Over the crib hung a colored photograph of the Taj Mahal, a lovely, white building that Mr. Whidden had always wanted to see. He also wanted to see Singapore, and the Straits Settlements, and the west coast of Africa, places that he had read about in books.

He was thinking about these places, and wondering whether little Conrad would ever see them, when his wife's voice rasped at him from the next room.

"Are you going or will I have to go?"

"I'm going, dear," he assured her in the manner of one who is tired.

"Well, hurry! Those men are a block away by now."

Mr. Whidden put on his coat, looked at little Conrad and at the Taj Mahal, and then started down the stairs.

There were four flights of them, and it was raining hard outside.

Twelve years later Mrs. Whidden (now Mrs. Burchall) sat sewing on the front porch of a pleasant house in a respectable suburb. It was a brilliantly sunny day, and the hydrangeas were just starting to burst out into profuse bloom on the bushes at either side of the steps.

"And do you mean to tell me you never *heard* from him?" asked Mrs. Lent, who was also sewing.

"Not a word," replied Mrs. Burchall, without rancor. "Not one word in twelve years. He used to send money sometimes to the bank, but they'd never tell me where it came from."

"I guess you ain't sorry he went. Fred Burchall's a good man."

"You'd think he was a good man all right if you could've seen what I had before. My *good*ness! When I think of the seven years I wasted being Roy Whidden's wife!"

Mrs. Burchall heaved a profound sigh.

"Ain't you ever sort of afraid he might show up?" asked Mrs. Lent.

"Not him. And if he did, what of it? Fred could kick him out with one hand tied behind his back. Fred Burchall's a real *man*."

She sewed in silence for a while.

"Of course, I *am* a little worried about Conrad. He thinks his father's dead. You see, we wanted to spare him from knowing about the divorce and all that. We couldn't have the boy starting out in life with his father's disgrace on his shoulders."

Shortly thereafter Mrs. Lent went on her way and Mrs. Burchall stepped into the house to see whether the maid was doing anything constructive. She found her son Conrad curled up in a chair, reading some book.

"You sitting in the house reading on a fine day like this! Go on out into the fresh air and shake your limbs."

"But, Mother——"

"Go on out, I tell you. Can't you try to be a *real* boy for a change?"

"But this book's exciting."

"I'll bet. Anything in print is better than fresh air and outdoor exercise, I suppose. You're just like your—can't you ever stop reading for one *instant*? I declare! One of these days you'll turn into a book. . . . Now you set that book down and go out of this house this instant."

Conrad went out to the front yard and started, with no enthusiasm, to bounce an old golf ball up and down upon the concrete walk that led from the front porch to the gate. He was thus engaged when a strange man appeared in the street, stopping before the gate to look for the number which wasn't there.

"Hey, sonny, is this Mrs. Burchall's house?"

"Yes," said the boy, "it is. Want to see her?"

The man was short, slight, and none too formidable-looking; although he was obviously a representative of the lower classes—possibly a tramp— Conrad was not in the least afraid of him. He had a rather friendly expression, a peaceful expression, as though he bore ill will to no one.

"What's your name?" the man inquired.

"My name's Conrad—Conrad Whidden."

Conrad wondered why the man stared at him so.

"I used to know your mother," the man explained, "before I went to sea."

"Oh, you're a sailor!" Conrad was obviously impressed. "Where've you been?"

"Oh, all over. I just came from Marseille."

"Gosh," said Conrad. "I'd like to go there. I've been reading about it in a book—it's a book called *The Arrow of Gold.*"

The man smiled.

"You were named after the man who wrote that book," said the sailor.

"I never knew that."

"No, I guess not. Your mother didn't know either."

Just then Mrs. Burchall appeared on the front steps, attracted perhaps by the suspicious cessation of the sharp pops that the golf ball had been making on the concrete walk.

When she saw her former husband leaning on the gate her first thought was this: Well, of all things! And here I was talking about him to Adele Lent not ten minutes ago. Then she realized, with sudden horror, that her son was actually in conversation with his father. She wondered whether that fool Roy had said anything . . .

"Conrad, you come here this instant!"

Conrad ambled up the concrete walk.

"How many times do I have to tell you not to talk to every strange man that comes around?"

"He's a sailor, Mother."

"Oh, a sailor, is he!" Somehow or other, that annoyed Mrs. Burchall. "Well, you just chase yourself around to the back and don't let me catch you talking to any tramps—or sailors either."

Conrad cast one glance toward the man who had come from Marseille, and then disappeared from view behind the house.

Mrs. Burchall walked elegantly down to the front gate and confronted Roy Whidden.

"So you're a sailor, are you?" she said, and surveyed him with deliberate satisfaction. "You look to me like a common bum. I always knew you'd never get anywhere."

"I guess you were right."

He smiled as he said this. Mrs. Burchall was irritated by the easy good humor of his tone, by the calm confidence in his eyes.

"Why did you do it?" she asked.

"I don't know. It was a rainy night, and I heard a foghorn out in the river."

"So you left me for a foghorn!"

"Yes—I knew you'd be all right. Your people had money, and I sent some."

"A lot you sent."

"I guess it wasn't much—but it was all I could scrape together."

"Well, what are you bumming around here for now? What do you want? More money? Well, you won't get it. Not one nickel. I told Fred Burchall if you ever showed up he was to kick you right out. And he'd do it, too! I advise you to make yourself scarce before *he* gets home."

"Don't worry, I'm going. My ship sails at six."

"Oh, your *ship* sails, does it! I'll bet it's a *fine* ship." She laughed harshly at the mental picture of any ship on which Roy Whidden could obtain employment. "How did you ever find out where I live?"

"Oh, I kept track of you through the bank. I knew when you got the divorce and got married again."

"Well then, why didn't you leave me alone? What did you come snoopin' around here for?"

"Just curiosity. I wanted to see what the boy looks like."

"Well—you've seen him."

"Yes, I've seen him. That's all I wanted."

He straightened up and started to move away. "Well—good-by, Em."

"Good-by, and I hope you enjoy yourself on that *ship* of yours."

He was walking away down the street when suddenly she called to him: "*Roy!*" He stopped abruptly in response to that well-remembered summons.

"There was something I meant to ask you," she said with an unusual hesitancy. "What—what was that extra about?"

He rubbed his none-too-smooth chin and thought for an instant.

"Let's see," he said. "It was something about . . . no, that was later. I guess I've forgotten."

"Was it about the world series?" she asked, as though trying desperately hard to prompt him. "The morning papers were full of it. Was it about that?"

He smiled with relief. "Of course—that was it! The Red Sox won."

WILBUR DANIEL STEELE

The Body of the Crime

THE HOUSE in which Daniel was born was the kind of which we say, as we drive past it in the elm-pillared margin of some New England village: "What a monstrosity!" One day, when the Antique has caught up with the Eighties, perhaps we shall say: "What a beauty! What noble bays and airy cupolas and richness of brown scrollwork! They knew how to build their houses in those days."

Perhaps, too, we shall have matured enough to say of men like Dan Kinsman, who was Daniel's father: "They knew how to build their lives."

When the young Daniel came home from his first year away to prep school and saw with his changed eyes the unchanging house, the weighing cornices and flying towers, squared bays, rounded bays, porte-cochere, all cocoa brown in the shadows of the chestnuts, "That's it," he thought; "it's not like other fellows' houses."

And when he studied this man, his father, it seemed for a while he had found the answer to the riddle as old in its secret wretchedness as the very beginnings of his memory. "And *he*, he's not like other fellows' fathers."

Other fellows' fathers, Daniel had found in his year, were men who arrived cheerfully from lifting their incomes and departed grimly to lower their medal scores. Forward-moving, tomorrow-thinking young elders, eager, industrious, mobile fellows fearful of nothing but of seeming to stand still.

But here was a father apparently content to be one year where he had been the year before, possessed of but the same possessions, the same small-town friendships, the same leisurely, half-patriarchal judgeship, the same pedestrian pleasures, books and dogs, pruning hooks and garden hoes and fishing rods. And he a strong, straight man alive, not yet fifty, with black hair thick on his head, and lungs to laugh with when he wanted. Strange!

Now it came to Daniel it must be because his father was so wanting in—that's to say, so strange this way—that he had always seemed to his son so—so—— Daniel groped for a word for a thing he'd never been able to give a shape or name, and had to finish lamely—seemed so "strange."

Daniel could have laughed for joy to discover, now he was grown up, that the trouble about his father was so little a one as this. For all the weight of his fifteen years, he could have skipped for lightness to know that here was a difference from other fathers he now could grasp, even learn to condone, yes, even admire, even fight for, with fellows with more—well—say—money-grabbing dads.

Yes. Daniel could have skipped for lightness on the deep cave-green turf of the hydrangea alley, where they walked and talked that first June afternoon at home, he and his father, while mother watched them with her pale smile from her long chair in her high window.

It was curious; Daniel had always loved his ailing, beautiful mother, easily, and been near her and told her everything tellable, easily, and not thought much about it. The one he would have given his life to be able to love as easily, to be close to, friends with, whole of heart, was this other, this darkly handsome man whom he himself was so absurdly like to look at, his father.

So today it was as if the year of forgetting had worked a good miracle. It was a dream come true to find himself sauntering and chatting with Dan Kinsman as affectionately at ease as though they had been but two fellows, gravely estimating the apple yield in the west yard and the hay chances in the back mowing, chuckling together over the antics of Spot's pups on the barn floor, waving answer to the view halloo of Doc Martin racketing by in the antique twin-six, and, wonder of wonders at last, arm in arm, man and man, marching indoors prepared to mount and demand of mother if supper were ever to be ready—as if she, poor fragile chatelaine, could know anything about that.

But, day of marvels! An elixir must have run in the air. For here in their sight came mother down the stairs to meet them, walking by herself, suddenly, subtly revivified, the flush on her cheeks and the shine in her eyes not more for their astonishment than for her own.

So tonight there were three at table in place of two, and it was like the sort of dream in which one wakes from an interior nightmare to find everything finished that was horrid, and everything at its beginning that is right and bright. Nor did it end with the supper table; afterward she would go out abroad with them, as if greedy to share in the marvel of those two men of hers who walked of a sudden as one and, by their walking so, seemed so suddenly to have made her walk again.

What a sight it was for the evening sun to see, level and bloody rose beneath the eaves of the chestnuts! Dan Kinsman, bemused, commencing words and swallowing their ends on half-choked chuckles, even as his eyes, quick for once, kept slant track of Vivian's every oddly exuberant gesture. Daniel, beatified, accepting wonders with a new omnivorous trust. And Vivian Kinsman, unbelievable, a princess freed from some evil enchantment in exile, returned to her kingdom, leading them.

In the east yard, hidden for years, the low, excited laugh was on her lips continuously. For this border, it was: "They're too gorgeous, Dan; I love them!" For that bed: "But there never *were* such flowers!" When she came in view of father's season's pride, the bastion of man-high crimson poppies, all she could do was put her hands to her heart.

Only when she caught sight of Spot and her puppies, taking the last of the sun at the barn door, was there a shadow of change in the exclamation of discovery.

"You're going to keep them all, Dan!" She drew father's eyes. "All, Dan!"

He would have temporized, laughingly: "Spot got away this time, and——"

"You're not going to drown them, Dan. I couldn't bear to think——"

The sharpness in her voice brought quickness to his.

"Why, no, of course not, Vivian. I shall keep them, of course—unless someone should want them very much—who'd give them a good home."

The sun touched distant woods. Father dared worry aloud at last.

"It'll be chilly in another second now, Vivian."

She turned back with a queer, mercurial docility, asking only, when they came to the porch steps, that she might have some of the crimson poppies for her room tonight.

"I should so love to see them in the morning, Dan, just three or four."

"You'll have an armful, that's what you'll have, dear; I'll go and get them now."

Daniel took her in on his arm, feeling tall, now his father was gone. She would go only as far as the living room for the moment, where a slender summer fire was laid, ready for the match. When Daniel had lighted it he studied the white figure lying back deep in Dan Kinsman's chair. He said: "You're happy tonight, mother."

She needn't answer. Her eyes, fixed on the fire, were alight with all its beginning, playing flames. And before he knew why: "Have you always been happy here with father," he demanded, "and with me?"

This must have seemed to need no answer, at first. But then she sat up and fixed the boy with her straight gaze. "Always, yes!" From vehemence it changed to mirth. "Whatever put it in your head, sonny—yes, yes, yes!" And sinking back, with a little gasp at the end of her laughter: "He's an angel, sonny, your father is, but he's an awful slowpoke; won't you go and hurry him along?"

Father had meant it when he said an armful; he had gathered a whole great sheaf of the poppies, and rather a pity, for the blooms were closed. But what matter, if Vivian wanted them; they'd open again at day. So he seemed to be thinking as he stood there, laden and bemused, in the falling night.

And so it was that Daniel, his son, came upon him, deep in a preoccupation of his own, halted a rod away, and, without lifting his gaze from the ground, said: "Has mother liked it here in Kennelbridge, father?"

Dan Kinsman had had a day of astonishments. Without turning anything but his head, and that slowly, he studied his dim questioner.

"It has liked your mother here," he said quietly.

The boy, given a riddle, raised his eyes to the man, who was no more than a shadow shape in the dusk now—and, as shadows may be, something distorted and magnified—between the blackening blood of the poppies he carried and the dyke he had torn them from. And Daniel forgot his riddle and widened his eyes. The father knew the sign of old. All afternoon he had been waiting for it, pulled between dread and the beginnings of an incredible hope. Now he wheeled, cried, "Ah, Daniel, son!" and held out his arms, careless of their sanguinary burden. And his son turned and ran.

What good is it to be fifteen and a man, instead of ten and a boy, or five and a child? When Daniel, fleeing, needles in his legs and an icicle up his backbone, reached the firelight where he had left his mother sitting, it was on the knees of veriest childhood he tumbled down, to hide his face in the chair bottom beside her, wind his fingers in her skirts, and sob it out in words aloud, at last.

"Mother—why am I—why am I sometimes—sometimes so fr-fr-frightened of my—my fa-fa-father?"

Mother had always answered his questions, till he asked this question. Her failure now, her complete, unstirring silence, doubled the magnitude of a terror till now his own shamed secret. And the doubled was redoubled by the sound of that man's feet on the piazza, coming toward the door.

He groveled. "Mother, please, hurry—hurry and tell me, tell me, mother! What—what's there about my father—what's he done that's such a—a horror?"

Still, for answer, no word, no gesture. And it was too late; a quiet door had opened and the feet were in the room. As Daniel scrambled up and wheeled, a defending courage suffused him. He stood his ground, and, not knowing why, spread his arms across the man's way, and, not knowing what, cried: "No! Don't! Don't come!"

Through the water in his eyes he began to see his father's face hung there before him, oddly gray, the stare of it fixed, not on him, but on her behind him. And he grew aware of two things fighting in that stare, the greater one like a stunned sorrow, the lesser like a reawakening hope.

As sometimes in crisis, it was of the lesser one the man spoke now.

"This, then, Daniel, is why you said what you said out there, and sobbed, and ran away back here? It wasn't that old queerness of yours coming back then, after all?"

The husband's shock was gentler than the son's, for all evening he had had in his mind as he watched Vivian the thought of a candle when it gutters, how it will flame to its old brightness for an instant at the last.

Not so with Daniel. When he turned and knew that the reason his mother had sat there and not answered him was that all the while she had sat there in the deep chair dead, he fainted.

Doc Martin had to mop his bald head with a troubled handkerchief many times in the following days. On the third, the afternoon after the funeral, stopping in at the Kinsmans' by right of the oldest and closest friend and finding Dan there all alone, he asked: "Where's Daniel hiding himself?" And if it sounded casual, and was meant to, already in the soil of the doctor's mind uneasy little roots of wonder had begun to set.

"Don't know; not far off, I guess." The answer was given with an averted face.

Why shouldn't it be? Men's faces, when they've just buried their wives of twenty years—why may they not wish to keep what's written on them to themselves? The physician mocked himself for a worrying idiot as he went on home.

But he had his head to mop again when he got to his own house and found Daniel fidgeting up and down the piazza, inarticulate and miserably mantling. It was all mysterious and awkward. He didn't know what he was to do or say, and especially was this so when the boy's dumbness, laboring, brought forth some mouse of words about the weather or the baseball standings. But finally, "Dr. Martin," it came at a rush, "was my mother happy, living here in Kennelbridge, with father—and me?"

It is unfortunate that at such moments men seem to think they have to speak in the manner of oracles. As Dan Kinsman, three days before, now Doc Martin:

"Well, son, she *lived* here in Kennelbridge, with you and your father, almost exactly ten years longer than I gave her to live. Does that mean anything?"

And thereafter he wondered why the boy's eyes, savagely troubled, followed him slantwise everywhere. He wondered more. Seeing the sun go and the dusk come, he wondered why the sensitive, naturally unobtrusive lad stayed on, apparently aimless and plainly wretched, and stayed, and made no move to go. It was after dark when Doc Martin appeared at the Kinsman place, to find Dan out in the east yard, standing, chin down, hands locked behind him.

"I thought, Dan, you might wonder where the kid was. He's over at my house. I'm afraid I've been—uh—keeping him."

Dan listened, stock-still, without comment. It became an ordeal.

"I don't know just how to say it, Dan. The boy seems badly upset. He has a lot of his mother in him, Dan—a lot of the thing that made us all love her—and—want to spank her, sometimes. That sentimental defenselessness—it went with her ailment, I've no doubt. That making a mountain of emotion out of a molehill of—not that I mean this is a molehill—but—

damn it, old man! The boy—this house—this night after the funeral—I've a hunch he'd more than half like to stay over with me. Thought I'd ask you."

"Yes."

The one syllable, it sounded rough in the throat. As he went away the doctor turned twice to study the figure posted there in darkness, head heavy, face hidden. Anger? Sorrow? What? Headless, tailless business! He told himself he wished he were dead and well out of it.

He wasn't. After that night any half plans there may have been of father and son going off for a summer of travel together were dropped. There was a camp in the Green Mountains where Daniel's school went, and he was packed for it by the second morning. Dan came to Doc Martin, unhappy, unused to lying.

"I wonder if you'll do something for me, old man? Drive Daniel over to the main line this noon. I shall be busy."

The doctor did it. What their parting was he never knew, for the boy had his bags out at the gate when he drove by, and the father was "busy." If the friend of them both was profanely troubled he kept it quiet, and set himself for a gallant hour of cheer and small talk. The problem of a book for the journey seemed a godsend. They went over the newstand's library with a mutual pretense of care, but, as if it were not bad enough that all the novels were detective novels, Daniel discovered after brief browsings that there was none he could be certain he hadn't read. As he accepted one at last, entitled *Murder!*, the physician had to stare.

"Lord, son! To look at you, anybody'd think you were as mild as a lamb. And here you turn out a glutton for crime. Don't you ever read anything else?"

Daniel went red—even redder, the doctor thought, than was asked for.

"Oh, I forget 'em faster'n I read 'em. If you asked me one single thing that had happened, a week after, I couldn't any more remember it than I could——"

He got no further. He had touched by chance on a pet dogma of the other's; and Doc Martin, figuratively, squared off.

"Couldn't remember? Bosh! Ever tried?"

"Tried?" Daniel was confused by this vehemence.

"*Really* tried, I mean. Rolled up your mental sleeves and taken pick and spade to the humus of memory, to try and turn up some one particular thing that's buried there? It's surprising. There are authenticated records of long-term prisoners, men in solitary confinement, who, simply for something for their minds to do——"

And here they came, the classic cases, served up with a zealot's gusto; the aged criminals reconstructing verbatim the nursery tales of infanthood; the old fellows repainting in minutest detail places passed through as children and thereafter wholly forgotten. And so forth. And so on.

The man with a hobby is not to be held accountable. Doc Martin, who had toiled to make talk—now his one fear was that the belated train would make up time.

"Can't remember! Actually, you can't *forget!* Nothing you've ever felt, heard, seen, no matter how tiny—you may mislay the record, but you can't lose it. No matter how dim, it's here in your cranium somewhere, indelible, forever."

The bent ear and big eye of his audience it was cruel to give up. The train wags in, but there was still the moment on the platform.

"Theoretically, Daniel, you ought to be able to remember the day of your birth. But it would probably take you as many as a thousand years, in a dark cell, and after all——"

After all, after the boy was up the step Doc Martin recollected something he had been two days thinking on.

"Daniel, listen! Your mother *was* happy. Her life here was a clear, quiet, happy life, with those she loved deeply. Believe me, Daniel."

It was good for Daniel he had the book called *Murder!* At the end of his emotional tether he must have escape, and the surest escape was here between these covers; he knew the taste of it beforehand, as the eater of drugs knows the taste of his drug. Escape, yes. And a curious, helpless, rather horrid surrender.

Half a year ago he would not have been ashamed to have the doctor remark it; it was only of late he had begun to have misgivings of this craving for the dark excitement that surrounds the body of a crime, a craving he could never remember not to have had strong in him.

Never remember? "Bosh!" For a little while yet he left the book unopened and thought of the mild old doctor and his ferocious expletive. But was it true, even a half of what he had claimed, about digging up buried things? . . . If you tried hard enough? . . . Took a pick and spade . . . to buried things? . . .

There were five hours to ride, more than enough for the book. Let it wait.

To remember things forgotten! By dim footprints in the mold of old fantasies, by broken twigs of sensation—this sort of sound disliked for no reason, that odor as inexplicably agreeable—by clues so thinner-than-air to be able to track back relentlessly—what?

"Bosh!" It was Daniel's own bosh this time. But the light in the deeps of his abstracted eyes burned no less steadily, nor did the color of a strange excitation retreat from his cheeks and temples.

There was a station. Express, the train only slowed, going through. On the flickering platform stood an elderly woman, back to, a stoutish figure glimpsed for a split second, gray-clad, with a purple hat with a tulle quill.

"Emma!"

But then the boy lay back and derided himself. It was that purple, forward-tilted hat. Emma, his old nurse, had been dead three—no, two years. It was three years ago she came to see him, from Albany, and that was the year before she died.

Yes, yes. She came in her nephew's car, and brought Daniel a sweater she had knitted for him. He could see her now, when he tried to get into it, there on the big circular side piazza, and her chagrin. "Mercy, when I was here last I never looked to see you grow so in two years. Remember when I was here last time, Dannie?"

"Course I do; what d'you think? And you said I used to be a caution when I was little, and you hoped I'd got over it."

"Bless you, Dannie, and have you?"

Had he? Got over what? Three years ago he'd known what, because three years ago he'd remembered what she'd said two years before that. Something about: "I declare, you always were a caution, Dannie. The first day ever I saw you . . . saw you . . . first day ever I saw you——"

Concentrate on it! Try harder!

". . . first day ever I saw you, do you know what you said . . . what you——"

In the Pullman, but unconscious of the Pullman, Daniel knotted his brows.

Don't give up. Go at it some other way. . . .

Well, they'd been in his room; he was ready for bed, and Emma had come up—she'd stayed overnight that next-to-last visit—and she'd sat there

in the blue rocker and talked and talked. Talked so long that mother had
called: "Daniel, Emma's tired, so you must stop asking her so many——"

But now he *had* it—the other thing—it was "question."

It wasn't "what you said." It was, complete: "First day ever I saw you,
do you know *the question you asked me?* Well, most three-year-olds, they'll
ask you like, 'What's a zebra?' or 'What's a airplane?' But the first thing
you asked me was . . . thing you asked me was——"

No, after all, not quite complete. Why did the light of recollection close
again, just there? Especially when, by thinking on it, that bedtime visit of
Emma's had grown as vivid as a thing today.

The expression of the boy in seat No. 5 was a set scowl. A flush colored
it, like anger. A "Bosh!" trembled on his lips. He had a book to read, and,
by hang, he'd read it now. A book called *Murder!*

"Murder!"

Why, now he'd got that too!

"The first thing you asked me—I was trying to get you to go into the
summerhouse and you were howling and pulling—and you asked me,
'What is murder?' And if you don't call that funny for a three-year-old
to be asking——"

Murder? Three-year-old? Funny? . . . But leave those, for the moment.

Summerhouse! What summerhouse? So far back as Daniel, by knotting
his brows to their tightest, could recollect, there'd never been at home any
such thing as a summerhouse.

Summerhouse? Latticework, probably. Light through it in squares or
diamonds, probably. Unless—ugh, it was chilly in the Pullman—there were .
vines. Vines?

The train carried the corporeal weight of Daniel Kinsman to White
River Junction that summer afternoon. But the part of him that weighed
nothing at all had started on an immensely longer journey, an incalculably
stranger quest.

At camp, for the first while, they let him go his own gait, without nag-
ging him or themselves. Aware of his shocking loss, they even let down
the rules a little—rules, fundamentally, of good fellowship—in his case.
Daniel, with his shut mouth, little appetite, and eyes fixed habitually on
nothing, was no good fellow for anyone.

This was all right for a certain period. But when a week and another
week had gone, and a normal youngster should have been getting some
hold on healthy life, and Daniel was still not less separate, but if anything

more so, physically torpid, colorless of expression, unmistakably if incomprehensibly not among those present, the responsible began to think of doing something about it.

At length the Head sat down and wrote a letter to the boy's father, who had shut up house on Doc Martin's plea and gone off with him to the Canadian woods. But that letter was destined not to be posted. Before a stamp was on it, word came in that young Kinsman had not been seen since lights-out the night before. At the end of a day and night of combing the woods, beating the hills, a telegram was dispatched to Canada.

Locked, bolted, and shuttered though the house was, Daniel knew a boy's way into it. One of the cellar windows was loose enough to let a lock-pick wire in.

Of all that Daniel had done, of all he was yet to undertake, this one act was the hardest. That he could, in the night, enter into that sealed, empty, pitch-black habitation, of which anyone might be nervous—and he, with his mother dead and his imagination whipped keen by a fortnight's flagellation, was horribly, icily afraid—gives the measure of the thing that was stronger than the house's terror, its pull.

If he were only in the house, only on the scene there, only at home! Day by day, night by night, the brown house of home kept the dragline taut on him, by innuendo, by promise, by command. Whenever a peephole, opened in memory, had closed again before the glimpsed stage could set itself with half the properties of old actuality—"Ah yes, but if you were *there* it might."

And now that he was here? Now that he was actually in, his feet weighing on sightless stairs, hands guiding him along blind walls? Now what was he to do?

Nothing. When he had reached his own room, at the end of gropings that brought sweat out of his neck, he pawed for his bed, found it, and laid himself down along the middle of the mattress. There, inert—almost as inert for hours at a time as a cataleptic—he remained. How long?

By calendar it came to four days. In his consciousness the lapse of time was not measurable, it was as well a dream's forty winks as a dungeon's forty years.

Of his rare actual moves he was to all intents unconscious. Luckily it was summer, and the water not turned off; from time to time he drank. Once he bolted raw oatmeal from a box in the pantry and was ill with it.

The electric current was cut, but there was the oil lantern he might have lighted long before he did, had he cared. Rather, perhaps, had he dared. Perhaps, more simply, had he felt the need. After all, his eyes were no longer concerned with this shuttered Here and Now.

They were concerned with the half-open door of a summerhouse.

Relatively, it may have been little more than a scratching of the topsoil; actually, in that blank-eyed fortnight away at camp, he had penetrated a surprising depth into the leaf mold of his fallen memories. Most important, he had caught the trick of it, learned the heft and balance of his tools, pick and spade, a dogged mental concentration working at one with a reserveless mental surrender.

So it had become child's play, literally, by fastening on some fag end of sensuous recollection—a barked shin of escapade, sting of a punishment, taste of the sweetmeat of some reward—to restore the outlines of whole episodes in the comparatively recent years of his sixes, fives, even his fours; to relive whole days, repeople whole scenes with shapes which began by having no names, or with names wanting shapes, and watch these phantasmal beings take on identities and lineaments—and lo! Auntie Prichard, of course, the doughnut woman! Or Mary Belle—who could forget the girl with wire on her teeth?

He had learned a lot about the creature of pranks and bush-beatings that is the mind. He learned, at a price, that no lead can be too paltry to follow. So it was, retrieving a boy's face plastered with freckles and banged with red hair, he had given three hours of his last camp morning to trying to find the face a name. A dozen times he nearly had it; the muscles of his tongue knew the feel of it, yet couldn't get the sound. It made him mad. "I won't give it up, not if it takes all day!"

And, "day," there it was. Georgie Day! Who could forget Georgie Day?

Accident? In the weird business Daniel was about, there's no such thing.

Georgie Day. Well, well! Immediately, fruitless hours fruited magically. A house suddenly sprang up around the freckled rascal, and around the house a tin-can-littered yard, and in the yard a tumbling barn, and in the barn, rabbits.

Rabbits? What about rabbits? Look! here's a rabbit running, bounding high with fright across a greensward in sunshine. No, none of Georgie's; he and his have vanished from the scene. This is a wild one, cottontail, surprised among berry bushes behind the home garden, retreat cut off, scuttling across the west lawn for all it's worth, and Daniel after it.

Run, cottontail! Run, boy! Bounce, bunny! Whoop, Dannie!

"Here, Daisy! Where are you, Daisy? Where's that dog?"

Daisy? Why, Spot's mother, of course, elderly, sleepy, all setter-red.

Yellow sunshine, green grass, little wild blue shadow, hunting, praying, for some hole. And a hole, a hole at last! Squarish aperture among massed leaves. Dive for it, bunny! Stop, boy! Into it, rabbit! Boy, stop dead! Don't go near there, youngster! Frown if you please, stamp, mutter; yes, you know you don't want to go near there. You know you don't.

Why not?

Pandemonium. Out comes rabbit, out comes Daisy, the lazy, surprised asleep in there. And the two of them fleeing, pursuing, flicker past the transfixed Dannie, and away, into limbo. For it's the squarish aperture in massed woodbine leaves, crosshatch of lattice in their gaps, lattice door ajar—it's this he's staring at.

So it was, by uttering the irrelevant words "if it takes all day," Daniel had found the way back to the summerhouse.

Two weeks it had taken him to reach its viny exterior. Had he had a hundred years, real ones, in place of the hundred hours he could command, who knows but that he might actually have succeeded in covering the rest of the journey—might have crept or leaped at last across that one remaining rod of grass, gravel, and doorsill, and been inside?

He started sanguinely. Only a rod left—the last dash—home stretch. Pooh! Thrown back from it, confused, he started again with the same assurance, only again to be set on his heels by a wall, impalpable as air, but impenetrable as glass. How many times did he relaunch the attack? In one hour of the clock he could live a score in recollection, a hundred, toward the end, when hunger and fever had whipped the pace. No longer sanguinely, but desperately, he tried one breach after another.

For now there were several; he had multiplied his points of attack. To the rabbit day he had added quickly the Emma day. It was no task by now to reconstruct that episode entire. He could commence with the breakfast table, where the new nurse was first introduced into the scheme of his cosmos. He could mount then to his room with her, suffer the change into denim play pants, come down, come out, and go towing around the yard at her arm's end, dazzled by the sudden wealth of her "What shall we play? Anything on earth you like, Dannie?"

So, not once, but dozens of times, he came to the spot where something in him balked, he began to howl, cleared Emma's grasp, let her go on. He

could see her face in all its mystification now—and see it, more was the
wonder, across the width of the rod he couldn't cross—in the doorway of
the summerhouse. And he could hear her expostulating still:

"What is it, Dannie? Nothing but a toad here. You're not afraid of a
toad!"

And he could feel something in his stomach's pit, that came up, and
was words.

"What is murder, Emma?"

Why on earth that? What was it in him, cold and hot—not shame, not
rage, not terror, alone, but like a misery of all three compounded? Or like
the feeling Daniel had to this day, immensely diluted, whenever anyone
in his hearing spoke of cycles or sickles or Seckles.

And, coming to that, why on earth that? Did it all come from "Seckle"?
And did that come from the pear tree, down past the east corner of the
barn, which, since he was recollecting, he recollected he had never liked?
Recollected, in fact, that when they used to play hide-and-seek at his house,
and Daniel himself was it, and one of the boys hid behind that Seckle
pear below the barn, he wouldn't go there to spy him, not if he stayed it
forever.

So? Why wouldn't he? Time and time again he made an effort to follow
that trace, but it was of no use; there was nothing there that was important, he had to tell himself; much better buckle down to business with the
shovel day.

The shovel day he had added to the rabbit day and the Emma day now.
Where it came in the chronology he couldn't say; though he judged from
the longer time it had taken him to dig it out it must have been earlier. At
any rate, it was the farthest back he could remember being frightened by
his father.

He had to work on it. Again, again, stubbornly again, he would stand
in a flushed twilight on the perimeter of that arc whose radius was a rod,
and watch the woodbine leaves put aside, and see his father emerge from
the dark interior, carrying a spade.

Well, what about it? What so fearful was his father doing? Going gar-
dening, probably, in the evening's cool; tools may have been kept in the
summerhouse. So, what? Look more deeply into this! But, try as Daniel
would, he couldn't. Each time, at sight of man and shovel, the child
gulped, turned, ran, with goblins grabbing after him, for the house and
mother.

Why? Why, oh why, oh why?

And now at last, time lost all count of—grown to months and years, it seemed, in the black house—now at last, let down by the caving of the body beneath it, Daniel's mind began to surrender to exhaustion. Daylight —what was actually the fourth daylight—creeping through the shutter cracks in slim fans of grayness, did not waken him for a long time from the sleep into which he had sunk near midnight.

When it did he failed to fall immediately, as his habit was, into his reminiscent reverie. Lying supine, staring at the ceiling, it was the ceiling he saw this morning. He raised himself on the mattress, intending to go downstairs, but with the act a dizziness took hold of him. He lay back again and listened to his teeth knocking together. It is one thing for a man, adult and idle, to starve himself for a while; for a growing boy it is another thing.

It was the first time there had been room in Daniel's brain for a thought of failure. Was it not possible that the end of the time he could hide and have solitude was approaching? No sooner the idea, than he repelled it. With a strength of panic he drove himself back to his task. Dig or die, now!

But the pick and spade, till now so docile, developed the balkings and crotchets of a curious sabotage. Today, when he summoned the old face of a playmate, straightway the features began to twist in the weirdest fashion, magnify, diminish, like the grotesque faces that dissolve in dreams. Or, coming on a new trail of old adventure unexplored, he found it leading him into extraordinary places, out of all color with the rest of his past —and realized with a start that it was something he had read, not lived.

And presently, frustrated, he slept again.

Each other day had been an age; this was but a dozen blinks long, a day wasted. How could Daniel know the incalculable value of that day his mind lay fallow?

It was night once more when he arose, went into his mother's room, and lay down on the bed there. It was nearly, if not quite, somnambulism. Certainly he was unaware of any reason for the move. Whether he fell asleep and woke up, whether he slept at all or waked at all, whether at any time he was actually, bodily, in the summerhouse, it would be now impossible to say. It can only be said that the thing till the end had all the stigmata of true nightmare.

The will to terror, to begin with. Terror sprung of its own seed, an effect wanting a cause, a shadow condemned to create the object that casts it. And with this, alternately, a weightless, boundless mobility, and a sense of being held from moving, arms pinioned, legs bound.

Nothing was very clear. Such moments as were lighted—less than pictures; mere rags of sight vignetted on the dark—were whisked away too quickly to be comprehended whole. Nor were these many. The pervading scene was a blackness in which blacknesses moved, giving forth but muffled sounds. Acts witnessed and no more, shadowy, separate, retreating rather than ever coming nearer.

"They're going away from the summerhouse, ma'am," or "carrying him away"—that adverb, "away," was forever recurring. And generally somewhere near it, whether before or after, blacknesses moved on blackness with a black burden; heavy breathing, soft feet.

It must be understood there was never an attempt at sequence. No act revealed itself whole at any one time; at divers times divers fractions of it would repeat themselves, mingled with stray fractions of other acts or utterances.

Take the one set of sounds. Sometimes it ran, out there—door creak, oath, blow, scuffle. Sometimes quite reversed. Sometimes—oath, blow, scuffle, door creak.

And that querying cry, coming from close above, thrown down—out of a window?—into the dark, now it would be, "Dan, what are you doing? Tom!" Then, like as not, next time it would be: "Tom, what are you doing? Dan!"

It is impossible to tell it, by a tenth, adequately. For by the very mechanics of telling, nine tenths of the formlessness is lost; fragments, released from the peculiar bedevilment of nightmare, inevitably fly together. Detached words, fractional phrases, flickering by, flitting back again; before they can be written here they must needs have formed themselves by some degree into sentences, no matter if the sentences are forever changing something of the forms. As, for instance, in the one, "Dan (Tom), what are you doing?" followed by, "Tom! (Dan!)"

There's the other sentence, into which at last the word "murder" has come. By the time it has crystallized itself into the sequence—"It was murder, Dan; I saw it; murder in cold blood!"—by that time the light around it has crystallized, too, in a pattern, a pattern of diamond-shaped pencils striking in through gaps of latticework. And the strait jacket of nightmare around one's limbs has taken the shape of the arms of the crier-out. And the crier-out is mother.

"Don't come in that door; I'm afraid of you, Dan! The blood on your hands is blood of brutal murder. Why? Don't tell me. Was it because I loved him? I love my child, here in my arms. Must I be afraid for *him* then? Must he be afraid of his father now, as long as the two of you live?"

And this cry, too, vibrant with hysteria, has a vision to go with it, a peephole vision of a close lantern, a red-flecked hand, a spade with earth spots on it, and the tight, white, terrible mask of father's face.

So, in the telling, already this big, close lantern light has extricated itself from the little lantern light at distance. But in the dream, if it was a dream, this very separation of the two became from the first the thing, intuitively, the dreamer fought for. Wrestled for with tied hands; ran after with hobbled feet; cried to with stopped mouth.

In the beginning it was equally the one or the other that might start it; toward the end of an aeon a kind of rule was established; it was the little light far off that began, and the big one then, too soon, that came and swallowed it, only to be swallowed in its turn by that blackness with black things moving in it, or the door-creak sequence, containing the scuffle, the oath, and the blow.

Perhaps it was because of this that the desire of the boy's dread centered more and more fiercely on that weakling spark, and he told himself it was there that whatever was hidden was hidden, and awaited its recurrence impatient of the other shadow plays. And when it came, and the voice of the second woman in the bedroom—a nurse?—began, "It's digging they are, ma'am, down there——" and with that the light began to swell, irresistibly, and stripe itself in the pattern that meant the summerhouse, Daniel fought with all his bitter, puny power against the re-enwrapping arms, the relifting hysteria of mother's "Don't come in that door; I'm afraid of you!" and the reopening peepshow of the red hand and the white face.

And he cried: "Yes, but go on with the other! Digging down *where,* down *where?*" till in the nightmare the lees of the sweat of his exhaustion ran in icy dribbles down his skin.

It was not till he gave up, beaten by weariness, that it suddenly gave in.

"It's digging they are, ma'am, down there under——"

"Under *what?*"

"—under that pear tree——"

"Pear tree?"

"—with the little pears, below the barn. By the light of the lantern, ma'am——"

Lantern! By the way, where is a lantern? Now, quick!

"—they're digging in the——"

Digging! Pick and spade? Where are they?

"—ground, burying something——"

A thing that is buried!

"—under the pear tree, ma'am."

Ever tried? Rolled up your sleeves, taken pick and spade—to turn up something that is buried there?

When Dan Kinsman and Doc Martin reached the house late that night, and found it black, the one last hope, which neither had dared confess to, seemed to have followed all its fellows. Red-lidded with sleeplessness, jaws ill shaven, clothing long worn, they looked the men they felt now, as, unlocking the front door, they went in.

"What's the good?"

It was the doctor that saw it, through one of the living-room windows.

"Hey! What's up there? Somebody with a lantern, down there behind the barn."

They started out of the door at a walk, but then ran.

They found a lantern, a spade, and a garden mattock under the Seckel-pear tree, and a sprawling trench dug, and a weazen-faced, wide-eyed boy to his knees in it, holding out toward them two brown bones.

Dan spoke. "For God's sake, what are you doing here?"

Daniel spoke. "For God's sake, what are *these* doing here?"

Doc Martin spoke. "For God's sake!" That was all.

It wasn't that Dan was obstinate; it was simply that he was dazed.

"What are you doing here, son? Tell me!"

It wasn't that Daniel was sullen; it was simply that his legs were going to go out from under him at any moment now.

"What are these, father? You tell me!"

"Son—sonny—you're sick."

"I am sick. Who was Tom?"

"Good Lord alive! Dan! look here. Be quiet, Daniel; wait till I get through with him. Dan, how long ago was it—I mean, how old would this kid have been, that night?"

"What night do you mean?"

"Come out of it, man! That night when you heard where Tom had been the week before, and called me, and I brought the chloroform over, thinking maybe, perhaps, the dog might——"

"Dog!" High in the roof of a boy's mouth, the one syllable, echoing.

"—and you, Dan, no maybe or perhaps about it, you got him in the head with the spade, thank God, in time. What I asked you—how old was Daniel then?"

"Not old enough to remember anything. . . . Daniel, who's been telling you——"

But Doc Martin wouldn't have it. "No, man, you talk to me. How old?"

"Two, perhaps. Not three. A baby. A babe in arms, actually, come to think of it. Vivian had him there in her arms."

"Where?"

"There in the summerhouse."

"Vivian—in the summerhouse?"

"Afterward. She—she had come there."

"You've never told me."

"No. I—it's something I—— Look here, Daniel, son, you'd best be——"

"No you don't, Dan. Talk! What's this about Vivian, and Daniel, and the summerhouse, afterward? Tell it, and tell it straight."

"She was ill, that's all. Frightened. And—and you know how she was about animals and things—and she didn't understand. Couldn't expect her to, not knowing anything. Hysterical. Went to the summerhouse to see—and bolted herself in."

"But when you explained?"

"That's it. I was a fool, I suppose. I tried to lie, at first. The mastiff was hers, from a pup; she adored him; it was all so sudden; I couldn't bring myself to say the word—hydrophobia. A fool."

"Yes, and a damned one."

"She said she was afraid of me, Doc. She said it was—it was——"

"She said it was murder, father. And—it was only—— *Father!*"

"Son! Lord! What's the—— Hey! Catch him, Doc, or he'll fall."

"Catch him yourself, he's yours. Pick him up, fool. Starvation; don't worry too much. Bring him along."

"But if he should come to, and me carrying him. I'm afraid——"

"Don't be. Not any more."

JOHN STEINBECK
Over the Hill

SLIGO and the kid took their forty-eight-hour pass listlessly. The bars close in Algeria at eight o'clock, but they got pretty drunk on wine before that happened and they took a bottle with them and lay down on the beach. The night was warm, and after the two had finished the second bottle of wine they took off their clothes and waded out into the quiet water and then squatted down and sat there with only their heads out. "Pretty nice, eh, kid," said Sligo. "There's guys used to pay heavy dough for stuff like this, and we get it for nothing."

"I'd rather be home on Tenth Avnoo," said the kid. "I'd rather be there than anyplace. I'd like to see my old lady. I'd like to see the World Series this year."

"You'd like maybe a clip in the kisser," said Sligo.

"I'd like to go into the Greek's and get me a double chocolate malted with six eggs in it," said the kid. He bobbed up to keep a little wavelet out of his mouth. "This place is lonely. I like Coney."

"Too full of people," said Sligo.

"This place is lonely," said the kid.

"Talking about the Series. I'd like to do that myself," said Sligo. "It's times like this a fella gets kind of tempted to go over the hill."

"S'posen you went over the hill—where the hell would you go? There ain't no place to go."

"I'd go home," said Sligo. "I'd go to the Series. I'd be first in the bleachers, like I was in '40."

"You couldn't get home," the kid said; "there ain't no way to get home."

The wine was warming Sligo and the water was good. "I got dough says I can get home," he said carelessly.

"How much dough?"

"Twenty bucks."

"You can't do it," said the kid.

"You want to take the bet?"

"Sure I'll take it. When you going to pay?"

"I ain't going to pay; you're going to pay. Let's go up on the beach and knock off a little sleep. . . ."

At the piers the ships lay. They had brought landing craft and tanks and troops, and now they lay taking in the scrap, the broken equipment from the North African battlefields which would go to the blast furnaces to make more tanks and landing craft. Sligo and the kid sat on a pile of C-ration boxes and watched the ships. Down the hill came a detail with a hundred Italian prisoners to be shipped to New York. Some of the prisoners were ragged and some were dressed in American khaki because they had been too ragged in the wrong places. None of the prisoners seemed to be unhappy about going to America. They marched down to a gangplank and then stood in a crowd awaiting orders to get aboard.

"Look at them," said the kid, "they get to go home and we got to stay. What you doing, Sligo? What you rubbing oil all over your pants for?"

"Twenty bucks," said Sligo, "and I'll find you and collect, too." He stood up and took off his overseas cap and tossed it to the kid. "Here's a present, kid."

"What you going to do, Sligo?"

"Don't you come follow me, you're too dumb. Twenty bucks, and don't you forget it. So long, see you on Tent Avnoo."

The kid watched him go, uncomprehending. Sligo, with dirty pants and a ripped shirt, moved gradually over, near to the prisoners, and then imperceptibly he edged in among them and stood bareheaded, looking back at the kid.

An order was called down to the guards, and they herded the prisoners toward the gangplank. Sligo's voice came plaintively. "I'm not supposed to be here. Hey, don't put me on dis ship."

"Shut up, wop," a guard growled at him. "I don't care if you did live sixteen years in Brooklyn. Git up that plank." He pushed the reluctant Sligo up the gangplank.

Back on the pile of boxes the kid watched with admiration. He saw Sligo get to the rail. He saw Sligo still protesting and fighting to get back to the pier. He heard him shrieking, "Hey, I'm Americano. Americano soldier. You canna poot me here."

The kid saw Sligo struggling and then he saw the final triumph. He saw Sligo take a sock at a guard and he saw the guard's club rise and come down on Sligo's head. His friend collapsed and was carried out of sight on board the ship. "The son-of-a-gun," the kid murmured to himself. "The smart son-of-a-gun. They can't do nothing at all to him and he got witnesses. Well, the smart son-of-a-gun. My God, it's worth twenty bucks."

The kid sat on the boxes for a long time. He didn't leave his place till the ship cast off and the tugs pulled her clear of the submarine nets. The kid saw the ship join the group and he saw the destroyers move up and take the convoy under protection. The kid walked dejectedly up to the town. He bought a bottle of Algerian wine and headed back toward the beach to sleep his forty-eight.

DONALD OGDEN STEWART

The Secret of Success

THE YOUNG MAN in search of employment came at last to the inner shrine in that temple of Modern Business known as the Ellsworth Products Co. As he stood hesitating at the portals, one of the high priests advanced to meet him, chanting the greeting of his order.

"Mr. Ellsworth is a very busy man. A *very* busy man," he droned, and at each pronouncement of the name "Ellsworth" the heads of the seven stenographic vestals in the office were reverently bowed.

Five times that morning in five outer offices had the young man been told that Mr. Ellsworth was a very busy man; five times had his letter of introduction carried him through the efficient obstacles which guard the inner temple from the eyes of infidel unbelievers. And now, his pilgrimage ended, for the sixth and last time he gave his name—Richard Kennedy, his business—an interview with the president regarding employment, his credentials—a letter of introduction from one of Mr. Ellsworth's friends.

While this letter was being examined, young Kennedy reverently surveyed the temple.

At one end was a huge mahogany door—the entrance to the throne room. His gaze fell next upon the seven virgins, busy at their consecrated stenographic tasks. One glance at these maidens told him that he was indeed on holy ground, for they were of such loveliness as belongs only in the offices of high executives. Kennedy had already, in the course of his pilgrimage, noted the significant business fact that standards of office furnishings and stenographic beauty increase progressively as one ascends in the scale of executive rank—exemplified in the present instance by the impressive early Georgian hangings and late Ziegfeldian typists of this office as contrasted with the plain, chaste furniture and plainer, chaster stenographers of the lower departments.

"Sit down, Mr. Kennedy," said the president's private secretary. "Mr. Ellsworth is a very busy man."

Young Kennedy obediently took the designated chair outside the throne-room door, from behind which he could hear at intervals a faint swishing noise. He idly wondered as to its cause, and one heretical thought which occurred to him before he could check himself was that it sounded somewhat like the noise made by the swinging of a golf club.

His eye fell upon a magazine lying on a near-by desk. *Efficiency,* it was called, *Efficiency—The Journal of Success.* He picked it up and was soon deeply engrossed in a fascinating article concerning a businessman of Tacoma, Wash., who had actually eliminated twelve minutes wasted time per clerk per day by the masterful ingenuity of having the fountain pens of his employees filled each evening by the night watchman.

The next article, entitled "How I Make Men Like Me," was by Abraham Nussbaum, sales manager for the Sutco Tire Co., illustrated with graphic and convincing photographs of Mr. Nussbaum caught in the very act of making men like him. "The secret of my success," confessed Mr. Nussbaum, "is personality. Personality and pep—that's the stuff, boys!" And farther on in the article he gave this advice: "Radiate magnetism! Envelop your customer with your personality. Practice at home before a mirror until you are sure that everything about you radiates personal magnetism."

Young Kennedy looked around for a mirror, but before he had time for any practice in the radiation of personal magnetism, the private secretary announced that Mr. Ellsworth was ready to see him.

The swishing noise had ceased; all was silent behind the mahogany door. The high priest took the young man by the arm. A bell was struck, the seven vestals bowed their heads, the door swung open, and the worshiper beheld the Great Man seated on his throne. He stepped forward, trembling; the door closed behind him.

Richard Kennedy stood alone before the president of the Ellsworth Products Co.

"Well, young man!" and President Ellsworth directed at Kennedy those keen eyes which, as described in the April number of *Efficiency*, seem to "look right through you."

"Yes sir," said young Kennedy. And then he added, by way of explanation, "Yes sir."

"Well, young man—what do you want?"

The idea of wanting anything suddenly seemed so incredibly blasphemous to the young man that for a moment he was silent. Then he ventured to give his name, his request for employment, and his letter of introduction.

Mr. Ellsworth adjusted an impressive pair of gold-rimmed eyeglasses to his nose and gravely examined the letter with that shrewd, keen glance which had so impressed the interviewer for *Efficiency*. His shrewd, keen comment, "You want a job, young man?" after he had finished the letter asking that young Kennedy be given a chance, showed that he had instantly grasped the fundamentals of the situation.

"Yes sir," replied Kennedy, adding apologetically, "I'm just out of college." President Ellsworth took off his eyeglasses. There was an impressive silence. Finally the Great Man gravely clipped the end off a cigar, lighted it slowly, and spoke:

"Young man, when I first came to this city I didn't have a cent. Not a penny."

He paused and closed his eyes to let the full significance of this fact sink in upon young Kennedy.

"Young man, listen to me."

The room was hushed. The smoke from President Ellsworth's cigar gradually settled around his head, covering him as with a cloud. Outside the building all noise of traffic had ceased. The sky was darkened. Suddenly there came a terrific clap of thunder, and from the cloud surrounding President Ellsworth was heard a voice saying:

"Young man, there are three rules for business success. The first of these is, 'Don't watch the clock'; the second, 'Don't be afraid of getting your hands dirty'; and the third, 'Work just a little harder than the other man.'"

As he finished, the cloud ascended and President Ellsworth sank back exhausted.

The young man, overcome with emotion, could not speak. It was one

of those rare moments in which words are superfluous; his heart overflowed
with joy that he, of all people, had been chosen to be the recipient of the
Great Man's secret of success.

It was Mr. Ellsworth who finally broke the silence.

"You will report to Mr. Augustus in Department 12 on Monday morning."

The young man's eyes shone with gratitude as he thanked his patron.
A bell rang, the door opened, and with bowed head he backed out of the
presence of the Great Man.

II

The following Monday he who had miraculously received the three
commandments descended from Mount Sinai and went to work as clerk
No. 4 in Section No. 8 of Department No. 12 of the Ellsworth Products Co.
at a salary of fifteen dollars per week. Inasmuch as Richard had never been
good at penmanship or long division, this was probably considerably more
than he at first merited.

At the commencement of his business career, in fact on the very first
morning, the young man came perilously near damnation; forgetting, in a
moment of weakness, the first commandment, Richard was just on the
point of *looking at the clock* when he remembered. It was indeed a narrow
escape, and he shuddered for weeks afterward every time he thought of it.

The second commandment also caused him a great deal of real worry at
first for, in spite of all his efforts, his hands were often quite clean.

The observance of the third and last commandment, "Work harder than
the other man," didn't seem quite so difficult; in fact, in Richard's department, it was almost suspiciously easy.

After a few weeks Richard's hard work combined with his college education began to have its effect on his superiors, and sometimes he was
entrusted with the addition of three and four columns of figures—a responsibility which the young man assumed with a modesty and capability
which greatly pleased the older heads.

Richard did not spend his evenings in idle pleasure, either, as did the
young men who had not been so fortunate as to have been entrusted with
the three secrets of success. He subscribed for the Benjamin Franklin
course in business administration, and after reading fourteen books he was
quite ready to take an executive position in any business. He knew what
caused panics and just how to prevent them; he learned that the cost of

labor and materials was apt to increase periodically provided that some other factors did not cause a decrease.

So they made him a clerk in the filing department and he was entrusted with the stamping of the word "Filed," with the date, on every letter.

This promotion did not, however, make Richard conceited, and his innate modesty won him many friends among the other employees with whom he was quite popular as soon as it became known that he was a friend of Mr. Ellsworth.

One day, after Richard had been working for six months as filing clerk, he conceived an efficient idea for saving time. This was no less revolutionary a scheme than to cease stamping both the word "Filed" and the date and simply imprint the latter in a certain definite place which would, of course, signify that the correspondence had been filed on that date. Richard worked hard in perfecting this idea; he figured out that it would eliminate 302 movements of the clerk's arm in a day, which, allowing for Sundays, holidays, and half days on Saturdays, would mean the saving of 87,580 movements per arm per clerk per annum.

When his idea was finally ready he took it to his immediate superior, Mr. Wilkes.

"That's all right," said Mr. Wilkes, for he believed in encouraging young men, up to a certain extent, "but the Routine Book says that the correspondence must be distinctly stamped 'Filed.'"

"But——" began Richard, and at that the patient Mr. Wilkes took down the Routine Book and pointed to the exact page, section, and paragraph which supported his contention. This closed the argument.

Or, rather, it would have closed the argument had Richard been a less ambitious young man.

But the more he thought about his idea the more efficient it seemed; he discovered also that in his previous figuring he had not allowed for the fact that the clerks worked overtime and all day Saturday during the winter months, which made his net total of saved-clerk-arm-movements per person per annum 92,365 instead of 87,580.

Fortified thus with an additional argument, this young Luther bravely contemplated nailing his thesis to the door of no less a person than President Ellsworth himself, but in several attempts he got no nearer that sacred portal than the office of the second assistant general manager, who coldly imparted to him the not entirely unknown fact that Mr. Ellsworth was a very busy man.

Then, in his hour of despair, Richard remembered Abraham Nussbaum
—the sales manager who had so successfully radiated personal magnetism
in the pages of the *Efficiency* magazine. Three hours a night for the next
five nights young Kennedy spent in front of a tall mirror, with a copy of
Nussbaum's article on "How I Make Men Like Me" spread out before him;
on the morning of the sixth day he was ready to try his skill. Behold—a
magnetic smile at breakfast, and the waitress forgot to charge him for
heavy cream on his corn flakes; another smile, through the window of the
café, and a street sweeper outside ran in and embraced him. This last was
rather embarrassing, and Richard deliberately shut off as much of the magnetism as possible until he could reach the office. But he was so charged
with personality that four newsboys, two beggars, a plumber, and a traffic
policeman followed him to the door of his office, overpoweringly attracted
to this magnetic young man.

In the office his progress to the throne of President Ellsworth was
triumphal; managers, secretaries, stenographers—all instantly liked him and
made way before his "Nussbaum" smile. But as he stood alone before
the president all of young Kennedy's magnetism was promptly short-cir-
cuited by the Great Man's patriarchal impressiveness.

"Well, young man?" said Mr. Ellsworth, fumbling among the papers on
his desk.

"Yes sir," said he. "I am Richard Kennedy, sir. I have a plan which I
have worked out for eliminating a great deal of unnecessary work in the
clerical department, sir. It will save 92,365 movements of a clerk's arm in
one year—and in ten years——"

During this speech the president had continued the search among his
papers.

Suddenly he fixed his shrewd, keen gaze on young Kennedy and said
"Humm."

Then, before Richard could reply to this, the Great Man pressed a button and a stenographer appeared.

"Miss Meyers," said the president, "did you see a little leather notebook
of mine?"

There was a minute's silence. Richard trembled as he thought of the
portentous possibilities of those notes—undoubtedly his complete record
with the Ellsworth Products Co.

The fatal little book was found and handed to Mr. Ellsworth. Young
Kennedy, in dumb suspense, watched the features of the Great Man for

any sign of hope. At last the president shook his head sadly and muttered, "I ought to have had an eighty-four easily. Six strokes on number twelve —a par-three hole—six——"

He looked up and saw young Kennedy. The shrewd, keen look returned instantly to his impressive features which, in the previous moment of forgetfulness, had carelessly become quite human.

"Well, young man?" he said.

"Why, sir," replied Kennedy in stubborn desperation, "I want to tell you about my plan for saving waste time in the clerical department."

President Ellsworth took off his gold-rimmed eyeglasses and listened thoughtfully as Kennedy unfolded his scheme.

When the young man had finished he sat lost in deep thought for some time, before he gave his answer.

"Young man," he said at last, "when I first came to this city I didn't have a cent. Not a penny."

He paused and closed his eyes to let the full significance of this fact sink in upon Kennedy before he resumed.

"Young man, there are three rules for business success. The first of these is, 'Don't watch the clock'; the second, 'Don't be afraid of getting your hands dirty'; and the third, 'Work just a little harder than the other man.'"

The Great Man paused—then added:

"I hope that answers your question, young man."

"Yes sir," said Kennedy gratefully as he bowed out of the room. "Thank you very much, sir."

III

Kennedy returned from his second pilgrimage to the Oracle greatly strengthened in his resolve to keep holy the three commandments on which hang all the laws of the profits. He realized more than ever before that it takes time and hard work to win true success. At the office he set to his task with added zeal; in the evenings he pored over his new correspondence course in Modern Business which guaranteed executive ability and a handsome set of nine books for sixty-five dollars.

But after a few months more he began to grow restless. He felt that possibly he wasn't getting ahead as fast as he should; somehow there wasn't at all the old thrill in adding figures, initialing correspondence, and in being efficient.

Furthermore, there had been a distressing visit to a Vocational Expert.

While perusing his beloved *Efficiency* magazine one evening, his attention had been caught by a full-page advertisement which demanded, in big type, "Young Man, Are You in the Right Job?" Under this was a photograph which Kennedy supposed at first to be a horrible example of a young man *not* in the right job; more careful study showed it to be Morris Stuttgart, A.B., Vocational Expert, who for twenty-five dollars would analyze your character and advise you at once as to your real lifework.

So Kennedy called on Mr. Stuttgart and, after sitting for half an hour in a strong light while the expert analyzed his character, he got a headache and the information that he had an unmistakable aptitude for a musical career. He thanked Mr. Stuttgart, paid his twenty-five dollars, and lay awake that night wondering why his parents had let him drop his piano lessons.

The next noon he sat at his desk, trying to concentrate on the chapter in his business course concerning "How to Write Effective Business Letters to Japan and China," when Mr. Fisher sat down beside him to pick his teeth. Mr. Fisher was a kindly chief clerk who sported three eighteen-karat molars and a fourteen-karat watch charm, the latter a present from his fellow clerks on the anniversary of his Twentieth Year with the Ellsworth Products Co.

"Well, Kennedy, what's new? Aren't married yet, are you?"

This was Mr. Fisher's daily question; Kennedy's daily answer was: "Well, not yet, Mr. Fisher. Can't get a girl to take me. How's Mrs. Fisher today?"

Kennedy had a sincere interest in the domestic welfare of his fellow employees and never faltered in his daily enthusiasm over the latest photo of the wife and kiddies.

Mr. Fisher shook his head mournfully.

"She had a bad night again with her stomach."

Mrs. Fisher's stomach was a subject on which the whole office got minute daily reports. Then he added, "What are you reading?"

"Why, it's the Dearborn Business Course. Pretty good, but I guess you can't get much out of books. It's the hard, practical experience that counts, isn't it?"

Kennedy possessed the modest attitude of amused contempt toward mere book learning which college men diplomatically employ when speaking to those who are unfortunate enough to have Henry Ford's cultural background.

"Well, the Dearborn course is all right. Not as good, perhaps, as some others," replied Mr. Fisher, mentioning three or four names.

"What, you've taken all those correspondence courses, Mr. Fisher?" said the amazed young man.

Here was something wrong; surely Mr. Fisher couldn't have absorbed all that knowledge as to how to be an executive and still remain a chief clerk.

"Oh, sure, I've read them all," was the answer.

"Well, tell me, have most of the clerks here taken the course?" asked the young man.

"Sure," was the surprising answer. "Long ago."

"Well, then, how about Mr. Schmidt?" The mystified young man mentioned the name of one of the highest officials; probably some handicap had kept the clerks from being executives; quite likely they had been "clock watchers" or, even worse, afraid of getting their hands dirty.

"Oh, Mr. Schmidt?" said Mr. Fisher. "Well, that's different. You see, he married Mr. Ellsworth's oldest daughter. Certainly a dandy fellow, too—Mr. Schmidt. Calls me Ed—always joshing me about my kids." And Mr. Fisher chuckled reminiscently.

"Oh," said young Kennedy. "He married Mr. Ellsworth's daughter. I see. And how about Mr. Spencer, the vice-president?"

It was Mr. Spencer who had patted Richard several times approvingly on the back when he had found the young man studying during the noon hour.

"Spencer—say, there's a regular man," replied Mr. Fisher. "Nothing stuck-up about him. He asked Bertha and I to his wedding—married Kitty Ellsworth, you know—the old man's second daughter. My, it was some swell wedding, I'll tell the world."

"Yes," said the young man, "it must have been."

Then there came to him the vision of J. D. Ellsworth battling his sturdy way from poor boy to president.

"But," he said to Mr. Fisher, "but how about Mr. Ellsworth? He came to this city without a cent, and by following three rules he won his way to the top. Told me so himself."

"Yes sirree!" said Mr. Fisher. "That's just what he did. I can remember when he first came. I was his boss for a while. Used to say to him, 'John, do this now,' or 'John, hurry up.' There wasn't any 'Ellsworth Products Co.' then; it all belonged to old Walter Kinnard, and when he died it went to his daughter, Ethel. I guess you've met her."

"Why, no—where?" said young Kennedy.

"She's Mrs. J. D. Ellsworth, the old man's wife, you know," was the answer.

The door of the office opened suddenly, and young Kennedy looked up at the sound of a woman's laugh. A plain young girl swept by them and passed into the inner sanctum.

"Say, isn't she a beauty?" whispered Mr. Fisher with awe in his voice.

"Why, no—I wouldn't pick her out of a crowd." The young man listlessly surveyed the book on business efficiency.

"Don't you know who she is?" said Mr. Fisher.

"Why, some stenographer, I suppose," replied Kennedy.

"She's Ellsworth's youngest daughter, Grace," said Mr. Fisher in the same tone of voice with which he would have mentioned the deity or John D. Rockefeller.

"What? Ellsworth's got another daughter?" cried the young man, clutching Fisher's arm.

"Sure."

"Married?"

"No—just nineteen."

"Oh," said young Kennedy.

IV

So he married her.

V

Thirty-five years later a trembling young man stood in the impressive office of Richard Kennedy, president of the Kennedy (formerly the Ellsworth) Products Co.

"Yes sir," he said eagerly to Mr. Kennedy. "I want to show you that a college man can start at the bottom and work up."

President Kennedy took off his gold-rimmed eyeglasses.

"Young man," he said, lighting a cigar, "when I first came to this city I didn't have a penny. Not a cent."

He paused and closed his eyes to let the full significance of this fact sink in upon the young man.

"But I made three rules which I always followed. They are the secret of success."

"Yes sir," said the youth eagerly.

"The first rule is, 'Don't watch the clock'; the second, 'Don't be afraid of getting your hands dirty'; and the third, 'Always work just a little harder than the other man.'"

T. S. STRIBLING

Bullets

AT THE DOOR of Munro's General Merchandise store in La Belle, Florida, Sawyer, the deputy sheriff, stopped an old Negro woman and the white man who followed her.

"You can't come in," he explained patiently. "They're holding an inquest in here."

The old crone quavered out that she knew it, that she was bringing in Slewfoot's lawyer.

The deputy looked at the well-dressed white man disapprovingly.

"I hope you're not stoopin' to defend a nigger cow hand that shot his own boss?"

"No, I'm neither defending nor prosecuting," assured the stranger.

"You have to do one or t'other if you're a lawyer."

"I'm not a lawyer; I'm a psychologist. I told this old woman if her son were guilty, my services would simply assure his conviction, that I would be a much greater danger for him than a jury itself."

The officer frowned and looked at the stranger as if he had not heard him aright.

"A psychologist," he repeated vaguely. "I don't exactly see how a psychologist would come in on a murder investigation."

"I'm afraid," snapped the stranger in Yankee impatience, "that I can't explain to you the connection between murder and psychology in two words."

"Well, that's all right," drawled the Florida man leisurely. "Take four words if you need 'em—take as many as you want. You ain't goin' to git in noway, so you've got all the time there is to tell me what you would do if you could get in."

The man gave the faint grin of a rustic who feels that he has put a city man in his place.

The psychologist turned away. The old woman began pleading:

"Oh, Mas' Poggioli, please don' fly off de han'l' an' leave Slewfoot by hese'f. Please tell Mistuh Sawyah whut you gwi' do inside fuh my po' boy Slewfoot."

The well-groomed gentleman controlled his temper, studied the guard for a moment as if reducing his thoughts to words sufficiently simple for the fellow to understand.

"Let me see. Murder—murder is a physical action impelled by some motive or motives, is it not?"

The deputy sheriff of Hendry County blinked his eyes.

"I mean," said the psychologist impatiently, "if one man kills another he has a reason for doing it, hasn't he?"

"Oh yes, yes," ejaculated the guard, suddenly seeing that this was what the first sentence meant.

"Very well; when you put a thought into action you leave traces of your motive in every object you have touched; do you know what I'm talking about?"

The deputy scratched his head.

"Tchk! Tchk! Listen: When you do anything, your motive impresses itself on everything you touch. You go through an action such as this murder, say. Very well; every trace you leave points to your mood, your motive, and your identity as plainly as a trail of torn paper. There is no way to avoid it."

The deputy became somewhat interested in what, up to this point, he had considered a meaningless jargon.

"Couldn't a man watch out an' hide his trail?" he inquired.

Mr. Henry Poggioli dropped his hands hopelessly.

"Don't you see what an absurdity your proposition involves? When you say 'watch out,' you mean 'take thought.' That introduces a second motive. This second motive produces results in its turn which are just as easily read as the first. In other words, no matter how many times a man goes over his own trail, putting out his own tracks, he must finally leave his last footprints quite open to view. Now, surely, you understand that."

Mr. Sawyer was astonished to catch a ray of light in the limbus of the psychologist's reasoning.

"Well, now, I'll be darned," he ejaculated. "That does sound reasonable. A man couldn't put out his own tracks, could he, because he'd make some more when he went back to put 'em out." He pulled at his chin. "Yes sir, that's plumb reasonable."

He paused, thinking, then started off with a new breath:

"Howsomever, this murder ain't anything so complicated as all that. Slewfoot shot old man Jake Sanderson twicet because the old man wouldn't advance him any money on his wages. That is, either Slewfoot or Finn Labby, a white man, shot him. They was both workin' for the old man an' both of 'em was in the store here when he was killed. Two shots were far'd, an' the jury has jest about decided the nigger far'd both of 'em."

"You knew both of these cowherders?"

"Shore—worked with 'em before I got app'inted deputy sher'ff."

"Was the Negro the sort of fellow who wanted to give orders, or was it his habit to wait and do what he was told?"

"He waited an' done what he was told—he was a nigger."

"Mm-m! Then if that was his mental habit, don't you think it reasonable to assume that he followed the lead of the white man in this as in everything else? Isn't it probable?"

The deputy frowned in a fashion that showed he was thinking.

"Now, by George, that's a p'int," he decided slowly, "an' a very plain one, too. I believe the jury ort to hear that."

"It's slight," disclaimed the originator.

"Big or little, I say it's so. Slewfoot was a triflin' nigger, an' if, for oncet in his life, that's a p'int in his favor, I say the jury ort to know it. Jest you keep this crowd back, mister, for half a minute, an' I'll step in an' tell 'em."

He called to the villagers in front of the door:

"Hey, you folks, this man's my deputy while I'm inside. Don't nobody come past him!"

With that he went inside to the jury at the back end of the store. The psychologist could see him talking and gesticulating, and presently he came back with a smile of satisfaction on his brown face.

"Well, they had to swaller it." He nodded. "They were fixin' to return their verdict that old Jake was shot by Slewfoot, but now they've changed it to either Slewfoot or Finn Labby."

"I believe you said Mr. Sanderson was shot twice."

"No, jest oncet."

"You will excuse me, but your original statement was twice," insisted Poggioli.

"No; I said they shot at him twicet—an' they did—but the first shot missed him. They jest hit old man Jake one time."

"And where did the other bullet strike?"

"In the wall."

"Were both bullets fired out of the same gun?"

"I don't know—how could you tell?"

"Cut them out and compare them; if they're the same caliber, with the same rifle marks on them, then one man shot both bullets and you can excuse the other man."

"Shore, shore, that's a fact, an' it runs right alongside ol' man Munro's argyment, too."

"Who's Munro?"

"The man who owns this store."

"What's his argument?"

"Why-y—er—derned if I know. He's got a clippin' out of a paper tellin' how this thing ort to be done. He's tryin' to git the boys to dig out the balls, an' Dr. Livermore is cuttin' the ball out of the body, but the jury figgers since the bullet in the wall didn't hit nobody, it don't make no diff'runce. I see now it does, an' I believe I'll step back an' tell the boys what you say about it."

This was carried out, and Poggioli was again placed in the deputy's stead at the door. The old Negro woman edged up to him and said in a shaky voice:

"See dah, Mas' Poggioli, you 'bout to git my Slewfoot out o' dis trouble wid one word."

"If the bullet in the corpse is different from the bullet in the wall, your son will be in worse trouble than ever," cautioned the psychologist.

"Why?" asked the old woman, mystified.

"Because that will show both men shot at Mr. Sanderson."

At this the old crone puckered up her brows and began a low praying that the two bullets would be alike when they were cut out.

"Aunt Rose, there is no use praying for the bullets to be something when they are cut out, because whatever they are, they are that now; and while the Lord might conceivably change a future condition, I should think it would be beyond even His power to change what has already happened."

"Yes suh, yes suh, Mas' Poggioli!" She then went on mumbling, "Oh Lawd, let dem bullets be jes' alike an' save po' Slewfoot!"

Her prayer was interrupted by a white woman attempting to enter the door. When the psychologist explained that no one was allowed inside, she said she wanted to do some trading.

At this a heavy old man with a square-cut face came forward and called to the psychologist to let her in, that his trade had to go on, inquest or no inquest. The woman bought a package of soda and handed the old man a dollar bill. The storekeeper started to his cash drawer, but paused halfway, turned, and came to the door.

"Any of you fellows got change for a dollar?" he inquired.

There was a general thrusting of hands into pockets. One of the onlookers produced a handful of small change.

The psychologist watched this incident without much attention when the old man looked at him and asked:

"Air you the stranger who told Sawyer to have them bullets cut out?"

The scientist said that he was.

"Well, by gum, I'm glad there's one man o' sense in this crowd. I been ding-dinging at them boys all mornin' to cut out them bullets. Suppose you come on back here with me an' tell 'em yourself why it ort to be done."

"Certainly, that suits me; I've been wanting to go in, but——"

He was following the storekeeper to the rear of the building when the deputy called out:

"Hey, there, mister, you cain't come back here. I deputized you as guard."

"Aw, thunder an' nation!" exclaimed the storekeeper. "This man's got good ideas. Let him come back, Sawyer, an' it'll save you prancin' up an' down the store ever' two minutes."

"Oh, all right, let him come on," called the foreman of the jury.

When Poggioli reached the rear of the store, the spokesman of the jurors asked just what he meant about the bullets being alike, and what did it mean if they were alike.

This was interrupted by old man Munro, the storekeeper, saying:

"Why, he means jest exactly what I was tellin' you boys. I got a clippin' that explains it. They call it—lemme see—they call it ballistics, don't they, mister?"

"I believe so."

"Well, the clippin' is right over here in my desk. I cut it out of a Sunday paper six months ago. I'll show it to you."

He shuffled to a tall desk near the back door and returned to the psychologist with a yellowed clipping.

Poggioli glanced at it out of courtesy to the old man, but he was really attentive to the scene before him. The dead man lay on the floor quite close to the counter. Over him stooped the village doctor, probing for the bullet.

The foreman asked the storekeeper:

"You say they was quarrelin' amongst theirse'ves when you left them in here for a minute, Mr. Munro?"

"Yeh, Finn an' Slewfoot was both devilin' old man Jake for some money, an' he kep' puttin' 'em off, sayin' he didn't have any."

"An' fin'ly they shot him?" questioned a juror.

"That I don't know. I reckon they did. Jest then ol' man Ike Newton drove up with a truckload of oranges. I went out to count the crates, an' while I was outside countin', I heard two booms in the store. They was so muffled I wasn't shore they was shots, an' me not expectin' anything like that either; so I finished my tally. When I went back in the store there was ol' man Jake down on the floor, openin' an' shuttin' his mouth, an' his two cow hands were gone. I run for Doc Livermore here, but when we got back, ol' Jake was dead."

The physician nodded at this and resumed his work.

"So it's a question of which of the two hired men shot him?" queried the psychologist of the foreman.

"That's right, sir."

"Were you jurymen acquainted with these two cow hands?"

"Oh yes, we're all cattlemen. Finn an' Slewfoot have worked for every man on this jury at one time or another."

"Then of these two men which was the more irritable and high-tempered?"

"Why, Finn Labby. He was always flyin' off the handle."

"Taking this case on its face value, then, gentlemen, isn't it probable that the higher-tempered man of this pair shot Mr. Sanderson? Isn't it reasonable that the waspish Finn Labby shot him and the easygoing Negro did not?"

The foreman of the jury hesitated for several moments.

"That sounds pretty good, mister," he said at last, "but if you must know—we think Slewfoot done it."

"Why?"

"Because he was jest the kind of nigger you described—easygoin' an' biddable."

The psychologist stood silent for several moments. Finally he said:

"Gentlemen, either my sense of logic is bad or my viewpoint doesn't agree with yours. I produce a reason which seems to me to clear my client; you gentlemen use the very same reason to condemn him. If we have no common ground of understanding, I think I had better withdraw." And he turned to the door.

The old Negro woman fell into a visible trembling and began praying aloud for God to cause the white man to stay and talk for Slewfoot. The foreman turned to the old negress.

"Don't be so noisy, Auntie." He then glanced at another juror and said, "S'pose we tell him?"

The juror addressed blinked his eyes.

"Well, all right—but there ain't a bit o' tellin' what that man'll figger out from it."

The foreman turned to the deputy sheriff.

"Mr. Sawyer, tell him."

At this the deputy beckoned Poggioli to follow him. He led the way to the back door, and when the two were out of earshot Sawyer nodded sidewise at the jury and said in a low tone:

"Them fellers think Slewfoot was put up to shoot ol' man Jake."

"Put up to it!"

"Why, shore; you know, pickin' a quarrel about money was jest one way to start trouble."

"Oh yes, that's why Slewfoot would have to be—biddable?"

"Why, of course," agreed the deputy. "An' it's dollars to doughnuts that one of them jurymen theirse'ves paid Slewfoot to kill ol' man Jake. Shoo! We jest know one of us done it—but we don't know which one; an', really, we don't want to know which one."

"Do you mean to say that just any member of that jury had sufficient cause of animosity toward Mr. Sanderson to murder him?"

"That's exactly what I mean to say, an' it's what I am sayin'."

"What did Sanderson do to infuriate everybody?"

"Why, ever' man on that jury is a cattleman, an ol' man Jake was what we call a 'open-range man.' If any of us fellers fenced up our pastures, he'd cut our wires an' let his own cattle range on our lands. He's treated dang near ever' man in La Belle like that from Doc Livermore an' ol' man Munro clear up to the Yankees that come in with the boom an' thought they could run things down here like they done up North, but ol' man Jake showed 'em they couldn't do it. No fences, that was his motto, an' he stuck by it till somebody paid a nigger to kill him."

Henry Poggioli grunted as the oddness of the investigation dawned on him. He stood looking out the back door. It gave on an expanse of creeping palmettos. The bayonet-shaped leaves bristled as high as a man's chest. Then he observed some tracks in the sand under the door. The prints were of hobnailed shoes and larger shoes with broken soles. The toes of these tracks were pressed deep in the ground while the heels scarcely touched the sand.

Poggioli called the deputy's attention to them.

"Have any of the jurymen come out the back door since the inquest began?" he inquired.

"Why, no-o, I don't reckon they have," said Sawyer. "One of 'em had to go across the street to the garage."

"M-m! Has the crowd out in front there been milling around this end of the store?"

"No; these scrub palmettos ain't a comfortable place to mill in. What are you askin' about that for?"

"I was just wondering if those tracks there were made by Slewfoot and Labby."

"Oh, shore, they're bound to be. That busted shoe is a nigger track, an' you know no nigger ain't been around here since ol' man Jake was killed. Yes, I noticed 'em there when I closed the door on the jury, an' I thought about layin' boards over 'em to preserve 'em for the criminal trial, then I thought ag'in, 'Now, they's no use in that. If you jest almost see one man shoot another'n with your own eyes, you don't have to go aroun' identifyin' his tracks.'"

Poggioli nodded slowly and grunted again.

The footprints visualized for the psychologist the two cow hands tiptoeing silently away from the store into the palmettos. But there was something about the picture in contradiction to the deputy's theory of the crime. The scientist was thinking about this as he turned and went back to the jury.

When he stood before the group again he saw one of the men with a chisel, about to cut the bullet out of the wall.

Suddenly the position of the corpse impressed itself on Poggioli. It lay near the counter, directly across from the bullet hole. A possible defense struck him, and he called out to the chiseler:

"Give me half a second before you dig out that bullet."

He drew a match from his pocket and thrust it into the hole.

"Gentlemen," he said to the group, "this matchstick is pointing in the direction from which the bullet came; straight across the dead man. But Mr. Sanderson is lying almost against the counter. The murderer, therefore, stood just behind the counter to fire that shot; do you agree to this?"

The jury assented, after a moment, by grunting and nodding.

"Very well; now, you men know Negroes. You have hired them, worked with them, been with them all your lives. Now I ask you as a group, did any man here ever see a Negro behind any counter in any store in La Belle?"

"I—I never did," drawled the foreman, looking around among the others.

"None of you ever did. Negroes don't walk behind white men's counters. They have been accused of stealing too many times when they were innocent for them to take a chance of being seen behind a white man's counter. Besides, there was no reason for Slewfoot to go behind the counter to shoot Mr. Sanderson. There was every reason for him not to go. Behind the counter he would have attracted the old man's attention. And when it came to actual shooting, he could have shot just as easily from in front of the counter. No, Slewfoot would never have walked behind the counter.

"With Finn Labby the conditions are exactly reversed. He was white. He had the white man's privilege to walk around for a bite of cheese. There's the cheese hoop. Once behind him, Finn could have shot his employer in the back of the head—where he *was* shot. This murder could have been a murder for anger, because Finn was high-tempered. This view of the crime, gentlemen, removes suspicion from any other man in Hendry County, and I recommend it to your discretion. Return your verdict that Jake Sanderson was shot and killed by Finn Labby. It will be a widely acceptable solution to this crime. I thank you for your attention."

This speech created quite a stir among the jury. They glanced at one another with relief in their faces. The old Negro woman began clapping her hands and praising the Lord and had to be hushed by the deputy. Then the officer came around to the psychologist.

"There's a lot to what you brought out, Mr. Poggioli," he said admiringly. "Of course a nigger wouldn't walk behind old man Munro's counter, an' of course Finn Labby would.

"Besides that, you send all these boys home with a clear conscience for each other. That was quite a stroke of yours."

"Thanks," said Poggioli.

The jurymen were standing up now, turning around and around after the manner of men who wish to retire for consultation but who have no retiring place selected.

"Suppose me an' Mr. Poggioli an' Mr. Munro go out front an' leave you men in this end of the store to ballot on this thing," suggested the deputy.

The foreman agreed.

"An' you go along with 'em, Aunt Rose," he directed, "while we free your boy from under this murder charge."

"Gemmen, I thanks you all. Oh Lawd, I thanks you!"

"Yes, yes, that's all right—just go along with Mr. Sawyer."

Sawyer, the deputy, was beside the psychologist and was still in a congratulatory mood.

"By George, I would never have believed you could get a Florida jury to free a nigger of a murder charge jest by stickin' a match in a bullet hole."

The scientist pulled his chin.

"I wish it were as clear to me as I made it to the jury."

"What do you mean?" asked the deputy.

"Those tracks at the back door, where the two cow hands came out——"

"Well, what about their tracks?"

"Why, both those boys went off on their tiptoes."

The deputy pondered a moment.

"Ain't that nachel, for 'em to go sneakin' away from their murder?"

"A man wouldn't try to tiptoe and keep quiet immediately after he had fired a pistol twice," said the psychologist.

"Well, now, that's a fact, too," admitted Sawyer, puzzled.

These observations were interrupted by a stir outside the door. Voices shouted out:

"Hey, Jeff, got one of 'em, did ye?"

"Where'd you ketch him, Jeff?"

"Slewfoot, what ye let the sheriff git ye for?"

A Negro's voice blubbered out. The crowd outside the door parted and a wool-shirted man entered, leading a handcuffed Negro.

When Sawyer, the deputy, recognized the Negro he shouted back to the jury to hold their decision as more evidence had been brought in. Old Aunt Rose looked at her son and wailed out:

"Lawd, Slewfoot, go an' git caught jess when Mas' Poggioli 'bout to sot you free!"

Slewfoot blinked at his old mother and said nothing. The jurymen who were standing now went back to their seats. The sheriff brought his prisoner before them, and the foreman motioned the black man to sit on a nail keg.

"Sheriff," asked the foreman, "did Slewfoot have a gun on him when you caught him?'"

"Oh yes," the officer nodded, "here it is." And he drew from his pocket an ancient single-action Colt revolver.

The spokesman took the weapon, turned it in his hand.

"Smith," he said, "better finish up your work chiselin' out that bullet. You've got yours, have you, Dr. Livermore?"

The surgeon indicated a pellet of lead lying on a piece of wrapping paper on the counter.

"Now, Slewfoot," said the foreman, "we want you to tell us exactly how old man Sanderson was shot an' who did it. No use in your tryin' to lie about it. If you did it, say so; if you didn't do it, tell us who did."

The black man became very frightened. He wet his lips with his tongue and stammered:

"W-wuw-well, Mistuh Tim, Ah di'n' do hit. Ah sho di'n' do hit!"

"Then who did?"

"Ah—Ah don' know."

"Wasn't you in the store here when he was shot?"

"Yessuh, Ah guess Ah was."

"An' you say you don't know who shot him?"

"N-n-no, suh, Ah don' know who shot him. Ah—Ah di'n' see nobody shoot him."

"Hand me that bullet, Smith, soon as you get it out," directed the spokesman, "an' let me have that one on the counter now."

The chiseler presently brought his bit of lead and handed it in. The foreman compared the two bullets with the revolver.

"Well, gentlemen, there you are," he said to the jurors. "Two old style thirty-eight balls shot out of this thirty-eight Colt." He swung the cylinder of the revolver to one side and added, "Here are a couple of exploded shells in his gun. The damn fool didn't even have brains enough to reload."

"Well, that ends the investigation," said one of the jurors.

"I think so," agreed the foreman.

At the sudden and simple turn of the evidence the old Negro woman began weeping and praying the Lord to save Slewfoot.

The psychologist called out above the stir:

"Wait, gentlemen—wait just a moment before returning a final verdict."

One of the jurors was impatient.

"Thunder! What more do you want? Here's the bullets that done the work exactly fittin' the nigger's gun."

"Still, I'm here representing the prisoner, in a way. At least let me have the opportunity to look over the evidence."

"Are you still thinkin' about the shot from behind the counter?" asked the foreman.

"I am; I am also thinking about Slewfoot's tracks just outside the back door. He didn't leap out as a man running away from a murder. His heels did not hit at all. He tiptoed away from the door. He was evidently under some sort of restraint."

"Restraint!" ejaculated a voice, and gave an incredulous laugh.

"Exactly; restraint—some sort of restraint."

The psychologist took up the two cones of lead and began examining them.

"I think this is a plumb waste of time," complained a juryman.

To this Mr. Poggioli made no reply but continued examining the two missiles that had been recovered. Finally he came to a pause, frowning in concentration over the pieces of lead. His expression caught the attention of the whole group.

"Now what in the hell d'ye reckon he sees in them two bullets?" asked a juror querulously.

The psychologist glanced up and answered for himself:

"One of the most intriguing mysteries it has ever been my good fortune to encounter," he replied gravely.

The foreman arose from his chair.

"What is it, Mr. Poggioli?" he asked curiously.

"These bullets. The one that struck the wall and the one that hit Mr. Sanderson—which one do you gentlemen think was fired first?"

"Why, the one that hit the wall, of course—he missed him."

"On the contrary, it was fired last. The bullet from the body has reddish rust in its old-fashioned lead grooves, but the one out of the wall is fouled with the black residue of smoke powder."

The coroner's jury looked at him in silence. Finally one of them said: "Well, what do you make of that?"

"I make this of it: The man who killed Mr. Sanderson first shot him down and then, for some reason or other, stood over his dead body and fired a bullet into the wall."

"Why, he may have shot at him twicet and jest missed the second shot," suggested the foreman.

"Impossible; Sanderson was shot in the back of the head. Death was instantaneous. He dropped like a beef. This old pistol is a single-action gun. The murderer had to recock his weapon, then he pointed it again and deliberately fired a bullet into the wall with his victim lying at his feet."

"What in the thunder did he do that for?" demanded the foreman.

Poggioli drew a long breath.

"Gentlemen, there could have been but one reason. The murderer wanted the bullet to be cut out and identified. He was afraid the ball in Sanderson's body would not be found, so he fired another into the wall. He had thought out his whole plan of action before he fired a shot."

"What would Slewfoot want to have his own gun identified for?" demanded a juror.

"Slewfoot didn't do the shooting. Such a plot was far over his head. The murderer gave Slewfoot this revolver after he had killed old man Jake. He had plotted to give it to Slewfoot; that was why he was so anxious to have the gun in Slewfoot's possession identified. He thought it would save his own neck."

At this the foreman of the jury got hastily to his feet.

"Here! Here!" he cried. "This way of savin' a nigger, first by stickin' a match in a bullet hole, an' then by punchin' a pin in the grooves of two bullets—they ain't no sense to that!"

"No, they ain't!" cried two or three voices.

Poggioli was about to protest this logical outrage when the spokesman of the jury nodded at him.

"Wait a minute, boys," he called. "Let me an' Mr. Poggioli have a word about this."

The session again had fallen into disorder. The foreman led the way to the back door. Poggioli followed him, wondering what would come next. When they were outside the door on the sand, the excited man asked in an undertone:

"Looky here, mister, do you know which one of us shot old man Jake?"

"Why, certainly," said the scientist.

"Well, which one of us—— No, no—don't tell me! I don't want to be goin' aroun' knowin'—— Yes, damn it, do tell me! I'd jest like to know the man that could think quick enough to bang another bullet into the wall."

"He didn't think that quickly," returned the psychologist. "He had been studying out that plan for over six months—ever since he clipped that article on ballistics out of some Sunday paper."

The foreman stood staring blankly at his companion.

"I'll be derned," he whispered. "Old man Munro!"

"Certainly. He had been holding a grudge against Sanderson ever since old Jake ran him out of the cattle business twenty years ago. He read this article on ballistics and made up a plan to murder Sanderson and place the blame on a Negro.

"His chance came. He shot his enemy and then told the Negro he would shoot him if he ever told it. Then he paid the Negro his pistol and all the cash in his cash drawer to leave the country. That is why he couldn't change a dollar bill for that woman a while ago. It also explains why these tracks here show two men tiptoeing away from the store and not running. They stole away with old man Munro whispering instructions."

The foreman stood shaking his head.

"I jest be danged," he said slowly. "You said a fellow couldn't cover up his tracks without makin' a lot more——" He thrust his head inside the door and called out, "Oh, Sheriff, has that nigger Slewfoot got any money on him?"

The officer called back:

"Yes, he's got a pocketful of small change. I thought it was cartridges when I first searched him, but it turned out to be nickels an' dimes."

"Well, then," called the foreman, "we'll have to turn Slewfoot loose, because you know he wouldn't have shot old man Jake for some money when he already had a pocketful." He looked at Henry Poggioli and winked. "You see, I'm a pretty good reasoner myse'f, when I git started."

"What are you going to do about old man Munro?" inquired the psychologist.

"Why-y—er—nothin', I reckon. A jury of cattlemen like us ain't goin' to give old man Munro any trouble for killin' a skunk like old man Jake Sanderson. We'll return a verdict that he died at the hands of unknown parties for well-known reasons. You see, out here on the Floridy prairies the law has its limits, an' old man Jake was one of them."

He gave the wink of a rustic who feels he has said something clever before a city man.

ARTHUR STRINGER

The Juggler

BENJAMIN SPINDEL had a Good Fairy. He was never quite sure what this Good Fairy should have been called. Sometimes she seemed best described as A-Sense-Of-Humor. More often, however, he preferred to know her as Fame.

For Fame, to Spindel, was something which came to you overnight, like a cold in the head or a milk bottle at the door. You simply woke up and found it there. The mere thought of it, waiting like a gnome on your doorstep, was something to send a tingle of romance through the small hours of the chilliest night, if you only made it a point to remember.

Not that Spindel ever quite forgot. For there were two things about Spindel that always surprised his friends. One was his industry; the other was his optimism.

Unlike so many others whose blood had been fevered by the virus of stage life, this doggedly industrious disciple of Romance never let the day be sufficient unto itself. Idleness, in fact, was luxury he could not afford. He was at least a plodder. And he believed, as he used to put it, in taking the bull by the horns.

So his immediate object in life was not so much to discover the fairy on the threshold as to keep the wolf from the door itself. Yet he nursed the entirely romantic delusion that Fame was something on which one might stub one's toe in the dark. Success was a sort of accident, the same as finding a dime on the street curb; you went to bed a plodding juggler of a dozen or two wooden puppets, and you woke up the Greatest Dramatist of the Age.

For Spindel's ambition, even when he came, a raw youth, from the Middle West, was not merely to be an actor. He nursed, in fact, an abhorrence for grease paint and call boards and dressing rooms and hydrogenated coiffures. He made no secret of the fact that his work on the stage was only a means to an end. Like an illustrious Elizabethan prototype to whom he often referred, he merely played parts that in the end he might learn to write them. For Spindel, like Shakespeare, wanted to be a playwright.

Like this prototype already referred to, Spindel was not essentially a man of letters. He prided himself on being one of the people. This claim was advanced, perhaps, in extenuation of certain oddities of orthography, for to the end Spindel was always a little weak in his spelling. But he was both adaptive and courageous, and no one could accuse him of not keeping his ears cocked and his eyes open. He nosed through life like a beagle nosing through bracken; he basked over street quarrels like a parent over a cradle; he blinked at park lovers like a hawk at a young rabbit, always hoping to scare up a new "scene" or a new "situation." So, while the weekly pay envelope of the actor was keeping the pot boiling, his experiences behind the footlights were initiating him into the tricks of the theatrical trade. He was devouring knowledge as silently and as persistently as any army worm devours herbage.

Yet after three years of playing small parts, and playing them none too well, he concluded that the back of the curtain had little more to teach him. He wanted to get out and see life "in the raw," yet nowhere, ironically enough, would he ever see its rawness less veiled than under the mask of the mummer. Here again, however, a sort of blithe practicality on his part kept interposing. He continued to mark time as a play actor, bending his neck to the yoke for the sake of a small but ever assured weekly envelope.

It could be called nothing more than marking time, for all his ardor, all his energy, was now being poured into his own secret pursuits. He was now giving his time and thought to the writing of plays—magnificently planned dramas which, by some odd mischance, never saw the light of day, and laboriously conceived comedies which, unfortunately, no one ever heard of.

His vocational hours, in fact, became a sort of somnambulism; he went through them with all the impersonal detachment of the sleepwalker. He was, by this time, living only in his writing. As his parts grew smaller and smaller, his pay envelope, in turn, grew thinner and thinner. But despair was unknown to Spindel. He still believed in the Fairy outside the door. He still passed vaguely elated and optimistic among his old-time friends of the stage, wearing the veiled smile of an adventurer who has learned the secret of some lost treasure.

"There's a guy they'll never grind down," said Gunderman's stage manager as he watched Spindel one day pocket his rejected script and trudge smiling and undaunted down to Broadway.

"They won't grind him down—he'll just *wear* down," retorted the apathetic Gunderman, to whom the years had brought wisdom and a weak digestion. And so fixed was Gunderman's mind as to this fact that he appropriated without hesitation a page or two of Spindel's third-act dialogue. It was nothing more, he argued with himself, than taking a plank or two from a passing derelict.

As Spindel climbed the stairs to that Twenty-second Street back room which he dignified as his "studio," his bearing took on an added touch of insouciance. He even whistled and affected a bit of a swagger.

And he had his reasons for this. For Spindel had been heaven-born optimist enough to bring a wife to New York with him out of the *terra incognita* of the Middle West. And that wife was young, and perhaps not always appreciative of the humoristic turns of overambiguous human destinies. She saw the script under her husband's arm, and she went to the window and looked out.

"My dear, those managers are positively *funny!*" blithely avowed Spindel as he put his play in its pigeonhole with the air of a victor putting his sword in its scabbard. "And all I say is, I'm thankful I can keep my sense of humor and see what a queer lot they are!"

"I wish they'd taken the play," said his wife, with the unimaginative immediacy of her sex, as she went back to her work of turning a last winter's skirt.

"But I'm getting closer to 'em all the time," chirped the indomitable Spindel. "I'm getting wise to their curves. I'm getting so I can humor 'em!"

And Spindel set to work writing a new play. He had to skimp and economize a good deal, by this time, for he could now get nothing more than an occasional "super" part to keep the pot boiling. But he accepted the dingy back-room studio and the meager meals cooked on a one-hole gas stove as calmly as an exiled prince accepts the exigencies of a banishment recognized as only a matter of time. He became oblivious of them. He went back to his play like an opium smoker back to his drug. He revised and rearranged and revamped. He closed his eyes, valiantly, and cut away whole act ends, at one grim stroke, like a surgeon operating on his own flesh and blood.

So he watched over his newborn play, and nursed it, and re-dressed it in epigram, and decorated it with a newer ribbon or two of fancy. Then he carried it off to the agencies and the managers' offices, with the blind pride of a mother carrying her first-born to a baby show.

That none of them could see any beauty in it struck him as ridiculous, as laughable. It almost took his breath away. But once more he came to realize, as he had so often tried to explain, that managers were a queer lot.

"If you can only keep your sense of humor at this game!" he persisted, with a wag of the head, as he read Gunderman's curt note of refusal.

So Spindel kept his sense of humor. He set to work again, as optimistic as ever. He once more became the prestidigitator; once more he laid out his worn and shoddy children of fancy, like a juggler laying out his "props."

Then he lost himself in his work. Once more he ruthlessly disemboweled and rearranged and rearticulated. Once more he shifted and sorted and pieced together. The result was something more wonderful, more Gothically embellished, than ever before. He once more buttressed it up and furbished and polished it, looking it over with contented shakes of the head.

"I'm learning the trick, my dear!" he jubilantly declared to his hollow-eyed wife as she stirred the veal stew on its hot plate next to the window. "I can see it coming closer, now, every day!"

And again Spindel began the rounds of the agencies and the managers' offices. And again the script came back to Spindel's dingy studio, and again it went out, and again it came back. Once more it moved the playwright to a mild and humorous wonder.

"Aren't they a funny lot? A rum lot?" he demanded. "Can't you see it, once you get a line on them and their ways?"

"No, it's not funny," said his wife, limp and listless in her chair by the window. "It's not funny any more."

He laughed as he put a hand on her thin shoulder.

"Just keep your sense of humor, my dear, and you'll see they *are* funny! Look how they contradict each other, even in their excuses! Look how one says, 'Cut down! Cut down!' and the other says, 'Build up! Build up!' "

It was Spindel's blind theory that if you kept at a thing you won out—you simply had to win out, in the end. And, such being his theory, he once more set to work. And finally, in vindication of this attitude, he actually went about showing a contract with a Western producing agent who had attached a "phony" curtain to one of Spindel's earlier first acts and converted it into a vaudeville sketch for a Chicago comedian.

This sketch seemed to bring new life to Spindel. He not only appeased an expostulatory landlord and a long-threatening gas company, but he also indulged in the extravagance of two Harz Mountain canaries, "to liven up the studio a bit," as he blithely explained to his wife, and he planned out intricate and extended shopping expeditions.

But the vaudeville sketch, after a run of three weeks, came to an abrupt and untimely end. Just why this was, the dazed author could never quite understand. And it saddened him a little to think that it had lived and died without once having come under the eye of its creator. Yet these one-act things, he cheerily added, were never worth worrying over. In fact, there was something humorous about it all, he still maintained. He thanked his lucky stars he could still see the funny side of it.

He refused to give it much thought, however, for already he had a new play to work on. This new play, like the others, became a sort of *pot-au-feu*, into which went every fragment that could be shaved from the bones of his past efforts, every shred of an idea that could be caught up from the passing moment. He wrote on and on, still believing in the Fairy outside the door. He sent out his script, still nursing the delusion that he was going to find Fame hanging by one hand to his mailbox down in the dingy front hall. And as he shuffled down in his tattered slippers, ten times a day, he thanked Heaven that he could still see the humor of it all, and went up to chirrup and whistle somewhat pensively into the swinging canary cage and then turn once more back to his writing.

It was one rainy morning when even the canaries refused to sing that the Ultimate Idea came to him. Times, he had to confess, were getting a bit tight. Things were no longer as rosy as they ought to be. It was too late for shilly-shallying; conditions seemed to call for a *coup de main*. And here he was with seven fine plays all about him, seven plays of his own. None of them could be all bad; even those human sheep known as managers confessed that one had a good scene here and another had a good curtain there and a third had a good idea somewhere else. But none had quite floated him out to the sea of prosperity. Then, demanded Spindel of himself, why not lash the lot together? Why not tie them up in one raft, cut away what was not needed, and let that one final venture swing out to sink or swim?

This amalgamative idea became first an intoxication and then an obsession. The work-worn playwright threw himself into the task with a fury that disturbed even his wife, who absented herself more and more from that unkempt and paper-littered back room, where Spindel strode up and down in his tattered slippers, enacting the roles he was reorganizing. She even upbraided him for scandalizing their neighbors with his enigmatically passionate utterances, with his frenzied self-altercations, with his climacteric shouts of scorn and triumph. He even forgot his wife and her existence. He uttered no protest as she took her departure for the day. He merely looked at her in his vacant and unseeing way when she, somewhat defiantly, told him that she was off to look for work of her own. He only nodded diffident assent when she somewhat challengingly informed him that her cousin, Jim Ecklin, was taking her to the Hippodrome.

For Spindel, in truth, was engaged in one of the most extraordinary juggling feats of all his feverish-fingered juggler's career. Into that one and final play he was crushing and crowding everything he had ever written, much like a shipwrecked traveler packing into one portmanteau the cream of all his belongings. He was molding his whole life into one forlorn amalgam. He was making that last play a sort of Irish stew of all his dead issues. He scraped the bones of each desiccated skeleton for its last enriching tatter of meat. He journeyed back through each abandoned structure for some last sustaining beam of action. He crawled over each devastated scene for some chance sparkle of epigram embedded in its ruins.

Then he once more polished it and furbished it, and so pretentious and flashing did that new façade stand to him that for the first time in his life he indited a peremptory letter in which he put forth certain peremptory demands, and sent both letter and playscript off to Gunderman, knowing only too well that this time it was all or nothing.

In the meantime winter had advanced, and the cold had set its teeth in the flank of the attenuated Spindel abode. The rigors of mid-December reminded the playwright that both the body and its habitation were in keener need of fuel. So Spindel took advantage of the holiday season and earned a few dollars as an extra ticket taker in a Fourteenth Street moving-picture house. The pay was not lordly, but his gas bills and his arrears of rent he could for the time ignore. Those more exigent claims which rose from the pit of the human stomach, however, could not be ignored. He also remembered that he had his wife and his two canaries to feed. He hated moving pictures; they were the darkest enemy of the dramatic artist. But he could live it down, once he had got started, once he had made his hit. And as he trudged homeward, with his half pound of hamburger steak, he looked more and more anxiously into the mailbox. But it always seemed to be empty.

Spindel wondered if even a sense of humor could not lose its elasticity in time. So one morning he took the bull by the horns, as it were. He made his toilet, such as it was, with the minutest care, and invaded Broadway and the Gunderman stronghold.

Gunderman, he was told, had been called to Chicago. He had either taken the script with him or mislaid it. But no word had come to the office as to its fate. And for a week or two nothing was likely to be done.

Spindel, that night, spent a long time over his task of feeding the canaries. His own hunger he appeased in a much briefer period. It was after nine o'clock when his wife came home, silent and self-contained. She told him, casually, that she had already eaten supper. But later in the evening, as she stood peering in the canary cage, she broke into tears, for no appreciable reason. It was the next day that Spindel began pawning things, surreptitiously taken from their dingy back room.

For some days he wandered about the city looking for work, as destitute of direction as a lost child looking for home. Late in the afternoon of the fourth day he trudged back to his "studio," a little dizzy in the head and a little weak in the knees. But he wanted to make sure the canaries were fed.

He found it hard to climb the steps. In the mailbox at the side of the shabby old hall he found two letters waiting for him. He climbed the stairs, step by step, and as he let himself into his room he saw a square of paper tacked on his door. He swung back the door and peered up at it.

He realized, as he studied it, that it was a "dispossess" notice. He slowly pulled it from the soiled panel, stepped into the room, and closed the door after him.

"Allie!" he called, for the light was not strong.

He looked about and saw with a deep breath of relief that his wife was not there. Then he slowly crossed the room and sat down by the window, under the canary cage. Then he put the letters on the ledge in front of him. He was very leisurely about it, yet he could feel his heart in his throat, pounding like an automatic riveter.

The first letter was in his wife's handwriting. He opened the envelope and slowly unfolded the single sheet it held. On it he read:

I've tried hard to stay with you, Benny. But a woman's got to have clothes and things. And I couldn't stand it any longer. I've thought it all over. I'm going to New Orleans with Jim this afternoon. Jim says he'll see I never want for anything. It's the only thing left for me. I hate to go this way, but I can't help it, and I can't stand it any longer.

ALLIE

Spindel read the penciled sheet for the second time. Then he slowly folded it up and put it on the window ledge in front of him. He sat there for several minutes, without moving. Then he turned the second letter over in his hand.

He found it hard to open, for his eyes were not clear. A yellow mist, like street fog, seemed to float between him and the paper. The first thing that struck him was the blue tint of the oblong enclosure. He looked at it, vacantly, for several seconds. Then he held it up to the light and saw it was a check. Then he slowly unfolded the letter and read it.

It neither startled nor elated him. He dimly remembered that it was from Gunderman's office. He was vaguely conscious that Gunderman himself was writing and saying that the four-act play, entitled *Fool's Gold*, by Benjamin Spindel, would be put in rehearsal the following Monday, for a New York production. It also, as far as he could make out, requested a receipt for the one thousand dollars in advance royalties, duly enclosed—but Spindel was no longer interested.

He slowly unfolded the first letter and slowly read it through again.

"I'm going to New Orleans with Jim this afternoon."

He read it aloud, as though the words were written in a foreign tongue, as though it were a text he could not comprehend. Then he looked at the blue oblong of the check. He looked at it for several minutes, without moving. Then he laughed, quietly, softly, without mirth and without emotion. He had lost his belief in the Fairy just outside the door.

He sat in deep thought for several moments. Then he pinned the two letters together and, taking a clean sheet of paper, wrote on it nine short words. Then he laughed again, quietly, but still without emotion. The words he wrote were: This is too much for my sense of humor!

He looked meditatively about and finally put the three slips of paper on the table in the center of the room. Then he carefully lifted the canary cage from its hook and placed it on the floor of the dusky hallway, outside his door. He locked the door, as he stepped inside, and again looked meditatively about the shadowy room. Then he took a number of newspapers and slowly tore them into strips. With these he carefully battened the cracks about the door and the joints of the loose window sashes. He did not even overlook the keyhole. Then, as he crossed the room, he reread aloud the words he had written: "This is too much for my sense of humor!"

He calmly drew the blinds. Then he groped his way back to where the green tubing, connecting the hot plate with the gas pipe, ran along the wall. He padded about until he found the stopcock. Then he turned it on, full.

He recrossed the room to the sagging spring couch, remembering to cover himself with the worn comforter as he lay down on the soiled bedding. He closed his eyes. He only knew that he was tired, very tired. Then he fell asleep.

Spindel, who so often dreamed that Fame was going to be left at his door, like a bottle of milk, woke up to find his wife there at midnight, crying like a frightened child.

"Oh, I couldn't do it, Benny; I couldn't do it!" she wailed, bathed in her tears of contrition, as he stumbled to the door and swung it open. She clutched at his dazed and silent figure. She clung to him in a self-immuring ecstasy of despair.

"Oh, Benny, what'll we do? What'll we do? What'll we do?" she wailed.

"Do? How?" asked the still-dazed Spindel.

"They've ordered us out!" she wept. "And we've no money. *And they came and turned the gas off on us this morning!*"

And Spindel, groping for her shaking body in the darkness, locked his arms about her and laughed.

JESSE STUART
Another April

"Now, PAP, you won't get cold," Mom said as he put a heavy wool cap over his head.

"Huh, what did ye say?" Grandpa asked, holding his big hand cupped over his ear to catch the sound.

"Wait until I get your gloves," Mom said, hollering real loud in Grandpa's ear. Mom had forgotten about his gloves until he raised his big bare hand above his ear to catch the sound of Mom's voice.

"Don't get 'em," Grandpa said. "I won't ketch cold."

Mom didn't pay any attention to what Grandpa said. She went on to get the gloves anyway. Grandpa turned toward me. He saw that I was looking at him.

"Yer ma's a-puttin' enough clothes on me to kill a man," Grandpa said, then he laughed a coarse laugh like March wind among the pine tops at his own words. I started laughing but not at Grandpa's words. He thought I was laughing at them and we both laughed together. It pleased Grandpa to think that I had laughed with him over something funny that he had said. But I was laughing at the way he was dressed. He looked like a picture of Santa Claus. But Grandpa's cheeks were not cherry-red like Santa Claus's cheeks. They were covered with white thin beard—and above his eyes were long white eyebrows almost as white as percoon petals and very much longer.

Grandpa was wearing a heavy wool suit that hung loosely about his big body but fitted him tightly round the waist where he was as big and as round as a flour barrel. His pant legs were as big round his pipestem legs as emptied meal sacks. And his big shoes, with his heavy good socks dropping down over their tops, looked like sled runners. Grandpa wore a heavy wool shirt and over his wool shirt he wore a heavy wool sweater and then his coat over the top of all this. Over his coat he wore a heavy overcoat and about his neck he wore a wool scarf.

The way Mom had dressed Grandpa you'd think there was a heavy snow on the ground but there wasn't. April was here instead and the sun was shining on the green hills where the wild plums and the wild crab apples were in bloom enough to make you think there were big snowdrifts sprinkled over the green hills. When I looked at Grandpa and then looked out the window at the sunshine and the green grass I laughed more. Grandpa laughed with me.

"I'm a-goin' to see my old friend," Grandpa said just as Mom came down the stairs with his gloves.

"Who is he, Grandpa?" I asked, but Grandpa just looked at my mouth working. He didn't know what I was saying. And he hated to ask me the second time.

Mom put the big wool gloves on Grandpa's hands. He stood there just like I had to do years ago, and let Mom put his gloves on. If Mom didn't get his fingers back in the glove fingers exactly right Grandpa quarreled at Mom. And when Mom fixed his fingers exactly right in his gloves the way he wanted them Grandpa was pleased.

"I'll be a-goin' to see 'im," Grandpa said to Mom. "I know he'll still be there."

Mom opened our front door for Grandpa and he stepped out slowly, supporting himself with his big cane in one hand. With the other hand he held to the door facing. Mom let him out of the house just like she used to let me out in the spring. And when Grandpa left the house I wanted to go with him, but Mom wouldn't let me go. I wondered if he would get away from the house—get out of Mom's sight—and pull off his shoes and go barefooted and wade the creeks like I used to do when Mom let me out. Since Mom wouldn't let me go with Grandpa, I watched him as he walked slowly down the path in front of our house. Mom stood there watching Grandpa too. I think she was afraid that he would fall. But Mom was fooled; Grandpa toddled along the path better than my baby brother could.

"He used to be a powerful man," Mom said more to herself than she did to me. "He was a timber cutter. No man could cut more timber than my father; no man in the timber woods could sink an ax deeper into a log than my father. And no man could lift the end of a bigger saw log than Pop could."

"Who is Grandpa goin' to see, Mom?" I asked.

"He's not goin' to see anybody," Mom said.

"I heard 'im say that he was goin' to see an old friend," I told her.

"Oh, he was just a-talkin'," Mom said.

I watched Grandpa stop under the pine tree in our front yard. He set his cane against the pine-tree trunk, pulled off his gloves, and put them in his pocket. Then Grandpa stooped over slowly, as slowly as the wind bends down a sapling, and picked up a pine cone in his big soft fingers. Grandpa stood fondling the pine cone in his hand. Then, one by one, he pulled the little chips from the pine cone—tearing it to pieces like he was hunting for something in it—and after he had torn it to pieces he threw the pine-cone stem on the ground. Then he pulled pine needles from a low-hanging pine bough and he felt of each pine needle between his fingers. He played with them a long time before he started down the path.

"What's Grandpa doin'?" I asked Mom.

But Mom didn't answer me.

"How long has Grandpa been with us?" I asked Mom.

"Before you's born," she said. "Pap has been with us eleven years. He was eighty when he quit cuttin' timber and farmin'; now he's ninety-one."

I had heard her say that when she was a girl he'd walk out on the snow and ice barefooted and carry wood in the house to put on the fire. He had shoes but he wouldn't bother to put them on. And I heard her say that he would cut timber on the coldest days without socks on his feet but with his feet stuck down in cold brogan shoes and he worked stripped above the waist so his arms would have freedom when he swung his double-bitted ax. I had heard her tell how he'd sweat and how the sweat in his beard would be icicles by the time he got home from work on the cold winter days. Now Mom wouldn't let him get out of the house for she wanted him to live a long time.

As I watched Grandpa go down the path toward the hogpen he stopped to examine every little thing along his path. Once he waved his cane at a butterfly as it zigzagged over his head, its polka-dot wings fanning the blue April air. Grandpa would stand when a puff of wind came along, and hold his face against the wind and let the wind play with his white whiskers. I thought maybe his face was hot under his beard and he was letting the wind cool his face. When he reached the hogpen he called the hogs down to the fence. They came running and grunting to Grandpa just like they were talking to him. I knew that Grandpa couldn't hear them trying to talk to him but he could see their mouths working and he knew they were trying to say something. He leaned his cane against the hogpen, reached over the fence, and patted the hogs' heads. Grandpa didn't miss patting one of our seven hogs.

As he toddled up the little path alongside the hogpen he stopped under a blooming dogwood. He pulled a white blossom from a bough that swayed over the path above his head, and he leaned his big bundled body against the dogwood while he tore each petal from the blossom and examined it carefully. There wasn't anything his dim blue eyes missed. He stopped under a redbud tree before he reached the garden to break a tiny spray of redbud blossoms. He took each blossom from the spray and examined it carefully.

"Gee, it's funny to watch Grandpa," I said to Mom, then I laughed.

"Poor Pap," Mom said, "he's seen a lot of Aprils come and go. He's seen more Aprils than he will ever see again."

I don't think Grandpa missed a thing on the little circle he took before he reached the house. He played with a bumblebee that was bending a windflower blossom that grew near our corncrib beside a big bluff. But Grandpa didn't try to catch the bumblebee in his big bare hand. I wondered if he would and if the bumblebee would sting him, and if he would holler. Grandpa even pulled a butterfly cocoon from a blackberry brier that grew beside his path. I saw him try to tear it into shreds but he couldn't. There wasn't any butterfly in it, for I'd seen it before. I wondered if the butterfly with the polka-dot wings, that Grandpa waved his cane at when he first left the house, had come from this cocoon. I laughed when Grandpa couldn't tear the cocoon apart.

"I'll bet I can tear that cocoon apart for Grandpa if you'd let me go help him," I said to Mom.

"You leave your grandpa alone," Mom said. "Let 'im enjoy April."

Then I knew that this was the first time Mom had let Grandpa out of the house all winter. I knew that Grandpa loved the sunshine and the fresh April air that blew from the redbud and dogwood blossoms. He loved the bumblebees, the hogs, the pine cones, and pine needles. Grandpa didn't miss a thing along his walk. And every day from now on until just before frost Grandpa would take this little walk. He'd stop along and look at everything as he had done summers before. But each year he didn't take as long a walk as he had taken the year before. Now this spring he didn't go down to the lower end of the hogpen as he had done last year. And when I could first remember Grandpa going on his walks he used to go out of sight. He'd go all over the farm. And he'd come to the house and take me on his knee and tell me about all that he had seen. Now Grandpa wasn't getting out of sight. I could see him from the window along all of his walk.

Grandpa didn't come back into the house at the front door. He tottled around back of the house toward the smokehouse and I ran through the living room to the dining room so I could look out at the window and watch him.

"Where's Grandpa goin'?" I asked Mom.

"Now never mind," Mom said. "Leave your grandpa alone. Don't go out there and disturb him."

"I won't bother 'im, Mom," I said. "I just want to watch 'im."

"All right," Mom said.

But Mom wanted to be sure that I didn't bother him so she followed me into the dining room. Maybe she wanted to see what Grandpa was going to do. She stood by the window and we watched Grandpa as he walked down beside our smokehouse where a tall sassafras tree's thin leaves fluttered in the blue April wind. Above the smokehouse and the tall sassafras was a blue April sky—so high you couldn't see the sky roof. It was just blue space and little white clouds floated upon this blue.

When Grandpa reached the smokehouse he leaned his cane against the sassafras tree. He let himself down slowly to his knees as he looked carefully at the ground. Grandpa was looking at something and I wondered what it was. I just didn't think or I would have known.

"There you are, my good old friend," Grandpa said.

"Who is his friend, Mom?" I asked.

Mom didn't say anything. Then I saw.

"He's playin' with that old terrapin, Mom," I said.

"I know he is," Mom said.

"The terrapin doesn't mind if Grandpa strokes his head with his hand," I said.

"I know it," Mom said.

"But the old terrapin won't let me do it," I said. "Why does he let Grandpa?"

"The terrapin knows your grandpa."

"He ought to know me," I said, "but when I try to stroke his head with my hand, he closes up in his shell."

Mom didn't say anything. She stood by the window watching Grandpa and listening to Grandpa talk to the terrapin.

"My old friend, how do you like the sunshine?" Grandpa asked the terrapin.

The terrapin turned his fleshless face to one side like a hen does when she looks at you in the sunlight. He was trying to talk to Grandpa; maybe the terrapin could understand what Grandpa was saying.

"Old fellow, it's been a hard winter," Grandpa said. "How have you fared under the smokehouse floor?"

"Does the terrapin know what Grandpa is sayin'?" I asked Mom.

"I don't know," she said.

"I'm awfully glad to see you, old fellow," Grandpa said.

He didn't offer to bite Grandpa's big soft hand as he stroked his head.

"Looks like the terrapin would bite Grandpa," I said.

"That terrapin has spent the winters under that smokehouse for fifteen years," Mom said. "Pap has been acquainted with him for eleven years. He's been talkin' to that terrapin every spring."

"How does Grandpa know the terrapin is old?" I asked Mom.

"It's got 1847 cut on its shell," Mom said. "We know he's ninety-five years old. He's older than that. We don't know how old he was when that date was cut on his back."

"Who cut 1847 on his back, Mom?"

"I don't know, child," she said, "but I'd say whoever cut that date on his back has long been under the ground."

Then I wondered how a terrapin could get that old and what kind of a looking person he was who cut the date on the terrapin's back. I wondered where it happened—if it happened near where our house stood. I wondered who lived here on this land then, what kind of a house they lived in, and if they had a sassafras with tiny thin April leaves on its top growing in their yard, and if the person that cut the date on the terrapin's back was buried at Plum Grove, if he had farmed these hills where we lived today and cut timber like Grandpa had—and if he had seen the Aprils pass like Grandpa had seen them and if he enjoyed them like Grandpa was enjoying this April. I wondered if he had looked at the dogwood blossoms, the redbud blossoms, and talked to this same terrapin.

"Are you well, old fellow?" Grandpa asked the terrapin.

The terrapin just looked at Grandpa.

"I'm well as common for a man of my age," Grandpa said.

"Did the terrapin ask Grandpa if he was well?" I asked Mom.

"I don't know," Mom said. "I can't talk to a terrapin."

"But Grandpa can."

"Yes."

"Wait until tomatoes get ripe and we'll go to the garden together," Grandpa said.

"Does a terrapin eat tomatoes?" I asked Mom.

"Yes, that terrapin has been eatin' tomatoes from our garden for fifteen years," Mom said. "When Mick was tossin' the terrapins out of the tomato patch, he picked up this one and found the date cut on his back. He put him back in the patch and told him to help himself. He lives from our garden every year. We don't bother him and don't allow anybody else to bother him. He spends his winters under our smokehouse floor buried in the dry ground."

"Gee, Grandpa looks like the terrapin," I said.

Mom didn't say anything; tears came to her eyes. She wiped them from her eyes with the corner of her apron.

"I'll be back to see you," Grandpa said. "I'm a-gettin' a little chilly; I'll be gettin' back to the house."

The terrapin twisted his wrinkled neck without moving his big body, poking his head deeper into the April wind as Grandpa pulled his bundled body up by holding to the sassafras tree trunk.

"Good-by, old friend!"

The terrapin poked his head deeper into the wind, holding one eye on Grandpa, for I could see his eye shining in the sinking sunlight.

Grandpa got his cane that was leaned against the sassafras tree trunk and hobbled slowly toward the house. The terrapin looked at him with first one eye and then the other.

JAMES THURBER

The Black Magic of Barney Haller

IT WAS one of those hot days on which the earth is uninhabitable; even as early as ten o'clock in the morning, even on the hill where I live under the dark maples. The long porch was hot and the wicker chair I sat in complained hotly. My coffee was beginning to wear off and with it the momentary illusion it gives that things are Right and Life is Good. There were sultry mutterings of thunder. I had a quick feeling that if I looked up from my book I would see Barney Haller. I looked up, and there he was, coming along the road, lightning playing about his shoulders, thunder following him like a dog.

Barney is (or was) my hired man. He is strong and amiable, sweaty and dependable, slowly and heavily competent. But he is also eerie: he trafficks with the devil. His ears twitch when he talks, but it isn't so much that as the things he says. Once in late June, when all of a moment sabers began to flash brightly in the heavens and bowling balls rumbled, I took refuge in the barn. I always have a feeling that I am going to be struck by lightning and either riven like an old apple tree or left with a foot that aches in rainy weather and a habit of fainting. Those things happen. Barney came in, not to escape the storm to which he is, or pretends to be, indifferent, but to put the scythe away. Suddenly he said the first of those things that made me, when I was with him, faintly creepy. He pointed at the house. "Once I see dis boat come down de rock," he said. It is phenomena like that of which I stand in constant dread: boats coming down rocks, people being teleported, statues dripping blood, old regrets and dreams in the form of Luna moths fluttering against the windows at midnight.

Of course I finally figured out what Barney meant—or what I comforted myself with believing he meant; something about a bolt coming down the lightning rod on the house; a commonplace, an utterly natural thing. I should have dismissed it, but it had its effect on me. Here was a stolid man, smelling of hay and leather, who talked like somebody out of Charles Fort's books, or like a traveler back from Oz. And all the time the lightning was zigging and zagging around him.

On this hot morning when I saw Barney coming along with his faithful storm trudging behind him I went back frowningly to my copy of *Swann's Way*. I hoped that Barney, seeing me absorbed in a book, would pass by without saying anything. I read: ". . . I myself seemed actually to have become the subject of my book: a church, a quartet, the rivalry between Francis I and Charles V . . ." I could feel Barney standing looking at me, but I didn't look at him.

"Dis morning bime by," said Barney, "I go hunt grotches in de voods."

"That's fine," I said, and turned a page and pretended to be engrossed in what I was reading. Barney walked on; he had wanted to talk some more, but he walked on. After a paragraph or two his words began to come between me and the words in the book. "Bime by I go hunt grotches in de voods." If you are susceptible to such things it is not difficult to visualize grotches. They fluttered into my mind: ugly little creatures, about the size

of whippoorwills, only covered with blood and honey and the scrapings
of church bells. Grotches . . . Who and what, I wondered, really was this
thing in the form of a hired man that kept anointing me ominously, in
passing, with abracadabra?

Barney didn't go toward the woods at once; he weeded the corn, he
picked apple boughs up off the lawn, he knocked a yellow jacket's nest
down out of a plum tree. It was raining now, but he didn't seem to notice
it. He kept looking at me out of the corner of his eye, and I kept looking
at him out of the corner of my eye. "Vot dime is it, blease?" he called to
me finally. I put down my book and sauntered out to him. "When you go
for those grotches," I said firmly, "I'll go with you." I was sure he wouldn't
want me to go. I was right; he protested that he could get the grotches
himself. "I'll go with you," I said stubbornly. We stood looking at each
other. And then, abruptly, just to give him something to ponder over, I
quoted:

> *"I'm going out to clean the pasture spring;*
> *I'll only stop to rake the leaves away*
> *(And wait to watch the water clear, I may):*
> *I shan't be gone long. . . . You come too."*

It wasn't, I realized, very good abracadabra, but it served. Barney looked
at me in a puzzled way. "Yes," he said vaguely.

"It's five minutes of twelve," I said, remembering he had asked.

"Den we go," he said, and we trudged through the rain over to the
orchard fence and climbed that, and opened a gate and went out into the
meadow that slopes up to the woods. I had a prefiguring of Barney, at some
proper spot deep in the woods, prancing around like a goat, casting off his
false nature, shedding his hired man's garments, dropping his Teutonic
accent, repeating diabolical phrases, conjuring up grotches.

There was a great slash of lightning and a long bumping of thunder as
we reached the edge of the woods.

I turned and fled. Glancing over my shoulder, I saw Barney standing
and staring after me. . . .

It turned out (on the face of it) to be as simple as the boat that came
down the rock. Grotches were "crotches": crotched saplings which he cut
down to use as supports under the peach boughs, because in bearing time
they became so heavy with fruit that there was danger of the branches
snapping off. I saw Barney later, putting the crotches in place. We didn't

have much to say to each other. I can see now that he was beginning to suspect me too.

About six o'clock next evening I was alone in the house and sleeping upstairs. Barney rapped on the door of the front porch. I knew it was Barney because he called to me. I woke up slowly. It was dark for six o'clock. I heard rumblings and saw flickerings. Barney was standing at the front door with his storm at heel. I had the conviction that it wasn't storming anywhere except around my house. There couldn't, without the intervention of the devil or one of his agents, be so many lightning storms in one neighborhood.

I had been dreaming of Proust and the church at Combray and madeleines dipped in tea, and the rivalry between Francis I and Charles V. My head whirled and I didn't get up. Barney kept on rapping. He called out again. There was a flash, followed by a sharp splitting sound. I leaped up. This time, I thought, he is here to get me. I had a notion that he was standing at the door barefooted, with a wreath of grape leaves around his head, and a wild animal's skin slung over his shoulder. I didn't want to go down, but I did.

He was, as usual, solid, amiable, dressed like a hired man. I went out on the porch and looked at the improbable storm, now on in all its fury. "This is getting pretty bad," I said meaningly. Barney looked up at the rain placidly. "Well," I said irritably, "what's up?" Barney turned his little squinty blue eyes on me.

"We go to the garrick now and become warbs," he said.

The hell we do! I thought to myself quickly. I was uneasy—I was, you might even say, terrified—but I determined not to show it. If he began to chant incantations or to make obscene signs or if he attempted to sling me over his shoulder, I resolved to plunge right out into the storm, lightning and all, and run to the nearest house. I didn't know what they would think at the nearest house when I burst in upon them, or what I would tell them. But I didn't intend to accompany this amiable-looking fiend to any garrick and become a warb. I tried to persuade myself that there was some simple explanation, that warbs would turn out to be as innocuous as boats on rocks and grotches in the woods, but the conviction gripped me (in the growling of the thunder) that here at last was the moment when Barney Haller, or whoever he was, had chosen to get me. I walked toward the steps that lead to the lawn, and turned and faced him, grimly.

"Listen!" I barked suddenly. "Did you know that even when it isn't brillig I can produce slithy toves? Did you happen to know that the mome rath never lived that could outgrabe me? Yeah, and furthermore, I can become anything I want to; even if I were a warb, I wouldn't have to keep on being one if I didn't want to. I can become a playing card at will, too; once I was the jack of clubs, only I forgot to take my glasses off and some guy recognized me. I——"

Barney was backing slowly away, toward the petunia box at one end of the porch. His little blue eyes were wide. He saw that I had him. "I think I go now," he said. And he walked out into the rain. The rain followed him down the road.

I have a new hired man now. Barney never came back to work for me after that day. Of course I figured out finally what he meant about the garrick and the warbs: he had simply got horribly mixed up in trying to tell me that he was going to the garret and clear out the wasps, of which I have thousands. The new hired man is afraid of them. Barney could have scooped them up in his hands and thrown them out a window without getting stung. I am sure he trafficked with the devil. But I am sorry I let him go.

JIM TULLY
Swirling Sky

It was my first year on the road. I was about fifteen.

Near my own age, though on the road much longer, Bill Nolan fastened his coat collar and said, "It's easy to get out of this burg."

"What do you mean, easy?" I laughed.

"Just what I said. Ain't we come all the way from California—over a thousand miles—without a hitch?" he asked. Then, drawling, "It takes a lonesome man to sing a lonesome tune," he added. "These mail trains are faster'n freights."

"Faster'n colder," I said.

"Well, nobody asked you to be a hobo," he said.

"No one said they did—I was born a bum."

We stopped on a bridge under which the trains ran.

"Now let go when I yell." Bill poised himself. "It's the Federal Limited —an' she don't wait. If you hit the roof, lie flat—so's the bridge won't knock you off."

Tense, we waited. The giant engine's lights went over the steel rails. When the train was under the bridge we dropped and laid flat. The smoke from the engine enveloped the train.

"Gee, that smoke's warm," Bill said.

"I'll say—I hate to leave here," I added.

The train swerved around a bend. Bill rolled with it.

"But I guess we'd better—or fall off," he said. We clambered for the blind baggage of the speeding train. "Anyhow, we're past the railroad dicks." Bill sighed. We rattled across another track. The engine whistle screeched. "Hold on," Bill shouted.

"What'd you think I'd do?" I asked, as we crashed by telegraph posts. "She's colder'n hell with the lid off." I held the blind baggage tighter.

"You said it," Bill yelled. "We must be goin' a hundred miles an hour."

We roared through a town.

"Casey Jones, that brave engineer, ain't wastin' no time. He wants to git home in a hurry. That smoke's warmin' anyhow." Bill blew on his fingers. "How'd you like to be in a nice warm bed?"

"Shut up," I yelled.

The country stretched flat as a pancake.

"Well, it's better'n them mountains—but let's get off at the first stop." Shivering, Bill gazed ahead.

"Okay," I said.

The engine whistle blew.

"She's slowin' up," Bill said.

Cramped, we hit the ground.

"What town's this?" he asked a working man.

"Elvan." The man paid no attention.

"Huh—two hundred miles without stoppin'." Bill shivered. "But enough's enough. We got all year to git where we're goin'. The Elvan jungle's not far from here—let's go to it. Maybe Bacon Butt Fatty's there," Bill said.

The east was blotted red. He looked at the rising sun.

"Maybe that'll warm us up," Bill said.

A factory whistle blew. A laborer came along, carrying a tin dinner pail.

"Maybe he's got something left—let's ask him," I suggested.

"No savvy," the man said.

We next pointed to the pail—then at our stomachs. The man held the pail upside down.

"Empty—thanks just the same," Bill sighed.

We walked along a river bed in silence. Insects droned tiredly.

"They're beginnin' early," Bill said at last. "She's sure a sultry mornin'."

"Yeap—kind of dark, too." I looked at the sky. "The sun's goin' behind a cloud—but it is warmer."

"I'm glad of that," Bill said. "Breakfast time for some, an' just warmer for others."

The water gurgled in the river.

"See that fish?" I yelled. "It's tryin' to breathe."

Bill shook his head.

An ant scurried across the road. He pushed its nest over with his foot.

"They're all out of the way. Something's wrong. You can't fool an ant. It knows too much about the weather. It's goin' to storm sure's you're a foot high."

"How do you know?" I asked.

"That ant told me—that's how," Bill said.

"How do you know it knows?" I persisted.

"Well, its people's been outdoors a billion years—maybe." Bill's head was down.

An engine whistle moaned, as if held under water.

"Goin' up the Elvan grade," I said. "It's purty steep."

The day became darker. The lightning streaked along a rail fence. The clouds rumbled.

The thunder roared louder. Large drops of rain cracked the earth.

Bill quit grinning. "Gee—that is cyclone weather. That ant knew. We'd better skedaddle."

It cleared suddenly. We stopped, out of breath.

"Not enough to settle the dust," I sighed. "All that runnin' for nothin'."

"What do you mean runnin' for nothin'? It's goin' to storm, I tell you." Bill sniffed. "That food at the jungle smells good anyhow."

A heavy man adjusted his bundle of umbrella sticks as he watched us approach.

"That's Bacon Butt Fatty all right." Bill's words were low. "He's the best scout in the business. You can't hide money from him. He don't miss nothin'. All the yeggs know it. Nobody gets nothin' out of him. Them umbrella sticks are a stall. He couldn't mend one if he got drowned."

"So that's Bacon Butt Fatty," I returned.

"I'll say," Bill said very low as we drew near.

Bacon Butt Fatty's eyes were narrow in his wide round face. He weighed nearly three hundred pounds. His rain-barrel body was short and squat.

"Hello, 'bo—how's chances to scoff?" Bill asked. "I was here comin' west."

"Yes, I remember." The man looked toward a table made of boxcar doors. Near it tramps prepared a meal. "It's okay by me—long as it lasts," he said. "We've been rustlin' the grub since yesterday. Just got in ahead of the rain myself. Glad it cleared up."

I stared at Bacon Butt Fatty.

An unerring scout for yeggs, the locator of banks that they might rob, the police did not connect him and his bundle of umbrella sticks with a daring robbery. Quietly strolling through alleys, his eyes on the ground, as if looking for cigar butts, he petted dogs as he passed by. He would not go near cities.

His brain was very quick. Clouds of doubt would roll over his huge moonface if the police questioned him. His words would come slowly and sincerely. "Gentlemen, I but seek to live in the only way I can. I'm just an old mush faker, a mender of umbrellas. Too heavy for other work, I keep the rain from the heads of other dear people." Immune from insult, he turned everything into laughter. A few silver dollars, presumably his wage for fixing umbrellas, was all he ever had on his person.

Bill knew all about him. "He just smells money in banks."

Bacon Butt Fatty walked slowly. In this way he missed nothing. He was never in a hurry. Wherever he happened to be at the moment was the hub of life for him. Freezing cold and burning sun were all the same to him. He smiled at Bill. "Who's the kid?" he asked.

"He's okay—the makin's of a good hobo," Bill said.

"All right." Bacon Butt Fatty dropped his umbrella sticks and sauntered toward a group around a keg of moonshine. We followed.

Soon his eyes slanted. "Look who's comin'. Did he follow you kids?"

"No. We ain't never seen him before," said Bill.

A boy shuffled toward us. His mouth was wide and loose. His straw-colored hair projected from beneath the torn edges of a faded cap too small for his small head. The short sleeves of his coat exposed his thin raw wrists.

His socks hung loosely over worn shoes. A black sateen shirt was open at his blue throat.

He looked for a second at torn pieces of slate-colored cloud drifting across the dreary green and yellow sky.

"It's been strange weather, hasn't it?" I said. "First it's warm and then it's cold."

The boy coughed. "Mighty strange weather. It's that time of year. It was colder'n a tombstone this mornin'." He glanced again at the sky. "It looks kinda funny now."

A road kid with dark hair snapped, "If you like them clouds I'll pull 'em down for you."

The boy looked at the other. "No—I don't want 'em," he said.

Bacon Butt Fatty smiled. "You look kinda all in, kid; have a drink." He drew a tin cup full of moonshine. The boy drank avidly, then shook his head.

"This'll put some vim into you. Have another cup." Bacon Butt Fatty drew more liquor.

"Gosh, it'll kill him," Bill said. "On an empty stomach, too—it's like drinkin' fire even after you eat."

The boy reached for another cup. He sang:

> "Out in this cold world,
> And far away from home."

He staggered and stopped.

"Go ahead'n sing—the birds won't care," Bacon Butt Fatty chuckled.

"Aw right." The boy rubbed his forehead.

> "Somebody's boy is wanderin' alone,
> Search till you find him, and bring him back to me,
> Far, far away, wherever he may be."

Then he stumbled. A badge flashed beneath his coat. Bacon Butt Fatty grabbed him.

"Where'd you get this?" he asked.

"Mail-order course," the boy hiccuped. "Seven lessons."

Openmouthed, the vagabonds looked. Fondling the badge, Bacon Butt Fatty smiled.

"We like detectives here. It shows our heart's right. Everybody's welcome," he said.

The wind rattled the leaves on the ground.

The boy staggered. "Tha's right. Room for everybody."

"Let's put him on trial," a hobo with two canes shouted.

"What for?" the boy asked.

"None o' your business." The man with two canes had his eyes on Bacon Butt Fatty.

"You be the judge—you'll be fair."

Bacon Butt Fatty chuckled. "Sure thing—I'll just be the judge. Everybody knows I wouldn't hang a man over twice."

I looked at Bill.

"Let them have some fun," he said. "It's only a kangaroo court where everything's turned around. The more guilty they find him, the sooner he gets free. It's better'n that liquor anyhow. It'll sober him up."

Bacon Butt Fatty glanced at the boy.

"I'm afraid this'll go hard with you, my lad," he said. "There's a law in this state against comin' into a jungle without the consent of them assembled. We were not consulted in the matter and you broke in upon our privacy, violatin' all the rights pertainin' to dishonest taxpayers the world over."

Bacon Butt Fatty looked toward the table. "How long before we scoff?"

"A half hour, maybe," was the answer.

"Huh," Bacon Butt Fatty said, "we can hang him and a coupla dozen others by that time. He'll hang easy, not bein' used to it." He looked around with legal dignity. "Now I'll appoint a court." Pointing to a chinless young tramp with one eye, he said, "You be the prosecutor—nobody'll believe you anyhow. You don't look dishonest enough." His eyes went over the other bleary men. "You defend him," he said to the man with two canes. "You first wanted to try him." His face became stern. "But you gotta remember, I'm a one-way judge—and I don't like people 'cause they're poor. If they ain't guilty they ain't got no business takin' up the court's time." His eyes narrowed at the youth. "Let's see your hands."

Now half sober, the boy held them, palms upward.

"Why," gasped Bacon Butt Fatty, "it's been years since you did any work—they're soft as mine—or any judge's."

"Dishonor," the vagabond with two canes cried, "in defendin' this man I wanna say I've had the misfortune of meetin' him at many a water tank an' I gotta tell you that he's guilty of the crime as charged in the excitement. As the defender of him before this bar of injustice, I further wanna say that he ain't only guilty but he stooped low enough one time to blow the safe in a Y.W.C.A. Yes sir, an' he got four novels about love in the dark. He's the lowest crook goin'."

Bacon Butt Fatty raised his hand.

"Halt," he said. "You have searched the prisoner?"

"It's no use, your mighty dishonor," shouted the man with two canes. "The cops searched him last night."

"Rob him again," advised Bacon Butt Fatty.

A comb was pulled from the lining of the boy's coat.

"A comb, dishonor." The searcher held it aloft.

"Why, this is terrible," said Bacon Butt Fatty. "This country ain't safe for society, with combs in the pockets of desperadoes. They might use them." He put his hands to his eyes. "Think of it, our wives and children at the mercy of such a desperate brigand. It's awful, awful." He sighed. "The laws of the nation are askrew." Bacon Butt Fatty looked sternly at the boy and thundered, "Have you anything to say which would further implicate yourself?"

"No sir," the boy replied.

"You see, dishonor," exclaimed the defending lawyer, "thinkin' judges are human, he 'sirs' you."

Bacon Butt Fatty's eyes went over the frayed assemblage, rested for a second on the boy, and then on the hobo with two canes.

"Not so loud in your defense," he warned. "My mind bein' already made up that he's guilty, I can quite boreful hear you between snores like any other judge, so I don't wanna be woke up."

The youth started to sob.

Bacon Butt Fatty pointed a thick finger at him. "This is real," he said. "Go easy on the tears. Bein' that you've no right here you can expect nothin' but quick injustice."

Again the youth started to sob. Bacon Butt Fatty looked concerned.

"Quit that," he cried, "or you'll make my heart colder. Ain't I tryin' to go easy with justice?" He looked at the moonshine. "My throat's dry—talkin' about justice. Hand me a drink." He smacked his lips, and continued, "I wouldn't like to rule in your favor, for if I did, some other danged fool would say I didn't know nothin'. I don't think you're guilty of anything but havin' no brains, an' bein' poor's the same thing. My heart would ache for you—if I had one—so—I won't sentence you to be hung—only to be shot."

The boy's eyes opened in terror. No one heard the wind.

"Let's hang him instead," suggested another member of the mock court.

"No—he's to be shot—bein' danged fool enough to come into this court with no money." Bacon Butt Fatty was firm.

A tramp's hand went up. "He has fits——"

"Shut up or we'll croak you before him." Bacon Butt Fatty glared. "Besides, how do you know?"

The boy's eyes dilated further. He shook with fear, sank to the ground, writhed in convulsions, and lay still.

"Get up, pardner," said Bacon Butt Fatty. "We were just foolin'." He put a heavy hand on the boy's shoulder. "He'll be all right soon," he said in the silence. "It's hell bein' a judge," he added with alarm.

"Well, what do you know about this?" the defending tramp said.

"Let's put him over under the tree." The mock judge turned to the boy with the dark curly hair. "We didn't do nothin'." He gulped. "There'll be the devil to pay for this just the same. It don't look none too good."

Bacon Butt Fatty's face was solemn. The vagrants looked at one another with concern.

The boy with the black curly hair placed the other under a tree. Bacon Butt Fatty watched.

The road kid said, "He can watch the clouds from now on."

"To hell with all this." Bacon Butt Fatty moved nervously. "Let's sing." He lifted his hand. "Now all together:

> "Nobody knows where the hobo goes,
> Where he bums his grub or gits his clothes—
> Nobody knows but Jesus.
> Nobody knows an' nobody cares
> Or gives a darn—but Jesus."

A wind whistled across the jungle and drove before it a spiral of dust. Leaves rattled down.

"I guess we're in for it." Bill's eyes went to the green sky. "It's cyclone weather all right. Let's go."

"What's your hurry?" asked Bacon Butt Fatty. "This wind'll blow over."

"I'm not so sure it won't take us," Bill shouted above the wind.

"Which way's it comin'?" I hurried after Bill.

"Every which way," Bill yelled over his shoulder.

"Then let's all go," Bacon Butt Fatty shouted. "Come on, men." He looked hurriedly around. "Gee, they're gone," he said. "I hope they beat the wind."

"They will," Bill said. "Follow me."

We rushed to a culvert beneath the railroad. Bacon Butt Fatty was even with us.

"Gee, you can run," I said.

"I kin when I have to," he said.

Stones of the roadbed flew along the tracks.

"Just in time," Bill panted. "I hope it don't blow the rails away."

I glanced at the other end of the culvert.

"It can blow us right outta here if it takes a notion," I said.

"Here's hopin' it don't take a notion," Bacon Butt Fatty grinned, "for I'm a-goin' to that end. They ain't room at this end anyhow."

The rain slashed for a second. Then it cleared. Bent low, we looked at the swirling sky. The clouds rolled angrily over and over. One of the muddy green ones hung down. The small end toward the earth, it swung like a mad elephant's trunk. The top spread wider. The little end bobbed up and down. Then, traveling swiftly, it circled.

Roofs were lifted from houses and barns. Horses and cattle neighed and bellowed through the air. A tree followed. There was a frightful clatter in the jungle. The boxcar-door tables blew above the culvert. A regiment of small clouds followed. The pendulum of cloud mounted higher. For a minute the bright sun dazzled the sky. The wind soughed loudly. The regiment of small clouds dispersed.

"The wind's goin' a thousand miles an hour," Bill choked.

"Those ants are safe." I tried to say more. The wind blew the words back.

There was a loud rumble as of thousands of heavily loaded freight trains going up the Elvan grade. The river was lashed into foam. Blending with the roar of the wind, its waves mounted high.

I held my ears. It was quiet on the blind of a mail train compared to this. The river overflowed its banks. The water was white far out. Trees crashed into it.

"The water's comin' our way. We'll drown like rats," I yelled.

"Let 'er come," Bill shouted. "We'll get up on the tracks."

"I'll go when you guys go," said Bacon Butt Fatty.

The water moved slowly. A lull came.

The tail of cloud remained motionless for a second.

"Who ever thought of this?" I asked.

"It ain't over yet," Bacon Butt Fatty said.

He was right.

"Here it comes again," Bill yelled.

The tail of cloud whipped suddenly up and down with the force of a sword in the hands of an angry, mile-high giant. Lightning jagged the sky. A loud roar of thunder followed and the rain fell hard for a second.

"I forgot my umbrella sticks," Bacon Butt Fatty shouted.

"It's a hell of a time to think of them," Bill screamed.

"Well, it's rainin', ain't it?" the fat fellow yelled:

Bacon Butt Fatty crawled toward us. The lash of rain and roar of wind continued.

Soon all abated. A dreadful calm followed. Warm and serene, the white sun went through the clear sky. We stood outside and looked upward.

"I think it's safe to go back now." I glanced toward the jungle.

"We'd better not be too sure"—Bill was wary—"but I guess it's all right."

"I hope so." Bacon Butt Fatty rubbed his forehead. "Here I was carryin' those umbrella sticks for nothin'. Now I'm wet as hell."

"So'm I," said Bill.

"But there's more of me." Bacon Butt Fatty looked at his huge frame.

Carefully we went toward the jungle.

Bacon Butt Fatty pointed. "Look at this. It's sure funny."

One wide path had not been touched. All around it wagons, parts of buildings, and iron chains had been whirled through the air and scattered on the ground. A horse lay dead, its harness stripped away. All that remained were the straps around its neck. Its wounded driver clutched the stump of a tree.

"Are you hurt, pal?" Bill asked.

Before the man could answer a lightning-struck tree fell. An owl flew blindly out of a hole in the top.

"Well, what do you know about that?" exclaimed Bill. "It never knew what was goin' on, but I'll bet the lightnin' burned its tail feathers just the same."

I looked at the fast-flying clouds and yelled, "Here she comes again."

Bill's eyes followed mine. "Nope—no more today. Let's beat it on to the jungle."

We started. The weeds were flat on the ground. The water ran over them.

"It never rains but it pours." Bill looked around. "This'll do the crops good next year."

Bacon Butt Fatty chuckled.

> *"More rain, more rest,*
> *More niggers in the west."*

The clouds raced across the sun. The jungle was a wreck. The keg of moonshine had crashed against a stump. Its staves were broken, its bands bent.

"Gee, an' I sure need a drink." Bacon Butt Fatty's head shook. "It's too bad to treat our home this way."

The sun threw shadows across a rivulet of yellow water in the center.

"Anyhow, we don't have to worry no more about that kid. The wind's took him away."

Footsteps were heard.

"Who's that walkin'?" Bill asked.

"It's me," was the answer.

The shirt torn from his body, the boy came toward us. Bacon Butt Fatty stared.

"We're mighty glad to see you," I said. "We thought you were dead."

"So'd I," the boy returned. "I thought I was a rolly coaster for a second. An' talk about a barber—it zipped the hair right off my chest. My hat's gone."

He felt his head anxiously to make sure the hair was still there.

"That was a close shave." He covered his shoulders with a piece of blanket from the ground. "No more moonshine." He rubbed his eyes. "What the dickens really happened?"

"Nothin' much," I said.

"I'm glad it wasn't longer," Bill cut in.

The boy looked at Bacon Butt Fatty. "An' everybody got away," he said.

Still staring, Bacon Butt Fatty said, "I hope so." He chanted:

> *"Home came the saddle,*
> *All bloody to see—*
> *An' home came the steed—*
> *But home never came he."*

A straw driven into an upstanding boxcar attracted the boy's attention. "Hey, lookit this," he shouted.

Bacon Butt Fatty's eyes narrowed in his large moonface. "That used to be a table," he chuckled, "till that darned cyclone blew our grub into the next county."

"Well," Bill said, "I'm goin' somewheres to eat." '

"Me too." Bacon Butt Fatty looked at the boy. "I'll take you all," he said. "I got some money. It's better'n bein' shot."

THORNTON WILDER

The Warship

THE SHIP *Trumpeter* which left London for Australia in the early eighteenth century with a hundred convicts and their families on board never reached its destination and no report of any survivor nor of any identified object connected with it ever reached the world. The ship's company did not entirely perish, however. The captain and the greater part of the crew were drowned in the storm that wrecked the vessel; many of the passengers and most of the children died in the hardships of the first few weeks thereafter; but finally over a hundred persons reached an island on the west coast of Australia. These survivors settled down upon the island which they promptly christened "England," but which in a few generations of oral transmission became "Inglan." In time the ingenuity of the colonists had established an agreeable mode of living; a church, a school, a parliament, and even a theater had come into being, and within a hundred years the population had more than doubled. It was greatly reduced in 1870, however, by an obscure disease which attacked the community, probably through some disproportion in the ingredients of the islanders' diet. A few years later the population was again diminished by the loss of a dozen of the ablest men who ventured in a roughhewn boat to visit an island which could be occasionally seen at sunrise on the northern horizon.

In 1880 a castaway reached the colony, a Finnish sailor, who had been drifting for many days in an open boat. It was several years before he learned sufficient English to tell the Inglaners about the outside world, a hazy account of the Napoleonic Wars, of an English queen, and detailed information about Baltic politics. This Finnish sailor never recovered from the ill effects of his exposure and died in the sixth year of his life on the island. No other visitor ever reached Inglan; no ship was ever sighted in the distance; and presently the Inglaners lost interest in maintaining the distress signal on the peak that rose behind their settlement.

In the original company of the shipwrecked there had been only a few men and women who were able, even imperfectly, to read, write, and compute, and they were already aged by the time the community came to feel a need for written records and had devised a substitute for paper on which to inscribe them. At the same time the colony was seized with a passion for recovering the lore of the outside world and particularly for anything connected with religion. Official scribes were appointed and all who could remember a passage or even a phrase from the Bible or the hymns contributed their share. In this way a brief anthology was committed to writing, including a synopsis of the *Pilgrim's Progress,* some fragments from the marriage and burial services, and a number of English and Scotch ballads. To this library the islanders went to school, where they likewise were given accounts of such things as animals, grains, and utensils. Geography consisted of vague maps of the world and the British Isles and detailed descriptions of London, Plymouth, and Bristol. At the beginning of the nineteenth century a gifted musician arose who fashioned himself some instruments and on the basis of the songs that had been retained made some new ones. Soon after a poet declared himself and versified copiously. A young woman who had gazed long at squares and triangles deduced the first books of Euclid from them and a school of mathematicians flourished for half a century.

Up to the time of the epidemic of 1870 the health of the community had been excellent, but thereafter it declined rapidly. The uniformity of the diet and the increasing bonds of consanguinity had a part in this, but chiefly a psychological factor that was an effect of the shut-in-ness of the island existence. The colonists were not aware of any desire to leave Inglan and view the outside world, yet they felt themselves lost, abandoned of God, and aimless. Vigorous personalities arose from time to time who found the opportunities and problems of even this restricted existence sufficient to justify a human dignity, but the majority relapsed into a fretful and listless submission to the passing of time. A large proportion of the children died

at birth or grew up sickly, unsocial, eccentric, and quarrelsome. A fer-
mented drink was brewed from the fruits on the island and intemperance
became universal. But most strikingly of all, in spite of the small size of
the territory and in spite of the fact that every colonist was many times the
cousin of his neighbor, the Inglaners divided themselves into factions and
lived in an atmosphere of distrust that frequently came to a head in strife
and bloodshed.

In 1910 there were only twelve adults living under civilization in Lunnon itself and they no longer made efforts to reclaim the few hermits who
had withdrawn themselves to the remoter parts of the island. Jonh Weever,
the captain of Inglan, as he was called, tried strenuously to inspirit his
community; he offered rewards for inventions, for writings, and for feats
of skill. His eldest son, Roja, felt the incitement beyond the others and
never tired of contriving improvements for the island; but at the same time
he distressed his father by continued speculation as to the nature of the
outside world. To Captain Jonh the existence of the outside world was a
matter lost in myth, tradition, and hearsay. Report said that hundreds, even
thousands, of human beings lived there in dwellings of extraordinary size
and beauty. Roja dreamed of finding a way to such a world, or of the
possibility of such a world's coming of Inglan. Captain Jonh would sigh
into his beard, shaking his head at such thoughts. "Whether that world be
still there," he would say, "whether it be better than our own or worser;
how far away it lies—these things we cannot know, neither be we like to
know. The best thing for us to do, my son, is not to beat our heads about
them, but to do our duty where we be." But Roja would not be put off.
He stirred up the men of Lunnon to renew the huge distress signal on the
peak. It was long and tedious work, but for a time the islanders were filled
with an unaccustomed excitement. The storms of the next two rainy seasons, however, tore the great structure down, and even when Roja became
captain in his father's place he made no effort to rebuild it.

One night when he had put his sons and daughters to bed and made the
rounds of Lunnon, Captain Roja descended to the water's edge and sat
down, gazing across the sea. He turned over in his mind the destiny that
had placed him there, the depleted colony, the rancorous spirit of his subjects, the difference that lay between today and the glorious days that his
grandfather had described to him, and he thought of the days that lay
ahead when his children would have survived him. And as he sat thinking
a strange sight appeared before him. A great ship came around the head-

land, hung with lights, festooned with two great rows of lights from stem to stern. Music came from it and the sound of shouting. Clouds of smoke hung in the quiet air behind it. Fore and aft two great skeleton turrets rose into the stars. For a moment Captain Roja thought of lighting a bonfire or setting fire to St. Paul's, but he paused. The vision was beautiful, but terrible. He knew that neither himself nor his companions could live in that world; all that power and energy was troubling and remote. He sat down again and watched the marvel pass into the distance, and the other shadowy forms that had gathered on the slope behind him gazed and trembled and went in silence to their homes.

CORNELL WOOLRICH

The Fingernail

INSPECTOR MORROW, retired, followed his friend to one of the little tables against the wall.

"This place is famous for its food," the other man, who was acting as host, remarked as they sat down, unfurled their napkins. "Ever been here before?"

Morrow looked around him uncertainly. "Restaurant Robert," he murmured. "Wait a minute, I remember this place! Before my retirement from Homicide we once traced a murderer as far as here—and then we lost him again. Remind me to tell you about it after we've ordered." He took up his bill of fare, studied it a moment or two. "You come here a lot—what's good?"

"Try one of Robert's famous rabbit stews," the other man suggested. "They're made separately for each customer, in little individual earthenware casseroles. It's Robert's own secret recipe, he won't share it with anyone."

"Sounds good to me," acquiesced Morrow.

"Two," said his companion to the waiter. "And tell Robert I have a new customer with me tonight." He turned to Morrow. "That'll bring him out in person at the end of the meal, to hear you praise his efforts—it always does. He's as proud as a kid of these rabbit stews of his." He leaned back comfortably in his chair. "It'll take a little while. Now what was that story you promised to tell me?"

"Oh yeah, that." Morrow helped himself to a piece of bread. "It's a good five years ago now. We found a man murdered one night. . . ."

Inspector Morrow, five years younger, five inches slimmer at the waist, climbed down the rickety iron steps into the basement antique shop. A younger man came toward the entrance to greet him, said "Hello, Inspector."

"Hello, Fletcher. What's the good word so far?"

"Well, I've got all the preliminaries over with," his subordinate said. "Weylin Hamilton's his name. He lived here alone on the premises, in back of the shop. It happened in the early part of last evening. Robbery motive. He evidently kept considerable money down here with him. We found the box he'd hidden it in busted open—and empty. No relatives or next of kin."

The place was even more grotesque within than it had looked from the outside. Technically it might have been an antique shop, but to Morrow's practical eye it looked more like a junk shop. It contained just about everything a person would *not* want, the way he felt about it. A suit of Japanese armor loomed terrifyingly in one corner. Scimitars, spears, and venerable flintlock pistols were affixed to the walls. There were squat Chinese buddhas, a South Sea war drum, even a Turkish water pipe coiled on a taboret.

"Look out, that's him," Fletcher warned abruptly as his superior was about to thrust his way between a couple of the overcrowded display stands. Morrow recoiled, just missing stepping on the inert bundle on the floor.

He gestured impatiently. "Move this trash out of the way and give me some room. That's better." He crouched down, peered attentively at the form lying there. "Now let's see what we've got here." The handle of an antique Florentine dagger, wrapped in felt, protruded from the dead man's chest.

"That came down off the wall over there," Fletcher pointed out.

"In other words, it wasn't premeditated. The guy didn't bring his own weapon with him. Hamilton came out of the back room, interrupted the guy trying to rob him, and the guy snatched down the first thing he could lay hands on and let him have it." He pointed. "What's this cotton wool doing wrapped around one of his insteps?"

"He was suffering with arthritis, the medical examiner says. Couldn't put one shoe on. Couldn't move around much, the last few weeks."

"Then it's a cinch he couldn't manage those breakneck iron steps outside, leading up to the sidewalk. Must have been sort of marooned down here." Morrow got up again. "Now let's see this box you think he kept money in."

"I know he did; there's a tiny corner of a dollar bill—or maybe it was a five or ten—got caught under the back of the lid and torn off in the murderer's hurry to get it out. I guess the old guy had it wadded in pretty tightly. Here it is."

Morrow eyed the tiny fragment of paper first. "Yeah, that's government paper," he agreed. "You can see the blue and red threads even with the naked eye." Then he turned to the box itself. It was of oriental origin, lacquered wood on the outside, but lined with a thin sheeting of copper on the inside. The lacquer was marred and gouged at all along the seam of the lid.

"He had a tough time opening this, even though it has no lock and key," Morrow pointed out. "You see, it operates by pressure; there's an unnoticeable sort of bulge in the wood. You press against that and that releases the lid. He didn't get the hang of it, must have kept digging his nail into the seam and trying to pry it up that way." He took it over closer to a portable reflector that had been rigged up, peered at the lining. "Then it shot up suddenly when he least expected it and his finger rammed home. He hurt himself on it, too. There's a thin dark hairline across the edge of the metal lining, where it peers above the edge of the wood casing—blood. Just where did you find the box lying?"

Fletcher took him over and showed him. Morrow got down and began to scan the floor. "Here's a drop here. Here's another. They must have escaped before he could wrap something around it——" He motioned imperatively to his assistant. "Gimme a piece of paper, any kind will do." He scooped at something with it, held the paper out to show him. "See what this is?"

Fletcher squinted at the little shell-like object. "It looks like—like somebody's whole fingernail."

"It is. He lost his whole nail. It must have been defective to start with to come off that easy, but the metal edge of that box lining caught under it and sliced it off. If it didn't come right off at once, he pulled it off himself to keep it from dangling. That was his mistake. It takes too long to grow a new nail for him to be able to cover up the loss before we've caught him." He wrapped and pocketed the queasy little memento.

"It was somebody that paid two or more visits—he knew just which box the old man kept his cash in, out of all the junk in here, and made a bee-line for it without disturbing anything else. Hamilton must have been incautious enough to haul it out once or twice in his presence."

"That looks like Hamilton paid *him* instead of him paying Hamilton for something he bought," Fletcher observed.

"Let's take a look at what that inside room is like."

It was just a cubbyhole with a cot and cupboard in it and not much else. Morrow glanced around with eyes trained not to miss little details that somebody else might have overlooked. He opened the cupboard, revealed several bottles of liniment and nothing else. He turned to Fletcher. "The medical examiner says he was suffering from arthritis lately and couldn't navigate the entrance steps. You say he had no relatives or intimate friends. Well, where'd he get his meals from, then? There's not so much as an empty cracker box in sight."

Fletcher scratched his head. "Gee, I never thought of——"

"He had them sent in, that's what he did. From some place near by where he'd been in the habit of going formerly, before he was incapacitated. That means a waiter or bus boy of some kind. And that's who killed him. It all checks. Repeated visits with a covered tray or hamper. And Hamilton took money out of the box to pay him, instead of his paying Hamilton. Now we're getting somewhere. We want a waiter with the nail gone from one of his fingers, who works at some place in the immediate vicinity, within a radius of about three or four blocks at the most." He blew between his hands, ground them together. "It's practically over!"

Andy, the junior waiter at Robert's, was nervous. He stood there in the kitchen with his back to the boss, while the latter cut up the skinned rabbits that went piecemeal into the famous stews, six casseroles of which were already slowly simmering on the charcoal stove.

Robert, a great good-natured hulk of a Frenchman, bald as an onion under his chef's cap, was rambling on, as he had a habit of doing whenever there was anyone in the kitchen to listen, no matter who. "Fonny thing happen this afternoon. Some guy he come to my door upstairs here in house, before restaurant is open, say he want to speak to me. I think he's policeman; you know, one of those kind without blue suit?"

Andy had stopped his work of trimming radishes, stood listening intently, head bent, with the paring knife held motionless in one white-gloved hand. He didn't say anything.

"He look at me close, like owl. He say, 'Which one of your waiters got sore finger, you happen to notice?'" Robert shrugged. "I say, 'How I'm going to tell you that? The one strict rule in my place is, all the men work for me they got to wear white cotton gloves, kip 'em on their hands all the time for to be clean and neat.'"

Andy just listened, neck rigid.

"He say, 'Never mind, I find out for myself. Kip it under your hat, eh?'" He gestured toward the dining-room door. "He sitting out there now; I see him when I come through. What you suppose is matter, eh?"

"I don't know," Andy said in a muffled voice.

Robert wiped his hands on his apron. "All right, ragout, they all ready now, just wait for to put seasoning in. I go down basement, bring up little spice. Kip eye on fire for me, eh, Andy? If she get too low, put on little more charcoal." He opened the cellar door that led down to the supply room, waddled clumsily out of sight down the steps.

Andy swallowed hard, as though he had a lump in his throat. He turned and eyed the redly glowing charcoal range. He went over to the sack of fuel slumped in a corner, scooped out a trowelful, carried it to the stove, crouched down, and spaded it in. Then he looked around across his shoulder. He was alone in the kitchen at the moment, and such moments were likely to be few and far between as the dinner hour got under way.

He unpinned something from the inside of his shirt. With furtive, trembling, white-gloved fingers he tore it across once, twice. He flung the pieces in on top of the flame-licked charcoal. One fragment escaped him in the draft, fell to the floor, lay there for a moment. The numeral "20" was engraved on it, in green and white, with red and blue threads veining the paper. He retrieved it, sent it in after the other pieces. Then he closed the stove flap. His face had been gray even in the ruddy glow beating against it.

He jumped furtively back to the worktable, just as the swing door flapped open and one of his fellow workers came bustling in. The latter loaded a tray without glancing at Andy, hoisted it to his shoulder, swung out again into the dining room.

Andy went after him, but only as far as the door. He steadied it with one hand, peered cautiously out through the glass inset near the top. There was a sprinkling of early arrivals already in the outer room. Most of them were habitués; he knew their faces. All but one. There was a man sitting by himself at a table against the far wall. He'd never been in the place before. Andy was sure of it. He didn't act hungry, he was ignoring the bill of fare. A waiter came over to take his order and the man said something to him. The waiter looked surprised, hesitated momentarily. The man repeated what he had said in a tight-lipped way that brooked no argument. Then Andy saw the waiter slowly strip off first one glove, then the other, poise his hands for inspection, palms down. The man nodded curtly and the waiter slowly began to draw his gloves on again.

Andy didn't wait to see any more. He left the door pane, fled swiftly across the kitchen toward the opposite door that gave on to the outside alley, stripping off his apron and flinging it behind him as he went. He pushed the door open, then drew up short. There was the motionless figure of a man outlined at the alley mouth against the street light beyond. He was just standing there waiting, effectively blocking all egress. There was no other way out but past him—in the other direction the alley came to a dead end.

Andy turned, floundered strickenly back into the kitchen again. He looked around him with agonized helplessness. Robert's slow, heavy tread was starting up the basement steps from below.

He had a minute left. It ended.

He was standing there, bent forward over the worktable, face ghastly white, when Robert came lumbering up into sight a minute later. Robert gave him a sudden, startled look. "What's matter, you sick? You got pain in stomach?"

"Boss, you'll have to let me go home for tonight," Andy whispered weakly. "I can't work any more." There was sweat on his forehead.

Another waiter came barging in. "One rabbit stew for the rich dame at number four table!"

Robert was a considerate boss. "All right, Andy, you go," he consented. "You no look good, that's a fact. You take over his tables for him tonight, George."

Andy's face was still deathly pale, but calm and untroubled now, when he tottered out to the alley mouth a moment later. The man standing there promptly reached out, pinned him fast. "Just a minute, brother, let's have a look at your hands."

Andy obeyed without demur. He held them out, shakily, palms downward. They were ungloved. The index finger of the right hand was a sodden, topheavy funnel of telescoped gauze bandaging.

"Take that off," growled the man.

Andy didn't have to. He just gave his hand a slight downward hitch and the saturated dressing flew off of its own weight. There was nothing to hold it, nothing under it, just a gory space between the thumb and the middle finger.

"It was him all right, eh?" Morrow's friend asked absorbedly.

"Sure it was him." Morrow scowled. "But knowing a thing is one thing, proving it another. He'd worn his white service gloves when he'd carted the tray over, so that did away with all hope of prints. The pair of gloves that had become bloody he probably destroyed. He admitted he'd taken quite a few meals over to Hamilton, but so had all the others. Hamilton had been seen alive after he called for and removed the tray that last night. The question was, which of them had sneaked back *after* the tray had been taken away, to rob the old man? We *had* to have that finger!

"I raised holy hell with them when they brought him in to me. 'You numskulls, get that finger!' I hollered at them. 'That's almost more important than he is!'

"We jumped right back to the place, all of us. Inside of ten minutes after it happened we were on the job turning the premises inside out. We put out the fire then and there, raked through the half-burned charcoal. We stopped the garbage before it had had a chance to go out, went through it with a fine comb. We emptied out all the flour bins and containers and what not they had around, we made a wreck out of that place. But the finger never turned up.

"*He* claimed it was an accident, of course. The knife had slipped and taken it clean off. He claimed he'd fainted with the shock, and was in too much pain when he came to to notice what had become of it.

"We ragged him for days after that, but it didn't do any good. We never found the money on him, nor any evidence that he'd spent it. We couldn't shake his alibi for the particular time the crime had taken place. He'd outsmarted us. We knew he was the guy. But without that nailless finger we couldn't prove it.

"It still burns me up, even at this late day, to think of it. It spoiled what would have otherwise been a hundred per cent perfect record for me. I still can't figure out what became of it, what he did to make it disappear so fast—and thoroughly."

"Here comes Robert, as I warned you, to find out how you liked his specialty," his friend remarked.

"Say, that rabbit stew was great," Morrow complimented the old chef. "I never tasted anything to beat it!"

"You like, eh?" Robert's chest puffed out like a pouter pigeon's. "I never had a complaint yet, in over twenty years——" He corrected himself conscientiously. "Just once, I remember now. One night fussy rich lady, who used to come regular, she send for me. This long time ago, we have a little trouble in kitchen that night. I get maybe a little excited.

"She say, 'Robert, are you sure that was *all* rabbit? I may be wrong, but the flavor at times seemed to vary a little. . . .'"

RICHARD WRIGHT

Almos' a Man

DAVE STRUCK OUT across the fields, looking homeward through paling light. Whut's the usa talkin' wid 'em niggers in the field? Anyhow, his mother was putting supper on the table. Them niggers can't understan' *nothing*. One of these days he was going to get a gun and practice shooting, then they can't talk to him as though he were a little boy. He slowed, looking at the ground. Shucks. Ah ain' scared-a them even ef they are bigger'n me! Aw, Ah know whut Ah'ma do . . . Ah'm going by ol' Joe's sto'n git that Sears Roebuck catlog'n look at them guns. Mabbe Ma will lemme buy one when she gits mah pay from ol' man Hawkins. Ah'ma beg her t'gimme some money. Ah'm ol' ernough to have gun. Ah'm seventeen. Almos' a man. He strode, feeling his long, loose-jointed limbs. Shucks, a man oughta hava little gun aftah he done worked hard all day. . . .

He came in sight of Joe's store. A yellow lantern glowed on the front porch. He mounted steps and went through the screen door, hearing it bang behind him. There was a strong smell of coal oil and mackerel fish. He felt very confident until he saw fat Joe walk in through the rear door, then his courage began to ooze.

"Howdy, Dave! Whutcha want?"

"How yuh, Mistah Joe? Aw, Ah don' wanna buy nothing, Ah jus wanted t' see ef yuh'd lemme look at that ol' catlog erwhile."

"Sure! You wanna see it here?"

"Nawsuh. Ah wan's t' take it home wid me. Ah'll bring it back termorrow when Ah come in from the fiel's."

"Yu plannin' on buyin' something?"

"Yessuh."

"Your ma letting you have your own money now?"

"Shucks. Mistah Joe, Ah'm gittin' t' be a man like anybody else!"

Joe laughed and wiped his greasy white face with a red bandanna.

"Whut you plannin' on buyin'?"

Dave looked at the floor, scratched his head, scratched his thigh, and smiled. Then he looked up shyly.

"Ah'll tell yuh, Mistah Joe, ef yuh promise yuh won't tell."

"I promise."

"Waal, Ah'ma buy a gun."

"A gun? Whut you want with a gun?"

"Ah wanna keep it."

"You ain't nothing but a boy. You don't need a gun."

"Aw, lemme have the catlog, Mistah Joe. Ah'll bring it back."

Joe walked through the rear door. Dave was elated. He looked around at barrels of sugar and flour. He heard Joe coming back. He craned his neck to see if he were bringing the book. Yeah, he's got it! Gawddog, he's got it!

"Here; but be sure you bring it back. It's the only one I got."

"Sho', Mistah Joe."

"Say, if you wanna buy a gun, why don't you buy one from me? I gotta gun to sell."

"Will it shoot?"

"Sure it'll shoot."

"Whut kind is it?"

"Oh, it's kinda old. . . . A left-hand Wheeler. A pistol. A big one."

"Is it got bullets in it?"

"It's loaded."

"Kin Ah see it?"

"Where's your money?"

"Whut yuh wan' fer it?"

"I'll let you have it for two dollars."

"Just *two* dollars? Shucks, Ah could buy tha' when Ah git mah pay."

"I'll have it here when you want it."

"Awright, suh. Ah be in fer it."

He went through the door, hearing it slam again behind him. Ah'ma git some money from Ma'n buy me a gun! Only *two* dollahs! He tucked the thick catalogue under his arm and hurried.

"Where yuh been, boy?" His mother held a steaming dish of black-eyed peas.

"Aw, Ma, Ah jus stopped down the road t' talk wid th' boys."

"Yuh know bettah than t' keep suppah waitin'."

He sat down, resting the catalogue on the edge of the table.

"Yuh git up from there and git to the well'n wash yo'se'f! Ah ain' feedin' no hogs in mah house!"

She grabbed his shoulder and pushed him. He stumbled out of the room, then came back to get the catalogue.

"Whut this?"

"Aw, Ma, it's jus'a catlog."

"Who yuh git it from?"

"From Joe, down at the sto'."

"Waal, tha's good. We kin use it around the house."

"Naw, Ma." He grabbed for it. "Gimme mah catlog, Ma."

She held onto it and glared at him.

"Quit hollerin' at me! Whut's wrong wid yuh? Yuh crazy?"

"But, Ma, please. It ain' mine! It's Joe's! He tol' me t' bring it back t'im termorrow."

She gave up the book. He stumbled down the back steps, hugging the thick book under his arm. When he had splashed water on his face and hands he groped back to the kitchen and fumbled in a corner for the towel. He bumped into a chair; it clattered to the floor. The catalogue sprawled at his feet. When he had dried his eyes he snatched up the book and held it again under his arm. His mother stood watching him.

"Now, ef yuh gonna acka fool over that ol' book, Ah'll take it a' burn it up."

"Naw, Ma, please."

"Waal, set down'n be still!"

He sat and drew the oil lamp close. He thumbed page after page, unaware of the food his mother set on the table. His father came in. Then his small brother.

"Whutcha got there, Dave?" his father asked.

"Jus'a catlog," he answered, not looking up.

"Ywah, here they is!" His eyes glowed at blue and black revolvers. He glanced up, feeling sudden guilt. His father was watching him. He eased the book under the table and rested it on his knees. After the blessing was asked, he ate. He scooped up peas and swallowed fat meat without chewing. Buttermilk helped to wash it down. He did not want to mention money before his father. He would do much better by cornering his mother when she was alone. He looked at his father uneasily out of the edge of his eye.

"Boy, how come yuh don' quit foolin' wid tha' book'n eat yo' suppah?"

"Yessuh."

"How yuh'n ol' man Hawkins gittin' erlong?"

"Suh?"

"Can't yuh hear? Why don' yuh lissen? Ah ast yuh how wuz yuh'n ol' man Hawkins gittin erlong?"

"Oh, swell, Pa. Ah plows mo' lan' than anybody over there."

"Waal, yuh oughta keep yo' min' on whut yuh doin'."

"Yessuh."

He poured his plate full of molasses and sopped at it slowly with a chunk of corn bread. When all but his mother had left the kitchen, he still sat and looked again at the guns in the catalogue. Lawd, ef Ah only had tha' pretty one! He could almost feel the slickness of the weapon with his fingers. If he had a gun like that he would polish it and keep it shining so it would never rust. N'Ah'd keep it loaded, by Gawd!

"Ma?"

"Hunh?"

"Ol man Hawkins give yuh mah money yit?"

"Yeah, but ain' no usa yuh thinkin' 'bout th'owin' nona it erway. Ah'm keepin' tha' money so's yuh kin have cloes t' go to school this winter."

He rose and went to her side with the open catalogue in his palms. She was washing dishes, her head bent low over a pan. Shyly he raised the open book. When he spoke his voice was husky, faint.

"Ma, Gawd knows Ah wan's one of these."

"One of whut?" she asked, not raising her eyes.

"One of *these*," he said again, not daring even to point. She glanced up at the page, then at him with wide eyes.

"Nigger, is yuh gone plum crazy?"

"Aw, Ma——"

"Git outta here! Don' yuh talk t' me 'bout no gun! Yuh a fool!"

"Ma, Ah kin buy one fer *two* dollahs."

"Not ef Ah knows it yuh ain'!"

"But yuh promised me one——"

"Ah don' care whut Ah promised! Yuh ain' nothing but a boy yit!"

"Ma, ef yuh le' me buy one Ah'll *never* ast yuh fer nothing no mo'!"

"Ah tol' yuh t' git outta here! Yuh ain' gonna toucha penny of tha' money fer no gun! Tha's how come Ah has Mistah Hawkins t' pay yo wages t' me, cause Ah knows yuh ain' got no sense."

"But, Ma, we needa gun. Pa ain' got no gun. We needa gun in the house. Yuh kin never tell whut might happen."

"Now don' yuh try to maka fool outta me, boy! Ef we did hava gun yuh wouldn't have it!"

He laid the catalogue down and slipped his arm around her waist.

"Aw, Ma, Ah done worked hard alla summer'n ain' ast yuh fer nothin', is Ah, now?"

"That whut yuh s'pose t' do!"

"But, Ma, Ah wan's a gun. Yuh kin lemme have two dollahs outta mah money. Please, Ma. I kin give it to Pa. . . . Please, Ma! Ah loves yuh, Ma."

When she spoke her voice came soft and low.

"Whut yuh wan' wida gun, Dave? Yuh don' need no gun. Yuh'll git in trouble. N'ef yo' Pa jus' *thought* Ah let yuh have money t' buy a gun he'd hava fit."

"Ah'll hide it, Ma, it ain' but two dollahs."

"Lawd, chil, whut's wrong wid yuh?"

"Ain' nothing wrong, Ma. Ah'm almos' a man now. Ah wan's a gun."

"Who gonna sell yuh a gun?"

"Ol' Joe at the sto'."

"N' it don' cos but two dollahs?"

"Tha's all, Ma. Just two dollahs. Please, Ma."

She was stacking the plates away; her hands moved slowly, reflectively. Dave kept an anxious silence. Finally she turned to him.

"Ah'll let yuh git tha' gun ef yuh promise me one thing."

"Whut's tha', Ma?"

"Yuh bring it straight back t' *me*, yuh hear? It'll be fer Pa."

"Yessum! Lemme go now, Ma."

She stooped, turned slightly to one side, raised the hem of her dress, rolled down the top of her stocking, and came up with a slender wad of bills.

"Here," she said. "Lawd knows yuh don' need no gun. But yer pa does. Yuh bring it right back t' *me*, yuh hear? Ah'ma put it up. Now ef yuh don', Ah'ma have yuh Pa lick yuh so hard yuh won' ferget it."

The first movement he made the following morning was to reach under his pillow for the gun. In the gray light of dawn he held it loosely, feeling a sense of power. Could killa man wida gun like this. Kill anybody, black er white. And if he were holding his gun in his hand nobody could run over him; they would have to respect him. It was a big gun, with a long barrel and a heavy handle. He raised and lowered it in his hand, marveling at its weight.

He had not come straight home with it as his mother had asked; instead he had stayed out in the fields, holding the weapon in his hand, aiming it now and then at some imaginary foe. But he had not fired it; he had been afraid that his father might hear. Also he was not sure he knew how to fire it.

To avoid surrendering the pistol he had not come into the house until he knew that all were asleep. When his mother had tiptoed to his bedside late that night and demanded the gun he had first played possum; then he had told her that the gun was hidden outdoors, that he would bring it to her in the morning. Now he lay turning it slowly in his hands. He broke it, took out the cartridges, felt them, and then put them back.

He slid out of bed, got a long strip of old flannel from a trunk, wrapped the gun in it, and tied it to his naked thigh while it was still loaded. He did not go in to breakfast. Even though it was not yet daylight, he started for Jim Hawkins' plantation. Just as the sun was rising he reached the barns where the mules and plows were kept.

"Hey! That you, Dave?"

He turned. Jim Hawkins stood eying him suspiciously.

"What're yuh doing here so early?"

"Ah didn't know Ah wuz gittin' up so early, Mistah Hawkins. Ah wuz fixin' t' hitch up ol' Jenny'n take her t' the fiels."

"Good. Since you're here so early, how about plowing that stretch down by the woods?"

"Suits me, Mistah Hawkins."

"Okay. Go to it!"

He hitched Jenny to a plow and started across the fields. Hot dog! This was just what he wanted. If he could get down by the woods he could shoot his gun and nobody would hear. He walked behind the plow, hearing the traces creaking, feeling the gun tied tight to his thigh.

When he reached the woods he plowed two whole rows before he decided to take out the gun. Finally he stopped, looked in all directions, then untied the gun and held it in his hand. He turned to the mule and smiled.

"Know whut this is, Jenny? Naw, yuh wouldn't know! Yuh's jus'a ol' mule! Anyhow, this is a gun'n it kin shoot, by Gawd!"

He held the gun at arm's length. Whut t' hell, Ah'ma shoot this thing! He looked at Jenny again.

"Lissen here, Jenny! When Ah pull this ol' trigger Ah don' wan' yuh t' run'n acka fool now."

Jenny stood with head down, her short ears pricked straight. Dave walked off about twenty feet, held the gun far out from him, at arm's length, and turned his head. Hell, he told himself, Ah ain' afraid. The gun felt loose in his fingers; he waved it wildly for a moment. Then he shut his eyes and tightened his forefinger. *Bloom!* A report half deafened him and he thought his right hand was torn from his arm. He heard Jenny whinnying and galloping over the field and he found himself on his knees, squeezing his fingers hard between his legs. His hand was numb; he jammed it into his mouth, trying to warm it, trying to stop the pain. The gun lay at his feet. He did not quite know what had happened. He stood up and stared at the gun as though it were a live thing. He gritted his teeth and kicked the gun. Yuh almos' broke mah arm! He turned to look for Jenny; she was far over the field, tossing her head and kicking wildly.

"Hol' on there, ol' mule!"

When he caught up with her she stood trembling, walling her big white eyes at him. The plow was far away; the traces had broken. Then Dave stopped short, looking, not believing. Jenny was bleeding. Her left side was red and wet with blood. He went closer. Lawd have mercy! Wondah did Ah shoot this mule? He grabbed for Jenny's mane. She flinched, snorted, whirled, tossing her head.

"Hol' on now! Hol' on."

Then he saw the hole in Jenny's side, right between the ribs. It was round, wet, red. A crimson stream streaked down the front leg, flowing fast. Good Gawd! Ah wuzn't shootin' at tha mule. . . . He felt panic. He knew he had to stop that blood or Jenny would bleed to death. He had never seen so much blood in all his life. He ran the mule for half a mile, trying to catch her. Finally she stopped, breathing hard, stumpy tail half arched. He caught her mane and led her back to where the plow and gun lay. Then he stopped and grabbed handfuls of damp black earth and tried to plug the bullet hole. Jenny shuddered, whinnied, and broke from him.

"Hol' on! Hol' on now!"

He tried to plug it again, but blood came anyhow. His fingers were hot and sticky. He rubbed dirt hard into his palms, trying to dry them. Then again he attempted to plug the bullet hole, but Jenny shied away, kicking her heels high. He stood helpless. He had to do something. He ran at Jenny; she dodged him. He watched a red stream of blood flow down Jenny's leg and form a bright pool at her feet.

"Jenny . . . Jenny . . ." he called weakly.

His lips trembled. She's bleeding t' death! He looked in the direction of home, wanting to go back, wanting to get help. But he saw the pistol lying in the damp black clay. He had a queer feeling that if he only did something this would not be; Jenny would not be there bleeding to death.

When he went to her this time she did not move. She stood with sleepy, dreamy eyes; and when he touched her she gave a low-pitched whinny and knelt to the ground, her front knees slopping in blood.

"Jenny . . . Jenny . . ." he whispered.

For a long time she held her neck erect; then her head sank, slowly. Her ribs swelled with a mighty heave and she went over.

Dave's stomach felt empty, very empty. He picked up the gun and held it gingerly between his thumb and forefinger. He buried it at the foot of a tree. He took a stick and tried to cover the pool of blood with dirt—but what was the use? There was Jenny lying with her mouth open and her eyes walled and glassy. He could not tell Jim Hawkins he had shot his mule. But he had to tell something. Yeah, Ah'll tell em Jenny started gittin' wiln fell on the joint of the plow. But that would hardly happen to a mule. He walked across the field slowly, head down.

It was sunset. Two of Jim Hawkins' men were over near the edge of the woods digging a hole in which to bury Jenny. Dave was surrounded by a knot of people; all of them were looking down at the dead mule.

"I don't see how in the world it happened," said Jim Hawkins for the tenth time.

The crowd parted and Dave's mother, father, and small brother pushed into the center.

"Where Dave?" his mother called.

"There he is," said Jim Hawkins.

His mother grabbed him.

"Whut happened, Dave? Whut yuh done?"

"Nothing."

"C'mon, boy, talk," his father said.

Dave took a deep breath and told the story he knew nobody believed.

"Waal," he drawled. "Ah brung ol' Jenny down here so's Ah could do mah plowin'. Ah plowed 'bout two rows, just like yuh see." He stopped and pointed at the long rows of upturned earth. "Then something musta been wrong wid ol' Jenny. She wouldn't ack right a-tall. She started snortin'n kickin' her heels. Ah tried to hol' her, but she pulled erway, rearn'n goin' on. Then when the point of the plow was stickin' up in the air, she swung erroun'n twisted herself back on it. . . . She stuck herse'f'n started t' bleed. N' fo' Ah could do anything, she wuz dead."

"Did you ever hear of anything like that in all your life?" asked Jim Hawkins.

There were white and black standing in the crowd. They murmured. Dave's mother came close to him and looked hard into his face.

"Tell the truth, Dave," she said.

"Looks like a bullet hole ter me," said one man.

"Dave, whut yuh do wid tha' gun?" his mother asked.

The crowd surged in, looking at him. He jammed his hands into his pockets, shook his head slowly from left to right, and backed away. His eyes were wide and painful.

"Did he hava gun?" asked Jim Hawkins.

"By Gawd, Ah tol' yuh tha' wuz a *gun* wound," said a man, slapping his thigh.

His father caught his shoulders and shook him till his teeth rattled.

"Tell whut happened, yuh rascal! Tell whut——"

Dave looked at Jenny's stiff legs and began to cry.

"Whut yuh do wid tha' gun?" his mother asked.

"Whut wuz he doin' wida gun?" his father asked.

"Come on and tell the truth," said Hawkins. "Ain't nobody going to hurt you. . . ."

His mother crowded close to him.

"Did yuh shoot tha' mule, Dave?"

Dave cried, seeing blurred white and black faces.

"Ah-h d-din-n't g-g-go t-t' s-shoo-oot h-her . . . Ah s-s-swear off Gawd Ah-h d-din't . . . Ah wuz a-tryin' t' s-see ef the ol' g-g-gun would s-shoot——"

"Where yuh git the gun from?" his father asked.

"Ah got it from Joe, at the sto'."

"Where yuh git the money?"

"Ma give it t' me."

"He kept worryin' me, Bob. . . . Ah had t' . . . Ah tol' 'im t' bring the gun right back t' me. . . . It was fer yuh, the gun."

"But how yuh happen to shoot that mule?" asked Jim Hawkins.

"Ah wuzn't shootin' at the mule, Mistah Hawkins. The gun jumped when Ah pulled the trigger. . . . N' fo' Ah knowed anything Jenny wuz there a-bleedin'."

Somebody in the crowd laughed. Jim Hawkins walked close to Dave and looked into his face.

"Well, looks like you have bought you a mule, Dave."

"Ah swear fo' Gawd, Ah didn't go t' kill the mule, Mistah Hawkins!"

"But you killed her!"

All the crowd was laughing now. They stood on tiptoe and poked heads over one another's shoulders.

"Well, boy, looks like yuh done bought a dead mule! Hahaha!"

"Ain' tha' ershame."

"Hohohohoho."

Dave stood, head down, twisting his feet in the dirt.

"Well, you needn't worry about it, Bob," said Jim Hawkins to Dave's father. "Just let the boy keep on working and pay me two dollars a month."

"Whut yuh wan' fer yo' mule, Mistah Hawkins?"

Jim Hawkins screwed up his eyes.

"Fifty dollars."

"Whut yuh do wid tha' gun?" Dave's father demanded.

Dave said nothing.

"Yuh wan' me t' take a tree lim'n beat yuh till yuh talk!"

"Nawsuh!"

"Whut yuh do wid it?"

"Ah th'owed it erway."

"Where?"

"Ah . . . Ah th'owed it in the creek."

"Waal, c'mon home. N' firs' thing in the mawnin' git to that creek'n fin' tha' gun."

"Yessuh."

"Whut yuh pay fer it?"

"Two dollahs."

"Take tha' gun'n git yo' money back'n carry it t' Mistah Hawkins, yuh hear? N' don' fergit Ah'ma lam yo' black bottom good fer this! Now march yo'se'f on home, suh!"

Dave turned and walked slowly. He heard people laughing. Dave glared, his eyes welling with tears. Hot anger bubbled in him. Then he swallowed and stumbled on.

That night Dave did not sleep. He was glad that he had gotten out of killing the mule so easily, but he was hurt. Something hot seemed to turn over inside him each time he remembered how they had laughed. He tossed on his bed, feeling his hard pillow. N' Pa says he's gonna beat me. . . . He remembered other beatings, and his back quivered. Naw, naw, Ah sho' don' wan' 'im t' beat me tha' way no mo'. Damn 'em *all!* Nobody ever gave him anything. All he did was work. They treat me lika mule. . . . N' then they beat me. . . . He gritted his teeth. N' Ma had t' tell on me.

Well, if he had to, he would take old man Hawkins that two dollars. But that meant selling the gun. And he wanted to keep that gun. Fifty dollahs fer a dead mule.

He turned over, thinking of how he had fired the gun. He had an itch to fire it again. Ef other men kin shoota gun, by Gawd, Ah kin! He was still listening. Mebbe they all sleepin' now. . . . The house was still. He heard the soft breathing of his brother. Yes, now! He would go down and get that gun and see if he could fire it! He eased out of bed and slipped into overalls.

The moon was bright. He ran almost all the way to the edge of the woods. He stumbled over the ground, looking for the spot where he had buried the gun. Yeah, here it is. Like a hungry dog scratching for a bone he pawed it up. He puffed his black cheeks and blew dirt from the trigger and barrel. He broke it and found four cartridges unshot. He looked around; the fields were filled with silence and moonlight. He clutched the gun stiff and hard in his fingers. But as soon as he wanted to pull the trigger, he shut his eyes and turned his head. Naw, Ah can't shoot wid mah eyes closed'n mah head turned. With effort he held his eyes open; then he squeezed. *Blooooom!* He was stiff, not breathing. The gun was still in his hands. Dammit, he'd done it! He fired again. *Bloooom!* He smiled. *Bloooom! Bloooom! Click, click.* There! It was empty. If anybody could shoot a gun, he could. He put the gun into his hip pocket and started across the fields.

When he reached the top of a ridge he stood straight and proud in the moonlight, looking at Jim Hawkins' big white house, feeling the gun sagging in his pocket. Lawd, ef Ah had jus' one mo' bullet Ah'd taka shot at tha' house. Ah'd like t' scare ol' man Hawkins jus'a little. . . . Jus' enough t' let 'im know Dave Sanders is a man.

To his left the road curved, running to the tracks of the Illinois Central. He jerked his head, listening. From far off came a faint *hoooof-hoooof; hooof-hoooof; hoooof-hoooof.* . . . Tha's number eight. He took a swift look at Jim Hawkins' white house; he thought of Pa, of Ma, of his little brother, and the boys. He thought of the dead mule and heard *hoooof-hoooof; hoooof-hoooof; hoooof-hoooof.* . . . He stood rigid. Two dollahs a mont'. Le's see now. . . . Tha' means it'll take 'bout two years. Shucks! Ah'll be dam!

He started down the road, toward the tracks. Yeah, here she comes! He stood beside the track and held himself stiffly. Here she comes, erroun' the ben'. . . . C'mon, yuh slowpoke! C'mon! He had his hand on his gun; something quivered in his stomach. Then the train thundered past, the gray and brown boxcars rumbling and clinking. He gripped the gun tightly; then he jerked his hand out of his pocket. Ah betcha Bill wouldn't do it! Ah betcha. . . . The cars slid past, steel grinding upon steel. Ah'm riding yuh ternight so he'p me Gawd! He was hot all over. He hesitated just a moment; then he grabbed, pulled atop of a car, and lay flat. He felt his pocket; the gun was still there. Ahead the long rails were glinting in moonlight, stretching away, away to somewhere, somewhere where he could be a man. . . .

Acknowledgment

A compilation such as this is impossible without the co-operation of a great many people—the men who wrote it, their representatives and publishers, and partisans who come up with suggestions in their fists. It is, therefore, dedicated to its many parents, an offering made here at the end so that if they haven't liked it, at least they will know that the stable was trying. Individual copyright credits on each entry follow.

MR. ARCULARIS, copyright, 1931, by Conrad Aiken, from *Among the Lost People*, published by Charles Scribner's Sons.

JUSTICE, copyright, 1929, by Louis Bromfield, from *Awake and Rehearse*, published by Frederick L. Stokes Company.

THE BABY IN THE ICEBOX, copyright, 1933, by the American Mercury, Inc.

THE SINGLE PURPOSE OF LEON BURROWS, copyright, 1944, by the F-R Publishing Corporation, from *The New Yorker*.

CORONER'S INQUEST, copyright, 1930, by P. F. Collier and Son Company.

FAREWELL TO CUBA, copyright, 1931, by Charles Scribner's Sons.

OLD BILL, copyright, 1943, by the Atlantic Monthly Company.

TWO SOLDIERS, copyright, 1942, by the Curtis Publishing Company.

A PLACE TO LAY ONE'S HEAD, copyright, 1945, by Waldo Frank.

THE HOUSE OF THREE CANDLES, copyright, 1938, by Erle Stanley Gardner.

FAME FOR MR. BEATTY, copyright, 1938, by James Norman Hall.

NIGHTSHADE, copyright, 1934, by P. F. Collier and Son Company.

WEIGHT OF COMMAND, copyright, 1940, by the Crowell-Collier Publishing Company.

CRIME WITHOUT PASSION, copyright, 1936, by Ben Hecht, from *Actor's Blood*, published by Covici-Friede.